MY FRIEND IS
MY ENEMY
Part II

MICHAEL J. COUCH

Although this novel is set in an historical context, the characters are entirely fictitious and any likeness in name or personality, to persons alive or deceased, is co-incidental.

MY FRIEND IS MY ENEMY
Part II

Copyright © Michael J. Couch

First published in Great Britain 1991 by Michael J. Couch
68 Chesil Street, Winchester, Hampshire SO23 8HX

Typeset in 10/11pt Baskerville

ISBN 0 9517531 1 8

Made and printed in Great Britain by
The Guernsey Press Co. Ltd., Guernsey, Channel Islands.

Further copies may be purchased by sending cheques/postal orders made out to M.J. Couch, 68, Chesil Street, Winchester, Hants. SO23 8HX.
Part I £4.99 plus 60p postage and packing.
Part II £5.50 plus 60p postage and packing.

This novel is dedicated to
my father
JOHN JAMES (JACK)

I wish to thank the following people who have been of assistance with research and advice.

Deputy Raymond Falla, O.B.E. — Occupation Essential Supplies and Commodities Committee.

Deputy Bill Green

Mr. R. Heaume — Occupation Museum

Mr. A. Benjafield and the Workers' Education Association

Mr. and Mrs. E. C. Robins

Mrs. D. Lawrence

Mr. A. Buckingham

Mr. J. A. McCormack

Mr. D. C. Maguire

Guille-Allès Library

Chapter One

During the scrub up the doctor, who had tended John from the nightmare tangle 'till the present time, had chance to impart his knowledge, and diagnosis so far, to the Consultant Surgeon.

"So, you're pretty certain we'll find some extreme haemorrhages in there, are you?" asked the Consultant.

"Absolutely," the Doctor replied, elaborating. "He was crushed right up against the steering wheel, there is extensive bruising of the abdomen and all the usual swellings associated with abdominal disturbance."

"Hmmph!" the Consultant mused, "seems as though we'll be late home for supper!" He smiled.

The doctor knew the Consultant would not have been so flippant if he had witnessed what he had, nor would he have talked of supper. Perhaps the doctor was not experienced enough of such disasters. Maybe he too, would be like the Consultant one day and laugh off, as routine, the devastation of a human frame. He did not have time to reflect or recriminate against the senior more.

"What else?"

"Pardon?" The question had come as a surprise.

"Any complications?"

"Yes, Sir."

"Well, elaborate please, Doctor. I don't wish to have to stop for 'Question Time' during the operation."

The Doctor elucidated the deepening shock and the fracture to the pelvis.

It was the Consultant's turn to be grave.

"So it has to be a very quick job, wouldn't you say?"

"Yes, Sir, in view of the shock, I would say, very quick."

"I agree with you, Doctor. If what you say is found to be the case then the quicker we have him sewn up the better."

1

The Consultant nodded, as he spoke, as though agreeing with himself.

"It will mean then, won't it Sir," continued the Doctor, "that the Orthopaedic Surgeon will not have much time with the pelvis, if at all?"

"What? Are you suggesting it is left alone?" the Consultant raised his eyebrows at the enormity of his own hypothesis, "send him back to Intensive Care with a passport to a wheelchair?"

"That's a decision only you can take once we're in there, Sir," was the Doctor's tactful reply.

"You're right, of course, though Doctor." He smiled above his mask. "Besides, we can't have Orthoes getting in the way, can we?"

*   *   *

Fifteen-year-old John Collins, civilian, forced worker for the Germans, in this, the second year of the enemy occupation in the British island of Guernsey, lay there. He was in his own bed, that much was clear to him. Yes, it definitely was his own bed and it was his very own mother who ministered to him in his fever. Dad was there too, both parents keeping anxious attendance.

It was still dark outside, the curtains were drawn and the candlelight flickered as his mother tended her son.

Still in the grip of fever, John was content to remain uncommunicative, while his parents fussed. Not for him was the necessity to speak of his recent experiences or to share their horror. No, his recall was personal, introverted, as he relived all that had happened, as the memories jumbled with his dreams. Nor was he to know yet what miseries and anxieties his parents had suffered during that period he had gone missing.

Who had been that man who had attended in the night? Had he been that evil S.S.? Possibly so, yet why had he administered a hypodermic, and why had Larry, his father, made no attempt to stop him? Well, the awful dreams and re-living had ceased after that visit, at least John could not remember any now.

Remembered? Yes, John, now awaking once more, knew

that there was something or someone he should have remembered, yet he was still confused. Perhaps he should return to his sleep to recapture his dreams, or was it his nightmare?

There they were now, those Germans, coming into his bedroom. What right had they to invade his privacy like that? And his own mother and father, the one who was usually so in awe of them, the other holding them in such contempt, did not protest, did not seem aware of their presence even.

"Go away, you bastards! Leave us alone."

Us? Yes, that was it. John now remembered. Where was his friend, Franz? His German friend. Yes, that was it, his enemy friend. What had happened to Franz? Had he really been there with John in a minefield, and had they been rescued together, or was that just a figment in John's troubled mind?

Had John Collins, lonely John, most of his contemporaries long since evacuated to England with the Intermediate School, really made friends with that lonely frightened German?

Was it Franz who had been reduced to a pathetic wreck when he had been caught in an R.A.F. raid? Was that how John had met him in the first place and had befriended him?

"Franz!" The cry which left John as he returned to yesterday to look for his friend, was barely audible to his parents.

"Franz, where are you? Are you all right?"

"I am here, John, right next to you. Don't move! Remember, we are in a minefield!"

So these Germans were rescuing them. Yes, there was that friend of Franz's, the one he had told John about; Corporal Schmidt. Yes, he was smiling, he had a kind look. Was he not the one who had told Franz it was all right for soldiers to cry, when Franz had told him how his father had been killed in action in Poland?

The Corporal's smile faded when he observed John.

"You are British, yes? You are with the R.A.F.? You do this to me!" shouted the man as he put his back to the youth.

"Father!" yelled Franz, as the other turned.

Franz screamed, his father had no face! It had been destroyed by the British R.A.F.

3

*　　　　*　　　　*

"He is still hot," said Frances, as she tended her son's brow. "Shouldn't he be less feverish by now?"

"He's O.K., love," replied Larry, "it will just take its course. The Doctor seemed quite happy, so that's all we can ask."

To Larry, John's father, to see his son now fevered and suffering, but retreating from harm's way, was far preferable to the awful prediction both he and Frances had projected when John had failed to return home last evening.

*　　　　*　　　　*

Both friends had been rescued from the minefield, and both had been separated, each to expect full retribution, not only for straying into a restricted area, thereby putting German property at risk, but also for their crimes against war, for fraternising with the enemy, for seeking to bring peace where hostilities should rightfully be.

Franz, now beyond the protection of his uncle Pieter, Gestapo Major, (for had that adult not threatened to disown him if he continued to associate with the peasants?), was taken to that very place where his uncle worked. Not to the comfort of his relative, however, but to be roughly inter-rogated by that same man's inferior, Lieutenant Hansel, fanatical Nazi Hansel, who so welcomed this opportunity to blacken his senior's name. How Franz, as he said the right things to stop the pain, envied his civilian friend, for John at least had parents to make sure he did not disappear, and as a civilian, would be protected by the Geneva Convention. No such comfort for Franz.

Ironically, John too had been taken to that same building. Not for him to be dealt with by the civilian office of the Feld-kommandantur, or to be handed over to the civilian police to expedite German justice, but to be dealt with as a German until such time as a policy could be decided how to treat a civilian who worked for the masters. Double irony in that John Collins worked as a messenger for the Feldkommand-antur, and his demise had befallen whilst delivering to outposts of the coastal military zone.

Not only had John befriended one the Wiermacht, presumably to corrupt that young soldier and to compromise him into crimes against his own side, but also, that same youth's father had provided the young Teuton with a bicycle for the day.

Yes, it was all very complicated, particularly as Larry Collins, the owner and lender of the bicycle, was suspected of being a subverter and distributor of property stolen from the Reich's forces. Added to this was the connection with the civilian priest, Father Peters, another suspected subverter who was recorded as having held telephone conversations with the Collins' family, to speak about Germans, and who had recently been caught out after curfew while carrying a message from young Franz to his Gestapo uncle. Oh yes, it was all so incriminating! It only needed the dedication of someone like Lieutenant Hansel to fit it all together in order to expedite the Führer's justice!

Not only did John wickedly associate with his enemy friend, but it was also against the direct orders of his master, the Feldkommandantur administrator, Herr Tropp. This same gentleman had recently delighted in pointing out to Major Pieter Müller the complete lack of good Nazi discipline the other was showing in allowing his young nephew to associate with civilians of occupied status. Fortunately, not all at Gestapo headquarters were as weak as the Major, not all sought to undermine mighty Adolf Hitler's ideals through their very apathy. No, Lieutenant Hansel's type definitely had to be cultivated for the greater glory of the Fatherland.

*   *   *

John was still hot; the hours in the sun as they had waited in the minefield for rescue, had turned him into a heat storage unit, as all that energy had now slowly to leave him, soaking his delirious bed with perspiration.

"Who's that, Franz?"

"Eh?" replied the German, resorting to the diction of a local. Who was that uniformed figure coming towards them?

Hüffmeier! Oh no, not that S.S. again!

"Watch out, Franz! Don't let him catch you!"

5

"What you say?" asked Franz, seemingly unaware of the unwelcome guest, "John, what is this 'catch you', please?"

Too late, the leering German was there, he had his arm across Franz's shoulder. As he tentatively placed his hand on Franz's thigh, John knew he had seen too much and, in his heat, willed away the uninvited intruder, to replace him with Uncle Bert, Bert Bisson, Police Constable Bisson, friend of the Collins' family.

"Why are you here, John?" asked Bert, "What have you been up to, young man, to be arrested like this and at the Gestapo and all? I've got better things to do with my time than to chase round after silly little buggers like you!"

Uncle Bert was very angry; he had been approached by Larry when John had not returned home, and he had bluffed a call to the Gestapo, hoping through the work he was often forced to do on their behalf that he was in some credit with the conquerors. Oh yes, they had John all right, but, far worse, thanks to Bert's well-intentioned but mistaken intervention, they had involved the Chief of Police too! No wonder Bert was angry, he with his black market connections too! No, Bert did not welcome attention drawn to himself, or his connections with John's father, in this way.

*   *   *

Franz woke in his windowless room with its weak, bare electric light bulb. No comfortable bed with flock mattress or feather pillows for him, just a thin straw pallet on a bare wooden floor, and a threadbare and bloodstained army issue blanket.

Franz's jaw ached and his ears were filled with a ringing pain. His bottom lip was so split and swollen that he could not close his mouth. He had the bitter, salty taste of blood in his mouth, but he had no mother there to minister cool water to him.

He remembered seeing John standing there at the Gestapo last night, but it had all been too quick and he had not managed, or had the courage, to speak to his friend. If only he had been brave enough to just mouth the word 'John' even. But his uncle had been there, and only last week he had threatened to disown Franz if he ever learned of his again communicating with 'the scum' as he put it. Well, Uncle Pieter would certainly find out now. What had the guard said as he had pushed him into the cell? Something about being up before the General on military charges. The coming day had little in store for Franz.

Franz so wished he had parents like John's, who had come to rescue him last night – at least he was not likely to disappear into the hands of the S.S. or that petrifying Lieutenant who had so cruelly treated him in the interview room.

He had not known what the officer had meant about the priest, he did not know Father Peters spoke bad things about Germans, but the infliction of pain seemed to stop when he agreed that this was so. He had not realised till last night that his uncle was a secret friend of the priest and had arranged for Franz and John to meet and become friends so he could have a chance to talk more with local people, but the smacking of his ears had stopped when he had said yes, that was so. Nor had he realised that he was not the only German to whom John's father had lent his bicycle for a day, in return for items of army property or information.

* * *

Keith had been dreaming. In his half conscious state he was aware that he was in bed, that it was early morning, not long since light, but his will power to raise himself from his restless bed, was manacled by lead weights of sleep-induced lethargy. He thought he had heard noises familiar, yet strange. Yes, that was it, the noise of the milk cart and hooves on the cobbled streets but that could not be, for it was long since that the population had had the luxury of early morning milk let alone deliveries!

Keith rhetorically shrugged his shoulders at his silly imaginings, turning back towards his pillow. It was always the way after a restless, sleep-starved night, that when he could have slept at last, it was time to get up.

There was Anne, sound asleep now but twitching and turning as though her dreams were just about to waken her to the more real nightmare of this new day. Soon she would wake to find the dreaded Friday had arrived, that their final

7

night had been used and that now all that was held for them was the uncertainty of the future. It would be this evening that the Gestapo would collect him for his follow-up session. Yes, it was tonight that Keith was to crack and, for the sake of the temporary expediency of cessation of pain, would sell the rest of his life and freedom to the conquerors. But it had to be.

He thought of their last night together. Damn it, how that expression had irritated him but, how it had dominated his thoughts. And how appropriate it had become, despite his resolve not to let it influence their final hours.

Now the dreaded day had come he almost welcomed it. He was glad. At last it had come! Yes, they could take him away now, do what they must and it could be over with, forever! But what would they do to him? Well, there would be the pain again, that awful seering pain which had so degraded him and stolen his manhood.

Until last night Keith had come to terms with his fate. He had decided that, as they would break him down any way, being no longer a real man, then it did not matter whether he told them what they wanted to know, before or after. Why go through that pain for nothing? With this resolve his last few days of freedom had been faced with more fortitude, he had been able to comfort his Anne more than days earlier. But last night it had been he, the weak, he the broken, who had stood proud once more and comforted and consoled, she the strong, she the resiliant.

And what a night it had been! Keith had been infected by Anne's philosophy that there is no point to a last time if there is never promise of more. She was imbued with the idea that the penultimate had to be the only realisation and that the final session had to be tainted as death itself.

So to bed they had gone, each mourning the death of their love. Keith had lain there, all the options so clear now, in his mind. He had thought of his boat, now impounded, of his wrecked trade and of the illegal dealings which had brought them to this pass. He thought of his dear one whom he was to leave behind, at best, alone for years while he rotted in a French prison, at worst a widow with no means of support. But she would get by, she would manage, for Anne was always the resourceful one. What of their child, he had thought, what of the unborn de la Haye? How would she explain to him that his father was alive in a French prison? His crime? That he stole from the Germans? No, his crime, that he was a coward and, in order to save his own life, had sold his friends. And what of those friends? How would they deal with Anne and the little one when they learned that it was he, Keith, who had been the cause of the break up of their own lives and the incarceration of their loved ones?

Keith so dearly wanted to see his little son. Would that ever be possible? Would he one day dandle him on his knee and take him out walking and swimming and far out to sea in his boat? And one day, would this bearer of the de la Haye name, hold his head up proud of that very name? Would he in turn, tell his own children how proud he had been of their grandfather, a grandfather who had borne interrogation and torture by the Gestapo but had not cracked and thereby gaining his freedom and saving his honour and the lives of his friends? Yes, Keith could imagine taking the little one's hands and proudly instilling in them the tales of the present which, by then, would be mellow with the passage of time and the passing of evil. Yes, that was it; the present was an evil era but, like all malignancies before it, throughout recorded history, would pass, as the bad dream passes away at the break of day.

So what if, when this evil had been removed from their lives, Keith could no longer feel part of the new order of good? What if he sold all that was good in his life, and the lives of all he knew, in order just to save himself temporary inconvenience? No, he could not despoil all that was of value in order to remove just one day. That's all it would be, one Friday, one bloody and horrible Friday, but it would pass and, with its passing, so his manhood would grow again.

All he had to do, he then knew, was to stand valiant against the tyranny. He had remembered then, he had heard of countless people who had stuck to their stories, passed the test of brutal interrogation and, through their resolve, had been released free with insufficient evidence against them.

There was no alternative really. What alternative was it to rot in a French prison, never to see his Anne again? How would it feel to be an imprisoned de la Haye and no longer proud of the name? How would he feel, thinking of his child growing up without him, not knowing whether it were a boy or a girl? How could he live with such lack of knowledge and such incompleteness? And what would the child think of its father? Would he, or she, even be allowed to think of him? Would the boy be ostracized at school for being the son of a traitor?

But, far worse, would he be told nothing of his father? Would the boy have a new father, a new name? Would Anne, his dear Anne, so disillusioned with her coward of a man, not even a man, find another? Would his darling call another one 'love' and his child call another 'daddy'? The thought was too horrible. Keith had tormented himself with thoughts of Anne lying, in this same bed, with another. It could not be contemplated. With this new loathing of his considered self and his newly pricked jealousy of the mind, he had, in the darkness of that final night, yet final no more, felt his manhood awaken. It was with such desire and urgency that he had taken her, and she had responded and worked with him, as he fancied himself a new man, and she forgot her fears, that they had made love as never before.

As Keith and Anne had united in love and repeatedly swept away the long hours in the rush of passion, so that they had become as transitory as memory itself, both had become born again.

Keith had been fearful that their love violence, with all the inventiveness of insatiable teenagers, would harm their unborn child. Somewhere in the far reaches of his mind he remembered the playground talk of sex and passion and of intercourse with pregnant women which would cause birth-marks on the visages of the unborn innocents. But Keith could not help himself for that all belonged to a past and forgotten world of dirty and furtive talk and guilt-ridden actions in the secluded parts of his boyhood education. None of that could be associated with his darling Anne who was clean and strong and beautiful and, like his angel, that she was, responded to his every pressure, welding herself round him so that their two bodies had become one, neither knowing where the one ended and the other began but both delighting in the feelings and sensations of the other. No, Keith and

Anne, in their love making, were perfect and clean and very very beautiful. Their unborn child could be nothing but blessed by their emission of love, time after time, through that long, short night.

Now, at this early hour of this summer morning, as Keith lay there pondering his lot, he realised that the ultimate had not been without its value. In fact he now realised the exquisite potential of a last time for he had now, built into his mind for ever the most wonderful memories. It was these memories which he knew would keep him alive and from going insane on this auspicious and bloody day. He now looked forward to his session with the interrogators. He knew he would not crack for now he was protected with the armour of his darling's memory. He had only to think of Anne, and of their last night, to know that he would pull through and come home to her again, the new man that he was.

Today was to be looked upon as a visit to the dentist, a dreaded affair but necessary in order to put behind him all the recent pain and to assure him of a perfect future.

The clattering of the hoofs outside was still there. Strange? What time was it? Hell, it was seven o'clock already, they must have loved each other to exhaustion. What blessed oblivion! He looked at Anne and thought,

'Once more? I am ready and armed, I am a soldier erect in all my splendour and she will want me and welcome me and, although we can never better last night, we can equal it a thousand times in a few Elysian moments. But no, why should I take her now? I have last night's memory to keep me sane and, I have her dearness there to draw me home again tonight.'

It was as Keith so resolved this, that the banging began on his front door. All his dreams broke, his body became rigid, Anne started, her eyes looking at Keith, flashing fear and bewilderment. She clutched at his wrist and was aware of his pulse. They looked at each other, her anger and fear countered by his sadness and resignation.

"Yes," he said, as he slowly nodded, "I think it's them, the bastards." There was no annoyance, no fear in his voice as his gentle words were drowned by a more insistent hammering. He made to get up. Keith was not sure if he heard her words, above the battering or if he read them, in Anne's pleading eyes, but she conveyed;

'No, don't go. Once more, just once more!' Her eyes screamed at him as her hands fumbled his responsive body.

Gently he lifted her hand and removed the heavenly sensation of her ministrations.

As the jackbooted heel finally broke the brave lock and the door flew open, its handle unwillingly but roughly hitting the panelling of the hallway walls, Keith kissed his Anne as he arched his body above her in order to make his escape.

"No," he said. "Tonight, my darling. Your fisherman will be home and he'll prove himself to you then."

She said nothing more but shrunk her nakedness under the sheet, as their heaven was transformed into an alien place, with gawping and gaping Aryans, while Keith stood there in his virile hairy nakedness.

"O.K., I'm ready," he said. "Bit early though aren't you? Bloody clock wrong or something?"

The menacing looks and gestures from his house guests showed they did not appreciate this early morning flight into British humour.

Keith completed his dressing in unhurried haste and with dignity. As he expected, when he went to kiss his Anne, he was prevented from doing so. He was glad in a way.

"Cheerie love," he said, almost nonchalantly, "see you tonight."

As the chains were attached to his wrists, he watched his darling bite her lip while she fought to hold back the tears which were already magnifying her beautiful eyes.

It was a relief to be bundled from the room.

*   *   *

John sat up in bed. His father stood at the end of the bed looking both irritated and edgy, as though he were not really sure he should be present. Frances, his mother, had her frequent anxious look and seemed about to leave the room at any moment. There must have been something in the atmosphere for even the respectable looking white haired gentleman, the only seated person in the room, crouching uncomfortably on the bedside stool, close to John's head, seemed agitated. He barely concealed his irritability as occasionally his questions penetrated John's dreamy state.

Yes, they were all anxious and worried, except John. He was conscious of their concern but felt quite free of it as though he were not really there at all. This man questioning him, who was he? Was he not part of last night's, so traumatic, scenes at the Gestapo Headquarters? But was he on their side or the Germans'? John smiled as he pondered the idea for it amused him, 'their side or the Germans'?' Was John himself German and were the Gestapo really the Guernsey people? Was it the Germans who were described by the collective 'swine', a word which seemed recently to have etched itself so much on to his vocabulary? Who was he?

'If I am German,' he thought, 'then this interrogator must be the enemy, he must be a Guernsey swine!'

Again he smiled, again the Chief Officer of civilian police looked towards Larry's direction, shrugging his shoulders helplessly.

'If however I am Guernsey, then maybe I am the swine and therefore this man is German?' John was terribly confused but quite enjoying his confusion. Yes, that was it, everything seemed so enjoyable now, since S.S. Hüffmeier had come, in the middle of the night, to inject his writhing body. From that moment of the injection of fear, all his nightmare had changed. Hüffmeier had become his old familiar doctor once more, Frau Borman had become his dear mother, and the myriad Aryans, who had seemed to slip through his very walls to invade the sanctity of his bedroom, had drifted away without trace, forgotten almost. John laughed out loud and the Police Chief got up to go.

'Is this Herr Tropp?' thought John. 'No, he cannot be for he is too quiet, too considerate.' Quiet, considerate people made him feel annoyed! Why could not this man be Herr Tropp? Why could he not be in command like a valiant German?

Feebly, so much so that the Police Chief, now with his back to the patient, was not sure if he had heard anything at all, John asked;

"Who are you?" he held out a weak hand limply on the end of an arm which no longer seemed to be within the control of his own body. The Chief turned, and both Larry and Frances leaned nearer as though, by so doing, their son would be encouraged to become more comprehensible.

John followed up his feeble start with:

"Herr Tropp, you are late for work, fill out a time sheet!" A pause and a giggle. "Major Müller, you're a hard man, give the Corporal back his face. Go on I say, Franz orders it!" More giggling as John sank down beneath his sheets laughing and sobbing like a child awakened from a nightmare. Frances immediately rushed to his side and comforted him.

"There," she protested. "Enough! Leave him alone! You can see he's in no fit state to talk to you, the injection is still having its effect."

The Chief ungraciously concurred with this sentiment and, looking more at Larry than anyone, but throwing out his statement to no one in particular, almost as a private observation said;

"I hope that's all it is."

As the Chief moved towards the door he said, almost apologetically, almost as if it were anathema to him:

"He'll have to speak to me soon, Mr. Collins. You know that, don't you? If he doesn't speak to me they'll do the interrogation. You do understand that, don't you? They won't worry about injections or the health of the patient."

"But what is there for them to know?" asked Larry in desperation and exasperation. "He got lost in a mine field from what I can make out. What the hell can they make of that?"

"My dear fellow," replied the Chief, "they can make what they want out of anything they wish and you, Mr. Collins, surely, should know that . . ." He paused, deciding not to follow that line further.

Larry took him up:

"What exactly do you mean by that?" he asked trying not to sound defensive.

The Chief looked him straight in the eye;

"Come now, Mr. Collins, please don't insult my intelligence. There's a war on, I've a job to do. Please don't make my impossible task more difficult than it already is. I suggest you contact P.C. Bisson when your son is fit to talk and I suggest that had better be pretty soon!"

With that he picked up his hat from the wash stand and, making for the door,

"I'll see myself out. Good morning!"

He was gone. Both Larry and Frances looked at each other with open mouthed expressions in their eyes.

John was snoring.

*   *   *

Keith stood in the entrance hall of Gestapo Headquarters, almost breathless from his forced march, almost at running pace, up The Grange. He did not mind that the hordes of early morning cyclists had seen him in chains, he was proud in fact. Was not he the brave fisherman who had withstood their torture and not divulged one name of the black market ring? He knew that he had to endure it just once more to be free to return to his beloved. What did it matter that they had come for him half a day early? So much the better, for the sooner he would be a free man once more.

The portrait of Adolf Hitler stared down at him. Strange how the man looked quite normal, trustworthy even, the sort of man who might have been your next door neighbour.

Lieutenant Hansel's face lit with a smile when he saw his victim, for he too was looking for renewed acquaintance in Interrogation Room Five, a room in the cellars conveniently soundproofed from the administrative section but just below the cells, where ghastly sounds could percolate to the detainees above. Hansel's anticipation was thwarted, however, when he learned that Major Müller had taken over the task, as he had threatened to do, with his boast of getting submissions and confessions without one bruise or the spilling of one drop of blood.

'The man must be insane,' thought Hansel, 'either insane or more deeply involved in this subversion than I dared to hope!'

The man was such a nuisance too, he had even discovered Hansel's ploy to get to de la Haye first. Life just was not fair!

When the Major arrived with the look of one who had either dressed hurriedly or whose uniform was a size too

15

large, he was delighted to observe his client, and began the psychology of surprise to soften him up.

"Good morning, Mr. de la Haye," said Müller, emphasizing the 'Mr.' which was not usually part of his English vocabulary when addressing peasants.

"I am sorry to have kept you waiting. Please to come with me to my office, where we can talk uninterrupted."

As Major Müller led Keith, by now quite confused at the contrast of anticipation with reailty, to his office, Lieutenant Hansel, having just relieved his frustration slightly by putting two slovenly sentries on an indiscipline charge, stood watching in amazement as his senior officer disappeared, seeming to treat the filthy fisherman as if he were a long lost friend. If Hansel had been able to apply any logic to this scene, it might just have confirmed his earlier suspicions.

"Well, Mr. de la Haye," scintillated Major Pieter Müller, effecting his most subtle manner, "please to sit down. Take that comfortable chair if you would be so kind."

Keith was completely abashed at the generous tone behind the ungenerous uniform, momentarily forgetting his most awful and dreaded Friday had begun, and that he was to keep his wits about him and steady his nerves as never before.

However, Keith had, in the past, read enough boys' comics and, until last year, watched sufficient American films, to realise that he was falling victim of that familiar ploy, 'soften 'em up then hit them hard!' He decided to keep as neutral as possible, only refusing to answer questions when that became necessary, in order to effect his resolve. He had to be as polite and non-committal for as long as possible. Keith expected that it would be just a matter of time before the Gestapo Major changed his tactics and sent for the professionals to do their work in the dreaded Room Five.

"Cigarette?" enquired Major Müller, benignly.

'That's it,' thought Keith, 'next he'll be offering me a light and talking about the weather or telling me what a beautiful island this is. (Was!)'

"I expect you will find it rather strong, Mr. de la Haye," said the Major smiling, referring to the Gaulois he had proffered, and which had been accepted cautiously. "It will taste very strange after your unusual local blends, so I hear."

Keith shrugged his shoulders, giving a little laugh.

"You must hear quite a lot Major, eh?"

"My dear man, yes. Let me light it for you, please."

Keith took a long draw of the French cigarette savouring its taste. During his dealings in the trade he had in fact acquired quite a liking for this particular brand. What was it he was now inhaling, he wondered? Four ounces of German bread, one egg, or half a pint of paraffin? Yes, that was about the going rate, although one quickly lost touch of the changing market. It had, after all, been some time now since he had had many dealings.

The Major observed Keith, with the satisfaction of one who has prepared a good meal and now watches the recipient enjoying it.

"I see you are enjoying this luxury," he said. "I am surprised you can take the real thing so readily. One might expect it to taste strange after such complete absence." This last statement was not uttered at all maliciously but more in jest as the Major's eyes sparkled.

'Bloody hell!' thought Keith. 'Is he out to trick me or something? Over a stupid little issue like that too! Hell, I'd better be careful. Maybe I'm getting too relaxed? Perhaps his schoolboy comic plan is really working for him?' He stubbed out the cigarette in the Major's ashtray and stood in annoyance, more at himself than at Pieter Müller, pushing the receptacle away from him.

"Keep the damned thing!" he exclaimed. "If that's your attitude, I'd rather smoke my colts' foot than your rubbish!" His eyes flashed anger, the Major's temporarily reflecting it, but he managed to control himself in order to save the situation.

'God's mother,' thought the Major, 'this peasant is certainly a touchy one, his nerves are bad. I do believe he'd almost be ready for Hansel's methods but I wouldn't give that dolt the pleasure. No, I must stick to my plan.' Therefore the Major swallowed his pride, in order to regain it, and made light of Keith's outburst.

"Just my little joke, Mr. de la Haye. No offence intended. You do understand, don't you?"

17

"I suppose so," grunted Keith, but nonetheless more defensive now and more on his guard.

"You must be missing your little fishing boat, yes? Especially in this excellent weather we are having."

Keith shrugged. What was there to say on the matter, after all? The Germans had taken away his boat and his livelihood and they also had it in their power to return the same. But at what price? That was the question.

"Yes, Mr. de la Haye, I think we must get you back to the sea once more. You would like that, no?"

Keith's reaction was to wish to readily affirm this but what was the point? He knew it could only be a trick. At best a cruel promise only to be dashed in order to further break his spirits, at worst a bribe to get him to traitorously sell the lives and freedom of his friends and associates, for personal gain. He tried to give a non-committal answer. The most non-committal he could think of was plain; "Yes."

"Very well then, Mr. de la Haye," continued Major Müller, "that will be arranged." He paused to gauge Keith's reaction to this. Although Keith's heart was thumping loudly, so that he could feel the pulse transmitting through his neck while wondering;

'Could it be true? Could it perhaps be possible? Could I have the old girl back and be able to go about my business to support Anne and the little one? But no, it's just all a dirty bloody trick, all a big lead up to get me to sell my friends.' He tried not to show the emotion he felt.

"Here is the licence you need, and here is my signature." The Major signed with a flourish, fumbled in his drawer for the appropriate rubber stamp and pad and, with great showmanship, completed the job.

"All that is needed now is for you to present this at the Feldkommandantur on Monday morning, in the usual way." The Major sat back beaming at Keith.

"Thanks."

"Is that all you have to say?" enquired Major Müller, somewhat surprised at the reaction of one to whom he purported to be so generous. "Do you have any questions for me, concerning this?"

Keith sighed a deep heavy sigh. This was all so ridiculous. It was not following any logical pattern. Here he was at the

Gestapo headquarters, ostensibly to be interrogated and beaten up so that he might divulge his mates who were involved in anti German activities, but what was happening? Not a mention of those activities, or of his previous session. Not a single question, just kindness, consideration and, what appeared to be, a return of his livelihood. It just did not make any sense at all!

"O.K.," he said, "so you're returning my boat. But why? That's not what I was brought here for, surely? Come on now, what's this all about? What do you expect from me?"

"Expect from you, Mr. de la Haye? Why, what could we expect from you? You are of no use to us." A pause, "Are you?"

"All right then, thanks!" almost shouted Keith in his frustration and bewilderment, but deciding to go along with the German's silly game, for better or for worse. He rose to his feet, eyes fixed on the Major, just waiting for the anticipated change of mood.

"I'm off then, O.K.?"

Dare he take the Gestapo authorization for a fishing permit? Dare he bring to an end the fantasy that this game they were playing, was for real? Well why not? It had to come to an end, it was all a big trick anyway. So what if he just picked it up and attempted to walk from the room? All it could do would be to accelerate the inevitable. The Major's mood would change and the anger would come, followed by the treatment in Room Five. But that was coming anyway. And yet, what if it were true? What if they were really returning his boat? And at no price? That would not be possible though, would it? Or, would it?

Well there it was, the permit lay on the desk while the Major sat staring at the polished surface, as though some sort of trap ready sprung to catch its victim, Keith, at his first move.

'Now,' thought Keith, 'now! I just grab it and go. All he can do is stop me, hit me, threaten, or just shoot me. I'm not afraid of any of those things. I've faced them all before. That's why I came today and why I'm here. It's what I've steeled myself for.' But, despite these rapid deliberations, he was no more able to move from his statue-like position than he could have, as a child, opened his eyes to look at the imaginary intruder in his dark bedroom.

Then, just as with final desperation, with heart pounding so that it was about to burst and spill up through his very throat, Keith was ready to snatch that piece of paper and rush from the room, the Major looked up. The lips of the stalwart old German, now in his second major war, moved, while the words took the slowness of an era to reach Keith, whose mind was in a turmoil of indecision. The fisherman must have hesitated a thousand times. As the words washed up on Keith's shore, and as he decided to jump from their feared destructiveness, they came crashing down on him with all their mighty force, a force seemingly not diminished by their very benign tone;

"Yes, Mr. de la Haye, please take your permit. It is yours. There is nothing we require from you, you are a free man." There was a pause then, as though it were an irrelevant afterthought, "We would however appreciate a little help from you as a gesture of gratitude."

"What help?"

"Oh, you know, Mr. de la Haye, just a few bits of information. Nothing much, you understand, nothing to implicate yourself in any way of course . . ." He stood as though embarrassed at the very idea while gesturing with his arm for Keith to pick up his document.

'As easy as that!' thought Keith. 'He can ask me to sell my friends and countrymen, just like that, for a simple piece of paper!'

Keith stepped towards the document while he felt every emotion fighting with him to move for the door without it. But oh, how strong was the draw of his little boat and the call of the sea. The sight, in his mind's eye, of nourishing food on Anne's plate once more, instead of swede and turnip watering their unwholesome tears, and the happy chattering of his unborn infant, seemed to dissolve the vision of his friends' suffering, as he had in Room Five, and to deafen his ears to their taunts and derision, to their hatred and scorn.

"And what if I don't help?" demanded Keith.

"If you don't help?" repeated the Major, as if puzzled, hurt almost, at the very idea of this ingratitude, "Well Mr. de la Haye, if you don't help, then I suppose you just don't help." He paused indecisive then continued once more in a hopeless tone. "It will just have to be on your conscience, that is all. Now go please. I have work to do."

The Major stood abruptly, making to end the interview.

Keith could not understand what was happening. He found himself picking up the paper while feeling elation and disgust simultaneously. As he picked up his boat, his career, his wife and son, his future and past, he felt a shock pass through his body. He heard the cries of pain of his friends and the anguish of their wives, he saw the backs turn, as he approached, and heard the infants called indoors and doors slam as he walked down the street. He felt the icy stares, as cold as death, while he drank alone in the crowded Golden Lion.

With his permit in his hand he strode for the door. The few steps seeming like a great field whose hedges get never closer on a hot exhausting day. Eventually Keith reached his exit and, feeling like a small boy, who has been dared by his peers to be rude to his teacher, turned to face the Major allowing his words to tumble out, hoping they would all reach the recipient in some type of logical order, before his resolve to so speak had changed;

"Thank you Major. I'll take what's rightfully mine. There is nothing I can tell you, and my conscience is perfectly clear. Good morning!"

"Good morning Mr. de la Haye, and good luck," replied the Major, almost jocularly, "I'm so glad your conscience is not troubling you. Please to remember me if it does." With that Pieter Müller sprang to the door and ushered out the completely puzzled Keith, closing it fast behind him.

Pieter then reached for his telephone in order to facilitate the fisherman's unhindered exit from the building.

*   *   *

Keith could have done with a drink. It was no good, however, for they were not open yet. Besides, he had not a penny to his name. In all probability he could have scrounged one from his many friends at the Golden Lion. Well why not? He'd scrounged enough this past week, one more wouldn't make much difference. Besides, on Monday he'd have his boat back and would soon be in the money once more. Then he could wipe the slate clean, so one more now wouldn't make much difference.

But it was no good, for no matter how badly Keith wanted a pint, it would not be possible until opening time and that was still an age away. It might as well never come, he thought, for the distance it was away.

Even if he had the money, or was soon about to have earnings in his pocket once more, could he really face the crowd at the moment? Well yes, probably he could. After all, he'd not sold anyone, he'd not given anyone away. No, that was true, he'd done his part, he had prepared himself for this awful Friday, going over and over it all in his mind since his last visit to Room Five. All the pain, all the anticipated suffering had been upon him for over a week now. And how his friends knew it! They had helped him through that past week, they had sustained him, listened to him as he'd sobbed in his cider, talked to him, encouraged him. They had filled his glass and, as they'd watched him get into that drunken oblivion each night, had conveyed to him, through their fearful eyes, that he must not give them away. The many true friends had proved themselves and had shared his load, which was indeed their load too. They had most certainly been in communion with Keith, the weak keystone of the shaky arch.

No, he had not given them away, had he? Well, he had his boat back. But no. Honour had been satisfied, he had taken back what was rightfully his, but had not helped the Germans at all, had he? No of course not! He had a perfectly clear conscience and everything was well. For the time being at least. But why, what was so special about him? Why had they returned his little boat for no cost at all to him, that was what he wondered. And that was what his friends would wonder too. Maybe that was their little game then, eh? Perhaps they weren't so stupid, or so kind, after all? Possibly it was all just a clever plot to put doubts and suspicions between friends? Damn them!

Well, even if that was the case, no one need think it until Monday and that was a whole three days away. No one had to know that in his pocket, Keith had this stamped Gestapo permit ready for presentation at the Feldkommandantur.

Yes, that was all right then. But, there again, it didn't really help at all, for the pub wouldn't be opening yet.

There was nothing for it really, but to go home. However, even that presented problems. How was he to approach Anne, Anne who would be by now biting her lips white and digging her nails into her palms in her imaginations and abject misery at what she feared was happeing to her poor man at this very minute? What would she think? Would she too, think that he had gained his freedom by taking the coward's way out? Yes, she was sure to think that at first, but he had to convince her that it was otherwise. Convince her? How could he do that? He had to keep trying to convince himself that this was so! He was totally confused now, and in his unexpected freedom, completely imprisoned in his loneliness and isolation. By God, he needed a drink!

                    *   *   *

"So! You really have done it now haven't you?" hissed uncle Pieter Müller to the cowering and dejected Franz who sat next to him on the plush black leather sofa. Uncle Pieter's eyes showed both anger and fear, although the other manifestations of such an emotion, the shaking hands and the empty feeling in his stomach, he kept well concealed.

The Major's anger was there without doubt. It was only this anger which helped to keep his fear at bay. He, a Major of the Gestapo, noted hero of the Great War, and trustworthy Party member, having to have his orderly life disrupted by the alien, or at least, almost forgotten emotion of fear! And for what? For this snivelling snotty-nosed wretch beside him! It was just too bad! Too bad!

To make matters worse, Pieter could not vent his anger. He would so like to be able to pick up this creature, this weed who, through a bitter twist of fate happened to be of the same blood as Pieter, bearing to his great chagrin and shame, the same surname, and shake him, and shake him, until his teeth clattered out and his eyes clouded with unconsciousness. Yes, he would even delight if the thing were passed to Hansel to be played with using his toys in Room Five. That thought so vitalized the already shocked Pieter that he almost forgot where he was, he almost indulged his feelings.

Pieter did however remember where he was, and he had to keep remembering for he must now fight for his very name, his very reputation, in order not to be dragged down with this worm.

To think, that Pieter once thought of Franz as a son! Now he would prefer to distance him with just 'F. Müller'. Better still, with luck, the reprehensible youth might soon not have even that title. The S.S. preferred to use numbers and even then might lose the person.

How could he have ever imagined himself in loco parentis? He recalled how the boy had always been special to him. Was it because he had genuinely wondered if he had in fact sired the child? Had his attentions to his young sister-in-law, while her own husband had tended the land, growing the food which was to build the Führer's forces to free Europe, really resulted in this putrefaction which now sat next to him?

Had he, he had tormented himself on many occasions, in fact, been the lad's father? He had no way of knowing. In his heart he had hoped so, even convincing himself that this was so. He had told himself that the woman believed it too, although they had never discussed the matter as she was only a female.

But Pieter had thought long and hard and the more he had thought the more Franz had looked like him. There was, after all, a marked difference between the infant and his older sister. The fact that she was a girl while his son was of the ruling gender had seemed somewhat irrelevant to a man who weighed all the evidence for and discounted doubts against his arguments. He could, he knew, have tackled the woman outright, when his brother went missing in Poland and when he, benevolent 'uncle', had done right by his 'nephew' taking him under his wing and under that of the all-providing Nazi system, for she had been very much beholden to him at that time.

Now this morning, waiting in the lavishly-furnished sitting room of the General's mansion, and surrounded by a rustle and bustle of the ever busy and ever smart to-ing and fro-ing officers, each of whom it seemed to Pieter, momentarily paused in their vital business, to stare and sneer. It was as though they knew of his shame as he sat beside the one who for so long had been his secret son, but was now just so much refuse, hopefully soon to be disposed of. He wished to release the doubts so long held captive in his subconscious, and to feel sure that this beside him was just the creature of his now putrefied brother and his despicable sister-in-law.

*   *   *

Müller, I see you have been a Major now for some time," lilted the General in the manner of a politician well used to making small talk.

"Yes Sir," concurred the much discomforted and highly nervous Pieter, while reflecting how unused he was these days to having to subject himself to the subservience of addressing higher ranks.

"Hmph!" half grunted, and partly growled the General, while considering the pair in front of him. He had been quite prepared that, busy veteran as he was, he would make the interview appear as unhurried as possible and keep its deliberations as civilized as he was able, in order to effect protocol and decency, as required from his high position, while imparting justice born from the wisdom of the Reich, incarnate in himself. And what did his good intentions and resolve in this regard bring him as their reward? Why, a snivelling looking wretch of a youth, the only German thing about him being his uniform, and a Gestapo Major completely lacking in personality and in no way able to warm to his charm, or be appreciative of his concern for a fellow Nazi, albeit of far inferior rank.

The busy General, hard pressed by difficult circumstances brought about by the belligerents, and over-worked in repressing a whole civilian nation, its population far in excess of twenty thousand, and known to house terrorists, not above spitting on the ground near a conqueror or of failing to adore the Nazi civilization and culture, and even to keep illegal wireless sets and on occasions cutting telephone wires, felt much irritated by this, knowing in his heart that, patient and socially aware as he was, he would have to give vent to his pent up anger before long, if only to save the honour of his slighted Führer who was personally insulted by what had come about.

25

"Müller, I'm a busy man, as you should be . . ." The General theatrically placed his monocle back into the puffy rolls of his tanned leather face. "I can only give five minutes of the Führer's valuable time to this, before I decide what has to be done. You will have a chance to say something once my decision has been made."

He paused as if waiting for the Major to attempt to interrupt. He was disappointed that there was no reaction for he would like to have snapped at the man. His disappointment helped to fire his anger which would soon, he knew, be turned from an act to a reality, especially if so readily fired by the one in front of him.

"I have considered the facts," these last words he almost shouted with glee at the prospect of what he had to say, "and I find your nephew guilty of a most serious crime against the Reich! He has undone much of Germany's work, work which evolved over years and years of national effort has been eroded in minutes by this traitorous act!" At last his anger was becoming real, he could feel himself being carried along by it now so that its power could take over. He no longer needed to think what he had to say. The words would just begin to come. He would not remember what he had said but they would be good words, angry words, and he would do Hitler's work with them.

*   *   *

It was a shocked Franz, a pale and shaken Franz, a Franz no longer there, no longer a living Franz but just a chained soul who floated there looking at his former self, days numbered, as he stared vacantly from the pebbled edged footpath, hat still clasped in his unreal hand, watching the rapidly shrinking staff car, bearing his former uncle Pieter, move away towards the reality of human existence, leaving him here with himself in timeless limbo.

Only moments before, the cowed and red faced Major, shaking uncontrollably with an amalgam of fear, embarrassment and anger, had almost run, eager in his wish to save himself and put away from him all that would associate him with the worst time he had ever experienced, from the presence of the General, now spent of all his angry tirade, back square to the two pariahs while feasting his adoring eyes on the portrait of the Führer, absorbing his master's gratitude for his recent loyalty.

*　　　*　　　*

Major Pieter Müller, oblivious of his shadow, his previous nephew and, heaven forbid, almost son, had rushed out of the building and stepped with one elastic movement into the back of his car. At last here was the familiar and the reality he had sought. Now he could close his mind to the incident and banish it from thought for ever. With the symbolic slamming of his door he had resolved oblivion, unaware that outside, only fractionally saved from a dismembered hand in a dismembering Gestapo staff car door, stood a thin pathetic replica of his very self, albeit separated by almost half a century.

As the dust settled and the sound of the receding motor was padded into silence by the oppressive still heat of that hot and humid summer morning, Franz's soul rejoined his helpless and hopeless body.

With great care the young Teuton placed his hat carefully on his head. The tears which almost brimmed into his swollen eyes, at the realisation of rejection by his own kin, receded as, with a loud sniff, a deep breath and the straightening of his previously bent shoulders, he decided that dead as he might well become, he was not dead yet and life was good.

Franz heard only the lilting cooing of pigeons on the tall granite walls opposite, along with the occasional comfortable sound of spade scraping stone as, somewhere in a walled garden, man was helping nature with the production of its fruits, and in the distance the soothing snore of the harbour fog-horns as they heralded the cool white sea mists which would soon cover and purify all that was coarse which did not belong to this beautiful place.

The General had shouted. The General had stamped. He had clenched his fists. He smacked his sides in his temper. Swear words he had uttered, whole streams of filthy oaths, the like of which Franz had never heard before. And while all these induced histrionics had been performed, Franz's

27

gaze had been held locked on to his verbal assailant's eyes as they sparkled with the excess moisture of fiery anger. So strong and piercing had that gaze been that Franz's fixedness had not even been momentarily broken when the General's monocle had dropped during the flicker of a twitch. All Franz could now really remember clearly were those eyes of National Socialist fervour and fanaticism. The ringing tones and the excited actions paled into insignificance as he watched still, those eyes. What he heard in his living recall was clear but almost irrelevant, as if intended for another and therefore of no great importance to him;

"You are a pervert! Yes that is what you are! You are filth, the scum, the refuse of our nation! You are not fit to be called a son of our beloved Führer. You are to Germany as a bastard of a Jew creature is to the human race . . ."

On and on had gone these momentous outpourings;

". . . You must be punished . . . purged of your heinous crime . . . your family . . . lost rights of consideration . . . fit only for . . ."

What was that? What was it Franz was remembering? He momentarily withdrew from his daze as his thought and recall had tripped that very switch of fear that he had, so very recently, completely repressed, for its tenor had been so terrible to him that he had felt compelled to treat it so.

He, like his close but distant friend yet enemy, felt the harsh clasping clamp of coldness contrasting with his hot and sultry exterior. Those words? Those ghastly purveyors of the abominable, now surged on him once more, engulfing him.

"Your bones will be crushed to make foundations for the tracks which will be used by our true German spirits, as they speed with bravery to their glorious victory, on the Eastern Front. You, loathsome coward, are to be part of our beloved Führer's victorious push into the heart of Bolshevism. But for you there will be no glory, no opportunity to prove your heroism, even if you were capable of such things. No, yours will be to starve in the trenches, to be placed in the heat of the onslaught, to be pounded by the death throes of the retreating Reds, your brothers, and to die for the country you, in your foolishness, have forsaken. Arrangements will be made for you to be taken to a camp of correction, to be prepared to die for the glory of your country. None of this glory will accrue to you. Think yourself fortunate that the S.S. have provided such facilities to rebuild you and purify you and your type, sufficiently to be able to die in such a way and in such battles as you are to witness. As soon as the necessary arrangements have been effected you will be collected and transported to the mainland!"

*   *   *

John, still unwell after his night of fever, so that now he shivered not only with fear but with cold, while outside his weak and racked frame the world sweltered in the humid, shimmering heat of a breezeless summer's day, stood nervously before Herr Tropp.

He had been summoned to his place of work, no doubt not to take up his employment, but to be dismissed for abusing his position of trust. It seemed inevitable that a messenger, a member of an inferior race who had such ideas above his station as to seek the friendship of one of the master race, in order to corrupt him into treasonable behaviour, should lose the privilege of working for the Reich.

Herr Tropp, the Administrator of the Feldkommandantur, well used to dealing with civilians, despaired at John's lack of self discipline. He entered into a lengthy lecture about the boy's lost opportunity to serve the master race and to help build a free Europe.

"Minefield indeed!" he expostulated, "And do you know what a mine costs? Supposing you had detonated one, what then?"

John was not cognisant of Herr Tropp's question, which only emphasised the master's point that the boy was not sufficiently motivated for such important work.

Herr Tropp had no qualms in telling John that his employment by the Reich was to cease, and that he was to be dealt with by other competent authorities regarding the consequences of the previous day's adventure.

All of Herr Tropp's lecture was lost on the Messenger, for he thought only of his friend, anxious to know his fate.

It was with great relief that John was taken from the building, hopefully for the last time.

*   *   *

Chapter Two

The incision was straightforward and the application of the clamps was purely routine. The only deviation from the norm, at this stage, was the unusual length of the wounding, but the search had to be quick and thorough.

There was much blood in the body cavity. The tubes were deftly placed to alleviate this problem, their gentle pumping and suckings being the only noises to accompany the metallic clatter of returned and replaced instruments.

The lights seemed brighter than usual somehow, while the unaccustomed marks of blood on their garb only heightened the sense of urgency.

The Consultant did a rapid exploration with his hands and grimaced as the nurse swabbed them. He turned to his task once more. There was still a lot of bleeding. He stole a glance at the instruments and the anaesthetist caught his eye. They both nodded.

With a series of grunts and well-rehearsed instructions, first one tool was passed, retrieved, then another, then aother.

Still the Consultant searched, still he looked grave. Still his hands were bloodied as the short ten minutes was intensified. He shook his head.

"You." He indicated the doctor, his word sufficient to tell his colleague that he should try. The Consultant stood back to allow the Sister to mop the perspiration from his brow.

"No?" he queried.

"No," conceded his colleague.

"Then, we must cut further," sighed the Consultant. "Anaesthetist, how are we doing?"

"You have had three and a quarter minutes, the pulse rate is increasing and blood pressure is falling quite fast."

"How's the breathing?"

"Reasonably stable, Sir."

"Good," grunted the Consultant. "And the heart?" He looked at the cardiograph to answer his own question.

The incision was lengthened. The precious time sped on.

John's shock was deepening alarmingly. They had little time.

*   *   *

Pieter Müller, unaware of Hansel's recent obscene dealings with the mind and emotions of his visiting fisherman, directed Keith to the vacant chair where he had sat less than an hour previously. It seemed to Keith that it had been only seconds ago, maybe that he had never left but had momentarily allowed his attention to lapse having only dreamed his recent trauma. Yet strangely it seemed that the interview earlier with the Gestapo Major, in which he had searched his own soul purging it of all possible guilt and had been returned his livelihood, his manhood even, had been an age ago. So long ago that it had not seemed part of his experience, just as his memories of the life of freedom and the life of plenty before the Occupation seemed.

"Well Mr. de la Haye, I am a busy man. We have here a lot of work to be done quickly, yes?"

Keith, bemused and as puzzled as he had been an hour earlier, almost effected a slight nod, to what, he knew not, giving credence to Major Müller's continuation.

"You are a free man. As you no doubt suspect we have here, in this building, your wife . . ." He paused and blew through his fingers clasped and crossed in front of his face.

'Here's the church, and here's the steeple,' thought Keith, 'open the door and see the people.'

"Your wife and . . .," hesitation, ". . . child, yes?"

Keith drew himself back from his musings. Hell, he must be going mad or something. What was he doing here? Was he playing child games with this German? What had Müller said about his child? What in the devil's name was going on?

"Mr. de la Haye, we want information from you, and you are going to give it, yes?"

There was no response. Keith had heard but it seemed to bear no relevance to the nursery rhymes he was trying to

31

recall. Or was he trying to draw back his present from the past?

"Mr. de la Haye, we have regulations. Under these regulations you have to tell us anything we ask of you, to which you know the answer. It is against the law for you to remain silent."

He waited for that to sink in, not realising that his words of erudition had just marched up to the top of the hill with the Grand Old Duke of York and were now half way down again.

"Under our regulations, we are allowed to punish people who do not tell us what they know and which we wish to know."

Humpty Dumpty was falling off his wall! Oh no, he was caught by Little Jack Horner. Little Jack Horner? No it was Georgie Porgie, Pudding and Pie wasn't it? No, what was it he did? . . . kissed the girls and made them cry! What was going on?

Keith broke in, unaware that he was interrupting the Major's lecture on the treatment of aliens in occupied countries.

"Where's my wife? I want to see her. Now!"

"Be quiet, man," said Pieter Müller, barely able to hide his irritation at being interrupted, "you will see her in due course. Or should I say, might see her, depending on how quickly we complete our business this morning."

"Eh?"

The Major continued.

"For failing to tell us what we must know, we can use all means at our legitimate disposal. Do you understand?"

Keith wasn't sure but inclined his head slightly. The Major continued;

"If all our usual methods fail we can have you sentenced under the law and sent to prison in France. I am sure you are aware of this, are you not, de la Haye?"

Keith nodded. He had not ever heard of such reasoning but he felt that with the Germans everything was possible. If they wanted to call black white then they'd pass a law to say so and, they at least, would believe it. But what in hell had all this to do with Anne?

"What's this got to do with me?" he interjected. "We had

all this out this morning. If you want to send me to France then do so but why the hell involve my wife?"

"Mr. de la Haye, please remain calm. We cannot effect our business if you keep interrupting me . . ."

"What bloody business?" Keith's anger jerked him out of his earlier lethargic day dream and, in a flash of mind, it all came clear to him. These creatures wanted him to speak and to give up all that he treasured, in his dealings with his friends and comrades, for the release of his wife and child from implied transportation to France. Hell, that was dirty! What a punch below the belt.

'Oh yes,' he thought, 'I can stand their Room Five, I can steel myself for it, live through it all in my mind and over-come it only to be released. Then they only have to mention the same treatment for her, for the very one with my unborn child, for which I'd bear the suffering, for me to collapse and sell all. But they can't! No matter what they think they've got on me they've got nothing at all on her. It's all one big sick bluff.'

"Mr. de la Haye, I am losing my patience," sighed the Major wearily so that either he was an exquisite actor at the part, or as more probably, talking the truth. "I cannot spend much longer with you and this is the truth. Look!"

Keith had no chance to reply. The Major pulled one of the inevitable Nazi documents from his drawer pushing it, almost reluctantly, towards Keith.

"Before I explain this to you, Guernseyman, listen and do not interrupt for I will only say it once. You have only one choice and, if you do not make it, I will carry out my duty, as written here, and do it for you."

He said these words with such sombre sincerity that Keith was completely stunned to the silence of incredulity, tinged with a mixture of intense curiosity and, for the first time in this whole Occupation, a growing sense of respect for the integrity of this first German adult he had met, who seemed almost human.

"As I said, we have the right in law to send you to France for your non-cooperation with the causes of the Reich. However, that, I think, would be a waste of time." He paused to collect his thoughts ready for his coup de grace. "If we send you to France it will do nothing for us. It would mean only that you would suffer a bit. Possibly you might die but that would be of no concern to the authorities here. On the other hand, you might live and you might return here one day, perhaps before, perhaps after, we have won this war. You would be a broken man, your health would have been destroyed in France and probably your spirit too but you would return to your wife, old by then, and one child who will run in fear from this thin old man with no teeth and hollow eyes. Both you and your wife would, by then, be too old to sire more offspring but you would be back to your freedom under the liberating swastika. That is no good to us, though. We are not vindictive, we do not want you to suffer if we realise right from the start that it will not aid our cause. No, we have a far more effective plan." Here he indicated the document once more. He beckoned Keith to move closer to observe its script thereby to reinforce his point.

"You see, Mr. de la Haye, you are a married man. Our country repects the civil laws of occupied territories, where they do not conflict with the aims of the Reich, or until such times as we can modify them to our superior legal system. As you are married then, under the laws existing both in my country and your England, you and your wife are one person. Whatever wrong you do is equally attributed to her and whatever action we take, or wish to take against you, we can do likewise, quite legally, to her."

Keith knew it. He had known it from the moment he had returned home, an hour before, to discover Anne gone and the house in a shambles. He had known it, when the old crone from next door had given him the tidings of malevolence, from the 'phone unplugged at the exchange and then re-connected so that the Gestapo could terrorize the unspoken fears growing like an evil cancer in his subconscious. Yes, he had known all along, though he had suppressed it, that they had his sweet one and would use her to make him act against his very nature.

He did not have to speak. He did not have to question the Major or scrutinize the document. His was now only to listen and to obey, to learn the terms of his unconditional surrender, as he sank back in his hard chair, shrinking into its angular frame, hands all of a shake, teeth chattering and eyes ready to brim with salt from the tears which would not rain. He shrank back and surveyed the king of the castle.

"Believe me, de la Haye, this is painful." The Major coughed in his sincerity. "I can see you are an intelligent man and have already, to some extent, worked out what could be inevitable."

Keith shrugged. He eyed the sparrow with his little arrow.

Major Müller was pleased with himself for he had used once more his not forgotten art of mental persuasion. Unlike his dolt of a Lieutenant, he had not used the physical. He was pleased, for it made him feel young once more, it linked him with bygone emotions of bygone times when he had felt the elation of success accompanied by pleasant fatigue. He now felt this, as Keith de la Haye, proud fisherman and loyal to his friends, was about to aquiesce and sell his very soul. Yet strange, Pieter Müller, National Socialist more of convenience than of conviction, an erstwhile bigot and admirer of elitism but now more a seeker of the quiet life and going with the strongest political tide to ensure an easy journey, felt a sadness as he watched the wretch in front of him. There was something about the man which he had admired for he had shown true spirit for his cause and his country right up until the last.

Now it was he, Pieter, who represented this man's loss, for it was he who was to destroy the man and make him, through love of his wife, sell the lives of his friends. He should have felt glad and proud for Germany, but he felt something which was very foreign to him, which only on much later reflection would he come to realise was a sense of shame.

The Major explained to Keith, the purport of the document on his desk. He spoke to him more as a brother, than as an alien. The document was a carbon copy of an earlier despatch to the General's inner administrative office. It had been coded 'Urgent' which would ensure the General's personal and immediate attention. In fact, it had to be dealt with by the General personally for, by its very nature, it flouted the Geneva Convention. Only Generals, like nearly virgins, could slightly disregard the breaking of this thin veneer of civilization painted onto the obscenities of war, with near impunity.

In it was requested the legalising of the removal to France, to a house of correction, at least 10km from the coast, of one Anne de la Haye, spouse of Keith de la Haye, withholder of the Reich's information; there to be kept indefinitely at the Führer's pleasure; the order to be operational from 1200 hours when the said woman would be handed to the transportation authority.

It was now 10.25. Pieter stated that once noon was reached the order would have all the force of law and would be irreversible. Even if Keith wished to change his mind, to speak, thereby releasing his wife, if it were after 12.00 noon it would be too late. The only way such an order could be rescinded, once Anne had been handed over, would be by Adolf Hitler's inner circle of advisers. Pieter Müller knew how non-existent such a chance would be as any such request would be kept from the Führer during such momentous times as these. The final appeal did not exist any more than the mercy of the S.S. was reputed to exist.

No, Keith had to do Judas' work now and do it quickly. He had no time for further soul-searching. All that had been done already.

He complied. One after another he sold his friends to prison, he gave the families of friends to anxiety and fear. He let their wives die over and over as they waited for non-existent news from the French mainland, where their fated loved ones served indeterminate sentences. He gave the children of his friends bitter salt-sobbed night-time pillows for comfort and hungry bed-time bellies. He gave himself over to doors slammed as he passed by, unseen bearers of rude calls in the street, to an exclusion by all at the Golden Lion, to vandalism on his boat, abusive 'phone calls and anonymous letters. In return he kept his Anne and his unborn son. She would have to learn to live the life of isolation too. Together they would have to support each other and she'd have to be bloody grateful. Maybe when the war was over, he could start afresh and move away to Sark or Alderney, to follow his trade. Perhaps he could even go to Jersey, for on a clear day he'd just be able to make out his homeland from there.

As he signed, Keith could not understand why. He just knew that he was fighting this whole damned war alone, that for the present all its evil and hate, injustice and hurt, were on him and were, through him, being passed to others. Keith, now by proxy an anti-Christ, sobbed as he signed his statement.

The Queen of Hearts retrieved her tarts.

Their business was finished at 11.25. The Major had now to work hard and fast to effect a stop to Anne's deportation order before it reached the transportation authorities. Maybe it was too late? If he had been Hansel he would not have been concerned for he had now in front of him what he needed. But, he was not Hansel and he now knew that if he did not get the man's wife spared he would personally destroy the evidence to hand and repress the information gained.

So Keith had lost much but, although late in years, Pieter had gained plenty. The island would be a little sadder now, thanks to Keith, but maybe the world would be a little better, thanks to the Major, from Keith's plight, new commitment to honour and respect of sincerity.

*   *   *

It was a silent couple who left Grange Lodge Gestapo headquarters at three minutes past noon on that momentous Friday.

Neither spoke, or wished to speak, nor knew what to say, or how to say it. Both Keith and Anne walked physically side by side, but spiritually alone. And both wanted it that way.

Keith hated Anne, for she was a woman, she was weak and she was pregnant and he had not been able to let her suffer. Keith hated Anne because he loved her, with a love so deep that he had sold all his friends to the evil of the German tyranny. He hated her, for now she was all he had, she was the only item of value in his life, for she was everything. There was nothing else.

Anne hated Keith for he was free and she loved him and she wanted him to be free. But she knew that his freedom must have been gained at the expense of others' suffering and incarceration. And she knew that he had sold all so that she would not be harmed, and she loved him for it. But now he would have only her and she, only him. How could they look each other in the eyes again and see the betrayal lurking in each other's soul? How could they ever talk again, or have any form of intercourse?

Each was fated to love the one they hated and to hate the one they loved for the two were one as victims and in their guilt. Each soul hated itself for living through such an impasse.

*   *   *

The silent walk home complete, Keith left Anne at her door. He could not enter, for it was her house. It was his house too, but he now knew it could never be *their* house.

Keith ran faster than any man has ever run. In seconds his body was transported from outside his house to the wide part of Rue des Forges, opposite Larry Collins' shop. In his fleeting, gliding errand he was out-running all evil and would warn his friend before the Nazis reached him. His pistons pumped as he heard his breath, in smooth motion with his arms and legs.

"Larry," he cried, "get out mate, get out quick, you old bugger! The Jerries are coming! I've told them everything. Quick mon vieux, quick! Go! Go! Don't worry about Frances and John I'll look after them, I promise. Just go!"

Keith pushed Larry from the shop, Larry unable to resist his pressure.

"Take my boat, she's in the careening hard. Go now, the tide's up. You'll just make it ... Don't worry about the boom, bluff it, look as if you know what you're doing ... Better to be shot than to go to France, eh? ... At least you've got a chance this way ... enough fuel to get you almost to Alderney ... Head west once you've passed Fort Doyle ... Oh bugger the reefs! I've told you, it's high tide ... Take a chance! ... Please for my sake, for Anne's sake, for my child's sake, go! A Royal Navy ship will pick you up ... You'll see ..."

Larry gone, Keith ran to the 'phone. All caution had gone now. What did it matter what the bastards heard now? They knew everything now, anyway.

"What's the number? Oh yes." That was good, all the numbers came to him, readily from his memory. The operator was so efficient, so helpful, so kind. She knew. She knew what Keith had done and wanted to help him put it right.

"Go, catch Larry at the Harbour, escape to England. . ."

"Peter? Clear off quick the Germans are after you . . ."

"George? . . . Can you? Good, then run like hell. . ."

"Frank, don't argue, just go. . ."

"Thank's Joe, I'm so glad you understand. I'll owe that pint till after the war".

". . . yes Bill, see you in England. Don't be long liberating us . . ."

The pummelling in his veins and arteries stopped, his hard breathing and so-vital momentum ceased, his moving limbs came to a halt, his heart stopped, his mind stopped. The 'phone conversations drifted away on this so-hot afternoon. The little boat just now, sufficiently lapped by the heavy clean salt water to be able to take Larry to his freedom, moved away. Larry moved away.

Larry, stumbling over the shop step through his forced and unexpected ejection, rocked and swayed from the blows and cuffs he had just received inside the door, as his assailant roughly manacled him to the chains which were to deprive him of the freedom, so recently awarded in Keith's thoughts.

There was nothing Keith could do now except become the failure his racing mind had tried so desperately to prevent.

He stood back, as the first of the many comrades, whose lives and freedom he had sold, was taken to what must surely be for all free people, a loss of freedom. All were destined to be deprived of anything which they found of value. Each had only to value something to know that its loss would be inevitable. Such was the way of wars, especially when they had beings like Keith to beam and focus the hate rays and kindle fires of evil which would gut the civilization of all its true values.

Keith's embodiment, as the catalyst for all that is odious, was crystallized, as bent and pain-stunned Larry saw him trying to seek mid-day shadows to hide himself, in the manner of Adam, vessel of none good. Larry momentarily noticed the one who had stood bruised and mortified in his shop only last week, the one who had cried and begged to his very soul for the mercy of quick passing time to bring old age in place of youth, in exchange for the removal of

39

these times. Larry saw him and knew that here was the man who, with his woman, on his belly would go, to feed his mind on dust for the rest of his days. Larry despised him and pitied him. He would go to hell rather than be in de la Haye's place now. And as such he no longer saw Keith, for the fisherman was no longer a person. He had become the mid-day shadow that he had sought.

Larry saw only the dark shadowed granite wall opposite as he lifted his shoulders and marched up straight, almost leading his captors. It was a Larry who now had no longer to concern himself with his destiny, or that of others, for all such considerations now were outside his control.

In his captivity Larry was free. In his freedom, Keith was imprisoned in his own mind.

*   *   *

Chapter Three

The car sped towards Winchester. Gerda sat in the back holding Frances' hand. Still she had not told her mother-in-law, still they got closer.

Their driver was silent.

Gerda had to say.

Gerda could not speak.

Gerda could hear, in her conjecture, Frances' questions as to why they were going out at this time and to where, and what was the urgency. She waited for the old lady to protest that they should not be out at this time for John would be arriving home at any moment. It was this very concept which motivated her.

'I'll mention it before the lights,' she thought. Down Andover Road they sped. There were the lights. Closer, closer they got! Still she had not spoken, but she had to.

Green, now red. Still they drove towards them. Yes the green filter and now their own light, they were going to make it!

Green lights, red lights, green, red, green, red. That was what had killed John, red lights! Red lights, red blood. Darkness, killed! Blood! Killed!

What was she thinking? Killed, he had not been killed! John was still alive. Hurry! Hurry!

*   *   *

Frances shivered. She said not a word. Gerda clutched her to herself while her friend drove on up the hill through a frosted window of tears.

They were outside the hospital now. All three of them shook. All three rushed from the car with nightmare slowness.

*   *   *

Frances was aware that she had fainted, and the throbbing in her head reminded her that she had hit her head on the kitchen table. There had been a lot of bleeding too, as old Gaudion from downstairs had tried to clean her up with her best tea towel. But she was all right, the pain in her aching head was nothing compared with the torment in her mind.

Old Gaudion must have had one of his most exciting days of the Occupation so far. All those comings and gongs! First, he'd ushered in Frances' sister Rita for one of her fleeting visits, then the Germans! Oh yes, he must have loved that, he never missed anything that would shame Frances and her family. He knew that the young German friend of John's had called the other night, and he too must have looked out from behind his curtains to see that angry S.S. man banging on the door the night John had run away from him. Frances had not understood what all that had been about, but she had heard Larry and Bert talking their 'men's talk' about it. That was another thing; old Gaudion must have seen Bert's comings and goings lately, and Bert in his police uniform too! No doubt the old man must have thought the family to be in trouble with the police!

The Germans, oh yes, how Frances was in awe of them. Not like Rita, who felt that as the authorities, they should be respected and obeyed (not that she ever said no to a tin of something or a bar of soap or a candle provided by her criminal brother-in-law). But for Frances it was more a fear than respect. And here they had been in her very own home, and what thoughts they had put into her poor mind.

"Both your husband and son will be standing trial for their crimes against Germany, and both will be found guilty," that German had said.

"It is a formality, both will eventually be sent to France for punishment, or even . . ." he had stated, purposely inconclusive. "We are going to release one of your men until their trials are arranged, the other must stay in prison." With an attempt at humour, he had gone on to say,

"It would not be wise for us to encourage two criminals into the same nest, if you understand."

Frances had been given the impossible task of choosing which of her two men she would have at home, her adored little boy or her beloved husband. That was her dilemma.

That was her choice, but yet, no choice. Her hour for decision was her hour of torment, forcing her to enter the timelessness of hell itself. An hour in which her two men vied in her thoughts, as though begging to be the one released.

"Mum you've been crying. Don't cry, mum. I don't like it when you cry. Please don't cry, . . . for John?", he had said, looking up at her with that disarming little smile which always melted her, always the unconscious prelude for getting his own way.

"I haven't been crying, my love, I'm so happy, really." She had paused, not knowing what to say further and not feeling the need, for she was happy and relaxed for this could go on for ever.

"Mum, why isn't dad here? Why is he still in prison?" She bit her lip. John felt the pain of that pressure, and his smile evaporated, replaced by the dark and angry look of a thwarted little boy. "You kept dad in prison didn't you?" he almost shouted this statement at her. "Why have you kept my dad in prison? I want him now! Why? Why? You wicked woman!"

Then she hated her son for she loved him so that she could not destroy him by telling him the truth. She should have left John in prison, never to be seen by his family and friends again, while she had Larry out, who would comfort her and make all the right decisions, shield her from this terrible guilt, telling her she had done the correct thing, the only thing to be done. Only thing?

"That's O.K. my sweet, just lie back, I want to love you again. All right?" His eyes bore down into hers and she saw the love and desire, feeling their will. It was hers too. How was it that their desire for each other's body was so complementary, so perfect? How was it that, although their oneness was not so frequent now, as first it had been, that always it was as perfect and beautiful and as natural as the sweet dawning morning with its cool purity, following the dream releasing tranquillity of night?

"Larry, oh Larry, make it last! Make it last for ever!" she gasped.

His eyes shallowed, his desire leaving them as his tranquillity and passion withdrew. A flicker of annoyance seemed to shadow his face.

"Not for ever," he snapped, "we've no time. Remember we've got John to consider!" Frances stiffened. All her supple parts became hard and stiff. "Why in hell you got me out instead of him I'll never know and that's the truth!" he shouted. "You, who were supposed to love that boy more than life itself! I just can't understand you Frances, you'd exchange your son's freedom for this!"

She almost ran to the sitting room to look at the clock. She knew it was important, for she only had so much time. For what? Oh, if only she could think clearly! But her head was aching and throbbing, she heard marching boots coming and receding through her skull. Coming and receding. She was inside her own head with then, the unseen sounds inside the great still dome. And she was lost in there. All was light green but there was not a window and no light, just a feeling that all was light green, enclosing her and stifling her and holding her in its viscous mucus so that she could no longer think clearly but only perceive the perpetual tramp, tramp, tramp, of boots as they inflicted their crushing pain.

The clock said only a quarter of an hour left. But a quarter of an hour till what? She couldn't think. Yes she could! The marching stopped. Yes she knew, it was to do with John and Larry. Or was it Larry and John? Just a flicker of insight, while both loved ones jostled for position as they had jostled for the past eternity of forty five minutes, while she had shuffled their freedom and imprisonment, unable to deal out the ultimate and final hand of declared love and pronounced rejection. The feet came pummelling down on her once more, as she closed her vision to the things of this world, welcoming the pain in her head, which took from her the torment of her inner hell.

Beautiful torment, longed-for agony, shielding her from thoughts and decisions with just an occasional cruel intrusion from John and then from Larry.

"Frances, I'm here. Do you hear? I'm in prison. Leave me here. Do you understand? Don't get me out. Get the boy out, he's got a life ahead of him. Get him out. Leave me here, never to be seen again, so they can take me to France and you can forget me. It's better that way. Think of the boy . . ."

The boy, what boy? She had no boy, she'd condemned him to prison. Her son was going to France to face goodness knew what, never to be seen again. Yes, he was off, for she'd deserted him with treachery so she could free the one who'd sired him to this world of misery and now to this non-world.

"It's O.K., mum. Really. I'll be fine in France. You'll see. I'm a grown man now, remember. Let me go, please. Please don't take me out of prison. Get dad out. I'm young and strong. I can look after myself. Get dad out of prison please, so he can look after you and cheer you up. I want to go, really. You wouldn't let me go away with the Intermediate, so now's my chance. I won't come home. Promise me you'll save dad. Promise, promise . . ."

The jar of the 'phone bell froze her with her indecision then quickly brought her to her senses, as all her thoughts rapidly shuffled into a card-pack of undecided priority. Maybe this bell could somehow save her from making her impossible choice? Perhaps it was the conveyor of some remote words of hope, someone who would say something to put off the evil which she had to perform.

'It's Rita,' she thought, 'Oh thank heavens. Rita can tell me what I've got to do.' She moved to the 'phone, confident that it could only be good at the other end. It could not possibly be bad news for she could not feel any worse than she just had. With shaky hand, she picked up the black solace, trembling in an effort to hold back the flood-gates of misery and relief that she had to control just a few seconds more for her sister's ear to share with her.

"Hello?" she enquired hesitantly, her voice charged to full tension, as the ripples of impending relief began to top her defences.

"Frances? – Listen . . .," the voice was a man's, it was not her sister! She was clutched with a cold cramp across her chest so that words were impossible, her disappointment revenging itself upon her, as its children of relief were held still-born. Her thoughts gave the unseen speaker many faces but all were men, all were Germans, none were human, or sympathetic or listeners. None were her sister to whom she could cry out the burden of her heart.

"Frances, is that you?" the voice hissed with insistence, almost urgency. It was not a German voice, it had once been kind, it came from before evil times and it called her Frances!

"Yes," she murmured, waiting for her hardly dared-for hope to be realised. "Who is that?"

"It's me, Bert. Now don't say anything. Just listen, O.K.?" Frances concurred as she bit her lip giving vent to a watery, shrouded smile.

"Look, I'm not talking on the 'phone but I've got to see you right away. Now you wait down by the front door, right. And let me in." He paused, wondering if he should explain his actions or not. Frances interjected quite irrelevantly;

"Larry's not here . . ."

"Yes, I know," said Bert, almost unable to hide his irritation at the introduction of the very subject about which his call was made but about which he was not prepared to converse on the telephone. "You just go down and in a couple of minutes I'll knock ever so lightly so's you can let me in. All right?"

"Yes," she faltered.

"We don't want 'you know who' to know do we?"

Frances was puzzled as she slowly lowered the receiver, almost vacantly, without deference to etiquette. 'You know who?' Who did he mean? 'You know who?' Did he mean the Germans? What a strange thing to say, for they'd sure to have been listening anyway. Maybe he meant Larry? She almost smiled as the thoughts chased each other and so kept her mind from her unthinkable consciousness. Well, why shouldn't she smile for she was going to be with Bert? Even if he brought bad news, she looked forward to it, for at least he would be there, and no news could worsen the burden she already carried. Bert would share it with her.

'You know who'? She was smiling as she almost daintily tripped down the wide shallow stepped ancient staircase past old Gaudion's open doorway, past 'you know who', who was having such an exciting day.

What had seemed to her would be an unbearable wait for Bert to make his way round the corner from the police station, as she rushed down the stairs, in fact flitted away, carried by her new hope. Hope of what, she knew not. Nevertheless hope, for any eventuality at variance from her recent trauma, could only herald such a state.

The gentle tap came almost immediately, its volume enhanced for her by her anticipation yet not sufficiently loud for 'you know who' to hear. She clutched at the handle, wrenching it so that the heavy door swung and pushed open, forcing against the drab walls, pushed by the invading light.

Bert winced at the sound, as he quickly stepped into the dark cavern, but Frances was unaware of his displeasure as she was unaware of his chasing out once more, by his frame, the sunlight so foreign to this place. Also she was not cognizant of the rustle behind her as, almost silent, but elated, Gaudion flitted via the passage, from one dark room to another.

"Oh Bert, come up quickly, love," she effected, as she tentatively touched his hand, turning to lead the way.

"Hurry!" he said gruffly, the unexpected tone of his voice taking her by surprise. The one word put her in her place, for it moved her back from hope to the anticipation and forboding of misery.

Once upstairs and in the kitchen Bert dismissed her attempt at niceties, trivialities as they seemed to his urgency, and she did not resist or protest.

"Frances," he began, "just listen. Don't say a word, don't interrupt, there's just no time. They've got Larry."

He paused momentarily, waiting for the anticipated fear and incredulity to pass from her face, so that he could rush on with the news and his urgent instructions. There was no upset, no display of fear, no distraught Frances. He was taken aback.

"Yes," she said, as the words smiled from her, "and they've got my little John too . . ."

It was Bert who now displayed all the symptoms of surprise, but there was not sufficient time to indulge in the luxury. This mystery had to be cleared, and quickly, so he could expedite his mission.

"What's that? They've got John? How do you know all this?" He almost shouted his question in his demand for rapid reply.

47

His tone was complemented by raised voices in the house below.

Both stood still. Both knew. They could only listen and wait alone in their togetherness, each with a different reason, for the sounds below.

As the tramp of boots and the gabble of voices grew louder up the stairs, the gutteral sounds of German commands, with the obedient grunts and mono-syllables of the recipients, intertwined with the insipid whine of Gaudion's voice, as he invited himself to the party, Frances knew that her hour was up and that she could still not give an answer.

With the abomination filling Bert's ears, he knew that someone had informed on him, of his visit here to illegally discuss German matters.

Both were wrong.

* * *

John entered the kitchen apace. His rush, almost a trip, as if he had been, as in reality was the case, propelled from behind. This sudden entry regressed Frances's thoughts to that moment, now so long ago last week, when full of excitement and glee, he had announced the R.A.F. planes were bombing the harbour. Now she stood with Bert, then she had stood with Larry. Both she loved, neither could she requite herself with. Then she had lived in her own mind-created fears of the unknown. Now she lived in those fears, and still all was unknown.

John now had no gasping excited smile on his face. This had been exchanged, in its boyishness, for that of a man. He had left this morning an agitated, impatient, self confident, if a little nervous boy, anxious to get the business over and to clear his self righteous name. He now stood there, all momentum stopped, bewildered and frightened. The light had gone out of his eyes and the youthfulness from his cheeks. His face showed he had lost his trust in the world. It was not just the superficial bruising of his lips or the swelling of his eye above his inflamed and lacerated cheek-bone, or the red-raw of his stinging ear. Nor was it his loose front teeth usually so beautiful and white, now yellow and stained from bleeding gums. It was more than these things, for they would pass and given time, would heal. Even the inner scars of fear would heal, in time, and by some grace might lend some of their excess healing to the irradication of bitterness and hate which now inhabited John Collins. No, it was more than all these things, for the John who had left his mother this morning had now returned a different person. The John who stood before her now was grown up. Her little boy had died while he was away. Her other man had returned.

"We have decided for you, Mrs. Collins," announced the kindly German who had helped Frances' second man so speedily into the room, followed in turn by his jostling minions and the invading curiosity of Gaudion. "He is well, as you see."

There was silence. Frances was unable to speak, having had her most momentous task of decision taken away from her in this way, but to no satisfactory conclusion. Bert and John were abashed to silence alike, neither understanding the purport of the German's words.

The German waited for some reaction then quickly, as though for effect, to stem what he had anticipated, but which had not come, continued as if it had;

"You see, Mrs. Collins, we understand mothers. We know German mothers would favour their sons rather than their husbands, for it is the duty of all Germans to select that which is more serviceable and to discard that which is of less use. We think the mothers of occupied countries, in the main, also think the same but perhaps pretend to agonize more. So, to save time, we have made your choice for you."

"Yes," was all Frances could manage. She stepped forward and reached for her grown-up son, putting her arms around him as if he were her lover. Thus she clung to her duplicate Larry, completely at one with the stiff unbending body, her face buried in his shoulder, as her racking sobs gave vent to her pent-up grief. John, now above embarrassment or the self consciousness of teenage boys, allowed his mother to sate herself while he relaxed himself and stroked the hair on her poor sobbing head. And in his new deflowered state, he too, allowed himself to weep with her for all the woes and miseries of the world which they carried on their shoulders.

49

The German looked away, embarrassed at the prospect, addressing himself to Bert.

"You are a civil policeman, yes?"

"Yes."

"Why are you here?" a question tinged with both genuine inquisitiveness and irritation.

"You tell me," replied Bert, in no mood to cooperate with the filth before him, the filth that had brought so much misery to his island and to this dear family in particular.

"I ask you," demanded the German, controlling his dignity. "What is your business here?"

"Visiting friends."

"Ah yes, I see," uttered the Teuton with gleeful sarcasm. "Of course, all policemen of the civilian force have friends in the criminal classes . . ."

"Leave off, won't you?" howled Frances breaking away from John's shoulder and turning her swollen eyes and misery stained face towards the two of them. "Haven't you Jerries caused us all enough trouble? Why can't you just go away?"

In tones, definitely more clipped than before, the German, affronted at this interruption, gave his final interdict.

"I go now, but I return. Mrs. Collins, you are to stay in this house with your son until you hear to the contrary. Is that clear? You may not have visitors until I have spoken with you again!" Here he looked at Bert studying him from head to toe. With a sneer in his voice adding, "We will be speaking together soon, policeman. Please to go about your duty now."

Bert said not a word, but it was clear by his actions that the full significance of the words had marked him. He simply stared at the German expressionless, signifying neither his inner hate nor disgust at all the creatures represented. Then, quickly and smartly, he picked his helmet from the table and leaned forward, kissing Frances on the cheek. Her hand went for his, to stay him, but he was too quick, too efficient.

Without loss of face, as if with one movement, in one stride, he completed his valedicton of Frances and giving John a reassuring pat on the shoulder, back turned to ignore the non-existent officer, he pounded from the room, all but Gaudion just managing to clear a way for him. The grunt, as he accidentally stepped on the old creature's foot, accompanied his memories of the scene as he descended the shallow stairs three at a time.

John and Frances stood shocked still, while a clatter of feet down the stairs passed, as an encore to Bert's hurried exit. Neither was quite sure how to interpret the past few minutes' events, for each had a tale of events different to the other's leading to the, now quiet, impasse.

Two flights down, the front door slammed shut and the harsh clipping of jackboots faded, the echoes dying away on the upper reaches of this vast old delapidated mansion.

A new sound assaulted their ears from far below, outside this time, rising and coming to them through the half open sash window. Now the boots gave their attention to the smooth granite cobble stones. They were accompanied by voices, the voices of command and the voices of obedience together with a general scuffle of activity.

John sidled to the window and looked down.

"They've got old Gaudion with them," he announced with a whistle, as their nosy old landlord was taken away.

*　　*　　*

51

Chapter Four

The whole lacerated and ruptured liver was exposed now. Each handling and turning of the flaccid organ further dampened it with the sticky dark red fluid.

"That is it," whispered the Consultant, "that is our impossible task."

The organ appeared too badly damaged to effect a lasting repair. They only had sufficient time for first aid. A miracle would be needed to effect success.

Time had almost gone now, the orthopaedic staff had almost tidied their task. At least, theirs was possible.

The pulse continued to quicken and the blood pressure to fall. More transfusions were following on from each other while all those present kept stealing glances at the instruments.

Sister bit her lip. The anaesthetist blanched. Soon he would have to advise his senior colleague that the patient could take no more, that if they continued, in their faint efforts to save him, they would in fact hasten his termination.

All were aware of this, not least the Consultant. What was his choice? Should he do his utmost to save a man, almost without doubt terminally injured, but not absolutely so, while miracles were sometimes in their gift? Or should the Consultant leave him to his termination without risking that he might have an untimely death, albeit numbered in hours, on his hands.

Between them the doctor and the Consultant did what they could. When a ship is badly holed and its eventual floundering is beyond most reasonable doubt, wise men patch the largest rents first leaving, if they must, the least devastating. So with this team.

The clamps were removed, swabs counted out, the stitches tied while still damp with bleeding from those lacerations that were outside the reach of time. And the great incision was closed and sealed, the cavity comforting its misery that natural darkness had returned once more where it had been so cruelly violated.

*   *   *

Franz, tired and dejected, Franz, his face still throbbing and aching with pain, demoralized, rejected, a miserable failure, returned to Town Patrol House. He neither wished to go there nor to stay away, for no matter where he might be he was destined to be clamped by the dark clouds of his depression because of his present circumstances and the inevitability that he was bound for the Eastern Front, which held no future for any of Germany's sons, let alone a traitorous, cowardly misfit of an offspring such as he.

Town Patrol House, which was his base from where he had been doing night patrols, was now likely to be his detention centre until his transport was arranged, for he would almost inevitably be confined to House in any off duty periods which he might have.

To make his misery complete, there in the entrance stood his Patrol Leader, as though he knew when the youth would return and was here now as a further part of Franz's punishment. One thing was for sure, he would not let the opportunity pass without taunting the lad and cutting him with sarcastic invective.

Franz was not only afraid of Patrol Leader Morten, but he also detested him. How could he forget the trouble this loathsome adult had caused between him and John when his civilian friend had been invited to the House's relaxation evening? How Franz regretted that he had become drunk and had appeared to John, when he arrived, to have been enjoying the attentions Morten and his S.S. friend and that womanish Frenchman were paying him. It had taken a lot of argument to persuade John that he had not been a willing party to the hand on his thigh or the caress which the other had witnessed. Even now, Franz felt a revulsion and horror at the memory.

"So our little flower has returned from his adventure!" laughed Morten, glad to observe the discomfort on Franz's face. There was nothing he loved more than to play with a victim and make him squirm. Well, to say 'nothing more' was not quite true; there were other things, but they always came well after a prelude of mental sadism.

Morten took such delight in confirming that Franz was confined to House..., "Never to see your dear friend again . . ." He filled his mind with tales of horror of what he was to expect in Russia, and how the S.S., with their exhaustive training, would prepare him for his ordeal, and how, most likely, he would not survive. He said how his friend S.S. Hüffmeier was determined to get to know Franz's friend John. Oh yes, Morten really enjoyed filling the naive young soldier, who stood before him, with precise details, dirty, filthy, perverted ideas of what was in store for John. Franz had heard of such things, but as they had never been in his experience or curiosity of thought, had never really understood, except that his instinct told him they were evil and not a thing for normal people to consider.

"And what a pity you won't be able to warn your friend," sneered Morten. "If only you could let him know, so he could avoid the danger!"

Yes, if only, but Franz realised how impossible such a course would be. Why was Morten saying all this? His tone was almost one of leading Franz to a point where he felt he could or should warn John, but why would he do that? No, Franz knew this was all just part of Morten's cruel game.

"Also, dear Franz, when it has happened, and your friend is full of hate, who do you think he will hate most? Will it be David Hüffmeier? Well you might think so," he effected gleefully, "but no, it will be you!"

He prodded Franz to make his point.

"You are the one he will loathe, for it will be you who brought him into contact with our nation, you who taught him to become friends with Germans. He will hate you for ever!"

There was only one way Franz could save his friend. Oh yes, Morten had prepared his ground well, and he knew that Franz, namby-pamby type that he was, the type who valued true friendship above self interest, (hardly a manly or military attitude) would try to save John.

Yes, if worked on carefully and with continuous sadistic mental cruelty, Franz could be persuaded to put himself in

place of John and become the sacrificial lamb, a sacrifice for
the sake of friendship. After all, Morten had the authority
over Franz's detention, having the power to allow or deny
contact between the two friends, and Hüffmeier did not have
to be gratified, the gift was the Patrol Leader's to bestow.

*   *   *

John could not stay in that house alone with his mother, her
very misery was destroying him.

No, the new man John Collins, through his experiences of
life, the boy transformed into manhood overnight, could not
stay to be dominated by his mother's morbidity. Not now,
not now he was a man with cares of his own!

Frances's distress was very real. John was aware of her
trauma. He knew her whole life was changing miserably
about her, that she was soon to lose not only her husband
but also her cherished son. It was not his place to comfort
her though, not at present. He was allowed to suffer too,
surely?

John had to get out, it was all too oppressive. He needed
to indulge his own thoughts. He had to reflect on the recent
past which would now inevitably colour his future. If he
could entertain such a concept?

No, if his mother was made still more unhappy by his
leaving her, then so be it! She would survive. He would not
be made to feel guilty, he too had the right to be miserable.
It would be better to be introspective while alone.

John left the house. He did not ask permission. He did
not even say he was going, that new man.

And now, here he was, out on those same ringing cobbles
that had only moments before produced the sounds of hate
on history. The ringing he heard now, in his memory, was a
mixture of departing Germanicness, with bitter recriminations
from his own mother who, in her disturbed state, had looked
on him as their only forlorn hope, at the same time berating
him, filling him with sharp recriminations which had pieced
his soul, causing the infection of guilt.

No, there was nothing for it but to look for uncle Bert. He
was sure to have up-to-date news of Dad.

Yes, uncle Bert would help.

* * *

Franz entered the daylight again, the sun was till high and hot. Strange how the sun still shone and gave its warmth, and the life all around went on as ever it did.

Only moments ago he had wrestled in the dentist's chair of Morten's private room, imprisoned by his own fear of the unknown, as he had waited tense for the moment the drill would touch nerves not quite numbed enough by injection. His few minutes had stretched for him like endless days while the surgeon had applied first one treatment and then another.

Franz shuddered at the memory while he felt himself physically shrinking with the untouchable filth he knew he had been party to. Again and again, as he revelled in the sun's warmth and real feeling, signifying the eternity of true and wholesome living, his mind darted back to that sunless room with its curtains half drawn.

He did not know quite where he was walking, all he knew was that his slow and rather listless footsteps now lacking in innocence, were taking him away from the evil hateful place whose darkness and coolness contrasted with the life on his cheeks outside.

Yet, even as he walked away, his thoughts involuntarily and wilfully kept returning to that vile place. To that room which was to haunt him for the rest of his days, to the place where the Nazi state, which till then had nurtured and built him, had completed his education.

* * *

It was strange coincidence, the like of which surround us, passing us by unnoticed most often, which brought the two friends together on this warm and humid day. It was perhaps the close proximity of these very two morbid souls which had helped, fixing them on the same path, the each heading towards the other as if to complement like the last two pieces of a puzzle. One light and speedy with worry and anxiety, the other dark and shaded with morbid introspection and guilt.

The meeting right outside the police station was the fulfilling of an unspoken need in each of them. John forgot his father in prison. In fact the encounter momentarily freed the parent who went about his mechanical trade as ever. Franz forgot his shame, the guilt and self disgust. For a few seconds he was the same virgin spirit who had first encountered this, his best friend, his enemy.

They both laughed involuntarily as they greeted each other. What did it matter who saw they were friends?

At that moment John's father was no longer incarcerated and Franz's soul was no longer tortured on that vile bed of unloving lust.

"Franz! This is absolutely marvellous!" shouted John, as he pushed his brother out from him to arms length, while still clamping his hand on the Teuton's shoulders. There were bruises yes, but no more than he had expected. They were both men now, they knew how to suffer bravely. Each wore his badge of bravado, each would heal.

Franz laughed;

"Oh John, you don't know how glad I am to see you, my friend. I too thought we would never meet again. And here we are! This is just too good! Come, where shall we go to talk?"

The words supposed that they were not complete here, there was something not quite right. If things had been right then why should they need to go elsewhere? What was wrong with here?

Each became aware now of the hiatus as both were imbued with an anger that the other was not breaking it.

The sound, as they simultaneously voiced their anxieties, to do the silence breaking task, which was really the other's, was the sound of embarrassment.

"Come on," urged John, "we can't stand here like this Franz. You know where we bloody well are, don't you?"

The question was rhetorical but Franz had raised his eyebrows questioningly as though expecting to be enlightened.

"We're right outside the police station," John hissed. "Look, I think we'd better split up and meet somewhere else, O.K.?"

The thoughts were whirling now, quickly through John's mind, as he took in the still-life picture of this pale and puzzled friend, tottering slightly before him in the warm bright sunlight.

Should he ask Franz to call round at his place? No, Gaudion would be sure to see him there! But no, Gaudion had gone off with the Germans so that was O.K.. But what of his mother? Well they could talk downstairs couldn't they? His mother wouldn't be likely to be coming down. Besides, if they heard her approaching, they could always move on down to the basement. At least they'd be out of sight of prying passers-by, once inside the dark passage of the old and musty house. Then Gaudion might return! With the Gestapo too. No, that wouldn't do! What about Candie Gardens where they'd first tasted the freedom of true comradeship, crossing the international boundaries of hate and division in this artificial war? Yes, maybe Victor Hugo would let them rest at his feet a while?

"Where John? Shall we go to your house maybe? You could go on that way and I could go. . ."

"No, not there. It's not possible! I'll explain later," interjected John with urgency.

"Well what about my house?" asked Franz. "There's no one in except Morten and he's not likely. . ."

"What?" interrupted John incredulously. "I can't go there! You know that! You're being damned stupid Franz! No, listen, we must meet in Candie Gardens, you know, where we had that fight, under 'You go's statue, remember?" His lips pursed into a sight smile as he realised Franz might well remember the statue but would most likely not recall the joke.

The urgent plan was still-born, rendered impossible by the appearance of the very contingency they were planning to prevent.

The policeman who stepped out of the station was no less than uncle Bert. That adult's face seemed to freeze into a gasp of amazement or horror. Or was it just plain disbelief?

John's immediate reaction was a feeling of relief for here, without further bother was the very man he had sought. His short-lived elation was quickly dashed as it turned to embarrassment while he realised, without the passing of words, the reason for P.C. Bisson's expression. And that focus, too, in the form of a guilt ridden and miserable Franz, having his feelings of being a less than human pariah, owing to the events which had scarred his character only minutes before, stood next to him.

Bert beckoned the two to him so that they would stand in close to the station wall with less likelihood of being seen from within.

"Uncle Bert," began John, but he was pre-emptorilly cut short.

"Shut up! What in God's name do you think you're up to?"

John was abashed. He wanted to grasp at Uncle Bert to tell him how glad he was he'd found him and to enlist his willing help but now here he was, feeling decidedly uncomfortable. He could not think why this family friend should be so uncharacteristically rude. Yet he knew why. The reason stood next to him.

"What?" asked John, not succumbing to a more polite form of enquiry.

"I said, why are you here like this when you've already caused enough trouble? Are you as bloody stupid as you make out? Haven't you any idea of what you're doing to your family?"

Bert's stream of rhetorical questions was accompanied by angry gestures, as he just managed to restrain himself from assaulting his so called nephew, in order to knock some sense into him.

John could not speak, he knew what was coming, for it was inevitable. With a feeling of heavy lead in the pit of his stomach he turned to Franz shrugging, as if to say, 'Sorry it's not my fault. I can't help what he says. You know it's not my fault. All this is just as bad for me as it is for you.' But his eyes did not complement his gestures of submission to the absurd. His eyes transmitted to the already miserable Franz that he was not sure any more. His eyes told his friend, 'I want you as a friend but you really are a nuisance. Maybe you'd be all right if you and I were what we seem but with you being a German, and . . . Well it's just a bit awkward for us to be friends at present. Maybe what uncle Bert is trying to say is for the best?'

"Why don't you go home to your mother? Surely she needs you now? How the hell can you go round with this, . . . with this . . ." Words failed him, as he contemplated the despicable son of the master race, inwardly writhing with hurt and unspoken embarrassment.

"What the hell you need to tell the whole world that you're a bloody quisling for I don't know! And for what? What is there so special about this little runt that you'd sell your family and all your friends?"

Franz was pale. It was true. He was nothing. He was a Nazi. Well at least he was the product of the Nazi state. Today he was nothing, he was not even masculine any more. Today his masculinity had been taken away from him by one of the elders of the very faith upon which he had willingly, or unwillingly, been weaned. All he knew was that he loved his brother John. He felt less than human, less than Nazi even. He was a non-person and as such was scum and filth like the same abhorrence he had just experienced.

As Franz stood pale, diminished to nothingness, so was John moving away. He could not in the short moments, exhilarated by his hitherto untapped adrenalin, rationalize the emotions he felt, but his whole physique seethed with a rising anger. His chest heaved and his breathing intensified as his cheeks flushed. He found his fists clenching while his anxieties for family and concepts of loyalty slipped away from him. He felt only the need to vindicate the status of his friend. In this momentary situation Franz became the only true focus of his attentions. Here was Franz shrinking and feeling as nothing, but his very feelings pulsing and, in their negativeness, transmitting to John; hiding from help, but in so doing eliciting his friend's support, to the final state of mankind, if need be.

John in his anger and Franz in his shame were united against a common foe which was neither fascist nor democratic but the foe of being from without, and in so being, from outside understanding, therefore not worth the effort now set in motion.

"Don't speak to me like that," ordered John in slow and deliberate words while his anger was reduced in inverse proportion to his efforts of self restraint. "I've come to look for you, Uncle Bert," he emphasized, the latter two words an unconscious attempt to imbue the policeman with guilt at his unthought out words, "to ask news of my father. I suppose I'm lucky to have found you. But I didn't come here to have my friend insulted in front of my face!" He paused to allow the slaking of his anger. He had wanted to tell Uncle Bert that he had not brought 'this German' with him, that he had bumped into 'this German' and that he would not have been so careless of his family's well being to be seen openly associating with 'this German' but his anger was such, at the recent outpourings from his uncle and the injustice of a half understood and regurgitated thesis by the same, that his instinct told him to defend his friendship with Franz would only be to cheapen it, imply it was wrong. He did not need to defend something which could stand with pride on its own.

"O.K.. O.K.! I haven't got time to argue the rights and wrongs. You've got to see to your own mistakes," said uncle Bert, "But just listen, John Collins, my lad. You're all in deep trouble, really deep. Did you know that, eh?"

John shuffled uncomfortably, looking at his shoes. All he could think was how damned dirty they were! They still had dust on and scratch marks from the cliffs, whatever age ago that had been. Even Franz's boots were uncared for! Hell, what sort of German was he associating with? He didn't even have the benefit of being clean, smart, brave and cheerful as their image had always led him to expect!

"You're in bloody trouble. Prison for you at best, France more likely. And your mother? Well she might get away with things. I doubt if they can pin anything on her, but they might try." He paused as if the thought of Frances suffering was more than he could bear. "Besides, how will she manage with you locked away, and your poor father?"

Again Bert's voice trailed off. He was filled with dual emotions as he addressed the miserable, foolish wretch in front of him. He felt terror and dread for his best friend Larry, knowing what he must be going through at this very moment, and what it would all amount to. It all made John's few months in the Guernsey hard labour prison, or the half year – year at most in an austere French prison, seem like nothing. Larry would be proven genuinely guilty of many crimes against the civil authorities, and many against the occupying forces, all of which could be substantiated by normal legal processes, let alone those employed by the tyrants. In the eyes of the world, such as which really bothered to keep a watchful eye on the fate of individuals, his treatment would be seen to be the expedient of justice. He would be erased from the lists of the legitimate human race and condemned to the list-less, there to be treated, or mistreated, with impunity, at the whims of the list-less keepers. Larry was about to be legally edited from the human race and there was no action, thoughts, prayers or processes which could be employed in its prevention. He would be edited, and corrected or erased. And no one would know, few would care and less would be caused permanent anxiety by it, for who can remember someone who has legally reached the status of no longer existing?

Bert felt also a guilt-ridden emotion of joy, the joy that is pushed from the mind as unclean and unnatural because it gives pleasure, therefore must be evil. With his best friend no more, he would have to comfort and console Frances in her time of need, and beyond. No, he must not have such thoughts, for this had much guilt-laden potential.

Larry or Frances? Frances or Larry? Larry or yourself? Yourself or Larry? It was all too impossible and had to be woken from. The waking salvation was the other state which embroiled them all.

"You're not the only ones, too!" he barked, his voice rising considerably so that it almost cracked into a sob of self pity at its highest reach. "I'm under investigation right now. Did you know that? Did you know that Uncle Bert is no longer a policeman?" He pulled off his duty band with dramatic effect, had been further going to heighten his actions by throwing it away to its fate, but saved himself from that course, through years of habit and respect. He carefully placed it into his pocket.

"Yes, I've been suspended. 'Not a fit person to work for the force to uphold law and order!' Law and order, I ask you? Uphold those filthy Nazi bastards. Sod the lot! Like you, I'm to go to court too. God help the lot of us!"

He gestured towards the windows above him.

"Yes, that lot in there! They're the ones who should go on trial, not you and me and Larry and . . .," he gave a slight pause as if through emotion, he had lost the train of his jumbled thoughts ". . . and him."

As Bert pointed to Franz, he looked directly at his face, so their two gazes met and locked, the younger with interest and clear ready to perceive, the older with anger and distraught with turbulence.

"We'll all be for it and that's for sure! We've all of us had it. Oh yes, they've seen us together now but that doesn't matter. It only makes a little quicker, and a little more sure, what is inevitable."

John broke in, as if he had been completely oblivious of Uncle Bert's inner turmoil or his propounded philosophies;

"What of Dad? What can you tell me? What's happening to him? Where is he? Tell me, tell me. I've got to know." He grasped at Uncle Bert's now unbanded arm, pleading for an end to the talk and conjecture. He needed news, for that was why he had come. He needed news of his father to take home to Frances. And P.C. Bert Bisson, albeit now suspended Constable Bisson, was able to provide it, good or bad.

Bert, not often given over to showing his feelings in public, took command of himself once more.

"Your dad's in there," he pointed to the grey granite prison walls across the road from the police station, "that is, that's where he is officially. . ." He trailed off. It was as if he was spacing his reply as part of some bizarre ritual.

"Eh?" replied John wrinkling his face in confusion.

"What I'm saying is, that is where he is supposed to be. That's where they want people to believe he is. Get it?" He paused for John to 'get it' but, seeing that he obviously had not, expanded;

"He could be anywhere, don't you see? He could be in there, he could be at your office in the Feldkommandantur, answering charges of his crimes against German civilian control. He could be up in the Gestapo for all I know."

"What do you mean, 'all you know'." voiced John with surprising vitriol, almost with sneering contempt. "You ought to know. You're in the police. You work for them and know their ways! Why can't you find out for sure?"

"Listen John, doesn't anything sink in? Haven't I told you I've just been suspended? Aren't I just about to be arrested, don't you think? And probably will be now. . ." He paused raising his hands with gesticulation, letting them fall once more, in a gesture of helplessness.

"Do you really think they're going to let me know anything

when they think, no that's not true, when they damned well know, I'm linked in friendship and dealing with your father? . . ."

"Yes but . . .," tried John, desperately trying to get some sense out of Bert's words.

"But nothing son! All you can be sure of is he's coming up for trial very soon and that's for sure!"

"So?" quizzed John, "and what's that go to do with it?"

"Now look here! Haven't you any damned sense in that brain of yours? If he's up for trial soon, and I mean soon, for the way they were all scrambling round and 'phoning and rushing here, there and everywhere for files and goodness knows what, and it's not like them to rush. . . Where was I?"

John was becoming exasperated as he tried to hold on to a thread of reality in Uncle Bert's seemingly rambling logic.

"You said 'if he's up for trial soon'. What do you mean? Are you telling me he could be just anywhere when he's about to go on trial? Shouldn't he be in the prison. Can't mum and I visit him? Can't we arrange an Advocate for him? What are our rights?" He almost shouted his last question.

"Rights?" laughed Uncle Bert. "You expect rights?" The words were painful for both John and Franz as the latter, who had stood in awful silence for some time, shifted uneasily, as his mind and that of his friend, transmitted the same memory which momentarily recalled another period of adversity. A period, which, by contrast with the present, now seemed halcyon for it had possessed a future then.

"What I'm saying is, if he's up for trial and Court Martial – and that is true, I saw the announcement and charges being drafted for publication – he can't disappear. Not permanently, that is. They can't lose him."

He almost smiled as he observed the look of creeping realisation invade John's face. "They can't harm a man who's going on public trial in a few days, can they? How would bruises and cuts and lost teeth look to those morbid creatures who've nothing better to do than inhabit the public gallery to watch their fellow countrymen condemned to degradation?"

"I see," issued John slowly, seemingly wondering why it

had taken him so long to reach this point of truth. "Yes, I see all that, Uncle Bert. Thank you."

John saw, he understood. He had been angry, now he was calm. He thanked Uncle Bert. Uncle Bert was in no better position to obtain information than he was, perhaps worse? So what had been the purpose of his mission and had it been fulfilled or left incomplete?

John was bemused. He turned to his friend and they both, as one, shrugged and in their gesture took away the whole weight of the impossible and injustice from the now defunct policeman.

As they turned to saunter away, the clouds of misery preventing them from the accepted conventions of politeness, the former reality of Uncle Bert tried to become real once more as he called;

"Wait. There is one person you might try, John! John, listen to me! John, try that priest, Father Peters."

John's departure halted at these words. He stopped suddenly, turning round to face his uncle.

'Yes, that's right,' he thought. 'Why didn't I think of Father Peters? He always knows what to do. He knows the Germans. He knows everything about them, he even visits them. He always knows the answer to everything!'

"But why . . .," he found his thoughts coming alive as he addressed his uncle. "Why do you know that?"

"Pardon?" replied Bert Bisson, puzzled. "I said, visit Father Peters. He's in all this, isn't he?"

There broke through John's subsconscious and into the deep reaches of his conscious mind, just sufficient to disturb his recently settled but highly unstable equilibrium, a feeling of horror, as he perceived some truth, some unspoken truth, in Uncle Bert's words. It was almost as though he knew what the donor was about to impart. He feared and knew what he was about to hear. He dreaded its portent but had no way of stopping its awful error, for he had nothing of logic in its stead.

"Go on," ordered John coolly, as if he were addressing one of the little boys at the Intermediate, almost beneath his contempt, "tell me something I don't already know."

The sarcasm, as much as it had been intended, was lost

on the recipient, who proceeded with an air of almost non-chalance.

"Peters, that priest from St. Luke's, is all mixed up in this, isn't he? It stands to reason, doesn't it? First there's those reports of his getting subversive 'phone calls from your father, then . . . No, you needn't look so shocked, just listen. Then he gets called to the Gestapo. You know that for a fact! And, I'll tell you, what's more, something you didn't know, and if I were still on service I'd not divulge, but now? What the hell!"

"Uncle Bert," John tried to interrupt but was cut off with only an uttered "but . . ." as P.C. Bisson concluded his thesis of Father Peters' involvement with the group.

"I was saying, there is something else about those 'phone calls. I've seen the report . . ." he bent his head low, almost conspiratorially, maybe in an attempt to exclude the alien Franz from the divulgence. "Father Peters was picked up a few nights ago, after curfew, and he was carrying a letter about your mate here . . ." He paused in order to shape himself into a look of contempt, before continuing. "What's more, there was something said, only a rumour mind, but that anonymous letters have been traced back to the type-writer at the Vicarage. So he's in it with your father, me, you, this, this . . ., person here."

"This is all bloody stupid!" emitted John, forgetting he was addressing an elder and a family friend, and that even though he considered it manly to use the language of Hill Sixty, now that he worked for a living, this adult, like his parents, would in most circumstances, take exception to it.

"You've got it all wrong, Uncle Bert, you really have! You must all be daft in there, you're as mixed up as them!"

He did not have time to expand on the misconception under which both police and Germans apparently laboured together in their uneasy marriage. Bert went on to conclude the interview.

Conspiratorially he conveyed to Franz that he should move out of hearing. To John's surprise and chagrin Franz, by now deeply dejected from all the trauma he had experienced, and the volatile talk he had witnessed, complied, moving slowly up into the shadow of the prison wall, while uncle

Bert addressed his captive so succinctly that he did not have time to blot out the words on points of offended principle.

"Besides, John, your precious priest is a double dealer. You know that and I know that. Half the force knows it. He hates the Germans and works against them. Or, at least, he gets others like poor Larry to do it for him. But, on the other hand, he's well in with them. He goes there and has afternoon tea with the Gestapo Major, would you believe? And what's more he's in league with that little creep de Bourgonnière who is the Germans' best informant if ever there was one and would sell his own children to do their filthy bidding if they so asked him to. . ."

John broke in exasperated, for he could take no more. What was the point of hearing all this? If he could not trust his own priest, the very one who had put his own freedom and livelihood at risk in order to save his friend Franz there, then who could he trust? How could Father Peters, a known hater of the oppressors, bring himself to help one of their weaker sons, if he had not been goodness itself? Or maybe, he secretly admired them? After all it was possible. It did not seem too long ago when John himself had admired these reborn Teutonic knights.

"You've got it wrong, I say!" stormed John, resorting to his old habit, stamped feet. "You're so wrong. It just can't be true! But I can't stand here and argue. You go on believing that if you like, but I'm off. I haven't got time to waste on explaining! Not now anyway. I'm off!"

"Where to?" asked a surprised and rather shocked uncle.

"Where else but up to Father Peters," explained John. "Come Franz, we've got to move!"

* * *

Franz could not say why, but he had been drawn to that formidable house in the Rue Marguerite. It had only memories of unhappiness for him, with all the portents that had projected to his now miserable present.

He had parted from his friend outside the prison wall, refusing utterly to accompany him up the main thoroughfare to the priest's house. A journey in itself which would have

67

been telling the world 'Look here we are; two enemies, friends. I am a traitor, he is a quisling.'

Franz had not been persuaded to accompany John. John had not argued, for he was excited at the prospect of visiting the priest. Yes, Uncle Bert had said Father Peters would have information about Dad. So, what if the priest were a double agent, as Uncle Bert had implied? Not that John really believed that, did he?

John was at present more concerned with the fate of his family than any strain a parting from his unhappy friend might place on his friendship with him.

So here was Franz, outside the door, a dull brown door, long since needing the compliment of a coat of paint. Just down the cobbled street he perceived the bent lamp clamped to the prison wall, while opposite, the small plantation at the back of the police station and court houses. It had been from there, its bushes all in complete shadow, that John's father had emerged in his drunken stupor, to salute the coming of the curfew hour which was to herald the beginning of his downfall. In fact the downfall of them all.

As Franz pulled at the bell ring which came too easily towards him to be connected to any interior wires, he remembered that recent dark evening, oh so long ago now, when he had held upright the staggering John, sagging and groaning from the vicious punch Curfew Patrol had just given him. He had not waited for an unanswered bell then, he had, at his friend's grunted behest, hammered on the wooden bastion. He did now, and in so doing crystallized the events even more clearly. His heart beat fast as he waited an identical repetition of that former encounter.

But there was no Gaudion this time, to breathe his vile tomato perfumed breath on him, no old man to look surprised and then to saunter away once more into the dark reaches of his cavern, while calling up above to herald Mrs. Collins, then to wait patiently out of sight, but well within hearing, to add yet one more chapter of nosiness to his fast receding life. No, this time Gaudion did not come.

Franz hammered again. He felt both agitated and frightened. He had to see John's mother. He could not contact his own mother, or his sister, come to that, and to approach Uncle Pieter was out of the question. No, a boy who had suffered, as he had today, needed a mother to be nice to him, to be kind and understanding and to elicit from him, against his conscious will, but in collusion with his subconscious wishes, all, well maybe not all, but most of what had been done to him. Yes, that was what it was, it had all been done to him, not with him. He had played no part in it, he had wished none of it, he had been forced.

Franz needed a mother who would understand and not condemn him. And he was frightened too. Why was he frightened? Was it that the neighbours might see him, a member of Hitler's valiant conquering army trying to make contact at the home of one of these occupied civilians? And was he afraid that some other neighbour of John's mother might see this and use it against her, or was he more afraid for himself? Maybe word would get back to Captain Weiss or even Morten. The thought made him shudder as he hammered all the harder.

As he knocked his most violent, the bastion upon which he rained his assault gave a slight judder as first it stuck and then slowly opened. There in the darkness of that shadowy place stood a still, silent figure of a woman appearing as a wax effigy. Her face was deathly pale as the intruding sun rays, hopelessly trying to invade the privacy of Gaudion's castle, lit upon the few silvery whisps in Frances's dishevelled hair. Her whole aura was one of old age with premature mourning, turned in upon itself in lethargy and misery.

Franz hardly recognised his would-be substitute mother.

*   *   *

Despite all the current upheavals in the routine of Father Peters, life, such as it was, still had to go on. Without the support of his dear wife, long since safely in England with the boys, the work of the parish had to be maintained.

The priest, dedicated detester of the Nazi imposition, was now, through an act of Christian charity, to love his enemy in the form of the helpless Franz, in deep trouble with the occupiers. Nonetheless, he still had to effect the work of the pastor to his flock.

It was at times like these when the priest almost questioned his own faith and wondered if he were deluding himself.

That very afternoon, he had to go through the motions of comforting a family of his parish with words of hope which he, albeit temporarily, could no longer make himself believe. did this make him as hypocritical as the very Germans he sought to belittle?

The insistent banging on the Vicarage door dispelled such thoughts.

*   *   *

"Who are you?" she rasped as the brightness temporarily effected her perception and Frances' view of the hot bright sunny exterior of the real world was rendered as clear as an under-exposed photograph, its fadedness matching the very same feeling of her mind and body, as she fought to control her disorientation, in order to face this caller from reality.

"It is I, Franz . . ." came the young soldier's hesitant reply, a reply he had rehearsed over and over whilst walking to visit John's mother and wondering how he might extend to fill the hiatuses from his primary introduction, his lack of initiative and anxiety at how the interview would proceed from here. His voice was also tinged by the emotion of hurt or rejection that he had not been immediately recognised. All this, together with shock at the dishevelled state of one whom he had set up, in his mind's eye, on a plinth, pedestal even, as being co-equal with his own mother.

". . . You know Franz, Franz Müller."

"Franz Müller? Oh yes . . .," Frances's reply was vague as the words spun out to the recipient's ear seeming exaggeratedly and uncannily lengthy in their journey. Her slowness of wit, exacerbated by deprivation of spirit, were suddenly cut short, as her mind and then her words were accelerated upon full realisation of who was at her unwelcoming door.

"Franz Müller? Aren't you that German? That one who's caused us all this trouble?"

Her question was more of a statement, as with its utterance, she summoned some vitality from her past, while in cold panic, tinged with irrational hatred, she tried to close the door; as if, by so doing, she could keep the recent past and all its portents for the immediate and inevitable future at bay.

"Go away! You can't come in here!" She pushed at the heavy bastion which juddered, sticking temporarily. "Go away! You can't come in, it's not convenient!" Again this slow motion fiasco with fast motion actions, as the door made one more move towards achieving her intention.

Frances had all but attained her futile aim when, as Franz, unthinking but in desperation, like a child rejected by its own mother, put his pale delicate fingers into the narrowing gap. Frances quite irrationally, in desperate search of some words to close the gap in invective, as surely as the gap in the door, added, "It's not convenient, we've got company!"

The door shut, except that this finality was rendered not quite possible, on the pathetic enemy's fingers so that his scream rent the air and seemed to colour the whole empty street with its agonising.

The heat of the day intensified, while the world stood still and silent beyond what Franz was able to ingest. Frances, realising her dastardly deed, stumbled back into the cool secrecy of Gaudion's downstairs entrance way.

*   *   *

"Oh John, it's you," said the priest, as he held the door only partly ajar, as if expecting it to be stormed at any moment by those who would do him harm. He hesitated. To John the voice shrouded an emotional response to his presence which was strangely uncharacteristic. The words were uttered in soft and gentle tones but they ill masked a certain insincerity and a wish that he had not been there.

"Come in, won't you?" continued Father Peters as he valiantly fought his annoyance so that it would not continue to show. "What brings you here this time?"

To John's susceptible mood, the 'this time', was clearly noticeable, as one of irritation, ill hidden. He, over-sensitive after the seeds of doubt had been planted so recently in his mind by Uncle Bert, reacted accordingly.

"We'd better speak, Father. Sorry to bother you like this but it's very important." John paused as he helped the priest put his welcome into action, assisting to open the heavy pseudo-perpendicular door which, intended to give

Regency charm and eccentricity, was rendered ridiculous in its pretentiousness, "I need your help and you've got a little explaining to do, too, I think."

The youth's manner was brusque for one needing help. The sentiments were not wasted on the angry and anguished priest who was already upset at being interrupted when he needed to be alone with his thoughts. How could he be his usual calm and patient self with this self-centred, puerile youth at a time like this? Hadn't he done enough recently? Hadn't he been sufficiently involved with the lad and his family? Too much, probably. His involvement in the cause of Christian justice and the turning-of-the-other-cheek, love-thy-enemy ethic had almost been too much, involving him in far too great a mental effort and soul-searching, far too much unwitting association with the forces of subversion and anarchy, for his own good. He had been rendered paranoid on learning he was a listed man. The priest had stepped outside the impositions of the unjust laws and for what? To save the friendship of a parishioner with one of the despicable enemy. And more than that, to try to retrieve from this affair some semblance of stability and security from the difficulties brought about by the silly boy's naivity and lack of discipline in the matter. Surely he'd done enough? And to what effect? None! All he'd achieved was a good beating up, a soiling of his reputation with the authorities and possibly less opportunity to help his flock once the mistaken word got round that he was in league with the Nazis.

"Come into the study, won't you?"

* * *

Larry reasoned with himself he had not languished long in the prison, yet, despite the logic of his circumstances, he did wonder. Could it be only this morning that he had been removed so brutally from his shop? Well, the tenderness of his bruises indicated they were quite new.

Larry had never realised how lonely a cell could be. He had probably never given it any thought till this day. This day? Had it only been today he had been arrested? It did not seem possible. Yet he could not recall receiving any

72

food. Surely even they would feed their prisoners, if only to create nausea by the vileness of the repast? Besides, why else the pail if they did not expect eventual outpassings from the generosity of sustenance? No, he could not remember any food or any visits by humans or Germans since they had roughly incarcerated him after his interrogation.

There was some light in this smelly place, just enough from the high barred hole above, to know night from day. Larry could not recall total darkness so, presumably, a night had not come.

Anyway he had the flies for company as they made their circuit in this place taking turns to infest and blacken his enamel pail waiting for his generosity so they too might feast or procreate. Yes, that was it, Larry could eventually record his time by the depth of his own filth. That is, if he could keep ahead of the appetites of his buzzing cell mates. What would one pail full represent? Three days, four, a week? Strange he had not learned such a table at school.

Those bastards had bundled him from the shop. Why had they punched so and twisted his arms up behind his back so that he had felt sure soemthing would break? After all he had not resisted. Well only verbally. He'd not have been so daft as to resist physically, not against six of them! So he supposed his angry words had annoyed them.

Strange though, that the twisted arms and the stomach punch, the clout across the jaw, which now so ached and much surely be puffing up well with rainbow swelling, was not a prelude. it was all the physical pain he had experienced.

Larry had been certain, as they led him manacled, past Keith, that weak pathetic sod, that he too was to experience the timeless agony of their Room Five interrogation. But no, his initial bruising was all he'd had. Perhaps it was still to come?

Of course they did not need much from him, anyway, did they? The pathetic fisherman had divulged all.

Oh yes, they'd read out Keith's statement. How had they got such detail from the fool? Well, Larry had had no time for introspection on the matter. He had not argued, there had seemed no point. Why fight them anyway? They knew it all already.

Now, in the loneliness of his cell, Larry had only the

73

prospect of his trial to look forward to. Well, he would still put up a fight there. Why not? Even though the Jerries had a few of his signatures, why not let the locals see Larry Collins struggling for justice? He might go to France, no that was for sure, but he'd go a bloody hero yet!

* * *

Chapter Five

The three ladies did not have long to wait. Reception had been alerted to their arrival and within long minutes a Houseman was at their side.

"Please come with me, ladies." He led the way without glancing behind, confident they followed.

They were taken to a small sitting room from which two porters, almost guiltily, removed themselves, with stubbed out cigarettes and half finished cups of tea.

"Please sit down." The Houseman was cognizant of their distress. It was his job to alleviate it and to calm them as well as possible. He did not know the full extent of what he had to say, knowing only the suspected complications and that their man was at that very monent in theatre. He was, however, experienced in such circumstances and felt they soon would be as relaxed as he.

*   *   *

Franz sat on the rug, his thin tense back resting against the legs of his new mother, as Frances gently and absentmindedly smoothed his hair, as she could no longer to her other son, who was now too grown-up for such attentions.

Both were coloured now, the one by embarrassment and shame at what he had had to tell his mother, and the other with anger at what had been done to her boy. Yes, 'done to,' rather than 'done with,' was how Frances had to see what had happened.

Frances, a woman, a housewife and mother, whose role was to make the home and look after her family, as all women of her age, was not expected to understand such things as she had just heard from the helpless little victim, and yet she felt she understood. The ways of some men could be dark and strange! No wonder men never spoke to their women in detail about such things, but just alluded amongst themselves, sometimes laughing or fooling to hide their own discomfort at the wickedness.

Franz too, still confused and in mental anguish, could not bring himself to understand all which had happened, and yet they both knew kindness and hugs and tender love, from his substitute mum, had been his contact with this good lady and had enabled his feelings of guilt and hurt to be lessened by sharing his ordeal with her.

Frances' feelings of tenderness and protection towards Franz now far outweighed any fear, awe or respect which she might have entertained for the German authorities. This was replaced by a detestation and anger at the outrage which had taken place.

Her fire of righteous indignation was not destined to be extinguished easily.

*   *   *

Father Peters had long been a good friend to John and his family. Seeing the youth obviously distressed and confused by what was happening in their lives, quickly returned the cleric to the skills of his craft. Dispelled now were his doubts and anxieties, to be stored away for another time. How could Thomas Peters, the good shepherd, entertain doubts while seeking to reassure this boy?

He talked John calmly through their present circumstances, not rising or being deflected by the youth's impetuousness, which at times, as is the way with teenagers, as yet unblunted by adult social graces, verged on brusqueness, almost insolence.

John conceded that there was little they could do for his poor father right now, and that events must take their course. Yes, he agreed that Larry had known the risks he had taken, and that it was just bad luck that he had been caught. The lad absorbed some of the priest's philosophical acceptance.

Of course there were moments when John Collins impatiently wondered why his confessor did not wish to get involved with Larry, as if he were afraid to have his name associated with that sinner. Larry was one of his parishioners, wasn't he? Surely it would have been quite in order for Father Peters to visit one of his flock? So, did this mean that he was a coward or something? Worse still, did it mean that he really was in league with the Germans, and did not wish to lose their respect by helping one of their enemies?

No, the longer he spoke with the priest and listened to his calm logic, John realised that this really was the Father Peters he had always known, not the stranger whom doubt and despair had tried to put in his place. He believed in his pastor once more, not only because of the forcefulness of that man's logic and argument, but because he wanted to believe in him. In his present world where around him all things and ideas of value seemed to be crumbling, he needed to have this one man he could trust.

The priest explained that if he were to visit Larry right now, it might actually do the prisoner more harm than good. After all, Thomas Peters was not exactly the German's favourite person right now, was he? Thanks to John and his involvement with his young Aryan friend, Father Peters was also under surveillance. He did not labour this point, however, for having agreed to help Franz contact his uncle during his time of previous trouble, he, in exercising his Christian duty, had brought the trouble on himself. It would have been better though had John not so foolishly and openly discussed that matter on the telephone. But that was all water under the bridge, water hopefully not to wash up its misconceptions where they might be observed and wrongly interpreted.

Between them, they reasoned that Larry was sure to have an example made of him, but he was a strong and fit man and should survive a spell in a French prison. After all, others has been known to return, subdued but unharmed. It was to be hoped that the Germans might not stress the military aspects of Larry's dealing, for they might well choose not to let the population at large know of weaknesses in their internal security. Perhaps he would be dealt with only for the civilian aspects of his trade, thereby showing the masters as guardians of the public good? It was to be hoped so, for French prisons, although reputed to be austere, had a better ring about them than the camps from which no one, to date, had been known to have returned.

The help of an Advocate was thought to be a most necessary idea, for the legal profession was still permitted to represent in the courts. The priest provided John with the name and address of such a person.

"But John, please do be sure to visit him. . ., not the 'phone, eh?" The weak smile on the youth's slightly flushing cheeks reassured the priest that John could indeed learn from his mistakes.

*   *   *

Frances was an amalgam of emotions. Recently she had been embarrassed, such a feeling quickly translated, through her empathy, to one of deep hurt and shame on behalf of her poor wronged German son. Her shame and sympathy had turned to anger, so that when dear young Franz had left her home, armed with the comfort and support of his adopted mother, to become a soldier once more, she had had to do something, and quickly, or be burned up by her inner rage.

Frances rushed down the cobbled streets not really knowing where her heightened emotions were taking her. Should she find the wrongdoers? Should she go to Franz's billet and demand to see who was in charge? What good would that do? Would it not be better to find the perpetrator of the crime and attack him? Perhaps she should find him in the street and shout out her accusations so that his comrades could hear it?

But this was all so silly, for she did not even know the person's name, and was not even sure which of the many requisitioned town houses was Franz's. Yes, she was a foolish woman and she knew it. Larry would have ridiculed her impetuosity. Oh, if only he were there now though, to admonish her.

'If only Larry were here, he would know what to do,' thought the silly woman.

*   *   *

Here she now stood, Larry's wife. Larry, now vindicated in his hatred of the Nazis. She stood here, in her new awareness, sad for her imprisoned man and angry for the injustices which had just been revealed to her.

78

There in front of her, within those very walls of the police station, somewhere, was Bert.

Somewhere in that building existed a man. He lived and breathed and thought and felt thoughts that were not all geared to his duty of law and order or the order of law, with its impositions of injustice for, and shielding on behalf of, the obscene master race. A man, who if she were able to face the reality of her thoughts, was her other love. Yes, in there, with all his faults and all his holding at bay that which would compromise his pre-occupation ideals of real truth and real pure justice and goodness, was her Bert. How she loved him! How she loved Larry! Larry was in prison, soon to be tried, and yet already found guilty, and at best to be sent to France for an indeterminate sentence, which to any in these times of subjugation could only mean for ever. At worst? A shudder could only answer that penetrating thought.

Bert was in the police station but already he was a marked, and by implication, finished man, impotent in his role as a protector of the people, a people whom he should be helping the Teutons to subjugate. But, by his very lack of pretence, he was himself about to be subjugated by the same system.

Frances' heart went out to her former and furtive lover in the same way that it had to her little enemy son, Franz. She loved Bert, her incarcerated and dear husband's best friend, in the same way that she loved one of the enemy she now realised she so despised. She loved Franz for he was her own John's chosen friend, chosen from the enemy itself.

And so she was a very mixed up lady in habit and in emotion, in reality and excursions of the mind.

To whom could she turn? There was no Larry any more. Any more? John had gone off in a frenzy, she knew not where. She could not follow. It was ever the anxious mother's lot to sit and wait in concealed misery until the afterthoughts of information might sweep her way as the scraps from the table might reach the patient fly. Her sister would only admonish with a wagging finger. Poor little Franz could hardly help himself to hold together with the dreadful trauma still attacking his consciousness. She had no close friends, all had evacuated, oh they were the fortunate ones!

No, there was only Bert. The very thought of him, her

only solace in extremis, drew her thoughts and longings to that so recent rejuvenation of thought in her kitchen, a kitchen which had transported her in time to the cliff paths, and summer smells and softnesses of the herbs and moist clean grasses, with the echoing cries of the waterline gulls. To the places, and touches and feelings, and smells, with hunger and longings of her youth. She had been transported to the very edges of heaven, a heaven into which she had looked but not stepped, time and time again since Bert had first taken her to the gate but had not, and never would, unlocked the door for he had, honourable man that he was, handed the key to Larry. Larry, who was now destined to be confined for eternity by other keys. The key of love passed to one, locked by the key of tyranny.

She was not really aware that she ran and yet the image of that awesome building enlarged so rapidly in her sight, and the stinging on her cheeks so intensified as with heightened pulse induced by her speed.

*　　　*　　　*

"O.K. Bisson just sit down won't you?" came the half irritated, half concerned request of one of Bert's colleagues.

"What's all this 'Bisson' supposed to mean?" came the dejected query of P.C. Bert Bisson, as he momentarily stopped pacing the small office to look quizzically at the duty Sergeant he had known on first name terms since he was a lad.

"I suppose you think, or him up there . . .," he pointed half heartedly in his attempt at theatrical drama, up through the ceiling to where he imagined the Chief's office to be, at the same time just managing to allay the slightest flicker of a smile, wondering if possibly he was a few degrees out and in fact crediting the Chief with a place in the upstairs lavatory. No it was not worth the effort to smile. ". . . I suppose he up there thinks I'm not worth my proper name any more. I suppose that's to make me feel inferior is it? All part of the breaking down process?"

The question just had to be rhetorical for he knew all the answers. Bert knew the interrogation methods and could predict their every move but it still hurt to find it being done to him, Bert Bisson, the unique and widely-respected constable.

The sergeant answered with the slightest of non-committal shrugs then, as an afterthought, as if some embarrassed explanation was called for, added;

"You know what it's like Bert, you know what it's like."

*   *   *

John's brief visit to the Advocate's office was almost over. The new man, now head of the Collins' household, had done a good and manly job. He had not become indignant at the lawyer's apparent indifference to his father's case, nor had he taken offence when asked to wait outside in the corridor, while a telephone call had been made to the Chief of Police.

"I cannot discuss the confidential business of a client in the hearing of another party," the Advocate had pronounced.

It seemed an age before the youth heard the office door open, and the hesitant words;

"You can come back in now. Well maybe you'll save both our time, I'll tell you here. I've been in contact with the Chief of Police who will deal with your father's matters personally. Your father is to be charged with serious crimes, as you no doubt expected. He is to appear in the Royal Court next Friday and further charges will be dealt with by Court Martial. I will no doubt see you there, Mr. Collins, if it is your father's wish for me to represent him. Oh and, Mr. Collins, you might be interested to know, your father is to be released from prison in half an hour's time. I think you might be a dutiful son and be at home to greet him, don't you?"

The advocate coughed almost subserviently and his wizened face seemed almost to show some prelude to benignity, before it returned to sobriety, in accordance with his profession. Then, as a parting gift, which left John with an impression of the impending awfulness which he and his family had no alternative but to face, he added with feeling, kindness almost;

"Your father is charged with serious crimes and they are not as you might expect. He is charged with crimes against

81

the Guernsey people. He's not going to need just my help but he'll need the crutch of support from the whole of his family. I'm afraid these devils know how to blacken people, it's their craft. Your father's going to find out who his friends are."

*   *   *

"So, do I take it you've got orders to keep me here, is that it?" came Bert's agitated question. "Am I under arrest or something, that's what I want to know? What's all this waiting business and hints at the Chief wanting me? Hell, I should be out on the beat by now. What's happening to . . ."

His concern for his unfulfilled role as a duty policeman was cut short by the day Sergeant, who, already embarrassed at the little sketchy information he had received about his charge, and the holding task, had clearly wished to change the subject.

"Look Bert . . .," he paused and corrected himself. One had to be scrupulously correct when meting out the law and following the regulations, especially as he was acting on direct orders from the Chief, ". . . Mr. Bisson, all I know is, the Chief wants to speak with you personally. I can't say much more but it must be importatnt as he's not entrusted the job to me, a mere Sergeant, or to the Inspector even. All I know is he wants you in his office as soon as he comes off the phone . . ."

It was Bert's turn to interrupt as with dejected resignation he interjected;

"So I'm for the chop then?"

"You said it, old son, you said it. Remember your theory training lad, 'No one is guilty until a court of law decides. He might look it, all the evidence might point that way but let the due processes of law decide.' Ours is not to interpret the law, just to help it along its way . . ."

"So you're saying there is evidence against me! Come on, spill it out, let me know what you know before I go up there. For Christ's sake, just level with me, won't you? Don't send me in there starkers!" His voice was beginning to take on a high pitched tenor as he became both angered and anxious. Anxious about what he knew, which logic dictated, had to be the outcome of his visit to the Chief. He had anticipated it all and yet in that anticipation it had all been for another Bert Bisson but not for him. It was the other imaginary Bert who had to take just desserts, not he. No, he had to hold on, he had to outwit that senior upstairs. He knew he could do it, or if not, he'd put up a bloody good fight and take a few others down with him, as he fell.

The Sergeant's need to answer and further involve himself in this problem, which brooked no solution, was removed from him. The Chief's telephone call with the Gestapo had obviously ended.

"Come up, Bisson, won't you?" came the ice cold steely request from one who was used to having his invitations treated as commands by all except the conquerors.

Bisson, a creature of habit, followed meekly, while wondering how important must be his present status for the Chief himself to have descended the stairs to fetch him personally.

*   *   *

The Chief was seated in a manner of studied relaxation as, with legs crossed high up, he tilted his chair slightly backwards, one elbow supporting on his desk, hands clasped under his chin. Bert remained standing at attention. It seemed an indefinite time before the bustling stopped and the hearty Inspector hastily retrieved his papers from a side desk, took his leave of the Chief and half heartedly with embarrassment smiled his acknowledgement to Bert. A smile partly of sympathy but partly manufactured disdain.

When the Inspector had left, the Chief, with weary resignation, stood, then went to the door which the hurriedly departing man had left swinging slightly ajar. He pushed it shut with deft firmness, accompanied by a sigh.

"Sit down, Bisson man, won't you." He signified wearily with his hand to Bert who, knowing what was coming, was almost excited as to what degree or line it would take. He was already playing out the various alternatives in his mind, with all the possible combinations of truths, half truths, red herrings and lies. He willed himself into almost so anticipating and enjoying his part that he felt he was to be the master of the interview. As he pulled up a chair, attending to the

Chief's bidding, he felt almost sorry for the man, German puppet that he seemed to be.

"Now, P.C. Bisson," began the Chief, in his rather arduous and somewhat awkward preamble, "let me see now, how long have you been in the force?"

It was a silly question, it was just a means to get the conversation warmed up a little. Bert recognised it as a complete nonsense for no one but a fool would undertake an assignment such as this, a Chief Police Officer's assignment, without first doing his homework. He knew that the Chief would have carefully scrutinized his records, and whatever hearsay he could have gleaned from the Germans, before even contemplating calling him here. The Chief too, knew that Bert must be thinking these thoughts as he smiled, almost nervously, as the correct P.C. Bisson enlightened him with the customary suffixual;

"Sir?"

"Well, don't you think you've put us all in rather an awkward spot?" came the Chief, unexpectedly straight to the point as if he had been dissatisfied with small talk or was just too busy a man, possibly too important, to waste his time leading up to what, after all, had to be expedited quickly.

"Pardon, Sir?" asked Bert Bisson in all innocence.

"I said. . ., Oh forget it Bisson. Don't play the stupid ass with me, man!"

"Sir?"

"Look P.C. Bisson, I'll come straight to the point. I haven't got the time nor the inclination to beat about the bush with you and I'd appreciate it if you'd make this as' easy as possible for both of us and not silly arse around with all this dumb insolence." His last statement was uttered more in mild irritation than in annoyance, being so intended.

"All right then Sir, if we're talking straight facts then I'll tell you what" (Bert heard his own words as if they were exuding from another; never had he imagined that he, as a basic Constable, would dream of addressing his Chief in such a way, almost as if he were his equal) " — you tell me exactly what I'm supposed to have done and I'll tell you personally, to the best of my ability, what I think of it. . ."

"What you think of it? That's big of you, isn't it!" came the Chief's almost sarcastic reply.

"Sorry, Sir, I'm not meaning to be rude, but I really would like to know what the problem is, then I can work out my response."

"Yes, I see," came that same voice from the Chief, slightly less charged with sarcasm this time, rather more aided by resignation, "so you're after some sort of deal are you?"

"No!" Bert's reply was almost petulant. Was he annoyed at the very idea or just annoyed that the Chief must have anticipated that this might be his ploy? He did not know, but he felt angry, rather like a school boy caught out before his fool-proof plan had even been put into action.

"Anyway Bisson, I'll tell you. Just let me say this however, that whatever is said between these four walls, at this stage, is off the record, O.K.?"

"O.K." Bert did not feel he was in any way compromised by his acquiescence to the Chief's plan.

*　　　*　　　*

Frances had approached the grey facade of the police station in haste, which had caused her blood to pulse and her cheeks to burn. And yet, she felt a strange inner relaxation that she had all the time in the world, and that her protracted movements were spun out and completely in the control of her own will. Was it due to the draw of her Bert, 'Bertram', as she now teasingly called him all those eons ago on the Elysian cliffs, that she had become timeless? Was she really now on an errand of mercy, of unheard-of magnanimity, to help one of the enemy? Was her cause just? Was she out to assist Franz or just to avenge the foul deed which had been committed? Was she really altruistic or were her hurried, and yet histrionically imprisoned movements, the response to her own indulgences? Had she come on behalf of young Franz, her adopted son, the potential downfall of them all, or had she come to meet her unrequited lover?

Bert temporarily, through the habit of unquestioning respect of seniority, brought low, wondering how he could climb from the trap of time, how in any way, once more, shape his own destiny, rather than have that act undertaken

85

for him, allowed his steps to take him laboriously and with the assistance of gravity, down the cool stone stairway, as he left the office of the Chief of Police.

As Bert and Frances met, each locked in their own dreams, the one of halcyon past with no present, the other with the dull lead depression of the present, oblivious to the past and with no future, flung themselves at each other emotionally, like an instant positive and negative charge. Their two separate miseries with hopes, non-hopes and fears became as one.

Oblivious to the world, they each shut off the phoney world of hunger and fear, war and tyranny, with its woollen Cobo dolls of status-quo policemen, and cardboard cut-outs of green-stained Wiermacht with colourless Gestapo.

Frances heard once more the crying gulls and smelt the sweet summer perfumes of the gorse and the myriad wild flowers scenting themselves in the heat of the day, as they made her cool cliff bed. Bert transported himself with the urgency of his past unfulfilled youthful lust, to that same place. Neither spoke but both knew.

It was far more comfortable, locked in the past than to step from the warm bed into the frosty unheated room of reality. As such they could have stayed joined in embrace for ever.

*　　　*　　　*

They made for the kitchen, still musty with smells of cooking from the years of plenty. The old smells mingled plaintively with the odours of more recent, less sumptuous meals, as they wafted from the linoleum, the distempered walls, the bare and serviceable table and chairs and the clean enamelled cooker.

The smell hung in the air, almost visibly in its density. All would have been somewhat alleviated by a good scrub and wipe down with carbolic and soda but gone long ago were the days of such luxury. Even the washing down had to be done with unheated water.

As if in accord with her current privations, and in moral support of the nasal assaults, Frances had been unable or

86

unwilling to break the habit of closing all windows whenever she left the house.

Why the kitchen? Why not? Bert would have preferred the bedroom but he knew that cause was lost. The guilt of the imagined adultery was already so heavy on him that to enter that room, even in his mind, would be to castrate himself morally from the human race.

Everywhere he could see Larry. Larry stared at him from the shadow of the gas globe in the ceiling. He was to be seen in the brown stain of the large rectangular sink. His face was in the black worn patch in the lino near the door. His smell too was in that room, the old black oil and paraffin smells.

Despite his lust for the demolition of his mound of unfulfilled and repressed desires from the past, Bert could no more give in to it than denounce his own best friends to the Germans. He knew that, if Frances had even suggested such a thing, if she had taken the initiative which he knew not how to, he would have degenerated to eunuch status, his own body and mind taunting and tormenting the other as if in an eternity of hell known only to, and feared by, men.

Frances, now that she had Bert here in her home, away from the sounds and eyes and ears of the uncaring and selfish world, did not really know what purpose it would serve. She recollected she needed Bert's help with her problem concerning Franz. She knew she needed advice about Larry and she needed someone to lean on. But what else was it she wanted? What had she so recently tasted which portended addiction at the very thought, despite the fact that all had been in the contemplations of her mind, rather than the fulfilment of her physical self? She was confused and utterly devastated emotionally at the unspoken, almost unthought of, and hastily dismissed, actions.

Frances was an animated hiatus while Bert was an indecisive action. Where else then than the kitchen with its one brass tap for cold water, its rarely used teapot, and just a little tea, for such occasions? What mattered it that Frances must surely by now be into next week's gas ration? She always was, wasn't she? Not long before the inspectors caught up with her misdemeanour but what threat or

87

deterrent could that pose to one who probably did not have a next week worth contemplating?

So tea it was, fresh tea, unused. Not the weak, re-used, dried on windowsill slop leaves, which Larry made her use on her sister. And still there was enough in the caddy for Larry if ever they released her darling.

Watching her bustle busily over this old routine, a creature governed by habit and unthought ritual in all her movements, Bert was brought back to the present stark reality.

The almost unfamiliar sounds of chinaware, rattling with cups on saucers, the splash of long dropped water into the thin old kettle, the click of flint and the dull thud explosion of gas ignition, all slightly anaesthetized the couple against their painful recognition that now was the real, the raw hard bitter truth. The other was just the dream, the never-to-be-fulfilled tantalization, akin to a nightmare in its unfulfilled frustration.

Before they knew it, the ritualistic mechanics of the brew had been completed and each eyed the other across the serviceable kitchen table, then each looked away, almost as if put off course by the jog of its uneven leg. Milk was poured, albeit skimmed, and the steaming liquid passed through the frayed wire strainer.

The longer they stayed silent, each hoping the other would break the hiatus, the harder it became to take the necessary start, so that the words came but more quickly drifted from the consciousness than they were created. With one will, determined not to allow this circumstance to prevail, they broke the silence as one. The sound of two simultaneous voices in this cavern of silence was akin to an explosion. Each sought ease in discomfort to react in their own way; Bert hesitantly stretched out his hand, tenderly taking Frances'. She put down the teapot, heavily, allowing her arm to become pliant as she looked away with what sounded to Bert like a laugh, but quickly converted to a sob.

Frances cried freely as her shoulders heaved. Gone were Bert's inhibitions but gone also were his fantasies, his main concern being now to comfort his erstwhile lover, but not to benefit himself.

"Love . . ." She looked up as his words poised in the air, her eyes pleading with him to say the right thing.

"Love, don't grieve sweet, we'll work it out. O.K.?"

"If you say so," she replied, the tears washing her wearied but still beautiful cheeks, seeming to belie her response. "If you say . . ." These last words issuing more as a sigh than a statement.

"It's Larry isn't it?" asked Bert grasping the nettle, "that's why you came looking for me?" He thought to himself how harsh and matter of fact his words sounded, as he lost the control of what came from him.

Frances' response too, was momentarily to react to him in similar fashion. Her "No!" was surly and petulant, more like that of an adolescent, than a mature mother, experienced with the tribulations of the times. She looked him straight in the eye, for a second her anger transmitting to him and receiving his shock and surprise.

"No?" Bert almost coaxed. "No? You didn't want to talk about Larry?"

"Yes . . . I mean, no. Oh yes, of course I want to talk about Larry but that's not imp . . ." She stopped herself, realising the purport of her incomplete word. She was both angry at herself and confused. How could words sound so awful and not be able to convey what she really wanted to say?

"Of course I want to talk about Larry, darn it! What do you think I am? Do you think I'm that terrible a wife that I've forgotten about him as soon as he's in prison?" Her stream of rhetorical questions helped her to unburden herself. Gone now was her self-consciousness tinged with guilt. Now, she was partially fired with anger, against whom she did not know, probably herself.

"All right," soothed Bert, "I wasn't saying you didn't care, I damned well know you care. I'd have to be a bloody stupid old bugger if I couldn't see it written on your face. Come on now, love, tell me what it is. What's on your mind?"

He went to move, awkwardly and angularly like one who, having sat too long in the same position, is prone to rheumatic pains. Frances, anticipating his comforting gestures and, unwittingly wishing to spurn them, or to cause them still-birth, moved her head so that she faced away from him, towards the open kitchen door.

Bert stayed. Frances spoke, at last she would unburden her soul.

"Heavens, it's hot in here!" she announced. "Is it always left to me to open and close windows?"

Her move from the chair, to accomplish the wish, was half-hearted. Bert made it first. The rumble of the well exercised sash window was the prelude to her saga, her plea for help. That hopeless cry which was tearing her heart until it could release itself.

"Bert, I need your help. I wouldn't ask, you know . . ." she hesitated, "but I am desperate."

Despite the gravity of her impending words Bert could not hide the flicker of a smile at her unintentional denigration.

"Go on, tell me. I'll try to listen."

"Bert, you know that German, eh?"

"That German?" he enquired benignly.

"Yes, you know, John's friend, eh?"

Now was not the time to lecture on the rights and wrongs of mixing with the enemy. He gave a shrug, grunting noncommitally, but his face remained kind.

"Yes, Franz, Franz Müller is his name. He's a nice lad you know." She paused, perhaps she was inviting a contradiction, perhaps she had to test Bert before casting her pearls? He did not reply, she had licence to continue.

"That Franz, that little German lad, so young, so innocent, such a shame, no father, away from his own mother, no one of his own age except my John," she rambled on.

"If it wasn't for his friendship with John I don't know where he'd be right now," she mused, almost as if she had forgotten Bert's presence but was just thinking out loud. "The poor little lamb. Where would he be? Where is he?"

The slight rise in the tenor of her voice brought Bert back into the participation and formed into him the thought which he consciously kept to himself.

'If it wasn't for the little bastard's friendship with John, perhaps none of us would be in the bloody mess we're in right now!'

"Come on Frances," he interrupted, his irritation putting just a slight edge to his voice. "What is it you want to say?"

"Bert, you've got to help him! You've got to, only you can!"

"Eh?"

"You're in the police, you can handle such things. I can't, Larry can't. He would but he can't, can he?"

"Can't he?" Bert was quizzical, "Can't what? What on earth are you on about?"

As his irritation and anger mounted with each question and unanswered query, so did Frances' urgency become the greater, although her expression of it was less than efficient through her vivant anxiety.

"Look, that innocent boy is a victim, just a plain ordinary victim! He was an innocent dear little orphan, it's not his fault there's a war on! He didn't ask for it. he is one of life's little innocents, another victim of those awful Germans . . ."

"Those awful Germans!" expostulated Bert, in a false laugh of indignation. "Those awful Germans you say? He is a German, Frances, he is a bloody German himself!" He felt his own words take her and shake her roughly from side to side as though she were a silly hysterical, blinded girl, needing to be shown how foolish she was.

"Yes," seethed Frances, now icy cold, still fresh in her mind the memory of the half understood pleas and confessions her adopted son had poured on her, "those Germans are filthy men, they are corrupting the innocent boy."

"Corrupting?"

"Yes corrupting." She became more rational now, more to the point. "Oh, I don't claim to understand the ins and outs of such things, but you know, men's things . . . You know Bert, you're a policeman." She was an amalgam of embarrassment, misery, ignorance and seething anger.

"I'm sorry, love. I'm not sure what you're getting at," replied Bert but already his policeman's interest was aroused, so that he sat straighter, waiting attentively for every word.

"They're using him, you know, for bad things."

A number of possibilities passed through Bert's now fully alert, mind. Were they using Franz in their black market exploits? Was there some truth in all that investigation farce? Had he perhaps been forced to infiltrate the ring and use John to implicate Larry? But why then, would Frances feel so for him? Who would have love to spare for one who had brought down her own husband and son and, come to that, Bert himself?

Was Franz some sort of spy or agent provocateur? Maybe the Jerries really did have something on Peters after all? But again, why should Frances wish to help him so? No, he could not quite make it out. He felt it must be other than these theses. He half suspected what was to come but was intrigued as he willed Frances on.

"Well?"

"Well? Sorry?" Bert remained outwardly puzzled.

"You understand, eh? You're going to help aren't you?"

"Frances, excuse me if I'm being a little slow on this," he was labouring at ensuring his words would not sound sarcastic yet he hoped the querulous patience would carry her along, "but for the life of me, I don't know what you're getting at, love. Are you telling me that this German really is in the black market lot, or a spy, or what?"

"No! No!" the exasperation was firing now. "No, you silly man! He's being used by them, can't you understand? They're bad men, you know? You know, don't you?" she looked at him begging him to know.

"You mean he's a queer boy?" he did not mean the sneer to sound in his voice. He should have been more considerate of Frances' feelings.

"Oh Bert!" she gasped as she heard the truth that lay unspoken and unravelled in her innocent and ignorant mind. "No, Bert, that's not it, exactly . . ." she hesitated until she sensed his recognition of her embarrassment, ". . . he's not the, you know, what you said, it's them."

" 'Them!' are you telling me, Frances Collins, that you think mighty Adolf Hitler's victorious German bloody army is full of nancy boys? Well that's ripe that is! What's new? Of course they're all damn cissies!"

"Oh," was all she could weakly manage, a very feminine and insecure 'oh'.

"So this Franz is one of their boys, is he?"

"Yes. No," she corrected herself. "Well, yes he is but he doesn't want to be. You know Bert he's being forced into this wickedness and he hates it and I want you to stop it!" There, at last it was out. She had reached her point, the centre of her plea for help.

"You are really asking me to poke my nose into Jerry's affairs and tell them how to organize their morals?" His disbelief was on the verge of a raging hilarity but he contained himself.

"And how am I to go up to some German Officer, or to present myself at the Feldkommandantur and say, 'Excuse me, Herr bloody Knackfuss but I think one of your young soldier boys is just a little bit on the queer side.' Or am I to say, 'I'd like to investigate some of your valiant army with a view to bringing charges of indecent assault!' Do you think I'm mad or something?"

"I don't know," said Frances "I just don't know, but you must help, please!"

"I can't!" stormed Bert, as he rose to his feet, his face angry and set hard against contradiction. "I can't, and I won't!"

There was a dreadful pause in which Frances knew he meant it. His voice and mood were intransigent. Bert was silent also. He did not wish to help any German, not that he was in any position to do so. Even if he had wished to, for his dear Frances' sake, he was completely impotent.

"Frances I wouldn't want to but I might have, even so. Just for you, my dear, but you see . . .," he looked down at his beat pounding boots, not exactly out of shame or lost pride, for he had become quite resigned to this emotion, but more because he was playing a part and, for most of his life, drama had not played very much of a role, "I'm no longer a policeman." He paused again, waiting the temporary solace her comforting might bring, while devouring her proffered empathy, knowing it to be a single sweet.

"I was suspended just before we met. I too am to await trial, date not yet fixed, just like your Larry and your John, thanks to your bloody little German snotty nose!"

Frances' gasp was transmuted into a wide opened mouth. Her eyes were clear and staring. Not the eyes for tears but the eyes of shock which reflect the possessors temporary trap in permanent timelessness. Her cold hands clasped his own, hot and tired as they were, more to steady herself than to give him solace, for he, if any, seemed the steady one, the one resigned and fatalistic.

"Yes, you can look shocked, my love, but now you'll understand won't you? This whole affair has gone too far to stop now. We're all ruined. I couldn't give a thought to some little Jerry wretch who hasn't got the guts to say 'no' to something he says upsets him. Even if I could, my hands are tied now. You do see that, don't you?" His rhetoric was superb, probably because there was no necessity for it to be so. Whatever he said in his present condition, had to be as he stated. There was no alternative.

"I understand." Frances' voice was cowed with dejection, but she understood and would not argue. She felt, with the latest revelation, the whole might of the German tyranny was directed on her feeble mind alone. She was the only one suffering, by proxy, for all her loved ones. She had to suffer for the four of them, suffer by watching them accelerate to their predestined fate. There was nothing she could now do except suffer.

Bert was up now and towards the door. It was best he should leave. He knew he would feel better once he was outside the house. Then Frances too could pull herself up from the pit of helplessness by herself. He knew she would press him to stay for the second cup of tea and he knew too, he would have to refuse but would probably acquiesce as the easier short term expedient, although a harder long term course.

Thus she did and thus he complied. It was just as inevitable that John should at that moment come in on this scene, a re-enactment of what had taken place only days before. The setting was the same, the props identical but the players now took on different roles. Frances was no longer being consoled but was resigned to the awful hopelessness of all their fates. Bert, formerly lusting in his previous memories, was now in opposition to this late mood and more anxious to extricate himself than stay on. Both principal players were seated well apart whereas before they had been caught in the act of breaking, with embarrassment, from their guilt laden embrace. But it was not these outward vast differences which caught the attention of John, it was the atmosphere. The atmosphere of unspoken thoughts and fears, an air filled with foreboding and doom, of resignation and helplessness.

John paused on perception of this feeling, foreign in his own home which, though often trespassed by anger and anxiety, withdrawal of conversation and sometimes surfeit of advice, was never the haven of such icy death.

Frances glanced at him slowly, as Bert looked up, then moved his focus as if the boy did not exist.

"I'm off!" stated Bert, his voice so loaded with venom that even he was surprised at its force. "I'll go before I regret my actions!"

He made to move, meaning that his exit should be accomplished for the reasons he had stated.

John, so shocked by the feelings of ill-will and distress in the air, knew without question that he was the focus for Uncle Bert's discontent. Before thinking, his response came at the policeman friend of the family, so that the unspoken shocks in the room could be broken.

"Why the hell are you here, Uncle Bert?" he demanded. Then, rendering the question rhetorical, he turned on his mother.

"And you've got more important things to do than to sit making cups of tea for him!" He pointed, deliberately, rudely, at the policeman.

"Now see here!" called his mother raising quickly to her feet, her anger breaking her from the mould of inactivity and misery. "You don't just come in here like that, my son, upsetting people and being so rude. . ."

"Oh shut up!" John shouted these last words, stamping his foot while revelling in the effect he had caused. He was passing on his own discomfort to others, thereby to some extent, alleviating his own burden.

This was too much for Bert. It seemed now, in retrospect, that he had never much liked this namby-pamby of a pseduo-nephew when he had been growing up, with his 'yes mum' this and 'no dad' that, his pleadings and begging against sanctions and, far too often getting of his own way. He certainly too hadn't at all liked the way the young fool had first worked for the Jerries, but to make matters worse, had gone round with them from his own choice. And what he'd just heard. Well? Didn't it explain a lot? Wasn't it often said of only sons, especially pampered, spoilt ones? So this John, this little quisling, who'd got them all into the most terrible trouble, trouble that was to alter all their lives and take away the little freedom they still enjoyed, was now going around with a German nancy boy! Well that really said it all!

"How dare you speak to your mother like that?" shouted Bert. He could gladly have hit the young devil. What right had he to come in here and speak to Frances as if she were dirt? He, of all people, had no rights after the way he had brought them all to this dangerous pass.

"You'd better bloody well apologize or get out of this house darned fast before I throw you out!" He meant it. John knew he meant it. Frances knew he meant it as she gasped almost imperceptibly, clutching at the air as though it were his very sleeve which she hoped to stay. She gasped at the reality of the present but also out of unspoken gratitude and admiration. Gratitude that someone should trouble so on her behalf, with admiration of Bert's forcefulness.

Their momentary shocked fixations were broken roughly with John's unexpected retaliation.

"And who the hell do you think you are?" the question starting in anger and changing in inflection to become a sneer, so that the donor felt much in advantage, as Bert felt himself shrink in stature by comparison with the rapid growth of his young assailant.

"We don't need you, Uncle Bert. We don't need help from you thanks!" The thanks implied anything but gratitude. The invitation not to involve himself was anything but friendly. It was probably unintentional, being unthought out in the heat of the moment, but the effect was to create in Bert a feeling of superfluity. Whatever help he might contemplate was just so much interference. The giver was made to feel the wrong-doer.

"John lad. . .,"

"I'll not be spoken to like this!" interrupted John, as he rudely cut off his uncle's attempts to extricate himself.

"Just go, please. My mother and I have a lot of serious matters to discuss and we need to be alone." His tone was now so rational and clear, so mature and self-assured even, carrying the weight of expediency, that Bert was able to absorb the recent slight, getting to his feet without a word or chance to feel any loss of dignity. Nor was it, it appeared, that any loss of face, or any advantage was sought.

Frances, involuntarily shocked into her acquiescence by

John's uncharacteristic manliness, yes that was it, manliness, an aspect never yet before observed in her off-spring, rose to her feet in unison with Bert but all the while looking at her son, no longer her little boy but now her young man.

Having silenced Bert, and in so doing relieved himself of some of his own speeding heat, John turned to his mother to impart his message. He knew now that this could be achieved without interruption. She was an expectant and captive audience. Despite his recent invitation to Uncle Bert to be less involved in their private affairs, John was somehow pleased to let him stay to hear.

A few minutes previously it might have been John's pleasure to shock and dismay his mother and, in so doing, by roughly passing on his own misery, share the burden, thereby lessening it on his own shoulders. Now, however, he was less self interested and more concerned for his mother's feelings and the way she might receive the news he was about to impart. Some of Uncle Bert's recent anger must have helped shape his present concern. He had to choose his words carefully, not for effect, but because he could not really bear the thought of hearing them coming out loud. To have to repeat them even, would be complete and utter anathema.

"Mum," he paused, "Mum you've got to know this . . .," John glanced at Uncle Bert, observing that person's studious gaze at his face, then quickly looked away to pretend he was not there. He addressed his mother alone.

"Dad's trial date has been fixed, I've just found out. He's to be tried in the Royal Court next Friday, and he's to be Court Martialled, charged with crimes against the Guernsey people. Mum. . ., Mum, did you hear that? Crimes against the Guernsey people!"

Crimes against the Guernsey people! What ignominy! Not even the glory of knowing the bitter price he would have to pay after the trial, that was to have been in the eyes of the free and democratic world, would have shown him as a martyr set against the tyrants. No, his lot was to be shown as a miserable little traitor who, in time of adversity, had worked for his own self interest against the good of his own community. What bastards these Germans were! What filthy, dirty bastards!

97

* * *

Larry was well-used to the nothingness of his new existence. Quickly he had learned to adapt to the timelessness of his circumstances. He would neither give thought to his status nor expect change. Yes that was it, he was no more so could effect nothing nor be effected.

The business of the unexpected visitor was brief and to the point. The official of the semi-independent civilian police was only there to put verbally the message of the document which he had carried, which the current regulations required him to do. The content of the papers had brooked no contradiction.

Laurence Collings of 12, Rue Marguerite, was summoned to appear before the Royal Court on Friday, 25th July, 1941 charged with crimes of dire theft from his fellow civilians, such actions being specifically proscribed by the competent German authorities. He was also to appear before a German Court Martial to answer charges of theft against the competent authority. He was also released from prison on bail, charged not to leave the island upon pain of military discipline for any such attempted breach. The conditions of his bail were that he should report daily to the civilian police station. He was in no way to seek contact or any form of communication with Keith de la Haye, Bertram Bisson, the Reverend Peters, any of the German forces except those specifically dealing with his case, and especially with one fifteen year old soldier viz Franz Müller. Although he was to reside at his own address he was ordered not to communicate verbally or in writing, or through any intermediary, with his own son, John Collins, punishment for any known deviation in this regard to be that either he or the said John Collins should be called into custody, the decision as to whom, to be made by the Chief Police Officer of the civilian police, in consultation with Colonel Brandt of the Gestapo.

The utter folly of the orders had been completely lost on Larry, in his euphoria that he was very soon to be with his sweet dear Frances, even though it was for such a short while. A short while as it speeds can be made long in its shortness in the pliant memory, when it is fully used. The prospect before of only fifteen minutes would seem an eternity in comparison with an eternity without fifteen such minutes.

Whether this had all been brought about by Father Peters' telephone call to the Advocate, followed, as directed, by John's visit to the notary's chambers, or whether it had been in the mind of the authorities to expedite Larry's release, none of the parties was ever to know. To them it was not a problem to be pondered.

* * *

Bert left 12, Rue Marguerite full of concern for his friend. He was, too, concerned for the shivering wreck of his other friend Frances, whom he had just left, still trying to absorb the awfulness of Larry's news. At least she had John there, to be kind for a few minutes, and soon she and Larry could unburden their separate miseries and be strengthened by sharing them jointly. Their adversity would strengthen their bond. For Bert there was only a lonely house with not a soul on whom to pour his miseries.

* * *

Chapter Six

The ladies, still agitated, sat themselves stiffly, Frances right at the edge of her chair. Gerda was desperate to batter the man with questions. He quickly caught the retreating porter then returned to inform the ladies of the nature of John's suspected injuries while the inveigled lesser mortal, strictly contrary to his job specification, went to organize four more cups of tea.

"Excuse me, Mrs. Collins," he inclined his head slightly in two separate directions, the one greeting thus serving both ladies, "but please bear with the fact that Mr. Collins cannot be visited at present. . ."

"Why!" gasped Gerda impatient and distraught at this news, unable to elaborate her concern or disappointment further.

"You see, ladies, Mr. Collins has been quite seriously injured and . . ."

Frances clutched at Gerda, their friend putting her arm across Gerda's shoulders. They knew, of course, that John had been seriously injured but they were destined to suffer this news fresh each time they heard it, as though hearing its terribleness for the first time.

The Houseman continued;

"He is at present undergoing an emergency operation."

Again the trauma of the first time re-enacted.

"And?" began Gerda, but unable to formulate her troubled thoughts into any semblance of ordered words.

"And, Mrs. Collins, it will be quite a while before you can see him, even after the operation. It will take a while for him to regain his consciousness and he will be in Intensive Care."

"What is his injury?" pleaded Frances. "Can you tell us if he'll be all right?"

The Houseman resisted a sigh. He resisted also a shrug of the shoulders. He could not answer such a question but it was his job to deflect it as best as possible.

"For your first question, all I can tell you is that he was involved in a very violent collision as you already know. When you do see him, please be prepared for a shock. A man does not go through such an experience and look as though he's just come from the South of France. . ." He effected to lighten the situation with an artificial laugh at his attempted quip.

The porter returned with a tray and four mugs of tea.

"Tell us the injuries," interjected Gerda.

"Well, you will see lots of cuts and bruises to his face. It will not be a pretty sight, so be prepared. However, the swelling will subside and those aspects will disappear."

"Yes?" asked Frances, willing him to come to the more serious aspects.

"He has a fractured arm and leg. You will find him plastered and heavily bandaged."

Frances imagined her little boy now with arms and legs contorted by pulleys and weights.

"Yes. Well, what else, doctor?" urged Gerda, as she took an overly large gulp of her very sweet tea. "Why the operating theatre?"

"We suspect internal injuries but what they are I am, as yet, not in a position to tell you."

"Oh!" Frances moaned, while Gerda's hand shook uncontrollably.

*　　　*　　　*

Frances did not know how to receive Larry. She had reached a point in her emotions where she no longer held a concept of pleasure. To her, to try to contemplate such a state would be the same as for a person, blind from birth, to understand sight. She knew the effect pleasure could have on those around her but she could not conceive of it herself. In fact, she was not so sure even that there was such a thing, it was surely a fallacy, wishful thinking, just as heaven had been to her as a child at Sunday School. She was not sure she had observed pleasure in any of her fellow humans for an eternity, for her recent days had been to her an eternity.

So now she was numb, her Larry was coming home, the very dream she had desired and longed for. But to what was he returning? He was coming home to an ex-wife, to Frances who could not fake joy or love or happiness for she no longer knew them, if she ever had. He was coming home to an ex-lover who was already mourning his departure, his death even, before it had happened. He was coming and she knew he would be glad, yet she would be a contrast to his enthusiasm. So already she was arguing and prevaricating with him before he had arrived.

Bert had left. How cold and empty she felt without him, how full of guilt. He had gone and with him had gone her youth, her yesteryear. She felt a stinging emptiness in the knots of her unfed stomach as she remembered that while she had been in his presence she had momentarily forgotten her Larry. In those few moments of shared nostalgia, and unspoken, if unrequited love, she had remembered her darling but it had been with love and longing, not with apprehension and guilt.

It had been Bert, dear good Bert who had given her such feelings of ease and had kept alive her marriage with Larry. Bert, the very one whose memory now seemed to imbue her with self-reproach and feelings of shortcoming. How could she not have responded to that dear man? How could she have left him unfulfilled, wasting their precious time with the silly pre-war ritual of tea drinking?

Frances knew now that she had wanted Bert. She now understood his unspoken thoughts and his self-manacled transmissions of love. Now, she would have translated his imaginations into words, his wishes into love.

This very feeling, recognisable in herself, only fired her ill feelings, fueling illogically, the fire within her which burned more and more chill.

*   *   *

John could not stay in the house. His father had returned, bounding up the stairs two at a time in the joy of his freedom and anticipation of his welcome. That same man, on temporary respite from incarceration, had quickly been brought down to the depths which helpless Frances had created, neither of them being able to respond to the other. Larry's charge had quickly been neutralized by Frances' discharge, so that both became caught in the negative miserable eternity of depression.

Here he was, at last, outside the front door. Inside were his two dead parents. The place felt like a tomb to him. Two parents whose past was dead and future could have no life. Two live persons trapped in a living death. The house sickened him. John suddenly abhorred it with its lack of sheen, its dull browns and greens, rotting window-frames, heavy doors, paint-peeled shutters and dark-eyed windows. The flagged patch at the front just reinforced his sensation that he was outside a tomb. He thought of the sunken walled garden at the back, with its crops of untended dandelions and docks, with its colonies of giant snails as they crawled over each other to form living, heaving mounds. How the discarded shells in this, the lesser creatures' cemetery, crunched sickeningly underfoot as his mind took him back and forth through the tomb and into its very depths even to the tomb keeper himself; Gaudion from the dark mists of the ground floor. John had to go, he had to find the living.

Franz was alive, wasn't he? That was for sure. Franz was under sentence of fate as his own father was promised to be. John too could expect the same. Yet, he was alive. True, a few hours before, his friend's face had been a picture of misery, but he had permitted it to flicker with relief when he had met John for those few minutes outside the police station. Oh yes, Franz would not let a little matter like impending disruption of all their lives stand in the way of their present enjoyment. Franz was an alive and real person, John's only friend. He, like John, would worry about tomorrow when it came, and not a moment sooner. Hadn't it been yesterday when they had both adventured and faced death together? But they had survived to live, to face death tomorrow. Well at least they could face it together for a little longer. Together for a while anyway. And that while had to be now so had to be good.

John would look for his friend.

*   *   *

Yes, he had done it, Bert had bluffed his way into Town Patrol House, even into Patrol Leader Morten's very office! Despite his no longer being a policeman, his uniform had belied his status, and the duty sentry had seen him for what he appeared to be, policeman, friend of the occupying forces, helping Germany to free Europe of its disease of democracy.

Bert Bisson had not intended to do anything about that little wretch of a Franz Müller. As far as Bert was concerned, the little nancy boy was getting what he deserved, for it was thanks to him that he and Larry and John, and goodness knew who else, were now in awful danger. Oh yes, Bert had made it quite clear to Frances that he would not get involved. Besides, he knew he could not, for, despite the Germans feeling they had a good relationship with the civilian police, Bert knew that the police had no authority, actual or moral, over even the lowest-ranking Teuton.

So why on earth was Bert here now, just hastening the day of his inevitable incarceration, for it would not be tolerated once discovered that he was an imposter, not only in this place but in his very uniform?

When Bert had left Frances and John, it had been with a heavy heart. How could he return to his emptiness of a house? He would not have been entering a home; it had long since been no such place since his wife had left him, probably never to return, using evacuation as an excuse. She had despised Bert's devotion to duty, a devotion which made him expect her to stay by his side and be invaded by the enemy. This same duty which had lost him his wife, and would now mock him if he went home, prevented him returning. Police work had been his solace these past months, and the signs of his trade would be everywhere to be seen if he had gone there. No, Bert had put off the moment.

As he had walked, he had thought of Frances, now so miserable, waiting for the return of Larry. Bert knew that what he had felt for Frances and what he felt sure she had for him in that brief moment of their embrace, could never really be. Poor dear, sweet Frances, poor lovely innocent sweet creature. She had flittered away their valuable few moments together worrying about silly things too. Sweet naivety that she was, she had asked Bert to help where he knew no help could be possible.

But Bert, in his misery, wanted to be true to their memory and to the unrequited dreams which were destined to forever be just in his imagination. Bert wanted to please his Frances as a small thank you for that which he now knew could never be. She would probably never be aware that he had acted, but P.C. Bisson knew that he would know, and the thoughts of his erstwhile angel would be gilded by the knowledge. So despite his professional logic, Bert had found himself here in the very office of the Nazi who had caused Frances such turmoil of mind.

The office was far smaller than Bert had imagined. The decor was the usual unimaginative, if practical, German military green and grey. The untidy desk could have been that of any minor office clerk in a small but busy office. There were piles of papers on spikes, flimsy documents held in position by a jackboot as a paperweight, with an ash-tray over full of butts to be that of a normally rationed soldier. The filing cabinet had all its drawers open while on the walls were charts pencilled and inked in uninteresting blacks and blues. The electric light burned, for there was no natural light in this room. All this was observed in the split second that it took the resolved and now angry Bert to step into the room unbidden, as he closed the door with all but a slam, watching the swarthy German behind the desk scramble awkwardly to his feet with surprise rather than deference.

Morten's annoyance percolated to his sallow face but he did not give vent to his feelings, for he was very curious. This was an island policeman who stood before him. One of the civilians who had perhaps got a little above himself. Morten wanted to control his feelings the better to drain his visitor of all details before he could muster his revenge for such an intrusion, in whichever way might seem most befitting, come that moment.

"You are the Patrol Leader known as Morten?" asked Bert, again trying hard not to sound too abrupt, at least at first. He had to remember his training.

The assailed nodded slightly but said not a word.

"I'm here about one of your younger soldiers, name of Müller, Franz Müller."

Morten was gripped by a clamp. It was disbelief mingled with recent memories, rather belittling memories where his manly pride had been hurt and the mere lad, whose name was now mentioned, had got the better of him (this time). Had the name evoked in him anger, shame, or was it guilt? Or was there a temporary, almost long-since forgotten emotion of fear, of being hunted? Forgotten that is for many years as he'd made good progress in the Führer's new military order. Did his nostrils for a moment take in a passing whiff of his own fear? His eyes darkened almost imperceptibly.

"Müller?"

"I think you know what I mean, Mr. Patrol Leader?"

"I don't know what you wish to say. May I remind you before . . ." Morten was interrupted in his search for words which would keep the subject at bay.

"I'm not here in an official capacity, I've just come to give you some friendly advice," continued Bert. "I can't cause you any trouble right now but you'd better listen to me if you know what's good for you."

Morten did not at all like the civilian's tone but he knew that while the conversation was kept within the walls of this office, especially with Weiss out of the building, he would not lose face, not with any Germans that is, so he decided to let the policeman have his say.

"Go on," said Morten.

"As I said, I can't cause you any trouble in an official way, but I think you're astute enough . . ."

"Say what you have to say," this time it was Morten to interrupt, "I'm a man of the world, I think we both know why you're here. Now say what it is!"

"Franz Müller; we don't want you to have any more dealings with him. You do know what I mean?"

"Yes," Morten paused, his mind flashing anger and fear at him simultaneously. This policeman had no rights to interfere in the dealings of the Weirmacht. Civilian law had no bearing on conduct within military establishments. On the other hand, this silly little policeman obviously knew too much. Morten could not risk having his boat rocked even if he could not be tipped out. He would dearly have loved, there and then, to have taught this self-important scum a lesson in his dealings with a senior German. He would like to have watched him squirm as his punishment would tenfold befit his offence. But all that would have to wait and would probably have to be done surreptitiously by proxy, without the pleasure of his personal participation. Now, the most important thing was to contain all this, right here. It must not get to Weiss for Morten had already pushed his indulgent Captain too far this week. No, he Morten, had to eat some humble pie and quickly.

"Yes, I know what you mean. It won't happen again."

"It can't!" shouted Bert. "You keep away from him, officer or no. Do you understand?"

"Yes. I gave you my word," answered Morten keeping anger at bay whilst sufficiently aware of his own fear to remain studiously calm. "And thank you Constable, for taking the matter so understandingly."

"I. . . ," Bert had been about to play his trump card and threaten Morten with divulgence to senior authority. However, he had discerned from the Nazi's tone that this action was no longer necessary. To act so might cause the satisfaction of seeing the German punished but could lead the quicker to discovery of him as a police impersonator. Better to leave the fellow a little self-disciplined by his own fear, than let him know that Bert had even less authority than his uniform supposed, therefore taking away any future restraints with the young Franz Müller. He completed his hesitant sentence;

"I, like you, German, am a man of the world. I shall have to accept your word on the matter. Good afternoon."

"Good afternoon." A rather shocked Patrol Leader attempted to see the civilian Constable out, but Bert was far too quick for him and was half way down the stairs before Morten gave up the chase, returning to his office, not a little shaken.

*   *   *

"I wish to speak with Franz Müller, please," asked John trying not to sound too surly, as he knew he most probably did, while trying to hide his self-consciousness. He had for expediency, and with little regard for the self-disgust his action caused him, taken his official arm-band from his pocket, and was now wearing it, desperately hoping the sentry man would recognise it.

"Franz, yes. . .," pondered the sentry. "Were you not here at our Relaxation last Tuesday? I seem to remember. . ."

His voice trailed off, to be cut into by a very pink-faced John who had nevertheless siezed upon this certificate of legitimacy;

"Yes! I'm a friend of his. I was with S.S. Hüffmeier".

The sentry was a little unclear as to his exact recollections of John's role on that evening for he, like all good Germans, when they have the liquid chance, had let the Relaxation live up to its name.

The mention of S.S. Hüffmeier might have caused John's stomach to heave but it had similarly brought quick recognition in the sentry. He stiffened slightly, calling all his senses into order, realizing that this supplicant to the Reich was as legitimate as the most recent one. He replied with almost patronizing enthusiasm;

"Yes, of course. I think little Franz is present. Please to wait. I will see what can be done."

* * *

"It's O.K. now," John reassured Franz, as they entered Candie Gardens. Franz looked nervous, but he too felt they had not been seen together, not by anyone who mattered of course. They knew from last Monday, (only four days ago?) when they had met on that problem-free, or at least problem-forgotten, evening, that this place was theirs.

There would be few civilians at this time of day but those that there were would be mothers too concerned with their infants to notice the illicit collaboration. Any Germans at this time of day too, would be off-duty and of lower ranks probably walking alone, the more aesthetic types liking to enjoy gardens or to just read or sit and look or listen. No, they would be fairly secluded from reviling tongues and looks here.

How sad that in this very beautiful place, where their

friendship had evolved to push hiatuses away, only four days previously, they now looked on it as a haven from the guilt of liaison for what was, despite war's rigours, just a good friendship.

The place was an Eden. Whatever the fruit was, which they had tasted, it made each aware that friendship now had to be clandestine for, to all the world, that which was good was called collaboration and treachery.

"Let's talk over there," indicated John as he moved towards the large secluded lawn near a path rarely used because of its almost permanent north facing shade.

Franz did not object but followed meekly.

Once they had sat on the grass it was difficult for either to break the silence. They had a lot to say to each other but it all suddenly seemed irrelevant and hopeless. John felt he had brought Franz here at great risk to both of them, for no good reason.

Franz too felt extreme anxiety and, despite his wish to unburden all his fears on John, was made dumb by the tightening prospect of what fresh troubles he would face when it had been discovered he had left the house.

"I'm sorry," apologized John with feeling. He heard his own words as he thought to himself that he was not far from the point of tears. He did not mind. He would not have cared if Franz had seem him cry. He hoped, in his helpless way, that his remorse would come across in his words and so legitimatize his apology.

"That is all right, John. It is I who have to be sorry."

"Eh?"

"Pardon me?"

"What do you mean?" asked John.

"I don't know," admitted Franz. "I'm just sorry you're sorry." He accompanied his words with a weak smile and John too, smiled.

Franz now put the house behind him. They could not find him here, well not yet, at least. It was better here with John, he could forget Morten. The war had stopped.

John, sensing the air lighten as Franz relaxed, began to see his own troubles more in perspective, mighty as they were, and to recognize that his friend too, was in dire straits. Had he not worried about the well-being of Franz the other day, and yesterday, and all through his troubled night? Only, with the fears for his father and during the upset at his parents troubled reunion, had Franz temporarily left his thoughts, but now he was here in thought and person.

"Who goes first?"

"What?"

"Who's going to speak first? We've both got a lot to say, eh?" pressed John, half hoping his gesture would allow him to be the first, but also prepared to be a good listener.

"Oh, you, John. Tell me how you get on with your visit to the priest." He remembered now, John had little time earlier, for that same visit had been pressing on him. He recollected how he had wanted his friend to stay to help remove the stain Morten had put on his mind. But Morten was behind him now. He would not exist while he listened to John.

John was glad of the opportunity to tell all and as he relived his visit with Father Peters, and as Franz sat taking in every word with the deepest and most sincere concern, the narrator passed through all the changes of mood that he had endured so recently.

There was the initial anger with the priest, then the sense of power as the cleric had come round to his point of view, followed by hope as he had made his way to the Advocate's chambers. Franz sensed how John had been awed by the Advocate's attitude but gratified that he had expedited matters with the Chief of Police. They both shared the shock of what they had both expected and yet could not face, the impending trial of John's father. Each held the unspoken thought that Larry Collins' predicament was only a prelude for their own separate troubles.

The happenings earlier today and now their recounting only helped them to accept their circumstances as no longer dream-like. Neither could waken from it. Nor, as they sat together, would they have chosen that course.

The implications of Larry's charges were not lost on Franz, the ignominy of being marked as a traitor against his own people, rather than a martyr against the enemy. He felt strengthened that he would in some way accompany John's father in this burden for this too was his lot. The hardest part for John was the meeting of his parents.

"I don't understand it Franz, I just don't!" His voice again held that bell-like sound as if close to breaking point. Franz remained silent.

"I've seen them argue before," he continued, "they've sometimes gone for days without talking. Mum's a right little sulk at times."

He paused while Franz looked up, presumably waiting for him to continue, but there was silence.

"John."

"Yes?"

"What is this sulk please?"

"It's nothing, forget it," then realizing it was better to go on talking, to encourage Franz to listen and then to speak himself, than to enter into an abyss of nothingness, more kindly added;

"Oh she would just go for days without speaking. You know, like a sort of little kid who's lost an argument and won't make friends again."

There, he had mended what could have been a rift between them. He felt better now, just as he sensed Franz did.

"So, maybe it is just the sulk now, yes?" ventured Franz, trying to smile and shrug off the problem for his friend. "Perhaps she will stop this sulk in a few days?"

"That's not the point, though, is it?" John faltered, but felt encouraged to continue. "She had nothing to sulk for, did she? Dad was coming home, and she wanted that, so why act like it? I tell you Franz, I can't take it. I just had to come and find you."

"Thank you. Then I am the lucky one." Franz realized, as the words left him, that they had two meanings. Had it not been for the gravity of his friend's mood he would have taken some comfort from this secret, yet also shared, meaning from his own statement. As it was, he kept the secret one to himself, not wishing to stem John's flow, but saving it for later if John should ask him to tell of his missing adventures. Maybe John would be too busy to make such an invitation? Perhaps John would not have time to listen to his own troubles? It didn't matter, it was good to be together no matter what the circumstances.

"What do you mean?" asked John, genuinely wondering, as breaking from his saga, to enquire.

"I'm lucky that you had to come and find me," explained Franz.

"That's for sure," added John, half in jest, so that they both smiled at his impertinence. They were not laughing today.

The silence was a comfortable one.

"She'll be all right John, you'll see" said the great philosopher, "she is a good woman, your mother."

"Lady," corrected John.

"Pardon?"

"I said lady. She's a lady, not a woman." John sounded almost petulant.

"Oh," came Franz's non-offensive, non-offended reply. He sensed he dare not explore the esoterics of this statement.

"It's O.K., Franz. Sorry, you wouldn't know. It's just in English you call ladies ladies and women are women, you know?" He wasn't explaining very well, but damn it, he wasn't a teacher, besides he had enough worries, didn't he?

"Anyway it doesn't matter, you can call her woman, for all I care."

"No," insisted Franz, "your mother is a lady, you must not call her woman." He could not understand the difference but he realized there was one, therefore Mrs. Collins had a choice and, in his eyes, she had to have only the best.

"Anyway, Franz, it must be getting late, aren't you on patrol or anything?"

Franz felt that perhaps John had tired of his company and was telling him he had better go. Well, maybe that would be for the best? Perhaps they should go off their separate ways now? But what then? What was there for Franz once they had parted? Back he would have to go and face that Morten. He did not feel he could face him again, or the trouble awaiting him when they discovered he had left the house.

What else was there for him? Only transfer to the Russian front. An unknown is always terrifying or at the least, causes worry. But the anxiety of action in the East seemed preferable to the known and dreaded Morten. Franz almost wished he could get posted immediately so that he would not face one more black night under the same roof. But then, of course, he would lose John.

Cold panic gripped him as he allowed his mind to explore such an eventuality. He could not let himself think of the inevitable. In fact, his misery had been so profound up till now that the thought had not entered his head. Maybe the relaxation of being with his friend was allowing his imagination to awaken once more?

Now, if he had a choice, what would be his decision? It was an awful concept, such as makes the perceiver imagine he will go insane if he continues to indulge. What would Franz choose? To go immediately to Russia and escape Morten's evil but lose his friend for ever, or stay with John and, as a price, have the nightmare of Morten's attentions?

Franz's insanity was not invoked as there was no choice, for the matter was not his to decide. He was just the drawing not the draughtsman.

"I spoke to you!" growled John, in mock annoyance, as he punched Franz on the arm. What fun if Franz would only retaliate, as he had done the last time. That luxury would be too much to ask for now that they were both wiser and both more drained by what this crazy world was doing to them. Both? Yes, that was true, since they had entered the Gardens, all it had been was John using Franz to pour out his own problems. But what of Franz himself, he must have his troubles too?

"Sorry?" Franz was feeling rather ill now. He knew they would soon have to part company and to do so was to ask him to have the strength of will to inflict a wound on himself. He did not think he could do it.

"I said, 'What about you?' " asked John, more concerned than irritated. "Have you got to go on duty or anything?"

"No, I'm off duty. How do you say, suspended?"

"That's good then, eh?" encouraged John effecting a nervous grin, but suspecting the portents were anything but good.

"Yes, it's good," shrugged Franz, as a wave of misery began to sweep over him. "It's good but . . .," he trailed off, looking out over the rooftops to where the distant cranes could be seen toiling in the harbour, their laborious grinding and clanking, every now and again, reaching their ears, as

113

the wind played with the sounds. That was where it had all started.

"But what?"

John sensed that Franz needed to unburden himself and needed to be cajoled into doing so.

*   *   *

Frances too, as though Town House were today a magnet, attracting all those who had been charged by the little German wretch Franz, found herself there trying to act, to do something positive to dispel the evil concepts which had inhabited her thoughts.

Larry's homecoming had been bleak in the extreme. He had deserved better than that. John, too, had been affected by Frances' mood and had left without a word.

Had it all been to do with Bert, or had it been something more? No, it had not been just Bert, with his reminders and arousals of some long-ago passions, so far in history now that they might not have existed, except as fantasies in the mind of a lonely woman.

No, it had all been to do with Franz and knowing that only she, his adopted mother, could, or was willing to, do anything to help this pathetic enemy.

"I wish to see Captain, whatever his name is, Weiss or something!"

She knew very well the Captain's name. She knew all the names which Franz had mentioned, for they were etched on her memory as if burned with a hot needle.

Captain Weiss had not been inclined to meet Mrs. Collins. She had heard his voice amplified through the ear piece which the embarrassed sentry had held back from his assaulted ear. The sound of explosive German had meant nothing concrete to her except that she suspected she was about to be refused an interview, this making her still livid anger much enlivened. The word Feldkommandantur was the only one she had recognized from the stream. She had been astute enough to realize she was about to be directed there, to put her matter before the civilian office. This she had not been prepared to accept.

114

"You, . . . man!" she had shouted close to the sentry's mouth, so that Weiss had been forced to notice her with her unthought out expletive.

Well it had worked and here she now sat, Weiss at his untidy desk and she on a small hard chair, dangerously rickety. The office was not used to entertaining comfort-loving civilians.

"Captain Weiss. I'm very angry! It takes a lot to make me angry like this, I'm usually a calm person. I can take a lot, but this matter is beyond me, quite beyond me!"

Weiss' whole instinct was to grab hold of her to forcibly evict her from his office. How dare this conquered hag come shouting at him, an officer of the Weirmacht, in his own office? He would greatly enjoy roughly pushing her out, or perhaps more seemly, letting some of his men enjoy the work. She could complain as much as she liked but who would listen to the stupid woman? She had already put herself outside the law, anyway.

The only thing which prevented his taking the angry course of action was a sense of curiosity as to why this person should have the audacity to be here in the first place. She had a very great bravery which could almost be admired, except that she was one of a vanquished race. Either that, or she was incredibly naive.

*   *   *

Franz wanted John to walk back with him to the house. In fact, he had insisted. John, shocked at Franz's bitter revelation, but drawn closer to him out of a sort of gratitude that his friend had trusted him enough to confide his darkest secrets, to off-load some of his guilt ridden fears, was happy to go along with him.

Neither of them cared too much now if people saw them together. They were both right and the rest of the world was wrong. Were not the hateful Morten and all the other person-alities who dogged their lives proof enough of this?

They both shared, although neither had discussed it, the sentiment that this walk together was probably to be their last meeting anyway, and if not the last, then the penultimate. The end was very near and when the end is near the remaining time is jewel-like in its preciousness and must be spent wisely. Wise to them was to do the things which most mattered for today, not the less pleasant actions which might provide a tomorrow. They had no tomorrow.

John had been horrified too, when he had learned of his dear friend's pending posting to the Russian front. He knew, full well, the implications of that, and although not voiced, he was aware that Franz also understood. What with Franz to be sent off to almost certain death, with no possibility of communication, or knowledge of whereabouts, and his own father destined, almost without doubt, to rot incommunicado in a French prison, it was all a ghastly coincidence. In his hurt mind, John felt that, by their fates, Franz and his father were to be drawn together. The actions, which had to some extent each contributed unintentionally to the other's downfall, had brought them together as one devastated spirit. Somehow Franz now seemed more family than ever.

As they walked slowly, to eke out the remaining few hundred paving stones, John's mind was full of his revitalized concept of brotherhood between himself and his friend. They had been through an awful experience together and they had each suffered alone. John would not have exchanged either of their separate sufferings for oblivion though, if it had meant they two had never know each other. He thought how angry he had been yesterday, that eventful day, when he had realized Franz had Dad's bike. He had not then been able to contain his jealousy and had felt no wish to share his parent. Now it was different; out of their sufferings had been forged a bond so strong that what was John's was Franz's equally and vice versa.

So, when Franz had recounted his trauma, reliving the misery with Morten, and explained how he had told this all to Mrs. Collins, John had not been annoyed as Franz had half feared, but had welcomed the revelation as further evidence of their bond.

"That is why Mrs. Collins is a lady, not a woman," Franz had said, "John, she is to me like a mother. . ." He had hesitated wondering if this would lose his friend once more, but it had needed to be said.

John's simple reply had been; "Yes."

At this, Franz had looked his friend directly in the face,

his wrinkled brow of expected rejection, smoothing gradually, as he had seen there in John, with his 'yes' a complete acceptance of what he had just learned.

"That's O.K. Franz, it makes us brothers then, doesn't it?." He had paused to allow Franz's sad smile to develop fully. "Brothers we are, mate, and brothers we'll stay for ever, eh?"

"That's for sure," had been Franz's reply, as the other had feigned attack for derisory use of one of his Guernsey expressions.

*   *   *

Weiss stood up, he was bringing the interview to a close. His mood towards the civilian woman, who sat on the rickety chair in front of his desk, was much calmer now. He was red in the face. Was it anger or was he actually embarrassed?

His curiosity had been sated now and he had learned things about his senior Patrol Man which he had always known. But, to hear them from a civilian, and a female at that, had been too much for him. Morten had really gone too far this time. Yes, Weiss was angry with his own man. Thank heavens he had decided, or events had ordained for him, to see this person. What would have been the outcome if she had carried her complaint to the Feldkommandantur, as at first he had wished? No, although Morten would clearly take all blame in this instance, and even though a civilian complaint about internal matters was not likely to succeed, it was sure to raise some eyebrows about Weiss' control of his own establishment. Questions would be whispered about the Captain himself. There were those who would delight in such gossip. He was wise enough to know how half the promotions and demotions and arbitary decisions, deeply effecting all their lives, were taken as a result of behind-the-scenes conversations, with no recourse to hearings or honesty or chance to put the other viewpoint. There was never another viewpoint, for Germany's system was strong and foolproof, it was not a weak democracy.

The Captain shuddered, partly with anger that Morten's deed had been so blatant and therefore foul, that it had given a civilian a low working-class woman even, the feeling that she had the right to question the very masters themselves. When the conquered felt they had some sorts of rights things must be bad, very bad indeed! His shudder was partly fear at the concept of what might have been while he temporarily allowed himself the indulgence of argumentative thought, where the unaccustomed concept of more than one outcome could be considered.

Mrs. Collins made no attempt to go. She had said what had needed to be said and now she felt drained. The Captain, although seething with anger and ruffled by fear, had not allowed these to transmit to her, as she had ferociously given vent to her feelings. He had remained outwardly calm, albeit getting visibly more crimson. His studied politeness and attention to all Frances had told him had impressed her and had taken the heat from her mood, so that she was now more passive.

"Well Mrs. Collins, thank you for coming." The Captain had coughed lightly. "As I am saying to you, I will fully investigate this matter. Please to take my word on this."

Frances, now realizing she was expected to leave, and finding herself now spent and more inclined to deference than she had been since hearing young Franz's tale, looked up. She forced her mouth to form some words intended to draw the Captain's attention to his other part of the promise but he, anticipating her demand, continued.

"You can contact me in a day or two, not by 'phone, and I will let you know what is to be done. Now please, Mrs. Collins, you must go. I am busy man."

Frances took the hint and far more puzzled, or just bemused, stood waiting to be directed out, to be told what was to come next.

Weiss turned the handle of his telephone barking some German into it.

"There, one of my men will show you out of the building."

Weiss was hesitant and ill at ease, as Frances waited for this chaperone, head bent and shoulders bowed.

"There is just one thing," he ventured hesitantly, just hoping its very mention would not inspire the person with an unthought action, "you must appreciate that this matter

118

must be kept completely between us if I am to deal with it. . ."

His words trailed, as she stared at him with cold emotionless eyes. A further cough.

"I am saying that you must not mention this to any of the. authorities, German or civilian. Understood?"

Frances did not deign to answer as the knock on the door heralded her means of exit.

*   *   *

They all but reached the point where goodbyes were necessary except that on this, possibly the last, occasion, John was prepared with bravado to accompany Franz right to the Town Patrol House door, right inside if need be.

They needed to arrange a further meeting, for life had to go on, even under sentence of death. The very planning for a future which could not be, would make the dream real and the inevitable irrelevant, with less force.

"This is it, then," hesitated John as he reluctantly made the first cut to sever this good meeting. "I reckon you'd better go on in, eh?"

"I don't want to," was the reply, not a statement of defiance but one of helpless dejection. "John, I don't want to go, I can't leave you now. I'll be all alone in there." His voice had taken on a shrill panic, as he allowed these last words. They emphasized his aloneness.

"Oh come on now, Franz," cajoled John kindly. "Look, just do it as we planned. Go on, eh. . . It's got to be done, make it easier for yourself."

John was not too sure that his words sounded very convincing but somehow he sensed that Franz had responded to the reminder of their earlier discussions.

"Yes, brother," came Franz's very faint and soulless voice. "Yes, if you say so, John." He held out his hand as if in a farewell shake, but could not bring himself to speak, as he reluctantly moved away from his friend towards the hydrangea bordered courtyard.

John did not take the proffered hand for it would have been admitting a finality. However he could not let Fanz leave without response.

119

"It'll be O.K., mate. We'll get together again soon, eh?"

They had been about to arrange, what must surely be an imaginary meeting. It was to be a charade really, but as such was far better than not even a dream prospect.

The imaginings and deliberations were rudely shattered for them when the front door of the house, until then so dead and unreal, like the unreal and unseeing sentry at the top of the steps, burst open to eject in a great explosion of hurry, a human dishevelled and in haste, like a green monster. Down the steps clattered the jackbooted, helmet-askew Morten, senior Patrol Leader of Town House, the devil in Franz's hell of terror.

Franz had no time to degenerate into abject fear, for Morten, upon seeing the two, the object of his haste, was at their side almost as quickly as they had seen him. His face was white, his expression divested of all human attributes. His eyes were black, shuttered against any attempts at exploring the thoughts he might hold. He breathed heavily, straightening his helmet, while standing glaring down at Franz. Franz was now all of a shake as he edged nearer to his brother in order to know that he, at least, was real in the presence of this evil one.

Morten had just been called in to see Captain Weiss and was still smarting from the verbal abuse he had received. The Patrol Leader was not unused to foul language or innuendoes but was not usually on the receiving end of such tirades. He had been forced to listen to his whole catalogue of misdemeanours with the hypocritical cant of how he had brought disgrace and ignominy on the whole German nation, how he would probably end up in a bad way and how he was to do his utmost to put everything to rights with the appearance of good and correct German order. And all the while, as he had been reviled and insulted, while he had to effect humble acceptance of all his misdemeanours and promise not to go further along that road, as the threat of the Eastern Front was paraded before him, he could only think of revenge. For him the eating of shame and confession and the undressing of his manly status in this way could only be put right by gruesome revenge. No matter if he was sent to Russia, revenge would remain sweet in his mouth while he suffered the rigours of a real war.

So here he was and here was the object of his vile temper. How he would enjoy himself! Caring not that Franz was accompanied by that little rat of a stubborn civilian boy, the one probably who had put Franz against him in the first place, in view of the sentry he proceeded. Morten, in his roused and belligerent state, could not temper his mood with moderation, even though Weiss was in that very building and quite possibly watching at that moment.

"Little scum!" he shouted as his forearm hit Franz across the side of the jaw, the meaning of the words lost on John but not their ferocity, and the sickening sound of flesh upon flesh.

Franz staggered under the blow, crying out as he clutched towards John. His brother instinctively stepped as a shield between Franz and Morten, cradling the young German's head against further assault.

Franz was only aware of an awful throbbing right through his head, accompanied by green and yellow pain. John heard only the crazy snorting breaths of the towering bully.

Insult after insult flew in German, all lost on the whimpering Franz.

John, who had saved Franz from any further immediate harm, felt himself picked up by his shirt, noticing, as if in the far distance, a ripping sound, and was roughly pushed aside so that, despite his resolve, he let go of Franz. He staggered, and, as he regained his balance, observed Morten shaking Franz so hard that it seemed his very skeleton would come apart.

"Stop that, you bloody bugger!" John shouted, as he jumped to Morten, trying to pull him away. It was as though he had no strength at all, for his actions had no effect. Morten only ceased because it suited him to do so.

And all the time the unreal sentry had remained unreal.

Franz, almost at the point of crumpling, was brought up to his true stature as Morten forced his clamp-like hand inside the lad's collar and began to march his prize towards the house. So quick was he, and so pliant was young Franz, that John realized he was being left behind, utterly impotent to alter events.

There was nothing else to be done but for John to follow. So he had the audacity, born of desperation, to enter the building immediately behind the two Germans, as if part of their group. Still the unreal sentry did not move.

Once inside the building, by a great stroke of fortune, they met Captain Weiss coming out of his office, still red-faced with lingering anger from his two recent interviews. By chance, he was looking for young Franz and was completely amazed to see him so firmly and roughly gripped by the Patrol Leader, especially as they had so recently had words. so surprised was he by this liaison that his whole concentration went to the two Germans while seeming unaware of John, a mere civilian.

Morten gave the Captain a smart hand salute accompanied by 'Heil', unusual in itself, for his dealings with Weiss, as Weiss' with him, were usually quite informal, not extending to such rituals.

Weiss did not respond to the salute, being too preoccupied with his matter in hand and not a little curious as to exactly what Morten thought he was doing. He did notice however, that the Patrol Leader was being formal. Perhaps he had taken some notice of the recent anger and was in awe?

"Well, Patrol Leader?" asked the Captain, as if the very statement should have some extended meaning to the man. He was glad to observe Morten looked discomforted.

"Captain?" replied Morten in quizzical tone.

"I'm asking for your explanation!" He indicated the supported Franz, noticing for the first time, the red wale across the boy's cheek with the puffed up swelling beneath his left ear.

'Perhaps this Morten is not incapable of learning a lesson,' he thought. 'Perhaps he's hit the lad as a disciplinary measure, to show that the other sordid business is over?' He almost chuckled out loud as he indulged himself in the thought that maybe this was how Morten treated his loved ones. A bit of cave man stuff. He ought to be in the damned S.S. like that sick friend of his, or leave from Alderney.

'On the other hand,' he thought, 'this Patrol Leader may well by trying to teach the young fool a lesson so that he'd think twice before spreading such slander again.'

Whichever reason it was, it did not really matter, for Morten could no longer expect any regard from one he had treated so harshly. Not that it mattered now anyway, as he had news for young Müller which would put an end to his nuisance value once and for all.

Morten was not unintelligent. His coming face to face with the Captain like this, had shocked some of the anger from him, to be replaced by an amalgam of awkwardness and defensiveness. He was not too experienced in either emotion.

"The boy?" he ventured, searching quickly for acceptable reasons.

"Yes, the boy! The two boys in fact," replied Weiss, again losing a little more of his anger in his enjoyment of Morten's appearing so ill at ease.

"Captain, I've been taking notice of your advice," lied the Patrol Leader. "Little Franz and I are going to have a talk together so that he will know exactly where he stands and how he's to respect the authority of this House."

"I see. That seems very good policy, Patrol Leader, but what of the other things?"

"Other things . . ., Sir?" The 'Sir' being as unaccustomed, to Morten's lips, as water at a Relaxation.

"Yes man . . .," the Captain was not going to let this creature get off without a little sweat, "young Müller's injuries, and this civilian you've brought in with you? You're not. . . .?"

He purposely let his question die, to full effect.

"Sir, you don't think . . .," Morten too was inconclusive but his superior immediately cut in.

"I don't think! God in heaven I should damned well hope not! That sort of behaviour's for your S.S. friends, not here, by an officer serving under me! Do I make myself clear?"

"Yes, Sir, you do." So clear was the Captain's meaning, Morten found himself doing a subservient heel click, as he replied.

"Well I suggest you see to your friend's face before you talk to him . . .," he loaded the word talk, ". . . and show this civilian here that we know how to look after our men. We would like him to go away with a good impression, wouldn't we?"

"Yes, Sir." Again an unaccustomed click of the boots.

All this while Franz stood still looking at the floor. He

123

was in great pain and shock, mixed with terror. Of all, terror had the greatest hold on him.

John had stood looking from one German to the other as the conversation had darted back and forth. He had not understood the words but, by following the directions of the eyes, the gesticulations and the tone of the voices, both masterly and subservient, he felt he had understood. He knew somehow, for the time being at least, things could only get better. The Patrol Leader, the arch enemy, seemed awed. John sensed the Captain was not pleased with Morten.

"Now before you go," the Captain took on a more measured tone, as he was about to change to something far more mundane, "I'm glad you're here Müller. I have news for you, young man. I'm very pleased for you, very pleased indeed." He allowed himself the luxury of a smile. Morten allowed himself a half smile wondering what would be the sting in the tail.

"You have caused me a lot of trouble one way and another, my fine fellow. You have taken up far more of my time than you are worth." He bent his head towards the glazed eyes of Franz, while John observed and listened, just hoping he would get opportunity soon to ask his brother what it was all about.

"So I am very pleased to learn this afternoon, and I'm sure your Patrol Leader will be too," he gave a knowing 'man of the world' smile to Morten, who deferentially reflected it, "you are leaving us, Müller. You only have a few days with us. You start your holiday in Ruskie Land next week!"

Franz, despite his preoccupation with pain and terror, choked a little at this re-affirmation and, without thought for the witness of his two senior countrymen, gasped, moving closer to John's side. John, not knowing the purport of the message, only understood the deadening effect it had on his friend and, also unconcerned at the appearance of his action, pulled Franz to him, to support him, as proof of his concern.

"Now Patrol Leader, this young soldier is yours until his posting. I wish to hear of no further complaints. I want all behaviour, including his, to be exemplary." He gave Morten a hard knowing stare which said 'He is yours but cause any trouble and you have had it, my fine fellow.'

"Müller, you are off duty until the aircraft takes you away

from us, for ever I hope. Usually people honouring their country in the front line of duty are given some sort of leave as a gratitude from the Führer. However, from what I've heard, I'm not too sure that you deserve to be treated as a hero. My conscience would not allow me to just let you wander and possibly cause the authorities more problems." He paused as though he had hoped to awaken some response, some argument or plea in Franz. All he got, however, was a further gasp, as the visage of the young soldier paled still more, contrasting with the redness of his cheek, which now took on a slightly purple hue. Franz realized his nightmare projections had begun. He was to lose John immediately and was to be given over to the evil one, as his prisoner, for several days of endless hell. The confirmation of this latest thought was the most damning blow.

"Senior Patrol Leader you must decide how this soldier spends his time. He is not fit to work. It will be your decision if he is to be kept in or allowed out. I wash my hands of him!"

*   *   *

As John entered Gaudion's dark portal, as light was excluded and the darkness of the downstairs passage of 12, Rue Marguerite, enveloped him, encasing him round with the musty odours and stale smells of cooked tomatoes from these past thirteen months, so did he temporarily forget the cares of his trouble world.

Rushing the stairs two at a time as he made his way up to the second floor flat, which was the Collins' home, John left behind his recent trauma. His whole rush home had been invaded by the thoughts and various computations of his and Franz' plight; yes, his as well, for were they not brothers now?

Only minutes before, Morten had helped John to the door of Town Patrol House, and so forcefully ejected him that he had almost stumbled down the steps into the bright light of the late afternoon sun.

John had not noticed the police station or the prison, or the plantation as he had rushed home. He had not been aware of one stone or one cobble or one fellow human being, such was his turmoil.

Was that to be it? Was that the last chance he would have to see his friend? Would the two never more meet and talk and walk and laugh and cajole each other? How he would miss serious Franz with his laboured enquiries about the meaning of English expressions. Never again was John to be asked;

"What is this 'penny for your thoughts', please?" or

"How you say . . ., this and that?"

How irritating his friend was at times, but oh, how he would be missed by John who, without his dear enemy, would have no contemporaries he knew in his whole island, all his friends from the Intermediate having long since been evacuated to England. Oh, so long ago!

Perhaps John could pass a message to Franz before he departed for the Russian front? Maybe one of the other patrollers would pass it on, but how? He did not know any of them, and how was he to go up to a complete stranger, and at a risk of being ridiculed, to try to effect this?

What about the post? No, letters were sure to be opened, and then Franz would be in more trouble, also his father would go wild when the Gestapo knocked on the door with yet more evidence of subversion.

The telephone was also out of the question.

No, it would have to be left to Franz to contact John. There had been just a hint that Morten could permit Franz to be out and about if that fine gentleman thought fit. Some chance! Franz would be too frightened. What if John himself sought Morten out and asked? No, John felt too proud for this. But what was the alternative, pride or lost friend? John knew if given the choice, it would have to be pride to be subjugated. But, even then, he reasoned, to let Morten know how much he wanted to see his friend would only further arm that evil one with the cruel weapon of withholding. It really was hopeless!

Only as John reached the top of the stairs, did the thoughts of his poor friend dispel, as the youth set his mind to the more imminent task, that of returning home to his mum and dad. What distress would that entail?

*   *   *

Chapter Seven

"I suppose the close relatives are here?" asked the Consultant Surgeon, as he and his assistant cleaned up. He looked tired now, haggard, his shoulders bent as if the rationed minutes of intense activity had drained him.

Despite his earlier lightness of approach, what had seemed almost irreverent flippancy to the doctor assisting, he had aged many years in those few minutes, as he always did when he saw the utter futility of his efforts which had reinforced once more the sometimes complete and hopeless fallibility of his craft. His question was asked of no one in particular, there just happened to be the doctor to receive it.

"They were sent for, I believe," replied the doctor as he allowed his overall to be removed to one of the silent minions.

"Then it will be my unpleasant task to inform them," sighed the Consultant. It had been a pointless remark for it was part of his job, but he needed to share the anathema with his colleague, even if just in prospect. There was no reply.

The hot water gushed. The steam rose to moisten his grey face. How he longed for retirement.

* * *

Franz was sitting alone on his bed. He had been only partly aware of the comings and goings of his fellow patrollers, but none had been able to penetrate the gloom which surrounded him. Nor was he particularly aware that they had tried. In his black mood, he viewed all his fellow countrymen with dark suspicion.

He wasn't even sure if he knew any of them. Not that he had looked any directly in the face, for he would far rather have had no contact at all at the present. Chances were that they were not the fellows he had last seen. How many days ago was it now? They had probably all changed duties and been posted elsewhere. Maybe they had all been victimized because they had been in contact with him, the pariah. He did not know and he did not care. Franz just wished they would go away and he could pretend he was all alone in that place, not having to be constantly reminded it was occupied by the Wiermacht of which Morten was a part.

Since John's departure, Morten had surprisingly left him alone, so much so that Franz allowed himself the luxury of fantasizing he had been forgotten or was no longer needed as a butt for revenge or worse. Despite his futile dreams, he still froze a little at the approach of each pair of jackboots. Involuntarily he trembled, unable to look up, whenever the wearer of the vociferous footwear paused anywhere near his bed.

Franz's uneasy peace was not to be for long. He only had minutes to contemplate his position, while thinking of his recent past shared with his friend; a friend who had probably now returned to find his parents happy once more and to forget his so-called brother for his last few days in this beautiful place. He did not think too much of Morten or of his posting to Russia, for both were awful and each to be preferred rather than the other. However, both were equally to be rejected as more foul a prospect than its alternative. Like a little boy running from a misdemeanour, to put off rather than obviate the punishment, he did not allow his mind to dwell upon the unimaginable.

The unimaginable was brought back to him by the sudden presence of a grim-faced orderly, demanding his presence immediately in the Senior Patrol Leader's personal room.

His room, not his office!

The orderly, with Franz close in tow, rapped hard on the door of Senior Patrol Leader Morten's private room. Franz felt lead like with misgivings as he remembered the misery he had suffered there earlier that afternoon. His every inclination was to run for it but the orderly had anticipated such an eventuality as he nervously froze Franz with his close scrutiny.

"Come in, Müller," was the Senior Patrol Leader's gruff invitation. Franz was now hypnotized in his complete control, fear and dread shackling him into obedience, as the orderly was dismissed with a flick of the hand.

"Look at me," demanded Morten in a voice, if not known to be that of his, might have sounded almost kind or caring in its tone, "Don't be afraid, little Franz. I'm not going to hit you again."

Once more the voice, unaccustomed as it was, seemed loaded with concern, or was its tone the prelude to more aesthetic pursuits? Franz felt almost relieved that Morten had not started off angry. His relaxation, with the reminder of violent assault, brought his pain to the fore as he groaned slightly.

"Ah yes, I see you have quite a nasty bruise there," noted Morten. He was not apologizing but simply being factual. "Anyway, little Franz Müller, I told you to look at me, didn't I? And that's an order." His timbre now seemed charged with almost a chuckle. Franz's nervousness subsided further as he hesitantly complied, his face contorting with the effort.

Morten was smiling now but it was not a cruel guise, for Franz did not want it to be cruel. No, it was a more friendly look than Franz could have imagined. There was a broad, teeth-gritted, grin so that the young soldier's face clouded at its enigma.

"Did the medic see to you?" Franz did not reply. "I asked if you've had your injury seen to." Morten stepped forward as if to touch the wound but stayed his hand as Franz involuntarily flinched.

"Yes he did," he muttered.

"Yes what?" The old harshness re-entered his senior's voice.

"Yes Sir."

"That's better! Now. . ."

* * *

Relief. The gas stove was not turned on, its clean dull enamel being in correct, unused order, Friday was not usually an oven day anyway. The tap was off. There was no damaged or disarrayed furniture. The cups and tea pot had even been washed and put away and the tea leaves spread

129

out to dry on a plate on the window-sill. Nothing was out of place. Neither were there parents present.

Back down the passage went John, cautiously turning the rattly knob on the sitting room door. Hesitantly he entered the large room only to find the same lack of evidence of anything untoward. He almost crept to the room's centre as the old floor bounced him to dance in time with the rattling of the sash windows. Even so, he could see no bodies either prone or hiding behind the sideboard or antiquated suite.

So, it had to be the bedroom. The door was closed but that was not unusual, for the family's privacy was enough impaired by giving passage to yet another flat above, and by being scrutinized by Gaudion, who shuffled his way up and down whenever he felt he would not be seen.

What if they were lying down? No that was impossible, how could he even imagine their wanting to lie down together so soon after the scene he'd witnessed earlier? No, it would take days, possibly a week, if it ever happened at all now! Nevertheless, John took the precaution of putting an ear to the door. Not a sound. He knocked timidly. Where on earth could they be?

*   *   *

"That's right, little soldier boy, you just watch your manners and do what you're told first time and we'll be able to send you safe and sound to visit the Bolsheviks."

Franz nodded. He did not really feel Morten had called for a reply. The longer that man kept talking anyway, the better. The door was still ajar too. What did he want?

"So we meet again so soon!" Morten's tone was mockingly smooth. "It seems only minutes ago we were here together, doesn't it?"

Franz responded with an involuntary shudder but he kept his eyes fixed on those of the cat who played with him.

"Why here, Franz?" was the Senior Patrol Leader's enigmatic question, "tell me that, eh?"

Franz did not know the reason for the question. Was Morten trying to trick him into some wrong answer to legitimize more anger?

"Excuse me Sir. . .?"

130

"Come Franz, don't be such a dolt! Surely you understand what I'm saying, you're not stupid are you?" His voice was almost a chuckle again. His smile looked almost genuinely benign.

"Why here in this room? Why have I invited you here?" His eyes darted fleetingly towards the bed as the gaze of the mouse followed to stare at the trap.

Franz understood.

*   *   *

Sure that no one would be in the bedroom, but still cautious, John began to open the door. It certainly was strange for both his parents to have gone out at this time of the day with no sign of a note for him and not even the gesture of food.

There, he was in! The room was quite dark with curtains drawn, rustling slightly by the open window as his opened door disturbed the air. There on the bed lay his mother fully dressed on top of the eiderdown.

As John accustomed himself to the shade, recovering from his surprise, he noticed his mother was awake. Her bright still eyes stared at the ceiling, as she lay on her back, deadly still. Was she awake? So still! She wouldn't sleep with eyes open would she? He'd never seen her asleep on her back anyway. She wasn't dead was she? Oh no, not that!

*   *   *

"Anyway, Mr. Müller, you're wrong you see!" exclaimed Morten with glee at what was intended to be his great jest. "I don't need you in here at all. Ha! That's a surprise, eh? Sorry to disappoint you, but there will be another time. Plenty of time yet! How many days is it. . .?"

Franz was not too aware of this monologue but just concerned with his own feelings. When he thought he had got the gist of the cat's game he had felt slightly light-headed. Now, he felt rather weak at the knees as the eternal throbbing in his cheek went right up into his ear so that it all but drowned out the meows.

"I suppose you're relieved to hear it, yes?" he purred.

"You thought. . . You do have a very bad mind, young man!"

The mouse began to feel dizzy.

With unaccustomed gentleness the cat caught the mouse, as it slid towards the floor, with not a squeak.

"Come Franz Müller, come on, boy. Keep on your feet lad. This is the German army not the cripple's camp!" His voice was kind again as he held Franz gently.

Franz could hear him and smell him and see him and feel him but it was not Franz.

Franz stood off to watch.

* * *

"Mum!" John's shriek shocked even himself. He was sure his mother was dead and had been laid out.

"What is it?" came her hoarse reply.

John was not sure which was the more shocking, his first misconception or its confounding.

"Mum, mum, you're alive!"

"Just about," was her miserable reply, the drollness being quite unintentional and not received, as John sank to his knees by his mother's side. He was at the point of tears.

She did not seem to have the energy to take him to task over his silly entry, with its ludicrous assumption. She was hardly aware of his mood, just that she had been disturbed in her still meditation.

* * *

"Come now, soldier boy, I think you have had a hard day, yes? Too little work and too much play is bad for you." Morten squeezed Franz's shoulder as he supported him.

The cat was docile now and did not wish to play. It chose to be generous in its outgoing affections.

"No, I really wanted to see you in my office but I thought the extra exercise of coming right up here would be good for you." There it was, an explanation. The nearest a cat can do to making an apology.

"Franz, look alive. I have serious words to make with you and offices are for words, not bedrooms!"

Franz seemed to quicken once more.

*   *   *

"Mum, are you all right? Where's Dad? What's happened?" John's outpouring welcomed him back from anxiety.

"Just quieten down a bit, for pity's sake," she whispered. "I've an awful head and I can't take all your questions."

"Sorry, Mum," John said, as he sat down on the edge of the bed unintentionally pushing her legs. The warmth of the contact reassured him and he was a little boy once more, exuberant in the early daybreak, asking to get in with his mum. She flapped her arm about aimlessly, as if unable to see, until her hand settled on his, her cold clasp holding him. With her other hand she shaded her staring eyes and began gently to sob with the relief of the first drops in a long-awaited quenching thunderstorm.

He let her sob for a few moments then, at the pity of the sight, bent down and kissed the hand shielding her pools. She thanked him by lightly squeezing the hand on his thigh using her smooth cold hand.

"It's O.K., Mum." John's words were half statement but partly question. "I'm here, Mum. Dad's back, everything's all right, isn't it?"

Frances did not answer but she unveiled her swollen eyes, biting her lip to give a watery smile. John too wanted to cry but he had ventured far enough back into his childhood already.

"Where is Dad?" he demanded, as if he had only just thought of this, while pulling his hand free from that of his mother's. He stood up and asked again, while he watched the watery smile dissolve and the tears of oblivion cease, leaving only the dried up rivulets on her flushed cheeks.

*   *   *

Morten was now business-like in his office. At last he was in control of an interview. He had begun to wonder if he had lost the skill and if he was always to be at a disadvantage in the talking game. But no, here he had a captive audience in the shape of little Franz. By the use of words, he could strike terror into his very heart or cause tears to spring. Just the slightest impartation could make the young weakling change his degree of paleness or bring out a visible shudder.

Morten realized he no longer had any great desire for this weakling, he had already caused the Patrol Leader so much trouble that he was not really worth the effort. He might have seemed a bit of a challenge at first, but Franz's act had turned out not to be a fabrication, it had been that of the real soft and, disdainfully pure, good boy.

No, there were others far more able to put themselves out a bit, astute enough to know that if they acted correctly they would advance and experience privileges. Wasn't that the way with a large section of Germany's new order, and no one could say it was weak? On the contrary! Someone like the stubborn and wilful civilian who had befriended young Müller and seemed, all credit to him, to have courage enough to stand by him, despite all the real dangers it caused him and his family. Yes, there was a true person worth cultivating. David Hüffmeier was right.

So desire was somewhat sated towards the snivelling wretch. After all, youth was not everything, there had to be personality too. Not that he would let young Franz off that lightly. No, there were several days yet in which he held the licence of all the disgraced soldier's comings and goings. Morten would think of a way of using this power to best advantage. Indeed he had been already inspired with an idea this very afternoon. Franz and John had provided him with his inspiration.

"Now, Franz Müller, I wish to have serious talk with you." He paused only to collect his thoughts, while making sure his captive was paying attention.

"Move those papers and sit down there." He indicated the covered chair which was to be moved up.

This having been done, Morten got quickly to the point. He prided himself on his logic and brevity in such circumstances.

"First Müller, we forget earlier this afternoon, for the time being at least. That's not to say it won't be called upon again but that is up to you." There, Franz Müller could absorb that information for a few seconds and become pleasantly softened up and receptive for the next stage of the thesis.

"People have been saying too much, much too much, and I don't like it! Do you understand?" Franz, by his twitch, seemed to indicate his understanding. "I won't apportion blame, this time, but, God in heaven, if ever I hear one of these words which I'm now telling you, get back to me you'll rue the day. Is that clear?"

"Yes, Sir."

"Good!"

"Now, I have noticed, as I'm sure many of our comrades have, how close you are with our enemy. In particular, that one who was with you this afternoon. What is his name?"

Franz suddenly felt very insecure, feeling himself threatened. He could not answer a question like that without knowing where it would lead. He was surprised to hear his own bravado.

"Why?"

"Why! You do not ask me why, just tell me his name!" Morten banged his clenched fist down on his desk to emphasize his earnestness. Franz became aware of his throbbing pain once more.

"He is John Collins, Sir."

"Thank you!" Morten was making progress. He had to keep the lad in his dishevelled state just a little longer.

"I too have noticed what close friends you are, if you see what I mean?" He was pleased to observe Franz stiffen in his seat at this further encroachment of his privacy with possible deprivation.

"Such close and loyal friendships are usually only to be seen amongst comrades and do not cross the enemy lines to become almost treason."

"Sir . . .," Franz felt he needed to try explanation but it would have involved all his own unthought out, just acted, incomplete philosophy on the matter so he gave up.

"What I'm saying, young Franz, is that such an action as yours and this native is truly to be admired. When we have won this war our new order will be built upon such foundations, mark my word. Just you wait and see."

Yes, Franz was showing some response, just a little excitement tinged curiosity was stirring in him to show in a hint of returning colour to his deathly pallor.

"I think you like this Britisher better than any German here, yes?"

Obviously a trick, but so what? Why should not Franz confess his true feelings?

"Yes, Patrol Leader, you are right."

"Ah, so!" Morten's face lit with a sudden glee. He was not angry or sarcastic nor was he vindictive, as Franz had feared he might be.

"So you would like to be able to meet him again before you go to Russia?"

Franz was so softened and surprisingly at ease by now that he could only respond in excited enthusiasm;

"Yes please, Sir."

Morten was delighted. He had scored his hoped-for point.

"Good Franz, good. Then this shall be arranged!"

* * *

Frances' tone was sombre and studied as, without emotion, she told her son the news of his father. John was puzzled by the detection of loathing and detestation in her voice. He did not have time to wonder if her disgust was aimed at Dad or at her own earlier reprehensible actions towards Bert.

"Your father is out, my dear!"

"Out? Well that's obvious isn't it? But out where?"

"Guess?" came the reply loaded with sarcasm and disdain.

"Oh, no! You don't mean. . .?"

"You've got it," she almost hissed, as she noted John's expectations for his father to be at the Golden Lion. "Nothing changes!" With bitterness she closed her eyes, as though signifying an end to the interview.

* * *

Franz was out of Morten's office now. He began to feel almost alive again. It had all happened; Morten had caught up with him, had dealt him a nasty blow, captured him so that he was now his prisoner awaiting posting to the Eastern

Front. Oh yes, it was all bad, but as Franz now realized that not everything was negative, there were still things in his life which could effect him with goodness and pleasure. Not everything had been taken from him. As he thought, he began to feel some pangs of guilt that he was indulging himself in the prospect of the good to come and was keeping at bay the evil day. At least it was not to be all evil today.

Morten had not hit him any more, had not shouted at him even. He had been a second time into Morten's private bedroom but he had not been misused. Franz even had the prospect of Morten's sanction for a continued liaison with his friend John.

It was a combination of the unbelievable, where the effected person almost dare not consider his good fortune in case it should evaporate, with the uneasy thoughts, not easily repressed, that there were conditions placed on his continued friendship with John.

That was it, that was why his joy at the prospect of his remaining days of freedom was marred. It was not the horror of the unknown Russia or even the likely return of hostilities at Town House but it was the unspoken yet implied drawing of his best friend into this dark and evil web, in order to keep him.

Very clear now was that conversation.

"Well, Müller," had said the Patrol Leader who, having realized his position to be so strong, had been able to be quite direct, "You may keep contact with that Britisher of yours."

Morten had watched the delight and near disbelief colour the young detainee's face.

"Sir?" Franz had been hesitant but his excitement had taken charge of his caution, "I can meet with John while I wait to go to Russia?"

"Yes, little Franz." Morten's eyes had melted slightly with amusement at the insipid wretch who had stood before him. He had felt almost good at having been able to use his authority so.

"You can go out with your dearest friend, whenever you like, so long as you tell me first."

Franz had gasped. His inclination had been to want to shake Morten's hand but he had stopped himself for the prospect of physical contact with that person had taken him back to the dark shades of reality.

"You can go out this very evening, if you so wish." Morten's intervention had prevented Franz's mind travelling further along the dark path of suspicion. "But remember to tell me where you will be and at what time I am to expect you back."

There had been a chill note in the reminder, but nevertheless Franz had anticipated more in it for him and his friendship with John than if the offer had not been made.

"So I can go now?" Franz was still expecting the words to have been just a cruel hoax.

"Yes, go, go!" Morten had gestured with mock severity, as he had ushered Franz to the door, while his victim had not been given choice in the matter.

"Oh, and Mr. Franz Müller," had called the Patrol Leader, so forgetful that he had only thought of it, as his charge had been leaving the office. "Try to cheer yourself a bit. Try to be a little friendly, to Germans as well as to the enemy."

Franz had almost stopped at these words, as they had come at him from around the open door, but he had decided it better not to answer than to try.

"Oh, and Franz," a pause for Morten's coup de grace. "It's Sunday Relaxation in two days, remember? We would like your friend John to attend, right?"

*   *   *

John was annoyed to learn of his father's desertion, but in all honesty, he was not terribly surprised. Dad's homecoming had not exactly been welcoming. The youth had not intended to be cruel or cutting, but he heard the reproach in his own voice, as though coming from another, therefore unable to stem the words;

"And why do you think he's gone to the pub, eh?"

"Eh?" enquired his distracted mother.

"I said, he's gone to the pub to get away from you, that's what I said!" replied John, "You didn't exactly make him feel welcome, did you?"

But there was more to be said as Frances was stirred from her introversion, as she almost gleefully sought to put the blame for Larry's departure onto some other cause, or at least to have the guilt of it shared.

"Well, let me tell you, my son," she raised herself, anger dispelling her depression, "You might think that. You can bloody well think that if it pleases you, but there are other reasons, you know!"

To hear his mother swear, and with such venom, shocked John. He learned of the other reasons.

With chill, he went to the already-opened letter which was addressed to him. His parents, despite all that he had been through, still treated him as a child. He knew what he was about to read even before he took out the contents. John now was no longer immortal, time his to dispose, for like all those who touched him, he too was capable of death. The little boy now knew that he too was to cease to exist, the very idea which up until then he had evicted from his consciousness, while he had sympathised with and for others in that predicament. Yes, John also had to step from the world of fantasy into life's reality, for now the final award of maturity was to be his; he too, John Collins, Esquire, had received his summons to attend court next Friday.

John's charges were similar to his father's, so that the population would learn of his ignominy rather than his heroism.

Ominously, the youth was also warned not to communicate with his own father, his priest or Keith de la Haye, fisherman.

Shaking himself from his detached stupor, John turned to his mother as though the news he had just absorbed were of no consequence and she did not already know its content. He asked casually with a smile;

"What is the date of Dad's appearances?"

Frances who had felt her sense of indignation sated somewhat by her recent observation of John's obvious trauma, was a little taken aback by her son's apparent calmness of reaction.

"You what?"

"When is Dad's trial?" His voice was slightly edged with impatience but it was more his act than his true feeling.

"It's the same as yours, son," she replied, at last some tenderness returning to her voice. "You'll both go together, my love." Her inclination was to move forward to clasp her precious love but she overcame it, stepping back slightly, appearing to totter.

"Yes, of course, I'd forgotten. You still read my letters, eh?" John's tone was intended to be recriminatory but he could not put any enthusiasm into it.

"Mum . . .," his voice was now piteous, "What will they do to me, Mum?"

Frances, now completely clear of her hurt and self-imposed barrier, as any other matron, at the plaintive cry of her off-spring, moved to her little boy and took him in her arms, rocking him gently as her sobs of temporary amorphous relief began to flow.

"Don't worry, love," she managed between sobs. "It'll be all right, you'll see. We'll make out, love, we'll make out."

John did not reason with her words. He neither accepted their logic nor rejected, he only knew that his Mum was speaking and telling him that she was now in charge. Mum was there, in control, so he did not have to give it a further thought.

* * *

He had to find Franz. Hadn't he supported and cheered his friend when he had heard of the horror of that young soldier's circumstances? Hadn't John lived through the misery with Franz, as the latter had tried to explain? Didn't the Civilian Messenger also go to the Eastern Front with his friend, and was he not prepared to be pounded and pulped there with him in order to stay with his best friend for ever? So now Franz had to repay. Yes, he must be prepared to go to prison with his enemy and to be exiled to a French prison, unable to communicate with his mother or his island. John had to share the malevolence and his personal misery with his friend, Franz Müller.

* * *

Frances was a mother again, her little boy needed her. She felt proud that she was the mother of this fine young man. Oh yes, he needed her and she would be there, just as she was for her other son. Everything would be all right; Mummy said so.

Here she was, alone with her thoughts. Frances had to

speak to someone, she could not bear to be alone like this, not when she had so much to share. John, her little one, had gone out to play with his new friend . . . no, silly woman, she was forgetting . . . out to play with her other son, yes, that was it, the two brothers had gone out to play. Larry was not available. What about her sister Rita? No, that was out of the question. Didn't Rita resent the fact that Frances had a son in whom she was proud, on whom she doted? No, Rita could be very pernicious at times, and Frances needed someone who could be kind, who was willing to listen to her and agree with her.

"P.C. Bisson speaking," said Bert as he absent-mindedly answered his telephone, years of experience and self-indulgence at the grandure of his position causing him to momentarily forget he was no longer the holder of such an esteemed title.

"Bert?" came Frances' hesitant reply, "Bert, is that you?"

"Yes," his voice was now loaded with annoyance, tempered with curiosity. Why should she 'phone him? What was the point? All that could be said had been said. Wasn't she aware that telephones were no longer toys for the amusement of the idle, but were direct links with the intelligence of the enemy? One-way links which could only take rather than give.

"Is that you, Frances?"

"Bert, dear, I want to talk to you," she paused. Then came the pleading tone as she implored, "Please Bert, we must talk, we must!"

"We can't," he declared with firmness. "You know we mustn't talk on the 'phone. Besides, there's no more to be said!" His voice was firm and decisive. Yes, that was what Frances wanted, a man, a real man who could make decisions and who could be brusque and commanding. Such a man would be willing to listen to her extolling the virtues of her son.

"Oh Bert, you must listen to me, please." She now spoke with a confidence that she would have her own way. "I'll meet you, we'll go for a drink or something."

"What?"

"A drink. We can meet up for a drink somewhere in Town can't we? The evening's young and it's a long time till curfew, eh?" Her voice now sounded almost coquettish. Bert felt his emotions were being trifled with. He could not understand. What on earth had got into her? He still felt a hangover from the days of freedom when ladies did not go into pubs, and even in those few places where they could get away with it, never would they with any but their own husband. Now she was suggesting a concept almost akin to adultery, especially contrasted by her earlier firm rejection of his desires, so that they had been still-born in him and he had accepted all the guilt of his fantasies.

"What about Larry?" he asked amost guiltily, wondering if he was to be party to or even included in this subterfuge.

"Larry? Oh he's not here." Frances sounded very vague, almost detached.

"Where is he?" asked Bert, feeling some slight relief that his friend was not witness to this conversation.

"Guess, Bert."

"No . . . , he hasn't?" Bert knew the Larry of recent weeks, he knew only too well. His feelings were of wanting to protect his friend and help him, while at the same time experiencing frustration that he should be the one to look after Frances, while she had so recently aroused such ambition in him.

"Yes he has. What else would you expect of him?"

"And what do you want to see me for?" asked Bert. "You don't want us to go off to the Golden Lion too, do you?"

"No love, don't be so silly, but I've got to see you. We've got to talk. Please, I'm lonely."

"I don't know," grunted Bert, but he knew that her wish was impelling. He knew that he was weak to her onslaught. "Does it have to be this evening? Can't it wait?" Bert knew the answer would be 'yes' followed by 'no' so had already acquiesced before Frances replied.

"Yes Bert, we've got to talk this evening. We must meet. Tell me where."

"O.K., O.K. Perhaps you'd better come here, if that's all right with you?" He found his hand shaking as he gave vent to these words. He hated the thought and yet his excitement willed their conception.

*　　*　　*

Chapter Eight

The troupe of actors had removed the patched and broken John to his resting place. Usually silent in such routine they all seemed more so this evening. The speed and efficiency was still its usual apparent smoothness, yet in their hearts and wills, although unspoken and unthought, most, to some degree, felt a lethargy of helpless hopelessness.

This man still breathing, was attended with all the skill of after-care. Despite its human resources with its finely balanced scientific machines and instruments, he was already dead.

As a baby from the utterance of its first cry, eager with the quest for life, is already a dead old creature on the ever-moving belt of time, so was John already a person past.

Along they had gone to Intensive Care, as if anything could save him now. Yet it was not theirs to question fate or future, just to obey the needs of present. No one was master of the present, not the Sister with her strident authority, the nurse still attending to the tubes and bags, as they swayed their accompaniment, nor the Consultant brought down to humility by the inability of his skilled trade, or the anaesthetist anxious that his patient would recover. Recover to what? Recover to be permitted to start the process of dying?

Soon the team departed to await yet other calls, quickly to forget the dying, not out of any lack of sympathy, but the better to serve those who could be saved.

One solitary nurse remained, her brief important. Hers was to tend to John's every need, albeit terminal.

The Sister had told her before she left. She knew all the procedures Sister had spoken of. Up till this night such actions had only been theory to her. Tonight she was to lose her virginity of successful nursing, to be rendered a helpless witness of failure beyond all their control.

*   *   *

John and Franz were out, freely walking the streets of Town, John in his best working clothes, Franz in his uniform. All the world could see them but neither cared. For each of them the war was over, it was not theirs.

John had not, until recently, shared his mother's and father's sense of a loss of freedom with the coming of the builders of the new Aryan order. He had found it all rather exciting and had almost dreamed himself into being a willing party to the exercise of historical greatness. Only in the past few days had his dreams been rudely shattered and his courtship turned into a nightmare; the rape of values he had hitherto not realized had existed. It was only recently that he had been aware of a loss of personal freedom, complimented by a feeling of degradation.

John's freedom now, like that of Franz's, was through detachment from all that effected and controlled their destinies. They no longer held their personal futures in their own power, so gave over also the concerns that went with them. Thus they were free, putting away any thoughts which could disturb this temporary tranquillity.

It could not effect John that his own countrymen might call him traitor or quisling, or any other insult they might whisper behind his back, or to his face even. He knew he was not any of these things but that soon he was to be tarred officially with such charges, for everyone to see. Why not let them have a prelude now?

Franz, too, no longer squirmed with embarrassment at the prospect of his soldierly comrades quizzing him as to his inferior acquaintances. What mattered it who he had associated with, be it a conquered Britisher or even a Jew, when he was soon to be only powdered bone and pulped flesh somewhere in a freezing trench in the Russian wilderness?

The exit from Town Patrol house had been surprisingly painless. Morten had seemed almost to encourage the liaison. John had been puzzled by the change in that bully but it had not been opportune for him to ask why it was so. Nor did he dare delve into any price or bargaining which Franz might have paid for such a passport.

For his part, Franz had not yet found the quiet moment needed to tell his friend how they must both remit the

144

charge of this evening by attendance at next Sunday's relaxation. Besides, Sunday was two whole days away.

Strange how John had not really been aware, until this evening, more than a year into the Occupation, how the shops of St. Peter Port no longer had wares to display. Most of the windows were divested of saleable goods, having only advertisements and dummy packages of items long since gone out of use. The shuttered and barred shops which no longer stayed open in the evenings, as once they had, now seemed to be making a rather futile gesture.

In The Pollet they paused on the cobbled street. Even in these days of shortage this place was hardly ever viewed so empty of milling people. It was a novelty for John to observe, probably for the first time in his life, how the road was perverse in that its tortuous route though overhanging and granite jowled buildings had a slightly inverted camber so that its clean gutter ran down the street centre.

It would have been good to have studied shop windows. At least it would have shielded their faces from prying eyes, even though they were studious in this being of no consequence to them. It was pointless to walk in order to talk.

They should have returned to Candie Gardens really, but somehow that place now held too many ghosts which might invade their calm to remind them of the dates which they had to keep at bay.

There is a crook in the wall just past the entrance to Lloyd's Bank. Here, with unspoken accord, they rested their backs, while watching from the shadowy retreat as the world passed by.

"Cigarette for you, John?" asked Franz tentatively, but almost as quickly retracted with:

"Oh no, I forget. You do not smoke."

"I bloody do!" exclaimed John in bravado as he snatched at the proffered gift, while grinning broadly, giving the lie to his voice.

"So, you are a man tonight?" teased Franz.

"Watch yourself!" had been John's reply as he had cupped his hands to receive a light.

Franz took a light from his friend's cigarette. Matches were scarce too, even for the victorious empire-builders.

145

"What shall we do, John?"

"Eh?" John did not know the reason for this question. It could mean right now, or it could have the deeper significance about the future. To either his answer would have to have been 'Don't know' so 'Eh?' had substituted his indecision.

"What are we going to do this evening?" repeated Franz, more explicitly.

"I don't know." John seemed almost irritable in his reply. He was quite contented as he was at present, relaxing with a cigarette, while indulging slightly at his little boy guilt at the act.

"Then I suggest we go to a bar. I've heard of. . ."

"No!"

"Pardon me?" queried Franz at this rather unexpected interruption of his preamble. "I was going to say there is a good place, I don't know its name but I've been on duty there. I could take you in . . . "

"No, damn you!" shouted John, more in frustration at his own broken peace of mind, than anger at Franz's attempt to organize the evening. "We can't go in bars, as you call them. We're not old enough to be served, besides. . ." He let his inconclusive statement die away for 'besides' was enough of a conjecture to evoke the unsaid.

"We would be served," insisted Franz. "I am in uniform. There would be no trouble, honestly, John."

Franz could tell from his friend's expression that he was not happy, and that the outcome of this conversation would be a veto, but now he felt equal with his friend, for they both had no further to sink until their individual and separate domesdays. So he felt justified in pressing the argument.

"Why not, John? Why can't we have a drink together? We are walking together now and it doesn't matter any more, so why not?" He found himself wanting to add John's curious Guernsey 'eh?' on the end of his question, so indulged himself.

John gave a whimsical smile but made no comment on the evidence of his friend's naturalization. His other thoughts were too damning for that.

"Look, I'll tell you why, you silly bugger! My dad's a bloody drinker and that's why! He's out now getting drunk and my mum's had enough of it."

He paused momentarily but, before Franz could react, continued:

"And what about you, eh? You don't know how to take drink. You know what I'm talking about, eh?"

Franz nodded. Both smoked out their cigarettes in silence.

John looked at Franz who had gone so serious and pale. He began to be aware of his friend's feelings. Franz could not have known about his father's problems. It wasn't his fault really. John began to feel guilty at the way he had verbally assaulted Franz. He had to try to put things right.

To go for a drink was definitely out but they had to go somewhere, that was for sure. They had to leave this black mood behind them to return to their forgetful carefree state of mind.

It was not easy for John to break the silence but, taking on the guilt of the upset, he felt he really had to try. In awkward discomfort at the embarrassing prospect, he began to fidget and shuffle while the other remained cold and still.

Whistling was no good for he was hardly accomplished in that art. He had however, to draw Franz out of the sombre state into which he had been plunged.

As he looked all around him, John's memory came to his aid. They were standing against Lloyd's Bank, with its impressive dome, visible from the three main streets of the capital. There was an opener for conversation which would be common to both their experiences.

"Look Franz, look where we're standing," he affected with enthusiasm.

"What?" came the almost non-interested reply.

"I said look, look at this building here," reiterated John, as he began to catch genuinely some of his own fabricated enthusiasm. "See, this is the famous Bank used by the Jerries, sorry, beg your pardon, Germans. . ." He paused deliberately to allow Franz time to absorb that his faux pas had been in jest rather than insult. "You know, don't you?"

The response was negative as Franz did not even trouble to deny knowledge of the matter, but continued to look as dull and pale as Aryan eyes.

"You take *The Signal* don't you?" urged John. "You know The Signal, eh?"

Yes of course Franz knew *The Signal*, the whole of free

Europe knew *The Signal*. What a stupid question! How could any one not know *The Signal* for it was printed, not only in the master tongue, but in all the minor languages of the liberated peoples, even in English!

"Yes I know *The Signal*." Franz seemed almost angry. Well at least he was reviving. "What do you want to say about *The Signal*?"

"Well this is the building they showed on last month's cover, eh? Did you get it, didn't you see it?" asked John.

"Maybe." Franz shrugged with disinterest.

"Well just you come over here, mate and I'll show you something." John tugged at Franz who offered no resistance as he was hurried along to Boots' doorway.

"There!" exclaimed John, with great satisfaction. "Now do you see what I mean?"

"No." Franz's dour mood, however, was beginning to evaporate. His curiosity was starting to evict his upset.

"Well, I'll just have to educate you then, eh?" chuckled John who actually evinced a slight smile from his friend.

"Go on, then, be my teacher if you have to," sighed Franz with false dejection.

"On the last *Signal*," John exclaimed, "on the cover, it showed this building," he indicated the full facade of the Bank, a miniature St. Paul's Cathedral, with copper green dome, "and your lot were marching past playing music. You know, one of your marching bands?"

"Yes, I see, that is very interesting," replied Franz irritatingly exaggerating his sounds of boredom.

"Yes, but you listen to this, mate," continued John, as all the emotions and conversations associated with the English language *Signal*, when it had recently been distributed, began to crowd his consciousness. How some people at work had laughed and derided the blatant propaganda. Some had fumed with anger, using the deception as further proof of the complete degeneration of the occupiers.

"They put a deliberate lie with the picture, that's what I'm saying."

Franz, despite his intention not to show interest, found his curiosity pricked slightly, especially as there was an implication that his race was being less than honest.

"What are you saying, John?"

148

"They said with the picture that it was German soldiers marching in London," pronounced John with glee.

"But that is ridiculous!" interjected Franz.

"Exactly!" John's excitement was complete.

"What do you mean, John? What for you say exactly? What is this exactly?" Franz sounded annoyed now for he was not sure if John was making fun of him or if he was being genuinely critical of the Germans.

"They said," announced John, with laborious patience, "that Germany had conquered Britain and their soldiers were in London playing their stupid Jerry music. Now do you understand?"

Franz was puzzled:

"But that is silly, John, you know it is. You know we have not won this war yet. We are still fighting your English people."

"That's what I said," was John's exasperated response, "and not so much of this, 'when we've won this bloody war' business, O.K.?"

"John, I think sometimes you are a very silly boy, yes?" replied Franz. "You say such strange things that I do not know if you have much sense!" He was not really angry but more petulant and puzzled.

"Come off it! It's not me who's silly. You're the one. You just don't have enough sense to see what I'm telling you."

"I don't care," replied Franz. "I don't want to talk any more about it. . ."

"Oh yes, I get it," cut in John, a voice exaggerated with sarcasm. "You always say that when you're losing an argument, eh?"

"No."

"Yes!"

"No!"

"Oh shut up, you stupid bugger! You argue like a little kid." John smiled as he said this for no real offence was intended, as it was as much against himself as his friend. Franz received the smile and accepted it as a cessation of hostilities.

"What is this little kid?" but now he was teasing as he burst out laughing at the stare of incredulity his question had created in John's face.

149

"All right, then, let's drop it, eh?" offered John. "Let's go."

"Go?" Franz shrugged but acquiesced. "Very well. Where shall we go?"

"I don't know, let's just walk, eh?"

"That is a very good idea, John. We will walk and talk."

So the two ambled down The Pollet, casually glancing at the empty windows and silently regaining their ease.

"I'm not staying out late this evening," said John. "You know, with all the trouble. I'd better get home to Mum and see if she is all right." He felt a little ill at ease, as if he were making an excuse, but Franz was aware of his friend's difficulties and selflessly made it easy for him.

"That is right, John. I think you should go home soon to be with your family. This is completely right." He smiled at John reasssuringly, as he sealed his sentiments by proferring another cigarette.

"No thanks, mon vieux, but you have one if you like." Franz put away the packet and continued to be the one to take the lead and make decisions. It was a good feeling for him to be in charge of the friendship, and it was good too for John to be the inferior for, despite his conquered state, he was usually the dominant one, being the natural host and Franz just the transient visitor.

"Come, John, I will walk back with you and we can plan when next we must meet."

John shrugged, it all made some sort of sense to him, for the pleasure was now slipping away from this evening, while the thoughts of his mother and father were invading him with their weapons of guilt. It really would be better to go home to cheer Mum up. There would be another day and another day and another day. That much was certain.

"Yes, perhaps you're right, Franz. Sorry." He shrugged apologetically while Franz slapped his back good-naturedly to hurry him along.

"So, we'll meet tomorrow, yes?"

"I don't know." John was in a quandary. "It's Saturday tomorrow and . . . "

"Yes, yes of course," jollied Franz. "You have plans. Well let us forget tomorrow, there are other days."

150

He was not annoyed or in the slightest vitriolic but the disappointment in his voice could not be disguised.

"No, it's not what you think," explained John, replying to a thought rather than a comment. "I'd like to meet up tomorrow, you must know that, but . . ."

"You've got to . . ," interrupted Franz, really hoping to make the excuse easy for John but himself cut off in his own interjection.

"No, you let me finish, Franz," came John sounding quite urgent. "I'm trying to explain why tomorrow is not possible, O.K.?"

"O.K." Franz shrugged but grinned also for he really did want the dreadful hiatus of earlier to end on a happier parting.

"Mum will probably want to visit my aunt tomorrow, you know, her sister."

Franz did not know but even he, slow-witted German that he was, had reasoned that the lady mentioned was either Mrs Collins' sister or that of her husband. Besides, the question was rhetorical. Franz had only to listen.

"Mum often goes out to her sister at St Martin's. It's usually on a Sunday afternoon with Dad but of course now, things might be a bit different." He looked at Franz, hoping to find some sympathy in his friend's face. It was there, so he continued, a little heartened, in his sad saga.

"Well I reckon maybe things will be a bit hectic tomorrow anyway. Dad's probably all haywire and Mum will be right down . . ," he shrugged helplessly with upturned palms. He really didn't know quite why he had to tell all this to Franz, but he'd started, so struggled on.

For his part Franz was not sure of the colloquialisms 'haywire' and 'right down' but he knew it was not the time to endulge his enquiring mind.

"So I'll just make sure she goes out there. It will do her good!" There, John had got through it, he had said what had needed to be said and he felt better for it.

"I do understand." Franz was humble in his dejection. John was able to contemplate a Franzless Saturday with clear conscience.

Up the steep alleyways they strided so that even their

151

hungered bodies began to perspire under the strain, as if they had both been perversely obese.

"Hold on, Franz!" called John, "I might have to get back but it's not that much of a damn rush. I don't want a heart attack, eh?"

Franz laughed. He too felt exhausted but would be glad to get past the top of the lane for he knew this way led past Town Patrol House and he did not wish to think of that place, at least not until the two of them had come to some definite arrangement about the remaining few days of their freedom.

Feeling that he might face a rebuff now but still cognizant that the need for definite arrangements was vital, Franz cautiously broached:

"Perhaps we two can meet on Sunday?" quickly adding, "if it is convenient for you and your family, John. I only thought . . . " He had been going to expound that as John was planning tomorrow for his mother instead of Sunday this would probably satisfy all parties. He still however, expected a rejection, in his pause preparing himself for it.

Franz's pause was taken up enthusiastically by John:

"Demme yes. That's a good idea. We'll do that, Franz!"

Franz was so relieved he could not go on. Indeed there was no necessity to.

"Franz, you call at my place on Sunday, will you?" Franz did not need to affirm. His smile was his answer. "What time, eh?" fired John.

"What time?"

" Yes, when can you get out and come to my house?"

"Your house?" Franz was surprised. John did not usually want him to be seen at his house but now, of course, things were rather different.

"Yes, you say what time you'll call and I'll be ready." It was Franz's turn to hesitate, for his life did not have a routine now. He'd not be on patrol any more, he knew that for certain. He just hoped he would be allowed out. There was a sort of understanding with Morten anyway.

Oh yes, and that was Sunday too. The Relaxation! He'd not yet told John of the price which had to be paid for these days of freedom! Well, the Relaxation was in the evening and that was two whole days away, too far to even consider, especially with the proposed day time to occupy their thoughts. Their thoughts? Oh no, God in heaven, he'd not told John yet! It would wait. He'd better make it early though, so the time could be long before the ordeal. At least it would not be such an ordeal with his friend present. If he came? Oh, he had to come, but he had to be told. Well they could talk about it early in the day. Why not?

"Franz?"

"Yes John, I was just thinking," came the pensive reply. "Do you think we could meet up in the morning?"

"Eh?"

"The morning, like eleven o'clock? Or earlier if you like?"

"Yes, yes I know what the morning is!" growled John. "But why so early?"

Franz immediately had the idea which had hovered near him for so long, that John did not really relish the idea of the meeting as much as he did. How could he explain the dire urgency for an early meeting, rather than one later in the day? How could he convince his friend without eluding to the, as yet unknown, pieces of silver of the evening, which was the price they would both ultimately have to pay? His trauma and indecision of quandary showed in his face so that John, sensible to their meaning, unwittingly, or subconsciously, saved the day.

"All right then, Franz, we'll meet at eleven o'clock. You come to my place at eleven . . ,'" he hesitated before proceeding with his ill-thought out plan but the end was important, the means just trivia which would have to fit with John and Franz, not vice versa.

"There is a slight snag though, but I don't think it's too bad?"

"Snag? What is this snag please?" Franz was not aware of complications but was stating his imperfect grasp of the English language.

"Oh, it's nothing," replied John, feeling Franz's query was with detail rather than with mundane translation. "No, you just come at eleven. Knock hard. I'll be listening and will come and let you in."

"Thank you," replied a relieved Franz, "but what did you mean, snag?"

Now John realized, and what had at first seemed an

organizational difficulty, but had now been reduced to true proportions, was easy to explain.

"Oh, don't worry. I was going to say that we usually have dinner at one so our time would be split up but it doesn't matter. You come for dinner too, O.K.?"

Franz was taken aback. Here was his friend inviting him into his home to a meal at a time when food was scarce, terribly scarce. Here was a gesture indeed! Both realized that details such as being seen together or calling at the other's residence were of no consequence to either now, as both fates were sealed. But the offering of sustenance was different, it did not just effect their personal miseries but cut into the rights and expectations of others, not directly involved in their personal privations.

"Dinner?" Franz was hesitant. Maybe he did not savour the prospect of Guernsey occupation recipes. Perhaps he was too shy? Possibly he felt he would be compromised by such a meeting?

"Yes dinner, you bloody idiot!" John mocked, half in annoyance but tempered in jest. "You know food, eat, you understand, yes?"

"I understand," was Franz's hesitant reply.

Was John really annoyed or was it just one of his strange jokes?

"You really have enough food for me to eat with you?"

Now John understood, Franz's reluctance had been out of concern for the privations of his family. John had not, up till this moment, even considered this aspect. Well, they'd make out. His mother always managed somehow, didn't she? Dad could moan as much as he liked, but nothing held much dread for John now. If the worst came to the worst he could always share his own plate with Franz. Sunday always seemed to provide more sustenance than week-days anyway.

"Yes, mate, you come round at eleven and we can decide then what to do. We can either go out before dinner and get back for one, or we can just listen to some gramophone records or something."

"That sounds good, John. What about your father . . ?" He left his thoughts unfinished but John received the idea which again pricked his sensibilities to the matter, so that almost harshly he replied;

"It will be all right, I tell you. Just you be there," adding a, "don't you let me down now, eh?" so that Franz really felt his presence was counted.

It was time to leave each other. They were now outside Gaudion's abode. Gaudion had probably noticed them and was even now watching from some curtain or the dark reaches of one of his musty rooms. But who cared?

It did not seem right to just go on in to the already dusk mellowing place, to leave Franz to make his own lonely way back to his miserable habitation, with nothing more than two days hence to keep in his mind. There had to be more. Something else had to be said, which words could then be transported with the Teuton.

"That's it then," shrugged John, "I'd better go in really."

"Go then," was the uncomplaining reply. "We have Sunday to look forward to."

John was inspired. The mention of looking forward and the prospect of anticipation, together with recollections and similarities with their previous last-minute conversations outside the prison corner just at the end of the street, now misty ages ago, brought back all of a sudden their inconclusive plans. Plans started on the night his father had been drunk, plans not concluded because of the intervention of the adventure and the dire trouble which was soon to deprive them of the capacity to make plans.

That was it, Franz could take back yet another arrangement with which to shield his thoughts and dismiss his terrors.

"Franz, next Tuesday?" John was so delighted at his sudden inspiration that he was not aware his thoughts were not conclusive.

"Next Tuesday?" Franz wrinkled his nose in his puzzlement.

"Yes, you know, you remember surely?" John's face lit with delight as little by little he let out the clues which would lead his friend to the same memory. Franz, still unenlightened with the thought, nevertheless began to reflect the enthusiastic smile.

"Tell me what?"

"Next Tuesday. You know, we talked about it the other night down there, outside the prison." John pointed. Franz's face darkened momentarily. He remembered that night well.

He held in his mind the black side, the drunken Mr. Collins, the brutality of his own countrymen, the noise and the pain of his friend, as he walked him to where they now stood. He would have to search for any memories of that night which might be such as to cause John to smile so excitedly.

"What was it?" Franz's voice was so sombre now that John had to stop this game.

"If you think, German, we planned lots of things that night; the pictures which didn't quite work out," he forced a smile now for he was returning his friend to calmness, he hoped, "and the other thing; you and me going to Boys' Club when it starts up again. Now do you remember?"

"Boys' Club? What is this Boys' Club?" asked Franz emphasizing the 'Boys' so that it appeared he had no concept of such a word.

'You and I are going to my Church Boys' Club next Tuesday aren't we?" John paused. Maybe Franz was no longer interested? Perhaps he felt, as a German, he was too much of a grown man for a Boys' Club? But it was only a word. Why was Franz not delighted and appreciative? Perhaps he should not have mentioned the idea?

"Oh," came Franz's pensive reply. It was a long drawn out 'oh' so that John found it impossible to gauge whether it was positive or negative. "Yes, I remember. Yes John, I do remember." The words gathered speed, attuned to his recollections as a slight smile could be detected.

"That I will like, John. We will make the plan on Sunday, yes?"

"Yes. Cheerie." John having given his colloquial farewell, rapidly took his leave, before Franz could change his mind or his mood.

"Goodnight, John," called Franz as he moved away watching the heavy dull old door push shut. Now he would think his way back to Town Patrol House. Now he could worry about the still unspoken price for their continued meetings.

*   *   *

'Mum might be in the sitting-room' thought John. As he had conversed with Franz outside in the gathering dusk he had been vaguely aware that no light had shone out from the kitchen or bedroom windows. That was not particularly unusual, however, as electricity and gas were so scarce it would seem a waste to use them on light when, for the price of a little eye strain, one could make do a little longer without.

No, there was no sign of his mother! John looked in all the rooms and even stood in the stairway calling pathetically as if his words could reach some place foreign to his eyes. He had expected her to be at home. She was always here. She had no right to go out without his permission! It was all too much like his earlier search when he had found her so still and wax-like in her darkened bedroom.

He was filled with that same fear of something foreboding. He knew not what, in this loathsome building which up till this evening he had always considered home. Now, the old house was perverse, it was hiding his mum from him.

He looked again from room to room, more carefully, in case his senses were playing bad tricks on him. No, there was no sign! Was she hiding? No, she was not here. He could not even sense her presence. He was now chill with anxiety.

Maybe she'd left a note? Surely she'd do that? Why would she want to cause him such worry? What had he done to upset her so? Hadn't he put himself out to come back early to look after her?

No, there was no note.

Would she have told Gaudion where she was going? She wouldn't like it if he asked Gaudion. Besides, she'd not speak to the old man. How could she speak to the creature about whom she'd been so vitriolic only a short while ago? Dad would raise Cain if anyone attempted to contact Gaudion anyway.

Ah yes, that was it! She must have gone out to Auntie Rita.

*   *   *

"Hello?" John paused, as his puzzled aunt at the other end of the line had time to gather her thoughts after the shock of such a late 'phone call.

157

"Auntie Rita?"

"Yes, is that you, John?"

Ah, thank heavens, she was expecting him to ring. Mum must be out there.

"Yes, Auntie. Is mum with you?"

"Mum? What, your mother?"

What a silly bloody thing to say!

"No, she's not here. Why would she be out here at this time? It's nearly curfew."

John felt his head thumping. He might be imagining it but the walls of the room seemed to buckle inwards, moving towards him in the half light, then wavering and moving out the other way.

"Are you still there?" His aunt's agitation brought him back from his reversed wonderland.

"Isn't your mother there, then?" Another damned stupid question! John could almost have laughed at the nonsense of it had he not been in the grip of such a panic from which there seemed no immediate prospect of release.

"Of course she's damned well not!" he shouted, as he slammed back the receiver. He now understood why Dad got infuriated with the woman.

Dad? That might be it? Mum might have felt bad about Dad and gone to look for him? That had to be the answer, there was no other possibility. Yes, Mum felt guilty at the way she'd treated Dad and had gone to find him.

So they'd both be at the Golden Lion now. Maybe even Mum was drinking? Perhaps it would do her good? John winced at the thought of his mother drinking in public.

Well, it was nearly closing time for soon it would be curfew. Should he run down the steps and find them together? What if they came up the other way though and he missed them? There were three long flights of steps, interspersed with stretches of steep high-walled alleys, leading down the cliff from their house into that part of St. Peter Port. John had nightmare visions of running up and down the hundreds of steps in the now near darkness with no street lamps and only shadowy people to bump into, as they made their silent ways to avoid curfew's hand.

Well, wouldn't they be home soon if he just waited? How could he just wait? Each minute would seem an hour in which to wonder where they were, how they were or what they were doing. Would they beat curfew? Would they be arrested? Maybe they were not together anyway? No, the prospect was too terrible.

'I'll 'phone the Golden Lion,' he thought. 'Dad won't like it but that's too bad. Besides, he'll probably be too drunk to even know I've rung.'

Where was the darned 'phone book? Oh no! He squinted in the fading light. No 'phone directory in sight! That was Dad! He'd threatened to get rid of it. He'd said he'd do it to discourage dangerous calls, and he had! Oh the stupid, stupid man! He didn't deserve to have people to worry about him.

What does one do when there's no telephone directory? What does one do when he's too lazy to look up a number even? The operator. He might be lucky, he'd come across helpful ones before.

"Number please?"

"Can you help me, please?"

"I'll try, Sir" came the efficient female voice. "What can I do for you?"

"Can you please connect me with the Golden Lion pub in Town?" Would she now tell him to look up the number himself? Would he have to explain all his reasons? Oh God, he hoped not.

"What is your number, please?" Thank goodness she was just going to get on with it!

"Central 2951."

"One moment, please." The moment had a potential of becoming eons.

"Hello?"

"Hello," exploded John, "Is that the Golden Lion, please?"

"No, this is the operator. Are you John Collins?"

"Yes."

"Could you hold on, please. I have a call for you?"

'For me,' he thought. 'Hell, it must be Mum!'

"Go ahead please."

"Hello! Mum, is that you?"

"John is that you, John?" it was not his mother's voice at all! It was Auntie Rita again!

"Yes, what do you want!" His tone was exasperated. How

159

dare she 'phone up to break into his private call? Why didn't she get off so he could keep searching for Mum?

"John, you're a naughty boy!" came the admonition. "You've had me very worried. Where is your mother?"

"I don't know! Why don't you just bugger off!" John pushed the receiver into his aunt's face, as he replaced it.

*   *   *

"I've got to go, love." Frances had just looked at the clock and realized how close to curfew she was.

Bert could not let he go, not now, not like this. But he knew she had to. There was Larry, his best friend, to consider, there was even that spoilt brat John, her pride and joy. Far more than both of these considerations, there was Frances herself. Frances' reputation had to be considered; it was paramount. And yet, he still could not let her go. He had to, but he could not; he would, but he would not.

Frances had been with Bert now for quite some while. He had been a good listener as far as he had been able but he had been too frustrated and thwarted in recent days, with memories long since mourned, revived and brought to the fore, old feelings long ago buried, beginning to rear themselves. The impossible had been paraded before his eyes, the unthinkable had been thought and now the unattainable had be attained. Bert was a bad man, Frances a wicked woman.

All evening Bert had wrestled with his conscience. He had pictured Larry drinking himself to oblivion in the Golden Lion. He had remembered the good times the two of them had shared as close friends, ever since Larry had come to the island at the age of eight. Myriad memories had flooded his consciousness, as with the myth of a drowning man seeing his past life run out before his throes, with the dream quality of condensing the whole into an almost timeless instant.

And all evening too, Bert had held other thoughts simultaneously. He had allowed himself to think what he had promised himself to be unthought. So damaged were his values, so pricked and teased were his emotions that, with his erstwhile true love in the house alone with him, his self-imposed barriers had burst and he had flooded his longing mind with his wife, safely kept from him now in England. She might as well have been on the moon. And yet, there she was. There they had all been, taunting him, deriding, begging, pleading, tantalizing and urging him. He had known loyalty to Larry was called for, respect for Frances who had, after all, freely chosen Larry and with Bert's blessing at the time. There was the consideration of love and constancy to his own wedding vows. He had known all this and accepted it, yet, with his heightening desires, which knew no quelling, their urgency so strong that they might self-destruct if not heeded, so did his logic give way to his animal need.

Bert the animal, as he now regarded his guilt-ridden self, had been devoid of blame while in the full flood of his sating, for his animal self had not allowed his conscience to function. All he had known, as he had taken Frances, was that it was all that had mattered in that timeless moment. They had been locked together for an instant. Yet it was eternity.

Even now, in his guilt, Bert knew that he would do it again. Theirs was for ever, the flowing of love so timeless and yet so instant had been such for them both that it had never been nor would ever be equalled.

How had it been for Frances, locked so tightly with love, as she had held within her and known his pulses slow and firm as part of her own eternal desire? She had been both young girl and experienced adult as she had willed it to happen, as she had moved and worked unconsciously to prolong the speedy ecstasy to full and monumental climax of physical extreme and emotional completeness.

Both Frances and Bert had been one in their adultery but had not known it as such for all thoughts had been excluded except their own glorious oneness, with its feelings of warm reds, yellows and oranges.

Neither had spoken of it before, during or after.

Both had eyed the other as they had undressed eagerly and without shyness, admiring in each other the previously only imagined unimaginable.

Neither had compared the other with the deceived partner, for deception had not been theirs to feel, their having no other thoughts than for the immediate coming together.

Bert, sure and steady, had experienced the burst of feelings as, almost imperceptibly, he had passed through hair and moisture and slipped into that part of the universe which was his heaven, the lack of which he was destined to find his hell. He had found his way without asking or staying as he had echoed the gasp that had eased from his other soul's lips.

Frances had never known such a pulsing and enlarging within her. For her the whole of her body had become that part of her which had been in union and she had known that this sensitivity, in its completeness of gentleness, and compelling firmness, was to hold this memory for eternity.

Why should either feel guilt at having united in their experience? Neither had deceived their partner, for with each the completeness of the act in its tender urgency had been a first time.

And now she wanted to go. She wanted to return to Larry. Bert would never see her or feel her or be inside her as part of her again. And yet she wanted to go. She wanted to punish him, for in so doing she would be punishing herself, for those who have ever been as one are always one. That is their blessing and their curse.

"Why?"

Frances was brought back from her evening and her feeling of inner contentment which had once more temporarily removed the sinfulness from her as she realized, to her delight, but also to her distress, that Bert wanted her to stay.

"I've got to, there's John and . . ." She could not form the words, she could not pin Bert through like some poor spent moth.

"You've got to go back to Larry, I know," he helped her out. "You haven't, you know?" He felt it was a helpless attempt, he could not hold on to what was not rightfully his.

"I have," her hand rested cool and tenderly on his. "We've both got to. You know that, just as I do."

"Do I?" Bert shrugged. "Maybe?"

"Let me go, Bert."

"How long for?"

"Don't ask me that. You mustn't."

Bert felt helpless. He knew it had to be this way but he could not bear to have his shadowy fears formed into words.

"Frances," he begged in his last desperate but helpless bid "it's too late, it's nearly curfew. Besides . . ."

"Besides what?" she asked kindly, in no way deriding or seeking to denigrate the wish she knew he had for her to stay.

"I was going to say; but it doesn't matter . . ." he ended prematurely like a small child wishing to be coaxed.

Frances, inexperienced lover, but very accomplished mother, acquiesced to this need in Bert.

"Come on, dear, say it. Besides what?"

Was there some slight hope that she'd stay? She at least was willing to listen to his argument. Should he convince her with it or should he just beg her or even resort to force? He felt he would be capable even of that to attain the right ends for both of them.

"I was going to say," he sighed, "that Larry won't be in anyway, will he?"

Frances could not answer that. She felt it to be true but in the light of her recent action against the man who had fathered her son and provided for her every known need all these years, she felt the urge to over-react in his defence, as some slight recompense.

"Well, he won't, will he?" urged Bert, the anxiety, which could so easily degenerate into anger, showing in his face. "You know he'll be on a bender and if you're lucky he'll be home if he escapes curfew. But he'll be no good to you, will he?" He hated the words he heard leaving his lips but they were now beyond recall.

"Don't say such things," implored Frances. "It's not his fault. Leave him alone!"

"All right, I'm sorry! I'm sorry, I shouldn't have said that, but it's true, love, isn't it?" He looked at her pleadingly. She could tell there was no malice in his words. She felt sorry for him, she felt sorry for both of them, but then that was good. It would, to some small extent, help atone the wantonness.

"I'm going, Bert, anyway. There's my little John, isn't there? I can't leave him alone, even if his father will be too drunk to know whether I'm there or not." She produced a light watery smile as she spoke. She did not feel the tenor of bitterness she effected, but such an attitude might just help Bert in the parting.

With the concept of Frances' darling John, Bert knew it was hopeless.

"I'll come with you," he said.

"You can't Bert, you haven't time, you'll break curfew! I'll only just make it if I rush like mad. Let me go alone, Bert. Please?"

She needed the ten minutes alone to move from one world to another, to prepare herself for the change of regime.

"No, I'm coming. I'll not have you out alone at this time of night with drunken Jerries on the loose. Get your coat."

Even as he spoke, he had tormenting pictures of the square-headed masters taking his Frances into some dark alley and forcing their way into her. Was she being forced or was she willing, as she had been with him? He'd far rather spend a week inside than have such scenes constantly raping his mind. It was a stupid idea, he told himself, for if nothing else the Jerries seemed very disciplined with the local women. He knew of no cases of rape, only 'Jerry bags' and they were always willing. But what if Frances were willing? What if she now had a taste for more? No, he could not bear it! Was this to be the torture of his imaginations now for the rest of his being? Well, at least she'd not be touched if he took her to her door. There was Larry of course, but that had to be. Larry had to be erased from his mind. Besides, Larry would not enjoy his virgin tonight. Larry would be impotent.

"Bert, I'll run if you like. You can't come though, dear. I'll be all right. You're in enough trouble as it is."

"I've got my uniform," asserted Bert, glad of the opportunity to think of anything but his torment, "They've forgotten to collect it off me," he laughed. "Good thing too. I don't think I've got another pair of trousers anyway."

Frances laughed also at this light relief. She laughed a little too loud and a little too long. Her voice was rather too shrill and the curfew hour ticked closer.

"No, love," she said at last. "You might have the uniform but they'll all know it's you. They'll be glad to get you into trouble, won't they? It will help their case. Don't you see that?"

Bert saw it but the prospect of becoming martyred over such a just cause helped to obviate his degeneracy. He was the insistent forceful Bert once more.

"Get your coat, woman. I'm coming, so don't argue!"

Frances loved this aspect of Bert but her fear for his safety did not allow her to revel in its strength.

As, mechanically she obeyed, putting on her coat, quickly tending a few stray wisps of hair at Bert's dressing table, she had an idea which could save both of them.

"Bert, you're right, love, but you're wrong too." He did not comment but just looked up vaguely interested, at least not wholly disinterested.

"Look, there's twelve minutes left. It takes ten minutes to get home, if I rush, so you just can't possibly get me there and then back yourself in the time. I understand you want me to be safe and I appreciate it love. Really I do, but I want you safe as well. Do you understand?"

Bert grunted. He understood but he would not be deflected from his plan, whatever she said.

"Well if we're quick and I ring John he can come half way to meet us. We can meet about the Canichers. What do you think?"

Bert gave in. He didn't relish meeting the brat but at least it deferred the torment of jealousy a little longer and it would save her upset. He couldn't bear to absorb her upset along with his other bad thoughts.

Frances rushed to the 'phone.

*   *   *

"The Golden Lion?" asked the operator. "Just one minute, please." John waited. It was a long wait.

"Didn't you try that number just now?" asked the operator, her voice loaded with what to John seemed like suspicion or anger.

"Yes," he replied in his most surly manner. It was not the same lady he'd spoken to minutes before, not the one who had cut across his call to allow auntie Rita to interrupt his business. John had not liked that, no he had not liked it one little bit. He was a grown-up after all, exercising his right to use the telephone. He did not expect to be treated like a little boy by some perfect stranger who felt she had the right to butt in on his private business, just because his aunt did not respect him as an adult.

"Just one moment, please!" Her irritation was ill disguised.

Just a minute? Just one moment? What was all this? Surely to connect him with the Golden Lion was straightforward enough?

"Hello, caller, er Mr. Collins," she corrected herself. "I'm afraid this is quite irregular." She coughed as John waited for the worst but said nothing. "You have to give me the number please. You must use your directory."

John had expected as much from the coolness of her tone. He was annoyed but the emotion of fear, that he might not get connected was the greater. Carefully, in order to hide his offended dignity, and to try to save the day, he began a studied explanation of his plight.

He might now be a young man exercising his rights to a telephone service but he was not used to so exerting his authority. All his experience at times of stress in all their occurrences in his life, up till now, had been to turn to adults for help and support. This he did now, as if it were the most natural course in the whole world. Without so planning he found himself almost pleading with the matron at the other end of the line. All his anxiety tumbled out as he began:

"Please help me," he whined. "Dad's hidden the directory. I must get in contact with him. Please, my Mum's out and I don't know where she is and I think they might be at the Golden Lion. It's too late to look for them, I might miss them. Please help me, I'm so worried." He stopped. Why did she not reply? She was a woman, surely then, she would help? All women helped boys in trouble? Why no answer?

"Ruth . . . ," another voice crackled into his receiver, it was the woman who had started off so helpfully before, too helpful as it had turned out, when she had allowed his call, at that time, to be deflected to receive one from his aunt. "Let his call go ahead, it's all right." Her firm but kindly voice had an air of authority. John had got his way.

* * *

166

"Golden Lion?" The man at the end of the telephone sounded very cautious. He did not like telephone calls at closing time. In fact he was suspicious of all telephone calls these days.

"This is John Collins here," gabbled John, anxious to state his problem.

"Who?"

John was stopped in his tracks. How could the name Collins be queried at such a place?

"John Collins," he continued, trying not to sound apologetic. "My father is Larry."

'That should do it,' he thought.

"What do you want?" The voice at the pub was low, almost a whisper. The words seemed antagonistic in their delivery.

"I want to speak to my father please. It's very urgent."

"Wait!"

John waited. At last he heard a clatter as the receiver was picked up.

"Dad?"

"Who is that speaking?" This was another man at the other end, his voice was aggressive. It sounded as if he would gladly have hit John if he had been there. There could be heard a muttering of voices in the background then deathly silence as if they had all been paying attention to this scene and been given some signal.

"I just said, I'm John Collins. I want to speak to my father, Larry Collins. Is he there, please?" John felt at the point of tears.

The man did not answer but John heard him confer.

"Says he's Larry's son. What shall I tell him?"

"Dunno," he heard one of the voices say, then all was lost in the general hubbub of conversation.

"You still there?" came the eventual reply. "You stupid young bugger! Haven't you been told not to use the 'phone?" The question was rhetorical for the caller went on to say, "It's too late now anyway, the damage has been done. Hear that, you Jerry bastards, if you're listening. Your father is here but he won't make it back tonight if you know what I mean?"

"Eh?"

"I said your old man's drunk. He won't be home. Legless, pissed. Understand?"

"But . . ." began John helplessly. Oh hell, no, he surely wasn't going to cry! He couldn't let those rough men hear him cry.

"There's no buts about it, mon vien, he can't walk. He either sleeps here on this floor or he gets taken in and spends the night in clink. You don't want that now do you?"

"No, but . . ."

"Well, then, bloody go to bed and forget the drunken old bastard . . . "

The speaker's voice died, someone else had taken over the mouthpiece.

"Did you get that son? Clear off. You're a trouble-maker!"

John still hadn't an answer to his unspoken question about his mother as the click cut into his ear.

Frantically he rattled the receiver until the operator came to his assistance. It was the first one, the kind one, the authoritative one.

"Yes dear?" She seemed concerned.

"I've been cut off. Get me the Golden Lion again please. Quick!"

She was also the nosy one;

"You weren't cut off, love, they hung up on you. If I were you I'd go to bed and forget all about your dad. He'll be all right. You'll see, he'll sleep it off."

"No, connect me again!"

"No dear," she said. "They're not in a mood to speak to you again, my love. They'll only start swearing again and you don't want that, do you?"

"But I want to know if Mum is there too," insisted John.

"Your Mum? She wouldn't be at the Lion my love, ladies don't go there. Goodnight. It will be all right, you'll see."

The 'phone was dead.

She had to be at the Golden Lion too. Mum just had to be! There was nowhere else she could be! John was all in a panic now. He knew where Dad was and he knew where Mum was not. More than that was incomprehensible. She just had to be at the Golden Lion. If she was not, then things were bad, very bad. That telephone operator was just stupid, stupid and nosy. How could she know his mother would not be at the Golden Lion? That woman could have no idea of the special circumstances that would have driven her to a place like that. She was talking out the roof of her hat as Dad would have said.

None of those men at the pub had said she was not there, it was just that John had not got round to posing the question. Dare he use the telephone again? Could he really face more insults, more swearing? Besides, would the nosy operator actually connect him? Could he really face explaining to her why he had not taken her advice? He did not think so.

So he had to make his way down to Town immediately for there was little time left until curfew. At least he was not likely to miss Dad on the way there for he was not likely to move from where he was by the sound of it. If Mum was there with him he'd not miss her either. If she was not with him it made no difference anyway.

Out John rushed, letting the door slam behind him, up the street, down the great stairways of granite steps set into the cliff-side, through canyons of dark old mansions and derelict slums. Not a soul in sight now. Curfew must have arrived.

*   *   *

"There's no reply!" Frances handed the telephone to Bert. Time was going by. She could only just beat curfew now if she ran nearly all the way home.

"You're right," said Bert, feeling as he spoke, that this was a ludicrous comment to make anyway.

What was to be done? Did Frances now have to make a decision or would it be left to Bert? Neither moved.

"Where can he be?" she almost cried in her despair. "Why isn't he home?"

Bert was at a loss, not that he had the same emotional interest in the little brat's well-being. His concern was that Frances would now leave him in upset. That she was to leave him at all was bad enough.

"Hello, caller?" came the anonymous voice.

"Yes?" replied Frances.

"I'm afraid there's no reply."

"No reply," echoed Frances in a detached way, as she replaced the 'phone.

"What now, Bert? I've lost Larry and now John's not there. What can I do?" She threw herself into his arms and began to sob. Bert, sorry for her plight, nevertheless revelled in this unexpected closeness. He could not answer her question but he could ease her pain.

"Bert, Bert what will become of us?" sobbed Frances. "Where will it all end?"

Bert held her at arm's length, looking into her beautiful dark pools. He felt the need to reflect their tears, so beautiful were they. This gaze was steady as her eyes locked on to his beam. Their two consciousnesses worked together.

"He'll be O.K.," he whispered, almost a grunt, as his passion roused to obviate all but the two of them. "John will live, Larry will live. All the worrying in the world won't change things."

Bert had not planned his logic but he knew it had taken root and was sound advice. He received the new vibrations of a calmer relaxed Frances. It had to be said again, it had to succeed this time;

"Stay Frances. For Christ's sake stay!"

Frances undid her coat.

*   *   *

What for John had started in panic-driven rush now ended in the oblivion of an exhausted sleep, for he was no longer master of his actions. It was with relief that he gave in to the inevitability of sleep in the austere cell. Yes, John really was now a fully initiated criminal.

The last few steps had been negotiated carefully and slowly as the blue-grey granite facade of the market had loomed before him. John has cautiously waited, listening for sounds of any curfew patrol. The Golden Lion, just a few yards around the corner, was his goal.

No, the night was quiet still, the fading light seeming to have subdued the alleys and streets of the town. Well, not quite true, John had become aware of some human sound. What had it been? Grunts or snuffles? Perhaps it had been intended to be singing? John had come across a drunken bundle, true to repute, lying as required in an appropriate gutter.

The youth's concern for the old Bacchus, having momentarily wondered if it were his own father, had been his downfall, as he had stood by transfixed, helpless, as the old wretch had vomited and begun choking.

It had been while trapped in this role of voyeur, frozen and helpless, as though a timeless witness, horrified as the man rocked backwards and forwards unable to catch his breath, that John's demise had come.

He had heard the clatter of boots from the nearby French Halles. It had all been so quick. Could he really have had time to close the gap between the patrollers and the Golden Lion, or would they have caught him anyway? Should he have run back and up the steps to lose the pursuers in the twists and turns of the dark flights and alleys? No, it had all been decided for him.

There had been no beatings, no rough handling, not even the glory of chains for all to see, just the handing over to two civilian police, to be taken away.

John was destined not to know the fate of his father or of his mother, John was wrapped in the shrouds of amorphous sleep.

*   *   *

Bert and Frances lay back. Neither spoke but each was deep in thought with feelings of guilt and self-recrimination. The only light was that of the night sky entering the one large open window. What light there was seemed to be directed into their secret corner by reflection from the hill which lay at the back of Bert's house and usually separated him from Frances, absorbing even any thoughts of her.

Frances was pleased now that she had declined to have the gas light on, with the curtains drawn. Initially her logic for this had been coolness. She had not been aware then, as she now was, of a need to keep from sight, Bert's untidy bachelor existence. Before, it had been somewhat endearing. Now she would find it positively irritating. How could he be so disorganized, so slovenly? He had obviously not made his bed for several days and there had been piles of very grubby clothes awaiting the next soap ration. She remembered how she had teased him about it earlier as they had both laughed, his lack of domestication having rather enhanced his sense of manliness. Now the acid smell of stale sweat was nauseating to her as she thought of her own immaculate home.

Bert was drained emotionally. He had tried hard, very hard but perversely; from the moment Frances had begun to unbutton her coat he knew that his dream and longing were going to vie with each other for place in his history. He had known from that second that he had at least to equal his earlier prowess or be forever damned to feel that what he had once experienced would never again be his. It would just be a dream, a figment of his imagination.

While Frances had been insisting on returning home to her cissy of a son and her most likely empty, well at least, unsatisfying bed, he had felt himself putting up a barrier and had begged her to stay. When she had acquiesced, his relief at this unexpected triumph had rendered the barrier unnecessary and it had been lowered.

For the past two hours or so Bert had been struggling with himself for revival. His wish was there, his whole zest for life, his present and future willed that he should perform. Yet his body could not put up the barrier that would prevent his manhood from evaporating. Having known how vital it was to succeed, for he was now like a cornered animal with only two possible outcomes, those being complete and eternal success or failure for eternity, he had been too emotionally tense and his body had been unable to respond.

Frances had at first accepted this, for it was probably the same for all men when a second time followed so close on a first. There were rarely any second times in her marriage these days and the firsts were becoming more rare. She did, however, recollect the early days of her marriage and recalled firsts, seconds and requests for thirds and how she had at times had to reject the advances. Gone were the days! It was something to do with the drink, she felt. Larry always assured her that it was the drink, not his lack of interest or need.

'There's always tomorrow, love,' he used to say. Poor

172

comfort when she had not the oblivion of drink to lessen the pain and emptiness.

But Bert? Bert did not drink. Why then, had he been unable to manage himself better? Had he not enjoyed her? Was she no longer attractive to him? Had she just been used that first time?

She remembered, soon after they had undressed in the dark and he had begun stroking her sides and brushing his hands up under her breasts pulling them apart, as if revelling in their firmness, and then brushing them gently towards the nipples which stood out firm like buds of sensitivity, how she had longed for him to enter her. She had not asked for all that stroking and fondling. She had wanted him right inside her. She had wanted once more that throbbing and pulsing. She had wanted to groan and cry out and to feel his increased ardour with each moan that signified her pain and pleasure were playing with each other, sometimes rough and sometimes gentle.

But what did she get? There was no urgent pressure at her glade, no gently pushing and sliding towards entry. Instead he continued to frustrate her by arousing still further her sensitivities as, while holding her lips with his, his hands had strayed deftly from her breasts electrifying her skin as they lightly worked to her stomach, explored her waist and then almost instantly her buttocks, sliding round her thighs. She had opened her legs slightly with such expectation and would gladly have sunk back on to his bed but he had held her upright in the near darkness, while his hands had continued to expore her silhouette.

As his fingers had reached the inside of her thighs and she had willed her legs to open further, despite her paralysis of expectation, his lips had left hers and taken their moisture down her torso, resting first on one nipple, then the other, so that she had gasped. They had continued their journey downwards as his fingers had probed upwards to tantalise his lover further.

She had been at the heights of expectation and, without being able to control her shudders or her actions had, as if willed by the other, begun to massage him in compliment to his actions. Her soft cool hands had darted swiftly down the nape of his neck and round to his hairy chest. She had just managed to reach his nipples, also erect as hers still were, while his bending low had almost burst her away from him.

She had felt his hot breath as he had explored her, and enlivened her still further. From this she imagined pangs of ecstacy where she willed a more complete union.

Descending from her upright position she had dropped to her knees, depriving Bert's moist probe of its goal. In her turn she had fumbled her hands towards his prowess. She felt it in her mind, she aleady experienced its bitter sweet wounding and longed for it for eternity, even before she had reached it with her ministering hands. So wonderful was the action in prospect that she was in ecstasy even greater than with the first time. She had known she would soon be complete and that completeness would be the zenith of her desires.

There had been nothing there!

Frantically she had searched and rummaged his hairy growth but her Bert was not there. She had found only an apology for a man. She had found an old, worn and sagging, drink taken, man who had insulted her thoughts and torn up her visions visible and tactile.

Her shock had been that of one dreaming in Elysian fields only to discover upon waking that the beauty and the ultimate delights did not, had not and never would again exist, for they were all of the mind, the cruel elusive, derisory mind.

She had only been able to react in one way: to laugh. A high crackle of a laugh which hid her inner loss and prevented her attacking Bert to scratch and tear him apart in his insult to her expectations.

And now she was haunted by that first laugh and the compounding effect of impotence it had caused her lover.

Frances heard it now in its cruel harshness as she felt Bert move away in the darkness. She listened to it as Bert tried to drown it while his horny hands clasped and cupped, cajoled and willed his inadequacy to abate.

It was no good. The harm had been done. What had been created for an eternity had now been destroyed. It would never bloom again. It was gone completely as was the past, its vacuum inhabited by their fresh guilt.

"I've got to go, Bert." Frances' words were partly statement but were also seeking an answer. She needed the reassurance that she departed with Bert's approval.

Bert's reply was to start dressing. He could not bear to speak; he wondered if he were still man enough to be able to be lucid.

"I said I'm going, love." The word love came with difficulty further enhancing Frances' feeling of guilt while heightening her panic that she should not be here. Her place was in her own home so that she could forget this whole episode with her infidelity. Also to forget the equally unforgivable cruelty to poor Bert.

Bert grunted. Well, at least he still had a deep-throated grunt.

Frances went to the curtains as Bert moved away elusively, in his shame. She drew the curtains shut with a wrench and stepped back, almost stumbling on to the bed.

Her dilemma quickened Bert slightly, as instinctively he went to save her but she had already found equilibrium rejecting his help almost brusquely with gesticulation. No words passed between them.

She had closed the curtains with the intention of dressing herself but of course here, there was no electric light. She needed Bert's assistance to light the mantle. She had to ask him to selflessly reveal his shame in order that she could escape to take her own with her.

She waited as Bert continued his covering, until she gauged he would be decent, before asking what he already anticipated.

"Bert, the light please, love."

"I know,' he replied. "Hang on a minute, won't you?"

His voice was definitely gruff. He was beginning to assert himself once more. Well he had at least covered his shame now.

Frances waited patiently while Bert made his way deftly in the dark to make the necessary motions with his rarely-used tommy lighter.

As the pale light grew, revealing the turmoil of the recent session, Frances hastened while Bert laboriously took his time, placing himself at the foot of the bed, his back to his erstwhile lover.

Then, more out of a sense of duty for memories past,

rather than from any moral conviction, Bert asserted himself with an order which brooked no contradiction.

"You stay here," he said. "I'll go out and see what's what. Don't argue; just do what you're told."

So forceful was his voice that Frances, by now physically exhausted through an eternal anticipation of what had not developed, and emotionally depleted, obeyed meekly. She even found that she could bring herself to watch Bert's movements as he completed his dressing.

She felt less pity now but more empathy. The more he covered his shamed body the faster her guilt receded, her love returned from hiding.

Sensing Frances was staring at him, Bert felt drawn to reciprocate. His actions speeded while she remained time locked half dressed, waiting as she had been bidden.

It was a revived Bert who, having completed his attentions to uniform, left a relaxed and reclining lover whom he knew would be still there waiting and wanting upon his return.

Bert now felt a great stirring as he carried out his resolve to leave. Frustrating it was to have willed and had ample time but not the implement, then to find the implement but no time for implementation.

But he departed with hope and a reborn knowledge that time was on his side.

*　　　*　　　*

Chapter Nine

The young blonde nurse busied herself about her work. There was no time for musing. She had to tend to the . . . No it was not the sick. It was not the living. She had to tend to the dying! She was the willing agent, the accomplice even, of death.

She breathed more deeply as John's breath faltered slightly. She had in her the power to speed this poor creature to his end, or to permit him to run the full race, even though he had lost. It was a good thing Sister had said she would be looking in frequently. She had the buzzer too. She could have immediate assistance if anything changed.

What changes were likely? Well, as just then, his breathing could falter. It could stop even so that the nurse might think expiry had come. But she knew a temporary, often lengthy, cessation was frequently followed by a reprieve. It was always the precursor though, of the eventual, last painless breath.

The nurse glanced at the dials. No, his heart seemed steady. Hadn't the two speedy operators said as much? Heart and lungs were fine under the circumstances. So, he would last a long time? Might he yet recover? Why couldn't they operate again to put right what they had had to leave unfinished? Couldn't this man be one of those rare miracles? Couldn't her first terminal duty be that miracle? Could she not by-pass the experience just this once?

Poor battered child, broken limbs and all. But no pain. No, they would not permit that. But surely he had to regain consciousness soon? It could only be a matter of time.

*   *   *

Damn! Bert had reached the front door of 12, Rue Marguerite but it was locked! Frances had assured him that it was always open. There was no need to keep it locked. Who had anything to steal these days? If the Germans wanted to get in, locks would not debar them anyway. So why the hell was it locked now?

Bert felt a slight panic. Although it was dark he was sufficiently used to such nocturnal conditions to know that he must be visible there in the starlight, as he stood self-consciously silhouetted against the white flagstones of the small front garden.

Well, this would not do. A locked door was quite out of character to this old house, layered as it was, into flats. It might possibly signify a Larry at home, so drunk that he had unknowingly locked the door. Or was it worse? Was it a Larry so angry that he was debarring all communications from the outside world, be it his own unfaithful wife or the bearer of news of her?

*   *   *

The relief of being in the familiar surroundings of his former work-place relaxed Bert. His anxieties drifted away from him one by one, as he looked around the room of the enquiry counter, taking in its chipped paint, the pre-war fashionable change of colour from dark to light half-way up the walls, and the worn dull, yet still spotlessly clean lino, on the floor. He did not feel threatened in any way as he waited to be on the receiving end of an interview. After all, it has been quite recently that he had taken a dressing down from the Chief when he had been suspended from duty. That had not proved too arduous and he had been spared the indignity of having a German present at the disgrace.

In a way Bert felt quite relieved to be here. True, a policeman himself, albeit suspended now, he had been arrested for breaking curfew. Probably more seriously, for continuing to wear his uniform, but at least he was with friends. He still had friends who worked in this building. They were not all collaborators. And now his destiny was temporarily taken from out of his own control which was a blessing in itself.

As he had stood knocking at Gaudion's front door, as he had witnessed the old man's cry partly of annoyance at being disturbed so late but partly out of fear at being confronted by a degenerate member of the police force, and as he had heard the inevitable whistle with the clatter of boots heralding his arrest, so had been taken from him, along with his so-called freedom, all the cares, indignities and shame of that night so far.

Bert had no longer been able to contact his friend Larry to make embarrassing explanations of his wife's absence. His was not to try to dupe his friend or to wonder how the words would form themselves into cruel recriminatory truths or unconvincing and soul destroying lies.

He could no longer find that snivelling John who still held, at his more than juvenile age, far too great a share of Frances' love and attention. He would not have to speak to the brat.

Nor, too, would Bert be able to return to Frances, to face his guilt and relive his adultery. This was good, for in her absence he was feeling terrible about the act of love they had shared, more terrible by its memory of its very complete-ness and absolute perfection. He had forgotten, probably because he had never in fact experienced, that the return would, in reality, push aside all the doubts and guilts because love is love first with morals and considerations second. By its very nature if love is what it purports then it can hold no second considerations which may be in conflict with its very being. Bert's soul, Bert's future persona knew this but he had not yet become aware.

Saved was he now from a repeated, self-imposed, impotence upon meeting up with his lover. No indignity, no shame. Yes, this familiar place which, since his wife had evacuated had been his only driving force, his wife, his mother, his sister, his lover, gave him oblivion deluding him with positive emotions so that, by contrast, the unattached exterior had to be negative. Hence he thought only of the negatives outside and would not indulge in the good thoughts.

To remember Frances ready for his return as he had left, only for a few minutes, fully intending his own re-satisfaction, befitting his rising spirits, did not suit his mood of artificial release. Thus he repressed the thoughts successfully and awaited his fate with equanimity.

So full was he of relief and self satisfaction now at what

179

had been, what had almost not, and what might have been, that he did not reflect how fortunate he was the German curfew Patrol, puzzled by a lone civilian policeman, had handed him over to his own people rather than deal with him themselves. It was a bizarre repayment of that same compliment so recently extended to Larry at almost the same spot.

"Well Bert? Explain yourself, man!" came the duty Sergeant's jocular, if slightly reproving tone.

Bert awoke from his musings giving his erstwhile colleague his willing attention with the customary,

"Eh?" of the ill-bred.

"I said you'd better tell me what you've been up to, you stupid old bugger." Again the reproving tone was exaggerated, Bert receiving it as a friendly comment. "Like why you're out after curfew and why you're still wearing the uniform, eh? Christ, the Chief will climb the wall when he hears of this!"

Bert shrugged. What did it matter? The Chief was the Chief, he was still a civilian policeman, and to be admonished by his senior had a pleasant aspect to it in that it gave Bert some attention, deeming him still a part of the establishment.

"You can shrug, but I tell you this, mate, you're for the chop!" The Sergeant was wide-eyed and earnest as he continued.

"For a start you shouldn't be here right now. We've got too much to do these nights, as you know, to have to look after our own. I'm for a right dressing down too, for not letting them take you over the road," as he indicated the Germans and the direction of the prison.

"So what's the chop going to be?" asked Bert quite conversationally.

The Sergeant just whistled through his teeth choosing to ignore such naivety.

"You're too busy at night?" quizzed Bert in derision, annoyed that his attempt at mateyness had not been reciprocated. "You don't look particularly rushed off your feet to me, I must say."

"Oh, come on, Bert," replied the Sergeant in a tone nearing exasperation. "You know what it's like at night, bloody hell! I'm here, half the force are out looking for chumps like you, the Super's upstairs and now they're getting the Chief out, the Chief himself is being fetched from his bed, mark me!"

"Wow!" emitted Bert in sarcasm. "The Chief himself, and out of bed too. Did they use valuable petrol to send a car for him? Are the Jerries going to collect him with a chauffeur? It must be important."

"You're a damned fool, Bert, you really are and that's for sure. He's coming out for you so you've had it now, my friend."

"For me?" mocked Bert. "Oh I thought maybe something unusual had happened like a crime or something. Or maybe someone had stuck two fingers up at one of the bastards and said 'Heil Churchill' or something. I didn't know that he was being called out because the whole fabric of our society was being threatened under the new order of the glorious German empire!"

"Shut up Bert, will you?" hissed the Sergeant looking furtively through the doorway to confirm that no passer-by could have heard such dangerous and subversive words. "You know better than to speak like that. You know the dangers. Anyway he'll be here soon. They rang him five minutes ago, so I'd better lock you away or it won't be just you they nail."

"They rang him?" Bert was incredulous as he stood to move off to his place of incarceration. "They bloody rang him? Oh come on, you can't be serious! Doesn't he mind police business being tapped? Is he really that happy at being completely under their control?"

Bert did not require an answer, he felt he knew it. The Sergeant for his part felt he knew it too. He just followed Bert as he led the way to his own cell.

"Just think, George," the recalcitrant said, as they reached the open door and he turned for a final word, "just think if the Chief's in a hurry and comes down on his bike. Wouldn't it be a damned laugh if one of their bloody patrols picks him up and takes him off to the nick for the night?" Bert guffawed at the humour of his conception and George, the Sergeant, joined in. The two men had to stifle their fits of mirth with great intakings of breath and snorts as they both interjected and added to the comedy.

"I'm the Chief of Police I say, let me go!"

"Oh yes, I see. Fritz, this one here on this bicycle says he's the Chief of Police . . . ."

". . . Oh yes Hans. Let me see now that must be the tenth Chief of Police we've had tonight. . ."

"Chief of Police are you? Prove it. Where's your uniform. . . ?"

". . . Oh yes they'd love that, they'd say that would reinforce why they're always pestering the silly old sod to wear a uniform. That would teach him not to allow himself the luxury of civilian clothes while on duty."

"The silly bloke must really think he's important or something. He must think Chief Police Officers must count for something still. He forgets we've lost this damned war."

*   *   *

The heavy cell door shut behind Bert, with it the joking and flippancy which had served to keep the minds of both, willing captive and not so willing captor, free from the serious business the war and enemy occupation played in both of their lives.

Now was silence, now was time to reflect and much reflection had to be done before the Chief arrived. Not that Bert cared any more, not that he had to devise an alibi. No, the truth would more than arm him with a self-righteous armour against those who considered themselves right and had earned such a status, by their very actions, against the right. They did not need to know of the areas where their recalcitrant was afflicted with guilt. Morals and dealings with one's fellow compatriots did not concern them any more. They were only interested in supervising the affairs of state, the Nazi fascist state to them. To them and their ilk power was state, power was right.

So Bert could relax in his innocence, with regard to the state, and the balance of unseen power. In his projected martyrdom he saw himself as strong and he saw the outcome as an obviation of his real sins. He could reflect for a few minutes, with incredulity, upon the importance the new order put upon such trivia; that he a suspended policeman found wearing uniform and breaking a curfew order of the

new masters, was thought worth pulling the Chief of Police
from his bed, to face the possible harassment of some of the
lowest ranking of the master race. A few minutes of quiet
introspection after the near hysterical revelry, was all he
needed.

But it was not to be.

"Who's there?" came the nervous question.

Who's there? Where was the voice coming from? Bert felt
he knew that voice, it was out of place here, just as he was,
yet it was familiar. It had to be the brat.

Yes, the voice was insistent and obviously came from the
next cell.

"Is there anybody there?"

What a damned stupid question! It was, without doubt,
John's voice. But why was he there? Bert had been relieved
to get away from all such influences on his consciousness
and now, here he was, imprisoned, to be subjected to their
bombardment. Bert chose to remain silent, to disregard the
intrusion.

*　　*　　*

Frances had been unable to sleep once Bert had left her. She
had looked at the clock before turning off the precious gas.
She could not remember a night of being up and dressed so
late since the Occupation had begun. There was no call for
it these days and parties, which had never held great
importance in their marriage, were all a thing of the past for
nearly everybody.

As the gas mantle had dimmed in her sight to first a blue
and then a pinkish and rapidly fading dark red globe, her
thoughts had become invaded. First she had longed for a
hasty return of her lover for it had been with mixed feelings
and a certain reluctance that she had dispatched him. Her
focus of thought, through her recently primed desires, had
been upon his reviving physical prowess, as he had departed.
There was a complimentary longing for his return which
would herald her fulfilment once more.

She was also an amalgam of other emotions, which, with
the slow passing of time in this new darkness, gradually

crowded her thoughts, injecting the self-inflicted wounds of anxiety, the anxiety of the guilty.

Would Bert find John? Would they have words? What if Bert harmed her dear boy? What if her dearest attacked her lover? Worse still, what if Bert found Larry? What would he do? Would they chat as old friends, the one deceived, the other the deceiver? Would Bert shame her and find his loyalties to his old friend so strong that he would denounce her, the wicked sinful seductress that she was?

The slow passage of time, which lingered even more intensely in the stifling darkness, brought with it more and more worries and unanswerable questions as her desire and her guiltiness vied with each other for her mind.

*　　*　　*

"Uncle Bert!" John had wrestled with the silence long enough. He was sure it was Bert next door. He did not wish to use the term of endearment but nor could he use the familiar Bert, not to a possible empty neighbouring cell, but definitely not if there was a possibility that it was not suspended Constable Bisson.

"Uncle Bert?" The voice was slightly tremulous but it had with it a quality of insistence that it would brook no refusal.

"Uncle Bert?" There, he was becoming stronger in his conviction. Anyone listening would know now that the caller had no intention of giving up.

"What?"

"Uncle Bert, that is you then?"

There was a very long pause. Bloody hell! This was the last person Bert wanted to contact let alone have intruding into his thoughts.

"Yes . . . ," his voice trailed off in almost meek acquiescence, ". . . what do you want?"

*　　*　　*

She could take no more. The torment of stationary time, the fear and anxiety, the guilt at what had passed between her and Bert and the way she had been unfaithful to Larry, at the time of his need, were all too much for her take in the timeless darkness.

What was the time? How long had Bert been gone? It seemed like hours, but she knew this was just a cruel deception of the mind. She had noted the time Bert had left and had realized that when she had evenutally put out the gas, her lover's departure had been only twenty-five minutes previous. Well, that had been bad enough, for she reckoned, with his ardent strides he would have reached his destination in about eight minutes. His return journey, spurred on by his pressing ardour, would have been even less. So, at the time of lights out, there had been an unaccountable ten minutes to which she had attributed all sorts of possibilities; polite conversation with Gaudion, a certain reluctance to enter during the hours of darkness, a building which was not his own, a search of the flat before eventually discovering drunken Larry in the darkness. Perhaps he had had to sober up his friend? Maybe even to clean him up? Perhaps Larry was too drunk to speak and Bert was trying to revive him? Possibly John had accosted him? What if John was in a bad way? Maybe strong words had lead to forceful action? What if Gaudion, on hearing this, had telephoned the police, or worse?

She went over and over, in her mind, all the eventualities. First down one path then another branching different ways. Always trying to be generous with her suppositions so that there continued to be valid reasons for the non-return of Bert.

But now, even more time had dragged by and reasons were harder to conjure. There had been no means of relighting the gas and she had resisted taking the mantelpiece clock to the starlight of the window. No, that would not have helped. But that resolve even, had been intruded by the striking of St John's clock. Bert was now far too late to fit any of her most generous fantasies.

What if he had found no one at all at the house? What if he'd gone looking towards the Golden Lion with its labyrinth choice of steps and alleys? If Gaudion had seen him, as he surely must have, and had made a 'phone call, as was his wont, then maybe by now Bert must have been picked up. Yes, that really had to be the answer. He'd have phoned her otherwise. He'd have rung from her house. If he'd made it as far as the Lion he'd have rung from there. He knew how anxious she'd be by now.

Yes, it all fitted; he was either in German hands, in which case he'd not have been afforded the courtesy of a telephone call, or he was with the police so he'd not have exercised his rights to request one for he'd not have wished to have heaped doubts and shame on her good name.

So having decided that this had to be the most logical outcome for his disappearance, she had to act. She could, of course, telephone the police station but then, they did not have to tell her anything. Much better, she felt, to make her own way there.

Armed with the feeling her premonition was right, Frances made her way deftly through deserted streets and alley-ways, pausing here and there in the shadows to listen for the tell-tale unison of night-time boots.

Crossing St Julian's Avenue was her most difficult manoeuvre. She dare not take the wide part of this, one of the island's main roads, for it was far too close to the Gaumont and the public houses in that vicinity which often offered after-hours hospitality to the troops, where one might expect a constant trail of late home-going parties of inebriated Germans. Besides, it was all too close to the White Rock, so the likelihood of being spotted by sentries at night-time barricades, was great. There were also even the occasional staff cars departing the Royal Hotel in the early hours. She had no personal experiences of such revelries but, holding the Germans in such low esteem as she now did, she would expect the higher echelons to indulge in waste and greed at the expense of the deprived islanders.

No, she had to deviate to take alleys and steps which brought her close by the Vauxlaurens Brewery and the Lunatic Asylum. Maybe, if caught, they'd even deem her an inmate on her nocturnal wanderings?

She waited in the cold shadows of the exaggeratedly bastion-like high granite walls, edging her way forward to the bend in the Avenue where she would have vantage of traffic up and down the full safe length of the road. The great trees were to afford her extra shadow.

The choice was hers; narrow streets, or the bushes of the

plantations of the South African memorial gardens leading her to Hospital Lane. She shuddered at the prospect of the canyon-like darkness of the former and slipped into the cool entirely encompassing plantation.

Never before had she broken the taboo of leaving the paths. Her sense of excitement was heightened as she forgot her cares.

Her progress became almost careless as if she felt immune from danger, having almost reached her goal. As she parted rhododendron leaves, picking her way carefully on the well-tended earth, she was suddenly aware of the presence of another human. It was not sound or sight, she could not feel the warmth of human company or smell the acid odour of another person, yet she knew in her stillness that she was not alone. Strangely, she did not feel fear but rather she welcomed this sensation of company, despite its awful portents. Her feeling was vindicated for, when she plucked up the nervous energy to move forward once more into the small clearing, turning her head slightly to the right, she realized she was in no way threatened.

A low German voice called helpfully:

"You will find Ludger just over there, Doris." This was quickly accompanied by a giggly voice of a local girl:

"Shhh! You silly man. That's not Doris. I don't know who she is . . . " Her voice trailed off into suppressed laughter, as the two chose to ignore their mistaken Doris; getting on with far more important things on this balmy night.

Well, she avoided Ludger. Rather flushed and excited, Frances made her way down Hospital Lane. Her upward final stage in Hirzel Street was almost a run. If a patrol came now she had a good chance of making the police station anyway and, if she did not, she could set up such a noise, if need be, that they would hear her and come to her assistance.

Her final steps were almost without incident. Almost, that is, until she all but reached the steps of the dark facade of the police station. She noticed suddenly, coming towards her from down the street, from the grimness of the prison shadows a striding lone figure. She stopped, as he did momentarily, but she had made it anyway. No one could block her entry to that door now, as she turned. He likewise followed her into the light.

The lone civilian, now behind, addressed her in a voice tinged with curiosity, with a sense of incredulity.

"Mrs. Collins, isn't it?"

Frances sensed the figure at her rear, raising his hat, as she recognized his voice as that of the Chief Police Officer so recently entertained in the early hours sick room of her John.

*   *   *

The Chief was very weary. His thin greying hair looked more grey than ever, his wrinkled face yet more wrinkled while his eyes seemed sunken back in dark sockets as if he were a very old man awaiting death. In his office, the constant flicker of the electric lights, flickers almost lengthy enough to be power cuts, did not make him feel any more at ease with his surroundings. Yes, the work place surroundings were familiar but work, at this time of night, was foreign to him.

It was true that as a Chief Police Officer he was one of the highest civilians in the Bailiwick, at least in the eyes of the occupying forces, if not in local society. As such, he was almost on a par with the lowest German and at times, when he did their bidding well and eased the passage of their justice, he was treated almost with courtesy, almost as if he were an equal. But the Chief was not a socialising creature, he was not gregarious, so did not particularly endear himself to that section of the hierarchy which would thrive under any regime. He did not gladly accept their invitations to parties or pleasures proscribed to the common islander by law or the force of circumstances. No, his qualities of a simple life with hard devotion to duty, which had been so admired by those who mattered before the invasion, were now rather a source of embarrassment to the authorities. They were stuck with him, however, so until there was another unambitious person, with enough ambition for the position, he would remain.

The Chief no more liked or courted the Germans than he did the States Controlling Committee who were, albeit now by proxy, his masters. He neither courted them nor actively disobeyed them. He was a true policeman to the end, despite his one self-indulgence of frequently refusing to wear uniform, revelling in the anonymity of it, just as the trained surgeon might in the revered title 'Mr' as opposed to 'Doctor'. Orders were orders. It did not matter who gave the orders, his was to see to their careful accomplishment.

So, what he had been required to do this evening was less painful than it was exhausting. He had been called to deal with Bisson. What a fool the man was! To continue to wear the uniform while under suspension was bad enough! The Chief permitted himself a wry smile at the prospect of Bert's statement coming out in court; He had continued to wear the uniform as he had no other suitable clothes. Knowing the man it was probably true, for he'd let his personal affairs go to pieces since the evacuation.

Anyway, this posed no real problem, for it was probably the truth and as such the Germans would probably edit it out of Bisson's statement as irrelevant. What mattered it anyway? Their system was crude, being at time less than fair to the recalcitrant, but it did ensure that the guilty did not go free. Perhaps the British would have a lot to learn from the Germans after this war?

Bisson's biggest folly, however, already a disgraced and marked man, was to be out after curfew. What had he hoped to achieve? It could only point to one thing, it was one more nail in the fellow's coffin, one further piece of evidence towards his eventual conviction and punishment.

The man, under cover of darkness, hoping the deceit of uniform would protect him, had sought to communicate with his partners in crime. It all pointed that way! Hadn't he been arrested outside the home of the Collins' family? It was all so blatantly obvious. Even without the lucky chance that the patrol had caught him at that moment, their man Gaudion would have complied. In fact the reprehensible creature had already been on the telephone about the incident quite independently.

But would Bisson confess? Would he hell! His statement would be almost blank had it not been for the Chief filling in the parts he knew to be true. What was the man's point in trying to cover up for the Collins family when all the circumstantial evidence pointed to their complicity. And circumstantial evidence was all the Germans needed, to convict a man.

Oh yes, they'd go through the ritualist dressing it up in legalistic terms for this was their delight. But in the end the accused knew, the prosecution knew and the military officials knew, it would always end in a sound and legal conviction.

Now, all that stood in the way of the course of justice was the lack of a signature. That was a minor incumbrance. Surely Bisson, even thick-headed, stubborn Bisson, not the easiest of men to get through to these days, would see that a signature would save him such a lot of trouble? He knew the routine. He would not submit himself to the Gestapo just for a forlorn principle or to cover for someone or some family who were lost anyway. No, the man might be stubborn, a donkey in the true tradition, but he was not a complete fool.

As if this had not all been enough, what had the Chief discovered as he had been taken to retrieve Bisson from the cell? The fellow in angry conversation with the inmate next door. Discipline was certainly getting slack in this building. There had to be some pretty thorough tightening up. That was bad enough, but who had the heated words of conversation been conducted with? Why, another Collins! That stupid young vandal, already in deep water over his trespass in German military territory. Yet a further indication of the complete complicity between the two families. Maybe his whole force was rotten right through to the core? Maybe they were all in it? Perhaps it was all one big plot against the Germans, against indisputable authority? Yes, probably the two had been put in adjacent cells and left to freely converse on purpose?

And now, the other complication. The Collins woman, who sat in front of him. How beautiful she seemed, how refreshing in his tired topsy-turvy world. Yet even she, beautiful, fresh, agitated creature that she was, was adding to the complications of his existence. If he had not been so utterly tired and deflated by his present existence, the Chief might have been cognizant of the whole coincidence of it all. As it was, part of his consciousness just fleetingly noted the oddity, filing it away.

"We meet again, Mrs. Collins." He effected a weary smile

which almost invited her to take over the conversation from that point.

"My regret is that I am unable to repay your compliment of a cup of tea," he shrugged, genuinely apologetic, seemingly unable to take himself from this course of small talk.

Frances was more agitated in her reply, "That's all right, thanks anyway. Do you think I could go please?" She looked up from her finger nails, staring the Chief straight in the face. The directness of her approach, and the naivety of her question, awoke him from his sleep, taking him by surprise.

"Go, Mrs. Collins?"

"Yes, either you let me go home now or just let me go off to a cell or whatever you do with wayward women."

The Chief was almost amused by this. He almost allowed his lips to crack open into a smile.

"It is not possible for you to go home, dear lady and . . ," he hesitated with a polite cough, "I really don't wish to think of you as a wayward woman."

"I see. Well, where does that leave me?" asked Frances, the hopelessness of her position firing her anxiety.

"You have some explaining to do, my dear, haven't you?" Despite his feeling of deep and lasting fatigue the Chief realized he was beginning to sound patronising and he regretted his words.

Frances too, was not prepared to be patronised.

"I've already told you why I came. What more do you want?"

"Well, for a start, I'd like to know your interest in Constable Bisson."

"Interest?" Frances seemed puzzled, almost angry. "My interest in Constable Bisson? What the hell is it to you?"

Even the Chief in his debilitating exhaustion and lack-lustre, picked up this response and felt it interesting enough to pursue. To the end if need be.

"Yes, that is what I said Mrs. Collins. Why were you here, looking for one of my suspended Constables? And, furthermore at this hour, after curfew? Why was it so important that it could not wait?"

There, he had presented her with some irrefutable questions! How would she wriggle out of those?

"I wanted . . . " She could not go on, none of it would make any sense.

"Yes, Mrs. Collins? You wanted what?" The Chief's voice was kind and patient, infinitely patient.

Frances gulped, trying to collect her thoughts.

"I don't want to bother you with it, really. I just wanted to see if Bert, er . . P.C. Bisson was here."

"Why?" The question was firm, decisive by contrast with his recent infinite patience.

"Why?" Frances was rather incredulous but at the same time she was desperately delaying her answer in order to think of a suitable reply, "I don't really need to bother you with it, Chief."

"But, my dear woman," he replied, "you were making for the police station when we met, were you not? So your intention was to concern us with your business. Am I right?"

"Yes you are . . ," she hesitated, "but I don't need to bother you with it personally. I just wanted to ask if Bert was here."

"Why?" Again that cold buffer.

"I don't see what it's got to do with you at all, it's none of your business!" Frances was tired now. Her anxiety had got the better of her. Why should she put up with any more of this? She stood up and made towards the door.

"Sit down, Mrs. Collins." The words were laboured and deliberate. "Come on, sit down. You are under police discipline now, you know."

There was an implication of hidden reserves of strength behind those words from the tired old face. Frances stopped and turned towards the Chief, waiting to be convinced.

"I'll tell you what," he said, "I'll tell you if Constable Bisson is in this building or not if you answer me one question." He paused waiting for her reply.

"What's the question?"

"Why do you keep referring to him as Bert, Mrs. Collins?"

"Is that all?" How she was beginning to detest this interview.

"It will do for a start," replied the Chief, smiling.

"Bert's a friend of the family. We've known him for as long as I can remember," then, as if she felt she were not convincing enough, adding, "Larry and Bert were at school together."

"Yes, I see," uttered the Chief enigmatically.

'He doesn't believe me,' she thought. 'Well so what?'

"Now, will you tell me?" She urged.

"Yes, he's here, Mrs. Collins."

She controlled her voice so that its stiltedness was apparent, "Is he all right?"

"Well, that's an interesting question," came the Chief's comment. "I suppose he is as right as can be expected under the circumstances." He hated what he was doing, he detested his craft.

"Circumstances, what circumstances?" Frances's voice was shrill and frantic. "Tell me, is he all right?"

"He is at the moment but, as you must know, he's in grave trouble. Constable Bisson has not helped matters by trying to contact your family tonight after curfew. That's what it was wasn't it? He wanted to warn your husband about events didn't he? That's why he came to your home at such a late hour?"

"No, that's not true," she cried.

"I'm afraid it is," sighed the Chief, "He came to warn your husband. It just confirms that they're both in it together."

"They're not, they're not!" Frances' voice almost begged the Chief to believe her.

"Why has your husband sent you here? Tell me that," he droned on. "Why wouldn't he take his own chances to come here?"

"I don't know," implored Frances as she sank into the chair once more in misery, covering her tired eyes.

"I'll tell you why," said the Chief, "because he's not at home, is he?"

"How do you know that?" Frances looked up startled and surprised.

"Oh, we have ways of knowing these things," the Chief was quite nonchalant, "but what about you, Mrs. Collins, you didn't know did you?"

"Yes, I mean no. Oh I don't bloody well know anything any more! Can I see Bert, please?"

"What about your husband, don't you want to see him too?"

What was this? Was he trying to trap her into confessions

of adultery? Well, so what if he was! She had come to the station with that as only a secondary consideration, Bert being her prime concern. She wasn't exactly likely to put Bert's career prospects in jeopardy by it, not now anyway. Maybe she should tell him all after all? Perhaps it might help dispel the false idea the Chief had formulated about Bert's relationship with Larry?

"I came here to ask if Bert was being held," she said with a deep sigh. "He left me ages ago and didn't come back." Frances now hung her head bending her shoulders in her disgrace.

"Yes, well," the Chief coughed delicately. "Yes, I see."

After a brief pause, in which he looked at his pocket-watch he added;

"Where did he leave you from, Mrs. Collins?"

"From his house, from his bedroom, if you must damned well know!"

"And your husband? Do you know where he is?" enquired the Chief kindly.

"No, I don't know, but you can rest assured he wasn't with us," she said with bitter bravado.

"Isn't he at home?"

"You just told me he isn't!" she snapped. The Chief moved his lips in a wry smile.

"I didn't say it, my dear, I just implied it. You did the saying for me."

"Then maybe between us we can imply where he is now, at this moment," was Frances' sarcastic reply. "I imply he's drunk somewhere."

"You could be right," agreed the Chief. "Perhaps I'll imply he's drunk at the Golden Lion, eh?" He was pleased to note that Frances was suitably impressed at this file of knowledge.

"Now, can I see Bert please?"

The Chief stood, making no comment.

"Mrs. Collins, that's not possible I'm afraid. The prisoner is asleep as you should be my dear, as I should be."

Her face betrayed her disappointment but she had expected it. The word sleep had a kind and tranquil aspect so that she was relieved Bert was not in any physical discomfort.

"By rights, Mrs. Collins, you should be charged under the

curfew orders. I don't bend the rules you know." He stared her hard in the face but evinced no reaction so continued:

"One might say you were out after hours helping me with police enquiries, mightn't one?" He smiled encouragingly, willing her to assent.

At her nod, he added:

"And who's to gainsay the Chief, eh? Nobody else knows, except you and I, what has been said in this room."

He felt very tender towards her as the delicate tears moistened her cheeks.

"I'll get a constable to see you home, my dear."

Frances was aware of this gentle consideration and she wanted to react to show her human gratitude. She wanted to hug this man of authority, but her other reaction held her at bay. She felt abhorence at the prospect of going alone and guilt-ridden, a harlot and thoughtless adultress into the house that was once her home, the home of her son, the home of Larry whom she had always called husband. It was not possible to contemplate such a course, not in the dark hours at least. She would rather have spent the night in a spartan cell, then attempt the journey in daylight.

She tottered momentarily in front of the Chief while the colour drained from her cheeks.

"Please," she gasped, "please no. I can't go back there alone . . . "

She stopped, letting the words reach the Chief, for she felt too emotionally drained to have to explain why.

He understood completely. He had brought her to this broken state where she had not only had to recognize her depravity, but also to make testimony of it to him. He had donned the roll of God while she, the sinner, had confessed. He now had to administer solace and, as far as was within his power, obviate, by absolution, the evil which she had placed within herself.

"All right, all right. Just calm yourself, please," he ordered, giving himself time to think. "Is there anywhere else you could go? A neighbour, a relative?"

Relative! That was it. Oh yes, how Frances needed her sister right now.

"Yes, my sister. I must go to my sister."

"Well, that's fine."

'At last,' thought the Chief, 'this whole beastly business can be put aside until another day.'

"I'll get someone to walk you to your sister. Where does she live?"

"Le Varclin, St Martin."

How could he now dash her? How could he tell her he had no cars at his disposal, that even he, Chief Police Officer had walked in? Surely she would not understand his hesitance at walking a constable through all those road checks? How would she realize that even the Chief of Police did not have such authority at his disposal to grant permission?

He could not disaffect her now. No, there was only one thing.

The Chief of Police had walked rather than be indebted to the Germans. He had not wished to feel in their debt for the right which had once been his to command. This was different, however. He was asking for Mrs. Collins, not himself. If he had to become a little subservient, then his conscience was clear, for it was the action of a gentleman helping a lady. He picked up the telephone.

*　　　*　　　*

Chapter Ten

"Can we go in to see my boy yet?" whimpered Frances, as she rose unsteadily to her feet, quickly accompanied by Gerda, who clutched her shaking frail frame.

The Consultant surgeon rose too.

"I think that will be in order. Please wait one moment while I check." He went to the telephone and busied himself.

Frances stared at her daughter-in-law but Gerda could not reciprocate. She looked down. She needed to be comforted as much as the old lady, but hers was to be the burden of the comforter. She could not permit herself any sadness or agonizing until it was all over. How long would that be? She could still hear the Consultant's words now. He had been kindness itself, no one could have said otherwise and yet his message had cut, with the deftness of a blade of sharp ice.

"It might just be a few hours," he had said, "but sometimes it goes on for a very long time, perhaps even a few days."

It had not mattered how long to Gerda, for those words had already killed her John. It was only the mourning which had to be postponed.

He had explained everything. For a busy man, with such important work, he had certainly not rushed. He had even had the time, almost casual time, to reiterate to old Frances that there was only one course. Gerda doubted that the old relic from youth, herself so long escaped the fate of the scythe, had understood or permitted herself to accept this. Another reason for Gerda only to suffer inwardly at this stage. She had the double tragedy of John and of his mother to stay calm for.

How Gerda had felt embarrassed for the man. It had been she who experienced pity for him, rather than self-indulgence of that emotion, as he had steeled himself to ask that she might donate her darling's kidneys when the moment

197

came. She had, of course. She had signed the forms almost gleefully. It had been a confirmation for her, a sort of contract, almost a wedding contract in the closeness it had caused her to feel with her departing husband.

Even in that discussion, Frances had not really seemed to be able to grasp that John was soon to be no more.

"Yes, ladies, you may go along to be with Mr. Collins now. A nurse will take you. I would like you to wait outside the ward and Sister will come and speak to you and acquaint you with the resting facilities."

"Resting facilities?" queried Frances half heartedly, yet more lively now in her excited anxiety to visit her son.

"Yes, Mum. We'll be staying with John till the end. It could be a long time. We will need to sleep."

"Will we?" Frances sounded quite vague.

*   *   *

John's early-morning rush home was in vain, just as his gently closing the gate to avoid disturbance, for he found the door locked and he had to summon the help of the old landlord, Gaudion.

No, neither his father nor his mother were in, the old man informed him. No one in, but there had been a telephone call.

"It's your aunt, you know. She 'phoned only twenty minutes ago. Lucky I was up. She wants you to ring as soon as you get in, said you'd not be long."

"How d'you know it's my aunt?" pouted John, "Did she say who she was?"

"No," chuckled the old man, "but I looked it up."

"I see," said John. "Did she say what it's about?"

"No, but I expect it's about your parents don't you?" he whined. "Both out and both in different places, and . . ," he stopped himself.

"And what?" asked John.

"And your uncle too," hesitated old Gaudion.

"My uncle?"

"Yes, that policeman you call uncle, he was here too. After curfew you know?"

"What?" John was amazed. Why the hell would P.C. Bisson have called here of all places after curfew? It didn't make any sense, not with his father missing and his mother missing too. So that was why he was in the cells. But it still didn't explain why he'd had to come hanging round here causing yet more trouble.

"I said he came quite late and the Patrol got him." The old man chuckled, or rather cackled, as he disappeared into his dingy quarters.

* * *

The 'phone was ringing now. John had got past that same nosy operator despite the agitation in her voice. Hell, was she still on duty? It seemed like days ago he'd had all that difficulty with her when trying to contact the Golden Lion. Something told John it was not right to ring anybody so early but then he'd been given the message and was only doing as he'd been bidden.

Mum must be there at Auntie Rita's, he thought, that would explain it all. But what if his aunt was just trying to continue the upset with him when he'd rudely hung up on her last night? What if she'd telephoned just now and found he was not at home so had resorted to Gaudion. What ructions that would all cause, especially with dad.

"Hello," it was his aunt.

"Hello, Auntie Rita?" John felt on the defensive, he had to try to make some sort of unsolicited apology for his actions. "This is John, I've just got your message from . . . "

"Good, thank God it's you, John. Where on earth have you been?" Her voice was acid and snappy as John was reduced to wondering just how he'd effect his apology while still asserting himself to making his own vital enquiries.

"No, don't bother to tell me now, just listen. Your mother's here with me. She's staying for a while. Have you got that?"

"Yes."

"Well then, where's that father of yours? Your mother's very upset, you know." John imagined so, but then he was not his father's keeper.

"Anyway, your mother's asleep now so I'll not bother her. You'd better come out to dinner, I suppose."

199

John was about to thank his aunt dutifully but could not get a word in.

"Bring your ration book with you, John. I can't do the impossible! And tell that no-good father of yours, if he comes he'd better not come empty-handed!" With that she put down the 'phone. John was left with a feeling of exasperation that his own aunt could be so concerned with trivia and not with the well-being of her family.

'I think I'd rather go hungry,' he thought, 'but we'll see. It's a long time till dinner time, a long time to think about nothing but food.'

So Mum was safe at least. And Dad? Well he was probably, right now, at the Golden Lion, getting up and preparing himself for a day's work. He might even call in here at any minute on his way? On the other hand, he might go straight to work.

For some reason, John did not really care any more. Perhaps it would help if his dad made the effort to telephone him? At least it would show he cared. Maybe he did?

Well, Mum was safe at least and John would probably see her at dinner time. Aunt Rita, despite her mean concern for coupons and supplies, was a good cook and John always managed to leave her table feeling full to the brim. One could swallow a lot of humble pie if it was accompanied by food too.

It certainly seemed strange to have no work to go to on a Saturday. It felt more like an early start to a Sunday or those long-ago, almost forgotten holidays when he was still at school and his island was free.

No, Mum was safe and could wait, Dad was of no concern and John had time to spare. Why not call on Franz? What harm would it do? No more trouble could be caused than he was already in. He already knew that Morten and, by now, the sentries would recognize him. At worst he'd not be able to see Franz but he felt positive he could at least leave a message then probably they'd meet tomorrow as planned.

He almost ran past the police station, having the sensation he was being watched from every window and that any moment constables would pounce out to return him to his cell. All those imaginary eyes at the back of his neck as he made his way to Town Patrol House. All the imagined unheard voices denegrating him:

'There he goes, bloody Jerry lover.'

'What's he up to now? Selling them back some of their stolen goods?'

'Perhaps he thinks his father's in there, or his uncle Bert?'

'Maybe he's going there to confess all or just to offer his services to do down the rest of his people.'

John, past the memorial now, was thankful that he was no longer in view. He only had to reach that door now and talk his way past the sentry, out of the rapidly brightening daylight.

*   *   *

Keith looked again at the unopened letter. It looked very official, type-written and embossed. One thing was for sure, it was not from England. There was a thought! No, this had to be the expected, the expected but still dreaded as if by its very unwelcomeness in his thoughts it might have ceased to have existed and gone away.

Of course he'd never before received a summons. It might just be a bill but he wasn't expecting any right now. Besides, they were usually handwritten and this letter was thick and official looking.

"Anne? Here a minute, love," he called. "I think it's come!"

"Eh? What was that, sweet? I didn't catch what you said," she answered from the back.

"I said my call-up papers have come!"

"What?" She rushed from the sink, hands still dripping, along the passage, looking aghast at what Keith held out to her.

"Oh Keith! Keith love!" she called out with an anguished cry which was of misery for him and self pity for herself.

They had both been expecting this, ever since they'd known of Larry's arrest and imprisonment, and now Bert's suspension. But expecting it and anticipating the trauma in no way lessened it when it came. Until it came there was always just the futile spark of hope that maybe it would pass them by untouched.

*   *   *

201

It was not to be John's day. The sentry, seeing him coming, as though prepared and anticipating the reason for the youth's visit, was rapidly on the telephone.

"No," stated the Teuton. "I have orders, you are not permitted to speak with Franz Müller."

No amount of pleading would deflect the man from his course.

"No, you must go please. That is all." The sentry clicked his heels with a certain finality.

"O.K., O.K., I'll go but can I please talk to the person you just spoke to? I wish an interview with Patrol Leader Morten."

The sentry winced at this name. How did this civilian know it was he to whom he had spoken? Maybe this boy was one of the Patrol Leader's friends? Perhaps he was wrong when he'd just 'phoned through to say here was someone waiting for Franz Müller?

As a friend of Morten's he really ought to be treated rather carefully. The sentry had better risk another call.

* * *

"It's all right, my darling. Calm yourself, calm down. It had to come, we both knew it would come, so why be upset?"

Keith clutched the shivering Anne to him, conscious that this very precious person was not just his darling wife but within her held his unborn child, the unborn wretch who might not ever see his father or, at best, might one day see the broken wreck, an apology of a man from whom he would run in fear when introduced, 'this is your dad, he went to France to be punished for trying to keep his family alive and trying to help his people survive.'

Strange, it was now he who was the strong one and she the weak, leaning one, needing all his support. Not too long ago it had been vice versa. He had been the potential wreck and she the stalwart.

* * *

"The Patrol Leader wishes to talk with you. Please to wait here."

So John at least would get his request listened to by someone who probably had the authority to grant it but who probably also possessed the perverse will to withhold it.

John began to feel nervous at the prospect. Why should he feel so nervous and so guilty, just because he had called to see his friend unexpectedly? What could he, a civilian, possibly have to fear from this military bully who had no direct jurisdiction over him? No, he could only state the reasons for his visit and pretend not to be too concerned if a meeting appeared unlikely to be permitted. He could affect nonchalance while hiding an inner bitter disappointment.

*   *   *

Father Peters received several letters these days. Invariably they were pastoral matters, letters from his parishioners. He received the occasional begging letters and letters pleading that he take up this case or that of abject poverty or hardship, with the German authorities. He sometimes felt that people must believe he had the ear of the Germans and that he was in league with them or something.

But what was this last official looking dispatch delivered personally? It was a stupid thought, it could only be one thing, hand delivered and all.

*   *   *

Morten was, as yet, unshaven. His uniform even looked a little dishevelled. He sat at his desk, his half-consumed breakfast of cold hard sausage, black bread and, what appeared to be and smelt like a cup of real black coffee, amongst his papers and administrative paraphernalia.

John had been unceremoniously ushered in only seconds before and stood looking at the despicable German as he munched his way impolitely through his meal, not even having the courtesy to acknowledge his visitor. Why did John still expect such consideration? Had he not yet learned better by now, or was it just that he found it difficult to unlearn or eradicate an earlier impression of the occupiers he had built up? Built up at a time when he'd almost believed them to be liberators?

203

The few seconds of being deliberately ignored by the munching bully, seemed too long and too embarrassing for the boy. He wanted to be greeted and told to find a seat, or at least to have his business demanded of him. But he had to wait.

Recognition at last. Between a mouthful of bread, not completely masticated, and a gulp of coffee, its true flavour if a little cool by now, unappreciated by the oaf, Morten effected a broad grin. John could not be sure if it was recognition and therefore pleasure at seeing him, or it it was just anticipation of being nasty to him. Since talking with Franz about the senior's proclivities and tendency for verbal sadism, John feared the latter.

"So, little English boy, you cannot live without me?"

"Eh? Pardon?" John corrected himself.

"I said," grinned Morten with twisted lips and sharp white teeth, intending to appear magnanimous, "You were here yesterday and now again so early today. This must be love."

"Love?" John screwed up his face. Was this German drunk or just plain stupid? Was he perhaps baiting him about his friendship with Franz?

The smile was withdrawn. Morten's face clamped as he pushed his empty cup aside, standing suddenly, both hands spread apart as he leaned on his desk, face thrust towards John.

"What do you want, Collins?" Gone now were the niceties of preamble.

"I want to see Franz," replied John with directness, adding hastily almost as an afterthought, "please."

"You want to see Franz?" mocked the Patrol Leader. "You want to continue this foolish friendship of yours which has led you to so much trouble? You are mad, boy! Mad! Completely mad!"

John stood there shocked still.

"If that is possible please Sir. Yes, I would like to see Franz."

"Well you can't, so you go now, pretty fast! You're trespassing on German military property."

That was the second time in a matter of minutes John had been informed this. He now knew he was being played with. A little of his boyish bravado returned. Why then not be a little cheeky with authority, just as he would have been before the Occupation, or even during its early days before the curtains of innocence had been drawn from his eyes?

"I'm not, this is my island."

"What did you say?" asked Morten not quite sure what John was intending. Was this some misunderstanding on the boy's part, or was he doubting the authority of the Reich?

"I said, I'm not trespassing, it's you who are. This is our island, we didn't ask you here." Even as he let the words pass, John realized he'd gone too far. Not for him now the friendly pretence cuff on the ear or the abuse of an older man who, despite his vile oaths, had actually enjoyed the game of jibe from one so young, making the recipient feel young as reward. No, he was dealing with a foreigner. Foreign in race, in language and in awareness of Guernsey humour.

God in heaven! Morten had never come across a boy like this. Never! What Hüffmeier had said was true. Here was an untamed animal. Here was one of the subjugated who still had spirit, no fear! And, so beautiful too! What a challenge and yet what barriers!

"You go, my friend," continued Morten with studied calmness. "Go before I arrest you for subversive talk."

Morton made his way to the front of the desk as if to show John the door.

John had accomplised nothing but he knew this was to be the case and he'd have to leave regardless. He regretted his false bravery and immaturity.

Before he knew it, Morten was between him and the door, his back to it, debarring his way, contradicting his own instruction.

*   *   *

Called to trial and Court Martial? This had to be a mistake! Father Peters had no idea that things had got this bad.

Oh yes, he'd been beaten and he had been kept in the Gestapo cell but his interview with Major Müller had ended amicably enough. There'd been almost a tacit agreement between the two men not to upset the life of the other. A

205

sort of gentleman's agreement. Surely that care-worn old Major, just out for an easy time, to finish his working days in the comparative easy peace of this place, while the actions of war raged elsewhere, had agreed not to implicate the priest, if in return the priest would not mention his nephew? The Major had, after all, noted and accepted the logic of Father Peters' position and knew that all the circumstantial evidence, for that was all it was, just circumstantial, did not stand the test of investigation.

Why, then, why? The Major was either terribly two-faced or he had been pressured from other sources. Was some informer working against the priest? But again, why? Father Peters had no enemies that he knew of. His only enemies were the Germans, this view being widely held by his parishioners, if not spoken of openly. He could not, or his faith in normal human nature did not want him to, believe that an anonymous informer, traitorous worker for the Germans, would denounce him. Particularly over things which were not true, just for money or privileges. Why him, friend of the people?

Perhaps Germans higher up were using this excuse to get rid of a nasty thorn in the flesh? Maybe the Major had been overruled?

They obviously wanted him out of the way because of his subversive talk.

Now was the time for soul-searching. With mind playing and weighing the concepts of good and evil, to confound or help an enemy, to hate all those of the evil side or to turn the other cheek, to allow head or heart to rule, to put self first or to be selfless? The priest made his way, summons in hand, to the Lady Chapel, there to place his dilemma into the hands of his Creator.

*　　　*　　　*

"Let me leave, please," asked John trying not to allow the quake he felt, sound in his voice. His face was very red, his pulse beat very fast, partly with fear but mostly tinged with anger and loathing.

"Let you go?" mimicked Morten. "Maybe," he mused. It seemed as if he might let John pass. John so hoped so, this was an awful place. Poor Franz, what hell to be imprisoned here.

Morten moved his horny hands towards the door knob, hands which seconds before had clasped the jaws of the unsuspecting John and pulled his innocent face to his unshaven vile visage. John still seethed inside with the imprint of that male kiss on his unsuspecting and virgin lips. The enigma was complete, he had derived no pleasure from the stolen embrace of a degenerate man who appeared scruffy and cruel and whose breath smelt and tasted of garlic. Well at least John had recognised the experience as reprehensible. At least now he knew that Franz likewise could in no way enjoy such things.

"So, just before you go, you know more now than when you came in, yes?" Morten's words held the ring of an enquiry rather than a statement. Perhaps they had the slight edge of doubt or worry.

John sneered as he replied:

"I knew already. Everyone knows you, you . . ," his words died unfinished.

"Then, if you are wise, my friend, what has happened here is kept here and goes no further. Yes?"

"What do you think I am?" shouted John in anger. "Do you think I'd want to talk about such things to anyone? You don't interest me, I just want to forget you. Now will you let me go?"

Morten opened the door with a certain feeling of relief. He was not concerned at the meaning of the words the boy had mouthed, many a boy had eaten such words.

"We will meet again."

"Will we?" came the still angry reply from a John red with embarrassment.

"Yes, we will meet on Sunday, which is only tomorrow of course."

John stepped out of the office ready to descend the flight of stairs which would take him back to his existence of decency.

"Why should we meet tomorrow? You don't make sense, mate!"

"Oh hasn't little Franz got round to telling you yet? What

207

a forgetful thoughtless boy." Morten clicked his tongue mockingly.

"Telling me what?" came John's aggressive response.

"Oh, it's nothing, really." Morten grinned again. "Why don't you just go home now and wait. I'll send your friend to you so that he tell you himself."

*   *   *

Berlin? Then what, though?

Pieter Müller sat back down in his chair at his desk with the brief memo, his memo, in his hand. All was his but not for long. Only the memo and its prediction for his unknown future, was his with certainty.

No more tennis club, no more challenge from Lilly Brown, no more restful peaceful nights, free from air-raids. No more days of fixed and easy routine, no more the dream of being spared the Nazi political machine in all its furious and fanatical intensity.

He realized now the loss that he would not previously have entertained. No more closeness to Franz, no family. The inhabitants of this island, whom he despised for their very apathy and acquiescent acceptance of the like of him, always lethargic through lack of supplies and yet always there and pleasant to look at, yes he'd miss them, for in Berlin their places would be occupied by the self-interested, frenzied, unreal people who always did what they were told, out of fear or respect, not because it was easier than to argue.

He would miss too, those walks to and from a quiet place of work, the little gardens, the lovely mellowed houses of the classical period, with their high walled gardens and magnificent flowering trees like the magnolias, camellias and rhododendrons. Where in Berlin would he find such beautiful lawns or such lovely colourful scented weeds dressing the mortar of granite walls?

His skin, now tanned from the gentle burning salt breezes of the daytime, and the chill blusters of the night-time, would soon return to pallor in the warring strife-torn capital.

Pieter Müller, Gestapo Major, all but lawn and hard-court tennis champion of this tiny island, which he now realized was home, now that it was too late, viewed with horror and dread, the prospect conveyed to him by the stark

208

impersonal memo he had just discovered on his desk. Or should he think 'the desk' for nothing in this island could now be his?

Perhaps this was just the beginning? Maybe nothing anywhere was to be his again? Soon he would be like the hapless Jews even, with no property, no rights, no state and no hope, only his memories and his desires to accompany and torment him?

Even the Jews had hope, things could only get better. But for him? Well he feared they could only get worse.

> 'Memo from Brandt, K. (Colonel)
> to Müller, P. (Major)
> Gestapo, The Grange, Guernsey
>
> 19 July 1941
>
> Your desk is to be cleared by Sunday
> 20 July. You are to hand over your
> duties to Lieutenant Hansel by that date.
> He will report to you for briefing this
> afternoon.
> Have your personal affairs put in order
> by Tuesday. Stand by for transportation
> to Berlin from that date.
> You are to observe civilian curfew hours
> until further notice.'

So that was how it was to be. No mention of past, no hint at future. There was no explanation, no reason, yet the Major knew such things were not necessary. He knew why. He understood how one such as he, one of failed family connections, was of no consequence to the machine and, as such, should not expect common courtesies.

What would happen to him in Berlin? Would he be reduced in rank? Would he be retired? Would his ignominy be translated into worse straits?

The only tranquillizer to his fears was the distraction of detestation, that his Lieutenant, the noxious Hansel, was to take over his comfortable job and that he would have the odious task of training the dolt. In some respects then, next Tuesday was to be welcomed.

*   *   *

Chapter Eleven

"Please don't get up," said Sister as she took old Frances' hand, gently guiding her back to her chair.

The two women had only been waiting a minute in the corridor, their friend discreetly gone on her sad lonely journey home.

Sister gave a brief but feeling smile to Gerda, as she crouched down to give her full attention to old Frances. The Consultant, astute from much experience, had prepared the unit staff that the old lady had walled herself round with delusion.

"Mrs. Collins, you can come in to see your son in a moment," she began, "but you have to be very quiet, he has only just regained consciousness."

"My boy!" called Frances, almost a yell, almost a wail.

"He may not recognize you, dear. He is very ill."

Frances clutched the Sister and raised herself again. She seemd quite unaware of the Sister's message.

Sister addressed herself to Gerda;

"Your mother-in-law does know, doesn't she?" She referred to the nature of the only outcome.

Gerda replied with a helpless shrug and a watery smile;

"I think so, but I don't think she has accepted it yet."

"I know, I know," spoke the Sister kindly. "It is often the case but at least she has you."

"Now, please be very quiet. We are quite near if you need us. We may ask you to go for a while in a few minutes but don't worry, first things first."

*   *   *

John went home as Morten had suggested. He did not do it out of any sense of duty to the Patrol Leader. He was not really sure why he did. His whole inclination was one of anger and disgust. He should have done just the opposite to that suggested by that evil man. He should have, but he could not, for there was another ingredient and that was Franz.

What had that sinister man meant? Meet on Sunday?

'Hasn't little Franz got round to telling you yet?' Franz would be round to tell him in person? It was all very puzzling, very sinister. Why should John have gone home to await Franz? What was it that Franz and Morten knew and shared, to John's exclusion? Why had whatever it was not been passed on to John?

So really it was partly curiosity which made John comply with Morten's instruction. Partly curiosity, but partly anger, for he wanted to get to the bottm of this referral to Franz knowing something concerning him which he had not taken the trouble to pass on.

Then of course, John had just had that awful experience. The shock was still stinging him, his whole face and neck were still red with embarrassment. How much worse it must be for Franz trapped there, subjected to it, or the fear of it, all the time? Perhaps Franz really liked it? Maybe he really enjoyed such attentions and had just pretended to John that the experience was abhorrent? No, that was just John's anger colouring his thoughts. He had to remember the abject misery his friend had been in when he had recently recounted his awful experience.

Therefore, by staying in at home, hoping against hope that Franz would arrive, and that this was not just a cruel jest by Morten, John felt he was helping his friend, for the errand would at least take the young German out of that evil place for a while.

Yes, John had to see Franz, he needed to talk and he needed to know his friend was safe and well. He too needed to unburden his recent upset on Franz.

"It's all right, Mr. Gaudion," he called. "It's for me. Go back." His last statement was almost shouted at the old man in what was very close to panic.

Old Gaudion, who had just reached the handle turned to John as he stepped aside to let his speedy passage.

"That's for sure, mon vieux. The visitor is for you, it's

your German friend." With that the old man shuffled back. He knew his place.

"I'm glad to see you." John's voice sounded distinctly cool, not matching the sense of his words.

"And I you, John," replied Franz as he fiddled nervously, passing his folded hat from hand to hand, waiting to be invited to state his mission.

There was a lengthy pause before John continued;

"We'd better sit down, eh?"

"Yes."

"Well, what have you got to say, Franz? Come on, get it out," said John deciding it was better to come straight to the point. His very directness provided him with some safety valve for the anger which was boiling up inside him now the immediate anxiety of whether or not Franz would come, had passed.

"You mean about today?" ventured Franz.

"Today?" John screwed up his face in disdain. "No, you know damned well I don't mean today. I want to know what all this business of tomorrow's about."

"Oh," Franz hung his head, "you mean the Relaxation?"

"Relaxation? I don't know anything about any bloody Relaxation! Is that what it's all about?"

John's realization had dawned at last and yet still he felt his anger flowing ever upwards towards eventual disgorging.

"I thought you must know. You visited Morten this morning and I thought . . ." Franz was interrupted.

"Thought? You thought? How was I supposed to know if you didn't tell me anything? Were you supposed to let me know or something?"

"Yes," replied Franz his voice low and miserable. "I should have said something yesterday but I couldn't, it was hard."

"Go on then, tell me now." John's voice was loaded with vindictive sarcasm, "Tell me now because your dear friend the Patrol Leader wants you to. You couldn't tell me for my own sake but you will for him. You do whatever he wants!"

"Shut up John, don't speak like that! You don't know what it's like." Franz felt desperation driving him towards anger too.

"I don't know what it's like? Is that what you think? Well you're wrong, mate. You're so stupidly wrong!"

Now John's sarcasm and anger became tinged with self pity, he had to spread his personal misery to his friend.

"I know all about your Patrol Leader friend from first hand experience from this morning, that's what! And now, I suppose you want me to come to your blasted Relaxation tomorrow to get another dose? That's it isn't it? That's the truth of it, eh?"

John's mood, his anger and annoyance had helped relieve him quickly of the words. He felt better for it. It was all up to Franz now, Franz could do the talking.

Franz was aghast, as he tried to take in everything which John had imparted. So Morten had been evil to his best friend too? It was no wonder John was so angry. Well, it was certain from his tone that he'd not accept the invitation for tomorrow so now it was already sealed in fate that they would never be able to meet again. He could not blame John for not going along. Would he, if he had the free will to choose?

This was to be their final meeting then, but what a way to part for ever, always to hold foremost in the memory a parting in anger, each disgusted at what had been thrust upon the other and consequently each bearing a doubling of guilt.

"I was going to invite you to the Relaxation, John. They said I had to."

"Did they now? Well you can just tell them from me that I won't be there. All right?"

"All right," murmured Franz. "I know John, I understand. What else could you say after this morning?"

"So, he's told you about what happened this morning has he? I suppose he thought it was a great joke?" came John's response, partly anger but towards dejection.

"No," replied Franz puzzled. "He tells me nothing. It was you who said. Do you think he tell me things like that?"

"Like what?" demanded John.

"Well, you know . . ." Franz's embarrassment caused him hesitation. "Like what he's done to you and me."

"Oh no, wait a minute, Franz!" retaliated John. "You've got things a bit wrong old son!" his voice sounded venomous

213

now. "He might get away with those things with you but he certainly didn't with me. What do you think I am? Do you think I'd just stand there and let it happen?"

Franz was completely mystified and beginning to feel a growing sense of hurt too. By all reckonings he was the wronged party but here he was being made to feel guilty and tainted, as if he were the instigator.

"And do you think I do?" shouted Franz standing up, stamping his foot, the urge great, to run from the room and end the friendship now before it became even more recriminatory. Instead he went to the window and stared sullenly at the sun reflecting between the haze which floated the distant paradise of Herm with its now historic happinesses.

John realized what he had said. He would gladly have taken back the words but it was too late. He could remove the knife but could not so easily heal the wound. He also stood hesitating. His one inclination was to move to his friend and to reassure him by his physical proximity that they two were all right, everything else outside of them was superficial. With these feelings and the positive urge for reconciliation, rather than destruction, his anger and self imposed hurt evaporated.

"No, Franz. I do understand what it must be like for you. Hell, I know it's not your fault. It must be misery for you."

Franz bowed his head to hide his face. He did not want his friend to see how he was effected.

John looked away. Now was not the time to acknowledge the other's need. Not now.

Some moments elapsed before John broke the silence. His voice was now calm. He knew his friend, back still turned towards him, face still cupped, was listening.

"Franz, I'm sorry for you. We're friends and I feel for you." He paused then continued.

"My experience this morning was bad enough but nothing like as bad as you have to put up with. So I do understand."

Still there was no reply, no indication that he was being received.

"Franz, I'm sorry, believe me. I've had nothing compared with you. He only . . ."The words were hard to express, he had for the sake of his friend, to use 'only' for what to him had been traumatic.

214

"Only?"Franz was attending.

John looked away so that both were now back to back at opposite sides of the room. His words came as a hoarse whisper;

"He only kissed me."

Franz withdrew his hands, wiping his damp cheeks as they passed. Turning towards his friend, stepping towards him, he addressed John's back;

"I understand now, John. I too am sorry. Of course this means you will not come tomorrow evening now. In fact I forbid it!"

Forbid it? Who was he to forbid anything?

"Who says I won't come?" John's voice had a little more of his usual lustre now.

"I thought it best,"answered Franz.

"And what if it is best and I don't come?" asked John. "What then?"

"Then we say goodbye now, my friend," was Franz's reply. It was a statement of fact; there was no hint of coercion. "I've been told if you don't come we'll not meet again before I go to Russia."

"It's like that, is it?" acknowledged John.

"It is."

"You stupid bugger!" shouted John suddenly with mock bravado. "We both knew the bastard would make things difficult for us didn't we? So this was expected, wasn't it, eh?"

"Yes, I think you're right, John."

"Then, stop pulling such a long face about it," ordered John. "We're not going to let a stupid little thing like a Jerry Relaxation stop us being friends are we, eh?"

John forced a grin. Time enough, how to handle the hurdle of ordeal later, but now they had to save what was good and forget the bad.

"You will come then?" asked Franz half in horror, but partly in eager expectation, that his friend would affirm.

"Of course I will and that's for sure," sounded John, taking encouragement from the sound of his own bravado.

"Oh good, John,"said Franz rather doubtfully, "but . . ."
John cut in;

"No buts, mate. How long have you got?"

"Got?"

215

"Yes, how long can you be out now?"

"I don't know," replied Franz. He had been given a mission to accomplish but had not been given any time limits. He didn't care any more.

"As long as I like I think."

"Good, then you and I are taking a long walk mon vieux, O.K.?" John was at his most insistent.

"O.K. John, but tell me one thing please?"

"What is it?"sighed John.

"What is this 'pulling a long face' please?"

Franz thought he knew, but was delighted to have it confirmed by his friend's great spasm of laughter.

*   *   *

The walk out to Auntie Rita's was a pleasant contrast to the shaded rooms and shaded thoughts which had depressed both of them at John's home.

The miles went quickly, as their light-hearted conversation thought not of tomorrow, for it was too distant.

Each was imbued with the same light-headed carefree feeling they had experienced all that time ago.

It seemed no time at all before they were at the gate of Auntie Rita's cottage set, in its country garden which was generous, by miniature Guernsey standards.

It was only now that John was brought to his senses. He had allowed feeling to rule reason but now he had to pay the price for his earlier generosity of spirit.

It had been easy, from the drabness of 12, Rue Marguerite, to invite his friend to walk openly with him through the quiet lanes, to share with him part of his family. It had been an easy and natural prospect, viewed from that space of distance and time. Why not share the joyous things? They were each later going to experience the miseries and projected privations of life, were they not?

Neither John nor Franz had instigated this stupid war nor the unnecessary Occupation, so why should they be made to feel different? Why should they not be friends even though their world told them they were enemies? It would do Auntie Rita good to see such bravado.

From home, John had half hoped she would begin to

imply criticism so he could then polarize his thoughts and invective to prove her wrong and, in so doing, prove the whole world in such a state, by proxy.

Now John was not so sure of his intended actions, as he hesitated, self-consciously at the gate, feeling that already the various family eyes had focused upon him and they were preparing their campaign of bitter words.

"Come, John. I like this place," broke in Franz upon John's hesitancy. "This house has a very big garden. I understand why you do not go hungry when you visit here."

"Yes," answered John vaguely. "They're lucky, all right."

Franz, in his excitement, turned the handle of the gate. Not for him the fears of recrimination or bitter criticism. Not yet anyway.

"O.K.! O.K.! Franz," said John, annoyed at Franz's eagerness, while still conscious of the stares and words emitting from within the cottage. "I'll go first, if you don't mind, it's not just any old house, you know? This belongs to part of my family." John did not intend the words to sound so vitriolic, but he was aware of their destructiveness as he grumpily allowed their passage. Franz, fortunately, did not receive them so deeply but responded by pulling a face of exaggerated subservience as he bowed to his master, ushering him in through the gate, before him.

"Very funny," countered John, forcing himself not to appear amused, but nonetheless relieved that hostilities had not commenced out here at least.

There was temporary relief as John led the way round the side of the rustic old granite cottage, hidden momentarily from the prying critical eyes. If only Mum would come outside to meet them. At least then he could get it out of the way with her before having to face his aunt and uncle.

One good thing, anyway, Dad's bike was nowhere to be seen.

"There's John!" Frances had exclaimed, as she got up quickly from the scrubbed kitchen table, delighted that at last her dear was safe and had come.

Although she had noticed he was with another, that had not registered in her thoughts at first. All her emotions had been for her boy. It was as though the night of misery and guilt, self-recrimination and loathing, had just been a fiction, figments of her imagination, drifting off now at the sight of her offspring, as the early mists disappear with the rising sun.

Shattered had been her thoughts when, in a high voice almost of disdain, Rita had asked forcefully, almost a statement brooking no answer;

"Who's that he's got with him? He's with a German! He's brought a blasted Jerry to our house!"

So he had. John had brought Franz. Well, Franz wasn't a German and certainly not a Jerry. Franz was her other only son. Franz was the other part of her John. How could Rita react so? How could she sound so black against Franz and, by implication, against John for bringing him here? It was the most natural thing in the whole world for the two youngsters, who loved her so, to want to be with their mother. Frances clouded out Rita's negative reaction.

"He's brought young Franz with him, Rita! Oh that's good, dear. Wait, I'll bring them in."

Before Rita had chance to react, or express any misgivings, Frances was up from her potatoes and peelings, making for the latch, while the knife clattered down on the table with her excitement.

*   *   *

John felt he had willed his mother to come out to them. The smile of love on her excited face dispelled all the doubts that had inhabited him, as he and Franz had walked down the path.

"John," she sounded, with delight, her arms open, as she rushed towards him, seeming and behaving younger and more carefree than John could remember.

"Love. Oh love, I'm so glad you've come." She hugged her boy, permitting the slightest trace of a tear to exude from her closed eyes.

John willingly allowed himself to be hugged, such was his relief.

"And dear Franz too," said Frances, as she opened her eyes from her ecstasy to view her other son through a curtain of distorting moisture.

Franz moved close, it all seemed so natural, just as he

had anticipated, while Frances put out her arm, pulling him into her trinity.

"Come on, boys. You'll be in time for dinner," said Frances, as she made a determined effort to release her catches. "Let's go in and introduce Franz to Auntie Rita."

John disregarded the second intention of his mother but flippantly countered;

"I should blooming well hope so! Franz and I are starving. You didn't think we'd walked all this way here for nothing, did you?"

Frances led the way.

Rita's reception was cool and stony so that all three, as they stepped from the sunlight, felt a rapid draining of their heat and euphoria.

"Rita, this is Franz I told you about, John's friend . . ." As she spoke she heard her own enthusiasm dissipating, as her sister's expressionless stare fixed on her.

"Hello, Auntie Rita," John greeted her, determined not to have his aunt dispel the good feeling. He'd known her like this before. Best to ignore it, as if it was not real, then it would seem less, at least. "Yes, this is my friend Franz."

Franz, hat already courteously off, as he'd bent his way into the cottage, stepped forward hand outstretched politely, his face a beaming smile. Here was the sister of John's dear mother. She had to be a lovely lady.

"This is a great honour," he began with all the charm he should have afforded a fairy-tale princess. "I've been so waiting to meet you, Auntie Rita."

His well-intentioned, and genuinely felt words were partly drowned by Auntie Rita's disapproving throat clearing as she chose to ignore the Aryan, either deliberately or by careless disregard, turning to her sister muttering;

"You'd better get these vegetables on if we're going to eat at all today. Larry will be here in a minute. Goodness knows what he'll make of it?" She left the room without further utterance, so that all three just stared at each other rather helplessly.

John felt angry for the slight placed on Franz. Franz was puzzled that the two sister could be so unlike, puzzled and disappointed. For Frances, the edge of annoyance had been taken from her at the mention of Larry's impending visit.

"This won't do," sighed Frances, half to herself. "This won't buy the baby a new bonnet. John, love, go out to the shed and get some more potatoes. And while you're there," she added, with a slight flicker of a mischievous smile, "you'll find an apple each for you and Franz on the shelf, but you'd better eat them out there."

"Thanks, Mum."

This time John bowed Franz through the outside door. Auntie Rita was elsewhere in the house and with her, for a few minutes at least, the aura of inhospitality.

* * *

The sense of the ludicrous controlled both John and Franz as they secretively remained in the lean-to shed against Auntie Rita's old cottage, munching furtively their stolen spoil. They both chuckled between bites.

Auntie Rita even seemed less austere to John in retrospect, while to Franz her ill manners were edited and re-written as the customs of a lesser people.

There was no need to rush this feast of body and spirit, for John had dutifully supplied his mother with the extra vegetables necessary for the repast, and still Auntie Rita had remained absent.

No, they could, in fact they ought to, stay in this cobwebby old shed, its wooden planking allowing whole chinks of the bright outside light and great eyes of luminosity through its gouged knots. Logs here, an old bench there, dust-covered piles of pre-Occupation magazines, rusty tools, a delapidated wheelbarrow, an earth floor worn hard and rendered hollow by much tramping in all seasons, musty old sacks, jars of nails, screws, nuts and bolts, tins of old paint long since used and saved but doubtless hard inside and of no further use. There was a creaky door which had long since forgotten to stand upright and would never again fit itself into the frame with which it had argued. Also a dirty, small-paned window, cracked with whole strips of emptiness where once had been putty. All this made their surroundings and the decor of their refuge.

"What is this, John?" asked Franz in curiosity, pointing to a rusty ornate frame hiding unobtrusively in the corner.

John's eyes followed in Franz's direction. He saw grey-white rollers and a wooden handle, whose metal piece still kept some of its original green paint, set in the dusty rusty frame.

"Oh that," John was dismissive, "that's an old mangle."

"A what do you say?" asked Franz moving to it, stepping on some logs and brushing his trousers against a pile of yellowed newspapers.

"A mangle, you know? Don't you have them in mighty Germany?"

"I don't think so," replied Franz scratching his head. "What does it do?"

"Oh come on," added John, amazed at so great a gap in his friend's education. "Everyone knows that! Besides, it doesn't do anything."

"It doesn't do anything?" Franz's voice raised with incredulity. "Is this one of your silly jokes, John?"

"No," replied John, pretending to pout at the very suggestion. "It does nothing, it's the women, who work it, who do everything." He laughed at his own wit.

"No, it's used when you wash clothes. You put the wet clothes through it to squeeze out all the water." John indicated where the clothes would be placed for the rollers to bite, while he almost tripped over Franz, just saving himself by clutching at his friend's arm.

"You turn this handle here," he added, once he had steadied himself.

Franz tried the handle. It was stiff. Moving it was not as easy as the apparent leverage would have suggested, but he saw the movement and thought he had understood what John had explained.

"Yes, that is very good John, I think I will buy this one from your aunt when this war is over, and take it back for my mother."

John suspected that it was he who was now being laughed at but one could never be sure with Franz. He had such naive ideas sometimes.

"What's your mum use then?" he enquired of Franz. "Don't you do much washing in Germany? Perhaps you're all so clean you don't need to wash things much?"

The sarcasm, albeit in jest, as lost on Franz, or was it? Franz replied,

"That is so, but sometimes we need to wash. Then we, the women that is, wring the clothes dry like this." He grabbed John's bare forearm clamping his hands on it, pulling the skin and flesh in completely opposing directions, administering what John would have called a Chinese burn. John was taken by surprise as the strange sensation, as akin to pain as tickling is to torment, filled his consciousness.

"You little bugger!" he shouted, "I'll bloody put you through this here mangle when I catch you!"

The chase had reached the garden path outside as Larry, bike held up with one hand, back towards them, gave his attention to fastening the gate.

Franz stopped on the path, his laughter, which had so recently filled the shed, now evaporated out of the garden. John stood behind in shock. What a way to meet up with Dad!

He knew he had to be the first to speak, to greet his father. He knew too that he despised the way his father had been treating his mother and that he would rather not have to speak to him right now. He also anticipated that his father's emotion would be one of incredulity and anger, once he realized John was here collaborating again. That same emotion which would be backed by his aunt and uncle inside and grossly exaggerated. And all this, when Dad's short dinner break could be far more usefully employed in attempting reconciliation with Frances. John froze, awaiting the storm when recognition would dawn on Larry.

The time it took Larry to turn from the gate seemed interminable, almost as interminable as it was for John to summon up his voice to give cracked and awkward greeting to his father.

"Hello, Dad."

Larry turned. His face was a dark glare, complementing his recent bruises, as he realized the insult, which to his instantly shocked mind, could only be intentional.

Slowly he wheeled his bicycle towards the pair, his face more angry, his voice unsounded. Only the noise of the free-wheeling, with its regular clicks, intruded on the seething storm he felt about to vent, which they knew to be coming.

Franz stepped involuntarily back to parallel John. The gap closed quickly yet with deliberate painful slowness.

"Get out of my damned way!" That was all the anger loaded Larry could say to the two recidivists who blocked his path. But his eyes, afire with anger and animosity at this very moment said it all for him.

What storm there was must obviously have taken place inside Auntie Rita's cottage, for John and Franz seemed mercifully, for the time being at least, spared from its destructiveness.

Both relieved and yet disturbed, the two boys waited, and both knowing that more was bound to come, as surely it must.

"Come in here, you two little bastards! Yes you, my so-called son, and you, you . . ," he searched for words of disdain to describe the German who had brought about their tragic downfall. "Yes, you too, come in, you dirty, no good Jerry!"

Larry's invitation, having been obeyed, the two friends found themselves inside, while Auntie Rita tried to bring calm and sanity where distrust and anger had invaded.

"Sit down everyone, please," pleaded Auntie Rita, "I'm going to. Let's just talk about things quietly and calmly."

"You can do what you like!" growled Larry. "I'm not sitting down with these two sods and that's a fact!"

"Why don't you just shut up," countered Frances. "We've had enough of all this shouting and bad temper. Why don't you think of Rita and Tom. They don't want any more of it either."

Frances' face was now livid. She had put up with Larry's torrent of rage for long enough and now she was waiting to have her say but she was restraining herself.

Larry sat down slowly, his height gradually sagging to an obedient stack while the others, as if dominoes, tilted and toppled, complementing his action, one after the other.

There was an angry silence, as each waited for the others to start.

Frances found her feelings of guilt and self-loathing multiplying in this charged atmosphere. Here was Larry, now in close proximity and yet all her feelings, although temporarily unthought, were for Bert. She saw, next to her on the sofa, the man she had loved since the day they had been introduced, loved past and still loved. Opposite, balanced one on the arm of an armchair in all its flower pattern cottage decoration, the other embarrassingly fidgeting, with his hat, sitting on an upright chair, the two boys she loved as one son. The one she loved even in his anger and her guilt, the others she loved even more intensely as they were the object of the former's loathing.

"Anyway, what I want to know is why he's got to be here?" almost cried Larry in his now calming heat. "Why's he got to be brought in to rub shit on us like this?" His voice was despairing. Larry was not aware of the shock and offence his invective was causing the gathered company of family and one intruder.

"Shhh!" urged Frances, but this was lost, absorbed by the horror.

"Don't shh me!" demanded Larry, standing suddenly, more in helplessness than in anger. "It's him who's brought all our troubles."He pointed to Franz, pale with head bent, while all eyes focussed on Larry's target.

"If it wasn't for that bastard I wouldn't be before the Royal Court and the bloody Jerry bench next Friday, to be sent off the France or worse. And he's . . .," continued Larry, addressing Frances as the mother of the reprobate, while inclining his head towards his erstwhile son, "also in difficulty. They'll even nail your spoilt little darling, thanks to him." The words came more ritualistically now than out of any pre-meditated anger, but to Frances, carrying her burden, as she did, they seemed cruel and unjust in the extreme.

"Now listen here!" she flared. "You can't blame it all on him! He wasn't the one to do all the stealing and upset the authorities in the first place. Just because he's a German . . ."

Rita's mouth was now wide agape as she witnessed her sister's righteous indignation and as Larry cut in.

"Just because he's a German? Just a German? Bloody hell!"

"Don't you swear at me!"

"Don't you tell me what to do!"

Uncle Tom shuffled in his seat but Rita, uncharacteristically remained silent and still.

It was John's turn;

"Why don't you all shut up and listen?" No longer was he the little boy answering back to his parents at the dinner table. Now he was a care-worn and seasoned adult, feeling entitled to an opinion and, through his self confidence, given a hearing. They all shut up and listened.

John did not really know what he was going to say but he felt the words would order themselves, so unfair was his father, with all the privations of the adult world heaped upon him and Franz.

"Look, Dad, we didn't ask for this war, Franz and I. We didn't ask to be enemies. It's your war, not ours!" Yes that was it, John had said exactly what was inside him, that said it all.

"Yes, that's bloody marvellous," sneered Larry. "You can just opt out of your responsibilities just like that. How I wish I was a damned kid again!"

John disregarded the slight about being a kid again. In fact, if it separated him from the despicable adult world, it was somewhat of an accolade. He needed to get right to the nub of Larry's disdain;

"Responsibilities, what responsibilities?"

"What responsibilities?" repeated Larry avoiding the question. "You ask what responsibilities? If you have to ask, if you don't know, then you're more damned stupid that I thought!" John stood up, incensed at this, his face pale, glaring with intense hatred on his parent.

"Come on, then," he demanded, "tell me what responsibilities I'm supposed to have opted out of." He breathed hard and loud in his anger, as his adrenalin flowed and he felt the old emotions of playground fights pulsing through him.

Larry too stood. he would not be spoken to in such a way by his boy, especially in front of the family. This boy had to be taught a lesson that showing off would not pay.

"You'll not speak to me like that, you cheeky young bugger! I'll smack you one!" Larry moved forward to carry out his threat. He had never been hotly violent with his son and rarely had he had to be physical with admonishings in his upbringing, on such few times the lesson being administered coldly and reasoned with a sense of duty rather than punishment.

225

This was not to say that he was above protecting his own interests with his peers and it was now that he felt his interests or his pride actually cut into by his own son. Never before had his offspring, the hoped-for reliving of his sire, got so near to reaching the real Larry and touching at the very centre of him, at his pride and fears, at his raison d'être.

"Come on, then," goaded his son bravely, stepping within reach of the inevitable assault, "damned well smack me one, but still tell me about my responsibilities."

John felt a death wish as he stood there receiving his father's blow. He felt the heat on his face, the distortion to his cheek and the temporary involuntary opening of his mouth with enlargement of his eye sockets. He heard his own gasp and great intake of air. He watched his own father, now discharged of immediate rage, move slowly back a pace as if a comic puppet. He watched himself from the ceiling as he froze stock-still, but the surround of unreal walls and furniture with their timeless images of human witnesses began to buckle, to shrink and swell, swell and shrink while revolving in opposition to each other, fast and slow, slow and fast, first in one direction then in another.

As the movements overcame him and the objects and images slowed, all towered over him, then he returned to himself to give vent to the shock and to express the pain occasioned by his father's mighty smack across the cheek. Now he wanted more than anything to scream out with the burning and stinging of the pain, as his eyes watered and his nose ran, while his mouth, agape, dribbled uncontrollaby down his chin.

He did not give leave to the sounds within him but, watery eyes of shock still on Larry, he stepped backwards slumping back into the deep armchair vacated by his mother who, having become real once more, guided his landing.

All came to life again as they turned to John; Frances, Franz, Auntie Rita and Uncle Tom.

Larry no longer existed as he made one slight hesitation, realized he was no longer in their thoughts, and turned, leaving the room.

*   *   *

It was a very subdued five who ate at Auntie Rita's table. The awkwardness which had infected them after the scene, and Larry's angry departure had somehow rendered the food tasteless, its devouring just a mere exercise or habit to keep hunger at bay. No one appreciated the whole week's fish ration used in one serving or the second helpings of vegetables, or the pudding with sauce which could almost have passed for custard, as host and hostess tried to make welcome their unexpected guest.

The meal dutifully over, thoughts turned to returning home. Frances was quickly disavowed of any idea she might have entertained about walking with her two sons.

The recent upset amalgamated with her guilt to sour her prospect of sharing youthfulness with her boys, and her bitterness could not be withheld.

"You can go home to your father and look after him by yourself. I'm not good enough to walk with you, so I'm not good enough to look after you!" There, she had got the words out. She felt better for it.

"You don't have to take it like that you know, Mum," responded John, trying to be conciliatory, realizing he'd unwittingly occasioned extra hurt and yet still needing to assert his rights of independence and privacy. He needed to walk alone with Franz. They had things to discuss.

"How else am I expected to take it?" Frances replied, yet slightly less displeased, through the detectable trace of concern in John's voice, than when she had first voiced her opinion.

"Go on, John. You go off to your father. I'll stay here."

No longer did the words come as threat or a sanction but where more of a logical acceptance of matters as they had to be.

"Go and make it up with your Dad. I'll come home tomorrow evening or Monday. Go on, dear. It's for the best really."

"Make it up with him?" queried John, aghast at the prospect.

"Yes, dear. You should, you know. he's had a lot to put up with lately," replied Frances, the significance of her own words beginning to kindle her guilt once more.

"I'd rather be seen dead than with him!" The ferocity of John's tone shocked all of them. The injustice of such a statement shocked even Frances, heaping yet more fuel on her fire of guilty infidelity.

"Now that's just not good enough, John, not good enough at all!" She always called him by his name when she was displeased. "He is your father you know! He was good enough to go out with last night, wasn't he. You were happy enough to go out with him then and let him buy you drinks."

"Eh?" John screwed up his face. "What are you on about?"

"You were out last night," stated Frances.

"Yes, what of it? So were you!"

Frances again felt a stab of pain in her conscience. Would it be like this for ever? Was she always to suffer for doing the thing which she had to do, which had controlled her?

"Well you were with your Dad, weren't you?"

There could only be one answer to this, it was rendered almost rhetorical. John was out all night so it stood to reason he'd stayed with Larry. On the floor of the Golden Lion, no doubt.

"No I wasn't, as a matter of fact," said John with satisfaction.

"Oh, where were you then? You weren't at home?"

"That's for sure," added John, almost smiling now at the prospect of the revelation which would serve only further to enhance his newly-acquired adult status.

"Well, where were you?" Frances' voice seemed on the verge of becoming frantic.

"I'll tell you, if you tell me where you were."

John knew where his mother had been, she'd walked out to Auntie Rita's but why shouldn't she have to confess with shame the way she'd left Dad, and treated him so badly, on the very night he'd been released? She'd have no cause to admonish him for being arrested once she'd attested to her own deficiency.

Frances looked at Rita. Rita's eyes darted from Frances' to John's.

Rita to the rescue:

"You know very well your mother was here last night! Now stop worrying her. She's got enough to put up with. Tell her where you were last night."

"O.K.," said John with artificial nonchalance, "if you must know I was locked up."

Both sisters gasped.

"You mean," faltered Frances, "locked up by . . . "

"Yes," interrupted John, "in a cell. You know, one of those places with bars on it."

Frances paled with the revelation. She took Rita's hand.

"Where were you locked up?" she asked tremulously. "Was it in the Gestapo again?" Oh, this was all too much for her! First Larry locked up, then dear Bert and now her own son, and on the same evening too.

There thoughts of Bert seemed some form of comfort to her in this added crisis. The fleeting images of him now were no longer loaded with guilt, they seemed somehow calming.

"Well, I was in the police station, eh?" enounced her errant son.

"Where?"

"The police station." Only the presence of Auntie Rita and Franz prevented him from being rude and enquiring if his mother was deaf or something.

"Why?" The question was the obvious one under the circumstances but it also covered her other secret enquiries and fears. He was in the police station last night. It was at the same time as Bert. Of course it was, it had to be. Had he spoken to Bert? Had Bert mentioned anything to John? No, that was silly.

Why had the Chief been so kind, so considerate? Had he done it for a purpose, had he got permission for that car, just to allay any fears she might have? Had he wanted her out of the way quickly to further investigate the links between the Bisson and the Collins families?

"Why?" repeated John, "I should think that would be obvious wouldn't it? I was out after curfew, that's why. I was looking for you and Dad."

"And what happened to you?" she asked.

"What do you mean, what happened?" came John's matter-of-fact-voice. "Nothing happened. I'm here, aren't I?"

"Yes, but what happened to you at the police station? What did they do? What did they say? What's going to happen about it?"

"Nothing, I said," replied John in exaggerated exasperation. "They just let me out this morning and said 'don't do it again, naughty boy'."

Frances began to feel some relief. Maybe he'd not been in contact with Bert after all? Oh, she must see him this evening or at least talk to him. She must, she must!

"I'll tell you something though," he added with a slight chuckle which was almost mischievious, so that Frances feared she knew what was coming. "Old Bert was locked up too".

"What was that?" asked Frances, feigning a casual response.

"I said Bert, sorry Uncle Bert, was in the cell next to me."

"Oh," said Frances, "and?"

She steadied herself emotionally for the upset to come. Rita knowingly flexed her fingers, giving her sister's hand a comforting squeeze.

"And nothing," continued John. "The miserable sod said he wasn't in a mood to speak to the likes of me and went off to sleep."

"John!" gasped Frances, in an attempt to sound shocked at his lack of respect, but glad of the chance to relieve herself of some of her tension. "Show a little more respect, please!"

'That's it,' she thought, 'I'm going home tonight. I'll not have John wandering round like that. I'll go home, and I'll contact Bert too.'

"That's it," she voiced, "I'm coming home tonight. Mark you me! No son of mine is going to bring constant disgrace on us. Police cells! Whatever next?"

There, it was out. If he knew anything, now he would say it for no one taunted with bad behaviour would fail to retaliate if he had the weapon to do so. Or would he? What did John know about her and Bert? Oh, the interminable hours until she could contact the dear man again! Would he also be free or would they have kept him? Time would just have to take its deliberate and tormenting course until she could know the answer.

"That's good, Mum," said John flippantly. "I'm glad you're coming home, we've got a visitor for dinner tomorrow."

"Who?" Frances' voice shook as her heart pounded. What was all this? Was her son playing some silly game with her? Was he in the know about her and Bert? Was that it, was he bringing his Uncle round for a meal? How awkward with Larry there and all!

"Franz," explained John, "I've asked him to dinner. That is O.K. isn't it?"

Frances' relief was great, she felt the wrinkles uncrease in her aged face while all the silver hairs left her head to drift away on her disappearing paranoia.

*   *   *

The two had almost reached Town, the pleasant walk having brushed past their consciousnesses, so that neither could have remembered what they had seen, as each had talked of trivial things and of the happy anticipation of the morrow with the Sunday dinner at John's.

Both friends had pushed from their thoughts the evening when they would have to pay for the pleasures of the day, by attending the Relaxation. They both knew the price would have to be paid, and both were aware that they needed to talk, yet neither wished to be first to broach the subject and thereby taint the dream.

John felt justified in letting Franz introduce the subject. It was, after all, his flipping Relaxation, wasn't it? John was only going to attend as a favour to help out this Aryan, wasn't he? No, he would let Franz squirm just a little, he would give him a hard time just so that he would realise what gratitude he owed his civilian protector.

Eventually Franz ventured, "Tomorrow night . . . ?" hoping his friend would take up the matter.

"What you talking about?" John was exaggeratingly brusque.

"You know?" urged Franz, "at my place."

"At your place?" John knew, he knew. Franz knew he did.

"Yes, you know, what you say this morning?" Franz was beginning to sound agitated.

'Good,' thought John.

"What I said this morning? What the hell are you on about, Franz?"

"Oh, come on, John," came Franz, half in pleading, partly bewildered. "This morning you say you come to the Relaxation tomorrow evening, yes?"

"Did I?" John shrugged his shoulders. He found he was spoiling for an argument.

"Yes, you did, John. You know you did."

"Well, I can't remember, that's for sure," came John's exasperating reply.

What had begun as a tease and a little cruel baiting of Franz was now becoming John's real mood. He found it hard to switch back from it, for he was being carried along on his act. He did not know why.

"Yes, you did. Come on now," urged Franz sounding very emotional. "This morning you say you are coming like I ask. You say you'd come so we are still keeping contact next week. I know you remember, John. You mean it then, so why change it all now?"

"Who said anything about changing it?" John's anger was almost real now. He really had to snap out of it. Here was Franz working himself up into a frenzy. It had gone far enough, they were nearly home.

"Well you are change it!" shouted Franz ill able to hide his misery.

"I don't understand, John, I just don't. This morning I tell you not to coming but you say . ." He seemed on the point of tears when John cut in;

"Oh don't bloody go on for God's sake Franz! Yes, I'll come. Now drop it, will you?"

"You will?" Franz was amazed.

"Yes, I just said so, didn't I?" John had to smile. Gone now was his manufactured mood which had temporarily taken him over.

"Oh this is good!" Franz sighed with relief.

"It's not," countered John, "It's bad very bad, and you know it!" He was not angry now, he was just stating plain facts and they both had a lot of talking to do.

Before they reached Town, they had come to an accommodation. Both knew that it was incumbent on their friendship that they should attend. Neither wanted to, yet Franz who had not option but to go did not wish to go alone. Nor did Franz wish to embroil his friend in the evil place just as John could not allow Franz to take the whole brunt of the German displeasure, if he, a civilian, exercised his prerogative not to attend.

After lengthy discussion, in which each assured the other that they were happy to let the arrangement stand and neither felt coerced by the other, they formulated a plan.

It was not a very good plan, they both knew that, but a bad plan was better than no plan and it would help to keep the evil prospect from their consciousness.

Franz knew that if the plan failed then John could always escape, for he was a civilian, while he, Franz, would just have to face a misery which was not unknown to him. If what Morten said was true, he could expect such things at the Eastern Front anyway. Franz knew he was a dead man, so why give in? Maybe it would get easier each time? The Patrol Leader said it did. Franz hated to think he might be right but that evil man seemed to have an uncanny way of getting his way in the end, so most likely his advice would always prove itself correct too.

"What we'll do then, Franz, is to stay together all evening. We'll never go away from each other's side. Do you understand?"

"Yes, of course, John," Franz replied to the very obvious course of action.

"Yes, but I really do mean all the time," reiterated John forcefully. "You don't go off with any of them for any reason at all. Do you understand? You don't go off and leave me alone."

"Yes, yes, I understand." Franz's voice sounded a little exasperated.

John had to be sure, he pressed the point even though he could tell his friend's tolerance was being severly stretched:

"You don't even go off to the lavatory without me, eh?"

Franz stopped walking and turned full face towards his friend. He was about to laugh but the humour left him when he saw the pale intensity in the other.

"Yes, if you say so, John."

"It's not if I say so, mate, it's deadly bloody serious!"

"I said yes," repeated Franz, "I said yes and I mean it."

233

"Well so long as you remember it," John found himself nagging. "It's just that your place is full of very strange people, as you know."

Franz's countenance darkened. He did not need to be reminded. It was all right for John. He did not have to live there. He felt the waves of misery sweeping over him again. He wished he could change the subject. Tomorrow evening would come soon enough.

"And there's another thing," added John. Yes, he was definitely becoming grown up now. He even droned on like an adult. He was the adult and Franz his child. "We don't touch a drink, eh?"

"Touch a drink? What is this, please?" Franz was puzzled. What was John about to embark on now?

"We don't touch alcohol at all. Surely you can see the sense of that, Franz?"

"Yes," replied Franz hesitantly, but he was not quite sure to what negative action he was committing himself.

"Well, don't sound so sure, old son." John's voice was getting angry again. But why should he be annoyed? Franz was saying yes to all his demands, wasn't he?

"You just see to it then. We can't afford for you to get in that bad state you got in last time, can we?"

Yes, now Franz knew what he meant. He shuddered.

"Yes," he affirmed. "I will not hold this alcohol."

"Touch, you stupid bugger! Touch it, not hold it. You can't hold it, that's your damned trouble."

Franz was puzzled. The discussion had been so serious, so charged, that he had forgotten this strange English ingredient called humour. Franz felt he was being criticized unfairly.

He retaliated by drawing from that halcyon summer day, now so long ago almost lost, lost in its innocence.

"You cannot say such things, Mr. John Collins. You do not know how to touch cider, do you?"

"Hold, you daft fool!" shouted John, as he pushed his friendly enemy off balance and into a holly hedge.

* * *

"Bert?" Frances whispered into the mouth-piece. At last Rita had stepped into the kitchen. How long she would be, she did not know. It was not as if Rita was not in the know but it was still better to pretend her sister was not aware of her shortcomings.

"Who is that? Is that you, Frances?" Bert felt a quickening of his heart rate.

"Yes love, I've got to be quick. Are you all right, dear?" She was longing to say how she loved him, how she missed him and how she still needed him. She could have blurted out her desire for them to meet this evening. She was, however, locked in trivial conversation and could not let herself be herself with Rita in such proximity.

"Where are you speaking from?" asked Bert, the concern shading his words. "Are you alone?"

"Yes, I am," she faltered. "Well, not exactly alone, but Larry's not here, if that's what you mean."

"Oh," Bert paused. Why did he have to be reminded of Larry right now? Why should the spectre of his friend haunt him with guilt only seconds after his great delight at hearing the voice of his lover? A delight which had temporarily removed all his cares from him, so that he had experienced a glimpse of heaven. Now she had spoiled even that impossible dream.

"Well, what do you want? Is there something the matter?" Bert sounded rather fraught.

"No, I'm fine. What about you though, Bert? What did they do to you?"

"What, at the station you mean? You knew about that then? I suppose John told you," he replied, trying not to sound too comtemptuous.

"I was worried," she whispered, "especially when I didn't hear from you."

"Well I couldn't exactly 'phone you, could I?" asked Bert exercising slight surprise at Frances' lack of logic. "What if Larry had answered?"

Now it was Frances' turn to feel the guilt and sin draining away her happy dream.

"Yes, you're right Bert, sorry," she said plaintively. "I must be quick." She felt she had to go quickly but still she had not reached any point that would further their liaison. She had to cut through the niceties to get to the point.

"Bert, can we meet this evening? Please?" Such a pleading could not go unheeded.

"What about him though?" asked Bert, referring to Larry.

"Oh I don't know, but we'll get round that. Just tell me where and when and I'll be there. You'll see."

*   *   *

Chapter Twelve

His eyes had opened, flickered for a moment then closed. She had been right. She had always known. His eyes were blue, the palest of blues like the coolness given to sight by the summer's sky.

So, he was still alive. Those eyes, so vital, so focussed, surely they were not of a man already dead by projection? He had seen, he had understood. In that brief contact with the world his brain had transmitted to her that he was fully alive.

Then he had been sick.

Sister had rushed in as the button had bidden. She was not annoyed nor even pretending not to be, at this intrusion upon her other work. She had simply endorsed approvingly what her young nurse had done. When she had left moment-arily, the young nurse had felt reassured. It had been good to know the Sister approved of her diagnosis. Her very lack of disapproval in the hurried contact had been approval indeed.

Then the patient with the pale blue eyes, the middle-aged man, battered and bruised outwardly by his recent adventures, and destined to die internally, but not yet avowed of this fact, had muttered. The nurse had left her futile observation of the charts and graphs for they only told what had already been ordained and provided no life-giving assistance. They only recorded the decay and destruction which was on its irreversible journey.

She had moved close to him and their eyes had met. In those seconds in which his eyelids flickered, as if unsure whether to open fully, or to stay permanently closed, she felt she had known her pathetic charge. He had no longer been a man just destined for the obscurity of anonymous death, he had become a personality. If he was with very little future, most certainly he had a great and interesting past. The fact that she was not part of that past, in no way detracted from it. His past had entered her soul but without her power of recall. However, he existed. He was.

What had he murmured so faintly, so intensely? Was it a name? She had been unable to make it out, yet she knew she had heard it and she knew she had undertsood, as surely as she now saw him as a living person, not as a projection of a corpse. She heard the name but it had gone too quickly. just as the recalled dream, which has influenced the dreamer's next morning, is recalled, in doses too fleeting to be held.

*   *   *

"Captain Weiss wants you," the door sentry informed Franz curtly.

Weiss? What did he want? What had Franz done wrong now? He wasn't late for patrol or anything, he was off all duties, surely? Unless this was another of Morten's cruel tricks to say he was off-duty then stand back and watch him get into trouble for acting on that information? Well at least it wasn't Morten asking for him. Franz did not know what he would have done if that man had started making demands of him again.

Franz dejectedly made his way to Weiss' office. At least the Captain acted correctly towards him. Had he not only recently prevented Morten hurting him physically? It was a pity that he didn't know about the other things but then Franz, who was now a nobody, signified by his disgrace in his imminent posting to the Eastern Front, could not expect any justice. He just had to be thankful that Weiss too, did not see him as fair game.

"Come!" barked Weiss clearly, through the heavy closed door. Strange how even when this man gave orders, or purported to be in an angry mood, his voice nevertheless belied this. He had an aura of gentleness about him despite his, by no means lowly, rank of Captain.

Franz at times felt he could almost have confided in the man. He probably would have, had it not been for his being adopted by his local family, his enemies.

238

Franz entered the office almost expectantly. Any time spent in house hours in this place was less time at the beck and call of Morten.

"Müller!" boomed the Captain, his attempt at harshness sounding almost convivial. "Where in heaven's name have you been?"

"Sir?" Franz was puzzled. What did the Captain mean? Had he done something wrong? Had they been looking for him? Why did Captain Weiss need to know?

"I asked you where you have been all day," explained Weiss forcefully. "Patrol Leader Morten tells me he sent you on an errand this morning and that was the last he saw of you. Look at the time boy! It's almost the middle of the afternoon! Explain yourself!"

Yes, Franz realized now. he had really forgotten his earlier anxieties that he was probably quite out of order in not returning straight away, back to Town House, once he had delivered his invitation to John. But of course, he had not got round to making the invitation until quite late in the interview, for John had pressed him into visiting the family with him, hadn't he? Besides, each time the worry had entered his thoughts he had pushed it aside, telling himself that he had not actually been ordered to return. It had worked each time, made easier by having John's company and that of the freedom of the conquered family, but each time it had left a little notch of anxiety in his subconscious. It was these notches, which now jolted and hurt his remnants of military conscience as he realized he had wilfully deluded himself.

"Sir, I did what the Patrol Leader said."

"What was that, Müller?"

"I went to my friend's home Sir and made the invitation."

"The invitation?" enquired the Captain, as if he were puzzled at the concept.

Franz began to wonder if they were talking about the same thing. Perhaps Morten had told Weiss something else? Maybe he was taking on the guilt of something other than he thought?

"Yes, Sir, the Patrol Leader's invitation to my friend to attend the Rel . . ."

"Yes, yes! All right, Franz!" The Captain cut across him, quickly correcting his avuncular tone to;

"Müller, I know all about it. Now tell me why you didn't return? The Patrol Leader is furious. He has asked me to speak to you."

"The Patrol Leader didn't say anything about me having to return Sir. He just told me to ask my friend about the Relaxation," was Franz's pathetic reply. As he said the words he realized how abysmally purile his excuse must sound.

"I see, so because you were not specifically told to return, you felt that gave you licence to wander off and not report back to the Patrol Leader?" began Captain Weiss with studied patience. "I suppose, if you were ordered to stay in this building you would remain in here for ever if you were not specifically told till when!" He thumped the table. Yes the analogy he had chosen, quite arbitrarily, to reinforce his sarcastic logic, had been a good one. By the expression on Franz Müller's face the lad looked as if he felt threatened by it.

"Well, what have you got to say for yourself?" Again the distant kindness, only shallow buried, seemed to burn in the officer's words. Franz felt he would be excused, the tone could mean nothing more sinister.

He dutifully hung his head;

"Sorry Sir, I didn't think . . ."

"That is quite obvious," came the Captain, "half the German army comprises people who 'didn't think'."

"Yes, Sir."

"Well," said Weiss, now feeling he had done all that was expected, he had taken the heat from Morten by saying he would reprimand the culprit, he had done all that was necessary. "You had better remember it in future, boy. If you're given an inconclusive instruction, think. Think, that's what your brain is for!"

Franz was sure now that his carpeting had climaxed and he was to be excused. What a relief, when all his anxieties had made him imagine dire problems. He felt quite relaxed.

"So you had better go to the Patrol Leader and inform him I have reprimanded you," concluded the Captain sternly.

"He wants to see you. Be sure to tell him I have been very angry with you."

The Captain almost smiled at the pathetic victim so that Franz sensed he must know what he had to face. So strong was this feeling in Franz that he felt he almost had an ally here, a protector even, who, if things got too unbearable, could be called upon for help.

"Yes Sir. Thank you Sir. May I go now please?" All Franz's instincts, all his inclination, was to stay here in the safety of this room with this jolly, almost non-militaristic officer, but he knew he had to face Morten and better to get that over with quickly so he could then have an unclouded view of tomorrow, with its visit to the home of his friends. Well at least he felt there was someone with the signs of decency under this very roof if things got too oppressive.

Weiss dismissed him, with the wave of his hand, while he appeared busy. He could not show his concern and yet Franz felt it, just as the cold weed feels the warmth of spring's promise while the winter sun still holds him in its frosty grip.

*   *   *

"So you have come back to Morten? I told you you would wish to come back for more! I will have you begging for me before much longer, my little boy," voiced the Patrol Leader most cuttingly, with a confidence that his crude directness could in no way turn back on him, for now he was lord and master, here in this room. His wish was law.

Franz had the appearance of one defeated and yet, in his thoughts, he held far better prospects. He was able to arm and protect himself with the prospect of better things to come. Morten was a bad man but he knew men, real men, true people who were not as this bully. He had only to think of them, and despise this perverted adult, to remain apart. Oh yes, Morten could put him through his evil distortions but he would never subjugate his will or his spirit while he held the knowledge of friends and strong characters such as John, his parents, that English priest and even Captain Weiss. Not all of the raised ranks of Germany's forces were depraved like this man. Corporal Schmidt had not been like

Morten. He had been a real man. Franz had only to think these good and positive thoughts to cause Morten and his ilk to shrink away to the minimal status they really were.

"Where were you all this time?" demanded the Patrol Leader stepping forward, grabbing Franz by the shoulders. Was he about to shake and terrorize the young person or was he going to effect tenderness? Franz would have preferred to be physically abused than to have received a sham of tenderness which would be a prelude to depravity. In his strength of resolve he found himself bravely removing first one arm, and then the other, from his shoulders.

Morten was amazed. Who did this person think he was? Did he not yet realize he was the property of the Patrol Leader alone to be treated as that person so decided?

"I have been out with my friend," replied Franz with the knowledge that his words carried a strength of conviction. Before Morten could react to his bravado he added with confidence, not in any way excusing himself or seeking the other's pardon;

"Captain Weiss has spoken to me and has told me to tell you he has reprimanded me. He said to let you know."

There, Franz had concluded all that was required of him so, now perhaps, he could go? He doubted it would be that easy. He was sure he would have to pay a toll for his dismissal but at least now, the proceedings were not of his making.

The unintentional assertiveness, borne unconsciously of Franz's acceptance of affairs, the lessening of naive concepts of the make-up of his fellows, transmitted itself to Morten, who read the reactions as those of one who was talking from a position of advantage.

Although annoyed at an inferior imbuing in him a holding back, he was nevertheless curious and a little more on his guard than would usually be his wont.

"And did your friend tell you to break the regulations of the German army?" stormed the Patrol Leader, as he prodded Franz so fiercely he was forced to step back: each prod administered in revenge for the slight of the boy's removing each hand from his shoulders.

"No he did not!" Franz asserted, with righteous indignation. Had he not already explained all this to Captain Weiss?

Did not the Captain seem to offer him support? What did it matter if Morten now took exception to this uncustomary response?

"So why did you not return till now?" Morten's face was clouded with anger at such insubordination and such a rearing of spirit in one who was usually his pliant subject.

"I've explained it all to Captain Weiss. Why don't you speak to him about it?" Franz was shocked at the bravery of his own rhetoric, hearing it as if the words were from a prepared script and not from himself. He knew as the words left him, that he had unleashed a storm which had no alternative now but to blow itself to a conclusion.

"You explained it to the Captain? You snivelling wretch. Why to the Captain, why not to me? Who sent you on the errand? Was it the Captain or was it me?"

All these questions. All this rage. Was it perhaps good? Would Morten now become violent? Would that be better than the other thing? Would it be neither or would the violence just exacerbate the other acts which then themselves would become more violent and loathsome?

Without conscious plan, Franz found himself seeking to placate the Patrol Leader. Maybe he had gone too far, surreptitiously seeking the support and sympathy of the Captain? Maybe Morten had a genuine grievance here which Franz ought to seek to lessen and put to rights?

"You sent me, Patrol Leader, and I have done what you asked." There Franz had said it, he had thrown clods of sand before the advancing rush of expiated waves. His fortress would stand a little longer. It would eventually fall but not on this particular offensive.

"What?" Morten had lost his train of thought and in seeking to grasp it had unwittingly permitted himself to expose this by allowing his confusion to show. "What did you say?"

"I said I've done what you asked, Sir," replied Franz, feeling more sure of himself with each word. "My friend will attend with us at tomorrow evening's Relaxation."

"Oh," Morten was silenced. There was nothing more to be said really. This must be where words end and actions take their place. But he was not sure of himself. Had not this boy just recently pushed aside his advances and summoned up the senior's anger, only then to as quickly defuse it? So, what now? He had achieved his objective, had he not? Why then risk spoiling tomorrow by an action now which might cause him loss of face? Better to wait, surely?

"Is that right, Sir?" asked Franz, rather dumbfounded by the other's apparent lack of response. "Did I do the correct thing?"

"Yes, oh yes," mouthed the Patrol Leader, vaguely looking his inferior directly in his pale young face. "Yes, that is quite correct. That is what you were told to do."

"And may I go now, please?"

There was a silence. Morten did not wish to answer such a question. Despite his logical deliberations, it was difficult to pass such an opportunity. His movement, as a prelude to blocking the other's means of exit, accompanied by the transfer of intention through his facial expression, registered with Franz. It came as a double blow, for he felt he had all but escaped.

"Oh no," cried the youth, "No! And I mean it!" and he did. "You try that and my friend does not come. I don't care what you do to me then, but it's 'no' if you want the arrangement to hold."

Morten turned his back as Franz took the opportunity to leave.

*   *   *

From the moment John entered the cavernous passageway of Gaudion's part of the house he felt the cold atmosphere of unspoken anger, and unconcluded hurtful words, enter his bones.

As he ascended the stairs, he had the force of doom and disaster falling upon him. It was as if an unseen trauma were just about to break around him, yet logic reasoned with him that it was not unknown, that he and his father had already sown the seeds of recrimination and created a gulf between them. There was more to it, for each must know, although dared not to think, that their actions past, now beyond reclaim, had shaped their futures.

Their present hostilities were only the scab on the festering wound which was soon to break out to sweep each party up and apart to their own individual and destructive destinies.

Neither could think ahead more than a few days, for the projections of the mind brought closer the trial which would herald the end of all that was familiar or palatable.

John knew it would be easier not to speak to his father once they met, than to risk conversation which could only lead to taking up, once more, the awful words which they had shouted at each other at Auntie Rita's. Better to stay silent, with all the knotting of the stomach and feelings of guilt that would entail.

Frances would return home before long and, as a party attached to both, with grievances against each for had they not taken her – the innocent, along in their personal and self-shaped destinies, accepting and uncomplaining at the futility of it – she would work hard at reconciliation. She would be the catalyst to unite the broken parts. Both knew they would be stronger as one whole yet did not have that burst of energy sufficient to act on their own.

Quite predictably, their third floor flat was chill with Larry's presence. The very rooms seemed more dark and shaded than they should be on a hot July afternoon.

John entered the kitchen where he found his father hunched over the table with empty cup and saucer. He appeared, in his gloom to be studying yesterday's *Star*.

Larry gave a slight, almost involuntary movement as he became aware of his son's presence. So slight that he was able to correct it and prevent himself from lifting his head in acknowledgement of his bitter offspring.

To John, it seemed the whole of his father had moved, then frozen, so it was as if he had not made an entrance and his father had just maintained a previously-held pose, as his eyes fixed somewhere at the far end of the scrubbed table, half way between the newspaper and the one whose presence he would not acknowledge.

This was how it had to be, it seemed. Yet, John, who had seen evidence of life, and had braced himself for the foray, would have preferred a re-opening of hostilities, initiated by his father, to a further clamping of hateful loathing which the parent's disregard of his son signified and endorsed.

John certainly would not take the leading role in any

belligerence but preferred to reverse himself from the open door to retreat down the passage to the sitting room.

His father abused him with his silence, as his glare lifted to the receding back. John did not observe the glare, but felt it. Larry did not hear John's misery but felt his own compounded, knowing that he had further set fences between them.

And so time passed interminably slowly for both the parties, each longing for the return of Frances who alone could put matters right.

Larry sat reading and re-reading passages from the paper hardly absorbing what he perused, as his thoughts kept darting to where John might be. He would get up, go and find the boy and grunt something at him. Yes that was the plan. Then, depending on the tone of John's reply, he could form some conciliatory words, or be justified in pursuing his angry course, once more. It didn't matter which course was taken, for the words would take care of themselves once that first barrier had been breached. But he could not get up. Each intention was as quickly followed by inactivity so that the pattern of staring, half reading while drumming his bored fingers, was continued. He even found himself thirsty but unable to make the decision to raise himself from the table, to move towards the tap. He was incapable of decision.

John felt miserable in the sitting room. He wanted to face his father and get the unpleasantness behind him. He was almost ready to apologize but for what, he was not quite sure. He would just go in to Dad and say the word 'sorry'. Yes, that was all it would take. It would just be the prick of the lance and then the boil would be soothed. But he did not have the courage to lance himself, despite the pain. The nurse would have to do it while he looked away, willing himself in future moments. He sat on the sofa not daring to get up even, to find an encyclopaedia to read, or to play the gramophone. It was a though it would be fatal to display any animation if his father were to enter the room. It would somehow alter the status quo and John was not sure in which direction it would take him.

The rattle of the door roused him from his sleep. His dream, vaguely to do with the sun's warmth, and peace with no discernible Occupation anxieties, yet shared with his friend, drifted from his consciousness so that all trace was gone in an instant, only to leave behind an impression that it had all been good, in contrast to what was now to be his lot.

Frances stepped inside, not really aware of her part in destroying her son's temporary oblivion.

"Oh, you're in then, love," she said pleasantly. "Have you seen your father?"

John was still slightly dazed, yet the feeling of his dream was enhanced by his pleasure that his mother had returned to bring warmth and light into the home again. Momentarily he could not speak but signalled that Dad was last seen in the kitchen.

Frances was relieved that they were both here for she too had been invaded by forbodings as she had approached the home. Now she knew that her anxieties had good foundation but that, at least, it was just a family matter upon which she could work. It was nothing external. That was a relief.

Frances left silently, making her way towards Larry. John sat forward on his seat to listen and wait.

Should he stay where he was and wait for them to come to him, or should he go and join them? What would they be saying right now? What if Dad would not speak to Mum? What if they too had angry words so that matters got worse? Maybe Mum would go off again and John would have to stay lonely in the company of his father? What could they be talking about?

Supposing Frances took Larry's side? Say they formed up against him and condemned his friendship with the enemy? What would happen then? John could not bear the prospect of both parents united against him any more than he could contemplate them both disdaining the other.

Should he go in now to prevent their formulating a policy against him? Would that help, or would it just put off the evil day? How would he feel if he did not go in now and thereby lost the opportunity to avert terrible consequences? What, on the other hand, if he went in now, only to break up a reconciliation which was including him?

John was in a quandry as he moved to the door, hesitated, returned to his seat, got up again and remained indecisive. At last he reached the door, easing it open gently to stand in the passage-way straining to hear what was being spoken about him.

This very action, of listening in, was reprehensible to him as he was imbued with a deep sense of the immorality of it, reinforced by a sudden irrational fear that he might hear things which he could not bear to know. With the dawning of this emotion he breathed heavily, noisily shuffled his feet and began to sing his breath through his teeth to drown out, and render incomprehensible, any words which might break through. So doing, he returned to the sitting room, noisily fortifying his ignorance with a hard pushed door and exaggeratedly heavy foot poundings on the springy old floor, as he made his way to the gramophone to play at full volume, the record left on its turntable.

* * *

"What the hell does he think he's up to?" demanded Larry, trying to sound annoyed yet somewhat relieved at having this excuse not to have to take the full extent of Frances' sudden entrance. "I've told him before not to have the records on so loud!"

"Yes, dear," said Frances, stepping back rather theatrically from her husband's outburst, her tone almost humorously patronizing. She was pleased. Larry seemed almost back to normal with his, albeit somewhat contrived, tirade.

She had just entered the kitchen and received the same cool treatment as John had. She had felt her guilt of infidelity pricked, yet also experienced a welling of warmth and love to this, her man, who had been reduced to such misery and inactivity by his own foolishness and that of his very family. She would not be pushed aside by his silence, for guilt governed her emotions. Her actions in not showing slight, would be one little way in which she could help to right matters and bring Larry back to his true self.

The semblance of his anger had made Larry more aware of himself. He had switched back into the present and here was Frances. Where had she been lately? What was going on? Why were they two so apart? It did not make any sense. Here she was, here he was. Their puerile offspring was in the other room and the best place for the little fool at

248

present, out of sight, out of mind. Here was Frances. She mattered, nothing else.

Larry raised himself. To Frances, his movement seemed painfully slow, almost indecisive, as she willed him to stay vital for her.

"Sorry, my darling," he began apologetically, "I didn't mean to take it out on you. It's just that. . . " He paused. He did not need to go into all that trivia.

"I know," she interjected soothingly, "I understand, love." She did not know what it was she was understanding but she knew her words were the right ones. Things had a chance of being all right again, for the present at least. And, after all, that was all any of them had any more, just a present.

Larry placed his hands on his wife's waist, smiling slightly as he pecked her on the cheek.

"I'll sort the little bugger out in a minute, but first I've more important matters in hand." He chuckled slightly, as Frances exaggerated feigned shock and dismay.

"Come on," he said. "How about a proper kiss now to celebrate your man's home-coming?"

Frances did not answer, as both forgot the volume from the adjacent room, for, with the uniting of the lips, with its symbolism an absolute proxy for all true union, nothing else existed, except their present moment with just the two of them.

After an age of ecstasy Frances pushed Larry gently away, her abdomen feeling cold at the loss of his pressure, as it re-shaped itself into conventional decency.

"That's enough of that," she admonished playfully. "It's only afternoon and it's not Thursday."

Larry's eyes, watery and softened with passion, received the admonition but questioned its sincerity.

'So,' said his eyes, 'it's not Thursday, but so what? You're here, I'm here, our bed is only seconds away.'

"And John's here too. Had you forgotten the noisy little 'b' as you called him just now?"

Larry remembered. He came back to reality and accepted this temporary defeat. He already knew the answer to his superfluous question as he heard himself asking;

"Later?"

Frances confirmed by slipping away, relieved that her husband had returned to normal, yet was considerate enough of her feelings to be restrained. She also felt a stab of disappointment that he had been unable to break their years of routine, succumbing so quickly to her call to reason. However, 'later' was now born in them as a reality, so 'later' could be included in their present.

*   *   *

The truce had lasted relatively well, mainly owing to the skill of Frances, determined not to leave the two protagonists together for even more than a brief moment, and ready to assist with a light-hearted change of subject whenever that seemed necessary. She felt quite exhausted, but it was the exhaustion of contentment, of a job well done, when John asked his matter-of-fact question at the end of their sparse tea.

It was more of a matter-of-fact statement than a request, just showing to what extent the past few days had aided his growing up. Nevertheless it was couched in conventional politeness, as when the authoritative person asks if someone will do something, meaning 'I am telling you to do it.'

"I think I'll go out for a while, if that's O.K.?"

Both Larry and Frances were rendered stock still by this, Frances sensing but hoping she was wrong, that Larry would be against the idea. Larry only paused to gather to mind some good reasons for preventing his son's absence, for none presented themselves readily, except that he wanted to go. If John wanted something then surely that was reason enough in itself to gainsay the matter?

Frances half hoped Larry would agree, for then maybe, after all, she could engineer their 'Thursday afternoon'. Larry wondered if he might take a stroll to the Golden Lion. Perhaps if John stayed in, to keep his mother company, he would not feel so bad at neglecting her again?

"Go out?" grunted Larry, "for why?"

"Eh?", queried John.

"You know what I said. I asked why. Why are you going out?" His tone was unreasonably aggressive, as Frances sought to placate once more.

"Go on, love, let him go. Not all the questions. Not now, eh?"

"It's not a case of 'let him go', damn it!" started Larry but already there was a detectable softening, or was that just in Frances' wishful imagination?

"You don't know what the stupid little sod will get up to! It's not as if. . ."

"Come off it!" shouted John rising suddenly from the table, almost knocking his crockery to the floor, "I'm not stupid you know? I'm no longer your little boy!"

Hostilities were about to flare again. In desperation Frances interjected.

"Let him go, dear. Please?" There was definite pleading in her voice, reiterated by her eyes as they fastened on to Larry's, willing a response.

"Let him go, it's 'Thursday afternoon', remember?"

Larry's silence was agonizing to Frances, as she awaited the verdict. She felt like the medieval wife selling her body to free her man from unmentionable misery, except that here it was all reversed and she would be selling herself and her regular strictures to the very one she had loved for so long and still felt she could love. The lover she would spare would be her son.

"Well, I'm going anyway," announced John. "You two can sort out your affairs however you please."

The spell was broken. However near Larry had come to acquiescing, his affronted authority now took over, as Frances knew she was about to become the whipping boy, to lose on two counts.

"You're not going out, damn you! While you live under this roof of mine you'll just bloody well do what you're told!" Larry thumped the table and stood up to prevent his son's exit. In so doing he caught the look on Frances' face. Looking past John his eyes told her 'You had your chance; you didn't take it so now you can wait.'

Frances bit her lip, fighting to hold back her tears. Tears of disappointment, tears of anger and frustration. She felt cheap. She had thrown herself at her husband only to be brushed aside.

"I am!" declared John, unaware of the secret conflict all around him. "Get out of my way, won't you?"

251

The very slightest of pushes removed John from his father's proximity, while he staggered back towards his mother.

"You're staying here with your mother and that's final!" ordered Larry.

'With your mother,' thought Frances, 'oh no! He's not going out and leaving me?' Her degradation and rejection felt complete.

Larry was gone, off down the stairs. His son dare not follow now. If he waited till Larry had gone on his way then so be it, but Larry, as father, had asserted his parental authority and his conscience was clear. Besides, he'd put the onus on the boy to keep his mother company, hadn't he? If Frances was now left alone she couldn't blame Larry. Oh no, she could only blame her precious spoiled son!

In his anxiety to leave the house and not to witness his son's disobedience, or to hear his wife's futile pleading, either to the boy or to him, he almost collided with two shadowy figures deep in conversation in the almost dark passage between Gaudion's rooms and the front door.

"Oh Mr. Collins," bleated Gaudion, "you're just the very one. This yer gentleman wants to speak to you."

Larry stopped and, adjusting his perception to the poor light, observed that Gaudion was in conversation with a member of the Occupation forces, wearing the black uniform of the S.S., no less.

Gentleman! Wanted to speak to him? What the hell was this all about? Larry felt a surge of paranoia and was almost oblivious to all but his own racing and panicking thoughts, as the creature in black interjected.

"Not so please! This is not the man I wish to see. I wish to see a younger man, his name is Collins, John Collins. I know he lives here!"

His voice of anger carried a ring of accustomed authority, and an expectation of obedience, seeming to presuppose that he was deliberately being denied access to the said John Collins.

In an instant Larry realized who this fellow must be. Was he not that purveyor of evil about whom John had, only nights before, confided his fears of how his so called friend was being mistreated? Was he not the one Larry had warned his son to keep well clear of? What then, was this bastard

doing here at his house asking for his son? Had John arranged
to meet this person? Is that why he was so anxious to go out
this evening? In no way would this be allowed to happen!
Larry's temporary paranoia was replaced with extreme and
icy cold anger towards the Nazi who confronted him.

"What is your business with my son?"

"Your son?" Hüffmeier was momentarily taken aback but
quickly composed himself. "My business is with your son,
not with you. Please to tell him I wish to speak with him."

"Look mate, anything to do with my son is to do with
me! We don't need your sort round here." Larry stepped
towards Hüffmeier who took a slight involuntary move
backwards while Gaudion was not sure whether to get closer
to better enjoy the shortly ensuing fracas, or to take shelter
in his lair, or just to go upstairs to fetch John, as had been
his original intention, thereby to fuel further the fires of
excitement.

"Mine is the business of the Reich!" screeched Hüffmeier,
sounding rather more terrified than authoritative now.

"Oh yeah?" sneered Larry. "So that's the Reich's business
is it? Well, we'll just see about that!"

With that he turned his head upwards into the stairwell
and bellowed;

"John, here a minute. There's a friend to see you!"

John, with Frances, having heard the commotion, were
out on their landing. John quickly tripped down the stairs to
stand at his father's side wondering if it was Franz who
would greet him.

He paled with the realization of who his visitor was.
Larry, whose eyes had accustomed themselves to the gloom,
was pleased to observe this reaction in his son.

Hüffmeier had time to correct himself and with enforced
confidence said, as if no others were witness;

"Ah, John Collins! You remember me, yes? We share the
same friend yes? Good!" He eyed John with his deathly
reaction, glanced quickly at the boy's father, who too was
for the moment subdued. He quickly continued;

"You will accompany me please? Yes? You and I must
this evening walk together and talk a little, yes?" It was
more of a command than a statement and that, with the
cold hard smile of his cruel nervous eyes, and the gleam of

253

his perfect teeth, was very sinister, so that John sensed the
goose-pimples forming on his arms and neck. He felt he was
back at the Gaumont being coerced to leave with the devilish
creature to he knew not where, but only with the vague
hope of meeting his friend. This time his innocence had
been lost; he now knew of the proclivities of this man. He
was not taking him to see Franz. His plans, half conjectured
by the semi ignorant John, were too awful to contemplate.
He was a little boy once more, the cat had got his tongue,
and he looked to Dad to take over, to save him from the
unimaginable.

"Do you still want to go out this evening, son?" asked
Larry angrily, but his anger was not directed at his boy.
John's reaction, upon recognizing Hüffmeier, had convinced
him that there was no wilful liaison there.

John could not answer.

"He's not going anywhere! Just you push off back to your
own sort!"

Larry stepped towards Hüffmeier.

John pressed back against the banister.

Frances took another step down the linoleum stairs,
Gaudion backed towards his door.

Hüffmeier grinned nervously, his hand moving slowly
towards his holster.

"I am an officer of the S.S.!" screeched Hüffmeier as his
hand touched his pistol. "Your son comes with me now. It
is German business!"

"No!"

Larry sensed Frances' proximity.

Frances took more steps.

John stepped behind his father.

Gaudion disappeared.

Hüffmeier drew his pistol.

"Frances!" yelled Larry, not sure which was the stronger;
his urge to protect his son on a matter of principle, the urge
to acquiesce and thereby continue his life, or the pressing
need to defecate.

"Yes?" her voice was close at hand but sufficiently far
from the madman's aim to put her out of any danger.

"Frances, go upstairs to the 'phone quickly. . . " Larry's
voice was quavering but so too was the temper-driven,

frustration-riddled, gloved hand, pointing the pistol at his belly. "Ask the operator to get you the Gestapo quickly. Tell them one of their S.S. men is here threatening us with a gun. Be quick!"

Frances' reply was her running steps as her shoes clattered up the stairs to do Larry's bidding.

But none of the parties heard her departure. All were enveloped by the encased explosion as the shot was fired.

All were enveloped in timelessness, trapping them in terror, as if moulded into a block of glass, immovable and helpless but all-seeing and spared nothing.

The ringing remnants of sound, which had been the shot from Hüffmeier's pistol, were all that had life for this extended moment. Their release came with the second aural assault, as the front door banged behind the rapidly exiting Hüffmeier.

Frances moved from the stairs to which she had been fastened. John raised himself from the bottom step where his father had pushed him down. Gaudion poked his pale wrinkled face from behind his door arch, while Larry lay still on the threadbare greasy carpeting of the passageway.

There was a jagged splintered gash in the bottom of the banister. The very wood, layers of old paint wrenched from its dried and shrunken sinews, cried out in its agony, as the smoke cleared painfully slowly from its wound.

Larry stirred. He felt no pain, he could move, his family were staring down on him, unsure whether to show grief or relief, their faces pale question marks against the grimy shadow encrusted ceiling.

Slowly realization dawned that he was still alive. Was he really alive or was he just witness to their mortal pursuits? Was he really without pain or was it just nature's amorphous shock, soon to be replaced with seering agony?

"Larry!" gasped Frances, now bent over him, her naivety providing the words. "Are you all right?"

"Dad! Dad!" yelled John. "Where are you shot?"

Larry, dazed and deliberate, did not answer. He had been prepared for death when the shot had fired. He had done all the correct responses, falling to the floor to knock his son over as he did. Yet he was not dead. So time had not taxed this son yet? Carefully, almost theatrically and comically, were it not for the serious prospects implanted in the minds of his audience, he examined himself from head to toe. First visually, then by hand. No trace of bleeding was to be seen, no malformation of broken bones, no ripped tissues. It could not be true! Hüffmeier's bullet had not hit him. It had hit only the elderly piece of innocent carved wood.

*   *   *

Mum and Dad had retired to their bedroom. It was still light, so John assumed his father was resting from the shock of believing himself mortally wounded, only to find himself the unharmed butt of Hüffmeier's angry, sadistic humour.

Frances had been in there a long time and John had thought it wise not to interfere. Should he go out, he wondered? No, he was too frightened that he might meet up with Hüffmeier.

What did Hüffmeier want? Why should he want to walk and talk with him? John shuddered, casting from thought the idea that the S.S. monster should be contemplating evil things for him just as had happened to poor Franz.

What of Franz? Was he safe right now? John thought not but what could he do about it? Franz had survived the privations up till now, hadn't he? Well, he only had till tomorrow then they would be both together during the day. They could each give the other moral support. What of the evening, though? What if Morten and Hüffmeier were both there? What a terrible thought! But that was too awful to contemplate, too far off. Besides, they'd made plans hadn't they? They'd made plans so they'd have to stick to them.

In his mind John went over the plans which he and Franz had formulated for tomorrow evening. They were very weak plans. So much could go wrong. They only had to weaken and take one drink, or get separated for both to be in danger. John knew he as a civilian, could always get out, but what of Franz? They would then be cruel to him as a revenge. But Franz could survive. Oh yes, but at what price? The thought was unimaginable to John, but to Franz there had been more than just thought, he had experienced.

Yes, and he was still alive and able to plan and rationalize.

These ideas were circling in John's mind, chasing each other and always coming back to the possibility of reaching the unknown tomorrow evening, and of his being forced to escape, to leave Franz to take on all the misery. And yet, that was how it would have to be if they were both to stay friends, in contact. Was friendship worth that price? Franz obviously thought so. If Franz felt so strongly then he was indeed the most true of friends and as such must be valued at any price, even at the price of allowing him to be abused in order to further prove his friendship.

John was dreadfully lonely. He was excluded from his parents' bedroom, he dare not go out and he had no friends who could call. He dare not visit Franz, for that could only spoil their day tomorrow.

All he had for company were his thoughts. Thoughts of Franz, of the good times past and times to come, yet constantly invaded by intruders; Hüffmeier and Morten. What if those two evil men were this very moment with Franz causing him further torment? What was worse; the real thing for Franz, or John's time-dragging imaginings of what might be happening to him. There, his thoughts were circling once more!

The telephone rang. Rescue from John's inconclusive thoughts. He waited. Surely Mum would answer, not Dad, Mum was sure to.

The telephone continued, its harsh call unanswered. Finally, John made his way to it.

"John! Answer the 'phone, please," came Frances' faint but urgent demand from her bedroom, as he picked up the black ebony.

"Hello?"

The end of the line was in silence.

"Hello?" again asked John in irritation and disappointment. "Who is it?"

He was about to put down the receiver when a crusted hoarse voice at the other end asked;

"John? Is that you, John? This is Uncle Bert. Can I speak to your mother, please?" The voice was plaintive and loaded with embarrassment as if taken aback that the 'phone had not been answered by Frances.

John, annoyed that it was only Bert, and slightly puzzled that he should want Frances, especially at a time like this, said in a matter of fact way;

"No, sorry, Uncle Bert. She can't speak to you at the moment, she and Dad have gone to bed."

"Oh!" replied Bert with effected nonchalance, while feeling that a javelin of jealousy had pierced him, striking his personality and aspirations to the ground, to die a lingering death. "Well, I'd better go then."

"Wait!" yelled Frances from the open bedroom door, as John bade Bert farewell. "Wait, John, who is it?"

Too late. The receiver had been replaced. Bert had been obviated. John felt some satisfaction. He could not tell why. Maybe it had only been because of the temporary cessation of bombardment by his thoughts.

Frances was agitated as she waited for the operator to answer. She was concerned also that John lingered near her in the passage and would possibly recognize the number or even ask her who she was 'phoning. Even if he did not recognize or enquire he was sure to listen in to her conversation. She should really have dismissed him but she had been so annoyed when he'd hung up on Bert that she had dared not admonish him for fear that her flood gates would have opened.

Her paramount concern, at this moment, was to put right what poor Bert must be feeling, for she had heard John's parting words. Strange now, that she felt guilty about the way she was being unfaithful to Bert where only hours before he had been the cause of the guilt between her and Larry. What would be worse; to have to feel guilt regarding both the men she loved or to feel, as they must surely each feel when they knew the truth, as know they must, that they had to share her with another? Each state had its misery but each its blessing too. The men could compensate themselves in their anger and jealousy while she, in having two men, both of whom she loved, had no such solace. But it did not seem to be working out quite that way. Yes, she loved the two but her enjoyment was kept from her by her guilt and the clandestine nature of her liaisons, legitimate and illegitimate. Worst of all was that she knew there was no

258

help for her condition, for love, with all its impossible demands, will take root wheresoever it chooses.

Yes, she had to put things right with poor Bert but how she wished John would disappear, and how she willed the operator to be quick. She so wanted to reassure her lover that all was well before Larry appeared from the bedroom. Already she imagined anxiously hearing Bert's voice and having to sound stilted and matter of fact, as if she were trivially discussing the weather, while, unbeknown to Bert, Larry stood listening. Then she would have to give Larry an excuse and she could not yet think of one. It would just have to form at the moment of need or she would be shamed and exposed for what she was, a guilt-ridden adultress.

"Number, please?"

"Er, Central 2689" whispered Frances all the time willing John to go away. He seemed to be standing there mocking her, as if he knew.

"Speak up, please, I can't hear you, caller," came the operator's agitated demand.

"Central 2689," Frances repeated, aware now that Larry was leaning at the bedroom doorway. It was exactly as she had predicted in her fear. She felt he was leering as his thoughts unpicked her unformed excuses.

"Trying to connect you."

"Hello, Central 2689." It was Bert.

"Hello," quavered Frances. "John said you rang."

"Frances, are you all right?" asked Bert. "Where are you?"

"I'm here at home, Bert with John and Larry. Yes, Larry's home too that's good, eh?"

She prattled on, not letting Bert get a word in. She had to convince him that this style was a deliberate ploy. She had also to convince Larry that this was just a friendly call on Bert's part. Yes, that was it.

"Did you want to speak to Larry?" She beckoned Larry to the 'phone hoping she might put the two into contact, to make some polite small talk.

Bert understood, but he was in low spirits. He had been waiting for Frances to telephone and, when she had not, he had been tormented by a variety of self-imposed fears; that she no longer wanted anything to do with him, or that Larry knew all and she had, despite her longings, decided that what had taken place had been only a temporary aberation.

When John had answered the telephone just now, his worst fears had been realized. Obviously the truth was out. What John had said had been loaded and venomous, designed for the maximum hurt. Frances had been back in bed with Larry. It hadn't taken her long. He must have changed too, to be in bed during opening hours! That was not the Larry of late. he was obviously claiming his rights and, in so doing, letting the other affected parties know without doubt.

Bert was unable to contain his misery.

"Frances, I need you! For Christ's sake come to me . . ."

She heard the words, despite the receiver taken firmly but gently from her grip, and she felt her whole body pulse with desire. She did not care if Larry had heard those words, which to him would be out of context anyway. All she knew was that she the discharge had to be charged before she imploded in her own vacuum.

"Hello, Bert. How's the world, mate?" enquired Larry in jocular vain. "Not too good, I reckon? What can I do for you?"

Hell, how Frances hoped Bert would take up the conversation and say something appropriate. She felt she had just enough love in her to sustain both men, if only she could prevent Larry discovering her shame and causing an almighty argument.

"Yes, Bert, I know that. Yes I'm sorry . . . Well, we've all got problems, my old son, you're not the only one . . . What you need, my friend is a good drop of cider inside you, that's what you need . . . Well it's up to you of course but I don't see . . . Now come on, mon vieux . . ."

Larry was becoming a little heated. He could listen to so much of his friend's moans but, damn it, hadn't he just reminded Bert that he too had problems. They all had problems! It wasn't the end of the world, well not quite. He'd been able to forget his problems just now with Frances. What Bert needed was a good woman, but he couldn't tell him that, could he? That would just be rubbing salt in the wound. Besides, he might just start taking an interest in

Frances like he had all those years ago in their youth. No need to open all that up again.

"I'll tell you what, Bert. I'm just off down The Lion in a minute. If you feel like it you come along, O.K.? No obligation . . . Yes, I know that Bert . . ., but . . ., well that hardly matters any more does it? We're in queer street now, so what the hell? . . . Yes I know that . . ., yes . . ., yes . . ., Bloody hell! Look, do you think I'd talk to you like this, over the 'phone, if I thought there was any chance of our getting off next week? Well anyway, like as I says, I'm at The Lion. You come if you like. I'll give you back to Frances now."

Without waiting for further conversation he thrust the receiver into Frances' trembling hand, muttering;

"I'm off to change. I'm going to the Lion. Don't keep Bert too long. He'll probably join me."

Bitterness and anger flooded Frances, as she took hold of Bert once more. She had just enjoyed Larry and now he was standing her up in favour of cider again. That showed his priorities! When Bert had come on heavy with desire, needing her, she had been unable to reply her similar need. Then, within a matter of seconds, he too had been seduced from his lust, to drink that vile stuff with Larry. What were her lovers but jars of cider!

"Yes?" she snapped cooly.

Bert now was aware that Larry was in proximity and tempered his conversation accordingly.

"Frances," he whispered. "Can you 'phone me when Larry's gone?"

"Yes Bert, Larry's just off in a minute. I hear you're going with him. It will do you good," she said, slightly exaggerated, for Larry's benefit, but also to sense the power of frustration it held over Bert.

"Frances, you know what I mean. 'Phone me dearest. I want you . . .," tried Bert.

"I might even see you there myself Bert. John's in. I might get him to walk me down later. We can all meet up then. Won't that be fun?"

Bert, not sure if Frances was being deliberately obstreperous, or if she was under some pressure of audience, tried;

"Are you trying to tell me something, Frances? Is it that you can't speak now?"

"Yes," she drawled slowly, in a matter of fact way.

"Well, will you telephone me when Larry's gone?" he begged desperately.

"Yes and no, you old silly," she said lightheartedly. "Now you really must go, Larry will be waiting for you."

"I'll ring you then?" he begged.

"Don't be silly," she replied teasingly. "John and I will walk. You are a fool, Bert; taxi indeed!" Frances laughed at her own conjecture.

"Frances?"

"Yes," replied Frances with exaggerated boredom.

"Frances, do you love me?"

"Cheerie, Bert," she affected cheerfully, as she put down the receiver.

*　　　*　　　*

"I'm off," said Larry, emerging from the bedroom fully dressed. "What was all that about?"

Frances shrugged;

"Oh I don't know, you tell me. I think Bert's feeling a bit low, that's all."

"Like the rest of us then," replied Larry unsympathetically and disinterestedly.

"He's coming to the Lion with you?" queried Frances.

"I doubt," replied Larry. "He's a bit of a stick in the mud. I doubt he'll come."

"Well, that's a pity," she said. "I think it would do him good to have a drop of cider in him."

"Yes, it might that," laughed Larry coarsely. "You know what they say about that Breton stuff, eh? Gives a greater drop than a spring tide, eh? That's half his problem I reckon, all tide and no shore." Larry guffawed at his own wit.

Frances deflected his conversation;

"Yes, I know what you mean. It's how you usually are when you come back."

"You're pleased to say," he laughed.

"Well, you were O.K. just now," Frances found herself

262

smiling lovingly at him. Larry pulled her towards him and squeezed her buttocks. Did he really want a drink?

"We'll have to get the bloody Jerries to pass a law to say there are two Thursday afternoons a week then, eh?" They both laughed.

"Larry?"

"Yes."

"Is it all right if John and I come down later to join you for a drink?"

Larry's smile was his answer.

*　　*　　*

Frances and John had almost reached the front door, on their way to join Larry at the Golden Lion. Frances thought she heard the 'phone ring. She knew it must be Bert. Why couldn't he have left it another minute? Should she go up and answer? What was the point? She would only have to say the same thing. 'No' was 'no' which ever way, or however kindly it was said. Besides, Bert would expect her to be out surely? Hadn't he listened to her when she said they were all going out? Maybe he thought she had just been saying that in order that the two of them could get Larry out of the way? Well, he would find he had been wrong wouldn't he? One of life's lessons. Maybe he would join them at the pub after all but she doubted it, just as she half feared he would and half feared he would not.

"What's the matter, Mum? Come on," urged John as Frances slowed to listen. "I want a game of darts with Dad."

"Oh, I just thought I heard the 'phone, that's all," said Frances quite detached, as they passed the mutilated bottom flight of stairs.

"I wonder who that could be?" mused John.

"Oh, it's probably just Uncle Bert again," sighed Frances. John looked at his mother strangely.

"If it's important he'll 'phone again tomorrow or he knows where to find us. Come on, dear, let's try this neaptide cider."

"Eh?"

*　　*　　*

263

Bert gave up. He had let the 'phone ring on as long as possible. He had counted twenty rings before the operator had interrupted;

"Sorry, caller, there seems to be no reply."

He had it in mind to ask her to keep on trying but he decided against it. He was disappointed that Frances had now answered. He had waited a half hour of self-disciplined hell, time sufficient to allow for Larry's departure. At each ring he had anticipated Frances' voice but he had also feared that of Larry or John. As the count had got higher so his disappointment had grown but also his sense of relief that he would not have to make some silly excuse as to why he had 'phoned a second time.

Well, at least he knew where they would all be. He could even join them there if he so wished. He could just take Larry's invitation at face value and go along. After all, Larry had seemed genuine enough just now and, as he had said, it did not really matter any more at being seen to associate with known or wanted dissidents. Neither of them had much more to lose, while those who had been denounced already knew it and awaited their fate just as they did.

So why not go? Well, John would be there. He made Bert feel uneasy. That teenage boy was far too close to his mother for a lad of his age and he seemed to have an uncanny sense that something was afoot between his mother and uncle. Bert felt quite inferior in front of John, more ill at ease than with the very man he was doing down.

Also there was Frances. Maybe her flippant tone on the telephone had not been just for her audience? Perhaps she really wanted it to say something to Bert. Possibly she felt a genuine sense of grievance at what had happened between them? Perhaps she, like he, was imbued with a crushing guilt at what they had done to Larry? Or worse, perhaps she no longer needed Bert? After all, she had just been to bed with her husband.

Bert knew this had to be, he knew, from the moment he allowed his desire to translate into reality, that he would be tormented by loss and jealousy, yet he knew he had not been able to stop himself. He knew that if the opportunity arose again he would grasp it, no matter what the consequences. He had to steal a little of Larry's wife again, otherwise there was no purpose to his life. Added to this, he had to know that she, too, needed him as much as he needed her.

He could not face going to the Golden Lion, as a friend of the family, to watch his darling playing the role of another's lover, no matter how legitimate.

Bert had to go to bed. The ever-growing rolls of distant thunder and the summer dancing of the lightening would be his companions if he made up his bed in the front. He could not bear to sleep in his usual bed, to have Frances' absence emphasized. They had both tasted of the apple. He was addicted, that force was now to dominate and subjugate his miserable existence.

*   *   *

The Golden Lion was full of life. Larry had been greeted with ribaldry as he had entered. He was reinforced by his memory of the recent reunion with Frances and the good feeling that he was still alive after that incident at the bottom of the stairs. Yes, he was alive and his wife and family were united as one once more.

"Hello, mon vieux, you old bugger! What's it to be?" asked one of his many pub friends. "A glass of cider or cider in a glass?" The locals laughed and groaned in their ritualistic acceptance of the sparsity and erratic supply of alcoholic beverage.

"My usual," shouted Larry who always forgot the cares of the world, when he was here with his mates, enjoying being the centre of attention. "And if there's any one here to whom I owe a pint . . ." he paused for effect, eliciting the pregnant pause he needed for his punch line, "then they can bloody well wait 'till we've won this war! I'm broke!"

Guffaws of laughter rippled all round as the genial general hubbub broke out again.

Amidst the general studied happiness of those drowning the day-to-day cares, a rather sombre voice reached Larry's ear. He looked and saw at one of the few tables, an islander accompanied by a female. Not unusual in this pub for it had an ill reputation and women were more a common sight than in most, but it was unusual in that the man sat with his wife.

Keith de la Haye, sitting with Anne, was calling to Larry in an attempt to be as jolly as the mechanic. His appearance belied his attempted tone, reflecting more the anxious careworn look of Anne, as he called;

"If they wait for that, Larry, it won't be you buying them pints. It'll be them buying you wreaths."

Larry stopped, turning to face Keith full on. The words had cut right into his mood of jollity. What he now replied was contrived and deliberate. He could not let this morbid defeatist prick the bubble of his euphoria in this place, even if the words he spoke rung true.

"If you don't shut your trap, my mate, it's not the end of the war we'll be waiting for, it's tomorrow someone will need a wreath!"

Everyone laughed and Larry realized he had turned his mood back from dirge to party.

Only Anne permitted the words to linger and enter into her consciousness, colouring them black and grey.

When all had forgotten Keith's interjection, and once Larry had completed the statutory niceties, the centre of the pub vitality moved from the bar, pint jar in hand, making his way to Keith's table. As he went, he knew he only had a few steps in which to change his personality from fun loving carefree Larry to anxious, cautious, care worn subterfuger that he really was in Keith's eyes.

"What's your trouble, Keith?" asked Larry as he nodded an acknowledgement to Anne, who looked as if she'd best prefer not to be noticed in particular.

"Oh, you know," shrugged Keith exaggeratedly dejectedly.

"Do I?" mused Larry, now sombre and wishing himself elsewhere, rather than having to face up to the realities that Keith's mood would surely try to force upon him.

"You've had yours?" asked Keith referring without doubt to the court summons. Larry was cognizant of what was alluded to.

"Had what?" he asked, with feigned ignorance.

"The summons, of course! What else do you think I bloody well mean? Come on now, I'm not daft!"

Anne clutched at Keith's sleeve. She had agreed to come

out with him, despite it being a new departure for her, in order to help cheer him and take his mind from the beginning of their end. She had not realized it would make him feel worse.

"Oh that? Yes, yes, I've had that. So what? I don't want to talk about that now. I've come here to forget all that and so should you. There's nothing we can do about it, is there?" Larry looked at Anne to evoke her support. She replied with a watery smile and the slightest shrug of the shoulders. He was preaching to the converted.

"Can I get you a drink, Mrs. de la Haye?" asked Larry, determined to change the course of this conversation. "I'm afraid there's only cider or brandy."

"No, that's all right, thank you," replied Anne, glad that Larry had steered the conversation another way. "Really, one is enough for me . . ." She paused then added, feeling an explanation was needed, so that she did not seem unresponsive to Larry's generosity;

"I'm not used to it, you see, and I don't want him to get used to it too early." She indicated the slightest of swellings in her abdomen and Larry understood. He knew now why Keith must be taking it so hard, poor bastard!

*   *   *

Thomas Peters, Reverend Peters, as those not of his parish deliberately insisted on calling him, but Father to his flock, found himself in the Lady Chapel of his Church. It was late, almost dark. Already the evenings were beginning to draw in and yet it seemed summer had scarcely come.

Strange, how in time of tribulation, upon looking back, time seemed to have galloped past and yet, the future and that very same past time, just months before, had seemed interminable in prospect.

Soon it would be their second winter under German occupation. A bleak outlook. The privations of food shortages and supplies were dismal enough, but a second cold and lonely winter, with a cold and lonely bed, and nothing more to look forward to than that of helping the less fortunate than himself, seemed to pall.

Even the lonely bed and the chance to go about his

ministry, now seemed in doubt to the priest. Who knew where he would be, come the spring?

He always came to the Lady Chapel at such moments of doubt. He felt at peace here, even though his world seemed to shatter about him. Here, he was always close to the host, the sacrament that was the centre of his Church, even though relegated to a side chapel by those in greater authority, who ever had an eye to the overall view, and perhaps less perception than the specialists of this particular high manifestation of the corporate Church. But not only was he in proximity with the bread and wine, turned flesh and blood through his directed and ordained ministry, but even more so, he felt he was close to his dearest wife and boys, for it was here he always prayed for them, and to them, and was with them.

It was good here in the gathering gloom. He could not, nor would not, allow even one switch for electric light, or to burn one candle more than the constant oil wick which the congregation permitted, through all privations, to hallow the presence. Always there was a provider for just that little drop more oil, to sanctify the presence, day and night.

It was this light now, shining and flickering through its red glass, as it floated serenely, making shadows short and long in this wholesome place, which kept the priest company, as he permitted his thoughts to shuffle and form themselves as in a relief-giving dream.

Materially all seemed lost, he had no future; and yet he was an optimist. He would continue till the end. Perhaps now that he knew when the end was to be he could be released from the anxiety, which had always seemed such a burden to him, of having to conform to the will of the occupying enemy. If he could have his final jab at them and, in so doing, know he was uplifting the spirits of his flock, while in no way adding to that same flock's burden, then he would do it, be it ever so small a gesture. If, as seemed likely, he was destined for a French prison, or even a camp in Germany itself, then he had nothing to lose.

He had with him tomorrow's sermon. He had learned to censor himself. After all, they always had their way so why prepare a sermon which would in any detail seem inflammatory? What object was there in trying to score political and moral points? Who would know he had made such a stand? Who would praise him or feel uplifted by words they were destined not to receive? No, he had just about managed to gauge what they could take and what they would reject. He still prided himself that sometimes he could subtly get a message between the lines that these square-headed oafs, even those of the Feldkommandant Intelligence section, who sat at the back of his Church, could not perceive. But then, of course, if he admitted realistically, the messages missed by the Germans, were probably above the heads of his congregation also. So it was not subversion that was his aim but a form of self-gratification. Yes, he was playing their game to a certain extent but he was cheating undetected, by using his own rules.

Yes, tomorrow's sermon was to be quite innocuous. Why not then just test them a little? What if he were to slip in the odd phrase, the odd reference against them? Would the two, so bored and indifferent, at the back of the Church, even notice? Did they really follow what he preached, as they purported to, or was it just a well-practised act? How about putting them to the test a little? What would they do? Would they jump up to stop the sermon? Would they call out? Would one remain while the other went to summon up a troop of sermon soldiers, or call the Gestapo to break up the subterfuge? Maybe they'd not even notice? Perhaps each would notice but hope the other hadn't so that no action unusual would have to be taken. Such things must, after all, be quite unprecedented in such a placid island as this – hardly a thorn in the Nazi flesh. Maybe they'd just note the deviation and report back to their office so that the matter could take its lethargic but legalistic course? Yes, this would most likely be the outcome, undramatic and unnoticed.

The peal of thunder agreed with him. Father Peters lowered himself to his knees, praying that what he was about to undertake would be more than a gesture, that it would at least uplift the spirits of his flock and help to keep them raised even when he had gone.

*   *   *

Chapter Thirteen

"Nurse, please bring in the two chairs from the corridor," asked the Sister.

Frances meekly sat on the furniture so fetched, while Gerda, aware of the courtesy shown and the unspoken kindness in the young girl's mundane act, just stood, her whole body trapped in a frozen grasp. It was not horror, it was not fear, nor disgust or misery, it was simply the only response she could make which was not a response.

"Oh John, John, my son," cried the old lady, rocking herself on her seat but unable to go to her child, and not receiving any attention from Gerda.

The Sister, who had other things to do, signalled to her junior. Quickly the young nurse returned to be with the two older women.

"I think he's regaining his consciousness," she ventured. "Perhaps you should talk to him. It might help."

Gerda moved close to John's face. Not for her the pale blue lights, just the shutters closed, but she did what was suggested.

"Come on, Frances dear," urged Gerda. "Come and talk to John."

Frances. That was it, the man had called her name! Strange for a son to call his mother by her name though. Some families did, however. She was sure that must be so.

Between them, the two women in his life spoke to John as he lay there motionless and pallid as the sheets. His only contrast to pale visage and greying hair was his bruising and his dark, smoothed lacerations.

Gradually, as they persevered, he began to move, to twitch and tremble. The nurse stood back, pleased that the man with the pale blue eyes might yet say his mother's name once more.

Poor Frances! She was tired now, already past her bed-time and brought to near exhaustion by her anxiety and the strangeness of their adventure.

"Frances, dear, why don't you rest like the nurse says? Go along to the bed and come back later. I'll stay. I'll call you if anything changes, I promise."

If anything changes? What will change? Will John suddenly get better? No, it will take a while but already he looks better as we have done what we were told. We have been talking to him and it is making him better.

"Look!" gasped Frances with near delight. "Look, Gerda, my love, he's woken up!"

John's eyes opened then fluttered shut again. But no, they opened wide, the large black pupils, dilated and reflecting the images looking in on him.

Gerda felt a stir of joy. Frances, no longer tired, knew her boy was getting better.

"There you see," she said gleefully, "he's on the mend. We'll have you out of here in no time, darling," she delighted.

*   *   *

Frances was cold as she slipped into her costume. She did not linger between bed and press. The night of storm, a culmination of days of summer heat, had swept away the sultriness and, with it, had kidnapped the blue skies which they had all come to expect these past weeks. Strange how one storm, one grey morning with wind and driven rain, cool by comparison with its prelude, could colour the whole recent memory so that the memorable days of heat and luxurious laziness and drowsiness were swept from mind. Only could be imagined and projected, the far greater damp and cold, with gales and buffeting of the next bleak winter, already reminding the vulnerable that it had not forgotten them.

Larry was still asleep . He had always enjoyed a storm at night. As usual he had insisted on the curtains being open and the window up so that the full glory and power of the atmospheric disturbance could be taken in. He had been charged with that power and predictably, despite the visit to the Golden Lion, had used it, translating it into his own,

271

subduing Frances while comforting her. She had not minded, or course, but had feigned fear of the booms and window-rattling crashes as the storm had passed overhead.

To say that Larry had overcome the springtide effects of the Lion was not wholly true, for had he not been very restrained at the public house? His intake had been definitely curtailed. It had seemed that he had derived more pleasure in having her and John present than in the usual substitute for his worries. Perhaps his anxieties had really lessened? Maybe he had been able to repress them at last to just be himself living for the present?

He had certainly been the life and soul of the gathering down there, no one could deny that. All those drinks he had had to refuse! Perhaps, when they had heard the distant build up of the thunder peals getting even louder and breaking through their most raucous of choruses, he had decided then that Frances was to be his again that night? Yes, that must have been it. He had not spoken the words but his eyes had said so, his smile telling her and his confidence transmitting to and singling out her attention and adulation in the crowded place.

And what was it he had said? Had he meant it or was it just the mood of the moment or the drink talking? Well, he had meant it at the time, of that Frances was sure. Even if he now gainsaid the idea she would not be too disappointed for, at the moment the words had been spoken, it had taken place in her thoughts. Even if he did not now come she would be happy with the knowledge that, for a fleeting moment, he had genuinely intended to.

"I'll come to Church with you in the morning, Frances," he had said. "I think it's about time I got a little bit in credit with God."

She had not been offended by the blasphemy, for no offence had been intended. Larry would not talk of going to Church, even if it sounded jocular, if he had not felt sincere. If she could understand that, then so would the Creator.

So here she was, shivering almost, anxious to see if in fact Larry would still be as resolute, delighted at the prospect of having him in Church with her, as in the old days. She desperately fought the ideas which flitted through her mind

272

like moths magnified, and opaquely shadowed on the screen, that this might be their last time at worship together.

Equally, in her chill state she would gladly have missed Church to bed up to her naked hairy man, to sleep on all morning, if need be.

No, she had got this far. She would quickly finish dressing into her very best clothes. She would probably have to look out her mackintosh. Mackintosh in July, it seemed almost laughable! Well, she would go and make a cup of something. Just enough for Larry as the tea had almost gone. Yes, that was it; from now on, only Larry would drink tea. Perhaps John too though, for his fate also loomed large on the horizon. She'd be quite satisfied with hot water, maybe a spot of peppermint essence as a special treat. The idea of self-sacrifice in that way appealed to her, her very negative role being symbolic, almost religious.

"What you up to, love?" It was Larry.

"Nothing, dear. You just lie back. I'll bring you a cup of tea."

"Sunday, isn't it?" he asked drowsily. "Where's my paper?"

Frances laughed, "It might not be too long, love, we've got to win this war soon." She hoped she sounded more convincing than she felt.

"Yeah," drawled Larry. "Once the Yanks come in we'll be O.K." He smiled, snuggling himself back down beneath the sheets. "I wonder if they'll bring me tea and papers in bed in France?" he mused.

"That's enough of that!" retorted Fraces with mock severity, wagging her finger at him.

"Who do you think you're speaking to? I've a good mind to get you back in here and give you a good spanking," he chortled.

The thought of the warmth and company were very tempting. Frances found she was almost forgetting her resolve to go off to Church.

"There's nothing more I'd like better," she replied with exaggerated hautiness, "but some of us have got to go to Church!"

"Oh, yes," commented Larry, "that's for sure! You've got a lot of sins to work off from last night, eh?"

"Stop it!" she exclaimed, grinning. "You're the one who's

got the explaining to do. All night long indeed! Comforting me from the thunder! That's a good excuse. I'm sure that would go down well."

She jumped back towards the door as Larry leaned out of bed and made a grab at her.

"It's no wonder you're staying there till I get back. You must be worn out!"

"Wait a minute," said Larry. "Who's staying in bed? I'm supposed to be coming too, aren't I?"

"Oh love! You really are?" Frances could have wept. He really did intend to come. She sat down on the bed and let him envelope her.

"Well, come on," she said at last. "We'd better get a move one. There's little time left."

"I'm coming," said Larry, as he jumped out of bed, turning his back on Frances to spare her embarrassment at his stormy state.

"You say I've a lot to confess. Well, maybe my going to Church will cause it to rain and with a bit of luck we'll get some more thunder, eh?"

Frances hit her man. She so loved him.

"Is John up yet?" asked Larry, sounding wide awake now and business like.

"John?" asked Frances, playing for time, rather fearing she knew the reasoning behind the question.

"Yes, my love, John. You know, our son, your little boy," he laboured.

"What of him?" she asked.

"Well, he's coming, isn't he?"

Oh no, this was it! Now Larry had to learn of Franz's visit. So he'd find out John was waiting in for his German friend and that this young enemy boy was actually going to eat at his table on this very day. How would that knowledge effect Larry? It could only make him angry. Possibly he'd rant and rave to spoil it for them all. True, he had to find out before long but far better that he did not know now. Much better to present him with a fait accompli. Not now! Not now, when he had almost got to Church.

"No, dear," she said with studied casualness. "He doesn't

274

always come, you know. Won't it be good, just you and me on our own?"

"Yes, I suppose so," he shrugged.

*   *   *

It was a long time since Larry had been to Church. He enjoyed the walk with Frances at his side, up The Grange. The rain had all but stopped and the fresh buffets of salty wind ruffled his thinning hair and made him feel young once more. He did not object when his Frances took his hand, just before Gestapo Headquarters, with the effect that he inclined her way and, in squeezing her hand, pushed the despicable place from his mind.

The old habits came easy, especially with Frances as his relaxed and confident guide. The water stoup, Frances' genuflection at the Lady Aisle while he awkwardly inclined his head, quickly turning away to receive hymn books and prayer books from the sidesman.

All were in their Sunday best.

Larry felt good to be dressed in his best suit once more, his shoes polished, a fresh shirt and collar, brass cufflinks and patterned tie. He sat easily in the pew, half way up the aisle, looking about him, while Frances pulled out a hefty hassock to kneel beside him. His gaze met several familiar faces evincing smiles of recognition and mouthed well-wishing.

Frances' lips were moving silently with fervour, her eyes pinched tight, her hands clasped around her closed missal, as her wrists rested upon the polished wood of the boxed pew in front. Larry thought he should join her in a token private prayer but he found he could not, not yet. And why should he pretend just for the benefit of those behind who might, or might not, be watching him? He owed them nothing, besides he sensed their charity. Who could feel anything but, in an inspiring place such as this?

Time drew near and all the preparations for Mass began to accelerate. The congregation moved to their places faster now, the chequerboard effect of the their former sparse seating now becoming lost to the placid observer, as more grouped up, people moved along and others stepped over friends who turned their knees sideways to allow passage.

Some, on reaching their habitual seating places decided to walk back or go forward in the central aisle and move to the side aisles to attain more easily their goals.

Soon there was hardly space to be seen, except behind the huge white round pillars. People began to spill into the side chapels.

Larry took in the light. How dismal it seemed at first but, as his eyes accustomed to the incense-laden gloom, he was aware of the stained glass windows, the round ones intended to represent rose windows and the pseudo-Gothic Perpendicular. How bright the reds and blues were with the daylight, even on this dull day.

A few lamps flickered near the sanctuary while black-cassocked beetles busied themselves, dashing from one vestry and another, placing service books for the choir, checking the lectern, fussing with the altar, collecting regalia and lighting symbolically one candle on each side of the stone table.

There was the organist. A few notes came. Yes, his organ still worked. He disappeared. Now the bell started to ring, summoning the late. What sweet sound as its regulated pace seemed to get faster and faster.

There was a shuffling with stamping and clattering behind. Larry, remembering his childhood, felt it wrong to be curious to turn and stare in God's house. Always, one had to look ahead. Today was different, however. He felt close to God through his own choosing and turned to confirm, looking over the heads of the pale and golden faces, some bent, others awaiting commencement, some with scarves, some hatted and veiled, all serene. Yes, the adult choir was taking its place in the upstairs gallery. Not for them the cassocks and cottas, for they were the unseen.

The bell stopped, an outbreak of expectant coughing waved around the assembled and the organist reappeared to fill and transform this upturned ship into a sanctuary of beautiful sound.

As the two vestry doors were creaked open, the one banging with an audible 'shhh!' from a petulant verger, Larry's gaze took him to the crucifixion scene set high above the choir steps, the sculptured characters pillared onto the great ornate and colourful beam. There, central, quite small, depicted in all the intricate detail of his agony, was the Christ on his decorative and carved cross, with his mother peering up on one side and his favourite disciple on the other.

Larry did not see the Vicar's procession with brass-encrusted crucifer, boat boy, thurifer and accolytes large and small leading Father Peters, his cope held out like a bird's wings, his biretta placed tilted on his greying hair. Nor did he see the red-cassocked choirboys pass down the central aisle, followed by the senior men in black, some boasting their own laced cottas, others their surplices with badges of blue material.

While the congregation stood for the entry hymn, Larry dropped to his knees and prayed.

The Creed completed, Father Peters had taken to the pulpit. There had been much incense-swinging and blessing, first of the sacred ministers then of the congregation so that now, as he sought to bless the words of his lips and dedicate them to the Holy Spirit with the sign of the Christian faith, the sunlight broke through. As the clouds parted outside the rays from the upper eastern-facing windows penetrated and accentuated the smoke.

Father Peters had taken as his theme, and introduced it with a number of relevant texts, the need to turn the other cheek and to forgive one's neighbour as many times as it takes.

The congregation was attentive, for the priest was a renowned speaker and usually tempered his words with the slightest of humorous references, partly to keep their interest, but also because he believed the world was a place to be enjoyed, and that false sobriety, for appearances' sake, was just so much hypocrisy.

There was a deadly hush when he asked rhetorically;

"Who is my neighbour? Who is this man or this woman to whom I must turn my cheek?"

He paused for effect. Now, he was about to depart momentarily from customary script. They were there all right, in the very back pew looking their usual bored disinterested selves.

"Some of you will say that I must now tell the story of the Good Samaritan, is that not so?" He waited, his question was not rhetorical now, his congregation was an audience. "Well I ask you, is that what you expect? Come on, answer

277

me, I am your priest, I am asking you a question. Do you want the story of the Good Samaritan?" There was a slight rustle in his audience. One or two looked one to another and there was a fidgeting and whispering. Time to turn them back into a congregation.

"Well, my children, you will be disappointed, for I am not going to tell you the story you all know so well! Ha!" He eyed them now, all faces turned to him, fixed, waiting his teaching whichever way he turned. Even the two Germans were now looking up.

"How can I tell you the story of the Good Samaritan? What relevance has it to us today, eh? It is not something that would happen here in this island, is it? There are none here who would do us harm. We have no enemies, no one who would knock us down, take what little we have and leave us for dead, have we?"

The intense interest of the congregation, now hungry for more, wondering where this strange dissertation was leading them, was now shared by the two enemy at the back. They both looked at each other, then turned their attention back to the priest. These words were not the expected priestly platitudes. What had happened?

"How could anyone expect to be unfairly or cruelly treated without the perpetrators of such a crime being deterred by the forces of good, or at least captured and punished for their misdeads, in our island today? Have we not got our rights and freedoms guaranteed for us now by our friends in authority?"

Thomas paused, He stood back to see what effect he was having. One or two of his flock were looking at each other in disbelief. Some grinned at the irony, quite a few shook their heads, while others looked shocked or embarrassed, but all showed reaction. Not least the two at the back who began to confer heatedly.

"Not one of you knows of a person robbed since our dear Germans came, no one has been beaten or hurt or wrongfully imprisoned. No one has gone short of supplies or hungry. Everywhere around us we see peace, enemy loving so called enemy. All turning the other cheek. We are all brothers, our German guests love us dearly, they have our best interests at heart with their new laws, and their information-gathering.

They are teaching us the evil of our ways, they tell us how wrong we have beens to have been to selfishly interested in democracy all these years. They are replacing all that for us. Praise be to our saviours!"

There was now a general muttering in the congregation. What did Father Peter mean? Was he really extolling the virtues of the occupying forces? Or was he just being droll? So convincing were his words that families seemed divided, unsure what was meant. People began muttering in groups, not least the two plain-clothed Reich's men.

Never before had Father Peters heard such a prolonged mutter during one of his sermons. Good!

"Soon, my children, you will no longer need to come to Church to be reminded to love your enemy as yourself, for soon we will have no enemies. All will go to the aid of the sick or the injured. They will be queuing up to help. No one will pass by on the other side or be afraid to do more than just look. If you doubt my words then only look ahead to the words of . . ."

Here it came. Yes the congregation was settling once more, they looked more relaxed now, more glazed by contrast with their recent enlivenment. Even the two Germans had ceased fussing, the temporary aberration must be finished. True they would have to report the strangeness of the sermon but there was nothing too subversive now, as they had at one stage feared.

". . . the mighty, the most glorious, the leader, the teacher of men . . ."

Dare he? Could he go through with it now? Could he shatter all their tranquillity and even their lives? He would definitely put a certain seal on his own fate.

". . . the honoured and revered and wonderful, who is the answer to all our life's problems . . ."

Now to pull the pin, now to explode the apathy.

"Mighty Adolf Hitler! He is our saviour, is he not?"

The silence was acute, the congregation frozen in spell.

"Yes, my children, when I am gone; for soon they will take me away. They will take me to one of their colleges of education in France or even to this heaven on earth, Germany, where I will be purged of my evil ways. Remember then my words. Do not lose heart, do not worry for me, do not pray.

You will have no need of me for you will have your new friends. Yes, my dear congregation, do not worry about earthly things but follow the holy words of wisdom . . ."

Now the shocked spell had ended, faces turned to faces and a muttering of anxiety broke out. Movement became increased. Some stood up but were persuaded by their families to sit once more. One of the flock even tried to interject;

"But father . . .?" His bleating was drowned by the mumble and the uncomfortable fidgeting. Thomas watched his family and wondered if it had been right so to disavow them. He felt what all parents feel upon forcing their offspring from the nest, the better to survive on their own. He took on all their suffering and shock, doubt and uncertainties. Was he doing the right thing?

"Consider the lilies of the field . . ."

One of the Germans stood up for a second time, his comrade trying to dissuade him from his declared course.

"They toil not, neither do they spin . . ."

A few of the congregation seemed to be preparing to leave, fidgeting with their books while edging to the ends of their pew.

"Yet I tell you, Solomon in all his glory was not arrayed as one of these . . ."

Now a handful stood, ready to lead a self-conscious but panicked exit.

"Please do not leave. Do not leave now," said Thomas, addressing the deserters. "You will come to no harm if you stay till the end to hear my words. You are not in danger, it is only I. They cannot tell your thoughts, they have not yet found a way to punish thoughts. They will, given time . . ."

There was a wry laugh from the midst of the gathering. Frances blushed as she poked Larry in the ribs, in response to her embarrassment.

"Stay, my children. This is not France, there are no machine guns outside, trained on the doors. They are not about to fire the building. Look, they are still here. No one has passed the word to our beloved occupiers yet." Father Peters pointed to the two intruders at the back and the congregation as a whole looked round to turn their eyes on them, focussing their hate and fear.

One got up and stumbled his departure.

The murmur rose. Some of the congregation began to follow. The other German stayed glowering back until the remaining heads turned to the priest once more.

"You must choose, my children. For you, times will be hard, but remember; your bodies may be imprisoned and you may be deprived of the necessities of life, but your loving Father in heaven will protect your minds and souls. No one can imprison your thoughts.

"The choice is yours. You can choose the modern saviour of this strife-torn world. You can choose the one who rids us of the sick and the handicapped and the mentally ill by taking them from us to kill them, or you can choose the Almighty God, The Father of all creation, who has seen such times come and go and are to him as the winking of an eye in the history of mankind.

"If you remain for the Mass you will have made your choice. God will take care of you.

"In the name of the Father, Son and Holy Ghost, Amen!"

*　　*　　*

As the priestly cortège left, the congregation bowing, Mass completed and with deeper significance to both priest and congregation, the choir singing its way to the rear vestry, with the devout sinking to their knees for parting prayers and the gathering of books, gloves and hats, Father Peters wondered what would await him at the Church door.

He felt strength and support in here with his flock, but how would he be, as first to the door to say farewell and enter into the usual after-service intercourse, when there alone? What would greet him in the outside world? How soon would it be before they came for him? Would it be in full view of his congregation? Could he face the martyrdom? Was he seeking it?

No, they would probably come secretly when all had left. He would be taken away and none would know until his absence was noted, first by the sick who would not be visited, and then by those who called with their problems, to find him not there. It would not be noticed until Evensong. Even then, they would probably not take him until darkness fell, so that his absence would not be noticed until the sparse early-morning Communion and then, only by a few of the parish, who were probably not aware anyway that he had even put himself in such danger today.

Perhaps there would be some who would pray for him nonetheless? He valued that prospect.

There were no machine guns at the door, no S.S., rifles trained on all the windows, no soldiers preparing to fire incendiaries at the roof, not a German in sight. Even the last remaining Nazi watcher brushed past Father Peters before the babble of those departing funnelled through the door.

No, the sun was shining again, the air was hot and humid, no wind now. Wisps of vapour rose from the last damp patches of the macadamed road, the birds sang, all was fresh and clean. Cyclists pedalled past. It was as if all his projections had been an intense dream, in which we had troubled out and sorted his own conscience, to wake at peace with his surroundings. It felt like a day for the beach. He should be taking his wife and boys after dinner.

It seemed all wished to speak with him as they left, some lingering and gossiping in groups, waiting their chance, others lucky enough to grasp the outstretched hand, holding onto it, to ensure their audience. No fleeting hand-slips today, no called goodbyes to those slipping past. The gathering did not seem to wish to run away.

Some used the ritualistic polite niceties and thanked the priest as they always did. Some were jocular, saying how Father had certainly given the Jerries something to think about. Others were puzzled, wondering exactly what the vicar had meant and, did they really have to choose between the Church and the Nazi State. Some were confused, not seeing that there was a choice, that the State could not impinge on their religion, could it?

There were a few who expressed anxiety that the priest was asking for trouble talking that way, trouble for himself and adversity for the whole parish.

Others asked the Father what was going to happen to him and when they would lose him and what would be their fate as a Church then?

Some were concerned for Thomas Peters' well-being, asking how they could help. Just a few; but there were some.

"Pray for me," he told them, "not for me the man, but pray for me, your priest."

"Hello, Mrs. Collins," he said, holding out his large hand and clasping her chill smooth fingers. "It's so good to know you were here this morning."

He let go of Frances, turning his attention to Larry:

"And especially you, stranger," the twinkle in his eye belying any displeasure.

"Thank you," answered Larry, uncharacteristically subdued.

"And what did you think of my sermon, eh?" he asked, squeezing Larry's elbow. "Did it strike a chord?"

"You know it did, vicar. I just hope . . ."

"Now, now!" admonished the priest, with mock severity. "There's nothing to be gained by going into all that, is there? We're both rather in the same boat, I think?"

"Yes," Larry sighed. "I'll be glad to get it all over with and that's for sure."

"Time will tell, time will tell," said the priest, sharing the empathy of his fellow man.

*   *   *

As John would have expected, Franz was punctual to the minute. This had not, however, prevented him from conjecturing myriad reasons why his friend might not come.

All the more reason, when he appeared, walking up the street with beaming smile, for John to run to his enemy, greeting him as though they had not met for ages.

They had enjoyed the private part of the morning. Time had not dragged and the dreaded hiatuses of having to entertain with ostensibly boring things, fell from thought.

It had been a case of Franz helping John to prepare the vegetables, playing the gramophone, admiring the full view of the harbour and Castle Cornet with all the islands, as the early drab greyness lifted to show all extra clear after the night purging of the air.

They had explored John's flat, even looking into Frances' and Larry's room, but mainly in John's own room which was large, always cool and on the floor below.

Franz had been excited when John had pulled countless

boxes from his cupboards, excited where John had feared he would have shown disdain. Not so, Franz did not effect bravado or assume false maturity with his friend. No, they had both become little boys as John had brought out saved childhood treasure after treasure.

There were the stone building blocks, the clockwork Hornby, all those lead farm animals and, most irrelevant, lead soldiers some with heads held in place by matches some with arms or legs so metal-fatigued that John no longer dared bend them back into position for fear of amputations. Soldiers which were in the dress uniform of the guards at Buckingham Palace.

Marbles had been rolled across the floor, snakes and ladders had been entered into and John had tried to get Franz interested in Ludo. But no, by far the greatest delight had been the collection of Dinky cars. Franz had zoomed around the room exaggerating the sounds appropriate to each model. He had adapted flying cars, taxis, lorries, vans and buses through space to land on a dressing table here, a window-sill there, down on to the bare varnished boards where the rugs did not reach, up on to John's bed to traverse the rough terrain. It had been of no use John trying conversation, for little Franz had been lost in play.

"John, could we not go outside with these?" Franz had asked.

"Where do you mean?" had been John's reply, fearing the humorous yet embarrassing prospect of the two of them, accompanied by Franz's sound effects, as they made their way down the public street.

"Oh, you have a garden, yes? Can we take these cars and make some roadways?"

That had been such a good idea! John had felt a thrill that here was a kindred spirit who would enjoy such erudite activities.

And so, despite the nagging worry that old Gaudion would view them — he probably knew of Franz's visit anyway — they went to the high-walled garden, Gaudion's private nature reserve for snails.

As always, the walls had been clustered with snails, snails upon snails. All the low dividing walls and paths, which had once divided cultivation from carefully-tended soil, had snails and silver trails. Dandelions and long grass grew in profusion, forming jungles in which were to be found the graveyards of the thousands of discarded shells.

"Wonderful!" Franz had exclaimed. "We can cut some roads through that patch and we can make some ramps here, see?" He had run about excitedly picking up bits of broken slate and flat pebbles to use as the tools of engineering.

"Look," John had ordered as he had taken Franz to part of his territory, "see?" He had stood back with pride, knowing how Franz would appreciate such things.

"That is absolutely very good, John," Franz had uttered in amazement, as he had viewed a network of Dinky car roads John had made only months before. There were cuttings and embankments, stone bases with carefully sieved earth turned into mud and laid as macadam surfaces. True, some of the intricate structures had been broken through by weeds like some giant trees, while some roads had been eroded by rain and others badly cracked by summer's heat. There were even aliens in the form of ant colonies unaware of the dangers of being run over. That did not matter, they would both enjoy the renovations and repairs.

"Let's get cracking," John had ordered. 'We'll repair these roads, eh?"

'Oh yes, this is such fun," Franz had replied. "You know, John, I must keep coming here. We can build more roads and your trains yes? And . . ." He had stopped, both had been dulled to the reality, for they had been just dreaming. They had no future about which to dream. There was only today.

*   *   *

Both Larry and Frances walked slowly back to Town. They were in silence but it was not an uncomfortable state for they were in contentment. The wind had dropped and the sun was warm on their Sunday clothes.

Frances was happy that Larry had gone with her to church. She was happy that it had been his wish. She was relieved too, that Bert was not pressing into her thoughts.

Larry had been stirred by the sermon. It was good to know that there were still people about, like Father Peters,

285

with the guts to stand up and say what they thought of the unwelcome occupiers. In some ways, he now felt his burden shared, having spoken to that brave man, a man who, if he had wished, could have kept quiet, done exactly what was expected and led a near normal life until all the hostilities were ended. Yes, Larry was in no doubts now as to the outcome of his trial. He knew his life was about to terminate, at least life as he knew it, but now he accepted this as inevitable. This was where he was different from poor Keith. Larry had been told when his life was to finish and had accepted this, therefore was able to enjoy each day remaining, whereas Keith could not face up to the truth. He clung to the hope that it would not happen.

It was only when they began the steep descent before the prison that Frances' tranquillity began to be evicted by her anxieties, for she had not yet told Larry they had a guest for dinner. She had to let him know and quickly, but it was too difficult to broach the subject, especially when they had both been so relaxed and calm.

Why should she be the one he would associate with his shock and disgust at the discovery? What would happen if she, as now seemed likely, did not mention the matter but just let Larry find out as a matter of course? Whichever way it was, there would be a scene, but maybe not as bad as yesterday's? Perhaps she could sooth Larry a little more quickly today?

So it was an agitated, guilty Frances who preceded her husband up the stairs, calling John's name anxiously. She had not mentioned Franz, hoping to at least act as a physical buffer between the encounter of the two.

"Jo-hon, Jo-hon dear," she coo-eed as she almost ran up the stairs. "We're home, dear. Where are you?"

There was not a stir, only the sound of Larry stomping up from below. John's bedroom door was open. Probably the two were in there? She quickly poked her head in. Oh, what an untidy mess! Well at least they were somewhere.

As she left the jumble of a room and closed the door, Larry had already overtaken her.

"John, John, we're home."

The noise of Gaudion's door was followed by his tendered information.

286

"They're outside, Mrs. Collins. The two boys are playing in my garden."

"Oh thank you, Mr. Gaudion," she replied, her heart thumping, wondering if Larry had heard. As usual the nosy old fellow had missed nothing at all.

Larry did not hear, but went straight into his bedroom to change into more comfortable clothes. He was beginning to feel hungry.

Frances turned and ran down the stairs, entered the cupboard door which led into a flight of stone basement steps, out through the washing-room and into the garden to greet their guest.

There they both were, two little boys lost to the world, shirt-sleeves rolled up with clothes creased and earth-marked.

"Hello love, hello Franz. How are you, dear?"

Both looked up, surprised to hear Frances in their private world. Franz smiled his pleasure, wiping his muddy hands on his trousers, as he prepared to step forward to proffer his handshake while John, less courteous or just more familiar, but most likely too trapped in his absorption, turned his attention back to the viaduct passing through a swampy jungle of last spring's bluebells. His tongue was out in his avid concentration.

"John dear, come on. Have you put the vegetables on? John!"

"Eh?"

"We're back, love. We're back from Church. We're hungry. Have you put the dinner on yet?" she said with great patience as she observed the glazed expression which told her the answer to her futile enquiry.

"No," was John's self-defensive, surly reply, in an attempt to cover his shortcomings. "I didn't know it was so late, did I?"

"It is my fault, Mrs. Collins," attempted Franz, "I made John . . ."

"That's all right," she cut across, smiling. "It won't take long anyway," adding jocularly, in a further attempt to put Franz at his ease, "It won't hurt his father to put things on will it? If he's hungry he'll have it all on the go by the time you two boys have washed your hands and faces and have come on up."

Franz laughed. Yes, he was at ease now. It was good to be called a boy too; it made Mrs. Collins seem more like a real mother than ever. Only Frances felt a temporary flutter of disquiet at the thought of Larry, as yet ignorant of their visitor's presence.

*　　*　　*

Larry, now more comfortable, thought he would follow his nose to the kitchen. No, there were no aromas or steam in there. No Frances either, come to that. Where could she be?

He looked in the sitting room. No sign of life there except a pile of records carelessly left to get broken and one out of its sleeve too. Hadn't he told John about that time and time again?

What was that sound coming from the garden? Voices, laughter. So that's where she was, hanging out clothes, no doubt. He wished she would hurry up and cook some food, as he moved his way towards the window.

He met her as she emerged from the basement, the two friends having stayed down to wash. She had not seen how Larry had observed them from above, or how he had paled and then turned crimson, how his fist had pummelled into his other palm. No, Frances had not witnessed the initial anger, tempered by hurt, but she now knew what fired her husband.

She had heard the clatter, reverberating through the shaky old building, as he had run and clattered down the stairs to find them.

There he was, breathless, still heaving with anger, frustration gripping him, as he had been denied simultaneous contact with all three. And here she stood, fortunately a brake on his rage, a delaying, cooling mechanism.

He stood glowering while his heaving breaths began to subside, his natural colour returning. Frances was still, unbelievably calm, as she let her heart rule her response. She put out her hand to take his wrist. It was to have been a communication which would have said it all. However, he flinched and pulled from her attempt.

"Well?" he growled at last. "Go on then, explain."

Frances was determined not to become defensive, she was

288

going to remain calm. She had definitely lost Larry's heart right now so she must accept that and just try to act as mediator, to help a very awkward hour to birth and on its way out of all their lives.

"I'm not explaining, dear," she said. "It's just a simple fact that John's invited his friend to dinner, that's all."

"That's all?" Larry sounded about to cry out in his inner rage. "That's all is it? His friend is a bloody Jerry. We're all for the chop thanks to their sort and he brings one of them here to eat our food! That's all, you say!"

"Darling . . ." Frances was still calm. She could hear voices from below. The two were about to ascend the steps. ". . . Please, dear, if for nothing else, just for my sake, be civil." Her eyes pleaded. She knew he would weaken, his anger would not stay, for he would be unable to sustain an act of annoyance. She had to help him to such a new course. The voices got louder.

"That's all very well," stated Larry, his voice now more that of a whine than of aggression, "but he is German, you know."

"I know," she replied patiently, this time her hand not spurned, "but he is just a boy, just like our John. You should have seen the two of them just now . . ."

Disregarding her argument he attacked from another direction;

"What about Gaudion?"

"Gaudion? So what? He's done his job, we know that now. It's too late to make matters any worse by Franz being seen here now, isn't it?" she reasoned.

"What about the food then?" The voice was calmer now, it was just saving its pride.

"Food?" she smiled. "I think Franz has brought us a tin of corned beef."

Footsteps were heard behind her.

"Please my love, please, . . ."

He briefly took both her hands in his and gave his answer. Without forethought he lifted her still delicate hands to his lips kissing first one and then the other. Then, without further ado, he about turned and ran on up the stairs, so that the meeting was deferred, as Frances stepped aside to let out her two prisoners.

As they joined her, unaware of the efforts she had made, of the labour pangs which had just been the birth of the new one-hour child, they heard the fast receding steps of Larry, without any concern as to why they were there at all. Only Frances heard the slam of their bedroom door, but, despite the intervening distance it was only the most modest of a slam. The baby had been slapped to make it cry for its first inhalation.

*　　　*　　　*

It was indeed a treat to have corned beef. How Franz had managed to get hold of it Frances did not know. Quickly she directed John to light the gas under the potatoes while she stood the smaller saucepan of carrots in the first to start its warming ready to take over the jet once the boiling potatoes were packed into the hay box to continue to simmer for half an hour. John busied himself laying the table.

Franz looked awkward, as there was nothing for him to do.

"Tell you what, love," she suggested. "You open the corned beef, eh?"

Already she was wondering if she would use just half the tin now and save the rest for later in the week. Tomorrow was Monday wasn't it? Maybe she could barter the other half for some fish in the market? Wouldn't that look rather rude though? Wouldn't Franz who, as a German must surely eat really well, or better than the civilians at least, be offended if they were so frugal? But what would Larry say? He might come out with something awfully embarrassing like, 'What's all this extra for? Why can't we just go on as we'd usually behave?' She imagined his response to the fact that Franz had been the provider of the luxury meat would be to say that the visitor didn't have to stay, if he didn't like it and besides he'd had a share of their vegetables and plums, hadn't he? Larry would not be conscious of the fact that Rita had deliberately slipped two extra potatoes, a carrot and three more early plums into Frances's bag just before she had left yesterday, for this very purpose.

"Open this tin?" asked Franz.

290

"Yes, love, let me see. It's one of those needing a key isn't it?"

"A key?" queried Franz. "What is this key, please?"

Frances almost snatched the tin from him, observed the tab where the key was to fit but there was no key.

"There," she said, pointing to the tab, John joining them with curiosity,

"You put a key on that and turn it to open the tin."

"Yes, yes, I know now. Yes I know what is this key," he replied delighted that he now understood.

"Well you see to it please, dear, won't you?"

"Yes, but Mrs. Collins . . ." Franz paused. John looked aghast in disbelief. He knew what Franz was about to say, "where is your key?"

"My key?" she asked, shocked. "My key, love? It's not my key, it's yours! Don't tell me you haven't got a key?"

John's fear had been exactly realized. Momentarily he forgot his mouth-watering and just absorbed himself in the utter humour of the situation. Frances, despite her anxiety, found herself joining her son in the hilarity of the ludicrous event, while Franz looked on, a stranger in this house, completely non-plussed.

"No," declared Frances at last, having rummaged right through all her kitchen drawers. "It's no use. We haven't got a key for it. You must have left it when you brought the tin Franz." The vegetables were almost cooked now, carrots beginning to boil and potatoes safely packed in their hay-box. The baby was getting hungry. It needed its first feed.

Larry came into the kitchen, made the briefest of nods towards Franz and grunted, then turned to go out.

It was learning its first words.

"Larry dear," called Frances staying her husband's departure. "Franz here has brought us this corned beef, see?" Larry raised his eyebrows exaggeratedly as she went on. "But he hasn't got a key for it."

"Bloody stupid then, isn't he," muttered Larry. Frances was not really taking notice of Larry's response but John knew it was said in shrouded humour. He also realized that Franz, as a German, despite John's recent attempts at training, would not realize the words were a prelude for jest.

Soon the little one would be smiling.

"Dad! Don't say such things. You know you're pleased."
John looked at Franz reassuringly as he admonished his
father.

The baby smiled.

"Not to worry," reassured Larry, while Frances juggled
with the sash window to allow the maximum current to
clear the vapoured room. "Pliers will see to it."

He left the room, quickly returning with the necessary
tool.

Already the new-born was learning its infant skills.

"Right, now. Stand by, we'll soon see . . ." he began, as
he gripped the tag, pulling slightly as with success they all
heard the anticipated in-sucking of air while each imagined
the aroma which would shortly set their insides all a rumble.

"Bugger!" The tab slipped from his worn pliers.

John laughed. Frances looked shocked but could not
suppress a smile. Franz grinned and Larry looked up with a
broad beam as he went to cuff the visitor mockingly on the
ear. He remembered the days when he had felt for the lad,
as if he were his own, when he was fitting him, all excitement,
for the loan of his bike.

Yes, the little one had uttered its first word!

Franz, suddenly inspired, and now feeling confidently at
home with all the family, quickly called John to him and
half whispered but audible to the parents.

"John! Come quickly downstairs to my jacket. The key
might still be in my pocket I think."

The two escaped and ran off with great sense of fun, as
Larry looked towards Frances, shrugging his shoulders.

"I can manage," he called after them, but it did not
matter, they had gone out from under the parents' feet.

Frances moved towards Larry. Both smiles melted into
one, as he pecked her on the lips.

The new-born child was loved by all the family. It had
its own dear personality.

And so the meal had been a very happy time. Franz had
found the key, rendered obsolete anyway by the time the
two had returned to the kitchen. He had found also, the
eight cigarettes he had brought for John's father and the
tiny bar of used soap for his mother.

The food was good. All the corned beef had been thinly

sliced so that each had received four slices, enough to cover their plates, the potatoes had been well mashed with nutmeg and pepper and creamed by a little saved milk while the carrots sliced thinly had added colour and luxury to their feast. The plums were sweet and yellow being enjoyed uncooked. All had left the table feeling more than full, thanks to Franz and Auntie Rita.

"Is the King drunk?" asked Larry, with a twinkle in his eye, enjoying the puzzled look on their guest's face, as he drew out one of the cigarettes.

"Don't worry," said John. "He's being funny, you know!"

"Oh? " Franz grinned. What strange people the English were! They could even be rude about their King and still call it funny.

"Yes dear, take no notice of him. He's just plain stupid sometimes," intervened Frances, as she collected pudding plates and laid her head on her darling's shoulder.

"I'm not," objected Larry, stealing a kiss.

The baby was certainly affectionate.

Frances explained the tradition of an official function, when smoking was permitted once a loyal toast had been taken.

"Oh yes, I understand," said Franz, "you can say the King is drunk and it is not rude."

"Well yes and no," she replied, but she was not prepared to go into the intricacies. Larry now had her on his knee.

What a strong child!

"You two had better clear off," ordered Larry, "or you'll end up washing up. Why don't you go out and enjoy this lovely afternoon?"

Frances looked at her husband.

Yes, the baby was ready for bed.

*   *   *

Bert was still in bed, the curtains closed. He had stayed awake right through the storm, thinking of what could never be again. It had seemed like hours of flashing and crashing emphasizing the hollow emptiness of creation and the cold vacancy in his bed.

Eventually, as the rumbles and lights had distanced

themselves to settle somewhere to the east of Sark, his misery had subsided into fitful sleep.

Daylight and a cold breeze had woken him at dawn. He had felt momentarily contented before the memories, with reasons and thoughts chasing each other, had crept back into his mind once more.

There had been nothing to get up for, nothing ever again. He had closed the curtains and escaped back to that other world, which for him would have to become the real one, spurning his present nightmare.

And so he slept, each time waking to have his anaesthetic removed but as quickly taken on again as he chose to return to nothingness.

*   *   *

Larry had offered his bike to Franz again. A source of great wonder and amusement to Frances and John who knew what great difficulty he had experienced in getting it back from the Germans. Franz was truly accepted.

The kind offer had been declined, as both friends had felt a walk would be better, for they could talk more easily and could take steps and alleys, lanes and paths less in the Sunday afternoon public eye.

Their walking took them where it willed for they did not really plan a positive course.

Rather, their route was negative. They could not go that way as there was a busy sentry point there. No, not that road, too busy, lots of cyclists and possibly German cars or lorries. This path? Well, what about courting couples? These steps? They lead to the First Beach. Won't there be lots of Guernsey families there on a day like this?

Eventually their tortuous course led them by quiet roads, flights of steps bent between high-walled terraced gardens, narrow streets high up on the cliff, with occasional glimpses of the sea and sand, and paths narrow and almost overgrown by brambles and gorse, to the sea level plateau on the other side of First Beach, which led to one of John's hallowed places from the past, to La Vallette.

Where they joined the road once more, it was quiet, there were no military vehicles, no cyclists and no ambling pedestrians. What civilians there were, and Germans too, were behind them now, on the beach.

It had been rather a torment to John to turn his back on the scene. The tide was half up so that the beach was quite small and consequently crowded. Already the high granite walls of the Esplanade backdrop, shadowed the greater part of the sand and give it a rather chill look. The water was unbelievably blue while the remnant of a chill breeze from last night's storm whipped the edge into pure white billows.

The crowd was almost entirely adult. How strange, in the first place to find this, one of the island's least attractive beaches, so full, and yet more strange still, to witness the dearth of youth.

There were one or two people in the water, while a few carefree souls paddled but, for the most part, people just sat or wandered aimlessly on the damp sand, which had been brought round from other beaches to hide the pebbles, courtesy of the German forces.

The sunny rocks were occupied by sun-tanned young men in bathers, obviously the masters, with the occasional brash and giggly female, most likely a Jerry-bag.

No, John led Franz towards the place further on where, as a boy, he had made his first unaided strokes in water over his height. They were heading for the pools; first the Gents, then the Ladies and then the Children's. John had not ventured this road since the beginning of the Occupation. He had not dared, for he was certain that it was out of bounds to the ordinary population. And to see visitors enjoying what was his by right, not being permitted to join them, would have been more than he could have borne.

Each step flooded him with memories, each picture taken in by his eye evoked deep thoughts and feelings he had taught himself to forget. The roughly-hewn rounded granite sea walls the red brick buttresses, so unusual in the island, the plant-covered granite drop from the plantations above, now overgrown, their gravel paths weed-covered, their shrubs a wilderness, all brought to him hot lazy summer days, homework left undone, meals not returned for, salt-encrusted sun-tans, laughs and shouts of friends, races, throwing in, ice cold water poured on sun-baked backs, seaweed cracking hard at pool edges, waiting for the ointment of high tide, eyes sore from underwater gliding over mountain ranges and fantastic forests.

Most of all, his childhood friends stared out of the stone and rocks at him and their voices drowned him in their babble. Where were they all now? Did he ever think of them? Why had he stopped thinking of them all, once Franz had become his friend? Did it make him a traitor, a quisling, a collaborator or a Jerry-bag? What would he tell them all after the war? Would they understand?

'Hello Vernon, how did you get on in England, eh?'

'Me? Oh, I stayed here and faced the Germans me!'

'What's happened to Cooky?'

'Cooky got killed fighting the bastards!'

'And Johny?'

'They took him prisoner. No one knows what happened to him.'

'What about you, John? Did you resist, did you give those Jerries a rough time?'

'Me? Oh, I learned to hate them.'

'How many telephone wires did you cut at night? How many road signs did you paint over?'

'Oh, that's stupid. All it caused was reprisals.'

'Reprisals? What did they do for those?'

'Well they took our wirelesses for a start and sometimes made our fathers stand sentry duty at night.'

'Big deal! Do you know what they did to prisoners who gave obstruction?'

'No, tell me.'

'No you couldn't take it, you like the Jerries too much!'

'That's not true!'

'Where's Brian?'

'He's around but he doesn't want to see you!'

'Why so?'

'He won't meet any one. He got shot down fighting the buggers. His face is like a melted blancmange he's so badly burned.'

'Beryl? How did she get on? I know she was going to be a nun like Jane . .'

'She's O.K. now. She went to France you know. The S.S. raped her!'

'Who's this, John? Who's your friend?'

'Oh yes . . ., I'll introduce you. This is my friend Franz. Franz, meet Vernon, we call him the Colonel, and Cooky, Terry to you. This is Egg Head, Allan really and this hyer's Johnny. Here's Brian, and David. Oh yes, and of course you'll want to know who these birds are. Well this is Jane, this one Joan, here's Beryl and this one is June, she's the shy one . . .'

'Wait a minute. Did you say Franz?'

'Eh?'

'Is your mate called Franz? That's a queer name, eh?'

'Why so?'

'Franz, it sounds like Jerry to me, eh, you chaps?'

'Yes, Franz is German, he's my friend . . .'

The bricks bricked up once more, the rocks became rocky, the granite solid and the plantation alive with its over-growth.

"Where are we going, John?" Franz's voice broke in.

"Oh we're nearly there, mon vieux. You'll see," replied John detachedly.

"We won't!" replied Franz, staring at his friend oddly. "Are you in a daydream or something, John? Look here!"

Across the complete width of the road, John having almost walked right into it, during his detached visit with the friends of his past, was a barrier consisting of a wooden frame strung with strands of barbed wire. Within this construction was an unfettered gate of the same construction, large enough to permit the passage of military vehicles. The barrier was untended.

"You were not going through there, surely John?" asked Franz incredulously.

"No," came John's defensive reply, "but I might just do that. It's up to me!"

"You can't, my friend, see here the notice!"

The words were in German but also in the inferior tongue.

"I can't read that! You know that Franz, I can't read bloody German!"

"But it is also here in English. See?" He read out loud the stark ultimatum.

"Restricted area. Passage permitted only for members of the Reich's forces. See, John. You are not allowed?"

"O.K. O.K.!" John was disappointed. Perhaps his friends were right about the Jerries? Maybe those futile gestures at cutting 'phone wires and daubing 'V' signs were to be admired after all?

"Wait, John. See here, there is another notice."

"I don't want to see any other of your damned notices!" replied John. "I'm sick to death of notices, notices, notices!" He turned his back on Franz hoping to get an accolade from the Colonel and all the rest of the gang. No, they had all returned to the past and the future.

Notwithstanding Franz read out loud:

> "Notice to all members of the civilian population
> and forces of the Reich:
> The German Command, with due regard for the
> well being of all its occupied territories,
> and as further proof of its care of all
> those for whom it claims responsibility,
> and in the continued promotion of excellent
> relations with such peoples, does invite the
> civilian population and the military to
> compete in a water gala of excellence, as
> brothers, on the afternoon of Thursday,
> 24th July at La Vallette pool known as the
> 'Ladies Pool'. For full details see La
> Gazette Officielle in your daily newspapers.
>
> Signed
>
> Feldkommandantur"

John was stunned. It could not be true! A gala? An excellent, fun-packed, exciting gala? Just like before the Occupation? Races, diving, clowns, cheering, laughing, swimming? A chance for John to shine again, to be the Boys' Champion that he once was? No, surely it must be a cruel hoax?

He read it for himself while Franz read the German version. They both looked at each other for a long time then suddenly John came to life.

"Yippee!" he yelled, jumping in the air like a young kid and throwing his arms round his friend. "Franz, there's going to be a gala! There's going to be a gala and I'm going to be a champion!"

When the initial euphoria had gone, and John was just plain excited once more, Franz was able to ask:

"John, what is this gala?"

John explained excitedly:

"Oh, I can't wait till tomorrow," he said, "to get hold of the *Press* and find out the details!"

Franz just humoured him and waited for the crumbs of information to be given condescendingly.

"Eh! It's a good job Boys' Club is starting up on Tuesday, eh?" announced John. "We might be able to get up a team from there! I'll bet Father Peters already knows about this. I'll bet that's why he's getting Club going again this week. I bet he's known all along and kept it to himself!"

Franz was bemused by all this sudden enthusiasm. If he was not careful his friend would be asking him to take part next. How could he disillusion him and say that, as an inlander, he could hardly swim, and at that, only breaststroke? How would his friend, who set such obvious store by the sport, take this shortcoming in him?

"You're coming to Club on Tuesday, aren't you, Franz?"

"Yes," Franz was hesitant.

"Well, that's good then, eh?"

"Yes, I think . . ," tried Franz, a little dubious as to where all this elation was leading them.

"Wait a minute," John interrupted. "I reckon your lot will make up some teams, eh? I suppose they've already been training up for ages! Demme that's not fair!" He paused, still grinning excitedly, his breathing harsh and active.

"I bet you already knew about this Franz? Go on, admit it! Tell me!"

"Tell you what?" Franz sounded rather defensive.

"You're already in a team of swimmers preparing for this gala?"

"No, I am not John, I have not even heard of this, what do you say, gala, till now!"

"Well, maybe you can join our Club team?" suggested John. "If you don't hear from your own lot that's the best thing to do, eh?"

"I must think," replied Franz seriously, then attempting to change the subject:

"Can we go now, please? We can't go this way and we came out for a walk, if you remember?"

John remembered.

There was nothing for it but to make for Father Peters' just to check if he had the details of the gala already. How could John be expected to wait for tomorrow's *Press*?

It was strange how, with his sudden thrilling and pacing of excitement, that he could hold only the one thought. Nothing else seemed to matter at this very moment.

For Franz, of course, not in any way imbued with this unimaginable enthusiasm for a sport which at best was arduous, and at worst positively miserable for him, he resented the way it had invaded their privacy to accompany them, uninvited, on their walk. Were they not going to make final plans for this evening? It was all right for John to get so excited. If he did not have adequate plans he could just leave Town House, just as he could, as easily, not even attend. Franz, however, had to live there. He would have to be there tonight after John had left. So to John, excitement about a silly sport was more important than what Franz would have to suffer! What he would have to suffer in order to remain in friendship. Remain in friendship for what, too? To be able to attend that Club. And there what to do? To make plans for this gala thing! It was too bad!

"Why must we go to this priest?" asked Franz in exasperation.

"You know why," mused John, not realizing the anger lodged in his friend's question.

'Oh, for this gala?" The sarcasm could hardly be missed.

"Yes, that's right. What's wrong with that?"

"Nothing." Franz sounded rather petulant.

The unexpected attitude from Franz pricked John momentarily, as he sensed some sort of opposition in his friend.

"Come on then, snap out of it!" he ordered, half gleefully, But with an edge of irritation. "What else is there to do?"

"Well, we are supposed to talk about this evening," started Franz glad of the opportunity to unburden himself. "If you remember it's this evening that will either . . ."

"Yes, yes! O.K.! O.K.!" snapped John. "We've already talked all about this evening. What else is there to be said?

It'll come soon enough. Now stop worrying."

Franz was very dejected. He could not really translate his fears into words, not now, it would just be wasted on his friend, for he would rather not understand. Submissively he walked with John up the endless uphill slopes until they reached the Vicarage.

To John the bounding journey was just energetic minutes, to Franz a painful exhausting boredom, accompanied by anxieties, as a prelude to this evening, this evening to be faced alone. John would probably be there but he would not share in the projected miseries. His loyalties were elsewhere at present. Franz had been sold for a stupid swimming gala and his own people had initiated it!

Such were the fears and miseries in the young Teuton, who was already bearing them alone, that, as they reached the Vicarage, he baulked and, even though he knew trying to break into John's private joy would only, and could only, lead to an unhappy scene, he had to try once more to be the master of John's attention.

"John, please. It is getting late now. Soon I must return to Town House."

"So?"

What was Franz trying to say now?

"Well, John," the voice was almost pleading, "we must talk, please. I am very frightened!"

"You what?" John tried to sound incredulous but it was a half-hearted act for he knew his brother too well now, not to understand the signs of tension and near hysteria. Fleetingly he was spirited from the races at La Valette to that first meeting in the entrance hall at La Porte.

"You mean about this evening?" the voice was more kind now.

"Yes, John. What will we do?" Franz's face creased and seemed too grey to be healthy.

For John the pool emptied, to be replaced by that noisy smoke-filled room.

"O.K., Franz. I understand. I promise we'll talk as we walk back. I'm sorry." He smiled unconvincingly. "I mean it. Look, we'll only be a couple of minutes in here and then we'll walk back a quiet way. Maybe through Candie Gardens. You remember?"

Franz nodded.

The knock on Father Peters' door was quickly answered. The priest was still in his black cassock. He looked relieved when he saw it was John, a little startled at the German uniform, but quickly realized who the stranger must be.

"Come in quickly," he ordered, leading the way into his study, John behind, leaving Franz to close the heavy door and follow down the mosaic-tiled hall.

* * *

"This is a surprise," mused Father Peters in an attempt to appear light-hearted as he relaxed into his chair. "All the Collins' in one day, must be quite a record." He signalled the two guests to take a seat.

The priest was wondering what the purpose of the visit was. He suspected more trouble, as John had his young German friend. He eyed the two, John all gleeful and active, right on the edge of his chair, as if he were about to jump up at any moment, the other by contrast, with miserable aspect, agitated, paying too great attention to the hat he twisted between his hands.

Thomas Peters could certainly do without the worries of others right now. He wondered how he might open the conversation the better to lead it to a quick conclusion. He had yet to prepare himself for Evensong which might, after all, be his last official function.

He need not have bothered, for John could contain himself no longer and, as a little boy full of expectation, blurted out;

"Father, have you heard about the gala? Yes, you must have."

"Gala?" The priest looked non-plussed. "What gala?"

"You know, at the Ladies' pool. You know, where they always are?"

Had the boy taken leave of his senses? Maybe all the recent strain had affected him?

"Excuse me, John," he asked, "let me get this quite right in my mind. Did you say gala? Do you mean swimming at the pools?" His voice sounded deliberate and patient in the extreme.

"Yes, that's it. So you do know!" John was up.

302

"Know what ?"

"The Germans are giving us a gala!"

"Nonsense!" was the priest's instant reply. "That lot don't give anything!" He suddenly realized the vehemence of his own voice and remembered Franz. He looked his way ready to show some sign of apology but that young man, who looked so pale and ill, did not seem to be paying any attention. He was more anxiously concerned with the clock on the mantelpiece.

John excitedly went on to explain what he and Franz had learned earlier that afternoon. The priest was certainly surprised but, even so John cajoled him that he had probably known all along and that the knowledge had been one of his prime reasons for recommencing Boy's Club next Tuesday.

At the mention of Boys' Club, quite forgotten by this man who felt he had no rights to share in any plans for the future, but nevertheless conscience-pricked by his inactivity in the venture, Father Peters pulled himself together. No, he had not heard anything about the forthcoming event but, like John, would wait to read details in tomorrow's newspaper.

He wondered if there really was any need to begin the club this week, after all. He had to confess that he had not been particularly organized about contacting possible leaders or planning a programme. John had been shocked at this and felt rather let down. Father Peters could sense the deep disappointment, beginning to wonder if the boy was being unreasonable. Hadn't he, as priest, suffered enough these past few days? Hadn't all the burdens he had been carrying for others infected him, and were now gathering in a great boil of evil pus, about to break out and destroy him? Why should the boy not realize this and indulge the adult a little? Obviously the young lad, so typically selfish at that age, was not aware of any of this. He could not know of the brave stand the priest had made against tyranny only that morning. So his parishioners had not discussed his earth-moving sermon at their dinner tables. So much so for bravery!

But then this was his job, was it not? This was his calling. He had known the consequences of his actions. This was the way he had wanted it to be. He was, it seemed, to be a subconscious martyr. So why take it out on the youngster? It was, after all, a treat to see a local showing anything greater than apathy, let alone one with apparent enthusiasm and drive. Just as Thomas would like to imagine his own sons in England.

The priest confessed his shortcomings, quickly trying to make amends with assurances, enlisting John's help in contacting the necessary people tomorrow. The two reassured each other that, even without detailed plans, the Club would thrive. There were still the table-tennis tables and billiard tables plus the gym with all its equipment. Yes, of course the priest was keen to get a team to enter into the gala, no matter how small. He wished to please young John to compensate for his temporary bout of disinterest. He even controlled his raised eyebrows at the concept of Franz coming along to the re-opening night, German uniform and all. They would just cross that bridge when they came to it.

At the mention of Franz, the two deliberators looked his way. He had been totally ignored for some time and was now glad of this key to loose him from the grip of anxiety.

Franz inclined his head towards the Vicarage clock to signify to John that they really must leave now, it was getting quite late.

John, unwittingly chose not to respond to this gentle and plausible invitation to leave. Was it the stubborn streak in him, which drove him to contrariness for the sake of it?

Franz got up. He had to stop a further long session of their discussing the unimportant.

"John, please . . .," Again he looked at the clock. Father Peters too, was concerned at the hour and was pleased to be able to say;

"I think your friend is anxious to leave?"

Franz nodded, grateful to the priest, but John would not take this.

"It's all right, Father. Don't be such a worry, Franz. It will only take ten minutes to get back to your place." The words were almost angry and the priest felt embarrassed for the uniformed creature even though he was only German. "But John," began Franz in desperation, "We must talk, you know that!"

"Oh that!" said John in irritation. "I don't see why it's necessary really, we've said all there is to be said."

"That's not true, John. You know it's not! It might be all right for you but for me it is so terrible!"

Franz was on the point of hysteria again, as he began to pace Father Peters' study, looking to the man for support.

"That's it, try to make me feel guilty!" shouted John. "Make it seem like all my fault!"

Franz's head dropped to hide his shame, he did not wish the two to see that he had been reduced to tears by the cutting tenor of the remarks.

John, feeling very bad, and knowing that he was in the wrong, stood studiously erect with his back to the other two.

"What is all this?" asked the priest in stern voice, edged with concern.

"We have a problem," said John briefly. "We've got a very bad problem and there is no way out of it."

Franz looked up despairingly. "It is so bad, minister, and we do not know what to do, and John won't even talk about it. What will happen . . . ?" He became racked with sobs so that John turned towards him once more and Father Peters became the Good Samaritan he had earlier declared not to be.

"I think we had all three better sit down and talk about it here, don't you?"

The two had assented gladly.

*   *   *

With little time to spare for Franz to be in Town House on time, and for John to be in time for tea, and Father Peters for Church, the two youngsters rushed from the Vicarage making their way via Les Rocquettes and La Gibauderie so as to be less in the public eye. There was nothing more to say. They both felt more calm about the prospect of this evening now, having poured it all out on the priest's willing patience. They knew now that events would be out of their control but, if they armed themselves with stern resolve, the eventual outcome of this conveyor belt away from life and freedom, would be a smoother journey, if nothing else.

The very fact that Father Peters had been so supportive of their efforts and their fears, and had not stepped back in horror, in the presence of one who had been defiled, had helped them both greatly.

They had even knelt, unselfconsciously, welcomingly really, in prayer, before he had sped them from his door with his blessing.

Father Peters had made light of the predicament and had gone along with the idea that they must stay by each other all evening and not accept alcohol. He had also agreed with Franz that if things got difficult then John, as a civilian, should leave. And he had encouraged Franz and John in the belief that if they parted company early this evening then Franz would still be welcome to escape on Tuesday and join them at Club. Even if that failed, there would be the gala where Franz's presence at the same time as John's could be legitimate.

Because the priest had so freely assented to all these plans, without apparent recognition of any great dangers he envisaged the two being subjected to, did not mean that he was not concerned. His sense of concern and horror was very great but he had hidden it, taking on this extra anxiety, rather than load the two with any more fears about an eventuality which, it seemed, had to be accepted, for it was outside their control.

What would the new Saviour of the world do about such occurences as this?

*   *   *

Chapter Fourteen

There it was again. That voice. Whose was it? John had almost forgotten where he was, or what he was doing, or even why. Did he like it here? Was it right to be here? It seemed quite good.

Was that voice, out there in the dark, the one he had been looking for? In the dark? When had he been in the dark? The dark? No that was not good! Why? What was wrong with the dark? Where had he been in the dark recently that was not good?

Recently? Perhaps? He had been in the dark but it was not this dark. Which dark had it been? It had been a horrible dark, frightening. He had been full of fear, but why? What was fear? He could not conceive fear now. How could he know what fear was, if he could not remember its grip?

The voice. That was it. He had heard a voice. Whose voice? Had he not just recently heard a voice? Was there someone here? Was it the same voice? Was it the person he was looking for? Was he really looking for someone, or should he be hiding? Should he be doing either? Well yes, everyone had either to do a thing or not do a thing hadn't he, or else that thing would not be there in the first place? What did it matter anyway? Nothing was real unless John chose to acknowledge it, or to do it, or not to do it.

Why then, was he in darkness? Darkness had upset him, he had not enjoyed that. Why now be in darkness, if it was not right? If he did not want darkness, then he would not have it, if he did not have it then it would no longer be there to dog him.

John opened his eyes. It was very bright. He had created someone. A person stood there with eyes fixed on his. He did not like it, it made him uneasy, he felt himself drained into that other person's soul. Who was it? He created the dark again. No, that was not good either. Just good to know he could retreat to it if he so wished to.

He opened his eyes.

"Franz," he whispered. Franz looked puzzled. He did not like his look. He closed his eyes again, retreating to his dark haven.

*   *   *

It was a very nervous John who walked up to the door of Town House. He was exactly on time, exactly as Franz had entreated him. It was rather important, in their plan, that they should be together right from the start.

As he walked up the steps, noting rather ominously that he was not challenged by the duty sentry, a sure sign that it was general knowledge he was expected, his stomach felt heavy, as if he had a surfeit of food and could never face eating again. Yet, it was empty and rumbling its emptiness.

He was concerned that he had crept out of his house not even saying where he was going, or even that he was going out. A grown boy could expect to go out without having to tell his parents, surely? But to go out stealthily, in order to avoid a confrontation, that was taking things too far!

So, part of his burden was that he knew his absence must have been discovered by now and that anxiety at home must be brewing. Also he felt very bad at his deceit and cowardice. Yet it had all been part of the sealed plan, it was all a necessary part of the pain that had to be endured in order to complete that plan. It was out of his hands. He had felt self-conscious too, as never before, making for that German place and he had imagined that more local eyes than could possibly have been out at this hour, had been boring into the back of his traitorous neck.

Not only did he bear the guilt and the embarrassment, but he had neglected to eat all his tea at home, sparse as it was, effecting by slowness to eat a lot while deliberately abstaining. Partly he reasoned that it was immoral to eat Mum and Dad's rations when he was soon to be filled with the enemy's plenty, and partly because, somewhere in the reaches of his education he felt he had heard that if ate while consuming alcohol, the effects would be lessened. Not that he intended any such inebriating beverage but then, he could not tell. It was best to prepare for all eventualities. Besides, if he ate a little at the tense Relaxation, it might be more likely to go unnoticed that he was declining drink. The secret, they had decided, was to keep a glass nearly full at hand all evening and if necessary, from time to time, surreptitiously to discard the liquid whenever opportunity presented itself.

He was greeted as he entered the door, although greet was hardly an appropriate description for the way he was received by his friend. Morten came down the stairs, followed close behind, although reluctantly, by Franz.

Morten's step was heavy as if he were exhausted at the end of a heavy duty. His leaden features formed into that smile which both John and Franz had learned to hate.

Franz, cognizant of John's presence, could not bring himself even to smile as, with what appeared some difficulty he took his downward steps, his face ashen, like one in a shocked trance. The look said it all. John knew then.

John wanted to go to Franz, to take him away and talk to him, to let his friend share his undoubted traumas with him, but Morten was there to see that such liaison did not take place.

Why had this John come after all? Why could he have not let the arrangement drop and let down his friend for once? Far better that he had not come, causing Franz only worry as to what reason this absence could be ascribed. Now, Franz would have, not only anxiety about his friend, but his friend's well-being, or lack of it, on his conscience. But, as with what had so recently been forced upon him, it was all completely outside his control. How could he be expected to take on the cares of the world when he had such problems of his own?

There was so much Franz needed to warn John as his erstwhile friend was bustled ahead into the Relaxation room, by a brusque and business-like Morten with affection and hospitality.

It seemed unlikely that they would have opportunity to talk alone, or even with just disinterested witnesses. No, Franz felt sure of that, just as sure in fact that if the case were to be reversed, and they were permitted unwitnessed words, that he would use John first to pour out all his personal sufferings. He knew he had to warn John, yet he was convinced that first he would indulge in his own abject misery. He just had to confide in someone in order to remove some of the layers of filth which seemed to attach to every part of his being. Besides, there was the pain. It seered across his buttocks where strap after strap had left their heavy wale.

The Relaxation room was much quieter and less smoke-filled than John had remembered on his last fleeting visit, but of course it was still daylight whereas last time it had been much later. He almost stumbled down the steps ahead of the Patrol Leader, aided by his convivial push. At the bottom step he looked round to seek the reassurance that his friend was still present. Yes, he was still behind Morten, but he had averted his eyes.

What now? Was it straight to comfortable settees to sit and be pampered with unsolicited alcohol? How soon before he and Franz would have to ward off the anticipated straying hands? Franz did not seem too perturbed. He looked almost not of this world, did he not? What had happened to him? John wished they could talk. Had it happened again, that evil thing? That was quick. Was the Patrol Leader unable to leave it alone for even a short time? John felt sick and yet it was Franz who had obviously suffered so. Just look at his face! It was as if he had already accepted that he was a dead person. Maybe he had already reached his hell?

John held back and, as skilfully as a footballer, deflected the Patrol Leader momentarily, just about reaching his friend's side, before Morten once more carefully manoeuvred his charge away.

It would have helped if Franz had shown some response, if he had stepped towards his friend or just shown a flicker of recognition or understanding of what John was trying to engineer. Instead, apart from a frightened upward look and a quick turning of his eyes, there was no response at all from the young German. As Morten firmly pulled John towards the far end of the room, the youth noticed the salt marks and black smears of unwashed tears on Franz's face, together with a lip, swollen where the other had bitten into

310

it in his agony and terror. Why was his friend walking so jerkily and stiffly as if the very contact of his uniform caused him discomfort or even pain?

As John was ushered, so did Hüffmeier raise himself from his shaded corner, to step towards the party with a look which might have been mistaken for the glee of welcoming hospitality.

Franz helplessly trailing behind, wanted to scream out now to make up for his muffled yells so recently as he had been gagged and held down in Morten's room. He had not seen Hüffmeir's smile at that time of misery but had been compelled to listen to his cruel laughter as he and Morten had indulged in the degrading beating which they had administered as a prelude to their other forced evil practices. Franz saw this smile as the visual sign of the aural intrusions.

How could he warn John? When would he have the chance to tell of the miserable plans he had been compelled to listen to? What opportunity to tell John of Hüffmeier's personal evil intentions towards him? How could a person, in just a few stolen words, tell convincingly enough to give the receiver sufficient courage to up and leave before the evil came to fruition? How could John, a free civilian, protected by laws, greater protection against such things than he as a member of the conquering race could expect, be expected to understand or even believe what Franz had to warn him?

Would John just laugh off as incredible that both Morten and Hüffmeier planned to aid his rapid drunkenness so that he could be spirited away unconcious at a point in the evening when nothing would be thought of it other than that the youngster had been too inexperienced, or too greedy of the free repast, to stay sober.

And what would be his attitude to the concept that while unconscious they intended to misuse him in turns, while forcing Franz to watch?

How could he be convinced that Franz was to be forced foully to abuse his best friend too? It was all too ridiculous to believe that John would listen to such things, even if there were to be opportunity to tell them. Yet Franz had to try, if only that John might remember his friend had warned him, when he awoke to reality, stinking inside and out in his wretched body, infected with lost innocence and tainted by evil. Would John not then surely hate his friend for being the German that he was? Who could love an enemy who emanates from a race that can evolve such perversion?

"Good, you see he did come!" grinned Hüffmeier, addressing Morten. "So we'll not have to. . .," he winked, "after all."

Morten nodded with sobriety, obviously wishing for a change of subject at this moment.

"Not that yours looks too bright," he added, to Morten's further chagrin. "I hope you won't wish to have a share of mine."

"Just shut up!" Morten continued in German. "This . . ." indicating John with the merest inflection of his glance, ". . . may not speak German, but baby boy here will soon tell him."

"What, my little Franz? Tell? Not so!" effected Hüffmeier, with mock patronage, as he stepped towards the terrified youth. "You do not pass on tales to the enemy do you, my sweet one?" His voice was now loaded and venomous, the last words almost sliding like snakes from his lips.

Franz's response was to step a little closer to John.

"Enough," interrupted Morten, in English. "We are ignoring our guest. Come Franz, we will sit. David, bring John with you."

No opportunity to speak, yet it had begun.

'This must be the time for our plan?' thought John, as the four of them were wedged into a large sofa to relax within the sight of the appetizingly displayed buffet. What great misfortune that he could not even sit next to his friend but found him separated by the two adults. Maybe it would have been futile to be next to Franz anyway? He certainly did not look too communicative. Even Morten had given up trying to engage him in conversation and now, much to the other's irritation, but to John's relief, kept trying to engage Hüffmeier instead. John was glad that he and Franz at least had this temporary respite. Also John did not have to suffer their childish talk, which was conducted in the master tongue.

When Morten attracted the attention of one of the orderlies, Franz suddenly came to life. The subject matter was lost on John but Franz had definitely become quite heated so that Morten too, allowed his voice to rise.

Hüffmeier, perhaps feeling that he had been ignoring his guest, and obviously quite unaware of the great pleasure such an omission caused him, turned to John quizzically asking;

"You too are not against drinking, are you, my little Englishman?"

Both Morten and Franz stopped their altercation at this, as all three awaited John's reply to the almost rhetorical question. Then John realized what the argument had been. Good, poor honest, trustworthy Franz, despite his obvious misery, was putting their plan into action. Up until now he had been bearing the burden alone.

John leaned forward as he answered and observed Franz's nod of approval as he said;

"No, I will not drink, thank you, not today, not on Sunday." That last clause had not been planned, it had just been inspirational, perhaps a gift from Sunday itself?

"But you must drink!" exclaimed Hüffmeier with mock affrontedness. "You are at the Relaxation. Drinking is part of the fun!"

"He cannot", suddenly interjected Franz quite unexpectedly but obviously controlled by the same inspiration. "It is Sunday; he has been to Church."

"So?" asked Morten, jabbing Franz in the ribs with his elbow. "Since when has going to Church stopped him?"

Morten was annoyed as he got up and whispered to the waiter. He was ready to make an issue out of this. Drink would be provided and, by the Führer, drink would be drunk!

The drinks were duly brought, the two youths accepted them protestingly. Franz could have done with something to dull his racing senses, for in his case alcohol could only have assisted him. But he realized that to John it would have been lethal. How long before they would be pressured into sipping the mixtures? Those first sips which would then lubricate the resolve into being less necessary.

There was nowhere to tip any of the potential danger. 'Maybe just a little would be harmless?' thought John as he lifted his glass, turning it, noticing how the mixture seemed filled with lines like myriad cracks in ice, all swirling in their miniature currents. Perhaps, if he took a sip, food would be

313

brought? The two men might be less attentive if they saw their hospitality was not refused? Maybe they would go off to fetch food then, if requested? Could they get away with drinking just a little and then maybe tipping some under the seats of the sofa or on to the carpets at their side? It had, after all, a clear water-like appearance.

Franz was aware of John's intention and, in his anxiety to communicate his displeasure to the far end of the seat, knocked Morten out of his temporary musing lethargy.

"What's up with you now?" growled the Patrol Leader, as Franz edged forward. "Why don't you just sit back and enjoy your drink? Go on, drink it. That's an order!" He turned his attentions to his friend David once more but S.S. Hüffmeier was already busying himself with his guest.

The pushing off of the hand on knee had been taken as just a game at first, all part of the lead up. Time was on their side;

"Go on, drink," cajoled Hüffmeier. "You cannot insult good German schnapps. It is too hard to come by, these days."

John just stared ahead. He heard the words but he was determined not to take any notice. It had started; the fight for his decency and self-respect had begun. He felt justified in ignoring conversation and disregarding polite convention with such a person.

How he hated this time. All the planning in the world could not have given him the slightest insight as to how he would feel right now.

With the removal of the hand his every inclination had been to get up and move away, to rush from the building and never come near it again. The very portents of Hüffmeier's action had opened for him a gaping hole into which he stared into a nothingness, an abhorrence of negativity. Yes, he could have left but where would that have put poor Franz? This was the beginning of the price he had to pay for friendship. This was the price and more, which Franz had already been paying for him.

The rejected hand slipped casually to the donor's side so that the full length of his lower arm rested alongside John's thigh. It burned there, against John's body, uncomfortably large, like a primed bomb. John's neck coloured, he felt the pulsing and he was imbued with intense anger which made his thoughts and senses more acute. As he squeezed further to the edge of the sofa so did Hüffmeier, still with all the time in the world, use the chance casually to turn his hand so that the fingers were better placed for the time that they should come out of hibernation.

John shuddered and without thinking took a gulp of his drink.

'Unwilling,' thought Hüffmeier. 'Good!' He liked a challenge.

'He's forgotten,' despaired Franz.

'David's the lucky one,' thought Morten.

'What have I done!' realized John, coughing and spluttering the burning liquid back into his glass, splashing his flannels.

Hüffmeier was quickly to the rescue, snatching John's drink from him and almost dropping it on to Morten's lap in his urgent endeavour to get his friend to take hold of it so that both hands could aid poor John.

"There!" he said brushing the loose liquid off John's trousers and placing his other arm across the boy's back to massage his choking.

"No trouble. You are all right soon." He stole the opportunity to brush John's clothing far more than was necessary, his hand straying compulsively far up into the boy's privacy, while he used the shoulder arm to slip behind him and pull him towards himself in a lustful hug.

There was no thought of plans, or of Franz, as John jumped to his feet, instinct of upbringing taking over his actions. So violent was his pulling away that none could have anticipated his sudden surge of strength, or have stopped him. Hüffmeier was pushed sideways so that he sprawled on to Morten who spilt part of both glasses on to himself and Franz.

John seethed. He wanted to run from the room, he wanted to turn on his molester and kick him. He felt the urge to punch and spit at any German who came his way, he wanted to cry out that Adolf Hitler was a queer bastard!

Hüffmeier too, was up. Gone now was his smile. He too was fired. He needed to smack this insolent dolt hard across the face, he needed to tell all the Germans present that he was S.S. They had to know that they were not permitted to question his behaviour. He wanted John's body!

The rough hands grabbed like clamps on John's shoulders. John was forced to stare into those loathsome, lust-filled eyes, into a face divested of any human attributes of decency. He felt the cold stare of all those present. Even the gramophone seemed to fade. All could hear, all would hear but only Franz would understand.

"Bugger off! Just bugger off, you filthy old bastard!"

The noises returned. Hüffmeier lost his thoughts. Morten quickly joined the pair and wrenched Hüffmeier away a few steps, while he signalled an orderly for help with the state of his clothes.

All the while Hüffmeier, who had pliantly, trance-like, moved to Morten's instinctive placation, stared at John. John looked at Franz and received his watery smile. It was all happening.

Franz took the opportunity of the temporary absence of the two men to move to the centre of the sofa. He was careless of the wetness upon which he sat as he willed his friend to join him.

"Good, John," he whispered, "now listen quickly. This is probably the only chance we get to speak alone." John listened. Never had he been so thankful for the proximity of a friend, as he now was.

Morten and Hüffmeier too moved away to confer, while the Patrol leader was attended to by a concerned waiter who was summarily dismissed.

"I'm sorry that happened, John, but that was nothing."

John stiffened. So that was nothing? Well he'd not put up with that again, not from anyone!

"John, you cannot stay. Let me warn you. These are dirty men. They have plans," began Franz excitedly.

John did not reply, he did not feel real, but he knew that Franz was aware he heard.

"John, they will make you very drunk and then when you are unconscious. . ." He, who had experienced the privations, did not need to describe what would follow, for he was already aware. Surely his friend must be aware too? Could he not now just use this opportunity to pour out his own

316

miserable history? John, surely, would make association and take the warning?

"I do understand, Franz!" John's words sounded, even to him in his justifiable anger, harsh and unworthy of one who was the recipient of a true friend's sacrifice.

"Sorry, Franz. Forgive my rudeness. What has happened to you this evening?" he asked in concern.

Franz's reply was to look away, aghast. John followed his gaze. Towering above the two stood the edifices of evil, Hüffmeier and Morten.

Hüffmeier rasped out the ultimatum. There were no niceties, no lead up, nothing left to the imagination or left to be filled in by any hope.

"You two friends will never again see each other, believe me, if you choose not to do as I tell you."

Morten looked at his friend but he would not stop the man who had sufficient mental acumen to put thoughts and wishes clearly into perspective.

"You, Collins, either come with me now and do exactly as I plan for you or you never again have any contact at all with Müller. You do understand?"

John understood, Franz understood. All their planning for a non-future had always been overshadowed by this fact but they had always been able to disregard it as unreal, just an ethereal nightmare.

"If you choose not to come now, then just remember this; in a few days you too will be in the prison for your crimes. Prisons can be lonely places. There is not always anyone around to hear prisoners. Prisoners can sometimes seem to ask for what happens to them. As a member of the S.S. I have free access to any prison or camp I choose to visit."

Franz clutched at John. The poor civilian friend was soon to be as non-existent as himself.

"And remember too, that if you leave here now, never to see your lovely Franz again, that he is ours and he has no rights. We will use him twice as much. There are two of us for only one boy when you leave, yes? Show your lover your precious buttocks, Müller!"

There was no choice. John could neither stay nor go.

"You have one minute to decide," was Hüffmeier's ultimatum. "You go now to put off for a few days more

317

what will be anyway, and you leave your dear one to us, or you stay and share his experiences with him, and keep him for a while longer. We go now to bring back drinks, four drinks to celebrate your decision."

"Go John, please," insisted Franz in his misery. "You must go. You are good, you are decent. Please go for me, John, for your mother, please!"

As if oblivious to the pleadings, John could only waste the rationed time, permitted for deliberation.

"What did he mean 'show your buttocks'?"

"It doesn't matter, John. You just go please!"

"I can't leave you to them, not two of them, not like that!" replied John.

"You must, John, you heard them. Can you take the things they want to do?"

John would not, could not, answer such a question.

"But they'll prevent us from meeting ever again," intervened John.

"No, they won't," urged Franz trying to sound more convincing than he felt. "There's our plan, remember? Tuesday and Thursday. Please go, my friend!"

Hüffmeier and Morten were returning, confidently.

"But you, Franz. How can you take it?" whispered John pathetically.

"Just go. I'm all right. I know what it is now. You get used to it," insisted Franz in his urgency.

The two stood, smirking grimly as they proffered drinks to the perturbed youths.

"That's true," mimicked Hüffmeier, "you get used to it. You certainly will, Müller, before this war has killed you off!"

"Get used to it?" questioned John in a daze. "If you get used to it, Franz, then so must I."

"Quite so!" concluded Hüffmeier. Morten clicked his heels and smiled. "Now we will all drink, yes?"

*   *   *

Franz was never to know why John made his decision, how he made his decision, or even if he made a decision. It was the same with John in some ways for he was, for the

318

remainder of his life, to wonder which of the impossible choices he should have made. For the eternity of years he was to be damned and condemned to think out first one course, then the other, but never to come to any conclusion to the inconclusive episode.

Franz was for ever to wonder if John, against all his instincts and all his upbringing of decency, would have, given that final choice, chosen his friend. Would he have indeed chosen to share that most awful fate with him? Would he have done so knowing what it would really have meant? Did he, at that moment, at the end of time, in the presence, not of God and the evil one, but in the presence of the two despicable and evil ones, decide that friendship must be carried to its ultimate conclusion of self sacrifice? Not for John, in the heat of forced decision, the calm logic that he would only be bringing forward an eventual horror, a horror which would stay with him for eternity, therefore its bringing forward, fatalistically would have been of no consequence, yet thereby keeping his friend for two days more. No, he would not have had time to reason thus. All his thoughts would have been basic and from the heart without the guidance of head. Likewise, with regard to fatalism, he'd not have had moment enough to reason that two more days with his friend was also of no consequence if they were in themselves to be a finality.

Perhaps then he, having had no time, would have heeded Franz's advice, his implored and begged counsel to leave while he still had chance, not to enter willingly or ostensibly willingly under coercion, into that act which he, rejected son of Germany, was to wrap round himself in disgust for the rest of time?

No, Franz was to remain tormented by the question whenever he had a moment for reflection. At times he was to hope John would have chosen the role which would have been painful to himself but nevertheless have been his greatest seal on their brief but lasting friendship. At other times he was to be angry and yet relieved that John had chosen to take his advice, thereby saving himself and giving his friend the gift of a memory of one friend etched in time, pure and unsoiled, one perfect who, out of love for his impure brother, had obeyed his heart-felt wish.

319

All was destined to be conjecture, however. Neither Franz nor John were ever to know the answer to the unanswerable, although both were condemned to play out both possibilities, in their merciless imaginations, for the rest of their days.

As for Morten and Hüffmeier, very likely all memory of the incidents, real and projected, which had caused such, and were to continue to cause such, traumas for the two enemy friends, were very likely wiped from their consciousness rapidly, once the youths had gone. They, neither of them, probably gave the two victims so much as a thought, not even when they pursued their evils with other innocents.

The impossible choices were not made. The drinks were never consumed.

There was a silence, real or imagined, like the immediate blast of concussion which follows an explosion. Ripples of unreality and silence seemed to pass through the whole of the assembled Relaxation. The four were caught in these waves of silence as they too turned their attention to the cause, to the spot which was to be the explosion.

On reflection when events, as not at the moment of observation, took on logical sequence, or that sequence which, to the retrospective observer seem conveniently logical. The start of the excitement was muffled noises rather like angry shouts from outside the door of the Relaxation.

These noises magnified dramatically as the door burst open rudely and in tumbled two men, civilians, quickly followed by vociferous and temporarily thwarted sentries. The whole assembly turned to stare. Only the gramophone continued, even that neglected machine deepening its voice as it was allowed, untended, to run down.

After the concussion the explosion. For John, and Franz, his father Larry and Father Peters were the explosion. For Hüffmeier, his shamed memory of pistol shot and degradation at the foot of Gaudion's stairway was his explosion. For Morten the expression on the face of Captain Weiss, who had followed the entry of this party, and who looked towards the Patrol Leader with malice, gave concussion.

*   *   *

Father Peters had been extremely concerned at what his two visitors had earlier told him. At first he had considered telephoning John's father to warn him, or to even cycle down to his house before Evensong in the hope of being back in time. Both plans had been rendered impossible, however, by the fact that John would have still been present at those times.

He had even considered cancelling Evensong, or as with any emergency, entrusting it to one of the Lay Clerks. The Bishop would not have liked it but, as his emissary the Dean had no possible way of contacting that Lord Spiritual, and, as Father Peters did not care for niceties in the face of the real evil of the Nazi disease, that was not a consideration. Again, to cancel Evensong might have got the priest to John's home far too early.

The outcome had been a compromise. Father Peters, without explanation or apology, had cancelled his sermon. He had simply gone straight through the service without break, to the great surprise of his small evening congregation. At the end of the shortened worship he had rushed from the Church, cassock and all, straight to the Vicarage, avoiding all chance of conversation on the matter, collected his bicycle, and quickly exited by the back way.

Thomas Peters had left behind a rather puzzled and shocked congregation, just a few of whom had earlier attended morning Mass, spreading the conjecture that their shepherd had been ordered by the Germans to omit his preaching.

Larry had been surprised to see Father Peters on the landing of the flat, such having been his urgency that he had not waited to be announced by Gaudion. The mechanic had noted the fraught expression on the cleric's face, and the way he had anxiously and hopefully enquired if John was out. Without reference to Frances, at Thomas Peters' request, he had taken the priest into the sitting room and listened to what he had to say. Already he and his wife had been charged with anxiety and worry at John's uncharacteristic disappearance, so he had been prepared for the worst.

Without even involving Frances, the two had slipped out and cycled immediately to Town Patrol House. Larry, who had an ear for such places, was almost certain he knew which building it was. His thoughts had proved correct.

"Collins!" he had barked at the sentry who had barred his way.

"Let me in. My name is Collins! You know that name, yes?"

His voice had been wild as he had pushed aside the thick-headed dolt at if he were just a model soldier and, without any regard or fear for his own safety, had led the way for Father Peters.

There had been shouting. Larry and the priest had stopped short, confronted by a number of closed doors and a flight of stairs. Larry had completely disregarded the threats of the sentry, who in the haste of the action, had been nonplussed and perplexed, unable to react other than to shout.

Larry's oaths and abuses, as he wrenched open first one door then another, finding another locked and resistant to his hefty kick, drowned the sounds of the Relaxation room and, in any case, caused the participants, momentarily to be dulled.

As he opened his fourth door to find the reward of his search, so did Captain Weiss appear, demanding unheeded;

"What in the name of Hell is going on?"

"Dad!" gasped John.

"Mr. Collins!" added Franz.

"John, are you O.K., son? Have these bastards harmed you?" Larry looked round him. He could have gladly killed the lot. Each piece of furniture, each armchair, the sofa, every ashtray on its stand, was a weapon for him.

John and Franz made towards the two newcomers. Weiss closed the door, all attention, waiting as the silence intensified. Morten, with the slightest of inclinations towards two of his men, signified an end to this impasse. Several relaxed Germans began of an instant, to move towards the two intruders, menace in their deliberate motion.

"No!" shouted Weiss in command, realizing what was happening. "You all get on with your own business! Now!" He paused, heaved his chest for a great intake of air and bellowed;

"You out!" signifying Morten. "Await me at my office!

You and you," pointing to Larry and Father Peters, "accompany me, if you please!"

He barked further orders, incomprehensible to Larry and the priest, but quickly various of the company stood by to effect the Captain's wishes, should any of them feel they were optional rather than obligatory.

"And what about my boy?" demanded Larry. "He's staying with me."

"It is not advisable, not possible," answered Weiss. Then, addressing John, "Go home to your mother."

"Yeah. and what about that dirty bastard?" shouted Larry. "Where's he going? I'm not having him following my son home!"

Weiss scowled. This man was in no position to make demands. Yet he was right. Who could permit an innocent to travel home with such a one at large?

"Very well!" announced the Captain at last, bowing to pressure. "You are ordered to stay in this room."

Hüffmeier, who had remained in shocked silence until this moment, suddenly baulked at the indignity of being ordered by a member of the Wiermacht. The flood gates of all his frustrations and disappointments opened as he replied;

"No! No Captain of the Army orders a member of the S.S.!"

"When you are here in this building accepting our hospitality you accept my discipline!" screamed Weiss.

"No! Go to hell, Weiss!"

Larry, unable to follow fully the course of this shouted conversation, but imbued with such hatred for the man in black, which hatred by contrast, gave him a feeling of warmth towards the officer, could contain his pent-up rage no longer. As an uncoiled spring and taking Weiss' obvious discomfort, at the insolence of Hüffmeier, as his release, he flew at the S.S. devil, knocking him to the ground, killing him in his mind. Killing him over and over again.

Father Peters put an arm round little Franz who was weak and sack-like, giving vent to his pent-up misery.

*　　*　　*

323

They now stood in Weiss' office, subdued and quiet in contrast with only minutes before.

Weiss made for his desk. Larry, Father Peters, Morten, Hüffmeier and John stood there in various states of disarray. The only missing person was Franz, who was, after all, of no importance anymore, just waiting his dispatch to serve his country in the East.

Hüffmeier, still bleeding from the nose, right eye already beginning to close, his manhood (his pistol) temporarily removed from him under Captain Weiss' orders, was ready, despite his pain and fear, not to mention the disgrace he had suffered, not only at the hands of a civilian of occupied status, but from an ordinary army officer and others who had bustled him roughly upstairs, to pour out his foul threatening invective once more.

"You will pay for this, Captain. No member of the S.S. can be treated so and expect to remain unpunished! And you . . .," he addressed Larry, ". . . you are a dead man! He struck a member of Germany's forces, you all saw. You know the punishment for that!"

"Be quiet, Hüffmeier, you filthy rat!" snarled Weiss. Why should he be intimidated by this creature now? Had he not sealed his own fate anyway? What was there to lose? His only hope remained now in keeping this person incommunicado long enough to try to get his own version of events into the right ears first. It was a faint hope but worth pursuing.

Weiss ordered the three attendants to wait just outside the door.

Father Peters and John were well aware of the consequences Hüffmeier had alluded to. They were subdued as they willed Larry to stay calm.

"So I'm to be shot, am I?" sneered Larry, "I'd gladly be shot again and again to be able to have another poke at you, you filthy pervert!"

"Give me back my pistol, Captain. I demand my pistol to do justice right now!" screeched Hüffmeier.

"You demand nothing, my friend," said Weiss calmly and deliberately. "If you say any more I'll have you locked up!" He meant it, too. Hüffmeier knew he meant it. The man was mad, a rat! What do rats do when concerned? They fight to kill. Hüffmeier, without his gun, was a frightened man.

"Now," began the Captain, having established his authority, "perhaps we can try to sort this all out." He seated himself at the desk. There were two hard-backed chairs in the office.

"Reverend, take a seat," he indicated casually, "and you," referring to Larry, "you sit there. Our medics will attend to your hand presently."

John, Morten and Hüffmeier were left standing. John because of his youth accepted this, Morten because of his disgrace in the eyes of his senior officer, demurred, Hüffmeier felt the intended insult. Weiss was delighted.

"Can I say something?" asked Father Peters, thinking to lead the course to as speedy as possible a conclusion, perhaps, with a little helpful background, taking some of the charge out of the situation.

"No thank you, Reverend," replied Weiss, but I think you will find I know more than you even suspect in this matter."

Morten eyed Hüffmeier and shifted his feet uncomfortably. Hüffmeier began to feel sick from the pain in his face.

Morten's anxious glance towards Hüffmeier had not gone unnoticed by the Captain.

"Patrol Leader, I think you had better leave. You and I will talk later!"

Larry was still in a daze, John was without understanding of the conversation but Father Peters had followed the gist so far.

As Weiss barked out orders to the door sentries, and Morten, leaden and dejected went to leave, John's interest was pricked. Where was he going? Perhaps he was going to fetch Franz? No, not him, one of the sentries would do that. Franz? Where was he anyway? No, surely Morten was not leaving this meeting, not Morten, free to revenge himself on Franz!

John looked at Father Peters, the fear darting from his eyes.

'Eh?' asked the priest's raised forehead.

"Where's he going?" whispered John, so huskily that it was like a rasp filling the room.

"He's not needed now," interjected Weiss, ready to get on with the matter in hand.

"But where is he going?" asked John in agitation.

"It is not your concern," dismissed Weiss.

Father Peters, fully aware of the very real fears which much be inhabiting John's thoughts, interjected quietly;

"Sir I think he is concerned for his friend."

"His. . .?" started Weiss, "Oh yes, I understand. Wait!" he barked, addressing the departing Patrol Leader.

"You are ordered to have no contact whatsoever with Müller. That's an order. Is that clear?"

The priest looked reassuringly towards John and nodded while trying to smile.

"Now, we will quickly deal with matters," announced the Captain, ready to run a quick agenda. "First you, you are this youth's father I suppose, yes?" he asked referring to Larry.

Larry assented with a nod.

"You struck a German in uniform, yes?"

"Damned obvious isn't it?" replied Larry, infuriated.

"My friend, I do not fancy your chances if you were to answer the Gestapo in such a manner. A wise man would at least deny it! Our laws are designed for justice you know. Even our quick efficient justice requires witnesses."

What the hell was he getting at?

Father Peters, without regard for niceties, lent over to Larry to whisper. Weiss, uncharacteristically, did not intervene.

"I think he wants you to deny it" hissed the priest.

"Eh?" Larry was confused.

"Not even Jerry likes the S.S."

"Oh?" Larry looked more alert. Father Peters sat upright, composing himself once more.

"What is this, Weiss?" demanded Hüffmeier.

"Captain to you, Hüffmeier," sneered the Captain.

"What is happening?" insisted the S.S.

"Just shut up or I'll carry out my threat to have you locked up," dismissed Captain Weiss, contemptuously. He meant it. Hüffmeier knew he meant it.

"Let us start again. Name?"

"Collins."

The Captain began to jot information. Quickly and systematically details were taken, identity card demanded, scrutinized and returned.

"Did you strike a German in uniform?"

"No."

Hüffmeier's wavering attention was focused once more.

"Are there any witnesses?" Weiss looked quickly from Father Peters, to John, to Larry.

"No? Good," as Hüffmeier, enraged and impotent, made one last attempt to divert this course from injustice.

"I told you . . .," anticipated Weiss, "that I would take no more nonsense from you!" He summoned a door-man, waited for his next statement to be clearly audible to the men outside, then continued;

"So there is no charge to answer, Mr. Collins. You obviously did not strike a German. There are no witnesses to this outrageous idea. This S.S. man is nothing but a trouble-maker, and more . . ." He let the weight of his words sink into all present. "I think he should be locked up for a little while to consider his position. Perhaps he will not make a fool of himself by making unsubstantiated allegations? Perhaps he will not wish the world to know his true nature? Take him to the cell on my personal authority," ordered Weiss with great pleasure.

*   *   *

Chapter Fifteen

John heard the voices. They were distant, but they were familiar and comfortable, comforting. Why did he need comforting?

John? Who was John. My son? Whose son was he? Was he anyone's son?

There was that other voice again. Should he come out of darkness to take another look? No, last time he had been disappointed. It had not been whom he was looking for.

He had been looking for Franz! Franz? Yes, that name meant more now. It had feeling to it just as the increasing pain deep down inside him had feeling. He wanted to find Franz. Franz was somewhere. Yes, he even remembered now who Franz was, after all these years. Yes, Franz was growing stronger in memory, more ardent in vision, expanding in pain which was spreading its agony from a seething broken inside, to his injured and strictured limbs and torn skin. Franz had gone off and left him to suffer alone.

And whose were those other voices, talking in such low tones? He knew the sounds as surely as he knew the increasing pain was his, and would not be shut away in his self-created darkness.

*   *   *

Keith was still in the habit of waking early. The good fisherman rises with the sun and takes the day to himself. Even today on this fresh Monday, when he had decided through depression at his state that he would not fish, he woke. He would not go to the White Rock, permit in hand, ready to ply his trade, frustratedly waiting for up to three hours for an accompanying German. Instead, he thought he would lie in, yet still he woke. Still the birds sang, despite the curtains drawn against the growing colour of the world outside.

This was his hell. His last few days of freedom. He could not bring himself to work, he had no future. All he had was a present, a darkened room, a beautiful wife, a forming child, a home and plenty of time. But he knew he was no more, for soon all would be gone. So already it no longer existed for him. For everyone else yes, but for Keith, no! He had no tomorrow, no next week, no next month, no next year, no hope, nothing!

*   *   *

Bert got up. It was late, much later than was his habit. He had slept surprisingly well. It was all the more a shame that he had had to wake at all.

How was he to fill his day? There was no structure to it. He could not even make himself a drink or attempt a breakfast, for his larder was empty save for the unused coupons in his ration book. How strange for someone to under-use these days!

The only reasonably presentable clothes he had were those of his uniform, so that precluded him from leaving the house. So what? What if he stayed in? He might as well be miserable inside as outside. At least inside he would not be forced to speak to people or wonder if he would bump into his lost Frances or be tempted to visit her surreptitiously. He could not face all the deception involved in paying a friendly visit to Larry's shop, to make certain he was there, before visiting or telephoning Frances. Besides, there was that boy of hers and he knew. Bert just could not face the self-imposed shame of it.

Frances knew where he was, what he wanted. If she had not contacted him on Saturday evening, yesterday or again today, well that was her answer and he must just face it.

He longed for the trial which would remove him from this island. He longed for the solace of a French prison or a concentration camp, where his will and mind would not be his to control, where destiny would be out of his hands. He quite welcomed the prospect of being shot if they would be kind enough to dispatch him from this present misery quickly.

*   *   *

Major Müller looked down. He hated aeroplanes, he had never quite got over his fear. Now, he did not mind too much, for he looked down impassionately on that shrinking parcel of colour which, for the past thirteen months had been his home. He realized he had not known the place at all. So small, so much glass, so much green, little valleys, trees, tightly-packed houses, pure white beaches and white ruffled reefs.

All he had known, he realized, now that it was being taken away from him, had been a sense of peace and contentment. For him the war had not existed for the past year. His war had been peace, relaxation and tennis. He had almost felt a family man too, with anonymous patronage of his kin, until that had been the cause of his present downfall.

'Downfall?' he mused, as the aircraft lurched, passing over the coast, 'more like upfall,' as the craft took him from the peace of this enemy land to the unknown terrors held for him in friendly Berlin.

What would await him there in the Fatherland? Would he survive the Fatherland's stifling love? Would he outlive the war? Could he ever return to that place which now was rendered only a dream, as his craft took him lonely and old into the clouds?

*   *   *

Morten was worried. Weiss had really gone and done it this time. He had put him on a charge. Insubordination he had called it, insolence to an officer. That was an irony, he thought. He had carried out his threat, so brave, so authoritarian!

'You touch that boy again and cause a scandal and you'll be in deep trouble,' he had said.

And what did he do? He charged him with insubordination. Oh yes, he had to save face, he had to carry out his promise but he had dared not charge him with the real incident. Oh no, Weiss had too much to lose if Morten wanted to drag him down too! Weiss knew it; he certainly was clever there.

Morten knew he would have to face this charge. Too many at the house were aware that he'd caused the Captain

330

a great deal of displeasure. He couldn't really put any pressure on Weiss, not this time. He knew he'd had too many chances. Besides, if he did involve the Captain then that man would only bring yet other instances of his own misdemeanours to light.

*   *   *

Hüffmeier had expected something like this! Morten had not been at their agreed meeting place outside the Market. Such a convenient place too, both could be observed to be doing legitimate duties of surveillance at such a busy venue. Hüffmeier was sure this was Weiss' doing. He had expected the self-righteous idiot to take some sort of revenge on his Patrol Leader. Had they had it too good, all their own way for too long? Surely not? David Hüffmeier was S.S. after all.

This was a rare emotion for self-centred Reich's elite, S.S. Hüffmeier to experience; concern for another. Yes indeed at times he thought of others, but more in the context of his own selfish self-gratification. This was different. Here he was almost worrying for the welfare of his army friend, Patrol Leader Morten.

Well, he dare not go to Town House. That would just invite Captain Weiss' ire once more. He might just be induced, fool that he was, to denounce him for some of his misdemeanours. Who did he think he was? A mere Captain of the army with such ideas above his station, who felt he could disquiet a member of the S.S., no less, over so-called moral crimes, and that only with a non-German of occupied status? If he were allowed to get away with such things he'd be supporting Jews next.

No, David Hüffmeier had a duty to his Fatherland, to break this man, to destroy him and his abhorrent threats which amounted to nothing more than blackmail. He knew, if he stood up to the Captain, ways would be resolved that his word would be believed and not that of Weiss. For the records his was of course, but unofficially, what? Yes, David might have the moral victory but what in the end would be the ultimate outcome for him? Wonderful to enjoy the destruction of Weiss, but not at any risk to himself. No, he

331

would definitely have to keep away and deny himself revenge for the time being.

David Hüffmeier decided to telephone his friend. He did not like this feeling of having to continue anxiety about another. It was not German. He would just get it out of his system rapidly.

"Town Patrol," came the weary answer of the duty man.

"Patrol Leader Morten. Quickly if you please!" demanded Hüffmeier.

"Wait, caller," the line went dead for a few seconds. Hüffmeier felt it was longer. He was unused to waiting or unused to being aware that he was.

Life came back into the line. A voice was about to speak. David Hüffmeier actually almost experienced pleasure at the prospect, pleasure on another's behalf.

"Yes? What do you want?" That was not Morten's voice, it was Weiss.

David put down the telephone.

*   *   *

Franz? Who knew of Franz? Who was he? Where was he? Did he exist? Who thought of him? Anyone, everyone, no one?

Franz knew who he was, what he was, who he was not, what he was not, but he had no idea where he was or how long he was likely to be there. The only positive thought that he had was that he was not at Town Patrol House, that he was still alive and that there was an absence of Hüffmeier and Morten. He felt suspended from life rather than passed by from it.

*   *   *

Father Peters set about his usual Monday routines, with a mixture of emotions. He still waited a visit from some officials be they Feldkommandantur or Gestapo, yet it was slow in happening. How could his sermon have been so disregarded? Were they just waiting the right moment to catch him without chance of witnesses? Was it their policy to leave him, to let him worry so that, at eventual arrest, he would

332

already have broken down his own resistance? Or were they just thinking that, as he soon would not be in a position to preach any more, they could just bide their time? Was it an attempt by them to let him think how unimportant he really was? Perhaps they were right, too. He was unimportant!

Unimportant they might deem him but in his heart he felt he did a job which was still very important, that of tending his flock. Not only his flock! Only last evening had he not been instrumental in saving one of the enemy's own sons from moral dangers? Pride! Yes, Thomas was proud; he would have to confess this before the trial but he was nonetheless proud of being proud.

And here was his biggest enigma, for Hüffmeier and that Patrol Leader had lent themselves to everything vile that he wished to associate with the occupying forces. This was how he had needed to think of them these past thirteen months, in order to sustain his bitterness and distrust. But what of that Captain, Captain Weiss? The priest had no option but to admit that here was a German willing to put himself in real danger in order to right a wrong. It would have been quite possible for his own side to ignore such a wrong under the circumstances, for it involved only one, who by their lights, was practically outside their own laws, or governed by their own law within the law and complete tenets of non-moral principles.

How could Father Peters ever again see things in such clearly defined roles of black and white, good and evil, German or non-German?

He was delighted for John, hopeful for Franz and yet perturbed now for his own view of the masters. How could he now go to trial, charged under their draconian laws, to be convicted, martyred in the cause of goodness against evil, if they too had goodness on their side? How long did he have, to examine his soul sufficiently?

* * *

Larry was at work. He had waited all last night for the announcement of a change of plan. He had expected a banging on the door in the middle of the night, the clatter of jackboots on his stairs, the jangle of manacles and rough handling as he was thrown into one of their cells. He was realistic, he had heard of people who had struck at the German uniform. He knew how they were treated. No need for a trial once such an act had been witnessed and recorded. Such criminals were fair game. What other civilian, or international opinion, would take the cause of one so hell-bent on self-destruction, through absence of self-control, that he could bring on himself such consequences?

He and John had parted from Father Peters very quickly after they had left Town Patrol House, by all appearances free men, as free as any could be under such an authoritarian regime. Father and son had journeyed home in silence, each full of his own pressing and mind-shaking thoughts.

Together they had faced the extremely anxious Frances and, although not planned, had acted in accord in the way they had involved her or skillfully managed not to.

Larry had spent a virtually sleepless night, his anxieties and anticipations magnifying proportionate to the passing hours of darkness. He had been aware of Frances' presence, but as none of this concerned her in any way, had felt her to be more of a hindrance than a help to his whirling concepts.

And so this morning, after a sparse and silent breakfast, feeling doubly disquieted that he now found it even harder to offer explanation to his wife, thereby imbuing her with guilt over matters which were not of her making, and outside her understanding, he had cycled to work, anticipating the grim arrest at the shop door. It had not come.

What were Father Peters' words?

'Not even Jerry likes the S.S.!' Incredible. He must be absolutely right there. So there were some Jerries who perhaps, although he could not like them, maybe he could respect for their very respectable response to real human circumstances? He could not like them and yet he almost admitted that he did like one, the focus of all the scenes yesterday, that little Franz. Yes, he had to admit that. It made Franz seem almost as if he were not German after all, sort of 'one of the family' as John would have said.

'I wonder what's happened to that poor little sod?' he had thought.

Well at least his problems had come to light now. Maybe that Captain person would protect him? Sure he would. If he could protect a civilian from the S.S. then he could not fail but to protect one of his own youth from the S.S. and the S.S.'s friend. Yes, that Captain seemed like a really decent type, more like a British officer really.

* * *

Franz was in a bare and cleanly distempered room. The only furniture was the bed upon which he lay and the chair upon which his uniform had been neatly folded. The door had no handle on its inside.

Was this a cell or an interview room? Well, it had daylight. True, the window had bars but it was quite large with clear glass panes. If Franz so wished he could come from under his coarse blankets and go to that window to examine the view.

He preferred just to lie there forgotten as the forgotten person he had been glad to become.

* * *

"Hello?" said Weiss speaking into the telephone. He had become more amenable as the morning had progressed, able to have a slightly less abrasive manner of communication, despite the fact that more work had fallen to him with the removal of Morten.

That was the second time the receiver for his outside line had gone dead.

What was this? Was it the Gestapo trying to unnerve him or something? Had that fool Hüffmeier actually pursued a complaint?

The Captain had fully expected a visit last night, either from his own Military Authorities, or from Hüffmeier with a group of friends, but when it had not materialized, he had wasted no more mental effort on the problem. They would have moved very fast, so they were not going to move at all. That S.S. bully had possessed enough sense of self-preservation to temper his lust for revenge.

Ah! Hüffmeier?

Captain Weiss turned the handle of the military telephone and waited, drumming fingers impatiently.

"Weiss," he announced. "Who was that call for. . .?" a pause, ". . . That call you passed through to me just now, you oaf?"

"It was?" His grin was partly relief and partly self-satisfaction.

"And what about that earlier one? Yes, yes, good."

One more question;

"Was it the same man? You are sure? Good!" he was about to end the conversation but felt sudden inspiration;

"If he asks again give this message, 'Patrol Leader Morten is in the hands of the Military Police awaiting Court Martial'. No, that is all, that will do!"

*   *   *

Frances was in misery. It was a combination of the events of last evening and the way she had felt excluded, not only this morning, but in her bed last night. The end of the Sunday had been doubly cruel and brutal by contrast with its beginning. It had been a complete reversal of recent days where family relationships had been at the depths, then had revived with careful tending, only to plunge again from ecstatic unity to these now dismal hopeless depths. There was so little time too for the enactment of reconciliation, while the hours lay interminably exposed before her for guilt and introspection.

So last evening John had left without word, deceitful almost. Larry, having agonised with her over this, had himself later, done exactly the same thing. She had only discovered from Gaudion that he had left with Father Peters. She had had no idea of what it could all be about but had been in very great fear, wondering if she would ever see her two men again.

And, what was worse she now had no one to turn to, to ask for advice. She could not contact her confessor. Her sister would have done nothing more but fire her anxieties or fuel her animosities, and how could she now bring herself to contact Bert?

Bert would have been the answer, but things had changed. Where previously with Bert a friend, she could have asked his favour and he too would gladly have tried to help, now

Bert was not the friend but the lover. That was different wasn't it? One does not ask a favour of someone one has refused. Once a lover, always a lover. No more acts done for friendship's sake. The very asking for help would be a recognition that the other still existed and burned as a light. The expectations so aroused in Bert would not be rationalized as reward, but as equal want. Bert was no longer a friend. Bert had to be forgotten, for he could no longer not be a lover, if he existed. How could Frances have a lover with Larry, as he had been, and with the end of their time being so close? Yet, how could she not have a lover with his demise also imminent? Did this mean that Frances could have neither? Did Bert now have to be eradicated from memory, as Larry soon would have to be?

*　　*　　*

As Franz lay there, the light getting brighter all the time, the blankets itching his bare legs and arms, he realized he was alive and well. Perhaps he was still a person after all? He had spent a whole night free of Morten. Yes, it was almost like waking refreshed from a fever.

As this day had certain absences which made it more endurable than the last, then perhaps it was an improvement? Perhaps life was a little better than it had been? At least it was not so bad.

So he was thankful, at least, for the absence of the evil privations. That did not help the feeling of loss which now grew in him, loss of his freedom, loss of his friend, loss of this beautiful place, soon to be loss of his life on the Russian front. He was dead of course but then, if he could disregard the losses of positive things and concentrate on the losses of the negative, then at least he was not dead at this very moment, just suspended.

Should he get up and look at the view to find out where he was held? Why had he been removed from Town House? He wanted to be there! Or did he? He wanted to be near his friend, near his adopted family. Yet why had Captain Weiss sent him somewhere else? Franz had done nothing wrong! It was not his fault Morten and Hüffmeier had used him so badly. Perhaps the Captain thought it was? Perhaps he

337

thought he had been a willing party? No, he had been too kind, too protective. Had he been removed then, for his own protection? That was probably it. Captain Weiss had not said why last night, just that he was going.

Why could he not have confided the reasons to Franz? Did he feel he had already shown himself as too kind, too unmilitary? He certainly had been harsh on the S.S. John's father would probably be kindly treated too. The same considerations had not been afforded to him. Yes, Franz was beginning to have feelings once more, sensitivities. He was definitely alive and for the present intended to improve his life, if only by thought.

If only the Captain had asked him. Would he really have chosen to stay in that place still to be at risk but to keep alive the hope of contact with his enemy friend? Could he have been as brave in his choice, as selfless, as John would have been in his choice, if he had made it last night?

No, Weiss had not even considered it. He had simply told Franz to collect his belongings, to be ready in fifteen minutes and that had been it.

Before he had known it, he had been driven from the house in a fast car, sitting alone in the back like an officer. The civilized streets and closely packed houses of the centre of Town had quickly been left behind and the larger stately mansions of the outskirts of St. Peter Port had been glimpsed from time to time in the lingering twilight.

Even the road-blocks had been lifted without question, as his car had sped him far out into the country so that it made its way by devious turns from main roads, which had quickly become tiny twisty lines, high-banked in green, over-shadowed by timeless trees like those grim and hateful in fairy stories.

He had been received by a young Lieutenant, without ceremony, in the courtyard of what appeared to be a disused farmhouse, lit only by starlight. He had shown him without speaking, first to the lavatory and then to his present room.

Once the flashing of his guard's torch had pointed to Franz's resting place, a camp bed, he had been left to feel his way and undress in the dark. Not a word had passed, not a word had been sought.

As he stood there, in his lonely room, in only his underclothes, aware that he was hungry and thirsty, lonely and in need of the lavatory once more, yet not anxious at the loss of any of these things, he looked at the view from his window and knew that for him this island now could only ever be a view. A view from a window, a view from his memory.

*   *   *

John had overslept. It was too bright outside to be early. Dad had not called him. There were no sounds from Mum above.

What day was it? Monday, yes it must be. Today he had to see his Advocate. Dad must be at work. Where could Mum be then? Usually she was up and busy quite early. Well, it was a strange feeling not having to get up for work on a Monday; he should have enjoyed the luxury of it. But no, it just enhanced his feeling of being unimportant, not quite grown-up, as he knew he had recently been. Being alone and bored, unaccustomed to this extra leisure, would only drag the hours to allow his mind to be invaded by doubts and unnecessary worries.

He should be worrying about something right now but he was not quite awake enough to know what it was. With mental effort he searched for his neurosis. Like a trap springing, it entered his rested consciousness, quickly focussing. If only he had gone back to sleep for an hour or two more!

It was Franz! There had been that awful choice which he had been required to make, and yet had not. Again he tormented himself with what might have happened if his father and Father Peters had not arrived when they had.

Yes, they had rescued him, but what about poor Franz? Had he been subjected to it yet again?

It? John could only half imagine 'it', yet 'it' had nearly been his to suffer!

That hand had been evil enough. How could he have taken more? Franz had had to. He shuddered. And all for him, for his friendship. It would have been better for Franz if he had remained an enemy. But could John be that selfless in his musings? If he had not gone to work for the Germans? If the

R.A.F. had not raided at that dinner time? If Franz had not been needing him at the Feldkommandantur? If Franz's uncle had enforced, more effectively, his ban on the two enemies liaising? If Larry had not softened and lent Franz his bicycle? All ifs, if! If! If!

No, Franz must be safe now. Hadn't that German Captain been harsh in his words to that S.S. bastard! How he had sent the Patrol Leader off in disgrace! Hadn't his father been lucky? No, if that Captain was so strong, so fair, such a good man, he would look after Franz. Yes, it just had to be, but John still had to worry. He could not allow Franz just to die from his memory. He had to be kept alive there, with all the possible and nonsensical potential hazards that might come to mind, until they came into contact again tomorrow evening.

Tomorrow evening? So far off!

What a good day it had been yesterday, until last night. All the memories of the earlier part of the day were gilded with pleasure, their flaws smoothed away. Even the Relaxation took on some positive attributes. At least, he had been there with his friend.

*　　*　　*

The house was still quiet. Larry had gone to work, John was not about. There was nothing for it but to act. Frances had to be quick. She had decided to telephone Bert. Had she swallowed her pride or were there other feelings gradually subduing her initial resolve, as the anxious minutes had begun to lengthen on these final few days?

The very act of surreptitiously contacting Bert, in this hurried way, helped to lessen her feelings of guilty introspection. It put her in mind of the silly schoolgirl antics from so long ago. It put a perspective on the whole matter, less intense than reality. She shielded herself with her retrieved feelings of youthfulness.

"Hello, Central 2689," Frances almost gasped at the anticipated voice. She wanted to giggle and whisper sweet nothings so her girlfriends, standing by, would be impressed and jealous.

"Bert?" If only they realized how passionate she felt, what

experiences she had had. And was still capable of? Poor girls, not for them.

"Frances!" What a shame they could not hear the gratitude in his voice or experience the huskiness of his lustful words. She would tell them a little, just enough to get them curious, then she could cut them off at the zenith of their enquiry.

"Bert, it's me." What a silly helpless little thing she was. "I need your help, Bert."

"My help?" She might even let the word out, to one or two other admirers, that Bert was infatuated. That would make them all the more ardent. It was good to be wanted, especially when you could enjoy saying 'no'. She might even hint to Larry. Larry?

The tone of Bert's voice had changed. How could a kind word like help sound so aggressive? What had she done to Bert, and to Larry?

"Yes love, your help." She waited, knowing that now she was alone, she was a mature woman, she had tampered with Bert's emotions and was about to have her guilt confirmed as he, poor man, shared his misery and bitterness.

"Frances, you need my help? Don't you think it's the other way round? What about me? It is I who need you! What the hell are you playing at, Frances? What are you doing to me?"

"Sorry." The tone of her single word confirmed the sincerity of her feelings and the hopelessness of her position. All was out of her control.

"Go on," sighed Bert. There was nothing in this for him except that he was at least speaking to her, wasn't he? She was there, he was here, they both existed. It had happened, nothing could take that away. He demoted himself from lover to friend. "Tell me all about it."

*　　　*　　　*

As a friend, Bert considered it was quite in order now for him to be visiting Larry at the shop. He had no ulterior motives as earlier conjectured, nothing to gain, only to give. Yes, that was the role of a friend.

Not that he needed an excuse to call. He nonetheless felt he should go armed with a reason. Friends do not need

341

reasons to call unannounced on friends but then, it was only in recent minutes that Bert had transferred himself back to that status. Although Larry did not know his visitor had been on a higher plane, Bert was very much conscious of it. Yes, perhaps he would now be a friend with Frances once more but his feelings towards the friend he had deceived could never be quite the same.

"Hello, Bert," Larry cried in genuine surprise. "What brings you in here, you old layabout?"

It was true. That was what Bert was, a layabout, and a very scruffy one at that. He felt selfconscious at the state of his very dirty old clothes. He really had let things go.

"Oh, I was just passing," said Bert casually. "You know how it is?"

Larry concurred. It must be miserable for Bert to have all this enforced idleness, especially one such as he, with no other outside interests, apart from his work.

"Well, it's good to see you anyway, especially looking so smart," added Larry feeling it was better to jest about it than to let the sight before him prey on his senses. Bert knew him well enough to be able to take it in good part.

"Anyway, I thought I'd better apologize for not taking up your invitation to the Lion the other evening. I don't know, I just don't seem to have any go in me any more."

"It's your age, mate!" Larry just couldn't allow himself to be drawn into deep conversation.

"How are things with you?" asked Bert.

"So, so," was the non-committal reply.

"Good." There followed an awkward hiatus.

"Frances well?"

"Yes."

"And John?"

"He's O.K. . . ." Larry seemed to hesitate.

What better for Bert to break awkward cessation in their conversation than to use small talk about John, without bringing attention to his real interest in Frances' troubles.

"You seem not too sure?" quizzed Bert. "Something wrong with the boy?"

"No, not really . . . well, yes and no."

"Go on, tell me," requested Bert with affected interest.

It was fortunate indeed that Bert had drawn Larry on the

subject, for it quickly put him into the matter from which his friend Frances felt excluded.

"Frances know about it?" he asked at length.

"No, that's the devil of a problem, old son. She ought to know but I don't want to embarrass the girl. Trouble is she knows something's up."

"That's for sure," added Bert, almost forgetting his role as double agent, quickly adding, "She's sure to know. Wives and mothers and all that. You'd better tell her then, eh?" urged Bert.

"Yep, I will," sighed Larry at the prospect. "I will, sometime."

"You do that, then, or I'll bloody well 'phone her up myself," Bert laughed casually.

"You'd be most welcome to, Bert," answered Larry, thinking that nothing could be further from his friend's mind. "It's what you might call the joys of being a parent, eh?"

*   *   *

"Oh, Bert," whispered Frances as if taken by surprise when the 'phone had rung, as if she had so many friends to ring her that she never knew which one might be at the end of the line.

"Look, Frances," urged Bert, desperate to discipline himself into keeping to the role of friend only, "don't tell Larry I've spoken to you, O.K.?"

Frances' heart began to pound. What was he leading up to? Oh no, not that again! She thought he had 'phoned as a friend and here he was being the furtive lover again.

"But I've been in and had a chat with Larry," he continued.

"A chat?" Frances was feeling slightly light-headed.

"Yes a chat. With your husband."

What was this? Why had he chatted to Larry? Oh no, surely no, not that? Not now? She couldn't face all the upset, all the disclosures, all the confessions and recrimin-ations. Her head began to swim.

"It's all right, Frances, my dear." Where was Bert's resolve slipping to now? "There's no real problem, not now any

343

way. I expect he'll tell you all about it later. There's absolutely nothing new to worry about. Is that O.K., Frances?"

She realized her misapprehension;

"Oh that!" she said with relief.

"Well, that's nice, I must say," grumbled Bert, not sure if he should be surprised or annoyed. "All the trouble I've been to and all you can say is 'oh that'."

"Bert love, sorry. I didn't mean it," said Frances, slightly alarmed. "I was thinking of something else. I'll tell you next . . ." What was she saying? Next what? She corrected herself;

"Bert, you are sweet."

The line had gone dead.

Should she 'phone him back? Had he been offended? Oh he was kind, he was such a dear.

Her feelings of warmth momentarily removed the state of the impossible which was weighing her down with guilt. She was able to think of her lover and enjoy her thoughts without the feeling of sin. She was, after all, just an ordinary human being and only able to entertain one concept at a time.

No, she would not 'phone now, but next time they spoke or met, it would no longer be with barriers set up by either. Somehow it would all work out.

* * *

When John got in for his tea, having spent his whole day busily doing very little more than visiting his Advocate and trying unsuccessfully not to let his thoughts chase themselves in circles, he found Dad waiting for him. He must have got home early.

"Hello, son." Dad was uncustomarily jolly. "You're a bit late, aren't you? Been working hard?"

"Very funny," laughed John. "It's not me who's late it's you who's early, eh?"

"You might be right, son, you might just be right," said Larry lowering his voice conspiritorially and continuing, "We two have got to have a chat to your mother and right now. It's no good putting it off. All right?"

"Oh no!" gasped John going pink at the embarrassing prospect. "Can't you just. . ."

"No, I bloody well can't!" cut across Larry, but his voice

did not sound as angry as his words. "Why do you think I'm in so early, eh? Why do you think Mum's got her feet up in the sitting room ready? Why is it that you and I are just going to take this tray of tea things in?"

Of course Frances knew that the two had plucked up courage to inform her but she could not let on that she was expecting such education.

She was very curious and just hoped they would get on with it. They were like a couple of shy youngsters just about to date their first girl.

Frances sat stock still. Her empty cup clattered in the saucer. Larry was uncomfortable but, with lots of false starts, had finally got out what he had wanted to say. John's face was a deep pink as he looked anywhere but towards his mother.

'If they only knew,' she thought, 'if they only knew I've heard it all before and in this very room.'

She looked first at Larry, that big, strong, handsome man, handsome in his ruggedness, in nature befitting his hairy chest. She loved him for his honesty. Oh, how she loved him, how she would miss him!

Then she looked at John, her poor innocent sheltered little child, such a bundle of emotions and embarrassment. How she wanted to rock him in her arms as she had done Franz. But her two sons were so unalike. John would have bored into the floor in his discomfort, whereas Franz had been supple and pliant to her.

And now, she was to lose both sons! Both sons and both lovers. She was the greatest loser of them all, she was losing all four, four she loved equally. Not one of them was to lose so many. Not one of them, except Bert was going to feel the guilt she had to feel. To feel guilt for love? Poor Bert. Poor Larry too, for she had been unfaithful to him and yet she knew in her mind, she could be again. Poor Larry, poor Bert. Was she not also unfaithful to poor Bert? Poor Larry, poor Bert, poor Frances!

*　　　*　　　*

"Yes?" Hüffmeier felt nervous. He could not rationalize why an officer of the S.S. should feel such an emotion, his very membership of the organisation precluded such a thing. But notwithstanding, he was the one who was not in control, as he telephoned Town Patrol House for the third time.

"Town Patrol House," drawled the bored lethargic man, suddenly stiffening as he recognized the voice. "Who do you wish?"

"Patrol Leader Morten."

"I have a message for you caller." He imparted the message with pleasure.

Hüffmeier's hand trembled as he slowly lowered the receiver, letting it drop the last inch.

*   *   *

346

Chapter Sixteen

The nurse stepped forward.

"Excuse me, please, Mrs. Collins. I must check your son one moment."

Those eyes opened again. John wore a frown.

His lips were swollen and dry. He moved them to vent his words and the pain stabbed at him.

The nurse bathed his lips and moistened them but the soothing sensation on his face just contrasted more, the unbearable growing torment inside. He winced, his grimace staying as a frown so that his blue eyes were pinched and the corners wrinkled. He was fully conscious now, able to recognize his visitors, able to receive pain completely.

"Mum," he whispered, "and Gerda, help me, please." His voice was low and self-pitying. He had not in him the ability to feel for others, not right now. His pain was his degradation.

"Excuse me," requested the nurse, "I must attend to the patient. Perhaps you could leave?" She had not chosen her words carefully as she moved to the button. She knew that she had just fired anxiety in the relatives. But, so they should be anxious. If not they soon would be, if they were subjected to John's bared excruciation.

"Leave?" mouthed Gerda puzzled, waiting some reassurance from the nurse. "You mean go outside? Is something wrong?"

Her question went unanswered, as Sister entered the ward.

Frances moved towards John again but he did not want to see his mother. His poor head moved from side to side in listless misery, as the groan broke from him.

The duty nurse did not need to elaborate. Sister was acknowledged and was in full control, having glanced at all the relevant dials and pointers on entering.

"Phone," was her calm instruction. Then, as the nurse left, she turned, still calm, still sweet;

"Please leave now, ladies. Wait outside if you will and I will come to see you as soon as I am able."

Frances' quavered attempt at questioning, and Gerda's nervous cough were both cut short by John's gasp, as he clenched his eyes and his moan became a tiny yet piercing cry.

The door was open, the two ladies out, door shut and Sister waiting, counting for the entry of the doctor with his hyperdermic.

*   *   *

Franz had spent the whole of yesterday in that small room. Surprisingly he had not suffered too much from boredom. The silent Lieutenant had brought him regular sparse but palatable meals and equally as regularly ushered him to the lavatory.

Franz had kept his thoughts, his memories and the view for company. He had spurned the association offered by his would-be companion, the future.

While it was true that Franz did not know Guernsey well he was aware that it was a small island and in the past short period of his freedom he had seen a lot of it with his erstwhile friend. In fact he had seen most of it, albeit a great deal of its twenty-five square miles from a distance. He did not however recognize this view. There was nothing familiar about its aspect. If he had not remembered that night time drive, he might well have imagined that he was on a neighbouring island except that it now seemed less attractive than those other islands viewed in prospect while in the company of his friend.

He was very close to the coast but there was no beach, just sea, deep looking, cold and uninviting. The rocks upon which the deep lonely waves broke were grey. The horizon was broken by no reefs and no beautiful islands. From his observation of the shadows the day before, he judged he must be facing north. Between his window and the coast there was growth enough, gorse spiked with bright yellow, stunted trees permanently leaning the way the wind had bullied them, and springy salt-soaked marsh grass. There was however a complete absence of creatures, human or otherwise; not even the gulls seemed to live here. The only evidence of life was a satire in that it was represented by a single strand of barbed wire staked along the summit of the mound which led down to the sea.

It had been good yesterday to feel free of Morten and Hüffmeier. He had slept a lot, each waking being a joyous confirmation that he really had been relieved. It had been good not to exist. Existence yesterday could only have meant existence with the evil ones. But that was yesterday, today was Tuesday, today he was not a nobody, today he was to be a Club Member, a member of John's Club, the Boys' Club. Today he was supposed to become a boy once more.

How was this to be effected? The Lieutenant still would not enter into conversation, he still only brought the meals and administered the lavatory with studied regularity. The view was still chill and uninteresting, remaining devoid of life and movement. He, Franz Müller, as he used to be known, continued forgotten, still not remembered.

*   *   *

John was anxiously waiting the time to set off for Boys' Club. It was so far off it seemed it would never come. His whole morning had been coloured pessimistically. The more he had tried to reason himself out of it the more he had sunk into gloom. Yesterday's stress had seemed like a bad omen for, when he had scrabbled the pages to find *La Gazette Officielle,* there had been no mention of a gala. He had read and re-read the official notices, German and Civil, but with no joy. He had even read each heading in each column in the tiny newspaper, including all the advertisements on the back page just in case, in error, the item had been misplaced. No, it had not been there. This very morning he had got hold of a *Star* with great difficulty but it was the same story.

His parents had made light of it, assuring him that the Germans would be in no rush to post the announcement. They knew the event would be fully subscribed, no matter how little notice they gave. Larry was sure it would be in tonight's *Press,* that is, if the boy had not imagined it all in the first place.

So John was torn. He wanted to go off early to be the first at the Club. The very thought of the pilgrimage seemed to put him closer to his friend and to create and strengthen the possibility that they would meet up. He was pulled also to stay and wait for Dad to bring home the *Press* and put him out of his misery. Well, at least these thoughts and contradicting influences helped to keep his other worries at bay.

He had even confided in Frances that he was going to the re-opening of Boys' Club this evening and she had accepted it calmly. It was the least he could do, after the way he had treated her recently. He had even told her that he would not feel like anything to eat, a most unusual state of affairs, and she had accepted it as if she understood. Uncanny, really. Mum seemed to be sharing the burden John felt without actually being told he felt it.

She suggested he should go down to his father rather than stay under her feet. John had taken her advice and sauntered down to the shop, albeit far too early in the afternoon for the *Press* to be out, but it filled the time. He could not resist a detour past Town Patrol House. That seemed a greater draw than the chance for an early glance at the newspaper. Besides, part of John was afraid to look at the paper in case it gave disappointment once more. Oh, he would feel so much better once Franz was safely with him at Club this evening.

* * *

Father Peters was hurriedly getting ready for Boys' Club too. He felt rather guilty that he had been so neglectful about the organization up till the present and now it was rather too late.

There had been a great deal on his mind; his own problems, problems foisted on him and problems of his own making. Maybe he was taking too much on? He couldn't fight this war alone! But then of course, the war was nearly over for him, as a positive force for good that is. Soon he would just be biding his time, having evil done to him or just good denied him. Soon he would not have the opportunity to alter things in the slightest manner. His power would be taken from him and he would be a living death.

Usually the Club had been self-perpetuating with competent voluntary leaders and a well-tried programme. It had all lapsed after the evacuation of 1940 for there seemed no more youth of the age it catered for. In fact the community suffered a dearth of all infants and young life. The leaders had quietly drifted and the facility had been withdrawn. Father Peters had been too busy coping with the shock of occupation, and half the population gone, to worry about the niceties of a cosmetic club which would seem only to imbue the new regime with acceptance and respectability.

It was only recently, as he had to some extent come to terms with the Germans, not loving them any the more, but feeling more contemptuous of their underlying inefficiency, despite their veneer of organization, and having the wish in some way to flout the spirit of their regulations designed to weaken association, that he had thought he would take advantage of their apparent lessening of draconian trivia. He had received a certain amount of success and self-gratification from making subtle comments against them in his sermons, so subtle that they had been pricked by them but unable to admit as much. This had fired his recent enthusiasm to re-open the club. He did not feel this was lending support for the masters, but just taking advantage of their foolish weakness.

Well, he just hoped John would be right, that even without any organization, the boys would amuse themselves with the games which were there.

He just wished he had made more effort to announce its recommencement to the Parish. He felt a sense of foreboding.

*   *   *

"It's no good upsetting yourself, my girl, just think of the child," admonished Anne de la Haye's mother with kind severity. "You upset yourself like this and you might harm the unborn precious, then where will we all be?"

Anne's mother longed to be a grandmother as much as Anne to bear her first baby. If only she could feel sure in her mind that the child would not grow up fatherless. If only her Keith had a future.

She could just about last out, soaking up all the tension generated by Keith and herself, until the trial took place. Yes, in that way, she could take on a lot of her darling's suffering. But what once the trial came? What would happen after sentence? Then he would be completely on his own with no one to help.

She could not let him know her anxieties, he was too taken up with his very justifiable neurosis and depression. She just had to keep it all to herself day after day after day.

Her mother knew what Anne was suffering but could not go forward to interfere. Some things a girl must carry alone. She had stood back suffering too in her own way, only able to help, as at this moment, when Anne came to her. Her every inclination was to smother her daughter with love, to compensate for the agony she was going through, but she knew that would be an unkind act.

"But I just can't cope any more, mum," she sobbed. "I feel so helpless, there's nothing I can do. I feel so helpless."

There was nothing her mother could say. All she could do was to hug her child and help the tears to flood.

"You know what he went through, Mum. You saw his poor face," she gulped out, as if fighting for her heartbreaking breaths. "You know how brave he was?"

Her mother nodded, she had observed and suffered for them both.

"You know how he took it all and would have gone on taking it? He's not a collaborator!" Anne cried. "He didn't want to talk to them. It was because of me and our unborn child . . ." She could not finish her thesis because of the trauma.

Grandmother to be knew exactly what Anne was saying. She understood the dilemma which was not of her making. She too was torn in her own way, the same as Anne was and as Keith must have been. The three of them still had, or had just possessed, the ability to choose but the choice had been an impossible one. For Keith in effect there had been no choice. It was now that he had to bear all the suffering he had suffered so much not to have to. Now he had to wait for the trial, carrying his weighty secret. It was there that he would see his friends and school-mates, his whole social entanglement destroyed because he self-indulgently had put wife and child first. He knew they would call him traitor, he realised that their families would ostracize his own. He knew it and Anne and her mother knew it. All three knew it but, until now, not one of the three had discussed it with the other. Their very conversation now was a further exclusion of Keith, a further putting him apart as different.

Anne so wished that he had saved himself by not considering her and yet she knew that he had given himself over to his present and predicted suffering, out of love for her and their child. She could not continue to loathe him for his bravery, while she was proud of his resolve. There was no answer now except the complete, but temporary, oblivion of tears.

* * *

Morten did not feel any particular disgrace at being held in military police custody. It seemed strange to him that, as a military person himself, he should be so kept, but really he felt it was quite immaterial. Whoever kept his freedom from him had to be looked upon as a temporary, if unnecessary expedient.

Weiss certainly had carried out his threats this time, he really had!

Anyway, the novelty of being in a cell was not lost on him. He had tried to get some sense out of the young policeman but only got something to the effect that they were just holding him until such times as his own section had a chance to deal with him.

The young policeman who was outside his unlocked, open-door cell most of the time either just watching Morten, or seeing to his needs, really did not seem to know what it was all about. Morten had wondered if he could just have got up and walked out of the building. Quite possibly, but why bother? Where could he go? Besides, the young man was quite pleasant to look at and was getting more friendly all the time.

He had time to consider his position carefully. His offence

was listed as insubordination. Insubordination with his good records, at worst would probably mean only a posting. Perhaps to Russia even? With Franz? Now there was a thought! Anyway the reasoning had not lodged long in Morten's consciousness, he was not one for worrying about events which were clearly outside his control. So, if it was being kept quiet at the top then surely that was a good sign? Morten was about to be the recipient of a covering-up operation.

As a side issue to toy with, if this young policeman did know of Morten's proclivities then he certainly did not seem disapproving. That, in itself, was rather good as Morten definitely liked the look of him, hardly more that a lad himself. Well, if Morten was not sent to Russia, but allowed to stay in this place, he might get to know this young man. He really could not lose, whichever way he thought of it. But then he preferred not to think. Much too tiring!

*   *   *

With John out of the house, and time on her hands, Frances had a chance to think. Larry was safely at work and would be for the next two hours. She knew he would come in for his meal, even if he did desert her again, this evening to flirt with his pint jar. Even that latter prospect did not fill her with too much concern for she now knew he was all right again and she was also. The two of them were in harmony once more. Well, at least they had been last night after the deep and frank discussion they had all held. It was true, things could change very quickly in the passing of twenty-four hours, especially when people were under stress. But it was convenient for her peace of mind to assume that the status quo would prevail.

Therefore she need not tease her mind with Larry or scourge her desires with the imagination that she might just be about to plunge into another of those interminable lows which, these days, far too quickly seemed to chase the high moments.

No, since speaking to Bert yesterday and benefiting from the result of his efforts with Larry, her mind could hold only him. It was a combination of the fact that the love was

354

illicit, that he was unattainable and she had a temporary lifting of the feelings of guilt. The very legitimate absences of husband and son, together with the attendant removal of her thoughts of them, dismissed her anxiety or clothed it in self-delusion. She reasoned, but repressed, the knowledge that an hour of reckoning would come to burden her with guilt once more but that all seemed so far off while the possibility of Bert could be so close, so real.

Should she 'phone him? No, even if successive sentences helped to eliminate, she could not take on a little bit of death she would receive from his initial words, as he tried not to allow his feelings to display or appear to take any course, for fear that she had made contact in order to hurt or deride him.

Why not walk down to his house? Already she fancied herself half running and skipping towards that far part of the town. He would be there looking so unbelievably miserable and she would delight in her power to control his mood and lift away his misery.

Yes, she could be there easily in fifteen minutes, ten if she almost ran. Quite unseemly of course, and Bert's neighbours would probably see her. It would not do for them to observe her haste, maybe, not to see her at all. So what? She did not know his neighbours, never would, nor wanted to. She skipped into the bedroom to fetch her hat and coat.

*   *   *

'Who now?' thought the priest as his front door was banged with urgency. He really did not wish to deal with any parish matters at present, not with the first night of Boys' Club so imminent.

It was certainly a very insistent banging, as if the person on the outside were in panic or fear. As he made his way to the door many people crowded into his thoughts as being outside. There was John again, and then that German friend of his. De Bourgonniere was there bearing bad news. He was replaced with that Gestapo Major. Then there was that enigma of a German Captain from last Sunday, so concerned, so good. What was his wife doing there? How

355

had his boys got over from England? Mother! What was she doing here in this place?

The suddenness with which the third round of hammering ceased, as he creaked open the door, swept away all his obtrusive visitors, only to have them replaced by two men, smartly dressed, hair cut short, faces unknown to his vast experience of local people.

They needed no introduction. Without knowing them, he knew who they were. His unwelcome visitors were plain-clothed Gestapo agents, an honour usually afforded only to the most serious of offenders, without hope of reprieve, so he thought.

Without bidding, both visitors stepped inside the hollow chill passage while Father Peters, as if propelled by some magnetic force, stepped backwards, keeping the distance from them constant. Neither of his guests removed their hats. One pushed the heavy door shut from behind him with a movement so sure that an observer would have thought it was well rehearsed and he was familiar with this place.

Father Peters did not speak. He felt more awkward than frightened. He was conscious of the silence and, like a nervous host, momentarily felt he should attempt to fill it, but he was at a complete loss for words. Then, realizing he was in a dream, from which he could will his escape, decided that it was not his place to order matters, but that he would just spectate and let them do all the thinking and talking.

"Priest, you know who we are?" asked the one nearest to the dividing magnetic field.

Father Peters did not answer. He did not even nod. There was no need to reply, for he was not there.

"We have been sent by the Feldommandant," continued the man, his lips hardly moving, as he lisped his errand. "You have to be spoken to."

*   *   *

There was Bert, exactly as Frances had imagined. Her every detail was correct. Or was it just that in retrospect, she shaped her remembered projections to fit what she found.

Well he was depressed. It seemed an age that he kept her at the door, neither of them moving. Like a rabbit prey, petrified and self-hypnotized, she stood there in the warm bright afternoon sun feeling his black mood devouring her body, as his mind perused her from head to toe, while moving not one jot.

Eventually, as if his mental machine had come to terms with this aberration, he stepped back inside his house and she followed meekly. Not a word passed between them but each knew the other's thoughts of unspoken urgency.

* * *

The two agents had led Father Peters to his own study, moving with confidence, as if they were familiar with his house, the one in front, the other silently behind. Perhaps they did know his house? Everything is possible in dreams.

It was not the priest's place to invite his guests to be seated. In fact it was he who was the guest, for he had come uninvited into their non-existence.

All three stood. None seemed uncomfortable at this.

* * *

Frances saw only his back, as Bert led the way straight up the stairs. He led her into the front room, the bed was less jumbled there. The windows were open wide, curtains flapping gently in and out over the sills in the light breeze. The whole neighbourhood of black-eyed, all seeing, windows could be seen from here. Bert made for the curtains to pull them, to shut out the prying intrusive eyes.

"No," Frances' gasp was little more than a whisper, but as such was a very definite syllable.

* * *

"Priest," started the only communicative one, "we have been sent to give you a message from the German authorities . . . ."

German authorities? Thomas Peters should have woken here. He was imagining all this. It was he who had brought the two unreal characters into his Vicarage and he too would now despatch them. Wake up! Wake up! No, it was

357

not possible. 'German authorities' could never be a dream to be moulded and shaped at will. Such things would never be entertained or held in the priest's conscious or subconscious mind for long enough to play a role.

"You are to be reprimanded prior to actions."

The second German, the silent one, stepped forward, taking Father Peters' elbow lightly from behind, as if nudging him back to reality.

"Reprimanded?" The second man ceased his nudging. The first stared the priest full in the face allowing his thin crack of a grin to dispel the remainder of Thomas' sense of unreality.

*   *   *

"No?" Bert turned to face his Frances. He did not believe it. There was not a 'no' in her. He was sure of it.

"No, not here!" her voice rasped, little more than a whisper, her throat flooded with the streams of desire welling up inside her. "Not here, Bert. In there, where we were before."

She did not hear his attempts at excuses or reasons, the mockery of his memory, his shame, the filthy uncared-for state of the room to be observed in daylight. She was busily undressing him, exploring his hairy body, touching every part of him with her lips, tasting his sweetness. She knew only that she was creating in her mind a happening which was soon to be reality, where all but their two bodies and minds would cease to exist.

*   *   *

"You are no longer permitted to preach in your church." The message was delivered calmly and without volume. The effect was stunning. Father Peters, who expected everything and would unwillingly accept it as being inevitable, swayed slightly, as the words ravaged his mind.

"Well?" grinned the plain-clothed Gestapo agent. "Do you have anything to say? Do you wish to make some insulting comments? Please do. I will gladly report them back to add to your case."

"What do you mean?" asked the priest, hearing his own

voice, as if from another, while thinking what a futile and ridiculous question he posed.

"We mean," continued his verbal assailant, with obvious satisfaction that clarification had been called for, "that you have lost the right to assemble together a group of more than two persons in a public place, as is the law in all Europe. Your permit to conduct services has been revoked. If you attempt to break the law in this matter then you will be immediately removed!"

The silent one drew out from his pocket the documentation to this effect and passed it to his colleague.

"But what of my Church?" Father Peters heard his plaintive voice beginning to plead. "How will my people be able to come to Church on Sunday?"

"That is your problem, friend," said the German almost gleefully. "You should have thought about such things before you self-indulged yourself in your stupid crimes."

"Crimes?"

"Nobody in free Europe speaks against the Führer and goes unpunished. You must know that, priest!"

"Yes, but how . . .?" Father Peters was not only pleading, but he was caught up by the impossibility of his position. Yes, he knew what had caused his demise. He had expected reciprocal action. He knew the tenor of the ban, but this was so sudden. It was not possible! There were too many unanswered questions, unfinished tasks, ambiguities. His dejection and pleading misery became imbued with a growing rage at the injustice and ludicrous nature of it all.

"How do I give my people their services? Their rites?"

"Rights? " asked the spokesman, "Who has rights? Did any of them prevent your subversion?" There was a chill cold sneer in his words. "You must work these matters out for yourself, it is all in here."

Without further ceremony he handed the manilla envelope to the shocked prelate and nodded to his companion. They both turned, leaving the house, their footsteps echoing in Father Peters' ears long after they had gone, leaving the front door ajar.

*   *   *

359

She completed her task in a trance. Undressing her lover was a work of art. Each exposed part of his so loved body equalled in reality all her fantasies. Yes, he was as good as her ideal.

She smothered him in kisses, urging his clumsy hands as he fumbled to remove her clothing, stopping briefly the hot kisses almost ill temperedly, to guide his foolish hands more quickly to effect her hot nakedness.

It was with pain and thwarted passion that she held back from his body to allow him enough access to her to fuel his desire, the better to satisfy her. For these long pauses her breaths lengthened and shortened with an apparent irregularity. She delighted in the coolness, as the air engulfed her exposed breasts, and longed for the cool swirling round the whole of her body, which was now on fire.

Restraining herself, she stood back regarding Bert as he too endulged himself. All the time she imagined the hot dry touch of his skin and the elixir taste of his sweat, while she was looking, not taking. Neither was better or worse, imagination or reality, for both were interwoven. Now, all her feelings were the same, as with her first time, for this was her first time again.

Bert, impatient, aware that time was rushing him on and that he did not have an argument with it, but would gladly take his desire right now, aided where Frances was tantalizingly slow, helped to expose himself to her view.

Ah, he was there, beautiful! Still she could feel, still the tastes, the smells, the magnification of sound, as fingers rummaged through hair and ran along skin. She felt all and sensed all, the past, the present and the future were all reality and she was the universe. She was the magnet for all the senses she drew to herself, real and imagined.

Bert's pulse was right through his body. He was the pulse, the throbbing. The pulsing and enlarging were part of his mind, while his body was just so many appendages. He was fighting himself for his second time, not for Bert a combining of first and subsequent in the thoughts. He had desperately to control and eradicate his thoughts now, in order to save himself for the essential moment which was to lift him, albeit momentarily, from the cares of this life.

As Frances viewed the focus of her desires, her mind and

impulses past and present interlocked, as soon their bodies would be, she knew that, for all her arousal, she had not within her a memory of the physical feeling that the great fulfilment had once granted her. She did not know how it would feel, it had not been retained within her experiences. She was oblivious, virgin to the projections once more.

The mind could not be sensuous without the physical accompaniment of body, of their two intense bodies. She had to will the entry in her mind and memory, to bring the union into her. She had to know what it was she was receiving. She had to know, not just see, and taste and hear and smell.

Pushing herself forward she made to effect the union. There were no hands for guidance as guidance was not necessary with this first time, which had had its first time prelude formerly to direct it. Bert gasped. He was holding back as she moved upon him and his moment of timelessness came with the initial contact. Not for him this time, the night-time struggling to effect the will of his desire. No, for Bert it was completed. For Frances, not begun.

*　　*　　*

John, back home, the *Press* under his arm, still unread by him. He had waited at Dad's shop until it had arrived, but not wishing to display his emotions or eagerness in front of his father, has asked if he should take it home.

Dad, knowing his son's anxiety, had agreed and had not discomforted the boy with any questions on the matter.

His first reaction, on finding an empty flat, was pleasure. Now he could open the newspaper to find his dream come true, of just to have his deep felt disappointment confirmed. There was no witness to either state.

He prepared himself to be confounded, turning the pages slowly, tantalizing his expectations.

It was there! It really was, a gala announcement confirming that what he had seen two days previously, had not just been in his imagination!

What was that?

> 'Civilians wishing to take part should arrive at La Vallette thirty minutes before commencement and report to the point marked Civilian Entry. . .'

No mention of Clubs being asked to submit teams. Ah well, what did it matter really? He would swim just the same. Perhaps Father Peters would give them more time for games at Boys' Club if they did not have to concern themselves with gala arrangements tonight?

Where was Mum? Despite his earlier resolve not to bother with a meal, John, in his excitement, now felt hungry. Where could she be so late, especially with Dad due home at any minute?

*　　　*　　　*

Frances, aware of Bert's withdrawal, her desires unsated, his depression at the realization of it, already clamped on her lover's face, could do nothing in her helplessness except cry.

As the tears slipped from her eyes and as predictably his ardour suffered, they both knew it was over, it would not now be a possibility today, if ever again.

The tears turned to bitterness and then to anger as she observed the shrinking which was to remain first in her thwarted desire and then in her mind, as her guilt and frustration were both to vie with each other.

She could not talk, she would not talk as she turned from him. Bert tried to grasp her shoulder, while moving his free hand to try to resuscitate himself but he knew, from the involuntary stiffening of her back, she would not be able to help his futile attempts at recovery.

*　　　*　　　*

What was he to do? Father Peters was in a quandry. The document was in German, quite brief but quite clear, even to his imperfect mastery of the tongue. He knew the laws about gathering in groups, how it was not possible even for a group of friends to stop to talk in the street, without a licence. He knew all this, and that where licences were granted, it was always with the knowledge that at least one German would be present, either surreptitiously obvious, as in the case of places of worship, or secretly, as in public houses or at concerts. He knew he had broken the law and now his licence had been revoked. But so suddenly!

What would happen on Sunday? If he were still free? Despite his pessimism on that matter he, like youth, felt he would survive. Death is for the old, for others, never for the youth himself. Should he 'phone the Dean? Should he try to get a fellow clergyman to try to help him out? They would not be too keen. They would say he had brought it on himself, he knew the game, he was aware of the rules.

Even if he got someone to help out, wouldn't they need a special licence for this particular congregation? Would he and the Dean have to go humbly to the Feldkommandantur or even the Gestapo? Was it all worth it? He may not have another Sunday anyway! Well he'd not think of it right now. There was the Club to open up. The other problem would not get any worse, nor would it go away if he tried to forget it for a while. No, he must live each moment as it came now. Now the moment had to be Boys' Club.

*   *   *

"Where's your mother?" asked Larry, mildly irritated that there was no sign of Frances. Her hat and coat had gone too.

"Don't know," shrugged John.

Larry picked up the paper;

"Did you find what you wanted?" he asked, not particularly interested, but attempting to make conversation.

"Yes," replied John, adding, "thanks," as a belated after-thought.

"Good, I suppose we'd better think about tea then, eh?" suggested Larry, unable to settle to the paper. It really was not good enough, Frances being out like this, with no mention of it, and not even a note! She should be here right now seeing to his needs after his hard day's work! She'd miss him after Friday! That was for sure! Then she'd wish she'd been better to him in his last few days.

"I don't want any tea thanks, Dad, I'm off up the Club," said John, breaking in on his father's thoughts.

"Not yet," said his father, beginning to vent his irritation on his son. "It's far too early."

"Well, I don't want any, anyway," replied John, unaware of Dad's annoyance.

"You'll have a drink at least, before you go, and that's finai," was Larry's response. "I'm not being messed around by two people at the same damned time!"

It was this loaded atmosphere into which Frances walked. To her it was her considered punishment for attempted infidelity.

"What's going on around here?" Larry demanded. "Where's my tea? I come in from work and what do I find but you not here. What the hell's going on?"

Frances, laden with guilt, feeling the whole world must, by now, be aware of her shame, could not answer. Where she would usually have given back abuse with equal ferocity, now she did not feel any justification. More so, she did not have the fight or the will.

Frances said nothing, she simply looked towards her husband, the one who needed her so and whom she had treated so badly. She almost welcomed his anger as some self-inflicted flagellation for her sins.

With her silence, Larry suddenly realized the enormity of his self-indulgence. He knew that he had broken a long-entrenched habit never to criticize, never to blame, but to take all life's little knocks and pains which came his way from Frances, either deliberately or unintentionally. It had always been the case that he had ended up apologizing and feeling in the wrong, even if he had started as the innocent party. He had always done this, since their early courting days. His swallowing of pride, to prevent or lessen the periods of hostilities, had become habitual. There had been a tacit agreement between them that it was done 'for the boy', that John, the symbol of their love, might not be exposed to that cruel fact of life, that parents did not always love each other as they always had.

"Love. . .," he started. "Sorry, love, I didn't mean. . . " She had gone! The sound could be heard of the bedroom door slamming.

"I'm off," said John, breaking into his father's shock.

"Yes, you do that," Larry absent-mindedly said, as he made his way to make his peace with Frances.

Within seconds John was out of the house and free of its cares, at least temporarily.

A few minutes later Larry also left. He did not travel so lightly. He carried the miseries of the whole family with him, down to the Golden Lion.

* * *

He knew that it could not be and yet he knew also that it was. John's way would not cross that of Franz, as he made his way up paths and lanes, up the sunbaked hills of history from St. Peter Port. But Franz was there. Part of John knew that they would meet, for it was formed in his imagination. He, the creator, had it in his power to make his creation perform to his will.

Inevitably and helplessly, far too early, John made his tortuous way to Boys' Club. He took the early detour away from his destination, past Town Patrol House. As in his dismal projections, the building was dead and silent, even the sentry was petrified. He saw Franz come from the great door and yet the hinges had not swung, the handle had not turned.

The warmth of the late sun burned on John's face as he turned his helpless journey westward. The heat, exuding from walls, passed into him and exhausted him with the tiredness of those who have not laboured. In that brief moment of the short walk, which would have invigorated the memory, had his hopeless friend accompanied him, he knew. He knew then momentarily that Franz, although alive, was dead to him. He knew that never would they meet again.

And yet, Franz was there. The Rue des Frères held part of him. Franz's memory, the trail of trauma as he had run from the raid, that raid, so long ago now, which had caused their first meeting, came out of the high stone walls, to chill him. John had not been with Franz on that race from hell but now he knew he had been. Rue des Frères, with its weather-washed and ancient tombs, landscaped into the hill, older than the very trees, penetrated his consciousness. He lived the evil, he knew the terror, which till then had been only words. When Franz had been with him he had sympathized without understanding. Now in the stark realization that all contact could only be retrospective, he understood and shared the suffering but could not ever tell the other so. John felt cold. Such thoughts would kill. He had to move on, for ever onward move.

La Port, St. Jacques, evil place of Feldkommandantur memories, and yet happy, loaded with that past where the two had once shut out the cares of the adult world. It was off the route and yet it was a pilgrimage.

The happy thoughts easily excluded all that was unacceptable. This self-indulgence was to shield the victim from the knowledge of his own thoughts. Not yet to suffer, although all past, John, unbeknown to him, still had a future.

* * *

John was first to arrive at the Club steps. Down he went, uneasily, into the concrete flight to enter the now shaded cool, uninviting building.

Was the place open? Was he too early? Would he be the only one there? Had Franz, too, excited at the prospect, got there first? Yes, that was it! Franz was already there, he was inside already, talking with the priest! Father Peters, despite himself, had to like just one German, he had to see that they were not all bad!

But what if Franz were not there? No, that was too silly for words! Of course Franz was there! At least he was there till John reached and opened that door.

John hesitated. He wished to stay a little with his dream, to keep Franz waiting there for him. Better to stay outside and know his friend was safe within, eventually to exit his way, than to go in, ready to share life with him, only to find his very entry had made his friend just so much dream to mock and taunt him.

"Ah, John!" Father Peters called from behind, greeting his parishioner, and sweeping Franz into eternity. "You and I are the first."

So Franz had not come, a club with just one member, just one leader. The waiting, with the anxieties allowed to surface once more. At least John could pour out his thoughts to the priest for he would understand.

366

"Hello, Father, I'm early," said John, rather stating the obvious, in his attempt to lose his mind in conversation. "Do you think there'll be many tonight?"

"How should I know?" replied the priest irritably. "Does anyone appreciate anything these days?"

"Eh? Sorry, pardon?" enquired John, the bitterness in his confessor's voice not wholly lost on his self indulgent misery.

"Oh it's nothing!" Father Peters sounded angry. About what was he angry? John had not said anything to cause offence. The man should be pleased that at least one person would come early. What did he have to be annoyed about anyway? He was a grown up, he had nothing to worry about. He had a safe easy job, didn't he? He wasn't going to France, was he? The Germans wouldn't dare touch him, a priest! His family was not about to be scattered. He did not have a friend who was an enemy. No, there was nothing complicated for the priest. Why then, should he, a supposedly good man, be irritable with John? John needed his help, that was the important thing. He did not wish the priest to express his own moods.

"Do you need some help, Father?" offered John, in an attempt to turn the contact energy back to his own problems, while Father Peters fumbled for the extraordinarily large bunch of keys, which he kept somewhere inside his shiny worn cassock.

"No," came the terse reply.

"Well, can I set anything up inside or anything?" asked John, determined not to be left feeling that he had in some way inadvertently offended the priest.

"Like open the canteen?" asked Father Peters, in bitter sarcasm. "There must be lots of bars of chocolate and ice-creams for sale, eh?"

John did not answer. He was not sure whether he should attempt to smile or just agree with the priest, in his bitterness about the privations of the Occupation. What did it matter if there were no food, no luxuries? There were still the activities, weren't there?

"Maybe you'd better go home, John. You won't want to stay here with me. That's not much fun, eh? A Club with one member?"

367

"There'll be more," attempted John, "Franz is coming. There are bound to be some more."

"Franz?" asked the priest. His voice was strange. Was it rage or was it disdain? "Who is Franz?"

"You know, Father, you know. . ."

"I know!" cut in the priest. "I know the German!"

What was that supposed to mean?

"Don't look at me like that, John Collins. You and your German friends! I just hope, for his sake, your Franz doesn't come here this evening!"

"Eh?" John was hurt but could not understand why.

"What's the matter, Father?" He was not sure whether to feel anger at the slight to his friend, or to try to placate this adult, who was showing all the signs of leading matters his way, rather than indulging John in his own problems.

"It's nothing, John. That's the whole problem. It's not for you to have to worry about the problems of this world. Don't take any notice of me. You wouldn't understand anyway."

John had lost control of how the conversation would go. He would have to subjugate his own important wishes to the lesser whims of the priest. Besides, he was curious and temporarily less conscious of Franz's absence.

"I thought you were pleased I could bring Franz," John almost whined.

"I am, yes I am that!" sighed the priest. "It's not your fault, John. It's just that we have problems," his voice trailed off.

Problems? We?

"I'm not being nasty or anything John, but probably it's a good thing your friend isn't coming," began the priest. The definitive 'isn't' jarring in John's mind, about to be ejected as some unwelcome foreign body from the respiratory system. "It's probably all for the best if nobody comes, if we just fold up the whole idea."

The priest went on to explain the visit he had received from the Gestapo and how he had lost his licence to gather groups together. He voiced his fears that the system would check up on them, in an attempt to catch them out. He warned John of the consequences, as if he did not know.

"If what you say is true, Father," said John partially

shocked, but in some way pleased that the priest's chagrin had not been directed at him, "then it doesn't really matter much anyway, does it?"

"I don't follow your argument," queried the priest.

"Well you're in trouble anyway, by the sound of it, and Franz and I are, that's for sure. So what more can they do?"

The logic could not be refuted. Father Peters concurred.

"John," said Father Peters, now less angry in tone, "don't you think you ought to face up to things a bit?"

He was sure that this young member of his congregation was deluding himself, that he could not come to terms with the truth that Franz was now gone, that the impossible friendship was at an end.

"What's that, Father?" asked John, his voice slightly quickened with defensiveness as if his subconscious knew and feared the purport of the speaker's message.

"Franz, John. You must know it's over." He tried to turn his hurtful words into kindness with his tone.

"'It' Father? What do you mean 'it'?" demanded John angrily, whilst trying to close his mind to the terrible things he was about to have to listen to.

"Your...," Father Peters hesitated slightly while he wrestled with the concept, finally subjugating his attitude in the cause of John's welfare, "your friend won't be here this evening. You must know that..."

John did not hear any more, as his mind screamed out to him not to heed this evil sound. What was the priest saying? What rights had he to talk about Franz? Who was he to say what was and what was not to be?

"Have you got the key to the games cupboard, please, Father?"

"He won't be permitted to come out any more, my son. Face it. At least he's..."

"The key please, Father!" John breathed heavily.

"Don't delude yourself, John. Please I'm trying to help you to face up to things. This war..."

"Will you give me the bloody key, Father Peters? Give it to me! The key, I want the bloody key!" John was stamping his foot with his demand. He had not listened, but he had heard. As the tears streamed from his eyes, he heard Franz say so clearly;

"It's all right for men to cry sometimes."

He looked up, proud of his tears. He observed the frosted concern on the priest's face, as he heard his friend coming down the steps.

There was Franz, he had come! There, he was entering the door. No detail, just a hazy outline through the hot tears, but it was Franz all right!

"Hello, Collins. You the only one here then?" came the most unwelcome voice of Vincent Carré.

* * *

Nobody else came. Father Peters did not have to be taken away for holding an illegal gathering. The so unwelcome other member gave up his attempts to get John to play billiards, eventually leaving grumpily, half-heartedly calling back, only partially received abuse, which was intended either for John or the priest; something to the effect that 'it' was all a waste of time.

"It's no use John, I'm going to have to lock up now," ventured the priest at last. "We'll have to go. No one else is coming."

John just stared helplessly at the doorway where the sun's brightness was beginning now to be replaced by the ever deepening shades of twilight.

"Come on, John. . . "

"I'll stay, I'll wait outside if you've got to push me out like this!"

The priest was not hurt for himself but he felt deeply the misery displayed in the other as he moved, trance-like, towards the door. Father Peters followed, relieved that at least he could soon lock this door for the very last time. He would lock inside out of mind, the scenes of unhappiness which had just emphasized all their helplessness this evening.

The turning of the key, the only sound on the now chill half-light, had a finality about it which entered deep into both souls.

"Goodnight, John," Father Peters hesitated. "I am going

home now. You had better go home too, eh? It's not long till dark now."

John waited. Yes, the offer was there. He had been waiting for it to be said.

"I'll walk with you, John. I will come to your door. It is all right for me to be out after curfew."

"Thanks Franz," he replied.

"John, I'm sorry," Father Peters was concerned. "Would you like me to see you home?"

What? What did he want now? Why couldn't he just bugger off? Why couldn't he just leave him and Franz alone? Why did grown-ups always want to interfere?

"John! Come on, I'll fetch my bicycle."

Franz had walked on. He was about to go round the corner.

"Wait, I'm coming!" yelled John, disregarding the priest. He pulled his bike from the wall, avoided the priest's steadying hand, and jumped on to the saddle.

His tyre was flat! That bastard Vincent! He'd let his tyre down!

*   *   *

Frances lay on her back watching the portion of the clear evening sky above the houses and prison wall opposite change imperceptibly through all the shades of blue to yellow then pink and gradually to violet. She lay there impassive, trying desperately not to think.

Bert was knocking at her mind again but she would not let him enter. He was pleading with her to let him in to talk with her but no longer could she contemplate such a prospect. Her guilt and self-loathing had changed, with the turning sky, to frustration and anger. And she had alienated her Larry also. She would not think of either, she would just try to close her conscious mind a little longer, to live only for the present.

*   *   *

A slightly relieved Father Peters, having done his best to console John and help the youth to accept the cruel fact

371

that, while this state of war existed, the two youngsters could not meet to continue their friendship, now prepared to send his young parishioner on his way. He felt he had done all he could.

"I'm off now, Father," stated John, standing suddenly, his voice without emphasis or its usual timbre.

"I'll call in at the Gestapo, on the way home. There's no need for you to come thanks. I'm O.K. now."

The Gestapo? Why would he do that? That should not be allowed to happen.

"The Gestapo John?" asked the priest as he too, face contorted in concern, got to his feet to fetch John's coat. "What's that for, eh?"

"I'm going to ask about Franz," asserted John. "Like we said, I've got nothing to lose by it. You never know, they might tell me how he is."

"I wouldn't, my son," ventured the priest, glad of this signal of John's acceptance of the circumstances, but worried that he might make matters more difficult for himself. "Why don't you sleep on it?"

"That's not possible, Father!" said John with studied bravado. "Not possible at all!"

"Well I strongly advise against you going in to the Gestapo, tonight at least," urged the priest.

"I'm sorry about that Father," countered John, "but if I don't go in to the Gestapo on the way home, where do you suggest I go. Shall I call at Town Patrol House?"

"Don't do either," was Father Peters' advice. "You'll only make matters worse."

"Worse? Why for, worse? It can't be worse! I'll tell you what, Father, I won't go to either place tonight if you do one thing."

John had not planned such words, they had just been inspirational, out of desperation.

Father Peters waited impassively.

"You contact them, Father. You get on the 'phone now. I've got a number."

The priest heard the words but was unable to equate them with logic. He knew John meant it.

"That's not possible, John. You must realize. . . "

"O.K., then," interrupted John, "don't. It's no skin off my

372

nose. You don't 'phone, I call in at the Gestapo now! It's as simple as that!"

Father Peters felt he was dealing with an angry dog who would not surrender its bone. He had nothing to gain or lose particularly, in letting John take his course, but his instinct told him that John stood to make matters very difficult for himself. John had to be saved from himself, even if the saving could only be accomplished by his involvement in the other's hopeless cause.

The priest succumbed to the emotional blackmail, the neglect of which would have kept his life less troublesome, the acceptance of which would add to his many problems. He could do nothing else. He would 'phone Captain Weiss, but in the morning.

It was agreed.

*　　*　　*

Frances heard John's leaden footsteps coming up from below. It was now almost dark, her room was chill and only the silhouette of the buildings opposite spoke of the endless sunset, now past. The steps paused outside her door. She entered back into time. He moved on.

She knew it was John. Was he not back early? Something was not right, she sensed it. She knew, although not sure she was supposed to have such knowledge, that he had intended a furtive meeting with Franz. She also now knew that this had not taken place. Her little boy was in distress about the plight of her other son.

She found him in the kitchen, helplessly groping his way through bare cupboard shelves, not wishing to waste the precious gas on light, while in the vain hope he might find food to placate the unbearable emptiness he felt.

"John, my love," she said, as she made towards him, not too quickly so as not to give away the concern she felt, carried by the quaver in her voice, "you're hungry, dear. Wait a minute, I've got something."

He did not answer, but remained staring at the fading light of the sky while his senses received each of the growing sounds of the night time cacophony, as curfew approached.

"Light the gas, dear," said his mother after what she had

considered a respectful pause, in deference to his obvious distress. "Here's the flint. I've got a little bread you can have."

"Don't put the light on, Mum. Please don't, it's better like this. Please!" he pleaded.

"Yes, all right, dear, but sit down. I'll sort you out. You must be starving. Didn't you have any tea before you went out?"

"No." His voice was sullen and lifeless.

Frances began to busy herself. There was no tea left but perhaps she could stretch the milk a little with some water. That would give him something hot. Should she ask him again about the light. Would he get irritated? It would help if she could see what she was doing. Besides, she wanted to have a good look at her darling. Even in this fading light she could detect his pallor reflecting the fading sky as if his face were the moon.

"Mum," he began hesitantly. "Could you sit down, please. I want to talk to you." The words came out with effort, as if he were in shock at the embarrassment of his intended conversation.

Frances was by his side now, sitting right near the table's corner, her back to the window. She took his hand. How cold it was. He began to shake.

"All right, dear. You just tell me everything. Take your time, all in your own good time, eh?"

With that, John fell forward and let his mother baby him. He was her little boy again. Even John could still be her little child, like Franz had been. Oh poor little Franz.

John, now lost in the comfort of his mother's protection, poured out all his misery. With his hot tears and rasped throat came relief. He knew, no matter what befell him or Franz that Mum would always be there. The world would not end, she would not permit it. All the impossibilities of their hopeless circumstances were now of no consequence, for temporarily John was outside their control. He was in timelessness, where no decisions could be made or enacted, without his mother's will.

As Frances listened to her son she absorbed it all. All the bitterness, all the misery and the hate, the self-doubt and the fears of the unknown. She equated his saga with her own. She knew many of the things he told her, for had not Franz confided and taken of her that same comfort for his own impossible lot?

The others she knew by instinct and experience. She knew the guilt and yet also she knew the deep and scourging anger which filled with rage at the injustice.

How could John feel outside the right for allowing a friendship of the heart to rule his head and judgements conditioned by the times, evil times? Why should she be condemned in her own eyes, and soon in the eyes of the world, for her impossible love with Bert? Why was it all so futile, all so impossible? John still loved his country, the cause of justice; she still loved her husband and yet both were branded in their country's sight and in their consciences, as traitors, for none should love more than one person or one cause more than another! Why, oh why, could not a person love more than one when that they clearly did? Why was this perverse?

Finally, when all talking had stopped, all heaving breaths and racking sobs ceased, only hot tear-stained cheeks now dried and sticky to the touch of each of them, did Frances, with the lead in her stomach, as though she now carried both loads, pull away. She had served her purpose. She had eased her other son. No more could be said.

"I'll put the light on now?" she asked as she moved with flint towards the mantle. John did not gainsay.

"There!" she uttered, as if for the first time ever, observing that blue globe guttering to turn to misty lemon as its pale light pushed darkness away to the corners and under shadows. "We're lucky, the gas is still on. They must have forgotten to turn off at the works."

John was silent. He did not care about the trivia of such privations. He was happy just to let his mother keep on chattering, to keep his thoughts at bay.

His pallor now had flushed, his salted eyes sparkled. It was Frances who now paled as she knew her turn had come to tell her own distress to someone. How, after such association of ideas, could she keep her own misery unshared. Who else could she confide in, except to her own little son, who would understand completely?

"John, dear," she phrased almost tentatively. "Thank you

for telling me your troubles. I've got problems too, you know?"

She waited for his reaction before she could steel herself to continue.

Mum? Problems? What problems could she possibly have apart from the obvious? Dad, he supposed, and the worries of the trials. What could John do about such things? He felt embarrassed at the prospect of hearing his mother's concerns. It was quite in order for him to load his matron, for that was her job, but for his own mother to have problems? No, that was not right! She was grown up, she was not entitled to such irregularities.

He resigned himself, wishing the moment past. He would try not to look as his mother undressed her mind with the light on.

*   *   *

He never could have guessed! Uncle Bert! Bert, no, he was not worthy even of that stark title. Bisson, plain Bisson, was better for him.

His own mother?

What about Dad? Poor Dad! How could his mother behave so? How could she, with him and Dad soon up for trial, to be sent to France? What was she thinking of?

Yes, there'd always been something about that person. He'd felt it all along; he was not quite right. There had always been something not quite right! John had been unable to recognize it until now. But now it all fell into place, all made sense!

So that was why he was always round here, always on the 'phone! That was why his poor father felt driven from the house, was always getting drunk!

It was too late. Frances' realization was confirmed, as her little boy no longer wished to be so, as he withdrew his recently purged and shared unhappiness back into himself, she sensing the exclusion. Gone now was the unity, now there was an icy barrier.

John withdrew perceptibly, emotionally and physically. She could detect disgust and disbelief on his soul, as his eyes saw right through her cloak of shame, into the nakedness of her infidelity.

John, without a word, left his mother as, in chill and shock, he went to his room.

* * *

Chapter Seventeen

The drama had been over in seconds and, once the doctor had administered his relief, Sister went out to explain to the two worried distraught novices.

"So sorry about all that," said Sister, genuinely apologetic. "There is no absolute knowing how long the morphine will last, you see. It is because of the constant transfusion."

She need not have gone into such detail, for Gerda had felt ill and was not listening, just fighting herself to stay conscious, to be fully ready to give herself to the last to her poor dying man.

Frances was pale, on the point of collapse. On her tired old face she had the quizzical look of a little girl.

"I thought he was getting better," she murmured, "so why does he seem so ill, my poor child?"

Gerda heard herself reply, as if listening to another, to a foolish woman unable to cope;

"He is, Mum. John is getting better, you'll see."

With the deception, Gerda aged almost to death's door with her husband, while old Frances was the beneficiary, reviving, ready to greet the recovery.

Sister interjected;

"I think you can come in now, but I would like you to go and rest quite soon."

"But what if . . .?" Gerda, who had been so recently such a silly woman, was not able to complete.

Sister, fully understanding, finished the sentiment for her;

"We will call you," she said. "Be assured, we will not forget."

Gerda was assured, yet still it did not seem right. Old Frances needed her rest though. She had to trust the Sister. She would trust her, but she could not. Not just yet.

They entered the ward once more. This time the nurse

was composed. She had time to flash a fleeting smile, an innocent light, almost of coyness. It seemed apt by recent contrast, for John too now lay calm, his eyes closed, his breathing more steady. The Doctor felt safe to leave.

Frances moved to her little boy. She smiled.

"Oh John, you all right now, my pet?"

"Yes, Mum," he whispered. He opened his eyes. "I'm just fine, me." He wanted to give his mother his arm but he did not seem to have one to give. It was a strange discovery, but it did not bother him. Nothing bothered him any more in this place. It was a strange place, so strange things would be the norm here. He smiled at the strangeness and old Frances, seeing him wince, smiled too. How strange. How awful yet how pleasant and how right it all seemed.

"Doctor . . ." Gerda heard herself talking again. The silly woman was just about to add to her ridiculousness, yet she knew she had to attempt to appear right, and sensible and caring, just this once. She had to be sure. She knew what she wanted to say, but the words would not come on their own.

The Doctor stopped in his tracks, glancing at Sister. Was this woman going to stop him from his duty? Had not Sister done her explanations? Perhaps he could afford to leave as if he had not noticed this plaintive cry? He did not need all this, he had work to do.

Sister knew what Gerda wished to ask. She knew too, that the Doctor thought her lax in her own task and that her nurse would feel the slight. All were sensitive of each other's thoughts and feelings. The presence of the dying heightens all the sensitivities, even of those assumed insensitive.

"Will he be all right?" she heard herself ask. She was doing it again. No, that was not what she wanted to ask. Of course he would not be all right. What a fool she was making of herself. How silly they must all think her? All except Frances and John, that was. So what did it matter? Before they could reply to their received misconception, she re-phrased herself.

"Sorry, Doctor. I know the position. What I really want to know is . . ."

Sister came to her assistance.

"Doctor, Mrs. Collins knows the outcome. She wishes to

379

know if she can go along to rest with her mother-in-law. I have assured her, but she would like to hear it from you."

The Doctor understood. The hurry was now gone from his exit, the disapproval from his face. The respect of his staff had returned to his confidence.

"Mrs. Collins," he explained kindly, almost leisurely, "it is quite all right for you to go to rest now, my dear." He glanced round him, confirming his reassurance, as he continued. "Nothing is likely to change imminently, and even if it did, we would call for you."

He paused. Gerda looked more relieved now.

Further reading the poor woman's mind, the Doctor added;

"I think it will be quite a long time, probably until late tomorrow. Now you need your rest for that, don't you?" His voice was kind, still unhurried.

He patted Gerda's hand, not waiting for a reply.

*   *   *

The morning came quickly for the priest, and with it the cold realization of what he had been inveigled into doing. Despite his now fast-diminishing last few days of freedom, he would gladly have turned back to sleep in his lonely bed, to return once more to his dear wife. But no, even though whatever he now did was soon to be erased, still he had to be true to himself and to his parish, he had to continue as though he still had a tomorrow.

The call was quickly connected, only for the priest to be greeted by the not too comprehensible master tongue.

"I'm sorry," he interrupted. "Could you speak in English, please?"

"Bitte?"

"In English," he sighed, "Sprechenzie in English, bitte."

"You are English?" came the gutteral reply.

What a dolt! Was it worth his bothering further?

"Give me Captain Weiss, if you please."

"Wait, please," was the reply. The line was dead for quite some time. Had they hung up on him? Was there some trouble with the line? Father Peters waited impatiently. He had time to catch a glimpse of his reflection in the hall mirror, as he stood. What a sight! Perhaps it was as well he would soon be removed from the community? Perhaps he might never return? Maybe, at the end of this war, his family would not have to suffer his lean and haggered, aged look?

Time is so precious when little of it remains, even if one only has plans for the trivial everyday routines. They take on a new significance, as precious, soon to be removed. How could he spend his time in such a wasteful way? Impatiently, without realization, he began to click the receiver for the operator. Just as he noticed his action the line came to life. Who was it, the operator or the Town Patrol House?

"Who speaks?" asked the voice at the other end. It was not the operator, it was definitely German and was male.

"I wish to speak to Captain Weiss," stated Father Peters for the second time, skilfully avoiding the enquiry.

"Who are you?" it had not worked!

"Peters is my name," informed the priest, "civilian priest. I have important business with the Captain."

How he would like to have given vent to his annoyance but how he realized the futility of such a course.

"Wait, please." Again the priest waited, again the line seemed dead. Once more he found his patience stretched.

"Hello?" Father Peters awoke from his fitful daydream.

"Yes?" Was this the Captain?

"Captain Weiss does not take telephone calls from civilians. You are to speak to the Feldkommandantur on civilian matters."

All that time to be told that! All that waiting! It was too bad! Father Peters was incensed but felt also a sense of panic at the hopelessness of the statement he had just received. It was true, he must go through the Feldkommandantur, he knew the procedures, but the very matter he had to discuss with Weiss must not involve them. Surely Weiss must remember him? Surely he must know why he had 'phoned? What a fool! How could he insist on rules and regulations in a matter of such seriousness? What fools these Nazi were! Even the one he had thought of as showing traits of goodness, turned out to be an idiot!

"I know that," began the priest, his anger ill disguised, "surely the man knows who I am? It's very very important, I can't. . ." He realized the line was dead.

*   *   *

There had been no Franz last night. John's mind was in turmoil. Why had his friend not come?

Had Franz just forgotten to come to Boys' Club, or had he not wished further contact with his enemy friend? Yes, perhaps that was what it was. Maybe, now that the German was safe from the evil Morten, he no longer needed John, he no longer needed his advice or his support, or someone with whom to share his misery? Perhaps John was already forgotten? Had Captain Weiss, the saviour of the young soldier, lectured Franz about his foolish involvement with a mere civilian, so that he now blamed John and his family for the terrible trouble he was in?

No, surely all the friendship which had passed between them could not be swept away just like that. They had known that their friendship was doomed, and yet they had continued it furtively, for the bond was stronger than the man-made strictures of war and propaganda. Such bonds could not be broken so easily. No, Franz must be being kept incommunicado. John knew his best friend would have come last night, just as he would attend with him at tomorrow's gala, where civilians and military would be permitted, no, positively encouraged, to mingle freely.

Yes, Franz was still his friend. They were brothers, were they not? Brothers cannot one moment be related and the next not. Brothers were forever. Franz would be in contact . . . if he could. If he could? What if he had already been sent away, though? No, such thoughts were too stupid to be entertained! Besides, wasn't Father Peters going to contact Captain Weiss this morning?

*   *   *

Father Peters knew why John had visited him so early, with the impetuosity of youth, expecting everything touching his all-important being to be expedited immediately. Well, at least the boy had learned something, and had not telephoned.

So Father Peters had not been able to carry out his promise! Well, that was just not good enough for John. Oh

382

no, his confessor would not get off so lightly. The man had said he would get news of Franz, and by golly, he would!

The combination of John's near frenzy and the priest's sense of failure, guilt almost, at not having been able to effect that which he had promised, persuaded him, albeit doubtfully and reluctantly, to try once more. Perhaps then his puerile parishioner would realize that failure had not been for the want of trying?

When the call was connected, fearing the predictable lack of success as previously, the priest steeled himself for some celestial deception. He could not concern himself with what effect it might have on the witnessing John's innocent soul. This was war, wasn't it? He had to employ wrong to fight evil sometimes, didn't he? Well, he could not enter into such introspection right now, there was no time. He could only play fleetingly in his thoughts, undertaking to try to right the wrong he was about to initiate in the cause of goodness's ultimate victory.

At the almost incomprehensible greeting he steeled himself, authoritatively stating, in his best Germanic accent;

"Weiss. . ." then adding, as if his confidence with the master tongue could convey his demand, with such brevity, "Feldkommandantur."

Almost immediately Weiss' voice was heard.

"Captain Weiss, this is Father Peters." The priest stopped, he sensed the chill in the atmosphere and was aware of the other's extreme anger in his silence, "No, do not put the 'phone down, Captain, please."

The hiatus was lengthy, before at last the priest was hailed with an anger seethed;

"God in heaven! You rang before, yes? You were told to deal with the Feldkommandantur, were you not? You are not permitted to speak direct with the Reich's forces! You have no right to knowledge of this 'phone number!"

"Now, Captain Weiss, you just listen to me," added Father Peters, trying to stay calm, just desperately hoping the German would not end the conversation. "You know there are some matters better not dealt with through the Feldkommandantur."

"What was that?" Captain Weiss sounded very defensive.

383

"I said, there are times when people have to break the rules, the procedures, is that not so?"

"Go on, priest, say what you mean," Captain Weiss' voice was cold, he sounded like a man in fear of what he might hear.

"I mean Franz Müller, that young soldier of yours," continued Father Peters, now more confident that he could keep the German's attention.

"Oh, I see," there was a definite relaxation of tension in the other's voice. "What concern is he of yours?"

Well, Captain, he is not my concern directly but like you, I feel involved in the lad's moral welfare."

"Like me? How, like me?" The Captain sounded almost affronted at the idea.

"You did save him, did you not? You showed protection of his innocence," stated the priest.

"Now look here, Mr. Reverend, who are you to say what I did for this boy? It is not your business to say such things to me, over the telephone. It is not your business!" Although his words were unfriendly, his tone belied it.

"Quite so, I understand," affected Father Peters, not wishing to compromise this good German's loyalty any further, "but could you possibly tell me if the boy is well, or even where he is? We are concerned, we would like to know."

'We'. What did he mean, 'we'? Why should a British minister concern himself with the well being of such a waif? What was there about that sickly underfed youth that brought out such good and unexpected responses in people? Even Weiss himself felt protective towards the naïve little fool. He had even helped him to his own possible detriment. Why had he bothered? Countless boys fell foul of the likes of Patrol Leader Morten and S.S. Hüffmeier, so why had he put himself at risk the way he had done? The young fool must have asked for it, and yet he had seemed so childishly innocent. Weiss had been unable to withhold his assistance, such as it was.

There must surely be some good in these conquered people too, some spirit, some fight left? It made the Captain feel they were not all contemptible, not when they too could concern themselves, and endanger their own lives, for a mere enemy youth.

"I cannot tell you anything," replied the Captain, but then, as if with second thoughts, rewarding the civilian's concern, "that is, I cannot tell you anything definite, only this. . ." He paused as though wrestling with himself as to whether he should impart yet more Reich's information to the curiosity of the enemy.

Father Peters' hope jumped, he was about to learn something. Maybe just speculative, but at least something.

John sensed the tension of expectation in his confessor's face. He concentrated to try to make out what was about to be imparted.

"The young soldier you mention is now out of harm's way. Will that do you?" asked the Captain, knowing full well that it would not, while preparing in his mind what next to say.

"You say he is well?" replied Father Peters, his relief transmitting itself temporarily to John who seemed momentarily to loosen all over his taut body. "Where is he, Captain?"

The Captain paused.

John too, was aware that conversation had ceased. What was it? What was wrong? Where could his friend be that was so difficult for the Captain to pass on?

"Minister, you must forget our young comrade now," came the Captain's reply. It was not intended to be unkind, on the contrary it was a gentle preparation for the shock he felt sure he had to reveal.

"You will not see him again while this war is on. Take that from me, please." Then, as if to forestall any anticipated protest, he added kindly, "Just be thankful that he is out of evil hands, if you understand my meaning?"

Father Peters nodded. John was puzzled and anxious at his side.

"I understand your meaning, Captain. Yes, we are grateful for that indeed."

Again John felt a flicker of unexplainable hope. All would be well. Why else should Father Peters say he was grateful? Perhaps Franz was soon to be released into circulation? That must be it, surely?

"Can we know what is happening to him please?"

Happening? What should be happening? Was he not about to be released? Hadn't Father Peters just expressed his gratitude?

The Captain sighed his resignation. This telephone call was most likely being monitored now. all sorts of notes were being made to be used against him, so why not complete it all? Perhaps if he told the priest everything, at least, the unthinking listeners and recorders might mention this revelation too. Such a conclusion might not hurt Weiss' prospects as seriously as if he were to remain inconclusive now? Besides, the subjugated man was a good person, perhaps he deserved to know, to slake his concern?

"Minister, Franz Müller cannot concern you anymore," he paused, he sensed his words would create unease. It was out of his hands but nevertheless, he felt he had to temper the stark statement with sensitivity. "Our young friend is leaving this island today. In fact he may well have left by now. All I know is, he is being transported by 'plane either to Germany or to some other part of the Continent. His destination is Russia."

How was the priest to tell John that already his pathetic friend was lost to him, at least for the duration of the war, but for ever perhaps? Was he to tell him the whole stark truth, or would the lad accept a vague explanation?

John knew from the tone of the one half of the conversation he had witnessed that at least his friend was well, he still existed, for he was still remembered, still known by all who heard his name. So that could not be bad, could it? At least Franz was still here in the island, at least he had not yet been sent to Russia. The very idea was ridiculous! No, Franz would not go to Russia yet, he would be here at least until John's own trial had taken place. Perhaps, once John had been dispatched to France, then Franz too might be taken to the Continent? Yes, that was most likely the case; it was symbolic somehow, both of them would travel to the mainland separately, yet bonded together by their common demise.

"So where is Franz right now, Father?" asked John, but already knowing he was safe here in Guernsey, probably doing duty on the cliffs. Well, the cliffs were not so bad. John was hardly cognizant of the priest's reply, as he imagined his friend sunbathing there at Pleinmont, while he peeled turnips and potatoes, as he listened to gramophone records. True, he would have the fear of the British commando raids at night, but surely that prospect was better than the horrors of the Russian front?

"Franz is doing duties, John. He will not be able to meet with you again," proffered the priest, breaking the news as gently as he could.

Well, that was obvious, wasn't it? John could not expect to meet up with his friend if he was now on the cliffs! But he would not be posted there for ever, would he?

"John, you will not meet up with Franz again until the war is over."

"Why?"

"Because . . ." This was so difficult. How could the priest enforce starkly the finality of Franz's departure, probably for ever, to speak of the inevitable with his posting to the Eastern Front?

"Because, John, your friend is on his way to Russia. You knew this was to happen, surely you must accept that?"

Russia? How silly! Of course Franz was destined for Russia! Franz knew that, John knew it, the priest also. Of course his friend was going to Russia, but not yet, not straight away! No, Franz was still here in the island, he had to be. John felt his friend's presence, he willed him to be still here. Sometimes Father Peters was just like his parents, like all adults; he had such stupid ideas.

*　　*　　*

It was good to cycle home, away from the stupidity of Father Peters. It was good to be able to break the rules and ride down The Grange two abreast with Franz. They even passed the Gestapo Headquarters in such a manner. What did it matter anyway, for the war was almost finished? The Russians had been beaten already, weaklings that they were. No need for Franz to go out there now.

The Americans wouldn't fight such a strong Germany. No, any day now Britain and Germany would sign a treaty of friendship and brotherhood. Franz and John had shown the world how it would work.

Russian front? How ridiculous!

That priest was certainly becoming very strange! Perhaps
it was his surfeit of hatred of Germany that made him so
odd? He seemed to have blinded himself to all the goodness
of the German people. How awful to be so bitter, so blind to
things happening around one!

"Come on, Franz. Let's see how those roads are which we
made on Sunday. I reckon there'll be some damage to
repair, eh?"

Franz chuckled.

"And you can stop bloody laughing, mon vieux,"
admonished John. "Just think yourself lucky I've caught you
up after that immature bastard let my tyre down."

The evening sun was hot on both their faces as they
cycled into the morning easterly breeze.

*   *   *

Franz wouldn't come upstairs to the flat. Well he'd gone
anyway. Perhaps he'd gone straight off down into the basement and out into the garden. He certainly made himself at
home! Well that didn't matter, why shouldn't he? It was his
home, after all. Didn't they share the same mother now?

The 'phone was ringing. Franz would be all right, alone
in the garden. John bounded up the stairs to answer.

"Yes, who is it?" he asked, waiving the formalities of his
own identification, in his haste to get back to his friend.

There was a pause at the other end of the line. John
remembered a similar incident quite recently. Before the
caller spoke he had steeped himself in annoyance that he
had neglected his friend for this.

"John?"

"What do you want?"

"John, this is uncle Bert. Can I speak to your mother
please?" The voice was hesitant, insecure, unsure of itself.

Speak to his mother? Strange, he had forgotten completely
last night's revelations! How could he not have held in his
mind that awful thing his own mother had told him? It was
almost as if he had been able to isolate that part of his
consciousness so that it would not impinge on the world,
with its relationships, as he wished it to be. Had not he just

388

now brought his friend back into his house, pleased once more to share his mother with him? How could he have forgotten his mother's confessions of infidelity and inexplicable deviation? How could he have contemplated forcing his friend to come under such a roof?

And now, here was the evil one speaking to him! That very man who had pretended to be his father's friend, who had worn a uniform as a badge of perfection, and all the time had cheated and deceived his father and him! How John detested this Bisson person!

"What do you want her for?" asked John, not attempting to hide his disdain.

"Eh," Bert was not yet aware of the other's animosity.

"I said, why do you want my mother? Why don't you stick to your friends? What's wrong with asking for my father? He's your friend, isn't he?" John very much enjoyed expounding himself in this way. He was spoiling for a fight.

Bert was somewhat nonplussed. What was the spoilt little brat getting at? He couldn't know anything, could he? Of course not, that was too ridiculous to imagine! How would he know anything? Frances certainly wouldn't have told him, that was for sure! Then maybe the little bugger just suspected something? Not him though, he was too much of a baby, he could not possibly begin to understand such things. No, he was just being rude, kicking against authority. Kids usually grew out of that sort of thing in their early teens, well before John's age. It just confirmed what a spoilt little immature brat he was!

"Look, John, your mother is either there or not. Will you please tell her I'm on the 'phone. I want to speak to her!" it was Bert's turn to be aggressive.

"Speak to her, is it?" sneered John, "Sleep with her more likely!" Sleep with her! Sleep with her, speak to her, speak with her, sleep with her, sleep to her?

The words spun round in Bert's mind. All his thoughts, his irrational fears, had somehow illogically come to fruition and what had just radiated from his mind now crashed back into his consciousness with a gravity exerted by subconscious guilts and fears.

"Get Frances," he gasped.

"You dirty old traitorous bastard!" replied John. "How

dare you bloody well tell me what to do? I'd not get my mother for you if you were the last person on earth!" His words were coloured crimson with his pulsing breast and were venomous in the extreme. He hated Bert as he had never hated anyone before.

"John?" asked the voice in the cold still silence at the other end.

"What?"

Bert did not know what. John cut off the silence as he pushed the receiver into Bisson's face.

* * *

Franz was nowhere to be seen. Not a trace of him in the garden. John had looked out, not a sign. He had raced down the stairs and into the cupboard steps leading to the basement and out into the now hot, mid-morning sunshine. The garden smelled of the thousands of dead snails rotting in their slime covered shells upon which their living descendants crawled their hot breeze-free existence.

No, Franz had not left a sign. He had not even touched their civil engineering project. John looked over at the roads which had given them such time-consuming pleasure only days before. Already blades of strong new couch grass were wreaking their havoc on the jungle roads and ants had despoiled the smooth surfaces upon which the two had laboured with such loving attention.

John kicked at the nearest viaduct, scattering it into so much stones and crumbling earth, as he turned his steps towards Gaudion's entrance.

No, of course there was no Franz, no bicycle. Of course, Franz did not own a bike. He had but only just for that one fateful day! Franz had not cycled home with him. Bert Bisson had seen to that! That corrupt policeman had sent Franz away. He of all people had lectured Franz on how to conduct himself! Just because he had been a policeman too, that filthy man, the thief of his own friend's wife, felt he could tell Franz what was right and wrong! And now Franz was gone, gone back to whereever it was he had been all along. Ex-P.C. Bisson had sent him back to his imprisonment!

* * *

What should he do? Bert was shocked and angry too. So John knew? How, he could not imagine. If John knew, then what about Larry? Perhaps he knew too? Bert doubted that. Larry would have been round, he'd not have stood for that!

Well, it was only a question of time now, before Larry did find out. How had John known though? Bert tried to go over in his mind the events of all the past few days, but he could not get his thoughts to run in sequence. He was incapable of reasoning the problem. All he knew was that he must contact Frances and very soon. Partly he needed to share with her the assault he had just received and to see to what extent she had been damaged by John's knowledge. Perhaps she could block the flood of innuendo before it became a disaster? He was not sure.

His overriding and strongest thought, however, was that which had been his original intention, to speak with his sweetheart, the only being who gave his life any structure and any recognizable proportions. He had not, after all, seen his dear one for almost a day and then it had been only to have his desires mocked by his own failure in performance. He could not enshrine as a final memory such an utter frustration. They had to talk.

What if John answered the telephone again? What did it matter? The boy already hated him. When a person hates it is not with degrees. He could not hate him more by having to speak a second time. But what if the second call just reminded John once more, causing him to tell his father? Well, so be it; that was inevitable anyway. Such an event would just exacerbate.

Besides, Bert could put down his own telephone if the brat answered. Either that or give him a mouthful of his own abuse to pay the child back.

Possibly John, hearing the ringing, and guessing it was just another attempt by him, would not answer. Then maybe Frances herself would come to the telephone? Perhaps Frances, even, was alone in the house now? John might have gone out? That would be good. Bert had nothing to lose.

*　　　*　　　*

The ringing started as John dejectedly climbed the stairs alone. He knew it was only Bisson; there was no point in answering. He did not enjoy arguing and today he had already been rude twice. Rude to two grown-ups and in one day too!

The sound was very persistent. The morning operator must be bored too, not to intercept till now. What if it were Franz trying to make contact?

John did not have chance to meditate on this hypothesis for at the umpteenth ring his mother dashed past him on the stairs, meagre shopping in her basket, desperately trying to reach the telephone in time, as if she knew, knew who, or hoped who, it was.

"Couldn't you have answered?" she gasped out, as she sped past.

"No need," was John's pouted response. "It'll only be Bisson again!"

"Yes?" she almost choked from her exhaustion, "Oh, yes, Bert it is." She felt a wave of relief swathing her, removing in an instant her exertion.

She was aware of John's prying eyes and alert and critical ears but far more important was that here was Bert!

"Yes," she said.

"Yes, he is." She paused, while listening to her lover.

"Mmm," she confirmed, "but it doesn't matter, love. Go on."

Again she listened, stiffening her back to John's aggressive intrusion. "I did, love," she said, "Yes . . . No . . ."

"No Bert, it doesn't matter really, not any more, it doesn't matter now."

Frances' voice was becoming tense. John made no move to go away. She turned to face him, a look in her eyes almost of fright.

'Why don't you go away?' her eyes pleaded to John.

"Just a minute, Bert I'll ask him to . . ., all right then I'll tell him . . ., I just said . . ., Oh, just wait a minute!"

Frances was now exasperated. It was not her fault John had been rude to Bert. She had not known he was going to take it so badly when she had told him. It was no good Bert being angry with her. What with Bert in a bad mood at one end, and John being such a nuisance, depriving her of her privacy here, it was very difficult. All part of the price she had to pay for her infidelity, she supposed.

"John, dear, do you think you could go off somewhere. I want to talk to Uncle Bert in private?"

"Oh yes, yes of course, Mum!" he derided, stepping forward and shouting loud enough for Bert to hear. "Yes, I'll just go on round to Dad's for a chat!"

"Frances!" They could both hear Bert.

"Just a minute," she snapped, dismissing Bert. "John, could you just behave like a good boy?"

A good boy was it? He'd show them who was a good boy. He snatched the receiver from his mother's hand pushing her harder than he intended, so that she stumbled back against the wall, with a cry of shock.

"Listen Bisson," he hissed. "You just get out of all our lives because if you don't . . ." He paused for effect, and Frances began to cry with a barely audible wail. "If you don't, you dirty old bastard, I'll tell Dad, and I mean it!" He slammed down the 'phone and looked with hatred at his mother who had shrunk into a snivelling heap.

For the first time in his life John had tasted power, power over others.

*　　　*　　　*

Strange how the old feelings quickly returned. With his putting on of uniform, Bert felt himself become a man once more. His freshly donned pride pushed out of mind all his shame, all his undermined self-respect. He was P.C. Bisson once more, respected by all, friend to everyone, upholder of the law. His new-found youthful pride, in contrast to his recent state of rejection and dejection, was tinged also with an excitement that he was openly courting danger and disaster. He felt important enough, once more, to be the object of someone's, or some organisation's, harm. He was now a real man, he was worth arresting. No longer would he waste at home, lonely and in unclean clothes, mocked by recent memories of euphoria, a euphoria which he knew he had experienced, but whose attributes he could not conjure in his imaginings. No, far better to go out with glory and pride. Much better to walk to the station as P.C. Bisson, there to be arrested for impersonating his former self.

*　　　*　　　*

Franz had not travelled in an aeroplane before. His entry to Guernsey had been by naval transport. He was petrified at the prospect, but it was completely outside his control. There was not one person to sympathize with him or understand what he was going through, as the final preparations were made for his ignominious transportation back to Germany.

His kit-bag had been packed in silence, including only the military necessities required for such a journey. He was not given opportunity to include any of his personal belongings. Not that he possessed many and those that he did own were back at Town Patrol House.

He had not even been told where he was being taken. His staff car journey had filled him with various speculations. At one stage he had imagined that perhaps he was on his way to his Uncle once more. Was it Thursday though? He really was not sure, it had seemed he had spent weeks in his lonely solitude. Besides, he didn't think it was afternoon yet. Hadn't he just recently been poked by the silent warder, to get up for the meagre breakfast and to ablute? Surely, Uncle Pieter only played tennis on Thursday afternoons?

Thursday afternoons? Wasn't there something else about that day? Wasn't he supposed to have some sort of arrangement with someone on Thursday? He thought he had, but what was it? Was it this Thursday anyway? What was he supposed to do? Who did he have to meet? Ah yes, that was it, he had to meet his dear friend John. Was it some club or other? He remembered where it was, well at least he pictured the place, nestled in the shade below the hill upon which John's church stood. No, that could not be right. He remembered clearly the upset he had felt upon realizing he had been compelled to let his friend down. Yes, that had been a long time ago. He had tried to reason with his uncommunicative gaoler, but the man had just shrugged off all Franz's pleas, as if he were out of his mind. Perhaps he was? Perhaps the man was right not to involve himself in the affairs of this strange young soldier who had such a pressing urgency to meet up with one of the enemy?

So it wasn't that club. John must have felt very let down, but Franz had been unable to contact him in any way. That had been doubly bad for, not only had Franz had to suffer the privations of lost freedom, but also, had to imagine how his friend would despise the way he had let him down.

But it wasn't that club. What was it? Ah yes, Thursday, that was it. Where had the two been, just prior to visiting the club building? That had been on a Sunday. Yes, they had walked. That was it, John had been all excited about something. That notice down by the swimming place. Yes, the notice of the sports event between civilians and Germans. John had wanted Franz to take part. He shuddered at the prospect. John had felt sure though, that Franz, as one of the Fatherland's youth, would be included in the competitions. How he had hoped not, but how he had feared John to be right. He would have had to have made himself look very inferior in his friend's standing, if he had been compelled to compete. Or he would have gone down in his estimation if he had opted out on the grounds that he, a superior German, was inferior, in this one regard. So maybe this was not yet Thursday after all, or he would have been enlisted, just to belittle his spirit further? Incarceration would not have been sufficient grounds to spare him the undoubted embarrassment.

He did not have long to wait to find out. In less than no time the car turned into the most drab and formidably fortified aerodrome, the only sign of vitality being the large swastika, uncamouflaged, flying stiffly in the strong easterly breeze, on the island's highest point.

*   *   *

"What the hell?" shouted the Sergeant, as he could not believe his eyes at Bert's entry, fully-uniformed, even the duty armband on his sleeve. His immediate reaction to this illogical happening, was that by some strange twist of justice, or the rules, or by some incredible German ineptitude, Bert Bisson had been reinstated. But that could not be, it just would not stand the test of logic.

"Watchyer, Sergeant!" affected Bert. "Surprised to see me?"

"That's for sure!" replied the Sergeant, scratching his head. "What the hell are you doing here, and like this?" He indicated Bert's uniform with incredulity.

"Just thought I'd nip along for a rest. I'm a bit tired, I've been on since six you know?"

Eh? Was he mad or something? Or was the Sergeant just cracking up a bit? Had Bert Bisson, or had he not, been suspended from duty, awaiting trial? What was this about being on since six? Oh no, surely the bloody fool hadn't been round Town like that? On no, that was just too much! Didn't he know what would happen to him now? Was this some sick sort of joke or something? Besides, how was it he could wander round Town so openly without the station knowing? Something was wrong there all right. either the Sergeant's duty team were incredibly inept or they were all in league together. Either way, heads would roll and the Sergeant felt sure his would be one of them.

"Come off it, you thick headed Bobby," said the Sergeant with more gravity than frivolity, while he picked up the 'phone, at the same time stepping towards the doorway, as though expecting the vision to try to evaporate through the opening, just to leave the duty man looking stupid.

"You are really for the chop now, aren't you, eh? What do you think they'll do to you now?"

"No idea," lied Bert. "Go on, tell me."

"They'll lock you up, you blasted fool," replied the Sergeant, really believing Bert was as naive as he pretended.

"Oh, is that so?" replied Bert, nonchalantly shrugging his shoulders and enjoying the strength of being completely powerless. "That's good, that's just what I want!"

*   *   *

No, not this! Not now! Oh not not yet, not so soon! Franz knew where he was. He saw the thick squat grey monsters which shrank into the skies and droned overhead on hot summer days. He saw them standing there stark and still and cold. He heard their droning and he felt the burning as their spilled fuel exploded and spread along the aprons, engulfing all he saw.

Not a 'plane! Not to Russia, not today. Not yet! Why was it so quick? Why had they not said anything? There had been nothing. No words spoken, nothing written. Was he just to be reduced into one of those insignificant dots in the sky? Did he have to enter that greyness and live out an unknown fear?

No, he would rather stay. He would do anything to stay. He was sorry, oh so sorry. Who could he say it to? Who would listen? To whom could he beg for mercy, for a reprieve? He couldn't leave this place. He could not leave this island, never more to see his friend or his adopted mother. Why were they doing this to him? What had he done that was so bad?

There must be someone he could talk to? Wouldn't they even let his friend John come to say goodbye? Why not, how would that harm anyone? No, he couldn't leave without a last word, to say farewell. He was going to Russia, wasn't he? He was going to Russia to fight and die for his country? He was too young to die. Why should he die? What was there about his country for which he should give his life? John did not have to give his life for his country, so why should he? John's people had lost the war, but John would live. Franz's country would win, but Franz would die, unwillingly, to make this so.

Couldn't John's father do something? He had hit Hüffmeier after all. He was a brave man to hit an S.S.! What about the priest? He seemed kind to John, he had put himself out a lot to help Franz too. Surely someone would help, but who could he reach?

His own uncle had disowned him. Not for Franz, the rescue this time. Uncle Pieter had carried out his threat all right.

What about Captain Weiss? He had been kind and understanding. Couldn't he help once more? Wouldn't he try to save Franz from the unknown terrors of death at the Eastern Front?

Unknown? That was it, unknown and alone. It was the unknown terror that Franz could not bear to contemplate. Even Morten seemed better than that prospect. At least he knew him, he was predictable. With Morten, Franz at least survived, he kept a regularity of surroundings. Now, it was as Morten had said, he was dead already, his grave was prepared.

Was he never to meet John again? Pale and aghast he followed the line of fellow travellers out on to the apron

397

where the grass weeds mocked the permanence of the Nazi concrete, by forcing through its cracks.

Helplessly he was engulfed, as the outer grey became an inner dismal tomb. On the floor they sat, several soldiers. No one spoke.

Franz had almost lost consciousness with the awful vibrations which turned him into part of the craft's very structure. How he had wished that death would come then. Where was his friend? Why had he let him down?

The prison rumbled down the bumpy track runway. It turned and first one engine revved and then the other until they seemed they would disintegrate, to crush Franz's mind. As it gathered speed, accelerating towards doom, ever faster, faster, faster, all the bumps and jolts fused into one mighty upheaval, so that all the floor-bound males were forced into an involuntary silent laugh, as jaws forced back and heads struggled for support. All that time Franz held just one thought, just as when Morten had abused his innocence. He held in his vision the picture of his friend, never again to be seen.

Suddenly the great jostle ceased and a leaden force pulled his stomach down on to the steel floor, while he lurched sideways. The craft was airborne. It had happened, he had died.

As the craft turned to pick its course he saw for the first time out of the small porthole. He was tipped towards the scene. How strange. Those were little houses, tiny glass lines of greenhouses. How small! How slowly they seemed to pass. Little fields like patchwork, earth bank hedges like so much binding of the material. There were trees and miniature cows. Not a person to be seen. A sudden lurch and the craft corrected itself. What was happening? Franz felt sick. No, he must not be sick. He breathed hard.

What was that? The fields got smaller, encroached by growth. It was the cliffs. The little headlands stretching down into their blue carpet, began to separate from one another, as the monster rocked over the currents of deep unspoiled valleys.

Far out on the carpet Franz could see other bastions of rock. Little islands. Was that not the place John had talked of where they used only horses and carriages, no cars, not even before the war? What was that place? Sark he thought. and over there. Was it? Yes it must be. There spread out like a large fish fillet its northern end banded in a thick white scarf of sand and shells, was his dear Herm, Herm where he and John had planned to visit soon. And there was that other round hill sticking from the sea with its two satellites for company. How inconceivable that only weeks before he and Corporal Schmidt had felt small, engulfed in the bracken of that tiny spot, near cliffs of deadly height. They had watched the gulls and puffins in the course of their duty.

All these thoughts, all these memories, nostalgia, trauma, newness of experience. Franz took all this alone. What news he would have for John! How he could boast and explain how he had done something his little islander had not experienced. But no, that was it. He would never ever share this with his friend. Franz had forgotten, the dead do not speak to the living, they cannot even write, they do not have the capacity to be held for long within the memory of the living.

Franz realized he could not even write to his friend, or to his new mother and father. He knew where they lived but he did not know a name for their address. After the war yes, he could visit them, but of course, after the war, he would be dead.

*   *   *

Chapter Eighteen

For Frances, the night passed excitingly quickly. She had always, since a little girl, had a sense of thrill from sleeping in a strange bed. Undoubtedly it was, despite her many years, because of the very rarity of such an occurrence.

She had spent most of her life in Guernsey and there, as was the custom of time and place, had rarely moved house. It was only in her latter years that she had come to see out her days with her son, and now, her daughter-in-law too. It had all been quite invigorating.

And now her little boy was ill, he needed his old mum once more. It was good to be needed. Good to feel so tired from being up so late, but to go to a well-earned rest knowing that she had done all that was required, that she had been there at his moment of need and that he was on the mend.

They had put Frances and Gerda in a little flat at the top of the hospital. Frances had been curious and had wanted to explore, like looking over the house of an acquaintance, really, but without fear of being noticed, whilst trying to see if they really lived up to the image they projected, or was as bad as the imagination hoped.

She had been too tired, really, other than to notice that they had three little rooms. A tiny sitting-room with a settee pulled down and turned into a bed. Leading off this had been a washing room with toilet, while in the corner, an open doorway leading to an alcove where there was a tiny sink, an electric kettle and a supply of tea, coffee and powdered milk.

Frances had been too tired even to wonder whose flat this was, or to whom she should be grateful or thankful for such thoughtful provision. She took in nothing beyond noticing that the bed was already made up, the sheets starched and brilliant, the covering of the chairs was at variance with the curtains and that the place was so old-fashioned, it did not manage a fitted carpet, but reflected its bright clinical light onto large seas of red linoleum.

It had been such a long day, so frightening at times, but now she could not even remember why she felt afraid, for she knew everything was going to be fine. She was starting on a fresh adventure, at her old age!

What fun this was, it was like going to stay at Granny's.

Gerda was quiet. Perhaps she was tired too? But she must be pleased as well, for she, too, understood that John was fine. She was a good girl, that one, such a help, just like a daughter. So good for her boy, she could not have wished better.

Gerda was busy in that little alcove. Making tea, probably. What a good idea. Yes, she was a sweet child. She would bring in her tea and help old Frances finish undressing.

Why, Granny had even left a nightdress on the bed for her, how kind she was. Two nighties. Oh yes, probably one was for Gerda. She would have to sleep with Gerda. It would be like sleeping with Rita, when they had been girls. Such a strange day, so many things from the past. Not intruding, but really quite welcome guests.

"Come on, Mum," urged Gerda kindly, cajoling the old lady, thereby keeping her own thoughts at bay. "Would you like some help, dear? I've got you a lovely hot cup of tea here."

She quickly got the old lady into bed, and watched her sink into almost immediate relaxation, her old face waxy and brown against the hospital sheets.

When Gerda returned from her wash, the old lady had gone to her dreams, her tea undisturbed.

*   *   *

Thursday was destined to be a strange day. It was the day of the gala. Probably for John this would have been the most exciting event of the Occupation. It had always been so before the invasion, so why not now? Was life so full of fun these days that happenings could outstrip a gala?

Well, of course, it was not so much that the prospect of a

gala could be any less exciting now, than last year. It was just that now, John was victim of a new element in his life. For the first time in his short span he was affected deeply with concern for others. So it was not so much that the event did not contrast with the drabness of his life, it was more that he could not give himself fully over to it.

His whole day consisted of rapidly changing moods and sentiments so that at one moment he would be high up and excited at the prospect of this evening's shining, while unaware of anything outside his immediate gratification. At the next moment he knew he could not anticipate any pleasure, for it was all stolen from him now. His alternation was further complicated by rare insights into what he imagined had befallen his friend. These varied from realizing that the two, as suggested by Father Peters, were unlikely to be able to make contact for the duration of the war, to the more palatable concept that Franz was really well, that nothing had changed and all would work out exactly as John's wishes decided to shape events.

It was easier for John to delude himself that his friend would somehow contrive to be present on this very evening, and to share in the pleasures of victory, when foes would be allowed to compete and applaud each other's victories, than to permit his anxieties to imagine any of the fears his priest had tried to plant in him.

"OK, Franz, mon vieux, just you watch me now and make sure you cheer for Guernsey, eh? For you'll be cheering for me!" John was excited, edging forward towards the marshalling area, just waiting for the announcement so that he could drop the towel draping his shoulders, to live up to the applause of anticipation, accorded to his team.

"Yes, John, perhaps you will win this race but we Germans will win this gala," replied Franz, teasing his friend. Oh yes, he was certainly learning a few things from mixing with the donkeys. He was getting quite sharp! 'We have won this war!' So what!

"So what, even if that was true?" retaliated John. "Whoever wins tonight wins for Guernsey not for Britain or for Germany."

"Yes," mused Franz, "this place is our home, both of us."

*　　　*　　　*

"Now this is it!" stormed the Corporal. "Scum, you go that way! You child, little pathetic cripple, you come with me!" Franz stood up, bemused by the flight and did as he was bidden. He no longer needed to think. He was in Germany once more.

*   *   *

John was in the water now. He had almost forgotten what it felt like to have the cold prying support chill him so. Now it all came back, that one hated moment, the necessary death each time, in order to enter the hereafter, the cold plunge of discomfort which would lead to the delight which each time, would erase the temporary discomfort. He shivered, as the cold contrasted with his sun hot torso, while he awaited the starter expectantly, so that he could lunge back and win his power-hungry backstroke race. Only once he had taken the signal, and knew that his fears of missing it had not been realized, would he relax and perform to win, unaware of any possibility of failure. Only then would the recurrent urge to urinate and warm his legs recede.

*   *   *

"No, don't sit, you putrifaction!" ordered the Corporal, as his victim momentarily sagged into the hut on the edge of some remote Fatherland airfield. "Don't get comfortable! You're not staying here. Once this aeroplane has refuelled you're off to the Front!"

So, he was off to the Front? So what of it? He was in Germany now, he knew how to obey. This was the Fatherland, everything decreed by the Fatherland was correct, it has always been so.

"You see, John, we are the master race. We win because we do not have to think and decide. Our decisions are made for us by men far more able to think properly than we are."

Franz was proud to feel Germany entering into him once more. It was as though he had never been exiled.

John did not answer. Franz knew why. John could not hope to argue against the success of mighty Germany. John knew a winner when he saw one.

*   *   *

"What time is this gala?" asked Frances.

"I don't know!" John was irritable. He had no real cause to be so with his mother but, on the other hand, there was no positive reason to be pleasant. Just as to sustain a smile uses more energy than to lapse into a basalt-like feature, so it was with responding to Frances. To be sociable with the one person who would always be there, no matter how badly she was treated, was all too much effort. Well, today at least!

"Sorry I asked," she added lightly. "I just thought you might know."

"Well I don't. Why don't you look it up in the *Press* for yourself?" he continued rudely, now trapped in the tracks upon which his mood had set him.

"There's no need for that," Frances admonished, genuinely hurt at his uncalled for sharpness. John knew she was right to be annoyed and he felt even more on the defensive now.

"Anyway, why are you so interested?" He tried to colour his voice with the slightest sneer of disapproval, without distorting his face. The meaning was not lost on her, as Bert flashed into her consciousness. The injustice of his statement cut her to the quick for she knew that what John was implying would have been a good plan, except that she had not thought of it until her own child had caused its birth. She was deliberate in her reply, not to allow her offspring to realize his power to hurt.

"I just thought you'd be meeting up with young Franz," she said. "That's all."

So Frances had recognized John's cruelty and had retaliated?

John too wanted to know the time of the gala and yet part of him would not allow himself to pursue an enquiry.

It would have to be an early event, that was for sure. No chance of wasting electricity on floodlights or of inviting attack by the R.A.F. What an irony that would be! No, it would surely be late afternoon, perhaps even earlier? It was a Thursday, after all, so everyone would be off work.

Frances had not responded to her bad-tempered son's invitation to look it up in the *Press*. She was being deliberately awkward. She just wanted John to feel bad, she knew what he felt like inside. It was her way of getting back at him!

Eventually, trying to appear nonchalant, and hoping his mother would not in fact observe his quest at all, he found the *Press*. Whistling casually, rather too studiously, he turned the pages, taking particular interest in everything but the announcements of *La Gazette Officielle*.

Suddenly, on an impulse, no longer able to resist the treat which was so enticing, and not caring if his mother did have the satisfaction of observing his lust, he turned to the penultimate page with such haste that any observer might have thought he feared its fading.

There was nothing for it now, but to plan and wait for the time, trying not to let it crowd his thoughts.

*   *   *

The time came eventually. Well, almost the time. Only ninety minutes before the registration time. Ninety minutes, an hour and a half: well, that was not too early to set off from home.

So, if he did get to the pool a bit early, even after walking round Town with ever accelerating pace, and watching the deadly stillness of a tideless harbour, and sauntering down La Vallette road at a subdued rush, what did it matter? He could wait. He did not mind waiting at the gate, even if it was closed up. At least he would be first in the queue, at least he would be there.

Even after his self-imposed delays, which seemed less and less essential to him as he curtailed them, he was first at the barrier, where he had been with Franz only four days previously. The barrier was closed, its inner pedestrian gate locked fast. Not a soul in sight, not even a German. Had he go the wrong day? No, of course today was Thursday. He reassured himself, counting back the days since he was last with Franz. That had been a Sunday. What a lot had happened since then.

John suddenly felt a chill. Franz? Yes this barrier, this notice. He heard Franz's voice, he heard Father Peters saying how hopeless everything was. Four days, he had not seen his friend for four days. He was going to meet him today however, and he was going to impress him! He had been sure he was going to meet him at Boys' Club last Tuesday, but it had not happened. Where was Franz? Where was everybody?

His fears that he had made some dreadful error, that John Collins the Gala champion, unable to read *Press* announcements properly, had arrived at the wrong time, or on the wrong day, were allayed for him as, with relief, he realised he was not to be alone. He heard voices coming from behind him, from the direction of Town. Yes, fellow Guernseymen and women, as if by some remote signal to coincide, were beginning to walk down the road on his side, towards him.

The first of the laughing, chattering bunch of typical fun-loving event types to reach the barrier were two police constables, armbanded for duty.

* * *

Only once he had changed was John in any way able to relax and turn his attention once more to matters other than the imminent event. Imminent? Well, it still seemed an age away!

Where was everyone? There were so few people. Mind, it must still be early. The time always had dragged like this for him, even before the Occupation. He was well used to arriving far too early for fear of being late, albeit the memory was almost two summers past now and, ostensibly, he had changed from boy to man.

No matter, they would come. Yes, more and more would-be victors, having registered outside, were now sauntering through the granite arch. All had that look of bemused curiosity about them, the outward sign of the inner emotion John had felt, as he had been the first to get in. Even a few spectators now began to trickle on to the rocks, seeking the best vantage point and combining it with greatest potential sun for company, as the evening began to assert its rights by casting rapidly advancing shadows from the tree-clad cliffs.

Where were the Germans? That was strange, not one German competitor in sight. John did not know all the locals round him but he knew them all by sight. Not one of these changed people was a German. They would have been as obvious as a pre-war visitor. Unless of course, some of these were German and John had absorbed their identification into his memory's files? That would be strange. It would mean that they really had established themselves and become part of the permanent order. Well, that could be the case of course, or probably would be one day, but John was dubious that it was so tonight. The Germans would have arrived in uniform. He would have noticed. Each uniform seen would have momentarily been a Franz and John had felt no reason to think of his erstwhile friend up till now. Besides, all these people round him were too pale to be the master race. All his fellow patriots were now denied access to the beaches with their heritage, the sun. Ironical that it was the visitors who were these days the tanned ones, while the Sarnians were pale. Perhaps that just emphasized again that these Tuetons were really and truly more than just visitors. They had brought about a complete change of role. So, similarly, they would reverse the whole order of their lives.

No, there were no Germans present, Germans would not change on the rocks and the shingle as these had done, adept at thwarting the air of their nakedness, as they struggled skillfully with small towels. The superior Germans would either come fully changed beneath their uniforms or seek the seclusion of changing rooms. So, they were still not in complete control, they had not become localized in their habits.

Perhaps then, it was another mistake? Maybe the competition would not include Germans? Could it be that they feared defeat? Surely not mighty Germany? No, why would they permit a gala to take place at all if they were not to make some capital out of it?

As John mused, still all his thoughts revolving round the exciting prospect of the laboriously slowly approaching event, yet more competitors arrived. Those who had already changed began, like him, to move from point to point, ensuring they did not miss any vital instructions or marshalling signals when the time came.

Despite knowing the faces of the people around him — many he had observed in the old Swimming Club days, albeit all less buoyant now after more than an year's strict rations — John realized that he stood out alone as being the only youngster. That was why he could not put names to faces or reply specifically to casual greetings. They were all older men and women who would once have seemed old beyond reach, when he had owned a surfeit of companionship of his own age. Of course this was bound to be, for all his friends had gone to England, had they not? All now were there in freedom, or dispersed around the world fighting whom they must assume as enemies, fighting the very people whom John was about to befriend in sporting competition.

He seemed to feel he had considered such thoughts only recently. Where had that been? Where and when? Had he not shared these thoughts with someone? Or was it that he had hidden them from that person? Yes, it had been Franz. He had felt disloyalty to his friends on that Thursday ride. He had compensated by excluding his new friend, their enemy, his friends' enemy and therefore, by association, his enemy, his enemy friend, from those private thoughts.

How long ago it seemed. How the contradiction of absolute anomaly seemed so irrelevant now. What ridiculous thoughts these adults had to contend with! What did it matter if they were all competing together, as if they were all human? Why should they not fraternize? Why should such a term of love and brotherliness be used as a smear to cast a stigma on the willing participants? The war was almost over, why could not the two nations unite in brotherhood? Each had suffered members killed by the other side, but not here in this place! Why should not this small part be set as a haven of peace in the strife-torn world?

Such musings kept the youth from the sense of let-down that his enemy friend had not yet arrived. But he would. Yes, that was for sure!

"Hello, John." There he was. John had only to think his friend and he was there!

"I thought I'd find you here too early. Are you getting excited or something?"

John turned to face Franz.

Father Peters stood there, the sun at his back, the silhouette of his threadbare cassock giving a sinister lie to John's fantasy. Why was it this priest again? Why was he always keeping Franz from him?

"Hello," said John, his voice surly and lethargic, as he turned his gaze of disappointment down to the priest's shoes. He could not make conversation with the intruder.

"Well, it's very early still," continued Father Peters with false jollity. He had been aware of John's disappointment, almost of annoyance, at realizing it was only him.

It did not matter, the young were like this, they never showed appreciation. They only took and never gave. Yet better to have a society of youngsters temporarily taking than to have a community virtually divested of its youth.

"What have you put your name down for? Everything, I suppose?"

"No." John's reply was terse. He realized the abruptness in his answer. He did not want this conversation, he wanted to indulge his thoughts once more, he wanted the gala to start so Franz could arrive to cheer him on.

The priest's face darkened but he quickly gained his poise.

"Not everything? My, you're slipping, Mr. John Collins," he affectedly smiled, realizing how patronizing his words must sound, but unable to extricate himself.

"I couldn't exactly go in for the ladies' races could I now Father?" John almost shouted his sarcasm.

Father Peters gave a shrug and manufactured a slight laugh;

"Well, aren't you going to ask me which races I'm in?" he continued.

"What races are you in, Father?" responded John, with studious boredom in his question.

"I'm not. I leave that to you youngsters," he replied, as if he had evolved a great witticism, but knowing as it had been formed, that it was still-born.

"We youngsters?" asked John incredulous. "Can you see any of we 'youngsters'?"

"There may be some. It's early yet, you know," suggested Father Peters with barely a trace of conviction.

"Like Boys' Club, I suppose?" Why did John have to be so aggressive? Well of course the mention of Boys' Club just confirmed the Priest that both their individual thoughts were converging on one specific outcome.

"Yes, well you're probably right," came the priest's reply of resignation. "As I told you the other evening, my son, we just have to face up to things. We have to accept the things we can't change."

Father Peters knew the problem, he was aware of the trauma in John's life. Yes, he, Thomas Peters, fully understood that the young John Collins who stood before him, had lost his only friend but had not yet been able to absorb this knowledge. The priest had done his best. Had he not prepared the youth that his enemy friend was destined for the Russian front? He had been blunt in his message, yet the boy had not been able, not willing to accept its inevitability. John was as one recently bereaved, with the knowledge of the parting but with the habit of expectation of the continued presence, still to the fore.

A small cloud drifted across the fast dropping sun and a breeze licked across the water to chill John's body so that his skin firmed and stiffened into goose-pimples. He shuddered.

"Where is Franz, Father? Please tell me."

Yes, it had to be Russia, Franz had gone to the Eastern Front. No longer could John keep his friend in Guernsey, on the safety of the cliffs, until such time as he was permitted to come to Town again.

Russia? Well, so what? Russia did not mean it all had to be the end of the everything, did it? Hadn't the Germans virtually beaten the British forces into submission already? Didn't the *Press* tell everyone that was the case? Was it not now only just a matter of time before the British saw the error of their ways and joined with their Aryan cousins? Yes of course, that was it! Franz had no need to worry. He would not be in any real danger for long. Soon the British Tommies would be fighting alongside the German forces, and the Russians would just collapse like all the non-Aryan Europeans of the continent had done.

No, John did not need words of encouragement from his confessor. He did not need to be told that the Americans would soon be coming to the rescue, just as they had done in the Great War. That was not necessary; it would only prolong things. Franz did not need the Americans. Britain and Germany could manage quite well enough without them.

So Franz was safe. The war would soon be over and both friends could share the glory of victory. No need for any Americans to share it with them; the Russians would quickly have to accept that their system had had its day.

Oh yes, Adolf Hitler knew what he was doing, Franz would be quite safe, his Führer would ensure that. Franz was lucky really, to be included in the glory. No doubt in just a few days John would receive a letter from his friend telling, with great excitement, of the great victory, then before he knew it Franz would be back in the island.

Yes, John Collins too would have such things to tell Franz about this evening. John knew now that he was just about to win his race, to win it for Guernsey and for Germany, to succeed for the Fatherland and for Great Britain. Brothers all!

*   *   *

John did not feel the chill as he slipped into the water, he was not aware of the silky green seaweed as he positioned hands and feet ready for the starter's signal. No anxieties about false starts this time, he knew he had won before he had started.

"Wish me luck, Franz! See if I can be at least two bodies' lengths ahead of the nearest Jerry, when I touch the finish! No! Sorry, Franz. I didn't mean it, honestly, I meant German." Franz smiled, he knew his friend had indulged in one of his English jokes.

"OK John, you win the race but we win this war, yes?"

John too smiled. What did it matter who won, for soon the stupid war would be finished and what would be the point of winning something which was no longer there?

*   *   *

There was no point in crying for no one would listen to him. Those around Franz in the darkness knew misery, just as

411

he, but they had learned not to cry for no one heeded. Crying would not take away his hunger or warm his from his damp chill aches nor would it give light or take away the awful odours and the terrible noises of this place.

No, Franz was a man now and in this place men did not cry. He remembered, as though it were a fast-fading dream, a time when he had been permitted to show his feelings to a true friend, when it had been all right for men to cry. He resolved to carry that place with him through this time of correction and right into the very Front, for they could not see into his thoughts.

He would keep these thoughts with him until one day they could become real once more.

No, they would not be able to remove his enemy friend and Franz was glad!

Jimmy's Hall

Written by Paul Laverty
Directed by Ken Loach

First published in 2014 by Route
PO Box 167, Pontefract, WF8 4WW
info@route-online.com
www.route-online.com

In association with Sixteen Films
2nd Floor, 187 Wardour Street, London, W1F 8ZB

ISBN: 978-1-901927-61-0

Cover design:
GOLDEN www.wearegolden.co.uk
From artwork supplied by Entertainment One UK Ltd

A catalogue for this book is available from the British Library

Printed and bound by CPI Group (UK) Ltd, Croydon, CR0 4YY

Contents

Paul Laverty
Writer

5

Sometimes an idea for a story can land in your lap like some benign present from on high, and you feel like thanking the lucky stars. *Jimmy's Hall* came this way, a long distant ripple from Nicaragua, via an old friend Donal O'Kelly, an actor and playwright whom I had the good fortune to meet there in the eighties while the United States was busy making carnage of the Sandinista revolution and its people.

Over three years ago, Donal and Sorcha Fox were planning a community theatre project in County Leitrim to highlight the plight of asylum seekers in Ireland, many of whom were held in limbo for years with the threat of deportation hanging over their heads. Donal imagined a theatrical/dance event with them, linking their plight back to the story of Jimmy Gralton, the only Irishman deported from his own country as an 'undesirable alien' without trial way back in August 1933.

The spark to invest so much effort in a story is always a question of the gut. As I read of Jimmy Gralton's life, I wondered out loud to Donal if it might make for a film in its own right. I was struck by the community effort to build a hall with voluntary labour on Jimmy's land where they could meet to debate, think, study, give classes, and of course sing and dance without interference from anyone, including the Church and the State which were intertwined around each other. Jimmy and his comrades were determined to build a free space in an increasingly authoritarian country dominated by the ideology of the Catholic Church, who insisted education was the sole preserve of Holy Mother Church.

It was both the conciseness, and the possibility of complexity unfurled, that made it such an attractive premise. The hall itself felt like a character. I spoke to Ken [Loach] and could sense the same gut reaction. I noticed that glint in his eye at the prospect of meat and mischief in a story. Rebecca [O'Brien] too was intrigued by the possibility of another film in Ireland, set a decade on from the period we explored in *The Wind that Shakes the Barley*.

With typical generosity, Donal and Sorcha were delighted that we were interested and encouraged me to begin research into the detail of Jimmy's life and the hall.

First stop was Effernagh in County Leitrim, and the sparse crossroads in the countryside opposite a pub called the Black Swan. By one corner was a wooden sign with the words, 'Site of the Pearse-Connolly Hall. In memory of Jimmy Gralton, Leitrim socialist deported for his political beliefs on August 13th 1933.' Though burnt down by 'persons unknown' on Christmas Eve 1932, it was still possible to imagine the outline of the hall in the overgrown grass.

It was a wet, miserable January day, and the only sound was that of crows from the trees opposite. But gradually I could hear in my mind the sound of feet tapping, and music drifting down over the 80 year gap. I couldn't help but smile at the thought of Jimmy's secret weapon in the battle against drabness: his stylish gramophone brought back from the States, and his collection of records. I was to hear stories of people travelling over 30 miles on their bicycles to hear the latest new record from across the Atlantic, while local parish priests fumed against the devil's music and the 'Los Angelization' of Irish culture.

I read news reports of over 500 people attending the Republican courts (in parallel to the boycotted British-run courts) held in the hall, set up during the War of Independence in 1921 to solve land disputes. To implement the court's decisions

Jimmy and his comrades formed the Direct Action Committee, which challenged not only the property rights of big ranchers, but upset the right-wing flank of the IRA. On one occasion the hall was surrounded by soldiers while Jimmy fled out of a back window. It was little wonder that he had to flee for his life to the States in those troubled times (May '22) leading up to the civil war which tore Ireland asunder.

As I stood there with the sermons by local parish priests O'Dowd and Cosgrove ringing in my ear from 80 years back, I remembered the words of a rich farmer from *The Wind that Shakes the Barley*, who told the two IRA brothers in the story that if their like were to win the war, Ireland would end up a 'priest-infested backwater'.

Beyond the site of the hall was Jimmy's family home, now abandoned and in a state of disrepair, set on a few acres of boggy land covered in reeds. It was not hard to imagine a tough life against the elements. The Plantation story was implicit in the landscape, with many humble Catholic families etching out an existence on poor land supplemented by trips to Scotland to pick potatoes. I imagined Jimmy's fierce sense of social justice forged against this backdrop, and nourished by politically aware parents.

In *The Wind that Shakes the Barley* we made a key decision. We tried to be truthful to the spirit of the times, but with fictional characters. In this story we were faced with a new challenge. There are key public events in Jimmy Gralton's life that we know from public sources, principally newspaper reports of the time, and word-of-mouth passed down through the generations. I owe a great debt of gratitude to Paul Gralton and his father Jim Gralton in particular. Jim's mother and father, Packie and Maggie Gralton, were both cousins of Jimmy from two different sides of the family and were very close to him. It was even Jimmy who suggested they marry, and he left the farm to Packie and Maggie after his deportation in 1933. Paul and Jim shared stories with me passed down through the generations, and I had a wonderful day with Jim who showed me the places where some key events took place, like the cattle drives to implement Republican court decisions in the 1920s, and the community action to force the return of the Milmoe family to their cottage (whose descendants are still there) after they were evicted from the Kingston Estate in the early 1930s. Jimmy was asked to speak to mark the occasion and his main point rings hauntingly true in the Ireland of today.

As I listened to Paul and Jim pass on their stories and considerable insight, it became obvious too that there is so much about a person's personality, inner thoughts, fears, vulnerabilities, imagination, and subtleties of relations with friends and loved ones that are beyond historical record. Likewise, there is much that is beyond the reach of subjective memories passed down from those who knew Jimmy (in their way), and then passed down in turn again to Paul and his generation.

In a film we have to grapple with the inner life, the contradictions, doubts and motivations, or we will be left with the damp squib of a public skeleton. So after discussion with Ken, another key decision was made: this would be a story 'freely inspired' by the lives and times of Jimmy and the hall. Our story doesn't pretend to be a conventional biopic. We know he brought back records of Paul Robeson from the States, but did he bring back Bessie Smith? Did a young and curious free spirit like Jimmy go dancing the Shim Sham and Lindy Hop at the Saxony hotel in Harlem while he lived in New York, the only place in the United States where black and white could dance together openly? Nobody knows if he did or not, but in our version we imagine he did.

Paul Gralton thought it feasible Jimmy might have brought back some blues from New York, so we have a jazz band playing in the hall instead of a record playing on a flimsy gramophone. (Not long after Jimmy was deported, there were anti-jazz marches led by priests in Mohill, not far from where Jimmy lived, so these debates were in the air.) We know about the boxing, painting and literature classes at the hall, but the personalities and mix of Jimmy's friends who taught at the hall, and helped him run it, are imagined. I read of the denunciations from local parish priests O'Dowd and Cosgrove, and others too, and the pronouncements of local bishops, and after weighing that up, and trying to imagine the times from the point of view of a local priest, we have drawn the fictional characters Father Sheridan and his curate Father Seamus. They struck us as more insightful than the priests of those crude sermons. We know Jimmy went to confront one of them. What he might have said, and how, are imagined.

I asked Paul Gralton if there was any hint that the unmarried Jimmy (he did finally marry in New York towards the end of his life, long after deportation) might have had a secret sweetheart given his personality and 'the catch' he would have been in those times having returned from abroad. Paul's reply struck a chord. 'You would never know even if he had.' So did this impulsive, generous man have a secret love? Who knows, but he does in our version, and she is called Oonagh. This is a freely inspired guess, nothing more, nothing less, sparked by the character that took hold as we tried to imagine the man in the round. Does that do an injustice to Jimmy? I hope not. And would the absence of that tenderness, the secret and the intimate, if that had been our choice, have been an even greater injustice to this charismatic ball of energy that Jimmy seemed to be? There are no arithmetical answers to these imponderables. I could only engage with the script if we dived in boldly, and if we have erred, I hope it is in the spirit of Jimmy's hall itself.

How can we know the depth and intricacy of his relationship

11

with his mother, Alice? Jim and Paul told me that Alice ran the local mobile library in the area. Did she read to Jimmy, a bright and curious child, and teach him to think, criticise and welcome ideas from beyond Leitrim? I relied on that to imagine the kernel of a loving relationship which in turn led to unbearable choices for Jimmy as the political pressure mounted on him. I can only guess that as a teenager who had the courage to desert the British army because of his political convictions, and challenge his superiors at such a tender age, he must have had some grounding from his family.

Of all the sources I came across, I was particularly struck by a transcribed interview with Packie Gralton, who helped Jimmy hide when he was on the run. He was asked what Jimmy was like as a person. I imagined an old man smiling at the memory of a soul mate: 'Ah... he was a free man... a free man.'

Taking the sources as a whole, what struck us, in essence, was a man who had seen the world, lived a full life, and with a generous spirit; who tried to bring the best of what he had learned and experienced back to this modest little hall in a country crossroads some 50 yards from where he was born. He had been a soldier, a sailor, a miner, a docker, a taxi driver, worked in bars and no doubt much else besides. He left school at 14 but, judging from the stories and how he wrote and spoke, he must have been a man who read and studied. He had a sharp tongue and no doubt this got him into trouble, even accusing Peadar O'Donnell, a fellow-traveller and supporter, of needing to be the 'bridegroom at every wedding and corpse at every funeral'. In a letter to Father O'Dowd after his deportation to New York, he wrote '...even the cloak of religion can no longer cover the imperialist hooligan that hides behind it'.

Having travelled the world, and witnessed the roaring twenties in the States, followed by the Depression after 1929, and the ripple of misery that flowed from there around the world, he must have seen tremendous poverty and brutality, but he never seemed to turn into a cynic.

I was struck by anecdotes of his generosity (housing a homeless man in New York who stole his trousers) and sense of humour. He was no sectarian. Jimmy was very popular with many of the nuns in a convent in the US where his sister was based. During a visit to Ireland, his sister attended the hall to enjoy the music until she was warned off by the local parish priest. Jimmy was intensely political, a committed socialist, but we had a sense of a man who appreciated that we need many types of nourishment, including fun and companionship. People travelled for miles to attend the dances despite the denunciations from the pulpit.

As well as digging into the secrets of the characters, another major challenge was trying to imagine the texture of lived experience of the 1920s in the flashbacks, and the quite different atmosphere of the 1930s after a decade of authoritarian rule of the Cosgrave Government; not from the safety of hindsight, but in the moment with the characters. Historian Donal Ó Drisceoil from University College Cork, who worked with us on *Barley*, was once again a bedrock of support to outline the political atmosphere of the times, fill in the details and answer endless questions – which he did with the sharpest of observations.

On a visit to the National Archives in Dublin, I confirmed what Donal had told me: the records relating to Jimmy's detention and subsequent deportation have mysteriously disappeared. What is intriguing, and what we couldn't find out, was when this happened. The vital question is how the decision was made in such secrecy and who was privy to it. It reminded me of the subversive first page of *The Book of Laughter and Forgetting*. Milan Kundera gives details of a famous propaganda photo of Communist leader Klement Gottwald on a balcony in Prague in 1948. In freezing weather, Gottwald's comrade Clementis gave his own furry hat to his bareheaded leader. Four years later Clementis was charged with treason and hanged. The Communist Party airbrushed him from the photo and history. But like the corner foundations of Jimmy's hall poking through sods of grass, Clementis's hat still remains. Kundera wrote, 'The struggle of man against power is the struggle of memory against forgetting.' It was not enough that Jimmy's hall was burnt to the ground, that he was deported from his birthplace – the official record of the events disappeared into nothingness too. Little wonder so few had heard the story of Jimmy Gralton, even in County Leitrim.

What attracted us to this story too was the physical courage of Jimmy and his comrades in intolerant times. I was reminded of this on Day 26 of the shoot when six people were set upon in Athens for distributing posters for a youth festival organised by the left. Fifty Golden Dawn fascists attacked them with baseball bats, inflicting serious injuries. On Day 29 of the shoot, on 17th September 2013 a hip-hop artist Pavlos Fyssas was chased by an armed group of 30 Golden Dawn members and then stabbed to death. While the circumstances were very different, and it would be specious to draw exact parallels – though the *Guardian* did mention Golden Dawn have been encouraged by clerics – it did make me reflect on the physical danger to our characters who refused to bow the knee before the Catholic elite in both Church and State, especially after the massive display of Catholic power following the Eucharistic Congress of 1932, when over a million attended mass at Phoenix Park in Dublin. It must have been terrifying for Jimmy and co. to be called 'anti-Christs' and the 'anti-God people' each Sunday from the pulpit, with hatred whipped up in an hysterical fashion. A mine was placed at the entrance to the hall, which did not explode because it was faulty. The hall was shot into (though in defiance they danced on) and I have little doubt Jimmy's friends must have feared for his life. It seems not much had changed, a decade on from Jimmy's first flight, when a crowd of 2,000 in Dublin, egged on by a priest, burned down the [James] Connolly House in 1932.

I hope this little tale will be an antidote to the instinct to conform and the tugging of the forelock to those in power. Between takes I found myself wondering who would be the modern day equivalents to the anti-Christs of Jimmy's time. Would it be Chelsea Manning, sentenced to 35 years on Day 7 of the shoot, for revealing torture and murder by US troops while the murderers go unpunished? Or Ai Weiwei, China's most famous artist who had his art studio – which was also to be used as an education centre – demolished by the Chinese authorities because they could not control his criticism or wit. Or Julian Assange, who finds himself facing serious personal allegations which, out of all sense of scale, dwarf in the public narrative the systematic crimes against humanity he and his collaborators had the courage to expose. Or Edward Snowden for revealing how the State and corporations collaborate on massive surveillance of our private lives. Or independent trade union activists risking life and limb in the maquila factories along the Mexican border, or the vicious sweatshops in China. Or gay activists in Russia, or women educationalists in Afghanistan, or those brave teachers in Greece threatened by Golden Dawn to have their ears cut off if they continued to teach immigrant children. Or those activists today in Ireland who demand a transparent accounting of deals done in private between politicians and financiers that have had massive repercussions in public services that will affect every level of life for the foreseeable future, or who have criticised Irish budget details discussed in Germany before the Irish cabinet even saw them. What a mockery of the democratic process.

It seems clear we need a Jimmy's hall of the imagination, whether material, virtual, or a combination of both, if we are to be citizens; a safe free space where we can meet to think, debate, listen, learn, organise and analyse the world around us, and examine how power is shared, or not, in our daily lives. If our resistance is to last we need the nourishment of mischief and friendship in the process. It was Emma Goldman who told the Bolsheviks 'If I can't dance I don't want your revolution' and the executed Nigerian writer Ken Saro-Wira who wrote, 'Dance your anger and your joys. Dance the military guns to silence. Dance their dumb laws to the dump. Dance oppression and injustice to death...' Somewhere, somehow, in every corner of the world, Jimmy's hall and Clementis's hat, reveal themselves, despite the brutality.

Sligo, Sept 2013. Revised Edinburgh, Oct 2013.

Jimmy's Hall
Screenplay

From 'The King of Ragtime' Scott Joplin, we hear his sparkly foot-tapping version of 'The Pineapple Rag' played on piano accompanied by the distinctive black-and-white archive footage of New York in the 1920s and 30s.

TITLES

Images of skyscrapers filling Manhattan island from point of view of workers at the top of the Empire State Building; understated nerve, balancing casually on planks of wood, bolting girder to girder, with the terrifying abyss below them.

Ships belching smoke sail towards the island, a sense of mass trade and movement.

Steam trains enter the island over massive bridges.

Manhattan draws everything to itself.

Down on street level now; hustle and bustle of a metropolis, streets with electric trams and cars, as jerky pedestrians dart between them.

We see men and women, rich and poor, their different styles, and many black faces too from Harlem.

Sense of the sheer energy of a massive city and its cosmopolitan nature. Armies of workers head into factories.

Now the tone changes; jarring black-and-white images of the Depression. Hundreds queuing for bread; soup kitchens; the old and disabled begging in the streets. Headlines of doom from the Stock Market. An emaciated worker has a handmade poster round his neck 'I want work, not charity'. Misery on the streets of New York.

Central Station disgorges thousands… but then concrete, tarmac, iron, and ragtime give way to a world apart…

1. COUNTRY LANES, COUNTY LEITRIM – MARCH 1932

…a huge expanse of green fields with mountains behind, and the silhouette of a single horse and trap in the far distance.

> CAPTION 1
> In 1921 the people of Ireland fought for
> independence from the British Empire.

The horse and trap clip along the narrow lanes and byways of County Leitrim.

> CAPTION 2
> In 1922 there was a civil war between those
> who accepted the Treaty imposed by the
> British and those who were against it.

More byways and open fields; people working on farms with basic implements or herding cattle.

> CAPTION 3
> The pro-Treaty forces, backed by Britain,
> won the civil war. It sowed great bitterness
> throughout the land.

More stunning scenery.

> CAPTION 4
> Ten years later a change of government
> promised a more peaceful future.

JIMMY GRALTON, a lean-looking man, mid-forties, sits quietly in the trap beside his lifelong friend MOSSIE (a powerful figure, with an unruffled quality) who has the reins in his hand.

There is a stillness to Jimmy, almost introspective, though his eyes are sharp and intelligent; he notices everything. His face, body, and hands are marked by a lifetime's hard work.

They pass by a few farm labourers who stare in curiosity at the stranger. By the time their faces show the shock of recognition, Jimmy is already passed.

CAPTION 5
County Leitrim, March 1932...

They pass by poor land with bogs and reeds on which there are modest thatched cottages made of stone.

MOSSIE
There'll be a crowd at the house tonight
Jimmy, word travels fast.

Jimmy just nods, but there is a sense that it is a burden.

JIMMY
When did they let you out Mossie?

MOSSIE
Just a month ago... after the new government
came in...

JIMMY
How long did you serve?

MOSSIE
Three years. Been very tough on Angela.
[Pause as he restrains himself] We had to
send our oldest... Katie... to her aunt in
Scotland... that cut deep Jimmy...

JIMMY

Is she back yet?

MOSSIE

I need work first... I have to make it up to
them by Christ.

JIMMY

You will Mossie.

They pass by a distinctive man with red face and silver hair who
stares at them as they pass. Jimmy gives him a wave.

JIMMY (CONT'D)

Jaysus! Fergus! He's still alive!!

Mossie chuckles heartily.

MOSSIE

Still swigging the juice...

JIMMY

And still telling the same story...

MOSSIE

...about his fecking bull!!

Gentle laughter.

Further along the road.

JIMMY

Have you seen Oonagh?

Mossie glances at him.

MOSSIE

She's well... teaches a bit... she married one of
the Malloys, did you hear?

Jimmy nods at last.

MOSSIE (CONT'D)
A decent lad... a struggle on that land but
she's a tough one... two beautiful children.

JIMMY
I know... that's good... very good.

Mossie looks across at him for a second, as if judging the moment.

MOSSIE
She was a sorrowful soul after you left
Jimmy... you know that?

Jimmy keeps his own counsel.

MOSSIE (CONT'D)
For a long, long time.

Jimmy doesn't flicker.

GRAVEYARD: Starkly beautiful and silent. Mossie leads Jimmy to a private corner and points to the spot.

MOSSIE (CONT'D)
Your brother's over there...

Jimmy moves to a recently placed gravestone. He stares at the name, Charlie Gralton, aged 54, and a few more biographical details. Jimmy is sombre and respectful, but there is no sign of the cross or whispered prayers.

BACK TO THE HORSE AND TRAP:

They approach poorer land, some of which is boggy and full of reeds.

They reach a junction and turn. They look down a long path to an isolated stone cottage beyond a little stream. Mossie glances at Jimmy as he takes a deep breath on approaching home.

Before reaching the cottage they move past a simple hall. It is clear that it has been unoccupied for several years. The zinc sides are beginning to rust. The double doors in the middle are beginning to sag with the paint curling. A wooden board has a sign saying 'Pearse-Connolly Hall'. Jimmy examines it as they trot slowly by.

> MOSSIE (CONT'D)
> A sorry state… me and Tommy keep an eye
> on the roof as best we can… a few ghosts in
> there eh?

Jimmy just stares without saying a word.

> MOSSIE (CONT'D)
> I still miss it.

They cross the stream and the cart pulls up in front of the family cottage.

Jimmy and Mossie jump down. Jimmy stops to take it all in as the memories rush back, while Mossie, with ease, pulls a few cases from the back of the trap. But one distinctive crate is particularly heavy.

> MOSSIE (CONT'D)
> Jaysus… what's in here? Gold bullion?

> JIMMY
> A state secret Mossie… my lips are sealed.

Jimmy looks up to see his mother (ALICE) come around the corner from the back of the cottage. A moment between them and then they rush towards each other.

They hold hands for a few long moments as she examines him.

ALICE

[Whispered] Oh James... too long, too long...

JIMMY

Yes Mam... sorry I didn't get back for
Charlie's funeral... just been to the grave.

ALICE

He was a good son... this farm is a mess
without him... Ah James... feared I'd never
see you again...

Her eyes moisten. Jimmy, barely containing his emotion,
embraces her tightly.

ALICE (CONT'D)

Thank God you are home son.

2. OUTSIDE ALICE'S COTTAGE – EVENING

A sizeable group of visitors have arrived to welcome Jimmy
home. They stand in groups outside the cottage while some of
the older ones sit on benches propped up against the wall.

Alice and a few other women dish out teas, sandwiches, and
there is a bottle of poteen being passed around too, and by the
rosy cheeks of some, clear it is having the desired effect.

In and among the crowd are Jimmy's closest old friends Mossie
(accompanied by his younger wife ANGELA), SEAN (a
literature teacher, sharp and articulate), DEZZIE (a dynamic
presence, warm and sociable), TESS (a vivacious art teacher),
and MOLLY (late thirties, with a lovely voice who used to help
out with music in the hall).

Jimmy seems slightly overwhelmed by all the attention. While
he converses politely he is distracted, and pays more attention

to OONAGH, a striking woman now in her late thirties, who criss-crosses before him in between bodies as she pours from a huge tea kettle. They catch each other's eye now and again as she moves from one person to another.

TOMMY GILROY (a pugnacious ex militant from the War of Independence, a hard man and joiner by trade) arrives at the cottage with a more contained character, FINN.

> TOMMY
>
> Where is that bloody rogue now?! Could smell he was back!

He bounds towards Jimmy and grips his hand firmly.

> JIMMY
>
> Ah Tommy yi old dog! Can't believe they let you out...

> TOMMY
>
> About bloody time, did you get lost?

Finn shakes his hand warmly too.

> FINN
>
> Sorely missed... great to have you back.

> JIMMY
>
> Thanks Finn... you just got married...

> TOMMY
>
> [Taking the piss] Some desperate women in Leitrim.

An older woman MARY beckons Jimmy.

> MARY
>
> Jimmy, come over here!

Mary takes him warmly by the hand.

MARY (CONT'D)

You must have been round the world twenty
times... Thanks be to God you are home with
your mother... she was a lonely soul here on
her own.

JIMMY

Well I'm here to look after her now Mary...
lovely to see you.

Jimmy catches his mother just looking at him, enjoying the
moment, through the bodies. Molly calls on him from the other
side of the room.

MOLLY

Jimmy... What are you going to do with
yourself?

The conversations drop. A momentary glance between Oonagh
and Jimmy.

JIMMY

Settle down back home with Mam... I've
missed the land... I want a quiet life now...

The incredulous silence grows from smiles to chuckles, and then
outright laughter among them all.

DEZZIE

I'll take bets on that!

JIMMY.

You're on! 10 to 1.

DEZZIE

Done!

JIMMY.
[Exchanging a quick glance with Oonagh,
more seriously] I mean it… I'm here to stay.

3. BY THE COTTAGE – LATER

Oonagh leaves the cottage and moves to her bicycle leaning up against the far wall. Jimmy comes out a moment after. He is holding three carefully tied up packages in brown paper.

There is a quiet tentative moment between them, and then he hands over two of the parcels.

JIMMY
For your children.

She is touched. He hands over another.

JIMMY (CONT'D)
For you…

She makes to open it.

JIMMY (CONT'D)
No Oonagh… by yourself.

It stops her in her tracks. A long moment as they get a first chance to look at each other.

JIMMY (CONT'D)
You look well Oonagh…

She blushes. She examines him in turn.

OONAGH
A bit greyer round the edges… but you're still
like a hungry whippet…

He catches that mischief in her for a second and he smiles.

OONAGH (CONT'D)
Why did you stop writing Jimmy?

JIMMY
You know why.

She holds his eye without answering.

JIMMY (CONT'D)
How are the children?

OONAGH
Healthy, full of spirit thank God.

JIMMY
And Fintan?

OONAGH
A good steady man, and loving father. [Pause]
And you?

Long moment between them, and then he looks to his boots.

JIMMY
Ah same as ever…

OONAGH
Nobody is the same after ten years Jimmy.
Nobody.

No answer.

OONAGH (CONT'D)
No sign of children yourself?

JIMMY
Who'd put up with me running round all
over…

She studies him for a moment.

OONAGH

Do you really want to stay this time Jimmy?

JIMMY

I had to come back... Mam on her own...

OONAGH

So, was it duty, or you?

Her sharp eyes hold his.

JIMMY

Do you always know the difference Oonagh?

They look at each other for a long moment.

OONAGH

I have to get back. Thanks for these.

She lays the parcels in her saddle bag. He watches her push the bike with one leg on a pedal and then swing the other over so elegantly and cycle off.

Her outline is still familiar, even after a decade.

He's relieved she turns round to glance at him.

There is a tenderness in his eye as he watches her disappear.

4. OONAGH'S ROOM – NIGHT

Oonagh enters her bedroom and lays the parcel upon the bed.

She looks anxious, and moves back to close the door shut.

She stares at the parcel for a moment, and then gently pulls the string bow which ties it. She is nervous as she unfolds the paper. She picks up a delicate flapper-like dress made of flimsy fine material of the best quality. It is a creamy gold, and has delicate little stones sewn into it in a charming pattern. It has short

31

sleeves. She savours the lightness of touch and rippling effect. She holds it up to herself in a full–length mirror on an old dresser. It has an elegant cut, and fits like a glove. She puts her arms round it, and stares at herself in the mirror.

Her eyes fill as she looks at her reflection.

Noise of children in the distance.

> FINTAN'S VOICE
> Where did you get the toy, Francis?

> CHILD
> Jimmy brought it back from America!

> FINTAN'S VOICE
> You lucky boy.

5. PEAT BOG, BY THE MOUNTAINS – DAY

A bunch of neighbours, a dozen or so men, look like black spots against an extraordinary landscape of bog land stretching for miles towards the mountains.

UP CLOSE: Tommy and Mossie are in a bog up to their chests against a beautifully cut bank, skilfully slicing bog with a slane. In turn they throw up turfs which are caught by hand by Jimmy who is above them. He carefully places them in a bog barrow. Jimmy looks thoughtful and withdrawn. Mossie and Tommy glance at each other.

> TOMMY
> Jimmy… a question… What did yi miss most
> when you were away?

He thinks for a moment.

> JIMMY
> Silence Tommy. I missed the silence.

The men watch him as he wheels the barrow off to a drying space. Jimmy up-ends the barrow and arranges the turf still with a confident hand after all the years away.

TOMMY

He's very quiet...

MOSSIE

Give him time...

Tommy and Mossie get back to work again, as Jimmy joins them once more.

TOMMY

A far cry from New York Jimmy eh? You
don't get this on Broadway...

Jimmy smiles and stares around him.

TOMMY (CONT'D)

You sailed the seven seas... from Rio to
Cairo... and here you are, back down the
same fecking bog in Leitrim... wet feet...

MOSSIE

...fleas in your pants...

JIMMY

...but nobody yelling orders... can't beat that.

They recognise a flash of the old Jimmy.

TOMMY

Have you been in the hall yet Jimmy?

Mossie can spot Jimmy's deep discomfort. He ignores the question.

MOSSIE
[Sharpish] Give the man peace now... don't
want to be stirring up a hornet's nest and the
fellow just back home.

6. LANE TO AND INTO ALICE'S COTTAGE

A forceful and energetic figure in his mid-fifties strides along the
lane and over the stream towards the cottage. The man's soutane
flaps as he powers along. FATHER SHERIDAN's dark eyes are
not best pleased as his corpulent frame avoids the puddles and
mud. He approaches the door, and knocks loudly. No answer.
In deep frustration he looks around.

He pounds again.

SHERIDAN
Mrs Gralton! Are you in there?

The door creaks open. Alice holds the priest's eyes without fear.

ALICE
Come in Father... would you like a cup of
tea?

The priest follows, and the door closes.

MINUTES LATER: The humility of the interior matches the
cottage from the outside. But there is one big difference. The
shelves are packed with books which Father Sheridan glances
at as Alice approaches with a cup of tea. She lays it on a simple
wooden table before him.

SHERIDAN
Thank you... [sipping] Word travels fast...
must be a relief to see your son again?

ALICE

It is.

SHERIDAN

Is he well?

ALICE

He is Father.

SHERIDAN

A lot of water under the bridge… New York
is a tough place… it will be a shock from city
life to our humble country ways… Do you
think he's… [looking for the word] matured?

ALICE

We all change Father… wouldn't you say?

They examine each other carefully.

SHERIDAN

God willing we all hope to change for the
better… do you think he'll stay?

ALICE

He was born in this house… I'll leave that up
to him to decide…

SHERIDAN

We have suffered great violence in this
country Alice… brother against brother,
neighbour against neighbour… scars on the
heart take a long long time to heal… but
I sense a new atmosphere… of change, of
forgiveness… Would you agree?

ALICE

There is always that possibility Father… if
there is mutual respect.

He can spot the steel in her.

> SHERIDAN
> Let's pray there'll be… [studying her]… no
> slipping back to the old ways.

Alice just holds his eye.

> SHERIDAN (CONT'D)
> Please tell your son… if country life gets too
> quiet for a man of action I have some excellent
> contacts in London who could find him a
> good job, which is always a relief to a mother
> in these times.

Alice just stares at him.

7. COUNTRY CROSSROADS – DAY

Jimmy, Mossie and Tommy are piled up on a donkey and cart carrying peat back home. A light rain has drifted in. Activity ahead captures their attention.

They come to a very modest crossroads under some trees where a bunch of youngsters, teens and early twenties, dance on the road accompanied by two friends who play a traditional tune on squeeze box and fiddle. Their rosy cheeked vitality challenges the elements.

Jimmy notices a long line of bikes leaning on the wall. As the cart slows he is intrigued by their dance and the simple joy of it.

The youngsters stand to the side to let the cart pass. Whispers and recognition among some of the youngsters as the cart passes.

An extroverted girl, MARIE (pronounced Ma-ri) 19 years of age, full of spirit comes up to the cart. She has a disarming smile and strong presence.

MARIE

Are you Jimmy Gralton?

JIMMY

And who wants to know?

MARIE

My name is Marie O'Keefe.

Jimmy's eyes flash at the name.

JIMMY

Daughter of Dennis O'Keefe?

MARIE

He hates you with a passion... nearly had a fit
when the priest came round to say you were
back.

She bursts out laughing which the others enjoy too. The squeeze
box starts up again.

JIMMY

You'll miss your dance.

She stares at Jimmy, obviously fascinated. She smiles and goes
back to the action. And how she dances.

At last Jimmy flicks the reins to the donkey and continues.

JIMMY (CONT'D)

Have you seen O'Keefe?

MOSSIE

...left the Free State army years back
after his first wife died and was on his
own with Marie... then he struck gold
and married into land... furious with the
change of government... calling de Valera a
communist...

TOMMY

Big shot now with the Army Comrades
Association... you know them... afraid they
won't be able to export to England...

Jimmy's eyes flash at the news.

MOSSIE

Bunch of fascists...

TOMMY

Keep well clear of him... nasty as ever...
[catching Jimmy's eye]... with a long memory.

As they trot along they become aware of a presence beside them.
First one, then another and then another... one panting red face
then more cycling like the clappers to overtake them. There are
over a dozen in hot pursuit.

MOSSIE

[Shouting out] What's this... the wild west?!

Marie O'Keefe has cycled her way to the front.

MARIE

Jimmy... Jimmy... can we have a word?

Jimmy pulls on the reins and finds himself now confronting over
a dozen and a half fresh faces in front of him trying to catch
their breaths. There is embarrassed shuffling among them but
still silence.

JIMMY

Well... are we under arrest?

That breaks the ice and some laugh. A big, curly-haired lad,
BRENDAN, who played the squeeze box, addresses the boy
beside him (AIDAN).

BRENDAN

You ask him…

AIDAN

No… you…

MARIE

The hall Jimmy… [Mossie and Tommy glance
at each other]… we heard all the stories…
[turning round looking for support] lots of
them…

Jimmy's eyes flash at Mossie and Tommy who are astounded.
Silence for a long moment. Jimmy stares at the youthful faces.

BRENDAN

My brother told me how you and Dezzie ran
the boxing there… he still does the training…

BOY 2

And your woodwork classes Tommy… my
uncle started his business after…

GIRL 1

And the art classes with Tess… I've seen some
of the paintings…

Their confidence grows and enthusiasm tumbles from one to
another.

BOY 3

We met Sean last night… all the poems he
taught… the newspapers… even books from
outside the country!

BOY 4

…said he'd do it again if you opened up!

BOY 3

Some of us have missed a lot of schooling
Jimmy...

GIRL 2

And the music with Oonagh, the singing with
Molly... I want to learn too...

Mossie studies Jimmy's dark face and knows he is suffering
inside.

BOY 4

There is nothing for us here Jimmy...
nothing! Hardly any work... and since they
changed the rules we can't get to America like
you did Jimmy...

A quieter boy's frustration eventually bursts out.

BOY 5

Will someone tell him!

They are taken aback by his vehemence. Silence for a moment.

MARIE

We want to dance... into the night... where a
priest or guard don't poke at us with a stick...
inside, where's it warm... [Pause] Will you
open up the hall again Jimmy?

Their vibrant faces make it even more painful for him.

JIMMY

It's falling to pieces... not even safe...

MARIE

We'll help you build it up again Jimmy... all
of us will!

They all voice their support and offer help. Tommy can barely contain his enthusiasm too.

> JIMMY
> [Sharp] You don't understand…

Muttered voices.

> VOICES
> Why not Jimmy? It'll be different this time… we'll all help… paint the place up! We'll start right now if you want…

> JIMMY
> I said no!! It can't be done!

> TOMMY
> Come on Jimmy…

> JIMMY
> Jaysus Tommy!! [It takes Tommy aback] You should know better…

> MARIE
> But why not?

> JIMMY
> Just can't be done! [It stuns them.] Work to be getting on with… now let me pass.

One by one they move to the side. As Brendan passes his frustration shows.

> BRENDAN
> So much for the Jimmy Gralton legend…

One last remaining bike blocks the path. Marie holds his eye.

MARIE

You better change the name of the hall...
[pause] James Connolly will be turning in his
grave!

This gets him through the heart and both Tommy and Mossie
know it.

They glance between each other. Jimmy's agony continues.

At last she moves aside. Jimmy swishes the reins and makes the
beast trot like hell.

8. INTO HALL – PRESENT

FROM INSIDE AND BLACK:

Warped double doors scrape open. Jimmy stumbles into the
gloom as the windows have shutters. He stares for a few moments.

Cobwebs float down. Jimmy moves to one of the windows and
opens up stiff shutters. Light shafts catch the dust all over the
wooden floor and his own newly made footprints. The sides and
roof are sealed with boards. There is a simple stage at one end.

In the gloom, from just one window, Jimmy walks around
slowly, taking it all in. He gets to the middle of the floor and
bounces a little to test the spring.

He stops again and stares around him for several moments; the
enormity of the decision weighs upon him.

He draws a finger over the dust on a cupboard door, and then
opens it to reveal a row of dusty books on various subjects from
the history of Ireland, including Connolly's, on exercise, boxing,
farming, woodwork, poetry and music.

He swivels to face the empty space... and a flashback of ten
years ago.

9. SEMI-CONSTRUCTED HALL – 1921

A hive of activity and considerable effort by many as they construct the hall.

A younger Jimmy shows off the progress to a local journalist dressed in a suit, with a notebook in his hand.

There is some tension as Tommy above supervises a delicate operation as they try to heave up a heavy part of the frame for the roof.

Tommy, frustrated and impatient, issues instructions to the three amateurs below, Sean, Finn and Dezzie, who don't pay best attention. The latter seems more interested in the food being handed out by Molly and Oonagh.

> TOMMY
> Easy now... higher, higher... Is anybody
> paying fecking attention down there?! This
> is a key part of the operation! It's the fecking
> roof!

It makes Oonagh and Molly smile, and entertains the journalist too.

> FINN
> It would help Tommy if you would just
> explain things calmly before shouting at us...

> TOMMY
> You never bloody listen! And look at him!

Dezzie has let go of the rope and wanders off for a sandwich.

> DEZZIE
> Just milked a half-dozen cows... I'm
> starving...

TOMMY

Jaysus Mary and Joseph give me patience!

RUARI

Come on Dezzie... [taking the piss] this is a
key part of the operation... do we need a roof
or not?

Their laugher infuriates Tommy even more. Dezzie wanders
back.

DEZZIE

Ready for action Tommy boy!

He sticks the sandwich in his mouth.

TOMMY

...higher... a little bit higher...

They heave on the rope and the frame swings higher.

TOMMY (CONT'D)

...down down... up up... up! Too much!
Jaysus! Do you clowns understand up and
down!! It's fecking simple!

The three lads get a fit of the giggles and the frame slips.

There is a sudden jolt, the frame collapses, and comes crashing
down.

JIMMY

As you can see, all master craftsmen...

The journalist laughs, a great mistake. Tommy's legendary hot
temper manifests itself once again.

TOMMY

Hey you! Which paper are you with?

JOURNALIST

Leitrim Observer...

TOMMY

[Brandishing his hammer] Any shit from you
and you'll get this hammer up your hole!

Jimmy can see the journalist's alarm, and beckons him further
away to safety.

JOURNALIST

[Whisper] Is that 'the' Tommy Gilroy... of the
flying column?

Jimmy nods and the journalists face darkens even further.

They move to the comparative safety of Tess (the art teacher)
who is painting up the name of the hall and putting the finishing
touches to the sign 'Pearse-Connolly Hall'.

JIMMY

The Tans burnt down the church hall in
Gowell about a year ago... so we decided to
build our own...

JOURNALIST

With whose money?

JIMMY

I had some savings from the States... and few
friends too...

JOURNALIST

So if it is your money and your land... must
be your hall?

Tess looks up sharply and intervenes.

TESS

No! Built by the voluntary labour of the
community... run by an elected committee...
I'll teach art... [nodding in their direction]
Oonagh and Molly the music classes,
Mossie, the boxing, woodwork, gymnastics,
literature... every penny will be put back into
the hall to buy musical instruments, books,
materials...

JIMMY

And we'll have the best damned dances in the
country...

JOURNALIST

Just spoke to the parish priest... not best
pleased... [looking over at the beasts] even
told me that every horse pulling sand would
die within a year...

JIMMY

Is he a priest, or a witch doctor?

TESS

[Overhearing] Is there any difference?

The journalist chuckles as he writes it down.

JIMMY

I'll offer him good odds if he wants a bet...

The journalist looks over Tess's shoulder as she puts the finishing
touches to the sign.

JOURNALIST

This will be a red rag to an angry bull... you
want to provoke him?

                    TESS

          Nothing to do with him... [still painting,
          journalist noting] Pearse was a visionary, a
          poet and great teacher ahead of his time...
          we're going to teach too... and Connolly...
          well... he asked the big questions didn't he?...
          And he was right... the poor still with us and
          not much has changed...

                  JOURNALIST

          [Writing it down eagerly] Big ideas for a tiny
          hall... but you better watch out... [chuckling
          at his own joke]... they were both shot!

Tess's eyes flash at him.

                    TESS

          But not forgotten.

Jimmy smiles to himself at Tess's conviction.

HALL – PRESENT: Jimmy sits down on a bench that hugs the
wall, and stares ahead of him again. He can hear music in his
mind, and the pounding of dancing feet.

10. HALL – FLASHBACK

Now a younger Jimmy sits in the same position as he watches
Oonagh supervise a small group of musicians in a traditional
reel with a group of young dancers; red cheeks, bobbing hair,
and concentration.

At some point they hurl each other around at speed. A young
muscular farmer nearly spins his partner out the door...

                  OONAGH

          [Chuckling] Easy Francis... yi nearly sent her
          flying...

Gentle laughter but the energetic reel continues; the young girl gives the young boy a run for his money on the next swing.

Gradually some of them become aware of a figure at the double doors. The musicians one by one fall silent, and Jimmy can feel the hall freeze and the nervousness on the youngsters' faces.

JIMMY
Come in Father, you are welcome.

SHERIDAN
Gralton. You come out!

Jimmy moves to the door but doesn't cross the threshold.

JIMMY
Mr Gralton to you, Sheridan.

The youngsters are stunned by defiance to a man of the cloth.

SHERIDAN
Who in the hell do you think you are…
running classes in my parish without my
permission?

JIMMY
No permission required! That's the point. We
built it ourselves.

SHERIDAN
Education is the exclusive reserve of Holy
Mother Church! Not semi-illiterates traipsing
back from America with big ideas… been
away too long.

Jimmy is about to rise to the bait.

OONAGH
[Quietly, cutting through] Jimmy, please…

49

It calms him down.

                    SHERIDAN
        I won't have a communist on my turf defy the
        Church.

                    JIMMY
        [Calmer] Days of tugging the forelock are
        gone... Sheridan.

Sheridan can barely control his temper.

                    SHERIDAN
        [Staring now at Oonagh] Short sleeves...
        hardly becomes you. Does your father know
        you are here Oonagh Dempsey?

                    OONAGH
        [Gently] If you would like to enrol in our
        dance class Father you are very welcome...
        doesn't cost a penny and we are all volunteers.

Jimmy smiles in deep satisfaction at her calm defiance.

PRESENT:

A swoosh of dust into the light as Jimmy blows the passing years
from a row of meticulously annotated files with clear headings on
the spines with dates from a decade back. Miscellaneous captions;
expenses, repairs, accounts, teachers, students, musicians, etc,
and then one catches his eye. He pulls it out and rubs his hand
over dust to reveal the title taking up most of the front cover.
'Republican Court', and underneath, 'Direct Action Committee'.

He sits down on a chair as he flicks through a bunch of newspaper
cuttings which brings intense memories flooding back. His
eye catches headlines and photographs from both inside and
outside the hall along the following lines; 'Noisy scenes as five

hundred attend Republican Court' and 'Republican Court solves complicated land case'.

He looks at an old photograph of himself, Sean, Tess, and others on a table underneath a banner 'Dail Court' inside the hall. He looks up at the very same banner, now fading and drooping, above the stage at the end of the hall.

As his eyes flick through a newspaper report he can hear a jumble of voices in his head above the sounds of an unruly crowd. He glances between the newspaper, and the old site of the actual court.

MAN 1

I am here to represent my neighbour Rory
O'Sullivan who is the rightful tenant... The
land has been in his family for over 26 years,
and due to ill health he fell behind on the
rent... despite repeated letters to the landlord
with a report from his doctor, the landlord
refused him a reasonable time to catch up and
threw him off the land...

SEAMUS CLARKE

My name is Seamus Clarke. I am the new
tenant...

VOICES

Shame on yi Clarke! Land grabber!

SEAMUS CLARKE

I rented this land in good faith and for a
fair price from the landlord, and I have the
contract here with me now for you all to look
at... Truth be told I have sympathy for Rory
O'Sullivan, but it has nothing to do with me...

51

ANOTHER VOICE
Come off it Clarke! You've had your beady
eye on that land next door for years!

JIMMY'S VOICE
Silence in court! Every man will have their
say!

Jimmy examines a newspaper. 'Parish priest supports furious
farmer who condemns Republican Court'. He flips to another
headline and can't help the smile coming to his face. 'Direct
Action Committee confronts IRA'. There is a photograph of
COMMANDER O'KEEFE (dressed in a smart Free State
army-like uniform in embryo as it is still pre civil war), a tough
figure DOHERTY (dressed in a trench coat, brawny, with
a striking handlebar moustache over a hard face), and Father
Sheridan in his soutane.

11. NARROW LANE TO FARM HOUSE – 1922

A cattle drive, implemented by the Direct Action Committee.

VOICE OVER SEAN
This court has reached a unanimous decision.
The tenant Rory O'Sullivan is entitled to
recovery of the land in dispute, and the cattle
belonging to Seamus Clarke will be removed
immediately...

Whistles, shouts, curses, instructions and barking dogs at the
heels of some nervous cattle. Jimmy, Tommy, Mossie, Dezzie,
Finn and several other recognisable faces from the hall, plus
several dozen from the community, march in front of the cattle
which are being driven up a narrow lane. There are another two
dozen behind the cattle, driving them on.

A teenager cycles at speed down the lane to meet them.

> TEENAGER
> Jimmy! Jimmy! O'Keefe's up there with the
> army! Doherty too with the Republicans...
> and the priest just arrived! They won't let you
> pass... you better turn back!

Jimmy glances at Tommy and Mossie.

> JIMMY
> Ah the Holy Trinity!... [To Tommy] Now
> easy Tommy... it's not the Tans we're fighting
> now...

> TOMMY
> [Ready for the fight] Fecking worse!

> JIMMY
> Promise me... keep calm. [Grabbing him by
> the arm] You're not armed are you?

> TOMMY
> [Shaking his head] Just my bare hands Jimmy.

Jimmy confronts Commander O'Keefe, a powerful man (dressed as in photograph of above) with a half-dozen men behind him in semi-militarised gear. On one side of him is Doherty in his trench coat, with two other toughs similarly dressed behind him, and Father Sheridan in his soutane.

The three burly men, blocking the gate to a sizeable farmhouse and yard, stare ahead as Jimmy leads the community and a dozen cattle towards them. The farmer SEAMUS CLARKE (new tenant of the land in dispute, recognisable from the newspaper cutting) stands behind his gate but in full view.

There is a stand-off with some ten yards between them. More and more men from behind the cattle join Jimmy at the front.

O'Keefe, Sheridan and Doherty, are outnumbered 6 to 1, and soldiers behind look very nervous despite their arms.

JIMMY

Open up Clarke! Here's your cattle back...
keep them off your neighbour's land...

SHERIDAN

Gralton! You sow nothing but conflict in a
peaceful community...

O'KEEFE

Go and join the Bolsheviks in Siberia and
leave us alone!

TOMMY

And you go and join the British!

SEAMUS CLARKE

I paid a fair price for that land! You have no
right to move my cattle!

JIMMY

You took advantage of a tenant in trouble...
you are nothing but an opportunist land
grabber! Keep your cattle off his land!

Doherty snaps out a document from his coat.

DOHERTY

[Shouting, nervous] I warning you now!...
This document was placed in my hands by the
acting OC of the IRA in this area... now you
better listen for your own good!

MOSSIE

[Fury] We fought the British too Doherty!

TOMMY

Can you read Doherty?

DEZZIE

Stick your orders up your arse!

Doherty shouts above their retorts, but some want to hear what
the document says and call for calm.

DOHERTY

[Reading] 'Certain evilly disposed and
unauthorised persons within the county of
South Leitrim have taken forcible possession
of lands to which they are NOT entitled...'

JIMMY

[Shouting] Yes, back in 1690!

A loud burst of laughter and then cheers which infuriates the
Trinity.

DOHERTY

[Even louder] Silence!! 'We order and declare
that anyone found interfering with the lands
to which the person has no claim shall be
severely dealt with!'

TOMMY

You threatening us Doherty yi bastard?!

JIMMY

We intend to implement the decision of the
Republican court! Stand aside!

O'Keefe snaps and pulls the revolver from his belt, shocking even
Sheridan, and points it at them.

55

O'KEEFE

By Christ, the first man that crosses that gate
will get a bullet in the head!

Tommy (stunning Jimmy) whips out an enormous handgun from inside his jacket and points it at O'Keefe.

TOMMY

You'll be first to hit the ground O'Keefe!!

Doherty grabs a gun from inside his jacket too… suddenly, several men from among the crowd appear with an array of weapons, including three shotguns pulled from under coats.

The soldiers behind O'Keefe grow increasingly nervous amidst the confusion.

JIMMY

We don't want to spill innocent blood! Stand
aside!

Silence apart from the mewing beasts. More men from behind the cattle (with farm implements or hurley sticks) now join those at the front. Sheridan can see the pluck on their faces. Another couple of men pop up behind walls with more shotguns.

SHERIDAN

[Leaning into O'Keefe] Bide your time
man… there's a time and a place… [Still he
won't back down]… Do what I say now…
both of you…

At last, O'Keefe, trembling with fury, lowers his gun. Doherty follows.

Both he and Doherty, profoundly humiliated, stand to the side as Mossie runs forward and opens the gate. The farmer backs off too. The animals are driven into the yard.

SEAMUS CLARKE
Gralton! What can I do with all my cattle?

JIMMY
I hope you're hungry... you can eat them one
by one yi fat bastard!

Their mirth infuriates O'Keefe and co. as the cattle are driven
into the farmer's yard accompanied by loud cheering. Open grins
in their direction, rub salt in the wounds.

The Holy Trinity have thunder in their eyes. Doherty leans
into O'Keefe.

DOHERTY
I swear I'll kill the fucker...

O'KEEFE
...if I don't beat you to it.

HALL – PRESENT:

Jimmy opens up another cupboard.

Inside, carefully hanging up on perches, are a half-dozen dusty
fiddles, an accordion and several bodhrans.

He picks up one of the violins and flicks his fingers across the
sagging and wasted strings.

He picks up a bodhran now and begins to tap it, gently, again,
again, and then... he can hear a beautiful voice singing which
drifts into the next scene.

MOLLY
I wish I was on yonder hill, 'tis there I'd sit
and cry my fill, And every tear would turn a
mill, Is go dté tú mo mhuirnín slán...

12. HALL – FLASHBACK (1922)

At the far end, Tommy and Mossie quietly lace up a pile of new boxing gloves. Jimmy sits at a small table near a window doing the accounts for the hall.

They enjoy a dozen or so young women, with Molly singing the lead part, practising a song without accompaniment, led by Oonagh who has the music in front of her. They sit on wooden seats in the middle of the hall between the men and the door. It is an old love song, 'Siúil a Rún' ('Walk My Love'), sang in part English, part Gaelic, which sounds like a lullaby.

> WOMEN TOGETHER
> [Chorus, but will be in Gaelic] I wish, I wish
> I wish in vain, I wish I had my heart again,
> And vainly think I'd not complain, Is go dté
> tú mo mhúirnín slán…

> MOLLY
> I'll sell my rack, I'll sell my reel, I'll sell my
> only spinning wheel, to buy my love a sword
> of steel, 's go dtéigh tú, a mhúirnín, slán…

The doors are kicked in. The women jump out of their skins. Commander O'Keefe and a half-dozen soldiers, now dressed in full Free State army uniforms, armed with rifles, barge in.

> O'KEEFE
> I want Gralton! He's under arrest!

> OONAGH
> What for?

> O'KEEFE
> No more anarchy in Leitrim!! No more of
> your kangaroo courts!

All hell breaks loose as the women recover from the shock and confront the soldiers led by Oonagh and Molly. Two women to each man. Tommy and Mossie rush over to Jimmy by a corner.

SOLDIER

There he is there!

O'KEEFE

Grab him! Now!!

OONAGH

Stop them girls!

Half the women grab the soldiers while the rest pick up their chairs and jab at them with the upturned legs. Oonagh grips a furious O'Keefe as he viciously tries to break free. Some of the young soldiers are intimidated, and in confusion.

OONAGH (CONT'D)

Where is your warrant?

O'KEEFE

[To soldiers] Come on you sissies! Give them a good smack if you have to!

By the window:

TOMMY

These bastards could shoot you Jimmy!

JIMMY

I can't leave yis…

MOSSIE

Or beat yi to a pulp… your life's in danger… move!

They manhandle him to the window and open it.

SOLDIER

He's jumping out the window!

O'KEEFE

Grab the bastard!!

Mossie and Tommy push Jimmy up and out as the first soldier breaks through but Tommy and Mossie are up for the fight.

Chaos in the hall as the soldiers and women confront each other. Three young women block the doors and fight wildly with the soldiers trying to get out.

VOICES

After him! Out the back! Chase the bastard!

A soldier is almost halfway out another window but a young lass grabs him firmly by the leg.

SOLDIER

Fucking whore yi... let me go!!

At last two soldiers break free and run into the yard.

Oonagh still grips O'Keefe's coat as his fury swells.

A soldier runs back in.

SOLDIER (CONT'D)

He's gone...

O'KEEFE

After him yi clown!

He catches Oonagh with a defiant grin. He whacks her across the face and sends her flying.

HALL – PRESENT: Jimmy smiles as he picks up a dusty old photo. He looks at Oonagh with a bunch of youngsters in the hall. She is laughing, and animated. He stares at her for several long moments...

13. STABLE, EVENING – FLASHBACK (1922)

Jimmy and Oonagh are face to face in the privacy of an old farm building and it's clear they've been talking for a while. Jimmy is in the same clothes as when he escaped the hall. Oonagh has a bruised cheek from O'Keefe's blow. Jimmy examines it with concern.

> JIMMY
> It looks a sore one… I'm sorry.

> OONAGH
> It's nothing… worth it to see his face, the
> bastard.

Her mettle makes him smile.

> JIMMY
> Will you say goodbye to Mam for me…
> they're watching the farm…

> OONAGH
> How long are you gone for Jimmy?

Jimmy shrugs.

> JIMMY
> Till things calm down… there's a few pistol
> boys keen to make a name for themselves…
> I have good comrades in New York who can
> find me work…

There is a moment between them and awkward hesitation.

> JIMMY (CONT'D)
> Mossie's waiting for me by the bridge… [He's
> about to turn, but blurts it out] What if I
> asked you to come with me Oonagh?

It knocks her. Silence for a moment.

OONAGH

[Whispering] What if my mother wasn't
fading… what if I wasn't the only daughter…
what if my father wouldn't fall apart… [done
in] what if I wasn't so trapped Jimmy?

JIMMY

What if, Oonagh?

She stares at him for a long moment.

OONAGH

And follow you about Jimmy?… One battle to
the next… can I take that?

Still she struggles.

OONAGH (CONT'D)

Are those the only clothes you have?

JIMMY

I hear they sell clothes in New York…

OONAGH

I suppose so… Jimmy Gralton.

It is unbearable for both. Jimmy stretches out a hand and strokes
her cheek tenderly below the bruise.

There is a whistle from Mossie in the distance.

Jimmy suddenly grabs her tight and embraces her.

JIMMY

[Whispering] Jesus Christ girl… you'll be in
my heart, no matter what, till the day I die.

He releases her just as suddenly and marches off without looking
back. Her eyes fill as he disappears.

14. HALL – PRESENT

Jimmy is still rooted to the spot with the intensity of the memory. Suddenly, with great energy, he strides round the hall, forcing open the rest of the windows and stuck shutters with considerable force.

At last he moves to the door, and with some difficulty manages to shove the other half of the double door open.

He looks up in some surprise. Tommy, Mossie, Sean, Ruari, Finn, Dezzie and Molly are sitting quietly on a bank. Some enjoy a quiet smoke.

Long moment between them as his eye jumps from one to the other. Jimmy is touched. He shakes his head and smiles.

> SEAN
>
> You just lost your bet.

At last they chuckle.

> TOMMY
>
> That fecking roof's never been right…

15. INSIDE THE HALL – PRESENT (1932)

Jimmy, taking his time and with great precision, gently lays the needle of an elegantly crafted gramophone on a record. (It is a stunning machine with a speaker in bold colours.)

> MOSSIE
>
> [Whispered to Tess] That's his fecking secret…
> nearly broke my back with all those records…

> TESS
>
> [In wonder at the gramophone] Wait till word
> gets out… We'll have them cycling in from
> miles…

63

As the static sounds, the youngsters from the crossroads gather round. The older faces from the hall are intrigued too.

It is an up-beat jazzy piano number that can only bring a smile; music that they have never heard before. It delights them beyond their imagination. It is slinky, and has an infectious bubbly rhythm. Their faces shine.

Jimmy, in some style, glides into the Shim Sham.

He catches Oonagh's eye, but she looks shy. He holds out his hand for her but she declines. She shakes her head. He beckons again with a roguish grin. She wavers a little. Marie pushes her gently... her reserve crumbles and she eventually takes Jimmy's hand and joins him.

Her confidence grows and they dance in an easy carefree style. The youngsters have never seen anything like it and are mesmerised by the novelty, the mischief, and above all the sense of fun.

JIMMY
[Over the music and to appropriate movements] And Shim Sham!!

Some laughter from old and young.

Oonagh steps over and grabs one of the lads as Jimmy takes Marie's hand. Jimmy beckons up others who join in.

They all have a crack at copying Jimmy and Oonagh. Some are quick and catch on, while others trip over their feet.

Mossie, Dezzie, Tommy, Molly, Alice and others look on from the sides; they are touched. The place is alive.

At long last they have their Jimmy and hall back.

Whoops of laughter and applause as the record ends.

Jimmy catches a glimpse of Oonagh's shining eyes.

64

16. FIELD

A single matchstick figure in a wide-open landscape.

In closer; Jimmy has a rake in his hands, and gathers up freshly dried hay. There is both concentration and satisfaction on his face.

He stops to wipe his brow and stares out over the open fields and mountains beyond. Absolute silence, apart from bird song. The peace and beauty of the place fill him up.

He goes back again to the quiet satisfaction of work.

A gentle girl's voice (ROISIN) drifts in above the sound of the countryside.

> ROISIN
> ...it had become a glimmering girl, With
> apple blossom in her hair, Who called me by
> my name and ran, And faded through the
> brightening air...

17. HALL, MOSAIC OF EVENING CLASSES

A. ANOTHER DAY: LITERATURE CLASS:

The spoken word from the previous scene continues. Sean, the teacher, is in the middle of a dozen new faces of mixed ages and gender while Jimmy does some paperwork by a corner.

A young women, on her feet, recites the poem 'The Song of Wandering Aengus' by W.B. Yeats. Though she has the sheet of paper in her hand, she closes her eyes and does it from memory, beautifully. From their faces, evident that each and everyone, young and old, are enchanted by her rendition.

Sean's eyes are alive too, and mouths the words to himself as Roisin recites.

ROISIN

...Though I am old with wandering, Through
hollow lands and hilly lands, I will find out
where she has gone, and kiss her lips and take
her hands; And walk among long dappled
grass, And pluck till time and times are done,
The silver apples of the moon, The golden
apples of the sun.

She sits down amid whispers of approval.

SEAN

Beautiful Roisin... thank you...

OLDER WOMAN

Oh my God... I hope he found her!

SEAN

Let's look at the beginning again... 'I went
out to the hazel wood...

One of the class, a big farm labourer, interrupts with spontaneous
enthusiasm.

BIG FARMER

'Because a fire was in my head' [Pause]
Jaysus... how did he think of that?!

Sean chuckles with delight at his raw enthusiasm.

B. BOXING:

Mossie coaches two powerful lads how to box, as several others
watch, skip, or do exercises.

MOSSIE

Left up... higher!... Protect your chin man!
That's better.

C. ART:

Tess supervises a class of some nine students who are doing charcoal sketches of a young freckly lad DIARMUID who is posing for them on a stool. He has a cap on at a particular angle.

Others quietly enjoy reading in another corner. Jimmy is among them.

Diarmuid can't resist an itch and scratches under his hat. One girl in particular SARAH is furious with him.

> SARAH
> [To Tess] He's done it again Tess!... Keeps
> fidgeting... [Frustrated at her work] Look at
> the mess...

> DIARMUID
> Just scratching my head...

> TESS
> He's trying his best... just relax Diarmuid.

> SARAH
> Never stops... have you got fleas?!

> DIARMUID
> Making me nervous...

Diarmuid concentrates with all his might as he tries to sit deadly still. He barely breathes, but something is amiss. Another itch begins to torment. He struggles not to move. He fights the urge. Very gently he tries to sneak his hand under his backside...

> AINE
> At his bloody arse now...

Diarmuid is humiliated as the others laugh.

18. PRESBYTERY

A newspaper is hurled down onto a thick wooden table in the dining room. Front page of the *Workers' Voice*, with emphatic headline face up.

Father Sheridan stands above the sitting FATHER SEAMUS, his curate, a gentle man who still has his youthful good looks at age thirty.

> SHERIDAN
> [Reading] 'The Pearse-Connolly Hall opens again!'

> FATHER SEAMUS
> [Reading]... a dance at the weekend too... perhaps we should pop along...

Sheridan is not in the mood for levity.

> SHERIDAN
> Advertised in a 'communist' newspaper... classes of every sort... defiance, that's what it is...

> FATHER SEAMUS
> With respect, best to ignore them Father... repression breeds belligerence... it's in our genes... Leave them alone and they'll wither away...

> SHERIDAN
> [Sharp] 'From each according to his ability... to each according to his need'. *The Communist Manifesto*... quasi religious, like 'love they neighbour as thyself'... the language of brotherhood... spreads like wildfire in a world of rampant greed! Do you realise

69

how attractive that is in the slums?... To the
poor?... The unemployed?... The landless?...
This Depression has destroyed lives around
the world... misery breeds desperation and it
only takes a handful of communists to set the
fuse...

FATHER SEAMUS

I think we may be getting things out of
perspective Father... there can hardly be more
than 200 in the entire country...

SHERIDAN

One man! One book, changed the world!!
Karl Marx!

FATHER SEAMUS

Gralton's just a worker...

SHERIDAN

His mother ran the mobile library... Never
patronise the self-taught man... especially
someone who has worked down the mines!

FATHER SEAMUS

A lightweight maverick...

SHERIDAN

[Shaking his head] Fire in his soul and a plan
in his head... You can't buy him off... not
greedy, not selfish... they remind me of the
first martyrs... have you read about those
union organisers in the States, the Wobblies...
entering towns and factories...thrown into
prison, lynched, murdered... If only every
priest had their grit...

FATHER SEAMUS

Not quite so dramatic here Father... just a tiny
hall in a country bog...

He studies the article again.

SHERIDAN

[Changing tone, thoughtful] With a
gramophone... he'll have then dancing first,
then reading... he'll work up from their feet
to their brains and that bloody book *Das
Kapital*! [Pause] I'm going to get one too.

FATHER SEAMUS

That bloody book?

SHERIDAN

A fecking gramophone yi bloody eejit!

19. CROSSROADS BY THE HALL – SUMMER'S EVENING

Saturday night exhilaration; dozens are on the march to the
dance hall. The age groups spans from children to older people,
but there are many young ones too.

INSIDE THE HALL: Jimmy helps the musicians arrange their
seats and instruments. Some are tuning up. Alice, Tim and other
volunteers are placing sandwiches.

Jimmy spots Oonagh arrive with her family. She holds the hands
of her two children and by her side is her husband FINTAN, a
warm ruggedly handsome man. Jimmy can feel his gut tighten as
the latter waves at him warmly and he goes over to shake his hand.

FINTAN

Time flies Jimmy... feels like nothing's
changed... been telling the children about the
old days...

71

He catches Oonagh's eye.

> JIMMY
>
> You look well Fintan… [To the children] I
> hope you're going to dance now!

> BOY 1
>
> Thanks for the toy…

> GIRL 1
>
> We want to hear your gramophone Jimmy!

Jimmy kneels down beside her.

> JIMMY
>
> Will you help me with the records?

She nods enthusiastically. He tussles her hair and studies the children.

> JIMMY (CONT'D)
>
> [To Fintan and Oonagh, touched] They're
> beauties.

OUTSIDE: There is a giddy sense of exhilaration especially among the young as they walk in groups or balance on their friends' handlebars.

Their smiles disappear when they confront Father Sheridan with a group of severe looking parishioners who stand by one corner, and Father Seamus, with others, at the other end of the cross. Father Seamus looks highly uncomfortable and almost ashamed of himself.

Sheridan calls out the names of people passing by to a middle-aged woman who writes them down in a notebook.

Father Seamus watches all the delight change to gloom as they spot him.

FATHER SEAMUS
[To parishioner by his side, sighing to himself]
Think we are doing more harm than good...

Several young women skip behind a group of boys and turn their faces away hoping not to be recognised.

There is great excitement as a car full of young people arrive with more bodies squeezed in than seats. It pulls up beside the hall as several crowd round.

Sheridan and a parishioner make a bee-line for the car and addresses the smart young driver.

SHERIDAN
Where have you come from?

DRIVER
Up the road Father.

PARISHIONER
Up the road where?

DRIVER
Up the road, and around the bend...

The attempts by those in the back seat not to laugh makes their mirth more explosive.

SHERIDAN
And which bend would that be young man?!

DRIVER
It's a fierce bendy road Father... [To the boys
in the back] Which bend was it lads?

They can't contain themselves, and it only infuriates him more. He spots Marie O'Keefe in the back seat between two young men.

SHERIDAN

Marie O'Keefe! What are you doing here?

She holds his eye and lets him have it.

MARIE

I am here to dance Father.

SHERIDAN

Is a proper parish dance not good enough for you girl?

She marches out leaving him behind.

SHERIDAN (CONT'D)

Does your father know you have been in a motor car with outsiders?

Father Seamus shakes his head and looks at his shoes.

20. HALL – NIGHT

The place is bouncing. Musicians are in full flow as the dancers do a traditional Irish dance. Young and old. Oonagh and Fintan are together. Delight all round.

Cut to a different dance, and another style. Many of the youngsters from the crossroads are now in action. Jimmy, by the side, has a big grin on his face. It gives him a kick to see them enjoy themselves so much.

Cut to a contrasting feel and rhythm; they now dance chest to chest in couples, with a quickstep or foxtrot. Marie shines as she partners the driver from the car.

Tommy dances with Molly making her laugh, while Tess dances with her husband. For a few brief seconds Jimmy catches Oonagh's eye through the bodies.

Delight and concentration on dancers' faces, as one couple after another glide round the room...

As the music begins to fade a strong voice bleeds in...

> SHERIDAN
> ...what is this craze for pleasure, this
> fascination with the materialist, the pagan,
> the Anglo Saxon, and most recently the 'Los
> Angelization' of our culture... what is wrong
> with being true to ourselves, to our deepest
> roots, our own pure Irish values?

21. CHURCH, SUNDAY MASS

The local church is full to bursting for Sunday mass and Father Sheridan is halfway through his sermon. The older members are shocked, and many of the youngsters (faces recognisable from the hall) are beginning to feel nervous and look to their hands as some of their parents and neighbours flick looks in their direction.

Doherty stands at the back of the church with several of his friends beside him.

Dennis O'Keefe and his family, including Marie, are near the front. Alice's eyes are hard and defiant. Mossie's wife Angela is there, as is Tess, the art teacher, who sits beside her husband and family.

> SHERIDAN
> Didn't Cromwell himself try to burn every
> harp in the land, murder our priests and
> expel our musicians... they tried to crush
> our language, our song, our dance... but our
> forefathers resisted... in hedge schools, risking

their lives... how they must turn in their
graves to see our youth debase themselves in
Jimmy Gralton's hall... jazz music, rhythms
from darkest Africa that inflames the
passions... pelvic thrusts and salacious body
grappling instead of the elegance and grace
of our own... and then... company keeping
under the stars, joy riding till dawn with
unsuitables, on the prowl from distant parts in
their motor cars... occasions of sin multiplied
beyond our imagination... but there is
something even more evil hatching in that
hall... Gralton and his crew are communists...
atheists, they deny the existence of God,
the Trinity, and the Virgin birth... Our
community faces a choice... is it Christ or is it
Gralton?

Father Sheridan picks up a sheet of paper and looks down at it
for a moment. Many young people squirm in their seats.

SHERIDAN (CONT'D)
The Church has not only the right but the
duty to protect the vulnerable... what I do
now is in the spirit of God's love... I will now
read out the names of those who attended
Gralton's hall last night... and other priests in
other parishes will be doing the same... they
will need charity and firm guidance in the
battle against the anti-Christs...

Many nervous faces and shuffling in their seats.

Some react with shame and embarrassment, while others stare
ahead defiantly. Family members react differently too, some

throwing dirty looks, some whispering, and some staring at
their hands.

> SHERIDAN (CONT'D)
> [Reading] Teresa Hanrahan, Kate Lynch,
> Paddy Kelly, Ciaron O'Reilly, Eileen
> Downey, Julia Downey... Marie O'Keefe,
> [looking up] joy riding too with unsuitables,
> Roseanne Maguire...

Marie, instead of shrinking into herself in shame like others,
smirks at a friend across the aisle who was in the car with her.
Dennis O'Keefe whispers viciously, but still she grins in defiance.
He loses his temper, jumps up, and grabs her by the arm.

There is general shock in everyone's face as she is dragged from
the front of the church as the litany of names continues to ring
out from the pulpit.

22. YARD TO O'KEEFE'S FARM – DAY

Dennis O'Keefe drives into his farmyard and screeches to a
halt. He jumps out of the car and, in a rage, yanks Marie from
her seat despite the shouting and protestations of his wife and
younger children.

> WIFE
> Please Dennis... just take five minutes to calm
> down... I beg you...

> DAUGHTER 1
> Daddy... leave her!!

> SON 1
> Daddy... you're hurting her! Leave her alone!

He is overwhelmed by his fury and violently drags a struggling

Marie to the stable. He kicks open the door, drags her in, and bolts the door against his protesting wife and other children. He grabs a horse whip off the wall.

> O'KEEFE
>
> Smirking at the priest… humiliating the
> family name! Contrary since the day you were
> born! The Bishop of Galway was right by
> Christ!

> MARIE
>
> I don't give a damn for your bishops!

> O'KEEFE
>
> 'Lay the lash upon their backs'! That's what he
> said!

He grabs her arm, rips the cardigan and blouse from her back and begins to whip her bare back as best he can.

But she doesn't give in; she kicks, pushes, and fights back in defiance. From outside the panicking family bang on the door and shout on him to stop.

> WIFE
>
> Dennis! You'll kill her… open the door! Calm
> down man!

Marie fights so hard the only way to control her is to grab her by the hair. Now his weight and strength gain the advantage; she can't escape. He pounds her bare white skin as the leather raises ugly welts and vicious red streaks break her skin.

> O'KEEFE
>
> Keep away from Gralton's hall! Do you hear
> me? Promise me!

She is now on her knees and her screams change to whimpers.

He whips and whips at her till his temper is gradually overcome by his own shame.

> O'KEEFE (CONT'D)
> Do you want some more? Do you hear me?!

More silent defiance. He gives her one last vicious swipe as Marie collapses to the ground.

Breathing hard, and trembling, he stops and stares.

Something catches his eye. His other daughter has pushed open a shutter and stares at him in silent tears.

Long silence. He stares at her wounded back now streaked in blood and marks.

> O'KEEFE
> Keep away from that hall.

He throws down the whip.

> O'KEEFE (CONT'D)
> Okay girl… that's enough… cover up…

He bends to try and help her up. She shakes him off.

> MARIE
> [Through her tears] You'll have to kill me
> first…

The disgust in her eye stops him in his tracks and he marches out of the stable with the rest rushing in to help Marie.

23. MOSSIE'S HOUSE

Angela, Mossie's wife, scurries around the far end of the kitchen making tea and laying out the scones on her best plate as her nervous eyes dart to the far side where Father Sheridan is speaking earnestly to Mossie.

Clear they have been speaking for some time.

                    SHERIDAN
          You had time to think long and hard in
          prison Mossie... [Pause] Do you want to
          end up on the wrong side of history again?
          An embittered old man with not a penny
          to your name? You have everything to live
          for... [nodding] a lovely spouse... [pause]... I
          could get you a job for life in the Council...
          [Mossie's eyes catch Angela's]... see your
          children grow up in security, educated...
          you're at a crossroads Mossie... you could even
          get little Katie back from Scotland...

It strikes home. Silence.

                    SHERIDAN (CONT'D)
          We have the Redemptionists coming to the
          parish on a mission... what if I brought round
          a Doctor of Divinity into your house to
          explain where Gralton is leading you astray?

Angela stares at Mossie from behind Sheridan's shoulder.

                    MOSSIE
          And what if I brought round a Doctor of
          Economics to yours Father, to explain how
          you go astray?

Angela tries to contain herself.

                    SHERIDAN
          Loyalty is a noble thing... but misplaced
          loyalty, for a man with children, is a tragedy...
          time's running out for you Mossie.

24. HALL

Jimmy and Oonagh as a couple teach about a dozen youngsters the Shim Sham that they demonstrated before.

Alice is at the other end of the hall preparing sandwiches.

The dancers are trying to follow the steps. They have learned enough to enjoy themselves and Jimmy and Oonagh (who dance brilliantly together) are delighted at their progress. Sense of enormous fun.

Jimmy shouts instructions above the music. He snaps his fingers to the music as he moves lightly on his feet.

> JIMMY
> [Demonstrating, with hands] Push... push...
> [with feet] Cross over... cross over... Push
> push... cross over cross over... now Shimmy
> Sham! [They all waggle their backside]...
> Shimmy it Brendan!

Some chuckle and others are lost in total concentration.

Jimmy moves over to Oonagh's side. They face the dancers. Nobody is behind them apart from Alice quietly working away by a corner.

She can't help but notice Jimmy and Oonagh hold hands behind their backs, in the tenderest most natural way, fingers intertwined, while the others are completely unaware.

She registers it for a moment, and then goes back to her work.

Marie bursts in through the doors. Tears streak her face. They rush over to her.

> OONAGH
> What's wrong Marie?

She can hardly speak.

> MARIE
> I didn't want to miss the class...

A friend lays a hand on her shoulder but she squirms.

> OONAGH
> What happened darling?

> MARIE
> I couldn't get on my bike...

She sobs with a broken heart.

HALL – LATER (AFTER WORD HAS GONE ROUND):

Jimmy, Oonagh, Sean, Alice, Tommy, Mossie, Finn, Dezzie, Ruari, Tess, Molly, and Marie stand around the stove at one end of the hall discussing what is the best thing to do.

> SEAN
> Makes the blood boil... you've shown real courage to come here Marie... I blame that hooligan in a soutane for whipping them all up!

Tess looks both emotional and ashamed.

> TESS
> Sheridan came round to our shop... [long pause]... said he'd organise a boycott... could ruin us...

> MOLLY
> What did Micky say?

> TESS
> He wants me to stop coming to the hall... we had a terrible fight... I'll have to give up the classes...

84

Molly beside her takes her arm in support.

Mossie watches her rub away a tear but doesn't say anything.
The others are shocked at her news.

> TOMMY
>
> He's been to the houses of most of the lads...
> other parishes doing the same...

> FINN
>
> Closing in like hounds... talk of bringing in
> the Redemptionists to preach fire and thunder
> for a week!

> SEAN
>
> A third of my class didn't turn up yesterday...

> MARIE
>
> He's been up to my father's too... with the
> Knights of Saint Columbanus... scheming...

> SEAN
>
> ...and he'll have your da and the fascists
> on one side... and the bloody Dohertys of
> this world on the other... at a safe deniable
> distance, both at each other's throat, only
> united by their mutual hatred of... us!

> DEZZIE
>
> Come on... we still have lots of support...
> people stop me all the time... half the lads in
> the Fianna Fáil think he's a fanatic...

> SEAN
>
> Spit licks!... who'll genuflect when the time
> comes...

> DEZZIE
>
> Good lads Sean! Some were at the dance!

TOMMY

My old brigade... most of them... and the
unemployed movement... they're behind us...
lots of the parents still solid...

TESS

For how long? He called us anti-Christs! And
I was at mass!

This intrigues Jimmy.

JIMMY

We have to see it from his point of view...
we are in his parish, so he must confront
us... his fellow priests, bishops, and the entire
Catholic community are watching him... he's
under pressure too... we have to get him off
our backs, without him losing face before his
supporters.

OONAGH

What if... [hesitating, which catches their
attention] what if we do the opposite of what
he expects... [she has their attention]... ask
the Reverend Father to join our board of
trustees? We can't be anti-Christs then...
we've always said everyone is welcome...

It stops them all dead for a few long moments.

MOLLY

Not a bad idea... what have we got to lose?

RUARI

Can you stomach that Jimmy?

JIMMY

I'll go to see him.

DEZZIE

Makes us look very reasonable… no matter
what he does…

FINN

We'll have him doing the Charleston yet…

It breaks the tension.

MOSSIE

If it continues like this we'll have an empty
hall… I feel for the lads… nothing for them…
after all this work…

ALICE

[With certainty] He won't rest till he crushes
us, or drops dead in the effort.

It stuns Marie and she is highly emotional.

MARIE

But we can't let them win… Oh no… if
they win… if… if… [struggling to find the
words]… it's the dreariness of it all…

She begins to sob and Oonagh puts an arm round her.

25. JIMMY'S FIELD

Jimmy forks hay from a cart onto a rick. He sweats with the
effort.

Alice approaches the cart with a flask of tea and huge sandwich
for him.

Jimmy joins her.

JIMMY

Thanks Mam… ready for that.

They are at ease, sitting on the cart, enjoying the moment and each other's company.

ALICE

Jimmy... do you want to settle down? [He shrugs] I won't be round for ever... it's a lonely place to be on your own...

JIMMY

Mam...

ALICE

You could be a great father... and many women would be glad to have you...

Jimmy takes refuge examining his fingers.

JIMMY

Who knows Mam...

Now they hold each other's eyes.

ALICE

I know.

Jimmy is confused.

ALICE (CONT'D)

Oonagh... you have to put each other at a distance... or run off together. No half-way house.

Her directness and accuracy stun him.

ALICE (CONT'D)

Otherwise you will break each other's hearts and you'll never meet anyone else. [Pause] I am truly sorry son.

She puts his hand on his. They sit together in silence as Jimmy confronts the truth.

26. STREET AND INTO PRESBYTERY

Jimmy walks towards the largest house on the street, by the church.

A pair of youngsters on the far side of the road greet him.

> YOUNGSTER 1
> Is there a dance at the weekend Jimmy?

> JIMMY
> Of course there is…

A wave between them, as Jimmy reaches the Presbytery, with a cross on the door. He rings the doorbell.

The housekeeper's jaw nearly drops as she confronts Jimmy.

> HOUSEKEEPER
> Oh my God…

> JIMMY
> No… just me.

> HOUSEKEEPER
> What are you doing here?

> JIMMY
> Thought I'd ask Father Sheridan to give up
> religion and join the Revolution… is he in?

She is still in shock and just nods, and stands aside to let him in. Sheridan is at the end of the corridor, and is stunned to see him too.

Sheridan strides towards him.

SHERIDAN

I'll be damned...

JIMMY

Don't lose hope Father... there's still time to
repent.

His sheer brass neck makes Sheridan chuckle.

He leads Jimmy to the study.

SHERIDAN

[To housekeeper] We'll have some tea Miss
McGatigan... brew it strong now... given his
views...

Jimmy's turn to smile. They enter the study which has a desk
and chairs, with a striking copy of a famous painting over the
mantelpiece which dominates the room. Jimmy glances at it as
he takes a seat. It is the oil painting by Sir John Lavery from
1922, 'The Blessing of the Colours'.

It portrays a Free State soldier, head bowed, clutching the
Tricolour in his hand. He is on his knee, bending before the
Archbishop of Dublin in the Cathedral who towers above him
on the step above as the latter blesses the National flag.

JIMMY

I know you have been busy on your rounds
Father... very busy... and other priests too...

SHERIDAN

Seems it wasn't in vain... otherwise you
wouldn't be here... What can I do for you?

It stings but Jimmy tries to keep his cool.

JIMMY

We want to invite you to join our board of
trustees who run the hall...

Sheridan stares at him.

JIMMY (CONT'D)

I am hopeful... once you come along and see
what we are doing with your own eyes... we
can put all this behind us... find common
ground.

SHERIDAN

So I will be the odd man out among your
hand picked 'comrades'... and no doubt when
it comes to choosing reading material we will
have a democratic vote?

JIMMY

Can you not at least...

SHERIDAN

A gracious offer Mr Gralton... at a time when
a quarter of the entire country is preparing
to travel to Dublin for the Eucharistic
Congress... the other 75% will tune in by
radio from Athlone... a country supremely
united, in faith, in love, and respect for
Christ's representative on earth.

The housekeeper enters with the tea and places it on the table
before them.

SHERIDAN (CONT'D)

Thank you Miss McGatigan... [As he pours
the tea]... Look at that painting. Look!

They stare up at it.

SHERIDAN

A democratic Irish State, true to its traditions,
in harmony with the people, under the
guidance of the one true universal apostolic
Church... that is the natural order...

Jimmy takes a deep breath.

JIMMY

You know my family are believers... my sister
is a nun... I said the rosary in solidarity with
fighters during the War of Independence...
love thy neighbour is revered in my book
too... in our hall we respect freedom of
religion and conscience...

SHERIDAN

You tell that to the Soviets who have
murdered Christians by the thousands! And
don't get me started on Joe Stalin's secret
prisons or famine on the horizon!

JIMMY

Don't get me started either Father! That's a
long debate to be had... but today can we talk
about our hall... just listen to what we have to
say...

SHERIDAN

I'm not a politician... no deals in dingy
corners... no half measures... no false
compromises... no...

JIMMY

[Almost exploding] A question please
Reverend Father!!... [It stops him] When was

the last time you really listened to someone
else?

SHERIDAN
Last night at confession... I listen to
the innermost fears and secrets of our
community... they open up their hearts to
me, not the man, but the priest, in a way
beyond your imagination... a true privilege...
What makes you think you are so important
Mr Gralton?

Jimmy stops to think and holds his eye for a moment.

JIMMY
Look at these hands Father... [thick calluses
on rough working hands]... dirt under the
fingernails... no scholar... I've been a soldier,
a sailor, a docker, a miner... on the seas and
underground... seen much and made many
a mistake... despite all our flaws I believe in
my neighbour, my fellow man... meeting
up and struggling to understand our lives
as best we can... all I know is this... on our
own, isolated, we perish... The hall is a safe
space where we can think, talk, learn, listen,
laugh and dance... it's a good place... if I
were a believer like you I would call it a holy
place... it brings out the best in us... Don't
be frightened... come along... meet us...
question us... but work with us... there is
enough misery in the world already...

Sheridan stares at him for a long moment.

SHERIDAN

You are a believer Jimmy... [use of Christian
name surprises him]... yes you are... and
part of me holds you in high esteem. Okay.
I will come along and listen to you and your
trustees... once you have brought me the title
deeds to the hall, and have them transferred
over to Holy Mother Church.

Jimmy looks at him for a long moment.

He turns to look at the painting just above his shoulder. He nods
at the genuflecting soldier below the Bishop.

JIMMY

I take it back Father... you do listen. But only
when we are on our knees.

Jimmy gets up and marches out. Sheridan sits there for a few
seconds in silence. On impulse he upturns his hand and he stares
at the soft skin of his palm.

27. CINEMA – EVENING

Straight to the screen. Jerky film footage and voice-over coverage
in a very plummy English accent.

The first images are six planes, in the shape of a cross, flying over
a ship bringing the Papal Delegate into the port of Dun Laoghaire.

COMMENTATOR

[Above the images]... flight of Free State
aeroplanes flying in the shape of a cross
escorting Cardinal Lorrie, the first Papal
Delegate to land in Ireland in over two
centuries...

From the projector's lights we can see Jimmy, Oonagh, Mossie, Tess, Sean and Tommy sitting along one row.

There is applause from some of the audience as the corpulent Cardinal, in sweeping cloak, arrives and begins an inspection of Free State troops led by de Valera.

> COMMENTATOR (CONT'D)
> …accompanied by President de Valera and his ministers he inspected his Guard of Honour accompanied by his retinue of Vatican officials in Elizabethan dress…

The light flickers on Jimmy, Oonagh and Sean's faces as more stunning images of the Congress are revealed. They secretly take each other's hand.

The roads to Dublin are thronged with tens of thousands.

> CARD
> A NATION KNEELS!! GREAT CATHOLIC FESTIVAL COMES TO IRELAND. SCENES OF ECSTATIC RELIGIOUS FERVOUR…

Next there are astounding images of over one million people attending mass at Phoenix Park in Dublin, accompanied by several hundreds of clerics in vestments, escorted by Free State soldiers.

More images of the multitude stretching in banks to the horizon, followed by cardinals at the altar with Free State soldiers below.

> CARD (CONT'D)
> A MILLION PEOPLE KNEEL IN WORSHIP!

More images cut between clerics and the faithful and then there is the image of the famous tenor John McCormick singing 'Panis Angelicus'.

More spontaneous applause from those in the cinema.

The cardinals bless the people.

CARD (CONT'D)
THE PEOPLE DEMONSTRATE THEIR
FAITH.

Images of young girls in first communication dresses like mini brides in the streets. Then more toddlers dressed in suits.

More clerics, and then the masses filling the entire length and breath of O'Connell Street with hundreds of thousands packing every square inch.

The Nuncio blesses the crowds. Fade, and warm applause.

As the programme changes to the next film and titles, a group of a dozen men several rows down below Jimmy and co. stand to join the queue and leave. They are all similarly dressed with white ribbons and distinctive badges of the Army Comrades Association – a Saint Patrick's cross, with red cross and blue background (precursor to the Blueshirts).

Mossie spots them first and whispers to the others.

MOSSIE
Bunch of fascists... keep your heads down...

But it is too late. One big beefy man spots them and the rest take up the challenge.

MAN 1
Gralton yi bastard!! Is that you... Go back to
your big Yankee pals!

MAN 2
Yi bunch of reds!... Mossie Maguire, Tommy
Gilroy! A shower of rats!

VOICES

Perverts! Communists! Anti-Christs! Shame
on you for coming here!… God bless the Pope!

Jimmy can sense Tommy about to spring.

SEAN

Easy Tommy… keep calm. There's far too
many.

They file past (continuing with aggressive insults) and out
towards the door as Jimmy and co. wait in their seats. One is
particularly nasty.

MAN 1

We'll be waiting for you!!

They begin to sing 'Faith of our Fathers' like a football chant as
they leave. Their voices fade in the distance.

Jimmy and co. remain behind, great strain and alarm on their
faces.

28. COUNTRY ROADS – EVENING

Mossie drives the horse and trap through the narrow lanes.

Sean is beside Mossie at the front, with Oonagh, Jimmy and
Tess in the back.

Mossie pulls up near the hall and drops off Jimmy. Oonagh
jumps off too.

OONAGH

I've left my bike at the hall… I'll make my
own way home.

MOSSIE

Keep your eyes peeled… they're going to
come after us now…

SEAN

The witch-hunt is on… I can smell it.

TESS

Be careful now… safe home.

They wave goodbye as Jimmy continues on with Oonagh.

29. HALL – EVENING

Jimmy opens the door and they step into the hall. Jimmy closes the door and waits for her. Oonagh heads for a cupboard and opens it. She is now behind the door so Jimmy can't see her.

OONAGH

Turn your back… [Jimmy is confused] and lock the door.

Jimmy does what he's told. He faces the door, waiting. His nerves tingle.

He hears footsteps walking now towards him. Slowly he turns.

He stares at Oonagh who looks terrific in the flapper dress he brought back from the States.

OONAGH (CONT'D)

It fits perfectly…

JIMMY

Why wouldn't it?

They stare at each other for several long moments.

They walk towards each other, take each other by the hand, and begin a gentle foxtrot without music.

All that can be heard are their feet twisting and turning on the wood. They begin to dance faster with more fluidity, throwing in perfect dips, her body arched back leaning on his arm, and then back again, chest to chest, and quicker steps. More chaffing

of leather, buffing the wood, with nimbler feet. Still no words, only the sound now of steps and growing breathlessness; faster and yet more intense...

They finish. Jimmy steps back a little to savour how she looks. Whiffs of hair curl over her reddened cheeks and the dress hugs her lithe frame just as he long imagined.

JIMMY (CONT'D)
You take my breath away...

They move closer and hold up their hands to each other; fingers intertwine; leaning forward they lay their foreheads gently one against the other.

OONAGH
Ah Jimmy... think my heart will break...

30. LANE OUTSIDE AND INTO HALL

Three tough-looking men cycle down the lane and stop by the hall (TAIGHE, DARAGH, KIAN). They join a gentle woman in her forties, along with her infant. The men go into the hall but the woman waits outside.

INSIDE THE HALL: The three men are in discussion with a group from the hall; Jimmy, Oonagh, Molly, Sean, Mossie, Tommy, Dezzie, Ruari and Finn. The atmosphere is tense.

TAIGHE
...it's about a man called Milmoe... that's his wife outside... he approached us as the Roscommon IRA after he was evicted from his cottage on the Kingston Estate...

DARAGH
We had an angry meeting last night... big split... a third of us want to reinstate him by

101

force... a third want nothing to do with it... a third sitting on the fence...

SEAN
Don't want to take on a big fish like the Earl of Kingston.

KIAN
...best of connections... guards, army, ranchers... politicians... and not just the small fry...

DARAGH
And he has some tough boys on the estate... his agent is a vicious bastard too...

The strength of the adversaries hits them all.

FINN
That's a fecking handful... Jaysus.

TAIGHE
But we can't have five children thrown on the street... she's breaking her heart out there... [hesitant] the truth is we have our backs to the wall... we're not strong enough on our own... fear in the air...

They glance at each other.

JIMMY
So what do you want from us?

TAIGHE
We need your help to reinstate them.

It's a bombshell, and it registers.

DARAGH
...we all know the history of this hall and

what it stands for... we'll get a big turn out if
we know you'll be there with your supporters
from Leitrim... it's all about confidence...

                    TAIGHE
But it's not just the reinstatement... it's the
why of it... that's more important...

Pause.

                    DARAGH
...why we need you there Jimmy, to address
the crowd.

Again it hits the listeners.

                    OONAGH
Can someone else not speak?

                    TAIGHE
They know Jimmy... he has a way with
words... trust him... no disrespect to the
others... but he'll draw people in...

Jimmy and Oonagh catch each other's eyes for a second.

                    JIMMY
What do you think?

Mossie rustles uncomfortably in his seat.

                    MOSSIE
...and we'll have every journalist in the local
press attend the event... note down your
words... spread like wildfire... be seen as a
direct challenge to landed estates throughout
the country...

                    DARAGH
It will... that's why we must win this one.

MOSSIE

And why they must win!... [To Jimmy] You
know what's going to happen don't you?

DEZZIE

Hard to judge... but they could go after you
again Jimmy... that's my fear.

Again Oonagh and Jimmy glance at each other.

MOSSIE

[Passion rising] Of course they will! And
they'll close down the hall. It's suicide.

Sean can feel his anger mount.

SEAN

How do we know for certain?! Mossie...
you've turned into a pessimist!

MOSSIE

A realist! I know what these bastards are like!
I'm still blacklisted after ten years, so don't
preach to me!

SEAN

It's an opportunity!... Here we have five
children thrown on the street by a Lord with
thousands of acres, all inherited after foreign
invasion. Who has the right to the land? One
rich man or the families who live on it, and
work it? What's the burning issue up and
down the country? The break up of the big
estates to landless labourers... We'll never get
a better chance...

Oonagh has difficulty containing her emotion as she follows the
arguments.

TOMMY

[Nodding agreement] We shouldn't let it
pass!... People are angry... desperate...
money has stopped coming in from family
in America with the Depression... we should
strike now...

MOLLY

Think before we leap. We forget the bishops
at our peril... they have never been stronger
after the Eucharistic Congress... remember
those crowds in Dublin. The Government
is in their pocket... they'll go for the kill...
make no mistake...

FINN

Or get some pistol boy thugs to do their dirty
work...

RUARI

If the ranchers don't beat them to it... they're
baying for blood... and ready to pounce...

DEZZIE

...and they're still hounding us from the
pulpit! Reading out the names... humiliating
the families... even spreading lies we are
running a whore house!

FINN

Even Tess!... [to the IRA] our art teacher has
been forced out... someone as strong as that...

Sean tries to control his deep frustration.

SEAN

They are going to come after us anyway! I say
we support this family...

RUARI

…but we have our supporters… there are
thousands of landless labourers outside these
estates… the rich are nervous too, fearful…
we've got to keep pushing… maybe this is the
spark we need… it's a tough one, but I'm in
favour too…

TOMMY

What is the fecking point of the hall if we
can't support them?!

Mossie's blood rises; his emotion is raw.

MOSSIE

We built this hall with our own hands!…
[Looking for the words] We've put our
lives into it… heart and soul… it's not just
a building… it's what we are… we need to
protect it for us and the youngsters coming…
it gives me life… [Eyeballing Sean]… I've
learned from bitter experience… If you bite off
more than you can chew… you fecking choke.

His depth of feeling impresses.

DEZZIE

I'm sorry lads… but that's my fear too…

MOLLY

Time for caution… they're too strong… too
wild just now… we need to bide our time…

FINN

I agree… I don't think Jimmy should speak…
we must protect the work we are doing here
for the lads…

JIMMY

Oonagh… you hardly said a word…

She tries to control herself and shakes her head.

TAIGHE

And you Jimmy? You'll be in the firing line…

He glances round them. He is struggling.

JIMMY

…they'll come after us… sooner or later…
how I don't know… Is it a price worth paying
now in support of principle or should we wait
till we are stronger? A question of judgement
between comrades… no right answer…
[Looking round them] I see we are split right
down the middle… [He struggles with it] It
would be tragic for the youngsters if they close
us down… it's their future too… I feel duty
bound to meet with them, listen to them…
think it through together, all of us, and let you
know as soon as we can… I'm sorry.

The IRA men are deeply disappointed but respect the frankness
of the debate. They look at each other in silence.

DARAGH

[To Jimmy] Will you tell Mrs Milmoe?

Jimmy's face darkens.

OUTSIDE THE HALL – LATER:

Oonagh waits for Jimmy some distance from the hall sitting on
a wall. The three IRA men too have moved off a little in the
other direction to give them some space.

She can see Jimmy try to console the broken-hearted woman clutching her child. She can't make out the words but it is excruciating to hear her pleas turn to sobs as Jimmy does his best to face her desolation. She grips onto his arm in desperation, as she cries louder.

31. THE LITTLE STREAM BY THE COTTAGE – LATER

Jimmy and Oonagh walk towards the cottage by the stream. Jimmy still suffers.

> JIMMY
> How many women and children have
> been thrown from their homes in this God
> forsaken land? Did yi hear her sob? I feel like
> a traitor…

Oonagh takes him by the arm.

They sit at a suitable spot by the river and stare into the running water.

At last Oonagh speaks gently to him.

> OONAGH
> I just couldn't speak… I could see it all unfold
> in my head…

> JIMMY
> I remember sitting outside the hall before we
> opened it up again… I knew this day would
> come… as it had to…

> OONAGH
> [Nods]… I blanked it out too… at least I
> could see you in safety… I know you…
> [Jimmy looks up at her]… If you see these

children thrown in the street... it will rot
your soul... and if you do speak... they'll
drive you out... your mother will be left
alone... and it'll break your heart... so it's
your soul... or your heart, Jimmy Gralton.

He ponders her words.

JIMMY

My heart's been broken a long time... can't
bear to see you... can't bear not to see you...
around and around and around it goes...

OONAGH

[Intimately] I know what you're going to do
Jimmy... It's why I love you... and why we
can't be together... your soul comes first...
it's in your nature... maybe New York calls
again... would that be a relief? To both of us?

He stares at her for a moment, recognising the truth of it, and her
intelligence. She sees that look in his eye again.

JIMMY

Oonagh...

She cuts him off as she barely contains herself.

OONAGH

Don't Jimmy... I can't bear it.

They reach out for each other's hand. They see Alice in the
distance leave the cottage and throw scraps to the chickens.

32. COTTAGE – EVENING

Jimmy and Alice sit opposite each other. Jimmy has a cup of tea and sandwich while Alice concentrates on trying to thread a needle to sew one of his shirts.

Jimmy looks up at her now and then between bites, and can't help but notice the fragility in her face, the deep wrinkles; hands, with a slight tremble, that have seen hard work. It gets to him. Her eyesight is failing too and she gets frustrated at her failed attempts with the needle.

> ALICE
> Sacred Heart of Jaysus! Thread that for me Jimmy...

Jimmy joins her. He holds the needle to the light and threads it in a second. He hands it to her.

> ALICE (CONT'D)
> Thank you son...

As he takes his seat again Jimmy does his best to settle his emotional state as he watches her sew his shirt.

> JIMMY
> If they drive me out again Mam... I want you
> to come with me...

She doesn't even look at him.

> JIMMY (CONT'D)
> I mean it Mam... I'll find a place for us
> both...

Long silence but she doesn't bite.

> JIMMY (CONT'D)
> Mam... maybe an easier place to manage...
> not so isolated...

She cuts him off.

ALICE

You need a new pair of boots son. They're all
worn... I polished them last night.

They hold eyes for a moment. At last he nods.

Jimmy notices the significant tremble in her hand as she stops
to pour the tea which nearly sets him off again.

33. KINGSTON ESTATE

A great hulking creaking cart, with the tenant's entire furniture
piled up on top, plus Mr Milmoe, an animated Mrs Milmoe and
their five delighted children dangling off various corners, are
escorted towards the lodge from where they were evicted. It is
pulled by two fine Clydesdale horses.

In front of the cart are some two dozen IRA men, and a dozen
Republican women, marching in formation, plus Jimmy and co.
from the hall (many of the youngsters' faces are recognisable too,
including Brendan and Marie). And behind the cart are around
some one hundred and fifty members from the community, half
of whom are pushing bicycles.

They pass by a spot on the lane with a wonderful open view of
the mansion house in the distance with a perfectly manicured
lawn between them. There is mirth among them as they see
what looks like the Earl in the distance on the steps to the
house, shouting instructions, while his workers scurry around
like panicked ants.

JIMMY
Ah there's His Lordship!

TOMMY
Shitting his breeches!!

General laughter, as the caravan moves on.

They get closer to a humble lodge; the doors and windows have been boarded up.

In a second the leading group split up and with great precision and energy the boards are pulled down with crowbars and hammers, the door is forced open, and they begin to carry in the furniture like an army of ants as the children and community cheer.

The Earl's steward, a compact man used to authority, accompanied by a half-dozen men from the estate move towards them.

By the cart Jimmy and several other men from the IRA (who attended the hall) hand down the last of the chairs.

The steward and his crew reach the cart. He can't believe his eyes, but he, unlike his workers, shows fury instead of fear.

STEWARD
This is private property! Get out now or we
call the guards!

Ruari, Finn, Tommy and a half-dozen of the IRA men (led by the three men who did the talking in the hall) aggressively surround them. Ruari, Finn and Tommy close in too. The other workers looked terrified, but the steward is still defiant.

TAIGHE
Shut your trap!

FINN
No more evictions without just cause!

STEWARD
No trespassing without just cause!

Ruari in a flash of temper grabs him by the scruff of the neck and forces him to his knees.

RUARI

On your knees yi lackey bastard, where you belong! Some of your own medicine!

Tommy moves in close and grabs him by the hair.

TOMMY

If you or the Earl or one guard lay a finger on this family... you know what's coming by Christ! That's a promise!

The steward, now humiliated, simply stares.

TAIGHE

[Shouting] Gather round now... We have asked Jimmy to mark the occasion.

They all encircle the cart with the steward and his group looking on too, still surrounded by IRA men.

Jimmy's sharp eyes take it in. He catches sight of a few journalists, including the one who attended the opening of the hall all those years ago, with their notebooks at the ready.

JIMMY

[Indicating] Who could not appreciate the magnificence of the mansion we passed... fertile land as far as the eye can see?... And the simplicity of this lodge... the Earl snaps his fingers and our brother and sister here, and their five children, are thrown on the street... This is the greatest lie they try to stuff down our throats... [Jimmy catches the steward's eye] that Ireland is ONE, that our Nation is

ONE, and that we are all ONE people united
in our beliefs with ONE common interest...
they build myths, quaint images and sing
sentimental songs of brotherhood and do
everything to preserve power in very few
hands... do you think the interests of a child
in the slum is the same as the rack renting
landlord?

VOICES

No!

JIMMY

Do you think the interests of a labourer are
the same as the Earl's?

VOICES

No!

JIMMY

...the interest of a miner or factory worker the
same as the owner, his lawyers, his bankers,
his investors, and the prostitute journalists
hired to write their lies?

VOICES

No Jimmy!

JIMMY

Do you think they give a damn for our old,
the unemployed, the hungry, the sick, the
homeless, those leaving our shores desperate
for work?

VOICES

No!

JIMMY

Look at that mansion we passed and those
who support them… Look at that lodge…
and we that support them! We have radically
conflicting interests! Can I remind the leaders
of Fianna Fáil, the trade unions, and even
the Church, of the words of Saint Augustine!
'Charity is no substitute for justice withheld!'
Do we want charity, or justice?!

VOICES

Justice!

JIMMY

Do we want the break up of these big estates
to the landless?

VOICES

Yes!

JIMMY

I saw the twenties in New York with my own
eyes, the wild speculation and the greed that
infected everyone… and then I saw the bubble
burst, the crash of '29 and misery in a land of
plenty… let's not forget how it spread round
the world, from a system steeped in illusion,
exploitation, and avarice. They try to pretend
it was destiny, or an act of God, but it was all
man-made, man-made to suit the rich!… We
need to take control of our lives again… work
for need, not for greed… not just to survive
like a dog, but to live! To celebrate! To dance!
To sing! As free human beings!

They applaud loudly, wild cheers.

Jimmy waves to the tenant, his wife, and his children on the steps of their home again.

JIMMY (CONT'D)

On you go… into your home!

Cheers as they enter. Molly starts a song, and the crowd join in.

Jimmy catches sight of the steward staring up at him, and then whispering into the ear of one of the journalists.

By the other side he looks down at Oonagh looking up at him.

There is a poignancy and warmth to her, the appreciation of a man alive to his talent, but she also senses the danger ahead for him.

They catch eyes and both understand.

34. INSIDE THE HALL – EVENING

The feet of a six-year-old girl; she does a solo traditional dance.

Aine, the 12-year-old, supervised by Oonagh beside her, plays the violin as a full crowd appreciate both young girls.

Suddenly there are loud cracks which burst above the music. Confusion and then shouts.

VOICES

Bullets! Live fire! Everyone down!

Everyone in the hall dives to the ground as another volley of bullets burst through the roof and high up on the wall, sending dust and bits of masonry flying on top of them.

There are some shouts of panic as some more bullets pierce the building and the music grinds to a halt. Oonagh smothers her nervous children.

All silence again. No more bullets.

> JIMMY
>
> Are you all okay? Anyone hurt?

Alice marches up to the musicians, and shouts out to the hall.

> ALICE
>
> I'd rather dance and be shot, than kneel before
> those cowards! Let's dance!

> VOICES
>
> You tell them Alice… Get up!

> ALICE
>
> Music please…

Loud cheers and a traditional song so all can dance.

Alice grabs Tim to dance, Marie follows with a youngster, as others take to the floor, and the band plays on stubbornly determined as Mossie, Tommy, Jimmy, Finn and Ruari run to the door and peer outside into the deserted darkness.

> MOSSIE
>
> It's started… the cowardly bastards…

> TOMMY
>
> Jimmy… watch your back. Hear me?

35. LOCAL CHURCH – DAY

The church has an other-worldly atmosphere as candles burn in the gloom and flicker on the outline of saints, the smell of candle wax permeates the church, and a pew of the faithful queue up in front of two confessional boxes.

Jimmy is among them, and he listens to distant whispers as sins are forgiven.

A woman leaves the confessional box and heads to a pew to say her penance.

Jimmy hesitates for a moment, and then heads for the confessional box. He enters, kneels, and pulls the curtain behind him.

He stares for a second at the mesh grill before him and then his eyes focus on the indistinct shape of a man's face.

JIMMY

[Gentle whispers at first] Bless me Father...
for I have sinned... it is over 25 years since
my last confession... [Pause] I would like your
advice on what I should do with the Pharisees
who from the safe distance of the pulpit have
told lies, incited hatred, and encouraged the
rifle squad to attack and endanger the lives of
innocent people...

SHERIDAN

What are you talking about?

JIMMY

I would like your advice on the sin of pride...
on those who assume they are the fount of all
knowledge, and yet do nothing but promote
ignorance and superstition...

SHERIDAN

Do you want confession?

JIMMY

...on those who try to destroy what is best
in us, our imagination, our sense of fun by
threats of damnation...

SHERIDAN

Who are you?!

                    JIMMY

    …but worst of all, those who try to kill our
    spirit by their miserable drabness… who have
    such venom in their hearts for everything they
    cannot control!

Sheridan forces open the mesh between them and stares at
Jimmy.

                    SHERIDAN

    Gralton!! This is a sacrilege.

                    JIMMY

    I'll tell you the sacrilege Reverend Father…
    when you have more hate in your heart, than
    love!

Jimmy holds his eye for a second, gets up, and strides out through
the church.

36. PRESBYTERY – NIGHT

Father Seamus leaves the sitting room and crosses paths with the
housekeeper.

                    FATHER SEAMUS

    Goodnight Mary…

                    HOUSEKEEPR

    [Hesitant] Do you think Father Sheridan is his
    usual self?

                    FATHER SEAMUS

    Barely said a word at supper Mary… I'll check
    on my way…

                    HOUSEKEEPER

    I blame Gralton… he's obsessed by the man…

Father Seamus reaches the bottom of the stairs, but is stunned by what he hears. Music. He moves up the steps at speed and hesitates on the landing.

Sheridan's room is open. Father Seamus moves closer, drawn by the delightful jazzy blues coming from inside. He reaches the door and peers in.

He is astounded to see Father Sheridan sitting in front of the gramophone with a sizeable glass of whiskey in his hand.

He beckons in Father Seamus, pours him a whiskey too as he takes a seat, and hands it over, as the rhythm of the music sweeps over them both. Sheridan is deadly still and gives nothing away.

There is some delicate clarinet, delightful saxophone and then the bursting energy of the trumpet followed by a black woman's beautiful voice. (Bessie Smith, 'Empress of the Blues'.)

Sheridan drains his glass and stares at Father Seamus.

SHERIDAN
What's wrong with that?

SEAMUS
I honestly don't know…

SHERIDAN
[Pause, appreciating]… A black woman's voice I suppose… [pause, sipping] quite remarkable…

Sheridan pours himself another drink.

SHERIDAN (CONT'D)
Gralton came today… had the nerve to leave these records in the porch. Had the guts to face me too… in confession! [Father Seamus is amazed]… Know what he said?… 'You have more hate in your heart than love!'

Sheridan takes a long sip of whiskey.

SHERIDAN (CONT'D)
What do you make of that?

37. HALL – NIGHT

[More beautiful blues from Bessie Smith over the scene.]

The roof of the hall explodes in a ball of flames as dark shadowy figures, their features unrecognisable, sprint from the hall.

They run to a truck and drive off.

The flames spread to the rest of the hall and a breeze sweeps the flames high into the sky.

Jimmy, pulling on his old jacket, sprints from the cottage towards the hall, with Alice just behind.

ALICE
[Screaming] Stop Jimmy! Could be a trap son!

The flames burst higher. Jimmy realises there is nothing he can do.

He stares at the ferocious flames consuming all their work and dreams.

Alice arrives beside him, and they both wrap their arms round each other's back as their figures are silhouetted by fire.

Tears streak their cheeks.

ALICE (CONT'D)
Ah Jimmy... is it you next son? I'm frightened
for you.

JIMMY
Don't worry Mam... we're not alone.

38. HALL, AFTERMATH – MORNING

Pan over the smouldering ruins of the burnt out hall.

People stand round the remnants in the foreground.

Groups of youngsters from the classes gaze at the wreckage of burnt out wood and twisted metal from the roof. Molly stands with them.

The blackened shape of the upright piano is barely discernable.

Tess arrives on her bike, and then walks towards Oonagh who embraces her.

Tess can't speak, holds her hands to her face and begins to sob. Molly moves over to her and tries to comfort her.

> TESS
> Couldn't believe it when they told me... a knife in the gut...

> MOLLY
> Like losing a loved one... that's how I feel...

Another spot. Mossie (deeply forlorn), Ruari, Sean and a few of the youngsters from his class stand around staring into the mess.

> SEAN
> [Glancing at Mossie] I didn't think they would go this far... I'm sorry Mossie.

> MOSSIE
> And all your wonderful books Sean...

> SEAN
> 'Anyone who kills a man kills a reasonable creature in God's image, but he who destroys a good book kills reason itself.' Milton.

At another spot. Oonagh stands with a few of the youngsters and Aine who played the violin. She clutches Oonagh's hand, and is deeply hurt.

OONAGH

What you have learned [kissing her head] is
inside here for ever... they can't destroy that...
we'll get you a new fiddle.

AINE

But why did they do it?

At another spot. Jimmy is surrounded by a few of the lads. Jimmy is transfixed by the blackened ash.

BOY 1

Can we start again Jimmy?

He doesn't lift his eye from the devastation.

JIMMY

[Almost to himself] Aye...

At another spot. Dezzie, Tommy and Finn and a few others. Dezzie looks out at their collective misery and tries to cheer them.

DEZZIE

Where was the fecking downpour last night
when we needed it... eh?

TOMMY

We should have learned a rain dance instead
of the Shim Sham!

It cheers some from their sadness, but Mossie and Jimmy are too steeped in their grief to respond.

Wide shot of the wreckage and the figures in the landscape.

39. O'KEEFE'S HOUSE, DRAWING ROOM – NIGHT

There is a group of five in a comfortable drawing room. O'Keefe, the local mayor, a senior guard (policeman), and the two priests. All bar Father Seamus drink from crystal glasses with a healthy measure of whiskey.

Father Seamus is unusually heated while Sheridan just sits quietly, watching everyone very carefully.

> FATHER SEAMUS
> Tactics of the Ku Klux Klan!… Cowardice, in the middle of the night!

> O'KEEFE
> Strikes me Father they were keen to avoid loss of life…

> FATHER SEAMUS
> [To guard] Do you have any idea of the culprits?

> GUARD
> Could hazard a guess… he has lots of enemies…

Chuckles among some.

> FATHER SEAMUS
> And many more friends, despite all our efforts! It's a disgrace! What are they going to do next? Burn down the cottage with an old woman inside? Could be a disaster for this community… sow hatred for generations and make no mistake, we will all be the losers…

> O'KEEFE
> Would be a tragedy if he's turned into a martyr… that would be a huge mistake…

FATHER SEAMUS
It would be a tragedy if a decent human being
is shot in the back!

O'KEEFE
Is it Christ or Gralton? I think those were the
words of several parish priests in this diocese!

FATHER SEAMUS
[Snapping] I suspect if Christ was here today
there would be several members of this parish
that would have him crucified again!

Tempers rise, and it seems to strike Sheridan.

MAYOR
Cut out that nonsense now. I expect he'll
scamper off in any event.

This infuriates O'Keefe.

O'KEEFE
He's a bloody communist! They don't
'scamper' off like you lot... they might make
a tactical retreat... they fight to the last
breath! Did you see what they are doing up
in Belfast?! Incredible! Read that! [Reading]
'The Falls and Shankill Unite!' Stirring
up fraternity between poor Catholics and
unemployed Protestants...

FATHER SEAMUS
And is that good or bad?

O'KEEFE
Twenty thousand strikers! They even fought
police issued with 800 rifles... two killed

Father, 70 injured… and over one hundred
thousand on the streets! Catholics and
Protestants, united, for the funerals! Workers
challenging their own trade union leaders as
sell-outs! That's reds for you…

FATHER SEAMUS

That's poverty for you!

O'KEEFE

God damn it, don't be so naive!

MAYOR

Calm down gentlemen please… [Pause]
Talking about Belfast… [a moment's silence]
Tom Mann…

It means nothing to them.

SHERIDAN

And what might that riddle mean?

O'KEEFE

Who the hell is Tom Mann?

MAYOR

A British trade union leader. He got his arse
kicked out of Belfast… no questions asked.

Father Seamus looks to his hands.

40. COTTAGE

Jimmy finishes off piling turf up against a wall from a cart
while Alice throws grain to chickens which she knows by name
scrambling around her.

They become aware of a truck driving up the lane towards them.

Six guards (policemen) move towards him; the senior officer, late thirties, has a letter in his hand, and he looks nervous. The others are even younger.

They march over to Jimmy and confront him.

GUARD 1
Mr Gralton... you are under arrest.

JIMMY
That's kind of you... [pause] What for?

GUARD 1
[Holding it up] I have an order signed
personally by a member of the Cabinet.
[Shock on Jimmy's face] You will be
deported from the country forthwith... as
an [struggling with the words] undesirable
alien...

There is total incredulity on Jimmy and Alice's face.

JIMMY
'Undesirable alien'? Have you been drinking
officer?

ALICE
'Alien'? He was born in this house... my son!

GUARD 1
But he has an American passport too...

ALICE
President de Valera was born in New York!
It saved him from the firing squad! Is he an
illegal alien too?

GUARD 1
I just do my job...

Jimmy takes the letter from him and examines it.

> JIMMY
>
> All the way from Dublin... from the Minister of Justice.

> GUARD 1
>
> It is...

> JIMMY
>
> What date is the hearing?

> GUARD 1
>
> There will be no hearing for you Mr Gralton...

> ALICE
>
> [Still struggling to understand] No... that can't be true... you can charge him with something... you can't just deport him... these are not the days of Botany Bay!

> GUARD 1
>
> We have our orders.

She is overcome and stumbles onto an old bench up against the wall. The guard looks ashamed of himself. He nods at the others who then grab Jimmy.

> ALICE
>
> For the love of God!... [Struggling] Let him pack his case... let me say goodbye to my son...

> GUARD 1
>
> I have strict instructions Mrs Gralton... I'm very sorry.

ALICE

Look at his old jacket… give an Irishman his
dignity!… Let him put on his suit… that's all
I ask. [Pause] I demand it!

A long moment as the officer struggles, glances at the others,
and gives in to her pain. Two guards stay by the truck, while
the other four march Jimmy into the house along with Alice.

INSIDE COTTAGE: Jimmy heads up the stairs to the upper
floor as a guard follows behind and stands by the door.

ALICE (CONT'D)

You'll all have some tea… I've still got my
manners.

BELOW: Alice lays out four cups on the table for them and grabs
the teapot from the stove. The three men look at her in deep
embarrassment as she shuffles around and pours the tea.

The senior officer glances round the room full of books.

GUARD 2

You used to bring books to our school Mrs
Gralton…

ALICE

Which school?

GUARD 2

Sacred Heart… was the best part of the
month… *Treasure Island*…

ALICE

Robert Louis Stevenson was always a
favourite…

GUARD 1

And *White Fang*.

It makes Alice smile.

ALICE
What's going on here son?

He looks to his boots again, and is deadly silent. The other guard nods at him, which gives him the impetus to continue.

GUARD 1
We were told the British deported Tom Mann from Belfast... some red trade union leader from Britain... over to help organise the general strike after those workers were shot... the police picked him up and deported him. Just like that. That's where they got the idea...

ALICE
[Still struggling with the enormity of it]
Expelled from your own home... not even a chance to have a say... Is that fair play son?

Ashamed glances between the men.

GUARD 1
I am very sorry Mrs Gralton... we're just following orders.

The guard upstairs by the door calls on Jimmy.

GUARD 3 – VOICE
Mr Gralton... are you ready yet?

No answer, and the faces of those below are wary as they move to the stairs. Loud knocking on the door above. Alice moves quickly to the front door, locks it, and sticks the key among her layers of clothes.

GUARD 3 – VOICE (CONT'D)
You'll have to come out now Mr Gralton...

131

Noise of the door being shoved and kicked.

Alice heads to the window (facing the opposite side of the cottage to where a police truck is parked) and a big smile envelops her face as she sees Jimmy, with same old jacket, running over the field and disappearing behind a wall.

GUARD 3 – VOICE (CONT'D)
He must have jammed it with a chair... [wild kicks and at last it bursts open]... He's climbed out through the fecking thatch! He's gone!

ALICE
[Whispering to herself] God protect you darling...

The guards above charge down the stairs and they all rush to the front door. They heave on it, but it is locked.

GUARD 1
Where's the key Mrs Gralton!!

ALICE
Now... where did I leave it...

GUARD 1
Shite! Smash it down!

Alice can't help but smile to herself as one attacks the door with his shoulder without much success and another tries to open a stiff old window.

GUARD 2
Fecking door! [Turning to her, desperate] Please Mrs Gralton... they'll have our guts for garters...

OUTSIDE: A stout guard, red faced, struggles to get out of the narrow window.

His fellow officers in front of the cottage stare at him in confusion.

> GUARD 3
>
> The door's locked!

> GUARD 4
>
> Where's the key?!

> GUARD 3
>
> Down her fucking drawers! Gralton's escaped
> out the back... after him!

He tumbles out. Shouting and bawling between them all. They run around like headless chickens trying to figure out in which direction Jimmy ran.

41. MOSAIC OF JIMMY ON THE RUN, HUNTED, AND IN HIDING

A. Jimmy is on a horse alongside Brendan (young lad from the hall) galloping down a narrow lane.

B. Jimmy walking through fields in heavy rain. He coughs, splutters, as he marches along.

C. Guard (police) raid on Mossie's house, door kicked in. Oonagh's house, her door kicked in.

D. Tommy rides by on a cart full of hay. A couple of guards block the crossroads where they speak to Doherty and a half-dozen of his men. Doherty spots Tommy and they pull him down from the cart. One of his men searches the straw with the pitchfork on the back, stabbing into the hay viciously. Nothing. They proceed to ask Tommy questions; he receives a nasty beating as the guards turn away.

E. Isolated shed: Sean and two youngsters from the hall arrive with some food for Jimmy. Jimmy, coughing and unwell, tries to eat. Sean hands him some newspapers too. Banter between them.

F. Marie and a whole bunch of youngsters paste up posters in favour of Jimmy in the nearest town. She sticks one cheekily on the main gate to the church.

G. Among isolated mountains. The rain hammers down in a freezing torment as Jimmy, Mossie and a big lad from the boxing class shiver on the back of an old cart among several sheep. Jimmy is hungry and worn and begins to cough. The cart stops and the men jump off. A worried Mossie supports Jimmy as he coughs and coughs, and spits up blood.

42. COUNTRY LANES AND BARN – DAY

Oonagh cycles down a country road and then into a smaller lane. Checking around her first, she turns into a small path by a river and cycles along.

She approaches an isolated barn.

She hears a whistle and then sees Jimmy on top of the hay waving at her.

Her heart jumps as she heads towards him. She arrives below and she stares up at him for a moment; he stares at her too. He doesn't look well.

> JIMMY
> Could see your bandy legs a mile off...

> OONAGH
> Could smell you before I saw you... need a
> good wash... [Joking over, concerned] You
> look worn out Jimmy...

JIMMY

Grand... nothing to fret about.

LATER: They sit opposite each other on old logs. The food has been spread out between them, and Oonagh has brought a bundle of newspaper for him to read too.

He enjoys watching her, listening to her, as she gives him an update on the news.

OONAGH

The Town Hall was packed Jimmy, two to
a seat, and every councillor was there... first
we presented all the letters of support from all
over Ireland... but what really infuriated them
were the petitions from America... the Mayor,
all puffed up... cursing Bolsheviks and their
Jewish backers... then red scares and one eejit
talked about a communist plot to nationalise
women and children... [Jimmy shakes his
head in amusement]... they didn't want to let
your Mam speak, but the whole gallery started
chanting 'Fair Play'... so they gave in...

She shows Jimmy the newspaper, and there is a photo of Jimmy's supporters [many known faces including the youngsters] outside the Town Hall with a banner, and then another, a striking photo of Alice's old face up close with the headline 'I blame myself'. Jimmy's face softens as he stares at the photo.

OONAGH (CONT'D)

Her hands were trembling Jimmy as she
gripped her notes... but her voice was
steady... you should have seen the look in her
eye...

Jimmy begins to read. He hears her voice in his head as Alice speaks. Oonagh sits quietly beside him giving him time.

> ALICE VOICE OVER
> What can a mother say, when about to lose
> a son?... Part of me wants to scream again
> as in childbirth... and part of me wants to
> ask... what is his crime? Why is an old tin
> hall so dangerous? Am I to blame for giving
> him books, teaching the boy to think and ask
> questions? He brought back the world, which
> he had seen, to the hall he built... is that the
> crime? If we can take a man, from his home,
> without a trial, and send him off because of
> what is in his head, I may lose my child, but
> Ireland loses much much more...

Jimmy's eyes moisten as he finishes off reading her words.

> OONAGH
> ...the gallery cheered Jimmy... a standing
> ovation... [pause] the Council ignored her
> and then they took the letters of support and
> burned them outside...

Jimmy listens quietly.

> OONAGH (CONT'D)
> ...all those meetings up and down the
> country... truth is... your support is confined
> to the usual friends... even the IRA are
> sitting on the fence and don't want to upset
> the Church... so the Government, and
> Opposition, won't move a finger and the
> deportation stands...

JIMMY

De Valera must have approved… [She nods] I
helped him in New York all these years ago…

She turns over another page in the newspaper to reveal a burnt
out building.

OONAGH

They burnt down the James Connolly
Workers' College in Dublin too… a mob of
two thousand… egged on by a priest singing
'Faith of our Fathers'…

JIMMY

They like to burn things… maybe preparing
for the afterlife?

Oonagh smiles sadly.

OONAGH

Not all of them… Father Seamus came to see
me… fears it will turn the youth against the
Church…

JIMMY

I prefer the Sheridans… at least he has the
courage of his convictions…

OONAGH

He's not the worst of them Jimmy… he said…
[she stops and tries to control herself] he'd go
over Sheridan's head to see the Bishop… even
go to Dublin… try to make peace…

She stops.

JIMMY

If…

A moment between them.

OONAGH

...if you promised not to build the hall
again... and lived a quiet private life...

JIMMY

[Chuckling ruefully] Like the temptation of
Christ in the desert... you can tell he's a man
of the cloth...

OONAGH

How about till your mother passes away?

It gets to him.

OONAGH (CONT'D)

Won't be long Jimmy... she's more frail since
you've been on the run... and she won't
budge.

He struggles for several moments. His hand reaches across and
presses on hers.

JIMMY

[Gently] A quiet private life... with you
Oonagh...

The deepest of sighs consumes him. He strokes her cheek.

JIMMY (CONT'D)

I wish, with all my heart... we had another
life to lead...

It hits her.

OONAGH

Ah Jimmy... they've drafted in more guards,
by the dozens... a matter of time.

They embrace each other.

> OONAGH (CONT'D)
> [Sobbing gently] It hurts so much…

Tears roll down their cheeks.

> OONAGH (CONT'D)
> Our last moments… I know it… I'll never see
> you again Jimmy Gralton.

> JIMMY
> [Whispering] Oonagh… Oonagh…

44. ROAD TO AND INSIDE COTTAGE – NIGHT

Eight guards march towards the lights of an isolated cottage.

As they get closer they split up and surround the house.

INSIDE THE HOUSE:

Jimmy reads by a lantern on a mattress in front of the fire.

He hears the dogs begin to bark outside, and he is already up
pulling on his trousers and old jacket.

Suddenly the door is kicked in and the guards come bursting in.
Shouts from upstairs as the owner comes running down.

> OWNER
> Who the hell is that? Get out of my house!

The guards surround him at gun point and put on cuffs.

> JIMMY
> What kept yi? Nearly died of old age.

> GUARD
> Yi bastard Gralton… you won't escape this
> time.

He is led out of the cottage and away.

45. POLICE BARRACKS, ROOM – EARLY MORNING

Jimmy stands by a barred window looking down below to the street as a senior guard fills out paperwork beside him at a desk. Another goes through the pockets of his old jacket, while another stands by the door.

Jimmy, from the window, watches a car pull up below him. Father Sheridan in his soutane, gets out of his car and stands on the pavement. A senior Free State officer, in full uniform, moves over to him and shakes his hand and stays to talk. Sheridan, sombre, does not look in the mood for idle conversation.

INSIDE: The young guard pulls out a few notes and coins from Jimmy's jacket and hands it to the Sergeant at the desk.

> GUARD 1
>
> That's three pounds 12 shillings and thrupence...

> SERGEANT
>
> That all you got?

Jimmy nods, as he sees a burly senior guard outside move to Sheridan, and Free State officer, shake hands and stays to talk.

> SERGEANT (CONT'D)
>
> The good news is, we don't confiscate it... the bad news is, it goes towards paying your fare!

There are chuckles between the three guards.

> JIMMY
>
> So how did you find me?

The Sergeant enjoys his power, and just taps the side of his nose.

OUTSIDE: Now the Mayor (from the meeting in O'Keefe's house) in a fine suit, walks over to join them, shakes hands, and stays to talk.

INSIDE: Jimmy still watches them. He sees Sheridan, not participating in their chat, look up at the window.

> JIMMY (CONT'D)
> Can I visit my mother to say goodbye?

> SERGEANT
> Not a hope in hell.

> JIMMY
> She's frail... my last chance to see her.

> SERGEANT
> Strict orders to get you out before the riff-raff
> come.

It is a heavy blow.

OUTSIDE: Dennis O'Keefe arrives, wearing a suit, shakes hands with Father Sheridan and the others, and stays to talk.

> JIMMY
> Where are you taking me?

> SERGEANT
> Direct to Cork, and then Cobh where the ship
> is waiting...

OUTSIDE: Doherty, with a fine trilby, and one of his companions walk over to join Sheridan and the others. He shakes hands with the priest and nods quietly at the others.

> JIMMY
> [Looking over at the Sergeant] Can I have a
> sheet of paper, to write her a note?

SERGEANT

Keep your tears for the crossing... there is a
fine postal service from New York.

A moment between them. He is as hard as nails.

SERGEANT (CONT'D)

Should have kept your big fat mouth shut
Gralton... always had to be cock of the
walk... you had it coming.

Jimmy looks down on the men, pillars of the community, in
their respective uniforms, in gentle banter among themselves
and enjoying their victory, although Sheridan is slightly apart
and keeps glancing to the window above.

Jimmy tries to disguise his vulnerability but he is rock bottom.

46. COTTAGE – EARLY MORNING

Oonagh cycles as fast as she can towards the cottage, jumps off
the bike and knocks on the door.

Alice emerges and looks at Oonagh's tear-stained face.

A long moment between them. Oonagh can't speak.

ALICE

Lost him... my beautiful son.

The two women embrace. Oonagh can't contain her sobs. They
grip each other.

ALICE (CONT'D)

God love you child... you should have been
together.

47. OUTSIDE THE BARRACKS – LATER

Jimmy, still in his old patched jacket and worn clothes, is frogmarched towards the truck between two burly guards who dwarf him. (The guard on his left has his right hand cuffed to Jimmy's left.) They push him onto the truck. Jimmy takes up a position on the right side of the truck with an open view.

He can now see Father Sheridan and associates stare at him like a caged animal. Dejected, crushed, he struggles to maintain his dignity.

They move closer to look at him.

> ARMY OFFICER
> Fine jacket... Charlie Chaplin!

> O'KEEFE
> Good riddance yi red bastard... you'll never
> set foot on this land again...

> DOHERTY
> This will cheer you up Gralton... the ship
> waiting for you is called the *Britannic*!

They, and guards who hear, all find this hilarious and they burst out laughing.

> SHERIDAN
> [Exploding in a fury] Give the man some
> respect! He's got more courage and decency
> than all of you put together!

It stuns them all to immediate silence. Sheridan strides over to Jimmy.

He struggles for a moment.

> SHERIDAN
> It was never personal Jimmy...

There is a long awkward silence. Jimmy holds his eye, without

a word said. At last Sheridan takes a step back and nods at the driver.

The truck moves off but suddenly stops some 25 yards down the road.

> DRIVER
>
> What the hell!!

A half-dozen bicycles pull up in front of them, and then more and more…

Some two dozen young men and young women, all on bicycles, (familiar from the hall) sweating, panting, and red cheeked from the rushed journey appear from nowhere.

Marie and Brendan are at the front, staring at them in defiance.

> DRIVER (CONT'D)
>
> Get out of the road!

They just stare at the truck and refuse to move.

> DRIVER (CONT'D)
>
> I'll run you down!

Sheridan and his collaborators stare in awe at the youngsters. Marie sees them, including her stunned father.

> MARIE
>
> [Shouting] You can burn down our hall… but
> you can't burn down the dance!

The truck pushes its way through them.

On each side of the truck young faces pound the sides and shout support for Jimmy.

> VOICES
>
> Be strong Jimmy! Thanks Jimmy! Don't let
> these bastards get you down Jimmy!

DRIVER

Feck off!

VOICES

The best dances in the country Jimmy! Send
more records... We'll keep dancing! Come
back Jimmy!

BRENDAN

Jimmy... Write to us!! We won't forget you!

The truck tries to accelerate off but, from inside, Jimmy can only
see an escort of youngsters pedalling like maniacs down the hill
on either side of him.

Marie struggles with all her might to catch up by Jimmy. She
desperately holds out a hand to reach him. He reaches out and
they touch hands for a moment.

MARIE

[Shouting] We'll keep dreaming... keep
dancing! I'll teach my daughters the Shim
Sham! We love you Jimmy!

It feels like a trance as he sees their hair blowing behind them
in the wind, their smiles, their freckles, their determination,
their effort...

Their zest for life fills him to the brim as he raises his hand to
wave goodbye.

Freeze frame on their faces.

And then music from the dance hall, pounding feet, squeals of
glee at spinning reels, laughter, and the thunderous rhythm of
the bodhran.

Fade... then drifting into the blues for last titles.

Jimmy Gralton

Timeline
Article in Workers' Voice
Letter to Irish Press
Letter to Fr. O'Dowd
Quotable Quotes

Jimmy Gralton Timeline

1886

James (Jimmy) Gralton is born in Effernagh, County Leitrim. His father Michael and mother Alice worked a small farm of 25 acres of poor land. He had four sisters and two brothers, one who died young. Two sisters emigrated to US, two married locally. His brother Charles stayed at home on the farm.

> Emigration was a central fact of life in Leitrim in this era. The population more than halved through emigration in the second half of the 19th century. 'Remittances', the money sent back by emigrants, helped to alleviate the widespread poverty in the area.

1900–07

Aged 14, Jimmy leaves school and becomes a shop boy. He moves to Dublin and works as a barman before joining the British Army. Based in Scotland and later Cork. Refuses to go to India to defend 'British imperialist interests' and serves a year in prison. Deserts following his release and goes to England. Works as a docker in Liverpool and a miner in Wales. Then travels the world as a stoker on a steamer. Returns briefly to Ireland in 1907, before emigrating to New York, aged 21.

1909

Having worked at various jobs, Jimmy briefly joins the US Navy.

1910-18

Gralton becomes politically active in New York. He is a member of Clan na Gael, the Irish-American support organisation for republicans in Ireland. He is influenced by the writings of James Connolly, the Irish socialist and republican who is executed for his role in the 1916 Easter Rising. Becomes active in the James Connolly Club in New York, established by Jim Larkin, a trade union leader and comrade of Connolly's who moved to the US in 1914. Campaigns against the First World War and in support of an Irish republic. He is an active trade unionist. In 1915 he applies for, and gets, US citizenship.

> Following the 1916 Rising there is rapid political change in Ireland as radical nationalism and trade unionism grow. Sinn Féin and the Irish Volunteers are organised countrywide, including Leitrim. The attempted extension to Ireland of conscription into the British Army to Ireland in 1918 is successfully resisted in a campaign led by Sinn Féin and the labour movement. Sinn Féin sweeps the boards in most of Ireland in the 1918 general election following the end of the First World War. The labour movement is stronger than ever at the war's end, but the Labour Party stood aside in the election to allow Sinn Féin a clear run. Meanwhile, the Bolshevik revolution in Russia in 1917 has offered hope to revolutionaries worldwide, and leads Gralton toward communism.

1919

Sinn Féin establishes Dáil Eireann, an independent Irish parliament, and declares an Irish Republic. The British refuse to recognise it and the War of Independence commences. The Volunteers become the Irish Republican Army (IRA). Jimmy is involved in support work for the republican cause in New York. Meets President of the Irish Republic, Eamon de Valera, who travels to the US on a fundraising and propaganda mission. Joins the newly formed Communist Party in New York.

1920

Black and Tans burn the Gowel Parochial Hall, the local, Church-run 'community centre', to the ground.

> The Black and Tans and Auxiliaries are sent by the British to take the war to the IRA and terrorise the communities that are seen to be supporting them. They attack civilians, trade unions, burn creameries and halls, towns and villages, and close down fairs and markets. The guerrilla war of the IRA intensifies, mainly involving ambushes by 'flying columns'. Meanwhile, a counter-state structure is created by the Dáil, including a court system. There is significant class conflict in town and country, and the republican leadership attempts to minimise it in pursuit of the single aim of driving out the British. Many court decisions favour the status quo.

1921

Gralton returns to Leitrim in late June 1921 and joins the local IRA. He brings money for the cause and trains volunteers. A truce is declared weeks later on 11th July. Taking advantage of the temporary peace, Jimmy offers to establish a new community hall on his father's land. It is built by voluntary local labour. The Pearse-Connolly Hall, named after two of the prominent executed leaders of the 1916 Rising, is opened on New Year's Eve 1921. It is run by an elected committee, including Gralton, who is one of three trustees.

> In 1920, the British government pass the Government of Ireland Act, which divides the island into Northern Ireland (the six north-eastern counties) and a twenty-six county Home Rule state called Southern Ireland. The independence movement rejects the act and fights on for a united independent republic, but the state of Northern Ireland is established in the summer of 1921. On 6 December representatives of the Dáil sign the Anglo-Irish Treaty with the British. This creates an Irish Free State as a British dominion. It consolidates partition

and maintains an overseeing British presence in the southern
state. This divides the independence movement and leads to
civil war seven months later.

In May-June 1921 the miners at Arigna, just over the border in
Roscommon, take over and work the mines for two months –
the so-called 'Arigna Soviet'. There are hundreds of 'Soviets'
in Ireland in these years, in creameries, factories, etc, but
the conservative Labour leadership refuses to coordinate and
lead workers' rank-and-file militancy. In the countryside,
the conservative republican leadership tries to minimise class
conflict, as small farmers and rural labourers engage in land
agitation.

1922

Jimmy throws himself into land agitation. Courts are held in the
Pearse-Connolly Hall to settle land disputes. A Direct Action
Committee gives effect to court decisions and organises land
seizures from landlords on behalf of tenants. Their actions lead
to the area being dubbed the 'Gowel Soviet'. The hall is also
used for dances. Because it is outside the control of the Church,
it meets with extreme hostility from that powerful quarter.
Gralton is condemned from the pulpit and rumours that the hall
is frequented by prostitutes are circulated. Music and education
classes are also held at the hall, further infuriating the local
Catholic Church, which seeks to monopolise schooling. The
hall is a direct challenge to their power. Gralton described it as
'a sort of revolutionary community centre'.

In May 1922 Jimmy and the Direct Action Committee are
confronted by Free State soldiers, supported by conservative
anti-Treatyites and the local priest, as they reinstate an evicted
tenant. They draw guns and the Free Staters back down.
Church and State are united in their determination to drive

out this 'troublemaker'. Both the pro-Treaty 'Free Staters' and conservative local anti-Treaty IRA leaders oppose the actions of Gralton and his committee. For landlords, large farmers and business people, he represents a serious threat to their position. He is condemned from the altar and is arrested by Free State troops. Protests lead to his release. Troops come to arrest him again at the hall on 24th May 1922. Gralton escapes, is later caught and briefly jailed, but escapes and flees back to New York weeks before the outbreak of civil war.

> Between January and June 1922, the independence movement split in two on the issue of the Treaty. The Catholic Church, business leaders and the mainstream press all support the Treaty. The labour movement takes a neutral position, weakening the position of socialists like Gralton within the anti-Treaty movement. The IRA splits irrevocably in March 1922. There is jostling for position across the country as the British leave. In South Leitrim, the pro-Treaty (Free State) faction prevails, but there is little conflict. On 28th June the anti-Treaty IRA HQ in Dublin is shelled with British-supplied artillery by the newly formed National Army and the civil war begins. Though initially numerically stronger, the anti-Treaty IRA lacks strategy and a clear programme to rally support. It holds out in Munster until August 1922, but is eventually defeated by the National Army's superior firepower and effectively surrenders in May 1923.

1922-32

Jimmy spends the next decade back in New York, working at various jobs in an era of high employment. He is active again in Irish socialist-republican solidarity work, supporting campaigns in Ireland such as that by small farmers against the payment of land annuities to Britain. He remains active in the American labour and communist movements, though they are in decline as American capitalism goes through a boom period.

While Church and State in an economically stagnant Ireland are creating a closed, repressive and exclusivist culture that frowns on and censors modern dancing, jazz music, Hollywood films and popular culture in general, Jimmy is living in the economically buoyant and culturally vibrant New York of the 'roaring twenties'. New skyscrapers reach to the stars, African-Americans become prominent in the arts and music, especially jazz, which is popularised through the new mass medium of radio and the burgeoning record industry. Dance clubs proliferate and new dances like the Charleston and the Shim Sham are born. In New York and other big cities there is an unprecedented mixing of different ethnic groups, and a loosening of the moral strictures that are being copper-fastened in Ireland.

The roaring twenties come to an abrupt end with the Wall Street crash of 1929. Mass unemployment and poverty hit the US from 1930. Jimmy and his communist comrades are temporarily energised, believing this to be the beginning of the end of capitalism. They are involved in organising the unemployed, fighting evictions and championing African-American rights. He stays in touch with events in Ireland, and sends regular subscriptions to support the new communist newspaper, the *Irish Workers' Voice*, and various workers' struggles.

In Ireland the pro-Treaty wing of Sinn Féin, now called Cumann na nGaedheal, is in government from 1922 to 1932. Anti-Treaty Sinn Féin and the IRA maintain their organisations and refuse to accept the legitimacy of either the Irish Free State or Northern Ireland. In alliance with the Catholic Church, the right-wing Free State government creates a very conservative society, characterised by censorship and repression. Economic structures remain untouched, policies favour big farmers who export cattle, and the urban working class and rural poor fare badly. The Labour Party is a weak and ineffectual opposition. In 1926 Eamon de Valera and his followers split from Sinn Féin – which refuses to take its seats in parliament – and forms

Fianna Fáil, which takes the oath of fidelity to the British crown that had been a major plank of republican opposition to the Treaty and enters the Dáil in 1927. They take advantage of the weakness of the Labour Party and the left and attract the support of workers and small farmers.

The IRA begins to shift to the left, but still has a significant conservative, Catholic tendency. Republicans join with the new Irish communist movement in a range of campaigns and groups sponsored by the Comintern (the Soviet Union backed international communist movement), including a radical campaign against the payment of land annuities to Britain. In the Depression following the 1929 Wall Street crash, these radical campaigns gather momentum. In 1931 the IRA adopts a socialist platform called 'Saor Éire'. This sparks a massive red scare and Church/State backlash. The IRA and a range of communist and radical groups are banned, the Catholic Church warns people about joining such 'sinful' organisations, and thousands are jailed. Fianna Fáil, promising to stop paying land annuities to Britain and to release the prisoners, among a range of other policies that appeal to the working class and rural poor, wins power in the February 1932 general election. Cumann na nGaedheal had tried to tar them with the red scare brush, but the party makes clear its Catholic credentials and reassures Irish capitalists about its intentions. Its economic protectionist policies are a major boon to Irish business interests. Fianna Fáil remains in government uninterrupted until 1948.

1932

Jimmy's brother Charles, who had been running the farm, dies. In March 1932 Gralton takes advantage of the new era in Ireland, with its short-lived atmosphere of hope, progress and political freedom, including a new Communist Party in the offing, to return home and help his aged parents. He immediately sets about establishing a Revolutionary Workers' Group in his area, as part of the network of such groups that would form the basis of a new Communist Party. He briefly joined Fianna Fáil in an apparent effort to force some investment into the area, but was soon expelled. His group attends demonstrations, local and national, and sell copies of the *Workers' Voice*. Meanwhile, he works the farm.

A number of local youngsters approach him to re-open the hall. Despite his reluctance to stir up his old enemies – the Church, local big farmers, businessmen and anti-socialist, conservative elements in the IRA, as well as the Special Branch (political police) – he eventually agrees, and forms a committee to run it. Classes and meetings and dances resume. His old enemies revive their demonisation campaign. Youngsters are warned to stay away from Jimmy's hall by the local clergy, who denounce him as a dangerous communist and agent of Satan. Names are taken of those who attend dances. The leader of the local IRA unit is hostile; stones are thrown at Gralton's house, hay is burnt and Jimmy is physically threatened. The formation of the fascistic Army Comrades Association adds to the menace. The local parish priest demands that the hall be handed over to the Church. The hall committee invite him to join the board of trustees, but he refuses.

In August, at the request of progressive IRA men from nearby Roscommon who have taken up the case, Jimmy makes a radical speech at the reinstatement of evicted tenants at the Earl of Kingston's estate.

In October, the British communist Thomas Mann, who has come to support the agitation against unemployment, is deported from Northern Ireland. The local parish priest in Gowel says in a sermon that all communists should be deported.

On 27th November 1932, shots are fired into the hall during a dance. Band and dancers hit the floor and no one is injured. The band play on and the people dance defiantly into the early hours. A landmine explodes near the hall in early December, and on Christmas Eve 1932 it is burnt to the ground.

Fianna Fáil withhold the payment of land annuities to Britain in June 1932 and spark off a tariff war that impacts most heavily on cattle-exporting big farmers. IRA support for Fianna Fáil in the election had led to the formation of the Army Comrades Association (ACA), former Free State army veterans under the leadership of the deposed head of the Garda Siochána, the fascist Eoin O'Duffy. The ACA grows in strength with the support of the disaffected ranchers, and become increasingly fascistic, adopting the blue-shirt uniform by which they became known in early 1933.

Strict censorship of films (1923-) is followed by a draconian Censorship of Publications Act in 1929. Bishops and clergy condemn modern dancing, 'jazz', motor cars and 'immodest fashions'. (In 1935, the Dance Halls Act brings dance halls under strict, usually Catholic Church, supervision and control.)

The Catholicisation of the new state is crowned in June 1932 when Ireland hosts the Eucharistic Congress, a huge international event that firmly establishes Fianna Fáil's Catholic credentials. Jimmy's sister Mary Ann, a nun in New York, travels to Ireland with thousands of others for the occasion.

The IRA, in the meantime, is in the process of distancing itself from communism and left-wing politics generally, which leads to a split in 1934 with the formation of the left-wing Irish Republican Congress.

1933

On 1 February 1933, Jimmy's father Michael dies. Two days later the police call to Gralton's farm to serve him with a deportation order; he is given one month to leave the country (he is described as 'an undesirable alien' – his US citizenship provides the basis for the order.) Jimmy escapes and goes on the run. A local and national campaign against the deportation – coordinated by the Gralton Defence Committee – is launched. It is supported by communists, socialists, republicans, trade unionists and writers. On 5th March a local church-gate meeting in support of Gralton is attacked by a priest-led mob, and the speakers, including prominent novelist and socialist republican Peadar O'Donnell, are driven out of the area. At a meeting of Leitrim County Council in July 1933, Jimmy's mother Alice addresses the councillors, condemning the deportation order and appealing for their support, to no avail.

On 10th August 1933, after six months on the run, Jimmy is finally arrested at the house of a poteen-maker near Mohill, County Leitrim. He is taken to Ballinamore barracks and the following day to Cork Jail. The next day he is put on board the *Britannic* at Cobh and sent to New York, with only the clothes he is wearing. His ticket is bought with money that was found on him when arrested. He is greeted by comrades as he disembarks in New York. He would never return to Ireland.

> Fianna Fáil was initially dependant on the support of the Labour Party to govern, and in late January 1933 called a snap general election and succeeded in gaining an overall majority. The final act of the party's first Minister for Justice James Geoghegan was to sign the deportation order against Gralton. Geoghegan was a barrister and long-time Catholic activist. It is probable that he was a member of the Knights of Columbanus, a network of lay Catholic professionals and businessmen who were vehemently anti-socialist, and that it was through this channel that the plan for Jimmy's deportation was hatched and executed, the idea having been formed following the deportation of Thomas Mann from Northern Ireland in October 1932.

1933–45

Jimmy Gralton immediately throws himself back into political activism in New York. He becomes the main driving force of the Communist Party-backed Irish Workers' Clubs (IWC) and of the Communist Party's (CP) Irish-related activities. The IWC supports left-wing struggles in Ireland and also organises Irish immigrants into unions and around various social and political issues in the US. In October 1933 Gralton stands unsuccessfully as a CP candidate in the New York Borough elections. He works at various jobs, and for a time runs a small food business. His last job is with a local radio station in New York. Jimmy marries Bessie Cronogue, from Drumsna, County Leitrim, shortly before his death on 29th December 1945. He is buried in Woodlawn Cemetery in the Bronx.

Compiled by Dr Donal Ó Drisceoil, historical advisor on Jimmy's Hall. *He is a Senior Lecturer in History at University College Cork and has published widely on Irish political, labour and radical history.*

Article in *Workers' Voice*
7th May, 1932

'Live Horse, and . . . !'
Farmers and the Annuities
by Jim Gralton

A vivid picture of the worsening condition of the Irish farmers and of the problems they are facing to-day is given in the following article to the Workers' Voice *from James Gralton, a Leitrim farmer who recently returned from America.*

The farms near Leitrim consist mainly of holdings of from three to twenty acres of bad land.

To-day we farmers find ourselves in a position where we are unable to balance our yearly budget, due to the reduced prices for what we have to sell, without a proportionate drop in [the price of] shop goods we are forced to buy.

This is not a new phenomenon. On the contrary, as far back as I remember, fathers of families went to Scotland or England during Harvest time, leaving young children that should be attending school, to reap and gather in crops at home. In this way, and through the 'Dole' received from relatives in America, we were able to pay rent and taxes and help generally in supporting a horde of people who never did a useful day's work in their lives.

For example, the farm I live on is part of a grant of land given by King Billy to Lord Abermarle for services rendered in the scrap against King James which ended with the fall of

160

Limerick. Since that time my ancestors have been paying rent to the original land thief or one of his descendants for the privilege of cultivating the soil to feed themselves and families.

Nor is this ended yet, for where the Abermarles laid off, the Irish Land Commission stepped in and is bleeding me yet.*

What I want to know from the *Workers' Voice* is how we small farmers will be able to maintain our already low standard of living in the face of the curtailed cheques from the United States due to the crisis there.

The reason I ask the *Voice* for this information is because as far as I know it is the only paper that interests itself in the economic problems of the small farmers and workers. All the other press are contenting themselves with advice, to be patient, and with giving vague promises of something in the future.

Live horse, and you'll get grass is their motto! It's not mine, nor the motto of my fellow farmers.

*A reference to the payment of land purchase annuities to the former landlords, collected by this Irish state commission from 1922. The land purchase annuities were a type of mortgage payment, paid each year by Irish tenant farmers against the amounts lent to them to purchase land from the landlords under the land acts, principally those of 1891, 1903 and 1909.

Letter to *Irish Press*

24th May, 1933

We have received the following letter:—

To the Editor, THE IRISH PRESS.

Dear Sir,—A deportation order was issued against me on February 3, and a wild scare was set up at the time, which made it hard for me to get in a word. Now, however, the fever has died down, and many who took part in the ramp against me are now a bit ashamed of themselves.

I came to Ireland simply because my brother's death left my parents alone here. Since then my father has died, and only the old woman remains. Naturally I want to remain here until I see her to her rest, so I am evading arrest.

I think I have a right to demand a trial, if there is any charge against me. If there is no charge I demand the right to live in peace, and look after my small farm. If the Government will not grant a trial I ask that some responsible national organisation or group of individuals will set up a commission and *sift the whole miserable story behind the order* otherwise a very dangerous precedent will have been allowed to get set up without being exposed.

I demand a trial or else peace. If there is no trial then thoughtful people should insist on having the facts, and they had better be got before the police get me.

JAMES GRALTON

Letter to Fr. O'Dowd, Gowel, Co. Leitrim
from Jimmy Gralton following his deportation in 1933

New York City, U.S.A.
n.d. (late 1933)

Dear Father,

Some time ago you stated in a sermon that you had gained a 'noble victory' in Gowel; that you did not want the credit for that victory, but shared it with Father O'Donoghue of Carrick-on-Shannon.

Now let us analyse this supposed victory of yours, and see what is noble about it. Let us see if there is anything connected with it that a decent-minded man might be proud of.

You started out a crusade against communism by demanding that the Pearse-Connolly Hall be handed over to you. You knew the cash that paid for the material was given to the people of Gowel by P. Rowley, J.P. Farrell and myself. You also know that the labour was furnished free, and that it belonged to all the people of the area, irrespective of religious or political affiliations. But despite this, you, with the greedy gall of a treacherous grabber, tried to get it into your own clutches. I put it to you straight, Father: is there anything noble about this? The people answered 'No' when they voted unanimously that you could not have it.

The hall was in my name; you knew from experience that you could not frighten me into transferring it to you, so you organised a gang to murder me. You bullied little children, manhandled old women, lied scandalously about Russia, blathered ignorantly about Mexico and Spain, and incited young lads into becoming criminals by firing into the hall. You did all these things because you could not close it, although you bragged Sunday after Sunday that 95% of the people were behind you. You are a noble man, Father; so is Father O'Donoghue for that matter. He went to Dublin but he did not succeed in having me expelled from the Drumsna Fianna Fáil club. Sure, he managed to have a few pounds relief money put at your disposal. By the way, Father, how many lads came to you cap in hand for the job? Answer: none.

The last act (perhaps) in your 'noble victory' was the deportation order, but you were only the local stool pigeon. By this time 95% of the people were with you, if your word is to be taken for it. Still, with all these people behind you, you did not come out in the open, but carried on like a thief in the night, and with the connivance of the government tried to railroad me quietly out of the country. Here again your 'noble victory' went astray, for it was only after six months, and after the case had got considerable publicity on two continents, that I was finally placed aboard ship.

You want to share this 'victory' of the Irish capitalists and British imperialists with Father O'Donoghue, but why stop here? Surely you got assistance from other sources? How about the Executive Council, the Knights of Columbanus, the firing squad, the petrol gang, the *Standard*, the gombeen press, the cads like Andrew Mooney and MacMorrow? And why forget the C.I.D. and the spies? In short, the whole motley crew who helped Buckshot Forster, Bloody Balfour, and the Tans to their 'noble victory'.*

Father, another such 'victory' and you will be of no further use to the criminal ruling class in Ireland (in Gowel at any rate)

– even the cloak of religion can no longer cover the imperialist hooligan that hides behind it.

Yours very sincerely,
James Gralton

(Published in the Irish Socialist, *February 1987)*

*The Executive Council was the cabinet of the Free State government; the Knights of Columbanus were a secret Catholic society that played a part in organising Gralton's deportation order; the *Standard* was a right-wing Catholic newspaper that specialised in red-scaring; Mooney, a Leitrim County Councillor and MacMorrow, a member of the Leitrim Board of Health, both spoke out in favour of the deportation; the C.I.D. was the Garda special branch (political police); 'Buckshot Forster' was William Edward Forster, British Chief Secretary for Ireland (1880-82) during the Land War; 'Bloody Balfour' was Arthur Balfour, Chief Secretary (1887-91), who oversaw the implementation of the notorious coercion acts; the Tans were the Black and Tans, the infamous police auxiliary force unleashed on Ireland in 1920.

Quotable Quotes

Fathers of this parish, if your girls do not obey you, if they are not back at the hours appointed, lay the lash upon their backs. That was the good old system, and that should be the system today.

Bishop O'Doherty of Galway at a confirmation service, 1924

(cf Scene 21)

Jazz is an African word meaning the activity in public of something of which St Paul said 'Let it not be so much as named among you'. The dance and music with its abominable rhythm was borrowed from Central Africa by a gang of wealthy Bolshevists in the USA to strike at Church civilization throughout the world.

Fr Peter Conefrey, 1926

(Conefrey was part of the agitation against Gralton's hall in 1932,

a precursor to his 'anti-jazz campaign' in County Leitrim in 1934.)

Gralton has been condemned without being given a hearing. He has been condemned by the very party which he supported in the last election . . . The people of South Leitrim are against his deportation. They ask why he should be victimised at the behest of his secret enemies. They ask why should a small farmer be deported while anti-Irish ranchers are allowed remain.

An Phoblacht, 25 February 1933

Gralton has been, for several months, the victim of a secret tyranny in his native Leitrim. An Amusements Hall he owned was fired into, bombed, and finally burned to the ground. His enemies work in the dark. Apparently they are few in number, but strong in influence. They have been able to silence TDs and get the active co-operation of the late Free State Minister for Justice, Mr. Geoghegan. Gralton's neighbours are friendly to him. Now the spotlight of publicity has been thrown on the terrorists who have persecuted him, they are coming to his aid. Fifty of them gathered to help him in his farm-work immediately the deportation order was served on him.

An Phoblacht, 4 March 1933

On Sunday morning last road surfaces in and around the town of Mohill were found to have been painted with such inscriptions as the following – 'Up Gralton', 'Justice Demands a Fair Trial', 'Down with Imperialist Coercion'. On Friday and Saturday last the Guards searched (without result) a number of houses in Mohill and Carrick-on-Shannon in an effort to capture Gralton.

Roscommon Herald, 29 July 1933

The arrest and deportation of Jim Gralton, which was carried out by Free State Peelers last Saturday, is one of the most shameful acts of coercion that has as yet been perpetrated in the interests of Banker-Rancher-Imperial Capitalism in Ireland. The fact that the Cosgrave-de Valera Coercion has been used in the first case against a Republican worker who has a splendid record in the Tan War should open the eyes of many an Irish worker to the 'Republicanism' of Fianna Fáil.

Workers' Voice, 19 August 1933

Telegram: NEW YORK, Tuesday: – Jim Gralton landed safe here. Delegations welcomed him from New York and Boston. Several American newspapers interviewed him. Mass meetings have been arranged.

Workers' Voice, 26 August 1933

Stone monuments were built in memory of men in the past. This is not the kind of monument Jim Gralton would want, but a world in which human beings can have security, be free from hunger and misery, and endowed with sufficient time to study art, music and culture. A world in which there will be no more wars, famine and depression in the midst of plenty.

John Mullally, Irish Workers' Club
Speaking at the unveiling of Jimmy Gralton's headstone,
Woodlawn Cemetery, the Bronx, NYC

Ken Loach
Director

Why did you want to tell Jimmy Gralton's story?
It is a story that brings so many things together: it challenges the idea that the left is dour and dispiriting and against fun and enjoyment and celebration. It also shows how organised religion will make common cause with economic power. They did it in the case of Jimmy Gralton and continue to do so. Church and State become agents of oppression. In this case – though it's barely mentioned in the film because of time – those who would appear to be progressive regressed, like de Valera, whom people thought would encourage open minds and tolerance. In fact, the first thing he did was to seek the approval of the Church and get them on his side. Principles were expendable in the interest of realpolitik.

Is it intended to be a companion piece to The Wind that Shakes the Barley *and if so, how?*
Well it's set just ten years later and there's a line in *The Wind that Shakes the Barley* where the Anglo-Irish landowner says 'This country will become a priest-infested backwater', and lo and behold, it came to pass. It's been a struggle ever since. The Church has now lost a lot of credibility because of the scandals. But when we were making the film, people absolutely understood the power of the Church and the power of the priest to determine who would be successful or not in the community.

To what extent is this film history and to what extent fiction?
The film is 'inspired' by the life and times of Jimmy Gralton. There isn't a huge amount known about the details of his life and personality. That's sad in some ways because clearly he was a brilliant man, but it gave us the freedom to imagine a private life and explore those choices he had to make. We wanted to give the audience a character that has richness and is a rounded person, not just a two-dimensional activist. That balance is very difficult and it always comes down to the details – can he have a relationship with someone? And then what might that relationship be? We can share and imagine the secrets. We did not want the priests to appear as caricatures, which would have been a danger if we had just dramatised the historical record. It was more interesting to imagine a priest who, while he was ferocious in his hostility, nevertheless had another dimension to him – he respected his enemy's integrity. Jimmy had real qualities that the priest couldn't ignore. What we tried to do was round the characters whilst being true to the historical facts.

What is the significance of the hall?
I think it's an embodiment of a free spirit, a place where ideas can be tested and expressed, where poetry, music, sport can all be celebrated, where people can express their talents and, of course, dance.

So what is the role of dance and music in the story?
It is an expression of freedom. Always dangerous to those who seek to exercise control.

How did you go about capturing dance and music on film?
You can do it in various ways. You can choreograph the camera and the dancers and make it very stylised, but that was the antithesis of what we wanted. People learned the dances to a

point where they could enjoy them and express themselves. Then we had to find camera positions and images that would capture that. I think it's to do with the angle you shoot at and it's to do with the lens you use: it comes down to technical issues. The images that I always have in my head are the Degas images of dance where you feel you're sitting in a box, alongside. It's not right in the middle of the stalls, where everything is straight on to you, he's at an angle, and he's slightly above the dancers, and you see not only the dancers but you see what's in the wings. You observe the dancers rather than being in the middle of them and you observe the joy and the comedy and the communication between them.

Rather than using a taped track you filmed your musicians live. Why?
Well because you've got to see the effort of playing. We've done that in our films for half a century – it's quite amusing that one or two people have started doing it now and it's presented as a breakthrough! It's the only way you can see people really playing, and the interaction between the musicians and the dancers, otherwise there's just something slightly wrong, slightly missing. It just needs to be live. It does mean that the editor has got to be good at cutting music and maybe joining two or three bits of music together. But Jonathan [Morris] is very good at that.

Why did you build the hall in situ, as opposed to using a studio?
Building a real hall was much easier. The landscape is very important – the landscape of that part of Ireland, the lives people lead because of that landscape and the bogs and the mist and the rest. The temptation in the studio is that you don't make it the actual size, yet the actual size imposes a discipline that I think you can sense as an audience. In a studio, walls can be moved and you get a shot you could never get in real life. In addition, the natural light in the hall is beautiful. Sometimes, Robbie

[Ryan, DOP] had to supplement it, but the reality was always there in the room.

And why did you choose to film it in Leitrim, where the original hall was situated?
We looked all over the west of Ireland but in fact Leitrim was the best, not only because it was the truest to where the story actually happened, but because it's quite an empty county so the impact of modern technical things isn't so great. It's also quite deserted. A lot of people have left because of the lack of jobs, so it's quite easy to film in. In the end there seemed no reason to go anywhere else.

How did the locals respond to you telling a local story?
They couldn't have been more welcoming. We had a lot of young people in the film and their commitment was very strong. What's great is that they weren't cynical, they were very open-hearted and generous and absolutely committed. They worked their socks off and their enjoyment was infectious.

What was the casting process?
We tried to keep a strong connection to the area, but there wasn't quite the range of people in terms of professional actors. So we had to spread the net a bit wider. It's just a long process – we see as many people as possible, anybody who shows interest. Kahleen [Crawford, Casting Director] is very good at drawing them in. We tried to cast as many parts as locally as possible because the sense of community is very important in this film – it isn't just one or two characters and a bunch of extras. Everyone who is in it became part of the process – and, I hope, felt embedded in the project. I think you can always tell when there are big scenes in films and people have been hired from a casting agency. They just turn up and they're placed by the assistant directors and the

176

director directs from a monitor. You can't do that. Well you can but it shows in the fabric of the film.

Why did you choose Barry Ward to play Jimmy?
Jimmy, as written, is politically very committed, he's got a genial spirit, he's got empathy with people, he's got a history of working class struggle, of working in different manual jobs, of travelling around the world. There's a warmth and a generosity to him as well as a shrewdness. Finding all those elements was quite tricky. We didn't want him too young and we didn't want him too old – in real life I think he was about 40 when this happened. So we saw lots and lots of people but Barry was the one who seemed to bring all those qualities altogether.

Who was Jimmy Gralton?
In real life he was a dedicated activist. I've met many over the years, dedicated trade unionists and organisers, people drawn to politics – once it gets its claws into you, it doesn't let go. When Jimmy came back to Ireland, having been kicked out ten years earlier, re-opening the hall was a big decision. Once the hall is re-opened they're going to be after him again. And once they're after him, he's either got to abandon the politics in order to stay or face the same huge battle as before. There was a feeling that the change of government would open possibilities but somebody with Jimmy's politics would know that a politician like de Valera would betray the interests of the working class. Jimmy understood class struggle, and that conflict is inevitable. So it's a very difficult question for him to dive back into politics when he's returned to be with his mother, to help look after the farm. He's exhausted after twenty years of travel and yet in the end what else can he do? If you're political you have no choice.

What parallels are there between Jimmy's Ireland and Ireland today?
Well I guess it's the same struggle. There was a financial crash in 1929 followed by a decade of depression and mass unemployment. That seems to be the case now: it's a huge struggle for the left to get any purchase in the political argument; it barely does. Politics is presented as a narrow discussion between different right-wing parties, and yet there is great hardship with the poorest taking the hardest cuts, lots of young people with no future, and in Ireland mass emigration to look for any kind of job security. So it's very similar in that respect: financial crash followed by economic depression.

Can film-making make a difference or affect the debate?
No, I'm not sure it can really, not much. By and large, films reinforce the status quo because those are the big films that get made and get the big budgets and get the most advertising. They either reinforce the status quo or they're just an escape valve. But I think that's pretty well always been the case. The medium is capable of much more but commercial cinema and the people who run it are not concerned with that. On the other hand, films can make connections, ask questions, challenge received opinions. At the very least, films can give value to the experience of ordinary people. It is through the drama of everyday life, its conflicts, struggles and joys, that we may glimpse the possibilities for the future.

Rebecca O'Brien

Producer

Foundations

At first I thought that *Jimmy's Hall* would be a nice, easy film to make. We had no idea that it would expand into the biggest film we've done. That's in terms of budget, production values, as well as cast and crew. We had a dance team, two different bands that we concocted ourselves, and of course we built a bloody hall in the middle of nowhere. I remember doing the budget and then thinking, 'Oh gosh, this is quite a big film.'

Fortunately our wonderful French supporters, Why Not and Wild Bunch, said, 'Let's do it again in the same way as we did *Looking for Eric, The Angels' Share, Route Irish...*' So, they came on board very happily in the same arrangement that we had before, whereby they cashflowed the production up front, trusting us to get on with the work while the legal process was still in train.

Because it was a bigger budget this time we thought we would probably need more money from other funders. So we approached the BFI, Film 4 and the Irish Film Board (because obviously it is a very Irish film, and needed Irish support) and all of them said yes. As usual, it was more complex wrangling three public funders – you've got three more sets of lawyers and financiers, and what one does the others want to do as well, so you end up with a lot of paperwork, but there was never a conflict. The financing was pretty straightforward because of the French funding.

We could not have made this film without their support from the very beginning because we had a huge prep period. We needed to be able to be in Leitrim, we needed to have location managers working early on to find the right sites, and we started casting in January and location recce-ing in the winter. We also had to train our actors in dancing, we were teaching people in Leitrim and Sligo for at least a couple of months before the shoot began. So, we had to think ahead of the game and that's obviously a bigger production number.

Our partners always leave us to make the film we want to make. I think it's partly to do with the fact that we are experienced. They know what they're getting; they have seen us deliver films within the budget and on time before. They feel safe enough that we don't have a completion bond for instance and they know how fiercely independent we are. Ken likes to work in the way that he does, without interference, and they've understood that over the years that actually it is best to leave him to it – they get a better film that way. Of course, it's generous of them to let us get on with it and it's quite brave of them too. That culture has got a lot worse in recent years. There is a lot of executive involvement in projects but with us they know that we don't appreciate it very much. We would much rather show them what we can do later.

'For peace comes dropping slow…' Filming in Leitrim
We chose in this case to film in quite an inaccessible place, yet it was always a real bonus that we were able to make it in Leitrim. The real Jimmy Gralton grew up in South Leitrim and though we filmed in North Leitrim it was still amazing to be able to do it in the right county. It was purely the coincidence of the locations being right – we would have filmed in Mayo if the locations were better there. But we needed places with as few modern bungalows as possible and we needed a town big enough to support us nearby, which was Sligo.

Sligo isn't the most accessible place but once we were there we were extraordinarily lucky – it rains for 50% of the time in this area yet we didn't lose anything because of the weather, not one day. To choose a place which is so wet, because it's so close to the Atlantic, is almost completely bonkers but the weather smiled on us. When you're building a hall on a bog it helps if it's not raining.

A lot of the cast were local as well, so it's actually been more of a community film than I ever imagined we could make. That has meant that the local people have been able to own the film in the way that you always want a film to belong to the area. That in turn makes it all the better because it's their film as well as our film. And I'd like to think it practises what it preaches, because everybody had a great time making it.

A companion piece, not a sequel

This film is a depiction of life ten years down the line from *The Wind that Shakes the Barley* and I think it's a bit more optimistic in a way. Historically it's a companion piece: it takes the same arguments and looks at how they evolved – the Irish Free State had been around for ten years by this time, and it's interesting to see where the power lines now lie. We consistently fail to learn from history – it's really important to re-visit, see where we went right and where we went wrong. Making a film like this gives you that opportunity to see what lessons we need to learn.

So long, farewell?

This is Ken's last big film, I think we can safely say that. There were a few teary people around on the shoot but I feel quite positive. For a start I don't believe it's Ken's last work because I'm sure he'll pop up with a documentary or something small. And I like the idea of having gone full circle with him. I started working with him on *Hidden Agenda* and the team that we've managed to put together can't last forever so it's nice to end it on a high. Or not even end it but to feel, 'Okay, here's a body of work.' One of my next jobs will be to sew all that together and find a way of using modern techniques to present that body of work and put the films in historical context. If you look at Ken's films they form a social history of the last 50 years. That should be preserved as well as it can and be made accessible.

Crew

Kahleen Crawford
Fergus Clegg
Eimer Ni Mhaoldomhnaigh
Robbie Ryan
Jonathan Morris
George Fenton

Kahleen Crawford
Casting Director

It's always great casting with Ken because he's happy to meet everyone, to be there. Some directors just want a casting director to say, 'Here are three. Pick one of them.' But we do almost everything together. We were meeting everyone in the right age groups and categories from all the theatre groups in Ireland, all of the colleges, all the actors' agents in London and the UK. We met people with long CVs, short CVs, people who had never done anything before. On Ken's work it's just about finding the right person and you can find them anywhere.

Ken's quite particular about people having the right voice from the area. It doesn't always end up that way but that's a good place to start narrowing it down. You do have a sense of what you think the person will look like. It's almost never where you end up because someone just captures you with something else. It's usually spirit and you find yourself gravitating more towards that than anything else.

We rarely end up using recognised actors. If the person was perfect that would be fine. We've met some actors who people would consider well-known and we've talked about some other people who are well-known. Everyone wants to work with Ken – I know that, though he wouldn't think that. But they just weren't right.

Barry Ward [Jimmy] came in for one of our very early casting sessions in Dublin. You can tell by his personality that he's right. It's easy to take an instant liking to him but he's also got a lot behind that – a lot of intelligence and he's well-read. I think he's got humanity, he's considered, and he's got great energy. He may be a bit different in real life to who Jimmy was but we gave him more script than Ken sometimes does to help him with that. It was a conversation we had – we said actually he's a skilled actor, he's done a lot of brilliant theatre and so let's let him work on the character. He's read a lot about Jimmy and that's helped. But he's also just a great person to have around. He's like the glue – he sticks everything together.

We fell in love with Simone Kirby [Oonagh] the first day we met her. She's a very still, engaged, engaging presence. You just want to look at her. Aisling [Franciosi, who plays Marie] is a bit like that too. Some really brilliant people came in and did improvisations with us but there was just something really special about those two.

Once you get one or two lynchpins you then start building up around them. It becomes a larger picture about how they fit in to the ensemble. The group dynamic has to work. We get to do a lot of chemistry casting – though Ken wouldn't call it chemistry casting, he would call it conversations. We had them in a gaggle for two or three days. You never really know until two or three weeks into the shoot if it's worked.

The problem is there aren't enough roles for everyone you meet. Paul [Laverty] actually wrote some roles in because we met some actors we felt we couldn't do without, like Martin Lucey, who also worked on *The Wind that Shakes the Barley*.

All the people we meet along the way – women's groups, local political groups, schools and colleges – we remember all these people and we stick them up on the wall of the office. So then maybe if we haven't got a little speaking part they'll be in our crowd. Some people are regulars in the crowd scenes – they've been out on eight or ten days' shooting. They are as much a part of the cast, genuinely, as anyone else. They all get along so well. It's like the kids that we put together to do the dancing – they were all going twice a week for rehearsals to learn dancing for six weeks before filming started. They'll be part of the heart of the film, definitely. They're a huge part of the energy.

Most of them are local. It adds to the flavour if you get the right voices and the right faces and it means something to them – it's their area. They know the place. They should be involved.

Fergus Clegg
Production Designer

What were your first thoughts on reading the script?
The main issue was having to build a hall – and one that we knew we had to destroy too. Normally Ken will, wherever possible, go to any extreme not to build a set; he will always use a location. But this would never be one of those cases, so from an art department point of view it was quite a big undertaking having to build this fully functioning dance hall in rural west Ireland. On the upside it was around the same period as *The Wind that Shakes the Barley* so it was a time and place we knew.

How did you find Jimmy's cottage in Leitrim?
We had several locations to look at in terms of the cottage, but none of them particularly worked well for me. They were slightly too domesticated when what I had in mind was something that was much more rural and in a much bleaker setting. The trouble was that we were trying to find the cottage very close to the location where we would build the hall but we couldn't find a cottage that had enough land. The other problem with the landscape was because a lot of it is bog, you literally are standing in a field and you start sinking. So we were up against geology as well as geography. We had a favourite cottage in mind, and we were on the verge of agreeing to use it when driving back

to Sligo I just happened to look out of the car window and saw this little spot on the landscape. We stopped the car, walked half a kilometre down a track and there was this amazing, pretty much untouched cottage. It was just a perfect location for me and then I realised also that the land around it was fairly suitable for building, or at least less boggy than elsewhere. That gave us the advantage of having the hall and the cottage being able to be seen in the same frame, not having to travel from one location to another.

But the hall obviously wasn't there at that point. What was the process of designing it?
I looked at as much reference work as I could: village halls and school buildings and that kind of vernacular architecture of the period. You end up with a quintessential hall that is basically like an agricultural building, clad in corrugated iron or tin and with a simple wooden frame that you build first. I built a computer model so that we could show it to Ken in 3D and then built a physical model. Then we changed the size so that it wasn't too large but it was large enough to film in – you always had that paradox of how you're going to make it look believable on the outside and yet like a Tardis, bigger on the inside, so you can fit the people and the crew and the camera in there. Ken always works with fairly long lenses, so he wants to get as far back as possible. You always end up in the corner of every room, filming with Ken, and he's always tapping on cupboards to see if he can get the camera in there.

Once we'd worked out all those parameters then we had to work out how we were going to build it because the land on which we were building was about a metre of peat bog on top of rock and it was at a slight incline on the field as well. We didn't want to make a deep impact on the landscape, and we wanted it to be semi-permanent, so it had to meet all kinds of strange specifications that a normal building wouldn't. Eventually we made up our own method by putting something down called bog mats which are these big, wooden timbers bolted together to form a mat. They're craned into position and they just leant on top of the bog and spread the load. They laid out these mats over the grounds and we built on top of those. We'd pre-fabbed the hall in a workshop in Glasgow in order to be ahead of the game. When it arrived on a big lorry from Scotland we had about two weeks of solid sunshine so the ground was dry and we could actually get on with the work. We were incredibly lucky, we managed to get the roof on in time before the weather turned. It was quite an epic build, but everyone really enjoyed it because for them they were building a building rather than a set.

Is working on a period piece more rewarding for a production designer?
Personally I find it much more rewarding working on a period piece because you do get to do different things and the research is much more interesting. This film was slightly more difficult than *The Wind that Shakes the Barley* because that was made in 2005 and after that there was another three or four years of the Celtic Tiger – three years of rampant build, build, build. Now a lot of the landscapes in Ireland are cluttered with modern intrusions, half-built grand design dream houses. The landscapes were littered with these unfinished dreams and it was very sad to see, but it made our job even more difficult because you were having to deal with trying to remove things.

What does Ken Loach look for in production design?
It's all about authenticity for Ken. The last thing he wants to do is have people look at the sets; it's all about looking at the performance and the actors. So we always play a background role in terms of supplying a space for the actors to work in. Getting a design message across is the last thing we want to do – it's just

about making it authentic and real for people. We do a lot of work that's never seen in terms of rooms that are decorated from ceiling to floor though you only see a section through the middle of it where the actors' faces are. We've had to replace flooring to make it look authentic and put the right sorts of carpets down just to make the actors feel when they walk in that they're in the right place. Here, when they walk on to the set of the hall, it's a real hall. For all intents and purposes, any passer-by will just think, 'There's a village hall there.' Apart from a few light stands and generators standing nearby, you wouldn't know it hadn't been there for 100 years, hopefully.

Eimer Ni Mhaoldomhnaigh
Costume Designer

How did you come to work on Jimmy's Hall*?*
I bumped into Rebecca [O'Brien, Producer] when she was over giving a talk in the National Film School where I also lecture. I knew she was coming so of course I door-stepped her, just because we'd kind of kept in touch a bit since I worked on *The Wind that Shakes the Barley*. She said they were coming back in the summer and would like me to do this so of course I leapt at it – working with Ken is a very special experience.

Where do you start with the costume design?
The script. I always start with the script. Once I know the story, I can talk to Ken about what he wants and start planning. It is not about saying 'I think it should all be blue'. A lot of it is about what we need to get – we have to dress 100 people and a lot of it is working out facts and figures as well, making sure it all adds up.

What are the characteristics of the clothing of the period?
I think that there is kind of a misunderstanding, even in Ireland, about Ireland in that period. I don't think it's right to say that people were fashionable because I don't think fashion was a huge concern. But just like every place else in Europe, and any place that's rural, it's not that people are suddenly completely isolated from what's going on in the big, bad world. Clothes have to be practical but at the same time, in Ireland there has always been this notion of the Sunday best. So people would have had their work clothes and one good set of clothing, mostly. It means we get to bring out the Sunday best for the dances and things like that – but it's not *Downton Abbey*.

What's really important about working with directors like Ken is first doing all the research, knowing what way it *should* look but then, at the same time, being able to make things look like somebody has got up that morning and put them on. There's an imperfection to the perfection that you're trying to create. So you are saying, 'It's okay if that hem is falling a bit.' It's about knowing where it's right to let those things go and to say, 'Well, he might be going to the dance but he's just been milking the cows so it's okay if he doesn't look spiffy and besuited.'

But at the same time it was the 1930s and there is a certain aesthetic and there are certain colours. For the men that means they're wearing a three piece suit but it's a suit that they've had possibly for a few years. They're heavy cloths, they're very durable with turn-ups on the trousers, and a waistcoat. The shirts would have spear point collars but very soft collars, skinny ties, and they would still be wearing flat caps – Ken calls them pancakes – but some of the men would be wearing trilbys.

Then for the women it's dresses and a lot of wraparound pinnies, aprons and a lot of cotton dresses. In the evening some of the dresses might be silk but not that much. They'd be in their Sunday best dress for the dances, pretty with small floral prints, lovely and fitted, and long. The whole silhouette is very flattering.

How did you dress Jimmy Gralton?
When I read it at first, I thought, 'Oh, okay, so Jimmy's coming back from America and he's been there for ten years so maybe he's going to have a slightly different look,' but I suppose for Ken it's very important that he's a man of the people and that he comes back and he blends in. When he arrives back he does have a good suit, but straight away, he's working on the farm and he's working in the fields. And so any kinds of notions I might have had about him being the returning Yank were dashed! One thing I did do that no one will notice is that on Jimmy's trousers the pleats are turned the opposite direction to the way they would be turned if it was a British suit. I did want Jimmy to look just a little bit different without it being in your face.

What about the dress he brings home for Oonagh?
Paul described it in the script as being a flapper dress, but by 1932, the whole kind of flapper thing has gone – it's just a word that's used as a generic term to describe a dress that's spangly and sparkly. I knew that Paul was saying this has to be a special dress, but I knew that Oonagh wasn't an ostentatious person. Jimmy knows her really well – he wouldn't buy her a dress that's beaded head to toe. But it is a dress that Oonagh would never buy in a million years. She just wouldn't have the occasion to wear it. The important thing is the whole dancing element – I wanted it to be something that would move when they dance.

How did you dress the priests?
Jim Norton plays this older, conservative priest so he's wearing the cassock, or the soutane from the time. He wears a homburg, which is like a trilby but with an upturned brim and it's edged

with a braid as well. It would have been a very popular hat but by the 1930s it's really something that's quite conservative. And then Andrew Scott who plays Father Seamus, he doesn't wear the soutane – he wears a suit. You're showing him to be a little bit more progressive, hopefully.

How does the costume design here differ from your work on The Wind that Shakes the Barley*?*
In *Barley* there was an awful lot of guerrilla warfare which meant trench coats, macs, ammunition belts, guns, flat caps, muck. In this, we've got a lot more happening indoors, in the hall with dancing. So I have set out to try and make them look like different movies. With *Barley*, there was a very definite colour scheme, which was a lot of beiges and creams; the colours of hay, barley when it's ripe. Whereas on this, I think the colours are much richer: it's browns and purples, trying to achieve a warmer colour palette.

Robbie Ryan
Director of Photography

What interested you about the story?
There was a community theatre-dance event that told the story, which was performed in Leitrim and a friend of mine wrote the music, so I kind of had a little bit of a connection with it already. Of course with Ken you don't actually see the script until you sign up for it so I was just hoping it would be something I'd like. I remember reading it and thinking, this is really well written.

What stood out as potential challenges?
I always look at the bigger scenes where there are a lot of people, but then having said that, Ken revels in those kind of scenes

because he can really get them quite succinct and without too much awkwardness. You also look at night-time scenes if there's any of those, and the locations that come up a lot which would have been the hall. It's anything that may involve lighting.

Is there an overarching look you're aiming to achieve?
In Ken's films it's all about an observed approach, as if you were somebody watching the whole proceedings from a bit of a distance. Working with Ken you soak up the way he sees a film and try and facilitate that.

How did this film differ to your work on The Angels' Share*?*
This was a lot more about lighting actually. Ken tries to keep it as natural as possible but we were able to embellish and augment a little bit. There were night-time scenes in the hall where Ken was hoping to try and do real candles and lanterns. We did have a few of those but you need a bit more on film so we needed to give it a little bit more exposure. That was quite a challenge because Ken shoots consecutively, so you go from one thing to another thing – sometimes you'd have to change the hall to go to night-time after it's just been day time and that's quite a big turnaround, so it was a busier job than normal for the guys.

There was also far more second camera work and possibly a third camera, because there are a lot of crowd scenes in this.

How did you shoot the dancing and musical scenes?
Again, Ken very much has a grand plan of how he wants that to work. That's when we had three cameras: Ken would get the whole thing going and then we'd concentrate each camera on certain things. One might be a wider shot of the room, another might be individual dancers going to feet and stuff like that, and the third one would be on the band. The great thing about that is it feels of the moment – because it is.

How much attention does the film give to the landscape?
It always revolves around the characters more than anything. There's one occasion where Jimmy's back home and he's out cutting in a field and I thought, 'Oh my God, we're getting a chance to do a wide shot!' Ken loves the landscape but it's not necessarily the prime focus. The general overall feeling is that we'll give you the odd nugget of this lush green space but you're not bombarded with it.

What was the most challenging scene to film?
The silent dance scene when Jimmy and Oonagh dance in the moonlight was a challenge because it was a little bit of magical realism. Ken let me express it a little bit more magically than realistically you know, and we had a lot of fun doing that. It's a really strong scene in the film, and I guess that's pleasing because it's a mixture of my stuff and Ken's stuff.

What was the technical set up for the film?
There are a lot of 'lasts' in this film. Supposedly it might be Ken's last film, it was probably the last film shot on Kodak, and it's probably one of the last films to be edited on a Steenbeck, which is a traditional editing process. It will more than likely be the last film to be finished photo-chemically in Deluxe laboratories, because I know for a fact they're closing down in May (in fact they have closed down a month early at the end of March so we've had to finish the film digitally). It's very sad and I'm hugely bereft at what's going on. I understand it's the natural progression but watching this film the other day at a screening it looks lusher than anything I've done in a while. It was projected on film from the negative directly and even though it was dirty and there were loads of edit markings on it, when it hit the right notes it looked gorgeous.

What have you learned from the two films you've made with Ken Loach?
I've learnt a heck of a lot. In this one particularly, I felt like I was learning more because I understood the approach better. So I was able to collaborate or to help a lot more. In general I would say I've learnt how to make a film better. He is a master at just getting what he wants and then moving on. He might rehearse for quite a while and then just shoot it quickly and move on. The guy's a leader and you know he's someone you just want to do your best for. And I reckon he's not finished yet: he might go and do something totally different but I don't think Ken ever says never again.

Jonathan Morris
Editor

What was the editing process on this film?
When Ken's filming, it's pretty much only Rebecca [O'Brien, Producer] and me who see the rushes. If he's concerned about something or there is a technical fault of some kind or another, he'll ring me up maybe in an evening after he's finished filming and say what do you think of this or that? The rushes for *Jimmy's Hall* came through in an interesting way because there are so many flashbacks. Ken generally shoots the flashbacks first because still, chronologically, in real time they do come first. So sometimes it's a little difficult to get a handle early on of the film itself.

And then when you get to the cutting room what happens next?
There's a lot of material! Ken tends to shoot more than other people because he prints everything, so if he's shot six takes, they'll all be printed. It's because there might be something in one take which is better than in another one.

There was a news story about you making an appeal in the edit for a specific type of tape. What happened?

We're probably the last people if not in the world, certainly in the country, to edit the way we do. There's a kind of plastic tape that you put on the numbering machine which burns the number into the picture and the sound, so that when I have a piece of sound and a piece of picture, I know exactly where the synchronisation is. We were running out of this tape, we made a public appeal for more and Pixar in the US came up with the goods. Apparently the editors there are all fans of Ken's films, and they had a box of the stuff. They also sent us a little cartoon of me and Ken as two *Monsters, Inc.* characters in the cutting room.

What is the actual editing method?

I physically lace up the film picture and sound on the Steenbeck. We view a scene and then we cut the scene. I mark up where I want to start the cuts with a Chinagraph pencil, drag it off the machine and slice it with a blade, basically. Then I join it to the next piece with sellotape.

What are the advantages of this method?

What's good about it is that we have the traditional atmosphere of the film editing room – it's less clinical than working on the computer. What's also good is the tactility of handling the film. But the main thing that's good is that Ken sees what I'm doing and he quite likes that. We also have a certain amount of thinking time imposed on us by the way in which you're working. When you get to the end of a roll of film, you have to either rewind it or you take it off and get it rewound. There is an amount of time spent when you're not editing. On the Avid it's pretty constant.

What were the major challenges in the edit?

There are quite a lot of music sequences and dance sequences in the film. Ken doesn't shoot with playback – which is when the music's pre-recorded so that it makes it much, much easier to edit than when it's played live. There must be seven or eight musical sequences in the film and all of them were shot to live music. So the challenge really was cutting music and picture, which I always quite enjoy. The first film I cut for Ken was in 1980 and it was a documentary about girls, dancers, and auditions. Probably 50% of the film was cutting dance sequences to music with no playback. So it's kind of full circle for me, really, with Ken.

Do you think that this is the end for editing on film, and if so, what have we lost?
It probably is. You can never say never, really. You'd be amazed at how many people were looking in our room whilst we're working. They're listening to the clatter of a Steenbeck, and people are getting a bit nostalgic for the old way of doing things. A whole generation who are younger than 45, I suppose, wouldn't even know how to start editing on film. That feels sad, somehow.

George Fenton
Composer

What was your process here – did you work from a script or from a cut of the film itself?
Usually, on the films I've done for Ken, I don't see the scripts – he likes me to see the film without any preconceptions. That's a good thing but in the case of this film I did see the script because of all the music that's in the film. We had to go through and find tunes to select and look at what kind of line up the band would be in the hall. Paul [Laverty] had done a lot of work about the fact that in the hall, when it was first opened, they played traditional music and they danced.

What research did you do?

The first time I went out to Sligo we had a lot of musicians who came to visit. We all met in a pub – they took it in turns to play and people danced, and then we hung out with them and chatted about the history of what they play. The most famous tradition in Irish music really is in Sligo and it's been passed down father to son, mother to son, father to daughter. It's like there's a legacy of fine traditional music. A lot of the musicians who are famous in Sligo went to America and then came back again, so the guys that played for us were all in some way connected with that tradition, either personally or through being taught. In the course of talking to them and looking at old photos and things like that, we worked out more or less what the line up would have been in the hall and then we chose the tunes they played and the musicians to play them.

More broadly, what is the role of music in this story?

The music that they play in the film has a very specific role, which is that the Church didn't like the free expression of the hall and in particular they didn't like the dancing – even the traditional Irish dancing that you see in the film. It's not what you associate now with Irish dancing. It's not like Michael Flatley, all contained, arms down by your side. It's much freer and looser – it looks much more like tap dancing. In any case, the Church didn't like that and then they particularly didn't like it when musicians came back from America and managed to borrow or buy instruments from the army that they could then play jazz on. When the jazz band plays in the hall that really is a statement. In fact it was right around this time that a priest in Dublin started a political party called 'The Anti-Jazz Movement', because jazz sounded so threatening.

Does your score attempt to echo the Irish musical tradition?
I don't ignore it, but I haven't written a score that is traditional Irish music. What I was more driven by, actually, was the music of Republican songs. They're basically old-fashioned songs like 'Come out you Black and Tans', songs that were written around that time. They're kind of 'Celtic' in feel, but *generally* 'Celtic' – they're melodies that are Irish, but could be Scottish, could almost come from anywhere really. I used a small group of cellos and basses, some percussionists and guitars and then fiddles, and tried to get a sort of earthy quality. Then there are some solo voices – Jimmy's story is introduced at the beginning with a solo trumpet which, of course, is not in any way Irish. But I did base the melody of it on a mode that's common in Irish music. The reason that I used a trumpet was because it had a sonic connection with the music of New York, and that's how the film begins, with imagery from The Great Depression, so it was quite nice to be able to use brass and it not seem peculiar. The trumpet line is like Jimmy's call, the thing that drives him. It comes at the beginning of the film, it reminds him of the hall when it was opened and then it returns when he is galvanised by the people who are evicted. It's when he decides to go, as it were, back into battle and put himself at great risk that you hear this same trumpet theme come back. So it's about both what he stood for and what he lost. The trumpet's quite good in that way because it sounds like something that's lost. It comes out of the air but, at the same time, it has a sort of determination about the sound.

You have worked on 17 of Ken Loach's films. How has Jimmy's Hall compared to previous scores?
It's been particularly rich musically. Whenever I have done films with him which have involved telling a story that is not an English story, like *Land and Freedom, Carla's Song, The Wind*

that Shakes the Barley and so on, it's always slightly different. In the case of this film, because there was music also in the film and there's both jazz and traditional Irish music, it feels like it's got quite a rich canvas musically – but it's delivered in the way that Ken always does which is very particular. It's not like working for anybody else. He's very exercised about music not being manipulative and that's quite hard, particularly today when we're all so used to music all the time. You have to really strip it down and say, 'Well, where does it actually have something to say? Can it say it very simply in a glancing way and reflect what you want without somehow soliciting that?' So it's always quite a challenge – particularly when I'd just finished doing a Disney film about grizzly bears, which couldn't have been more polarised than this!

Cast

Barry Ward
Simone Kirby
Jim Norton
Andrew Scott
Francis Magee
Mikel Murfi
Martin Lucey
Seamus Hughes
Aileen Henry
Aisling Franciosi

Barry Ward
Jimmy

How much did you know about Jimmy Gralton before you began this film?

There's very little about Jimmy Gralton out there in terms of literature, so I found what there was and that was effectively a couple of pamphlets really. Even when Paul [Laverty] was researching the story for the writing of the script, he sifted through government documents on the deportation and they've been totally obliterated: 'Let's have no trace of the fact that we have deported a man without fair trial.' So you can't find a great deal of information about it. We spoke to some of Jimmy's family – cousins and nephews – and they're all still keeping the legacy alive. He's very much alive in local folklore, but hopefully this film will bring Jimmy Gralton to a wider audience.

Aside from his political beliefs, what sort of man do you think he was?

I think he was a very enlightened human being, very sympathetic to people's plights. I think it physically pained him to see anybody treated in an unjust way. He was always sticking up for people and he was an incredibly generous man. Every report I read, he was forever dishing out money. He didn't have a lot but when he came home from the States he brought with him a gramophone and some records, for the people to experience some of the great stuff that was going on elsewhere in the world. The really nice detail was when he finally was deported to the States, he sent back a load of money to the people who had housed him while he was on the run – with strict instructions to have a party.

What was the casting process?

Ken brings people in for a ten minute meet and greet chat. The auditions entail improvs about subject matters, scenarios and scenes that have nothing to do with the film. For the whole duration of the auditions you have no idea what it might be for. Now, obviously word was out that it was a movie about Jimmy Gralton and the Jimmy Gralton story. But as to whether he was the main guy, or not, or whether it was around the fringes of that scene, nobody knew.

What do you think Ken saw in you?

I've not really spoken to him about it, but I think it's something of the everyman in Jimmy that he wanted, rather than casting a big star. Obviously Jimmy Gralton is a very attractive man – a lot of people listened to him, went to him, followed him. But he was also an everyman and everybody has a bit of Jimmy Gralton in them. So I think he went for an average Joe.

How important is dance in this film?

The authorities, namely the Church and government, didn't want Jimmy stirring up a hornet's nest. It suited the powers that be to keep people subjugated and keep them down. He was the antithesis of that. He thought, 'Let's rise and let's live and celebrate, let's dance and let's sing.' One of the things that he had brought back from Harlem was this kind of provocative dancing: things like the Lindy Hop and the Charleston that involve closer proximity than people would have been used to. When Church and government saw that, they just thought sex, wildness, booze and cavorting. Without ever attending the classes themselves. It was fun and it was exercise; it was soulful and joyous. Yet it was something they felt they couldn't control.

How is your dancing?
To say I'm passable would be putting it kindly. We had about four weeks of rehearsals in London before we came out to Ireland, which was tough. I just couldn't get the basics. But it's like anything – you spend enough time doing it and you'll pick it up. By the time we got to shooting the scenes I was flying.

What is the significance of the hall to the local people?
It works on two levels; one is the fact that they could go and have fun and celebrate and dance. Because in an earlier scene you see me come across kids at a crossroads dancing, and they're dancing outdoors – it rains in this part of the world for 300 days of the year or thereabouts, so it's very restrictive. For them to have somewhere where they can go and do the things they love and listen to new music and read new literature and experience the world from the safe confines of a hall, that's a big, big attraction.

On another level, the political situation here was far from stable. There was a lot of capitalist exploitation and wealthy landlords who were being very, very harsh on their tenants, evicting people at the drop of a hat, all in the name of money. Within the hall they set up a land league and a court where they were trying to implement real justice – several cases came to them as a last resort. There was a properly established court where they would sit and listen to both sides of the case and give what they deemed to be a fair ruling. And then, with the help of the community and locals, they would implement it by sheer force of numbers.

How would you describe Oonagh and Jimmy's relationship?
I think it's really sweet and powerful but unconsummated – circumstances drove a wedge between them and they never got together really. Simone [Kirby, who plays Oonagh], Paul, Ken and I had lengthy discussions about this. Here are two young,

single people and it's written in the stars they are going to get together. In 1922 he flees, they continue writing to each other, but Jimmy has no intention really of coming home. Oonagh has to get on with her life, she meets someone, marries, and they have a family. And that's the end of it. So when Jimmy comes back ten years later, their love is still very, very strong. But their hands are tied, there's nothing they can really do about it. It's got to be put down as a lost opportunity.

Is Jimmy the leader of this gang or just the man who speaks for them?
Ken stressed from the very beginning that there is no real leadership in this. Although people look up to Jimmy for advice, it was very much a democracy at work and each man has an equal say. I think Jimmy made sure that that was seen to be the case. Because even though the hall was largely built with his own money and savings from the States, and indeed it was on his own land, in fact it belonged to the community. Everyone built it with the fruits of their own labour, so anyone who chipped in had an equal ownership of it.

What has it been like making this film?
I had friends who worked on *Barley* that told me incessantly about the day-to-day runnings of working on a Ken Loach movie. They loved it. So I kind of knew what was in store – but at the same time I never knew what was coming up in the script so there was always that brilliant element of surprise every day. That's very conducive to a good performance and it's very, very actor friendly because you're experiencing it as the character is – you have to live it in the moment.

You're from Dublin; do you know Leitrim?
My family hail from here; my dad's Roscommon and his grandparents are Leitrim. So in many ways it's a returning to

roots. I had two weeks in Drumshanbo, which is Leitrim as well, before official rehearsals and the rest of the cast arrived. I was working on local farms and I just met the kindest, warmest people. They thought I was half mad because I was looking for a scythe to practise when they were cutting grass with tractors. But that's what I needed to do. Now I can cut and foot turf as well as scything and raking.

Have you played a role like this before?
No, it's my first lead in a movie. And I've been dying to work with Ken, as most actors and anybody into film would be. So it's a dream job. I'm not even speculating on what it will do career-wise – you've just got to enjoy it for what it is now. Before this I'd done bits and bobs, TV and film. This is my fourth or fifth feature but in the last three or four years I've been doing lots of theatre. Mostly Dublin based – I've been very fortunate to have done quite a number of shows at the Abbey National Theatre in Dublin. I was chugging along quite contentedly.

Simone Kirby
Oonagh

Describe your character
I'm playing Oonagh who is Jimmy's love interest. In the 1920s they were sort of a couple we think, and then he leaves, comes back ten years later and she's married with kids – but they still have this very strong bond. She's also on the board of trustees for the hall and she teaches dancing there.

How do you imagine her past?
In the 1920s when Jimmy leaves he asks her to come with him but she's the only daughter, her mother is fading and her father

would be lost without her... you can tell that she's probably one of these women who's been taking care of everybody and the house for a long time. She's probably a very hard worker and has had a lot of duties and responsibilities from quite a young age I think.

Is she based on a real life figure?
Not in Jimmy's story but I did say to his relatives that I was playing the love interest and we were thinking perhaps Jimmy might have had his eye on someone – someone who had their eye on him.

How did you come to be cast?
My agent in London sent me for a meeting with Ken and we just had a five minute chat. Then I was asked to come back a couple of weeks later to do some improvisations, then after that I did another round in London and then I came for two days to Dublin, so it was a long process. Even when I had been offered the part I didn't know my character's name. We knew it was built on Jimmy Gralton so we were all looking online to see who this guy was. I had seen very little about his personal life so I asked Rebecca [O'Brien]. Ken called me back just to say, 'Okay let me just explain a little bit who you are, it's a fictional character, it's not a biopic,' and that's when I let go and went, 'I have no idea so I'm just not going to think about it anymore – I'll just turn up and play whoever they want me to play.'

How did you find playing period?
I knew from quite early on in the auditions that it was set in the 1930s, and that's around my grandmother's times so that interests me. It's lovely to do a costume thing.

Much of your previous work has been in theatre. How has this differed?
It's actually more like theatre than it is any film or TV that I've done before; Ken's much more involved with us in my experience than any other director in film. So it's actually more my theatre experience that lends itself to this than anything else.

What effect does not having read the full script have on your performance?
I find it really liberating actually – I'm not playing for something that I know is going to happen to her in the future. I can only play what I know now. It makes total sense to me: just play what you know. Even though we try and do that anyway as actors, it's a bit of a gift to genuinely not know what's round the corner.

Have scenes gone in unexpected directions as a result?
Yes. The very first day I didn't have any lines. The camera was quite far back and it was sort of hard to get a grasp on it – I'm used to being told where my mark is and things like that. I was feeling a little bit like I didn't really know what to do with myself. Then Mikel Murfi started throwing in lines that were not in the script that he had been told to throw in and I got a bit of a shock. I laughed, completely out of character, and then I realised, 'Okay this is the beast – I have to be on my game all the time with this.' Any surprises after that I've been able to react to properly. I was reminded just to stay in character for them.

How have you found the singing and the dancing?
When we were in London, Barry [Ward] and I were immediately sent off to learn how to dance together. We had three classes a week and then we went to a ballroom once. I love dancing so I revelled in it. Luckily I did some step dancing when I was younger, so I picked that up quite easily – she's supposed to be a big dancer in the room so it would look terrible if I didn't know step dancing. Then I just loved learning the Lindy Hop, though

they're not supposed to be experts at Lindy Hopping, they're just supposed to be able to shake a leg. Actually, I was a bit sad once the big dance scenes were over because we were learning for ages and then we didn't have to do them anymore. The Riverly ballroom is around the corner from where I live in London, so we've already said we are definitely going to go some night and do some more Lindy Hopping!

What is the Lindy Hop?
When you see old videos of them doing it in America, they are flinging each other around the place. It's really athletic actually. We are doing a much, much tamer version with basic spins and twirls. The thing is, unlike step dancing, you're pressed against each other a lot more, which is why it was controversial at the time.

How active is Oonagh in local politics?
Jimmy's the one flying the flag, and some of the boys are much more active, but Jimmy and Oonagh are very like-minded politically. They'd had discussions with each other about politics. It's not just that they fancy each other – they actually connect on that level. They're socialists – it's all about helping some of the underdogs really, helping people who've been ousted, picking people up and making things more fair.

What is your background in theatre and film?
I'm from Ennis originally, I moved to Galway when I was 17 and I did youth theatre and then I trained properly a couple of years after that in Dublin. I lived in Dublin for another few years after that then I moved to London for work – I wanted to do more stuff like this really. The irony being now I have come back to Ireland for what's been probably my biggest role.

Jim Norton
Father Sheridan

Describe your character

Father Sheridan is the parish priest of this small community. He is very rigid in his beliefs, but he is, I think, essentially a good man. He's doing the best he can from what he knows – he's following the dictates of the Catholic Church at that time, which were very tough and obsessed with controlling the moral life of the people in the community.

When Jimmy Gralton returns to Ireland and rebuilds the hall, what does that mean for Sheridan?

It's a huge threat to his position because he obviously knows Gralton by reputation and he knows there's trouble ahead. At that time the church's Parochial Hall was the centre of cultural and social life. Suddenly someone is coming back and it was like opening up an alternative entertainment. Not only that, but Gralton is bringing his socialist ideas which, of course, as a Catholic priest he would have been very frightened of. And then there's the dancing. The Church was obsessed with dancing – they used to say that dancing in the dance halls and not doing the pure Irish dances was dancing on the hobs of hell. They were afraid of giving these people their freedom, giving the young people the opportunity just to be who they were, to be young.

But you say that you feel that he is a good man at heart?

Yes, I think he is, though it's hard to know; I'm ambivalent about it. It's always difficult playing someone that you're diametrically opposed to – and I am diametrically opposed to everything that he says and does. But I think deep down he does have a genuine vocation and he does think that he is doing the right thing.

Is there also a personal clash with Jimmy, rather than just a moral one?
Yes, I think he's threatened by him; he's threatened by the fact that he is a bright, intelligent, articulate young man with very strong ideas. Father Sheridan sees that as in conflict with his authority. It's hard for us to understand today the power the Church had over people's lives. It wasn't just about morality and Catholicism, there was also a political element as well, still very much aligned with the government and with the people who were for the Treaty [of 1922]. Gralton obviously was from the other side; he was a Republican and also had been to America and was bringing back ideas and attitudes that the Catholic Church didn't want.

What is Sheridan's response?
Father Sheridan is quite devious in the way he goes about trying to find out if Gralton is going to stay. He goes to his mother and says, you know, 'Is it likely that he's going to stay or maybe he'd be better off in London.' He actually offers to get him a job in London – anything to get him out because he can see trouble ahead. He can see that not only is his authority going to be questioned but what Gralton is bringing in to the parish are not qualities of life that Father Sheridan wants to see.

Yet we do see Sheridan listening to jazz music himself at one point…
That tells us that there is an element, a part of his personality and his emotional life that he hasn't even investigated. It's kind of frightening in a way to him to find that he's responding to this rather wonderful music. He has been told that this music that comes from Africa is jazz and jazz means sex and sensuality. That's part of his conditioning. Yet there he is, having had a few whiskies and listening to Bessie Smith and being quite moved by it. Maybe in that scene he begins to understand what it is that the young people see. And also begins to realise what he has missed in his life.

You mentioned earlier that it's hard for people today to understand the complete power of the Church in Ireland at that time. Did you experience that yourself?

Well I grew up in Dublin in the 1940s and 50s and I was sent to what my parents assumed was the best possible school, the Christian Brothers, which was the most hateful, dreadful and deeply unpleasant period of my life. I spent a long part of my life undoing the damage that I felt was done to me by these people who were put in charge of what they laughingly called my education. If education is a preparation for life it wasn't, from my point of view, a very good one. It was based on fear and abuse and violence and I ended up as a very angry person when I left school and regretted the fact that I didn't stand up for myself more than I did. This was in the 1950s – can you imagine what it was like in the 1930s, the power, the condition reflex that people had to the Church and to their authority? This is why now in present day Ireland there are young people who would be amazed to know how teenagers at that time were so deeply affected by the power of the Church.

This is the second time you've worked with Ken Loach...

I worked with Ken 20 years ago; we did a film called *Hidden Agenda*. It was interesting because I was actually working out in Los Angeles at the time when I was cast. I remember flying in from LA on a really cold, wet winter day and meeting Ken on Albert Bridge. I was dressed in denims, I'd just got off the plane with my suntan and we were there shivering. We went along to his office and we just talked about the film. The next day I was on the set and it was just a magical experience. Even then I was very well aware of his work and a big fan of his but I just loved the way he worked. I loved the trust he gave the actors and, working with my mate Brian Cox, we had a really good time – and it was a good film as well.

How did the part in Jimmy's Hall *come about?*

I was rehearsing Conor McPherson's new play *The Night Alive* in Dublin and I knew that Ken was casting the movie. I also knew a bit about Jimmy Gralton because my grandmother came from Clones in Monaghan. I remember as a child hearing a talk about this man who had been the only Irish person ever deported from Ireland. When I read about the movie in the paper, I said I know that name, so I got in touch with Ken and we had a chat and a meeting and a discussion about Father Sheridan. A few days later they rang and said we'd love you to do it. At that point I had no idea who the character was and as we are talking now, I still am finding out – that's the great journey that you make with someone like Ken.

Andrew Scott
Father Seamus

Describe your character

I play Father Seamus who is a young priest in the village and the junior priest to Father Sheridan. He is an example of a more modern, benign and accessible Catholic Church, a representative of the new Church that would have been emerging at that time. Probably slightly less intolerant and less paranoid and maybe a bit more humane and modern, trying to introduce arts and culture and that kind of thing to local communities.

What is his relationship with Sheridan?

Although he's evidently quite different from Sheridan, I think he's actually very fond of him. I think he tries to understand him, to understand the motivation behind what's political for Father Sheridan and what is personal. These priests used to live together in the same big houses, with housekeepers and everything. So, there would probably be quite a balance between them in a way. I think that goes slightly awry when Father Sheridan starts to take some rather extreme decisions. Seamus is not belligerent, and he's not particularly powerful, but I think that while trying to remain within the confines of his job he tries to make his point.

And what does he make of Jimmy Gralton?
Well, I suppose they are probably a little bit more similar in age and I think they share a great love of the arts and culture and all that comes with that. Seamus is not as scared of culture and music and the arts; he doesn't see it as something to be frightened of. So, I don't think he's as scared of Jimmy as Father Sheridan is. In fact that's what Father Sheridan's chief problem is: it's that he's actually intimated by Jimmy.

What appealed to you about this film?
Well, that answer is the same for everyone – it's Mr Loach, there's no doubt about it. He's kind of a hero of mine so I was happy to. I would have done the catering to be perfectly honest, even though that wouldn't have been good for anybody because I'm a terrible cook. But, yeah, the idea of working in that way, with a script as a basis but having the opportunity to improvise in a lot of stuff, is wonderful. It's so enjoyable to be able to make films in that way – to strip them back and be involved in a story where you don't necessarily know what the outcome is going to be. That's really, really exciting. Maybe some actors might find that a little discomforting but I think other actors find it really exhilarating. Certainly for me it was extraordinary.

What stood out for you from the shoot?
The extraordinary calm and passionate way that Ken goes about making films. It shows how if you concentrate on what you should be concentrating on, which is to try and make the drama

as dynamic as possible and as truthful as possible, then you can make brilliant performances out of people who aren't actors and very truthful performances out of other actors. I suppose I had that really rare feeling when you just absolutely trust everything he says. There was a very nice atmosphere but not an overly serious one, which I think is always good for creativity, even if the subject matter can sometimes be serious. And my family are from that part of the country. My father is from Mayo and my godmother lives in Sligo where we filmed. It was just lovely to spend a little bit of time in that beautiful, beautiful part of the country as well.

Have you worked in this way before?
I've done a little bit of improvisation in the theatre and a little bit in comedy as well. What's unusual in this is that we don't know how the story will turn out – which is truthful, because as human beings we don't know the outcome of our stories. I think that's what the very free thing about working with Ken is about. You just play the truth of the scene. You play it day by day, which means you don't think 'Oh God, I've got that big scene two on the 17th' because you don't have a schedule in the same way you do on other films. So, you don't feel pressure in that way. In a strange way it's really relaxing.

What was it like playing a man of the cloth?
You're very aware of the Church's power. I've already played a couple of priests in my time for some reason. I do have a lot of questions and doubts about organised religion – a lot of Irish people do. Particularly in the light of the way the Catholic Church has conducted itself in the past 20 years. What they do very well with the priests in this film is to realise that they're trying to act in the best way they know how. They had enormous power at the time – and some of them abused it, there's no doubt about it. But I think a lot of them are just trying

to keep going with something that they were taught to do by the previous generation of priests before them, and they before them. Growing up in Ireland in the eighties I probably would have known some of these priests, or at least my mother would have. Someone like a Father Seamus would have been an old man then. So, I would have known a little bit about what they were like. They were at least trying to be modern but it's very difficult, to try and break through. I think it's very important in our culture to have questions; for everything to be questioned in order for things to be healthy. The Catholic Church wasn't questioned at all. That's very regrettable.

Francis Magee
Mossie

Describe your character
I'm playing Mossie Maguire, one of Jimmy's oldest pals and a stalwart of the whole movement. He's a down to earth, dependable geezer from the area, and a good family man – he has his wife Angela and two children, one of whom, because they're so poor, they've had to send her to Scotland with an auntie. He's been in jail for quite a long time for his political activities. He fought in the War of Independence – he's used a gun before and he would do it again – but he's kind of disillusioned now that the British haven't been kicked out, and the situation for people like him hasn't changed a bit: the Church still all powerful, the wealthy hanging onto the wealth and not sharing it with the rest of us.

What does Jimmy's return mean to him?
First and foremost Jimmy and Mossie are personal friends, so that means a lot. Mossie would stop a bullet for Jimmy, I think. It just re-awakens a lot of hope and optimism, Jimmy being back

on the scene: he's one of those guys that has the charisma that the rest of us lack. And he gets things done; we'll follow him but we're not leaders really.

What does the hall itself represent for Mossie and the community?
Well, Mossie has a line where he says, 'It's more than just a building, it's what we are; everything. This place gives me life.' So it's just hope, optimism that things can be better. For Mossie, who runs the boxing classes in the hall, to see the young ones dancing and having fun, as well as learning, it means it's not all dour socialism. It's a place of entertainment as well and that's so valuable for this rural area.

How did your casting come about?
I initially met Ken in London when they were just seeing who was around. Then I met him in Dublin some weeks later, did improvs and heard nothing for a while. When I heard I'd got it I was delighted – and scared. Ken is very much an actor's director. I never know what he's going to come out with next, but that keeps you on your toes.

Have you been victim to any surprises on set?
We were doing a scene in the hall, a singing lesson for the ladies. We did this scene for hours from this angle, that angle, we do it one more time and then suddenly from the back of the hall the door was kicked in and in comes the Free State army. Hardly anyone knew that was going to happen. I had an inkling, actually, because I saw them outside. But the point is any shock that's on the faces of whoever the camera's pointing at is real.

Did you get to dance?
He's a bit of a mover but Mossie's more of a singer. They had me do a solo – I've never sung on a film or a TV show, so that's a first.

Mikel Murfi
Tommy

Describe your character
I play a guy called Tommy Gilroy. He's the ex-head of the Flying Column in the War of Independence. Tommy might not have necessarily spent any time in jail, but he'd have been very anti-English, probably would have gone all round the place, leading the Flying Column, shooting Black and Tans whenever he could, then fought in the civil war on the anti-Treaty side. He's a good pal with Jimmy and Mossie and they'd be close allies. They don't always agree on what's going on with the hall, but they work it out.

Is he a fighter or a thinker?
I think he's bought into Jimmy's philosophy wholesale, in the sense that he won't want to act in a violent manner, unless he thinks it's absolutely necessary. I think the political climate at the time was such that people had fought each other in the civil war and figured that that was enough of that. If we could stand arms down and get people to bear with one another for ten years, five years even, at peace, that might start something. People could settle down and then politics might take over.

How did you come to be cast?
I'm the only one of the core cast around Jimmy who's from Sligo. I imagine that was an attraction to Ken in the first place. I guess, also, that when you meet him and you're improvising those meetings, in the audition period, that there's something in you that he sees – something that fits with what they think is the closest they can get, in an actor, to the character. A lot of the work that you're doing is just intuitive, rather than things that you could go away and craft as an actor.

What did you know of this story beforehand?
I never knew it beforehand and I was not particularly interested
in history, but in a very short space of time, during the rehearsing
period, with Ken and with Donal [Ó Drisceoil], the historian,
talking to us, you build up a very quick, efficient composite of
what was happening in that locale at the time.

You're a Sligo man. Does this feel like a particularly local film?
Oh yeah, absolutely. I mean, the authenticity of it is superb, but
that's Ken, and Kahleen as well, the Casting Director – between
the pair of them they've auditioned and interviewed every extra
on the thing. The people they've brought on board for the dance
hall sequences are all local and they're magic. Aileen [Henry] is
from over the road and she would have danced in dance halls in
this locale not long after the time. It means the woman sitting
there beside you, who is from this place, could have been in this
hall, just as easily. It's very affecting and it's lovely for people in
the locality to know that, somehow, this person Jimmy Gralton
is being honoured.

Sorcha Fox
Molly

Describe your character
Molly lives and works on a farm. She has aging parents that are
not well, so she looks after them. She loves music, so though
she hasn't had any training, she teaches music in the hall. She
wouldn't have had a formal education, but she would have been
very interested in books and would have read a lot, so I think
she's educated herself about politics. The hall means everything
to Molly, because what it represents is a glimpse of an alternative
Ireland, where there is real equality, and real justice. And also for

a woman in rural Ireland at the time, and a subsistence farmer, the freedom of expression through dance and through music and literature would have been an absolute lifeline.

What sort of a person is Molly?
I think she's probably passionate rather than angry. Yet she's cautious insofar as I think she realises the potential threat they're under from the forces that they're opposing. But she has decided that it's worth it, because to not do anything isn't an option for her.

What was your favourite scene?
I do a bit of singing so it was lovely to be able to do that in this film. Molly sings a song called 'Siúil a Rún', which means 'Walk My Love', that she's teaching the children. It's kind of a slow, beautiful song, half Irish, half English. Ken and all the crew and the cameras were out of the way. And at one point I was looking down the hall and only the class were in front of me and I could see the Leitrim hills out the windows of the hall, and you could see nothing else apart from the world you were in. That was magical.

What is your background and how did you come to be involved?
I'm from Dublin originally, but I moved seven years ago to just down the road in Leitrim so I would be local. Myself and my partner at the time, Donal O'Kelly, did a piece called *Jimmy Gralton's Dance Hall*. I think Donal had sent a little poem that he'd written about Jimmy Gralton to Paul [Laverty]. So Paul got over and saw the thing we did and started researching the story and I have been involved ever since.

What would you say is at the crux of this story?
The hall. It wasn't just a political place, and it wasn't just a dance hall. It was a combination of something that really gave people

the image of an alternative. It offered freedom in the forms of physical freedom and dancing, and then the freedom that comes with education. And so it was actually a truly empowering place. But at the same time plugged into an international movement, and I think that's why it was so dangerous to the powers that be.

Martin Lucey
Dezzie

Describe your character
Dezzie is an old friend of James Gralton from a working-class family. He's very enthusiastic about the education of kids and about getting the rightful owners back on the land. Basically, he is interested in fair play.

What does Jimmy's return mean to him?
It's like a new light again. He remembers how it was. He remembers how good it could have been. Dezzie fought in the War of Independence. That was his primary concern at the time, to get complete freedom from Britain. And that didn't fully materialise. The middle classes got their land and their lives back together. But the hand-to-mouth farmer like Dezzie did not get anything and it doesn't look like it's going to improve. So that's why I want Jimmy back because I know he's a good leader. He's charismatic. He has the energy and the intelligence to rally people. And I know that that's what we need.

What does the hall mean to them?
The hall signifies a place where like-minded people can meet. And it's a place that's of benefit to the working class, to the education of the poor. The rich get worried when the poor get educated. Dezzie's very aware that education is important – he

takes part in the literature classes. He's there in the class to learn himself, but he's also there to make sure that people are coming in to organise and to help in any way he can. He's very, very enthusiastic about the hall.

You were in The Wind that Shakes the Barley. *How did you come to be cast in this film?*
I heard that Ken was casting and I rang Kahleen [Crawford, Casting Director]. Word had it with all the other *Wind that Shakes the Barley* actors that he wasn't casting anybody from that film. So when I was called again, if I got half a day's work I would have been just over the moon. But to get seven weeks was a dream come true. I went home and told my wife, it's like meeting family. It's so comforting – there hasn't been a voice raised in either production, not once. Nobody ever had a cross word with anybody, or any of the stuff that sometimes goes on in other sets. Whether you're in for a day or whether you're playing James Gralton, everybody's treated the same. We all get ready in the same place, we travel with the buses, we eat at the same table. It makes it more than a film, it's an experience.

Are you a Leitrim local yourself?
No, I'm from Cork. Ken did say to try and tone down the Cork accent because it's very strong, especially when I get excited. So I've been trying to be aware of that. But though the landscape is definitely lovely Leitrim, I think the story is Irish. James Gralton just happened to live in Leitrim but when the English left, the Church took over and that was all over Ireland. We're only just getting out the other end of that now.

Shane O'Brien
Finn

Describe your character

I'm playing Finn, who would have been one of Jimmy Gralton's closest friends. Finn would've been a friend back in the 1920s as well, in the early days before Jimmy headed to America for the first time. So they'd be pretty tight. Finn was in the same brigade as Tommy. Tommy would've been my superior officer. But I think Finn's a bit tired of military action, and he's newly married, so he's enjoying the whole time in the hall and what Jimmy's all about. While Finn agrees with putting people back into their homes, if they've been evicted, or been abused in any way, I'm not the all-out militant that the likes of Tommy would be.

And what is his role in the hall?

His background is as a creamery worker, so he's quite good with his hands. He can do a bit of manual labour, so he helped with building the hall, and the carpentry and so forth. Outside of that, really he's just kind of a handyman.

What is the nature of the community we're seeing here?

It's mainly a farming community, I'd say. Trying to make a living on two or three acres, very little money, some of them tenants living on the property of the local landlord. They're the type of people that would be in Jimmy's group and that he represents.

Why has the hall become so important to them all?

I think the beauty of the hall is it's a free space where people can express themselves, and it isn't under the control of the Church. In those days, they pretty much controlled every community activity, or had some say in it. In the hall people can be themselves. They can dance and express opinions, they can learn new skills, they can learn how to box, or sing, or paint, or dance. The Church has no say in it, and that is why they fear Jimmy.

Why do people like Finn gravitate towards Jimmy?
He's a man that's willing to make a decision. He's a leader. A charismatic man, very likeable, very gentlemanly, with a very strong will and a strong backbone. And he's travelled a bit as well, he's been to America for ten years so he has seen horizons beyond Ireland. There's a colour to him and people like that.

How did you react when you first learnt Jimmy Gralton's story?
I'll hold my hand up – history-wise I had a very, very basic knowledge. It did anger me a bit learning about what they did to him. But look, I'm all for moving on – it's good to know your history, but not be shaped by it completely. I believe times have changed, and we need to change with them.

Seamus Hughes
Ruari

Describe you character
I'm playing Ruari. He was one of the lads that came to the hall in the 1930s. He probably wouldn't have been around in the 1920s because he was too young. So he'd be a very enthusiastic supporter of the hall and the principles of the hall. It's the times that have politicised him – there's a bit of anger there. He was probably someone who was looking for a little bit of leadership, like many people back in the day I imagine. It wouldn't have taken much to get like-minded people to come together behind the likes of Jimmy Gralton. Ruari would have heard about him, because he'd gone away. Then Jimmy comes back with a bit of an aura, has seen a bit of the world – it's just what people need.

What does the hall represent to the local people?
People are disparate. They can only see themselves coming together under the auspices of the Church or a political party. Not for themselves, by themselves. It always seems to be on someone else's terms. This hall represents our terms, for us. They've rebuilt this hall themselves. They have pride and ownership of it. It's a bubble of freedom in an otherwise rather repressive life and state.

What is the dynamic between Jimmy and his friends?
It's socialist and democratic. Everyone's voice must be heard – that's the principle of the entire hall. Even when we have our meeting about whether or not to take direct action Jimmy says we need to speak to the youth as well. It is their hall because they would stand to lose out also. So there is that genuine democracy that is fostered between women and men of all ages.

What did you know of this story beforehand?
I had actually heard of Jimmy Gralton. I've always had an interest in history – probably since school. I always thought that what they don't tell you was more interesting than what they do! I knew Leitrim was a hotbed and that Jimmy was one of the instigators at that time. Once I knew what this film was about I had access to several books written by family members and biographers. But most helpful was being up in Leitrim, meeting Jimmy's cousins, family friends, seeing exactly where he was from. I learned a lot about what the time was like. And of course the accent is something you're listening out for – I'm from Galway City and a Galway accent is different from a Leitrim accent. Even then it's complicated – it depends where you are from in Leitrim; and it depends where you are in Galway!

How have you found working with Ken Loach?
Ken lets you find your way in to scenes and allows whatever your honest reaction is to happen. From there the character emerges. There's a sort of village feel to it all – when you spend time with these people the character emerges. It's a wonderful process.

Aileen Henry
Alice

Describe the character you're playing
I am playing Alice, the mother of Jimmy Gralton. She's lived through very hard times and she has buried a son, so she is very pleased to have Jimmy home. She's a very strong woman, intellectual, fond of books. She would've brought Jimmy up to be upright and thoughtful and to love his country and she would've taught him all the values of life.

How does she feel when he comes back and she sees how the story starts to unfurl?
Well I think she would've been very, very proud that he saw the needs in the area and he started up this hall. He built this on his own land. He put all sorts of activities in there that were educational and good for the local community.

What do you think Alice wants for Jimmy?
Well I think she wants him to be happy. She doesn't wants him to make a hasty decision that might affect the rest of his life. She feels that if he goes down the road of Oonagh, it may become a disaster and he might never find anybody else for himself. I'm sure she's glad he's back, but I'm sure, like every mother, she wouldn't see much of a future for him in a country that's in dire straits.

Where do you come from?

I grew up in this parish, in a small town, so I know the hardships that there were. I was a psychiatric nurse when I was young, but married women couldn't be employed, so when I got married I had to leave. I ended up living on another small farm down in North Sligo; which myself and my husband built up from nothing. When my husband was made redundant, I went out to work in a healthcare company for about 25 years. I was a union activist there and became involved in an awful lot of things. I've never been idle.

How did you come to be cast?

I have never done any acting before. I got a phone call from our local union office to say that they were doing a film but me in my naivety thought it was something to do with union activities because it's the 100 year anniversary of the foundation of the union in Sligo. I went in there and I met Ken Loach and I wasn't aware who Ken Loach was, not being a film person. I just did what I was asked to do and I didn't ask any questions.

How does it make you feel learning about Jimmy Gralton's story?

I'm very sad and very upset. Jimmy was young but his elderly mother that had to see him deported already after burying her husband and her son – how any mother would feel going through that kind of drama I don't know. I think it's a heart-rending story. They shouldn't have allowed it to happen. There seemed to be no consideration for his mother either and I find that terrible.

How have you found working with Ken Loach?

Well it's an experience never to be forgotten: his gentleness, his attitude, just listening to him. He makes everybody comfortable – all the actors, all the crew, everybody will tell you the exact same thing. It's been fantastic, absolutely, I've never seen a frown on anyone's face.

Aisling Franciosi
Marie

Describe your character

My character is Marie O'Keefe. She's about 18 years old, and she's quite feisty and rebellious. Her father Dennis is very much a Free-Stater, quite conservative and on the side of the Church. Marie is going through a rebellious teenage phase, and so she goes against everything that he believes in. When she hears that James Gralton is back, and sees her father's reaction, and how angry he is, obviously this intrigues her – she wants to know who this man is. She's heard about the dance halls, and she's a young, spirited girl, so she wants to dance in a hall, as opposed to just by a roadside, so she urges Jimmy to re-open the hall. That leads her in to a little bit of trouble with her father as a result.

How much did you know about this period, and about Jimmy Gralton, beforehand?

To be honest, I only had a limited knowledge from junior school, so I was actually really grateful to get an opportunity to find out about such an important part of our history. I did lots of reading, and we had history lessons before we started. I learned that it was such a complicated and fractured time. Ken really pushed the point as well that it was not like there were good guys and bad guys. Everyone had their reasons for doing what they did. It was also nice to learn Sean-nós dancing, because I hadn't had any experience of Irish dancing, and not even that much of Irish music really. Doing this has kind of opened me up to all that.

Where are you from in Ireland?

I'm from Dublin, but until I was about five I grew up in Italy, and then moved over to Dublin with my mum and brothers.

How has it been working on this film?
The only way I can describe it, and it's not actually an overstatement, is life-affirming. There have been days where the atmosphere is amazing. Ken walks the walk, you know, he doesn't just talk the talk. He knows everyone's name, he's so respectful, and there's a really loving, caring atmosphere, from everyone from the crew to the production to the actors. Apart from my finger it's been the best experience.

Your finger?
We had a scene where my father is disciplining me. We were doing the scene, I fell over at one point – that was part of the scene – and then on the second take, I came outside, almost fainted. I couldn't understand why, because I'm not a fainter at all. They force-fed me chocolate biscuits, and then I was fine. When I regained full consciousness, my finger was really sore. But I wanted to finish the scene because the energy was just great. At the end of the day, I went to get my finger checked and I had fractured the knuckle. I think that it will add to the scene, at least!

Film Credits

Director:	Ken Loach
Producer:	Rebecca O'Brien
Screenplay:	Paul Laverty
Executive Producers:	Pascal Caucheteux
	Grégoire Sorlat
	Vincent Maraval
	Andrew Lowe
	Ed Guiney
Production Designer:	Fergus Clegg
Photography:	Robbie Ryan
Recordist:	Ray Beckett
Sound Editor:	Kevin Brazier
Casting:	Kahleen Crawford
Costume Designer:	Eimer Ní Mhaoldomhnaigh
Assistant Directors:	David Gilchrist
	Michael Queen
Production Manager:	Eimhear McMahon
Editor:	Jonathan Morris
Music:	George Fenton
Production Companies:	Sixteen Films
	Why Not Productions
	Wild Bunch
	Element Pictures
Funders:	BFI
	Film4
	Bord Scannán na hÉireann/
	Irish Film Board
	France 2 Cinéma
	Canal +
	Cine +
	Le Pacte
	Les Films du Fleuve
	Longride Inc.
	France Télévisions

Jimmy	Barry Ward
Mossie	Francis Magee
Alice	Aileen Henry
Oonagh	Simone Kirby
Stella	Stella McGirl
Molly	Sorcha Fox
Dessie	Martin Lucey
Tommy	Mikel Murfi
Finn	Shane O'Brien
Tess	Denise Gough
Father Sheridan	Jim Norton
Marie	Aisling Franciosi
Journalist	Seán T. Ó Meallaigh
Sean	Karl Geary
Commander O'Keefe	Brían F. O'Byrne
Doherty	Conor McDermottroe
Seamus Clarke	John Cronogue
Ruari	Seamus Hughes
Father Seamus	Andrew Scott
Fintan	Michael Sheridan
Mrs. O'Keefe	Rebecca O'Mara
Mossie's wife	Diane Parkes
Roscommon IRA	Padraig Fallon
	Chris MacManus
	Donal O'Kelly
Steward	John O'Dowd
Young Dancer	Anna Crossley
Young Violinist	Róisín Judge
Mayor	John McCarrick
Senior Guard	Hugh Gallagher
Guards	Colm Gormley
	John Colleary
	Shane Cullen
	Joe Lafferty
	Tom Colsh

and

Catherine Bell, Kieran Brennan, Aideen Burke, Maggie Carty,
Sarah-Louise Conlon, Johnóg Conlon, Shane Cronogue,
Anna Crossley, Martina Crummy, Rosemarie Dolan, Emma Duggan,
Faye Dunne, Marian Edwards, Killian Filan, Paul Fox, Fiona Gallagher,
Amy Gilligan, Breffni Gorman, Jennifer Healy, Brendan Joyce,
Martha Keaney, Deirdre Kerins, Niamh Kerins, Grainne Langton,
Deasun Lyons, Kerrie-Ann Murtagh, Dermot O'Connor,

Rory O'Dowd, Eoghan O'Neill, Darragh O'Malley, David O'Reilly,
Christian Pinder, Colin Pryal, Kevin Sheridan, John Sweeney,
Claire Tansey and many others…

Production Supervisor	Noëlette Buckley
Production Co-ordinator	Susan Holmes
Assistant Production Co-ordinator	Zeke Lawless
Production	Bernard Hayes
	Margaret Moggan
	Ann Cattrall
	Jack O'Brien
Historical Advisor	Donal Ó Drisceoil
Dance Choreographer	Chantelle Carey
Irish Dance Instructor	Edwina Guckian
Irish Music Co-ordinator	Édaín Ní Dhomhnaill
Script Consultant	Roger Smith
Script Supervisor	Susanna Lenton
Stills Photographers	Joss Barratt, Bernard Walsh
Location Manager	Niall Martin
Unit Manager and Key Scout	Kieran Hennessy
Locations Assistant	Jim King
3rd Assistant Director	Daire Glynn
Trainee AD	Fiona Bonnie
Crowd Casting Assistant	Nicola Conlon
Transport	Tony Clarke
	Paul Fox
Daily AD	Stephanie Barnes
Focus Puller	Andrew O'Reilly
Clapper loaders	Joachim Philippe
	Léo Lefèvre
Camera Trainee	Tommy Griffin
Additional Camera Operators	Matt Fisher
	Sarah Cunningham
Additional Focus Pullers	Ron Coe
	Louise McEllin
Additional Clapper Loaders	Rory O'Riordan
	Rob Flood
Boom Operator	Pete Murphy
Sound Trainee	Macdaragh Lambe
Gaffer	Andy Cole
Best Boy	Simon Magee
Electricians	Laurent Van Eijs
	Martin Holland

Art Director	Stephen Daly
Assistant/Standby Art Director	Judith Hynes
Assistant Art Director	Christine Fitzgerald
Prop Buyer	John Neligan
Prop Master	Noel Walsh
Dressing Props	Daragh Lewis
	Dermot Blighe
Standby Props	Chan Kin
Trainee Props	Jeff Dolan
	Zack Vymazal
Assistant Prop Buyers	Sinéad McGoldrick
	Naomi Britton
Props Drivers	Michael Cassidy
	Liam Maguire
Greens	Matt Gardner
	Lee Guckian
Thatcher	Jimmy Lenehan
Horse Wranglers	John Reynolds
	Niall McManus
	Caillin Reynolds
Cattle Wrangler	Eddie Drew
Armoury	John McKenna
Vehicles	John Malone
	Brendan Bradley
Cinema Playback	John Parsons
	CAVS
Construction Managers	Chris Higson
	Danny Sumsion
	Nicky MacManus
Carpenters	Alex Robertson
	Jake Drummond
	Gabriel Coates
	Alan Finglas
	Jim Finnerty
Painters	Perry Bell
	Bobby Gee
	Norman Duff
	Wendy Moore
Stagehands	Joe Clifford
	Eddie Arkins
Set Construction Glasgow	Jason Strachan
	Sam Curren
	Stewart Cunningham

Standby Crew	Paddy Treanor
	Kristian Tighe
	Tommy O'Shaughnessy
Hair Designer	Lorraine Glynn
Assistant Hair	Sevlene Roddy
Hair Dailies	Malvo Karpats
	Linda Gannon
	Maureen Smith
	Lyndsey Herron
	James Synott
Make-up Designer	Lynn Johnston
Assistant Make-up	Catherine Biggs
Make-up Dailies	Elaine Finnan
	Emma Moffat
	Kate Donnelly
	Tara Gannon-Carr
	Martina Byrne
	Blue Evans
Wardrobe Supervisor	Judith Devlin
Costume Assistants	Caoimhe Stack
	Cathy Young
Costume Trainees	Bébhínn McGrath
	Slawomir Narwid
Stunt Co-ordinator	Paul Heasman
Special Effects	Real SFX
Senior Production Accountant	Tina Shadick
Accountants	Evelyn McLoughlin
	Habib Rahman
Auditors	Malde & Co.
	Crowe Horwath
Catering	Gary Walsh
	Daniel Patachi
	Cziko Marius
	Nicoleta Rosu
Rushes Courier	Gus Meehan
	Aerfast
Camera Equipment	Eye Lite Group
	Vast Valley
Lighting Equipment	B&L Lighting
	Teach Solais
Insurance	John O'Sullivan
	Media Insurance Brokers
Script Clearance	Seeling Lafferty

Post Production Script	Sapex Scripts
1st Assistant Editor	Paul Clegg
Effects Editor/Foley Recordist	Robert Brazier
Dialogue/Foley Editor	Ben Brazier
Foley Artist	Rowena Wilkinson
	Sue Harding
Sound Transfers	Steve Carr
Cutting Room	Goldcrest Post
Editing Equipment	Salon Editing Equipment
Titles Design	Martin Butterworth
	Creative Partnership
Archive Researcher	Jacqui Edwards
Digital Post Production	Molinare Post Production
Colourist	Gareth Spensley
Online Editors	Nick Anderson
	Gareth Parry
Post-Production Contacts	Len Brown
	Louise Stewart
	Steve Knight
Film Stock	Kodak UK
Laboratory Services	Deluxe Laboratories
	iDailies
Neg Cutter	Steve Farman
	PNC
Re-recording Mixers	Ian Tapp (CAS)
	Andrew Caller
Sound Mix Technician	Rolf Martens
Re-recording	Pinewood Studios
Music recorded and mixed by	Jonathan Allen
Pro Tools Operator	Lewis Jones
Recording Studio	Abbey Road Studios
Orchestration	Geoffrey Alexander
Music Preparation	Samuel Pegg
Orchestral Contractor	Isobel Griffiths Ltd.

Score Musicians

Irish Flute Andy Findon, *Clarinet* Barnaby Robson,
Trumpet Andrew Crowley, *Percussion* Frank Ricotti and Paul Clarvis,
Guitar/Fiddle Seamie O'Dowd, *Guitars* John Parricelli,
Guitars/Banjo Steve Donnelly, *Violin* Dermot Crehan,
Harp Skaila Kanga, *Celli* David Daniels and Tony Lewis,
Double Basses Chris Laurence and Richard Pryce.

'Sugar Foot Strut'
Written by Charles Schwab, Henry Myers, Billy Pierce and Georges Matis
Used by kind permission of Carlin Music Corp.
Performed by Louis Armstrong & His Savoy Ballroom Five,
courtesy of Sony Music Entertainment Inc.

'Goose Pimples'
Composed by Jo Trent and Fletcher Henderson
Published by Music Sales Corp. and
EMI Music Publishing Ltd / EMI Mills Music Inc.
Performed by Bix Beiderbecke & His Gang,
courtesy of Sony Music Entertainment Inc.

'I'm Lonesome, Sweetheart'
Written By Davidson C Nelson and Joseph Oliver
© Peer International Corporation 1929
Performed by King Oliver & His Orchestra,
courtesy of Sony Music Entertainment Inc.

'Weeping Willow Blues'
Written by Paul Carter
published by CR Publishing
Performed by Bessie Smith,
courtesy of Sony Music Entertainment Inc.

TRADITIONAL IRISH MUSIC
'Bridie Morley's' arranged and performed by
Gearóid Devane, Stephen Doherty, Thomas Doherty,
Sarah Egan, Fiachra Guihen, Cónan Marren,
Liam O'Connor, Fiachra Ó Maolagáin

'Stack of Barley' arranged and performed by
Gregory Daly, Colm Gannon, Gerry Harrington,
Ben Lennon, Brian McGrath, Shane Meehan

'Moving Bog', 'The Sailor on the Rock',
'Bank Of Ireland', 'The Taproom'
arranged and performed by:
Harry Bradley, John Carty, Mary Corcoran, Charlie Harris,
Mossie Martin, Seamus O'Donnell, Seamie O'Dowd, Jesse Smith

JAZZ BAND
'That's a Plenty' written by Lew Pollack and Ray Gilbert
Courtesy of Carlin Music Corp on behalf of Redwood Music Ltd &
Music Sales Creative on behalf of George Simon Music Co.
'Boogie Woogie' written by Davidson C Nelson and Joseph Oliver
© Peer International Corporation 1930
Arranged and performed by Jimmy Higgins Snr., Frank Kilkelly,
Stephen Kohlmann, Eddie Lee, Seamie O'Dowd,
Kieran Quinn, Cathal Roche, Ciaran Wilde

ARCHIVE
British Pathe, Clips and Footage, Corbis, Critical Past, eFootage,
IFI Irish Film Archive, the Father Browne Collection,
ITN Source/Reuters, Kinolibrary, Producers Library,
The WPA Film Library

'The Blessing of the Colours' (1922), Sir John Lavery
The Bridgeman Art Library

THANK YOU
Donal O'Kelly, Jim and Paul Gralton, the Gralton Family,
Johnny Gogan, the Curneen Family, the entire McMorrow Clan,
Betty Purcell, Francis Purcell, Des Guckian, Block T,
Blue Raincoat Theatre Company, Brenda O'Callaghan, Chloe James,
Clarion Hotel – Sligo, Clive Noakes, Deirdre Bynre, Eamonn Murphy,
Emmanuel Esposito, Frank Kistemann, Fabien Snoeck, Finian Joyce,
Fr. Tom Hever, An Garda Síochána - Sligo and Manorhamilton,
Glasshouse Hotel – Sligo, Glenview Folk Museum, Killenummery Hall,
Lá Nua Project – Ballinamore, Leitrim County Council,
Lough Bo Shooting Centre, Love Leitrim, Mary Jordan,
Melody Urquhart, Moorlands Equestrian Centre, Nico Linul,
Patrick O'Rourke, Philip Delamere, Risteard O'Domhnaill,
Sharon McGourty, Sinn Féin offices - Ballinamore and Sligo,
Sligo County Council, Sligo Fire Department, Sligo Folk Park,
Sligo Jazz Festival, Susan O'Keeffe, Therese O'Loughlin,
the editors at Pixar Animation Studios,
Dixie the horse, Cabundie the donkey
and Homer the three-legged dog.

BIBLIOGRAPHY

The Gralton Affair by Pat Feeley;
Deported: The Story of Jimmy Gralton by Des Guckian;
My Cousin Jimmy by Margaret Gralton;
Down with Jazz RTE Radio Documentary;
Audio recording: *Margaret Gralton – Jimmy Gralton
and the South Leitrim Soviet*;
Labour and Local History: the case of Jim Gralton 1886-1945
by Luke Gibbons;
Pakie and Maggie Gralton interviewed by Evelyn Kelly 31st March 1991

Lawyers	Stephen Grosz
	Bindmans LLP
	Jonathan Kelly
	Philip Lee
For Why Not Productions	Etienne de Ricaud
	Pauline Bénard
For Wild Bunch	Carole Baraton
	Marie Besançon
	Emmanuelle Castro
For Element Pictures	Paula Heffernan
	Mark Byrne
	Darragh Noonan,
	Chelsea Morgan Hoffman
	Vicky Owens
For Les Films du Fleuve	Delphine Tomson
	Naziha Chahed
	Tania Antonioli
For BFI	Ben Roberts
	Natascha Wharton,
	Fiona Morham
	Amanda Pyne,
	Will Evans
	Virginia Burgess
For Film4	Tessa Ross
	Sue Bruce-Smith
	Louise Long
	Gerardine O'Flynn
	Hannah Saunders
For Bord Scannán na hÉireann/ Irish Film Board	James Hickey
	Mary Callery
	Cian McElhone

Produced with the support of
investment incentives for the Irish Film Industry
provided by the Government of Ireland

and

Brahim Chioua, Valérie Boyer, Bertrand Hassini-Bonnette,
Laurent Hassid, Nathalie Coste-Cerdan, Myriam Hacène;
Anne Flamant, Claire Squara, Arie Chamovni; Jean Labadie;
Avec le soutien de Tax Shelter Films Funding
et Tax Shelter du Gouvernement Fédéral de Belgique
Dirk Beckaert en Wim Hoeckman, Victor Buyck Steel Construction;
Baudouin Decamps et Sophie Decamps,
Etablissements Baudouin Decamps;
Daniël Daniëls, D.S.S.V.;
Noémie Berenbaum, L'Immobilière Dimo;
Artémis Productions

Collection Agent   Freeway CAM B.V
International Sales   Wild Bunch S.A

Filmed on location in County Sligo & County Leitrim, Ireland
The principal public events and incidents depicted
are based on the historical record.
Some scenes have been altered for dramatic purpose
and certain characters are entirely fictional.
The private lives of the historical characters have been imagined.

A British / Irish / French Co-Production under the
European Convention on Cinematographic Co-Production
© Sixteen Jimmy Limited, Why Not Productions, Wild Bunch,
Element Pictures, Channel Four Television Corporation,
France 2 Cinéma, the British Film Institute and
Bord Scannán na hÉireann/the Irish Film Board 2014

Other titles in this series

The Angels' Share

Route Irish

Looking for Eric

For further information on these books,
and other titles from Route please visit:
www.route-online.com